THE FACE OF DECEPTION

THE KILLING GAME

THE SEARCH

IRIS JOHANSEN

Bantam Books

NEW YORK TORONTO LONDON SYDNEY AUCKLAND

2013 Bantam Books Edition

Published in the United States by Bantam Books,
an imprint of The Random House Publishing Group,
a division of Random House, Inc., New York.

BANTAM BOOKS and the rooster colophon are registered
trademarks of Random House, Inc.

The three novels that comprise this omnibus were
originally published separately in 1998, 1999 and 2000
by Bantam Books, an imprint of The Random House
Publishing Group, a division of Random House, Inc.

Excerpt taken from *Flight to Arras* by Antoine de Saint-Exupéry.
Translated from the French by Lewis Galantière,
Harcourt Brace & Company, 1942.

ISBN 978-0-385-36424-9

Printed in the United States of America

www.bantamdell.com

1 2 3 4 5 6 7 8 9

Cover design by Christine Kell

BOOK ONE

THE FACE OF DECEPTION

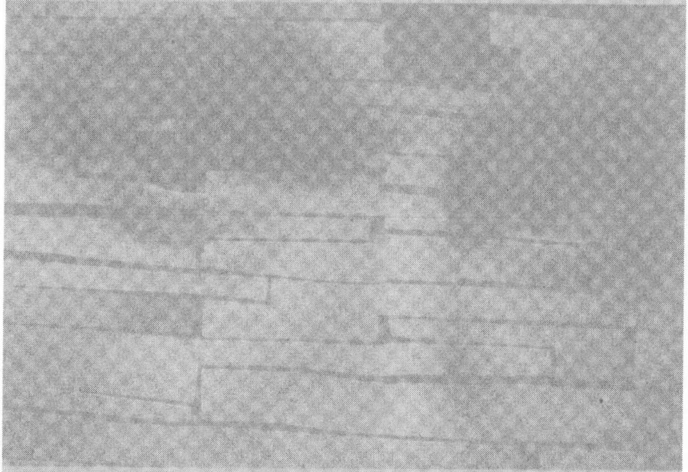

IRIS JOHANSEN

BANTAM BOOKS
NEW YORK TORONTO LONDON SYDNEY AUCKLAND

ACKNOWLEDGMENTS

My deepest and warmest thanks to N. Eileen Barrow, Research Associate and Forensic Sculptor with the FACES Laboratory at Louisiana State University. Her generosity with her time, help, and guidance was invaluable in writing this book.

Also a very sincere thank-you to Mark Stolorow, Director of Operations of Cellmark Diagnostics Inc., for his patience and kindness in helping me with the technical aspects of DNA profiling and the intricacies of chemiluminescence.

THE FACE OF DECEPTION

PROLOGUE

DIAGNOSTIC CLASSIFICATION FACILITY
JACKSON, GEORGIA
JANUARY 27
11:55 P.M.

It was going to happen.

Oh, God, don't let it happen.

Lost. She'll be lost.

They'll all be lost.

"Come away, Eve. You don't want to be here." It was Joe Quinn standing beside her. His square, boyish face was pale and drawn beneath the shadow of the black umbrella he was holding. "There's nothing you can do. He's had two stays of execution already. The governor's not going to do it again. There was too much public outcry the last time."

"He's *got* to do it." Her heart was pounding so hard, it hurt her. But then, at that moment everything in the world was hurting her. "I want to talk to the warden."

Quinn shook his head. "He won't see you."

"He saw me before. He called the governor. I've got to see him. He understood about—"

"Let me take you to your car. It's freezing out here and you're getting soaked."

She shook her head, her gaze fixed desperately on the prison gate. "You talk to him. You're with the FBI. Maybe he'll listen to you."

"It's too late, Eve." He tried to draw her under his umbrella but she stepped away from him. "Jesus, you shouldn't have come."

"*You* came." She gestured to the horde of newspaper and media people gathered at the gate. "*They* came. Who has a better right to be here than me?" Sobs were choking her. "I have to stop it. I have to make them see that they can't—"

"You crazy bitch."

She was jerked around and found herself facing a man in his early forties. His features were twisted with pain, and tears were running down his cheeks. It took a minute for her to recognize him. Bill Verner. His son was one of the lost ones.

"Stay out of it." Verner's hands dug into her shoulders. He shook her. "Let them kill him. You've already caused us too much grief and now you're trying to get him off again. Damn you, let them *burn* the son of a bitch."

"I can't do— Can't you see? They're lost. I have to—"

"You stay out of it, or so help me God I'll make you sorry that you—"

"Leave her alone." Quinn stepped forward and knocked Verner's hands away from Eve. "Don't you see she's hurting more than you are?"

"The hell she is. He killed my boy. I won't let her try to get him off again."

"Do you think I don't want him to die?" she said fiercely. "He's a monster. I want to kill him myself, but I can't let him—" There was no time for this argument, she thought frantically. There was no time for anything. It must be almost midnight.

They were going to kill him.

And Bonnie would be lost forever.

She whirled away from Verner and ran toward the gate.

"Eve!"

She pounded on the gate with clenched fists. "Let me in! You've got to let me in. Please don't do this."

Flashbulbs.

The prison guards were coming toward her.

Quinn was trying to pull her away from the gate.

The gate was opening.

Maybe there was a chance.

God, please let there be a chance.

The warden was coming out.

"Stop it," she screamed. "You've got to stop—"

"Go home, Ms. Duncan. It's over." He walked past her toward the TV cameras.

Over. It couldn't be over.

The warden was looking soberly into the cameras and his words were brief and to the point. "There was no stay of execution. Ralph Andrew Fraser was executed four minutes ago and pronounced dead at 12:07 A.M."

"No."

The scream was full of agony and desolation, as broken and forsaken as the wail of a lost child.

Eve didn't realize the scream came from her.

Quinn caught her as her knees buckled and she slumped forward in a dead faint.

ONE

ATLANTA, GEORGIA
JUNE 3
EIGHT YEARS LATER

"You look like hell. It's nearly midnight. Don't you ever sleep?"

Eve glanced up from the computer to see Joe Quinn leaning against the doorjamb across the room. "Sure I do." She took off her glasses and rubbed her eyes. "One late night does not a workaholic make. Or something like that. I just had to check those measurements before—"

"I know. I know." Joe came into the studio lab and dropped down in the chair beside the desk. "Diane said you blew her off for lunch today."

She nodded guiltily. It was the third time that month she had canceled out on Joe's wife. "I explained that the Chicago P.D. needed the result. Bobby Starnes's parents were waiting."

"Was it a match?"

"Close enough. I knew it was almost a certainty before I started the superimposition. There were a few teeth missing from the skull, but the dental check was very close."

"Then why were you brought in?"

"His parents didn't want to believe it. I was their last hope."

"Bummer."

"Yes, but I know about hope. And when they see the way Bobby's features fit the skull, they'll know it's over. They'll accept the fact that their child is dead and it may bring closure." She glanced at the image on her computer screen. Chicago P.D. had given her a skull and a picture of seven-year-old Bobby. Working with visual equipment and her computer, she had superimposed Bobby's face on the skull. As she had said, the match was very close. Bobby had looked so alive and sweet in the picture it was enough to break your heart.

They were all heartbreakers, she thought wearily. "Are you on your way home?"

"Yep."

"And just dropped by to yell at me?"

"I feel it's one of my primary duties in life."

"Liar." Her gaze was on the black leather case in his hands. "Is that for me?"

"We found a skeleton in the woods in North Gwinnett. The rain unearthed it. The animals got at it, so there's not much left, but the skull is intact." He snapped open the case. "It's a little girl, Eve."

He always told her right away if it was a girl. She supposed he thought he was shielding her.

She carefully took the skull and studied it. "It's not a little girl. She's a preteen, maybe eleven or twelve." She indicated a lacy crack on the upper jaw. "She's been exposed to the cold of at least one winter." She gently touched the broad nasal cavity. "And she was probably black."

"That will help." He grimaced. "But not much. You'll have to sculpt her. We don't have any idea who she is. No pictures for superimposition. Do you know how many girls run away from home in this town? If she was a slum kid, she might not have even been reported missing. The parents are usually more concerned with getting their crack than keeping track of their—" He shook his head. "Sorry. I forgot. Open mouth, insert foot."

"A habit with you, Joe."

"Only around you. I tend to lower my guard."

"Should I be honored?" Her brow knit with concentration as she studied the skull. "You know Mom hasn't been on crack for years. And there are a lot of things I'm ashamed of in my life, but growing up in the slums isn't one of them. I might not have survived if I hadn't had it tough."

"You'd have survived."

She wasn't so sure. She had been too close to going under to take either sanity or survival for granted. "Want a cup of coffee? We slum kids make great java."

He flinched. "Ouch. I said I was sorry."

She smiled. "Just thought I'd take a jab or two. You deserve it for generalizing. Coffee?"

"No, I have to get home to Diane." He stood up. "There's no hurry with this one if she's been buried that long. Like I said, we don't even know who we're looking for."

"I won't hurry. I'll work on her at night."

"Yeah, you have so much time." He looked at the pile of textbooks on the table. "Your mom said you were studying physical anthropology now."

"Only by correspondence. I don't have time to go to classes yet."

"For God's sake, why anthropology? Don't you have enough on your plate?"

"I thought it might help. I've tried to find out all I can from the anthropologists I've worked with, but there's still too much I don't know."

"You're working too hard as it is. Your schedule is booked up for months."

"That's not my fault." She made a face. "It was that damn mention your commissioner gave me on *60 Minutes*. Why couldn't he keep his mouth shut? I was busy enough without getting all this out-of-town stuff."

"Well, just remember who your friends are." Joe headed for the door. "Don't go moving away to some highfalutin college."

"Don't talk to me about highfalutin, when you went to Harvard."

"That was a lifetime ago. Now I'm a good ol' southern boy. Follow my example and stay where you belong."

"I'm not going anywhere." She got up and set the skull on the shelf above her workbench. "Except to lunch with Diane next Tuesday. If she'll have me. Will you ask her?"

"You ask her. I'm not running interference again. I have my own problems. It's not easy for her being a cop's wife." He paused at the door. "Go to bed, Eve. They're dead. They're all dead. It's not going to hurt them if you get a little sleep."

"Don't be stupid. I know that. You act like I'm neurotic or something. It's just not professional to ignore a job."

"Yeah, sure." He hesitated. "You ever been contacted by John Logan?"

"Who?"

"Logan. Logan Computers. He's a billionaire racing on the heels of Bill Gates. He's been all over the news lately because of the Republican fund-raisers he's been throwing out in Hollywood."

She shrugged. "You know I barely keep up with the news." But she did recall seeing a picture of Logan, perhaps in the Sunday paper the previous week. He was in his late thirties or early forties with a California tan and close-cut dark hair with a dusting of gray at the temples. He had been smiling down at some blond movie star. Sharon Stone? She couldn't remember. "Well, he hasn't been soliciting me for money. I wouldn't give it to him if he did. I vote Independent." She glanced at her computer. "That's a Logan. He makes a good computer, but that's the closest I've ever come in contact with the great man. Why?"

"He's been making inquiries about you."

"What?"

"Not personally. He's going through a high-powered West Coast lawyer, Ken Novak. When they told me down at the precinct, I did some checking and I'm almost sure Logan's behind it."

"I don't think so." She smiled slyly as she punned, "It doesn't compute."

"You've handled private inquiries before." He grinned. "A man in his position has to have left a trail of bodies on his way to the top. Maybe he forgot where he buried one of them."

"Very funny." She wearily rubbed the back of her neck. "Did his lawyer get his report?"

"What the hell do you think? We know how to protect our own. Tell me if he gets hold of your private number and bothers you. See you." The door shut behind him.

Yes, Joe would protect her just as he'd always done, and no one could do it better. He was different from when they had first met years before. Time had hammered every trace of boyishness out of him. Shortly after Fraser's execution, he had resigned from his job as an agent in the FBI and joined the Atlanta P.D. He was now a lieutenant detective. He'd never really told her why he had made the move. She had asked, but his answer—that he'd wanted to jettison the pressure of the bureau—had never satisfied her. Joe could be a very private person, and she hadn't probed. All she knew was that he had always been there for her.

Even that night at the prison when she had felt more alone than ever.

She didn't want to think about that night. The despair and pain were still as raw as—

So think about it anyway. She had learned the only way to survive the pain was to meet it head-on.

Fraser was dead.

Bonnie was lost.

She closed her eyes and let the agony wash over her. When it eased, she opened her eyes and moved toward the computer. Work always helped. Bonnie might be lost and never be found, but there were others—

"You've got another one?" Sandra Duncan stood in the doorway, dressed in pajamas and her favorite pink chenille robe. Her gaze was focused on the skull across the room. "I thought I heard someone in the driveway. You'd think Joe would leave you alone."

"I don't want to be left alone." Eve sat down at the desk. "No problem. It's not a rush job. Go back to bed, Mom."

"You go to bed." Sandra Duncan walked over to the skull. "Is it a little girl?"

"Preadolescent."

She was silent a moment. "You're never going to find her, you know. Bonnie's gone. Let it go, Eve."

"I have let it go. I just do my job."

"Bullshit."

Eve smiled. "Go to bed."

"Can I help? Make you a snack?"

"I have more respect for my digestive system than to let you sabotage it."

"I do try." Sandra made a face. "Some people weren't meant to cook."

"You have other talents."

Her mother nodded. "I'm a good court reporter and I nag damn well. Will you go to bed, or do I have to demonstrate?"

"Fifteen minutes more."

"I guess I'll allow you that much slack." She moved toward the door. "But I'll be listening to hear your bedroom door close." She paused and then said awkwardly, "I'm not coming home right away after work tomorrow night. I'm going out to dinner."

Eve looked up in surprise. "With whom?"

"Ron Fitzgerald. I told you about him. He's a lawyer in the district attorney's office. I like him." Her tone was almost defiant. "He makes me laugh."

"Good. I'd like to meet him."

"I'm not like you. It's been a long time since I've been out with a man, and I need people. I'm not a nun. For God's sake, I'm not even fifty. My life can't stop just because—"

"Why are you acting so guilty? Have I ever said I wanted you to stay home? You have a right to do whatever you want to do."

"I'm acting guilty because I feel guilty." Sandra scowled. "You could make it easier for me if you weren't so hard on yourself. You're the one who's a nun."

God, she wished her mother hadn't decided to go into this tonight. She was too tired to cope. "I've had a few relationships."

"Until they got in the way of your work. Two weeks tops."

"Mom."

"Okay, okay. I just think it's time for you to live a normal life again."

"What's normal for one person isn't always normal for another." She looked down at her computer screen. "Now, scat. I want to finish this before I go to bed. Be sure you drop in tomorrow night and tell me all about your dinner."

"So you can live vicariously?" Sandra asked tartly. "I may or may not."

"You will."

"Yeah, I will." Her mother sighed. "Good night, Eve."

"Good night, Mom."

Eve leaned back in her chair. She should have noticed her mother was becoming restless and unhappy. Emotional instability was always dangerous for a recovering addict. But, dammit, Mom had been clean since Bonnie's second birthday. Another gift that Bonnie had brought when she came into their lives.

She was probably exaggerating the problem. Growing up with an addict had made her deeply suspicious. Surely her mother's restlessness was both typical and healthy. The best thing that could happen to her was a solid, loving relationship.

So let Sandra run with it, but watch the situation closely.

She was staring blindly at the screen. She had done enough tonight. There could be little doubt the skull belonged to little Bobby Starnes.

She noticed the Logan insignia as she logged out and turned off the computer. Funny how you never paid any attention to things like that. Why the hell would Logan be asking questions about her? He probably wasn't. More than likely it was a mistake. Her life and Logan's were at opposite ends of the spectrum.

She stood up and moved her shoulders to rid them of stiffness. She'd pack up Bobby's skull, take it and the report to the house, then ship them out the following morning. She never liked to have more than one skull in the lab at the same time. Joe laughed at her, but she felt she couldn't give her full attention to the job she was working on if she could see another skull silently waiting. So she'd overnight Bobby Starnes and the report to Chicago and the day after tomorrow Bobby's parents would know that their son had come home, that he was no longer one of the lost ones.

"Let it go, Eve."

Her mother didn't understand that the search for Bonnie had become woven into the fabric of her life and she could no longer tell which thread was Bonnie and which were the other lost ones. That probably made her a hell of a lot more unstable than her mother, she thought ruefully.

She walked across the room and stood before the shelf bearing the new skull.

"What happened to you?" she murmured as she removed the skull's ID tag and tossed it on the workbench. "An accident? Murder?" She hoped it wasn't murder, but it usually was in these cases. It hurt her to think of the terror the child had suffered before death.

The death of a child.

Someone had held this girl as a baby, had watched her take her first steps. Eve prayed that someone had loved her and given her joy before she had ended up lost in that hole in the forest.

She gently touched the girl's cheekbone. "I don't know who you are. Do you mind if I call you Mandy? I've always liked that name." Jesus, she talked to skeletons and she was worried about her mother going off the deep end? It might be weird, but she'd always felt it was disrespectful to treat the skulls as if they had no identity. This girl had lived, laughed, and loved. She deserved more than to be treated impersonally.

Eve whispered, "Just be patient, Mandy. Tomorrow I'll measure and soon I'll start sculpting. I'll find you. I'll bring you home."

MONTEREY, CALIFORNIA

"You're sure she's the best choice?" John Logan's gaze was fastened on the television screen, where a video of the scene outside the prison facility was playing. "She doesn't appear all that stable. I've got enough problems without having to deal with a woman who doesn't have all her marbles."

"My God, what a kind, caring human being you are," Ken Novak murmured. "I think the woman might have cause to appear a little distracted. That was the night the murderer of her little girl was executed."

"Then she should have been dancing with joy and offering to pull the switch. I would have been. Instead, she pleaded with the governor for a stay."

"Fraser was convicted for the killing of Teddy Simes. He was almost caught in the act and wasn't able to dispose of the boy's body. But he confessed to murdering eleven other children including Bonnie Duncan. He gave details that left no doubt he was guilty, but he wouldn't tell where he'd disposed of the bodies."

"Why not?"

"I don't know. He was a crazy son of a bitch. A last act of malice? The bastard even refused to appeal the death sentence. It drove Eve Duncan frantic. She didn't want him executed until he told them where her daughter was. She was afraid she'd never find her."

"And has she?"

"No." Novak picked up the remote and froze a frame. "That's Joe Quinn. Rich parents, attended Harvard. Everyone expected him to go into law, but he joined the FBI instead. He worked the Bonnie Duncan case with the Atlanta P.D., but he's now a detective with them. He and Eve Duncan have become friends."

Quinn appeared to be about twenty-six at the time. Square face, broad mouth, and intelligent, wide-set brown eyes. "Only friends?"

He nodded. "If she's gone to bed with him, we haven't found out about it. She was a witness at his wedding three years ago.

She's had one or two relationships in the past eight years, but nothing serious. She's a workaholic and that doesn't lend itself to enriching personal relationships." He looked pointedly at Logan. "Now, does it?"

Ignoring the comment, Logan glanced down at the report on the desk. "The mother's an addict?"

"Not any longer. She got off the stuff years ago."

"What about Eve Duncan?"

"She was never on dope. Which was a wonder. Practically everyone else in her neighborhood was sniffing or shooting, including Mama. Her mother was illegitimate and had Eve when she was fifteen. They lived on welfare in one of the worst areas of the city. Eve had Bonnie when she was sixteen."

"Who was the father?"

"She didn't list him on the birth certificate. Evidently he didn't claim the child." He pressed the button to start the tape again. "There's a picture coming up on the screen of the kid. CNN really wrung the story for all it was worth."

Bonnie Duncan. The little girl was dressed in a Bugs Bunny T-shirt, blue jeans, and tennis shoes. Her red hair was wildly curly and there was a smattering of freckles on her nose. She was smiling at the camera and her face was alight with joy and mischief.

Logan felt sick. What kind of world was this in which a monster could kill a kid like that?

Novak's gaze was fixed on his face. "Cute, huh?"

"Fast-forward."

Novak pressed the button and the scene was back outside the prison.

"How old was Duncan when the kid was killed?"

"Twenty-three. The little girl was seven. Fraser was executed two years later."

"And the woman went bonkers and became obsessed with bones."

"Hell no," Novak said curtly. "Why are you being so rough on her?"

Logan turned to look at him. "Why are you being so defensive?"

"Because she's not— She's got guts, dammit."

"You admire her?"

"From her head right down to her toes," Novak said. "She could have given up the kid for adoption or gotten an abortion. She kept her instead. She could have gone on welfare like her mother and repeated the pattern. She kept the baby in a United Fund nursery during the day while she worked and did correspondence courses at night. She was almost finished with college when Bonnie disappeared." He looked at Eve Duncan on the screen. "That should have killed her or sent her spiraling back where she came from, but it didn't. She returned to school and made something of her life. She has a degree in fine arts from Georgia State and is certified as a computer age progression specialist at the National Center for Missing and Exploited Children in Arlington, Virginia. She also received advanced certification for clay facial reconstruction after training with two of the nation's foremost reconstruction artists."

"Tough lady," Logan murmured.

"And smart. She does forensic sculpting and age progression as well as computer and video superimposition. Not many people in her profession are experts in all those areas. You saw the clip from *60 Minutes* on how she rebuilt the face of that kid who was found in the Florida swamps."

He nodded. "It was incredible." His gaze returned to the video. Eve Duncan's tall, thin body was clothed in jeans and a raincoat and appeared terribly fragile. Her shoulder-length red-brown hair was soaking wet and framed a pale, oval face that held agony and desperation. The brown eyes behind her wire-rimmed glasses reflected the same desolation and pain. He looked away from the screen. "Can we find anyone else as good?"

Novak shook his head. "You asked for the best. She's the best. But you may have trouble getting her. She's pretty busy and she prefers to work on lost-children cases. I don't suppose this has anything to do with a child?"

Logan didn't answer. "Money is usually pretty persuasive."

"But it may not mean that much to her. She could be making a lot more money if she took a university appointment instead of working freelance. She lives in a rented house in Morningside, an area close to downtown Atlanta, and she has a lab in a renovated garage in the back."

"Maybe a university hasn't made her an offer she couldn't refuse."

"Maybe. They're not in your league." He raised his brows. "I don't suppose you'd like to tell me what you need her to do?"

"No." Novak had a reputation for integrity and was probably trustworthy, but there was no way Logan could risk confiding in him. "You're sure she's the only one?"

"She's the best. I told you that she— What's bothering you?"

"Nothing." It wasn't the truth. The whole damn prospect of having to choose Eve Duncan bothered him. She was a victim already. She didn't need to be put at risk again.

Why was he hesitating? No matter who got hurt, he had to go through with it. The decision was already made. Hell, the woman herself had made it for him when she'd become tops in her field. He had to have the best.

Even if it killed her.

Ken Novak tossed his briefcase on the passenger seat of his convertible and started the car. He waited until he was past the long driveway and out the front gates before he picked up the car phone and placed the call to the private number at the Treasury Department.

While he waited to be put through to Timwick, his gaze wandered to the Pacific. Someday he was going to have a house like Logan's out on the Seventeen Mile Drive. His house in Carmel was sleek and modern but nothing like the mansions here. The people who owned them were the elite, the kings of business and finance, the movers and shakers. That future wasn't out of Novak's grasp. Logan had started out with a tiny company and built it into a giant. All it had taken was hard work and the ruthlessness to forge ahead no matter what the odds. Now he had it all. Novak had worked for Logan for the past three years, and he admired him tremendously. Sometimes he even liked him. Logan could turn on the charm when he—

"Novak?" Timwick was on the line.

"I've just come from Logan's house. I think he's settled on Eve Duncan."

"Think? Don't you know?"

"I asked if he wanted me to contact her. He said he'd do it himself. Unless he changes his mind, she's a lock-in."

"But he won't tell you why he needs her?"

"No way."

"Not even if it's a personal matter?"

Novak's interest was piqued. "It has to be personal, doesn't it?"

"We don't know. According to your reports, the things he wanted investigated are a mixed bag. Some of them may have been red herrings to throw you off."

"Possibly. But you thought enough of them to pay me a princely sum to find out more."

"And you'll be paid even more generously if you give us something we can use against him. He's raised too much money for the Republican Party in the last six months and the election is only five months away."

"At least you have a Democratic president. Ben Chadbourne's popularity numbers are up again this month. You think Logan wants to make sure the Republicans take Congress again? They may do it anyway."

"And they may not. We could take it all next time. We need Logan stopped in his tracks."

"Sic the IRS on him. That's always a good way to discredit."

"He's clean."

Novak had suspected he would be. Logan was too smart to fall in that trap. "Then I guess you have to rely on me, don't you?"

"Not necessarily. We do have other sources."

"But none as close to him as I am."

"I said you'd be well paid."

"I've been thinking about the money. I think I'd rather trade in favors. I've been considering running for lieutenant governor."

"You know we're backing Danford."

"But he's not being as helpful to you as I am."

There was a silence. "Bring me the information I need and I'll consider it."

"I'll work on it." Novak hung up the phone. Nudging Timwick had been easier than he'd thought. He must really be worried about the upcoming presidential election. Democrat or Republican, all those political insiders were the same. Once they got a taste of power, they became addicted, and the smart man used that addiction to move himself up the ladder to a place on the Seventeen Mile Drive.

He followed a curve in the road, and Logan's Spanish palace on the hill was once again in view. Logan wasn't an insider; he was that rare commodity, a true patriot. He was a Republican, but Novak had even heard him praise the Democratic president on that negotiation with Jordan three years earlier.

But patriots were often unpredictable and could be dangerous.

Timwick wanted him brought down and, if he worked it right, Novak could parlay that need to the governor's mansion. He had little doubt that whatever task Logan wanted Eve Duncan to do, it was personal. He had been too secretive and on edge. Secrets regarding skeletal remains were usually a pretty fair sign of guilt. Murder? Maybe. He had led a pretty rough life during the early days when he was trying to build his empire. It appeared that sometime in Logan's checkered past, he had stubbed his toe big-time.

He hadn't lied about his admiration for Eve Duncan. He'd always liked tough, take-charge women. He hoped he wouldn't have to bring her down with Logan. Hell, maybe by bringing Logan down, he might be doing the woman a favor. Logan was planning on aiming that characteristic ruthless intensity on her, and she could be trampled.

He chuckled as he realized how he'd rationalized betrayal into gallantry. Damn, he was a good lawyer.

But lawyers served the royalty that lived along this drive, they weren't royalty themselves. He had to move up from the station of adviser to the throne.

It would be nice to be king.

TWO

"You look beautiful," Eve said. "Where are you going tonight?"

"I'm meeting Ron at Anthony's. He likes the food there." Sandra leaned forward and checked her mascara in the hall mirror, then straightened the shoulders of her dress. "Damn these shoulder pads. They keep shifting around."

"Take them out."

"We all don't have broad shoulders like you. I need them."

"Do you like the food there?"

"No, it's a little too fancy for me. I'd rather go to the Cheesecake Factory."

"Then tell him."

"Next time. Maybe I should like it. Maybe it's a learning type thing." She grinned at Eve in the mirror. "You're big on learning new things."

"I like Anthony's, but I still like to pig out at

McDonald's when I'm in the mood." She handed Sandra her jacket. "And I'd fight anyone who tried to tell me I shouldn't do it."

"Ron doesn't tell me—" She shrugged. "I like him. He comes from a nice family in Charlotte. I don't know if he'd understand about the way we lived before— I just don't know."

"I want to meet him."

"Next time. You'd give him that cool once-over and I'd feel like a high school kid bringing home my first date."

Eve chuckled and gave her a hug. "You're crazy. I just want to make sure he's good enough for you."

"See?" Sandra headed for the door. "Definitely first-date syndrome. I'm late. I'll see you later."

Eve went to the window and watched her mother back out of the driveway. She hadn't seen her mother this excited and happy in years.

Not since Bonnie was alive.

Well, there was no use staring wistfully out the window. She was glad her mother had a new romance, but she wouldn't trade places with her. She wouldn't know what to do with a man in her life. She wasn't good at one-night stands, and anything else required a commitment she couldn't afford.

She went out the back door and down the kitchen steps. The honeysuckle was in bloom and the heady scent surrounded her as she walked down the path to the lab. The aroma always seemed stronger at twilight and early morning. Bonnie used to love the honeysuckle and was always picking it off the fence, where the bees constantly buzzed. Eve had been at her wit's end trying to stop her before she got stung.

She smiled at the recollection. It had taken her a long time to be able to separate the good memories from the bad. At first she had tried to save herself from pain by closing out all thoughts of Bonnie. Then she had come to understand that that would be forgetting Bonnie and all the joy she had brought into her and Sandra's lives. Bonnie deserved more than—

"Ms. Duncan."

She stiffened, then whirled around.

"I'm sorry, I didn't mean to frighten you. I'm John Logan. I wonder if I could speak to you?"

John Logan. If he hadn't introduced himself she would have recognized him from the photo. How could she miss that California tan? she thought sardonically. And in that gray Armani suit and Gucci loafers, he looked as out of place in her small backyard as a peacock. "You didn't frighten me. You startled me."

"I rang the doorbell." He smiled as he walked toward her. There was not an ounce of fat on his body, and he exuded confidence and charm. She had never liked charming men; charm could hide too much. "I guess you didn't hear me."

"No." She had the sudden desire to shake his confidence. "Do you always trespass, Mr. Logan?"

The sarcasm didn't faze him. "Only when I really want to see someone. Could we go somewhere and talk?" His gaze went to the door of her lab. "That's where you work, isn't it? I'd like to see it."

"How did you know it's where I work?"

"Not from your friends at the Atlanta P.D. I understand they were very protective of your privacy." He strolled forward and stood beside the door. He smiled. "Please?"

He was obviously accustomed to instant acquiescence, and annoyance surged through her again. "No."

His smile faded a little. "I may have a proposition for you."

"I know. Why else would you be here? But I'm too busy to take on any more work. You should have phoned first."

"I wanted to see you in person." He glanced at the lab. "We should go in there and talk."

"Why?"

"It will tell me a few things about you that I need to know."

She stared at him in disbelief. "I'm not applying for a position with one of your companies, Mr. Logan. I don't have to go through a personnel check. I think it's time you left."

"Give me ten minutes."

"No, I have work to do. Good-bye, Mr. Logan."

"John."

"Good-bye, Mr. Logan."

He shook his head. "I'm staying."

She stiffened. "The hell you are."

He leaned against the wall. "Go on, get to work. I'll stay out here until you're ready to see me."

"Don't be ridiculous. I'll probably be working until after midnight."

"Then I'll see you after midnight." His manner no longer held even a hint of his previous charm. He was icy cool, tough, and totally determined.

She opened the door. "Go away."

"After you talk to me. It would be much easier for you to just let me have my way."

"I don't like things easy." She closed the door and flicked on the light. She didn't like things easy and she didn't like being coerced by men who thought they owned the world. Okay, she was overreacting. She didn't usually let anyone disturb her composure, and he hadn't done anything but invade her space.

What the hell, her space was very important to her. Let the bastard stay out there all night.

She threw open the door at eleven thirty-five.

"Come in," she said curtly. "I don't want you out there when my mother comes home. You might scare her. Ten minutes."

"Thank you," he said quietly. "I appreciate your consideration."

No sarcasm or irony in his tone, but that didn't mean it wasn't there. "It's necessity. I was hoping you'd give up before this."

"I don't give up if I need something. But I'm surprised you didn't call your friends at the police department and have them throw me out."

"You're a powerful man. You probably have contacts. I didn't want to put them on the spot."

"I never blame the messenger." His gaze traveled around the lab. "You have a lot of room here. It looks smaller from outside."

"It used to be a carriage house before it was a garage. This part of town is pretty old."

"It's not what I expected." He took in the rust and beige striped couch, the green plants on the windowsill, and then the framed photos of her mother and Bonnie on the bookshelf across the room. "It looks . . . warm."

"I hate cold, sterile labs. There's no reason why I can't have comfort as well as efficiency." She sat down at her desk. "Talk."

"What's that?" He moved toward the corner. "Two video cameras?"

"It's necessary for superimposition."

"What is— Interesting." His attention had been drawn to Mandy's skull. "This looks like something from a voodoo movie with all those little spears stuck in it.

"I'm charting it to indicate the different thicknesses of skin."

"Do you have to do that before you—"

"Talk."

He came back and sat down beside the desk. "I'd like to hire you to identify a skull for me."

She shook her head. "I'm good, but the only sure ways of identification are dental records and DNA."

"Both of those require subjects to match. I can't go that route until I'm almost certain."

"Why not?"

"It would cause difficulties."

"Is this a child?"

"It's a man."

"And you have no idea who he is?"

"I have an idea."

"But you're not going to tell me?"

He shook his head.

"Are there any photos of him?"

"Yes, but I won't show them to you. I want you to start fresh and not construct the face you think is there."

"Where were the bones found?"

"Maryland . . . I think."

"You don't know?"

"Not yet." He smiled. "They haven't actually been located yet."

Her eyes widened in surprise. "Then what are you doing here?"

"I need you on the spot. I want you with me. I'll have to move fast when the skeleton is located."

"And I'm supposed to disrupt my work and go to Maryland on the chance that you'll locate this skeleton?"

"Yes," he said calmly.

"Bull."

"Five hundred thousand dollars for two weeks' work."

"What?"

"As you've pointed out, your time is valuable. I understand you rent this house. You could buy it and still have a lot left over. All you have to do is give me two weeks."

"How do you know I rent this house?"

"There are other people who aren't as loyal as your friends at the police department." He studied her face. "You don't like having dossiers gathered on you."

"You're damn right I don't."

"I don't blame you. I wouldn't either."

"But you still did it."

He repeated the word she had used with him. "Necessity. I had to know who I was dealing with."

"Then you've wasted your efforts. Because you're not dealing with me."

"The money doesn't appeal to you?"

"Do you think I'm nuts? Of course it appeals to me. I grew up poor as dirt. But my life doesn't revolve around money. I pick and choose my jobs these days, and I don't want yours."

"Why not?"

"It doesn't interest me."

"Because it doesn't concern a child?"

"Partly."

"There are other victims besides children."

"But none as helpless." She paused. "Is your man a victim?"

"Possibly."

"Murder?"

He was silent a moment. "Probably."

"And you're sitting there asking me to go with you to a murder site? What's to stop me from calling the police and telling them that John Logan is involved in a murder?"

He smiled faintly. "Because I'd deny it. I'd tell them I was thinking of having you examine the bones of that Nazi war criminal who was found buried in Bolivia." He let a couple of moments pass. "And then I'd pull every string I have to make your friends at the Atlanta P.D. look foolish or even criminal."

"You said you wouldn't blame the messenger."

"But that was before I realized how much it would bother you. Evidently the loyalty goes two ways. One uses whatever weapon one's given."

Yes, he would do that, she realized. Even while they'd been talking he'd been watching her, weighing her every question and answer.

"But I've no desire to do that," he said. "I'm trying to be as honest as I can with you. I could have lied."

"Omission can also be a lie, and you're telling me practically nothing." She stared directly into his eyes. "I don't trust you, Mr. Logan. Do you think this is the first time someone like you has come and asked me to verify a skeleton? Last year a Mr. Damaro paid me a call. He offered me a lot of money to come to Florida and sculpt a face on a skull he just happened to have in his possession. He said a friend had sent it to him from New Guinea. It was supposed to be an anthropological find. I called the Atlanta P.D. and it turned out that Mr. Damaro was really Juan Camez, a drug runner from Miami. His brother had disappeared two years ago and it was suspected he'd been killed by a rival organization. The skull was sent to Camez as a warning."

"Touching. I suppose drug runners have family feelings too."

"I don't think that's funny. Tell that to the kids they hook on heroin."

"I'm not arguing. But I assure you that I've no connection with organized crime." He grimaced. "Well, I've used a bookie now and then."

"Is that supposed to disarm me?"

"Disarming you would obviously take a total global agreement." He stood up. "My ten minutes are up and I wouldn't want to impose. I'll let you think about the offer and call you later."

"I've already thought about it. The answer is no."

"We've only just opened negotiations. If you won't think about it, I will. There has to be something I can offer you that will make the job worth your while." He stood looking at her with narrowed eyes. "Something about me is rubbing you the wrong way. What is it?"

"Nothing. Other than the fact that you have a dead body you don't want anyone to know about."

"Anyone but you. I very much want *you* to know about it." He shook his head. "No, there's something else. Tell me what it is so I can clear it up."

"Good night, Mr. Logan."

"Well, if you can't call me John, at least drop the Mr. You don't want anyone to think you're properly respectful."

"Good night, Logan."

"Good night, Eve." He stopped at the pedestal and looked at the skull. "You know, he's beginning to grow on me."

"She's a girl."

His smile faded. "Sorry. It wasn't funny. I guess we all have our own way of dealing with what we become after death."

"Yes, we do. But sometimes we have to face it before we should. Mandy wasn't over twelve years old."

"Mandy? You know who she was?"

She hadn't meant to let that slip. What the hell, it didn't matter. "No, but I usually give them names. Aren't you glad now that I turned you down? You wouldn't want an eccentric like me working on your skull."

"Oh, yes, I appreciate eccentrics. Half the men in my think tanks in San Jose are a little off center." He moved toward the door. "By the way, that computer you're using is three years old. We have a newer version that's twice as fast. I'll send you one."

"No, thank you. This one works fine."

"Never refuse a bribe if you don't have to sign on the dotted line for return favors." He opened the door. "And never leave your doors unlocked, as you did tonight. There's no telling who could have been waiting in here for you."

"I lock the lab up at night, but it would be inconvenient to keep it locked all the time. Everything in here has been insured, and I know how to protect myself."

He smiled. "I bet you do. I'll call you."

"I told you that I'm—"

She was talking to air; he'd already closed the door behind him.

She breathed a sigh of relief. Not that she had the slightest doubt she would hear from him again. She had never met a man more determined to get his own way. Even when his approach had been velvet soft, the steel had shown through. Well, she had dealt with powerhouse types before. All she had to do was stick to her guns and John Logan would eventually get discouraged and leave her alone.

She stood up and went over to the pedestal. "He can't be so smart, Mandy. He didn't even know you were a girl." Not that many people would have.

The desk phone rang.

Mom? She had been having trouble with the ignition on her car lately.

Not her mother.

"I remembered something just as I reached the car," Logan said. "I thought I'd throw it into the pot for you to consider with the original deal."

"I'm not considering the original deal."

"Five hundred thousand for you. Five hundred thousand to go to the Adam Fund for Missing and Runaway Children. I understand you contribute a portion of your fees to that fund." His voice lowered persuasively. "Do you realize how many children could be brought home to their parents with that amount of money?"

She knew better than he did. He couldn't have offered a more tempting lure. My God, Machiavelli could have taken lessons from him.

"All those children. Aren't they worth two weeks of your time?"

They were worth a decade of her time. "Not if it means doing something criminal."

"Criminal acts are often in the eyes of the beholder."

"Bullshit."

"Suppose I promise you that I had nothing to do with any foul play connected with the skull."

"Why should I believe any promise you make?"

"Check me out. I don't have a reputation for lying."

"Reputation doesn't mean anything. People lie when it means enough to them. I've worked hard to establish my career. I won't see it go down the drain."

There was silence. "I can't promise you that you won't come out of this without a few scars, but I'll try to protect you as much as I can."

"I can protect myself. All I have to do is tell you no."

"But you're tempted, aren't you?"

Christ, she was tempted.

"Seven hundred thousand to the fund."

"No."

"I'll call you tomorrow." He hung up the phone.

Damn him.

She replaced the receiver. The bastard knew how to push the right buttons. All that money channeled to find the other lost ones, the ones who might still be alive . . .

Wouldn't it be worth a risk to see even some of them brought home? Her gaze went to the pedestal. Mandy might have been a runaway. Maybe if she'd had a chance to come home she wouldn't . . .

"I shouldn't do it, Mandy," she whispered. "It could be pretty bad. People don't fork out over a million dollars for something like this if they're even slightly on the up-and-up. I have to tell him no."

But Mandy couldn't answer. None of the dead could answer.

But the living could, and Logan had counted on her listening to the call.

Damn him.

Logan leaned back in the driver's seat, his gaze on Eve Duncan's small clapboard house.

Was it enough?

Possibly. She had definitely been tempted. She had a passionate commitment to finding lost children and he had played on it as skillfully as he could.

What kind of man did that make him? he thought wearily.

A man who needed to get the job done. If she didn't succumb to his offer, he'd go higher tomorrow.

She was tougher than he'd thought she'd be. Tough and smart and perceptive. But she had an Achilles' heel.

And there was no doubt on earth that he would exploit it.

"He just drove off," Fiske said into his digital phone. "Should I follow him?"

"No, we know where he's staying. He saw Eve Duncan?"

"She was home all evening and he stayed over four hours."

Timwick cursed. "She's going to go for it."

"I could stop her," Fiske said.

"Not yet. She has friends in the police department. We don't want to make waves."

"The mother?"

"Maybe. It would certainly cause a delay at least. Let me think about it. Stay there. I'll call you back."

Scared rabbit, Fiske thought contemptuously. He could hear the nervousness in Timwick's voice. Timwick was always thinking, hesitating instead of taking the clean, simple way. You had to decide what result you needed and then just take the step that would bring that result. If he had Timwick's power and resources, there would be no limit to what he could do. Not that he wanted Timwick's job. He liked what he did. Not many people found their niche in life as he had.

He rested his head on the back of the seat, staring at the house.

It was after midnight. The mother should be returning soon. He'd already unscrewed the porch light. If Timwick called him right away, he might not have to go into the house.

If the prick could make up his mind to do the smart, simple thing and let Fiske kill her.

THREE

"You know you're going to do it, Mama," Bonnie said. "I don't understand why you're worrying so much."

Eve sat up in bed and looked at the window seat. When she came, Bonnie was always in the window seat with her jean-clad legs crossed. "I don't know any such thing."

"You won't be able to help yourself. Trust me."

"Since you're only my dream, you can't know more than what I know."

Bonnie sighed. "I'm not your dream. I'm a ghost, Mama. What do I have to do to convince you? Being a ghost shouldn't be this hard."

"You can tell me where you are."

"I don't know where he buried me. I wasn't there anymore."

"Convenient."

"Mandy doesn't know either. But she likes you."

"If she's there with you, then what's her real name?"

"Names don't matter anymore to us, Mama."

"They matter to me."

Bonnie smiled. "Because you probably need to put a name to love. It's really not necessary."

"Very profound for a seven-year-old."

"Well, for goodness' sake, it's been ten years. Stop trying to trap me. Who says a ghost doesn't grow up? I couldn't stay seven forever."

"You look the same."

"Because I'm what you want to see." She leaned back against the alcove wall. "You're working too hard, Mama. I've been worrying about you. Maybe this job with Logan will be good for you."

"I'm not taking the job."

Bonnie smiled.

"I'm not," Eve repeated.

"Whatever." Bonnie was staring out the window. "You were thinking about me and the honeysuckle tonight. I like it when you feel good about me."

"You've told me that before."

"So I'm repeating it. You were hurting too much in the beginning. I couldn't get near you. . . ."

"You're not near me now. You're only a dream."

"Am I?" Bonnie looked back at her, and a loving smile lit her face. "Then you won't mind if your dream stays around a little longer? Sometimes I get so lonesome for you, Mama."

Bonnie. Love. Here.

Oh, God, here.

It didn't matter that it was a dream.

"Yes, stay," she whispered huskily. "Please stay, baby."

The sun was streaming through the window when Eve opened her eyes the next morning. She glanced at the clock and immediately sat up in bed. It was almost eight-thirty and she always got up at seven. She was surprised her mother hadn't come in to check on her.

She swung her feet to the floor and headed down the hall to the shower, rested and optimistic as she usually was after dreaming of Bonnie. A psychiatrist would have a field day with those dreams, but she didn't give a damn. She had started dreaming of Bonnie three years after her death. The dreams came frequently, but there was no telling when she'd have them or what triggered them. Maybe when she had a problem and needed to work through it? At any rate, the effect was always positive. When she awoke she felt composed and capable, as she did today, confident that she could take on the world.

And John Logan.

She dressed quickly in jeans and a loose white shirt, her uniform when she was working, and ran down the stairs to the kitchen.

"Mom, I overslept. Why didn't you—"

No one was in the kitchen. No smell of bacon, no frying pans on the stove . . . The room appeared the same as it had been at midnight when she'd come in.

And Sandra hadn't been home when she'd gone to bed. She glanced out the window, and relief rushed through her. Her mother's car was parked in its usual spot in the driveway.

She'd probably gotten in late and had overslept too. It was Saturday and she didn't have to work.

Eve would have to be careful not to mention she'd been worried, she thought ruefully. Sandra had noticed Eve's tendency toward overprotection and had a perfect right to resent it.

She poured a glass of orange juice from the refrigerator, reached for the portable phone on the wall, and dialed Joe at the precinct.

"Diane says you haven't called her," he said. "You should be phoning her, not me."

"This afternoon, I promise." She sat down at the kitchen table. "Tell me about John Logan."

There was silence at the other end of the line. "He's contacted you?"

"Last night."

"A job?"

"Yes."

"What kind of job?"

"I don't know. He's not telling me much."

"You must be thinking about it if you're calling me. What did he use as bait?"

"The Adam Fund."

"Christ, has he got your number."

"He's smart. I want to know how smart." She took a sip of orange juice. "And how honest."

"Well, he's not in the same category as your Miami drug runner."

"That's not very comforting. Has he ever done anything criminal?"

"Not as far as I know. Not in this country."

"Isn't he a U.S. citizen?"

"Yes, but when he was first establishing his company he spent a number of years in Singapore and Tokyo trying to improve his products and studying marketing strategies."

"It seems to have worked. Were you joking when you said he probably left a few bodies by the wayside?"

"Yes. We don't know much about those years he spent abroad. The people who came in contact with him are tough as hell and they respect him. Does that tell you anything?"

"That I should be careful."

"Right. He has the reputation of being a straight shooter and he inspires loyalty in his employees. But you have to consider that all of that is on the surface."

"Can you find out anything more for me?"

"Like what?"

"Anything. What's he been doing lately that's unusual? Will you dig a little deeper for me?"

"You've got it. I'll start right away." He paused. "But it's not going to come cheap. You call Diane this afternoon and you come down to the lake house with us next weekend."

"I don't have time to—" She sighed. "I'll be there."

"And without any bones rattling around in your suitcase."

"Okay."

"And you have to have a good time."

"I always have a good time with you and Diane. But I don't know why you put up with me."

"It's called friendship. Sound familiar?"

"Yeah, thanks, Joe."

"For digging out the dirt on Logan?"

"No." For having been the only one holding back the madness that had clawed at her during all those nights of horror, and for all the years of work and companionship that had followed. She cleared her throat. "Thanks for being my friend."

"Well, as your friend, I'd advise you to go very carefully with Mr. Logan."

"It's a lot of money for the kids, Joe."

"And he knew how to manipulate you."

"He didn't manipulate me. I haven't made any decision yet." She finished her orange juice. "I've got to get to work. You'll let me know?"

"That I will."

She hung up the phone and rinsed out her glass.

Coffee?

No, she'd make a pot at the lab. On weekends Mom usually came down in the middle of the morning and had coffee with her. It was a nice break for both of them.

She took the lab key from the blue bowl on the counter, ran down the porch steps, and started for the lab.

Stop thinking about Logan. She had work to do. She had Mandy's head to finish and she had to go over that packet the LAPD had sent her last week.

Logan would call her today or come to the house. She hadn't the slightest doubt. Well, he could talk all he pleased. He wouldn't get an answer from her. She had to find out more about—

The lab door was ajar.

She froze on the path.

She knew she had locked it the previous night as she always did. The key had been in the blue bowl, where she always threw it.

Mom?

No, the doorjamb was splintered as if the lock had been jimmied. It had to have been a thief.

She slowly pushed opened the door.

Blood.

Sweet Jesus, blood everywhere . . .

Blood on the walls.

On the shelves.

On the desk.

Bookcases had been hurled to the floor and appeared to have been chopped to pieces. The couch was overturned, the glass on all the picture frames had been shattered.

And the blood . . .

Her heart leapt to her throat.

Mom? Had she come to the lab and surprised the thief?

She strode forward, panic making her heart race.

"My God, it's Tom-Tom."

Eve whirled to see her mother standing in the doorway. Relief turned her knees weak.

Her mother was staring at a corner of the room. "Who would do that to a poor little cat?"

Eve's gaze followed hers and her stomach lurched. The Persian was covered with blood and barely recognizable. Tom-Tom belonged to their neighbor but spent a lot of time in their yard chasing the birds attracted by the honeysuckle.

"Mrs. Dobbins is going to be heartbroken." Her mother stepped into the room. "That old cat was the only thing she was close to in the world. Why would—" Her gaze had moved to the floor by the side of the desk. "Oh, Eve, I'm sorry. All your work . . ."

Her computer had been smashed, and beside it lay Mandy's skull, shattered and destroyed with the same cruelty and efficiency that had been used on everything else in the room.

She fell to her knees beside the pieces of the skull. It would take a miracle to put it together again.

Mandy . . . lost. Maybe forever.

"Was anything taken?" Sandra asked.

"Not that I can tell." She closed her eyes. Mandy . . . "They just destroyed everything."

"Vandals? But we've got such nice kids in the neighborhood. They wouldn't—"

"No." She opened her eyes. "Will you go call Joe, Mom? Ask him to come right away." She looked at the cat, and tears rose to her eyes. He was almost nineteen and deserved to have a kinder death. "And get a little box and a sheet. While we're waiting, we'll take Tom-Tom to Mrs. Dobbins and help her bury him. We'll tell her he was run over by a car. It's kinder than telling her that some mindless savage did this."

"Right." Sandra hurried outside.

Mindless savage.

The destruction was savage, but it was neither mindless nor random. Instead, it was thorough and systematic. Whoever had done this had wanted to shock and hurt her.

She gently stroked a piece of Mandy's skull. Violence had touched the girl even in death. It shouldn't have happened to her any more than brutality should have ended the life of that poor little cat. Both were wrong. So wrong.

She carefully gathered up the skull pieces, but there was no place to put them. The pedestal across the room was smashed like everything else. She laid the pieces on the blood-smeared desk.

But why was the skull on this side of the room? she wondered suddenly. The vandal had deliberately carried it over before smashing it. Why?

Then the thought flew out of her mind as she saw the blood dripping from the top drawer of the desk.

Oh, God, more?

She didn't want to open the drawer. She wouldn't open it.

She did.

She screamed and jumped back.

A river of blood inside and, in the middle of the sticky pool, a dead rat.

She slammed the drawer shut.

"I've got the box and sheet." Her mother had reappeared. "Do you want me to do it?"

Eve shook her head. Sandra looked as squeamish as Eve felt. "I'll do it. Is Joe coming?"

"Right away."

Eve took the sheet, braced herself, and then moved toward the cat.

It's all right, Tom-Tom. We're taking you home.

Joe met her on the doorstep of the lab two hours later. He took one look and handed her his handkerchief. "There's a smudge on your cheek."

"We just buried Tom-Tom." She wiped her tear-stained cheeks. "Mom's still with Mrs. Dobbins. She loved that cat. It was her child."

"I'd want to kill someone if they did anything to my retriever." He shook his head. "We dusted but didn't come up with any prints. He probably wore gloves. We did find partial footprints in the blood. Big, probably belongs to a man, and only one set, so I'd bet it was a single perpetrator. Is there anything missing?"

"Not that I can tell. Just . . . destroyed."

"I don't like it." Joe glanced back over his shoulder at the wreckage. "Someone took a long time to do that thorough a job. It was pretty vicious and it doesn't look random to me."

"I didn't think so either. Someone wanted to hurt me."

"Any kids in the neighborhood?"

"None I'd suspect. This was too cold."

"Have you called the insurance company?"

"Not yet."

"Better do it."

She nodded. Only the day before she'd told Logan she wasn't worried about leaving the lab unlocked. She hadn't imagined anything like this could happen. "I feel sick, Joe."

"I know." He took her hand and squeezed it comfortingly. "I'll have a black and white keep an eye on the house. Or how about you and your mom coming to my place for a few days?"

She shook her head.

"Okay." He hesitated. "I should get back to the precinct. I want to check records, see if there's been any similar crimes in the area lately. You going to be all right?"

"I'll be fine. Thanks for coming, Joe."

"I wish I could do more. We'll question your neighbors and see if we come up with anything."

She nodded. "Except for Mrs. Dobbins. Don't send anyone to her house."

"Right. If you need me, just call."

She watched him walk away and then turned back to the lab. She didn't want to go inside. She didn't want to see that violence and ugliness again.

She had to do it. She had to make sure nothing was missing and then call the insurance company. She braced herself and then walked in. Again, the blood struck her like a blow. God, she had been so frightened when she had thought that blood might be her mother's.

Dead cats and butchered rats and blood. So much blood.

No.

She ran out the door and sank down on the doorstep. Cold. She was so cold. She clasped her arms around her body in a futile attempt to banish the chill.

"There's a police car parked outside. Are you all right?"

She looked up to see Logan standing a few feet away. She couldn't deal with him now. "Go away."

"What's wrong?"

"Go away."

He looked behind her at the doorway. "Something happened?"

"Yes."

"I'll be right back." He went past her into the lab. He was back beside her in a few minutes. "Very nasty."

"They killed my neighbor's cat. They smashed Mandy."

"I saw the shattered bones on the desk." He paused. "Was that where you found them?"

She shook her head. "On the floor beside it."

"But you and your mother weren't hurt?"

Lord, she wished she could stop shivering. "Go away, I don't want to talk to you."

"Where's your mother?"

"At Mrs. Dobbins's. Her cat— Go away."

"Not until someone's here to take care of you." He pulled her to her feet. "Come on, we're going to the house."

"I don't need anyone to take care—" He was half tugging her down the path. "Let me go. Don't touch me."

"As soon as I get you to the house and get something hot inside you."

She pulled her arm away from him. "I don't have time to sit around having coffee. I have to call the insurance company."

"I'll do it." He nudged her gently up the steps and into the kitchen. "I'll handle everything."

"I don't want you to handle everything. I want you to go away."

"Then be quiet and let me get you something to drink." He pushed her down into a chair at the table. "It's the quickest way to get rid of me."

"I don't want to sit—" She gave up. She was in no shape to do battle just then. "Hurry up."

"Yes, ma'am." He turned toward the cabinet. "Where's the coffee?"

"In the blue canister on the counter."

He ran water into the carafe. "When did it happen?"

"Last night. Sometime after midnight."

"You locked the lab?"

"Of course I did."

"Easy." He measured coffee into the coffeemaker. "You didn't hear anything?"

"No."

"I'm surprised, with all that damage."

"Joe said he knew exactly what he was doing."

He turned on the coffeepot. "Any idea who did it?"

She shook her head. "No fingerprints. Gloves maybe."

He took a cardigan from a hook on the laundry room door. "Gloves. Then it wasn't done by amateurs."

"I told you that."

He draped the sweater over her shoulders. "So you did."

"And this is my mother's sweater."

"You need it. I don't think she'd mind."

She did need it. She couldn't stop shivering.

He picked up the phone.

"What are you doing?"

"I'm calling my personal assistant, Margaret Wilson. What's the name of your insurance company?"

"Security America, but you don't—"

"Hello, Margaret. John," he said into the phone. "I need you to— Yes, I know it's a Saturday." He listened patiently. "Yes, Margaret. It's a terrible imposition. I'm duly grateful for your forbearance. Now, will you shut up and let me tell you what I need?"

Eve stared at him in surprise. Whatever she had expected, it was not Logan browbeaten by one of his employees.

He grimaced at Eve, still listening. "Now?" he repeated into the phone.

Evidently this time the answer was an affirmative, because he said, "Make a report to Security America for Eve Duncan." He spelled the last name. "Break-in, vandalism, and possible theft. If you need details or verification, call Joe Quinn, Atlanta P.D. I want a claims investigator out here right away, and arrange for a cleaning crew. I want that lab spic and span by midnight." He sighed. "No, I don't want you to fly out here and do it yourself, Margaret. Sarcasm isn't necessary. Just take care of it. I don't want Eve Duncan bothered with anything more than signing her name to a claim report. I also want a security force out here protecting the property and Eve and Sandra Duncan. Call me if you run into any trouble. No, I'm not doubting your efficiency, I just—" He listened a moment more and then said gently but firmly, "Goodbye, Margaret." He hung up, then reached into the cabinet for a cup. "Margaret will take care of it."

"She doesn't want to."

"She just wants to make sure I never take her for granted. If I'd done it myself, she would have accused me of not trusting her to take care of it." He poured hot coffee into the cup. "Cream or sugar?"

"Black. Has she been with you a long time?"

"Nine years." He set the coffee down in front of her. "We need to go back out there and collect anything that you don't want the insurance investigator going through."

"I don't think I need to hurry." She took a sip of coffee. "I've never seen an insurance company work that fast."

"Trust Margaret. Someone will be here soon." He poured himself a cup of coffee and sat down opposite her. "She'll regard it as a challenge."

"I don't know Margaret, so I can't trust her. Just as I can't trust you." She met his gaze. "And I don't need any private security force out here. Joe's going to have a police car keep an eye on us."

"Good. But a few extra precautions never hurt anybody. They won't get in your way." He studied her as he took a swallow of his coffee. "Your color is better. I thought you were going to flip out."

She did feel better. The shaking had eased a little. "Don't be stupid. I wasn't going to faint. I deal with horror stories every day. I was just upset."

"You had a right to be, and this particular horror story hit very close to home. That makes a difference."

Yes, her private life had been serene and free from violence since that night at the prison. She hadn't been ready to have this ugliness erupt. "It's more than that. It makes me feel like a victim. I swore I'd never be— I *hate* it."

"I can see that you do."

She finished her coffee and stood up. "If you really think someone from the insurance company will be coming out right away, I'd better go back and finish checking out the lab."

"Take a little more time. Like you said, there's no hurry."

"I want to get it over with." She moved toward the door. "My mother will be coming home soon and I don't want her to feel that she has to do it with me."

"You're very protective of your mother." He followed her down the steps. "You're close?"

"Yes. We didn't used to be, but now we're good friends."

"Friends?"

"Well, she's only sixteen years older than I am. We sort of grew up together." She glanced over her shoulder. "You don't have to go with me, you know."

"I know." He opened the lab door for her. "But Margaret would be very upset with me if I made her work and didn't do a thing myself."

FOUR

"Lots of blood," Logan said matter-of-factly. "But the cleaning crew will take care of it." He nodded at the pile of articles on the floor by the smashed bookcase. "Why don't you check for anything there that can be salvaged? I see a couple of photographs."

She nodded and knelt by the bookcase. Being here was easier with Logan, she realized in surprise. His matter-of-factness lightened the darkness. There was blood; it must be cleaned. There was destruction; probe to see what could be saved.

And the pictures of Bonnie and her mother could be saved, she saw with relief. Only one corner was ripped on each. "It's okay."

"Good. Then whoever did this isn't as clever as I thought. He didn't realize how tearing up the picture might hurt you." He was at the desk. "I'll check the drawers and see if there's—"

"Wait! There's a—" It was too late. Logan had already opened the drawer containing the dead rat.

The rat was gone. The police must have taken it, but the drawer was still brimming with blood.

He grimaced. "I'm glad I opened this before the cleaning crew did. We might have had some trouble keeping them here." He pulled out the drawer and carried it over to the door. "I'll get rid of it for you."

He hadn't even displayed a flicker of surprise. "You seem to be taking all this in stride."

"Remind me to tell you what happened to my office after my first major takeover. At least no one defecated in here. Keep on looking. I'll be right back."

There wasn't much else to look through. The books were ripped, the hourglass her mother had bought for her at Six Flags was broken, the base of the pedestal was chopped into two pieces and—

The pedestal. Mandy.

Why had Mandy been carried to the other side of the room before being shattered? The strangeness of it had occurred to her before, but she had been too dazed to have it sink home. Everything else about the destruction seemed coldly calculated. What had been the purpose of the skull . . .

She got to her feet and moved quickly to the other side of the desk. The only object that had been smashed in that particular spot was the computer. And the skull had been brought from the pedestal to be destroyed with it.

She stared down at the computer and suddenly made the connection. "My God."

"I thought you'd get the message once you thought about it." Logan was standing in the doorway, watching her.

"You knew it."

He nodded. "Once you told me where the skull had been found. He tried to make it clear, didn't he? The Logan computer. The skull. A warning."

"Who?"

"I don't know. Evidently someone doesn't want me to use your services."

Her gaze traveled around the room. "And that's what this is all about?"

"Yes."

She looked back at him. "And you weren't going to tell me?"

"Not if you didn't figure it out yourself," he said bluntly. "I was afraid it would tip the scales against me. This was meant to frighten you, and it did."

Yes, she had been frightened. She had been scared and sick and saddened. Besides the destruction of property, Tom-Tom's life had been taken and Mandy's identity had been forever stolen.

And all of it had been done to manipulate her away from a certain path. Fury burned through her as she remembered Mrs. Dobbins's face that morning.

"Damn him." Her voice was shaking with anger. "Damn him to hell."

"I'll vote for that." Logan's gaze was narrowed on her face. "I hope there's some significance to the fact that you're damning him and not me."

"Vicious bastard." She strode out of the lab. She couldn't ever remember being so enraged except the day Fraser had been caught. She wanted to *kill* someone. "He didn't care. People should care. How could he—" She knew how he could do it. He was probably a crazy freak like Fraser. Cruel and cold and without mercy. "I want him to pay for it."

"Then I'll find out who it is for you," Logan said.

She whirled on him. "How can you do that? Did you lie when you said you didn't know who he is?"

"I don't know him but I know who probably hired him."

"Who?"

He shook his head. "I can't tell you, but I'll find out who did this." He paused. "If you'll come with me."

"Tell me who hired him."

"You'll find out yourself if you come and do the job. Why not? It will take time to set up a new lab. You'll just be spinning your wheels now. I'll up the money for the Adam Fund another two hundred thousand and throw in the son of a bitch who did this to you."

A sudden thought occurred to her. "Maybe *you* had this done to push me into going with you."

"It would have been too chancy. You could just as well have jumped the other way. Besides, I don't kill helpless animals."

"But you're willing to take advantage of what's happened."

"You bet I am. Is it a deal?"

She looked around the bloodstained room, and once again rage rushed through her. "I'll think about it."

"What if I raise the—"

"Stop pushing me. I said I'd think about it." She picked up a box from the floor that had once contained printer paper and began to put Mandy's skull fragments inside. Her hands were still shaking with anger, she noticed. She had to be calm. "Go away. I'll call you when I've made up my mind."

"I need to move fast on—"

"I'll call you."

She could feel his gaze on her and expected him to continue to try to persuade her.

"I'm at the Ritz-Carlton Buckhead." He paused. "I shouldn't tell you this. It compromises my bargaining position. But I'm a desperate man, Eve. I have to have your help. There isn't anything I wouldn't do to get it. Call me and give me your price. I'll pay it."

When she looked up, he was gone.

What would make a man like Logan that desperate? If there was any desperation in him before, he'd kept it well hidden. Maybe the confession of vulnerability had been a ploy.

Well, she would consider that later. She needed to get back to the house so her mother wouldn't come looking for her here. She picked up the pictures and Mandy's box and started for the door. She could try to put the skull back together. Even if she couldn't get a completely accurate structure, it might be enough for computer imaging—

Another wave of helpless fury washed over her as she realized that couldn't happen. Joe had told her they had no idea who Mandy could be, so how would they find a photograph? Her only hope had been of building the face and using that face to lead to someone, anyone, who could identify her. That hope had been crushed by the bastard who had deliberately smashed the skull to warn her off.

"Eve?" It was her mother walking toward her down the path. "That was the insurance company on the phone. They're sending a claims adjuster out right away."

"Are they?" Evidently Logan's Margaret had prevailed. "How's Mrs. Dobbins?"

"Better. Do you think we should get her a little kitten?"

"Not for a few months. Let her get over the first hurt."

Sandra's gaze went to the lab. "I'm sorry, Eve. All your files and equipment."

"They'll be replaced."

"This is such a nice, quiet neighborhood. Things like this never happen here. It kind of makes you scared." She frowned. "Do you suppose we should get some kind of security system?"

"We'll talk about it." She opened the kitchen door. "There's coffee, would you like some?"

"No, I had a cup with Mrs. Dobbins." She paused. "I called Ron. He suggested we go out for lunch to get my mind off it. I told him no, of course."

But it was obvious she wanted to go, Eve thought. Why shouldn't she? She'd had a hell of a morning and she wanted comfort. "There's no reason for you not to go. You can't do anything here."

"You're sure?"

"I'm sure. Go call him back."

She still hesitated. "He asked you to go along too. You said you wanted to meet him."

"Not now. You said the insurance people were coming."

"I'll come right back."

Eve set Mandy's box down on the kitchen counter. "Stay out as long as you like."

Sandra shook her head and said firmly, "Two hours. No longer."

She waited until the door shut behind her mother before letting her fixed smile fade. It was stupid and selfish to feel this abandoned. Sandra had done everything she could to help. She just didn't realize how alone Eve was feeling.

Stop whining. You are alone. You've learned to deal with it. Even Sandra was sometimes more of a responsibility than a companion, but that was okay. She wasn't going to start feeling sorry for herself just because some slimeball had tried to scare her.

Fraser.

Why did he keep invading her mind?

Because she felt as helpless and terrified as in those days after he had invaded her life. He had killed her daughter and she had been forced to plead with the authorities not to execute him. She had even gone to see him at the prison and begged him to tell her about Bonnie.

He had smiled that charming smile that had lured twelve children to their death, shook his head, and told her no. The bastard had even refused appeal so the books would be closed and the children would never be found. She had wanted to tear him apart, but she had been trapped, caught by the words he wouldn't say.

But she wasn't helpless now, or powerless. She didn't have to be a victim. She could take action. The knowledge sent a rush of fierce satisfaction through her. Logan could find who destroyed the lab for her.

If she paid his price.

Was she willing to pay it? She hadn't been sure before. She had been going to think rationally and unemotionally about the proposition before she gave him her answer.

Logan was probably banking on the fact that she didn't feel rational or unemotional now. He would take advantage of every weakness she showed him.

Then don't show him weakness. Take what you need and avoid the traps. She could do it. She was as smart as Logan and, as she had told him, she knew how to protect herself.

She was not a victim.

"I'll do it," Eve said when Logan picked up the receiver. "But on my terms. Half my fee up front and the entire amount going to the Adam Fund deposited in their account before I leave this house."

"Done. I'll do it by electronic transfer today."

"I want proof that it's been done. I'll call the fund headquarters in four hours and make sure they've received it."

"Fair enough."

"And I want my mother and my home protected while I'm gone."

"I've told you that you'd have security."

"You also promised me you'd find out who destroyed my lab."

"I've already got someone on it."

"And if I find out that what I'm doing will make me an accomplice to any crime, I'm bailing out."

"Okay."

"You're being very agreeable."

"I told you to name your price." She was going to *do* it. Hell, he would have promised her the world. "Pack a suitcase. I'll be around to pick you up later this evening."

"*If* I receive the confirmation from the Adam Fund."

"Exception noted."

"And I have to tell my mother where we're going."

"Tell her you'll be moving around and you'll call her every other evening."

"*Will* I be moving around?"

"Probably. I should be there by ten tonight."

He hung up the phone. *Yes.* He had her. After he'd met Eve and gauged her toughness, he'd been afraid it would take much longer. He might still be arguing with her if the break-in hadn't made her so angry. Maybe he should thank that bastard Timwick. Authorizing that stupidity had been exactly the wrong thing for him to do. There had been enough violence to anger Eve, but not enough to completely scare her off.

And the incident had warned Logan that Timwick was suspicious and possibly had inside knowledge of his actions. Interesting.

Timwick was smart and didn't often make mistakes. When he learned that Eve had not been scared off, he would correct the error and up the ante.

And next time he would make sure it wasn't a cat that died.

A block from Eve's house Fiske smiled as he pulled the electronic listening piece out of his ear and laid it on the seat beside him. He'd always loved gadgets, and particularly admired this powerful X436 amplifier. The concept of hearing through walls was so intriguing. Actually, in this case, it was through panes of glass, but the feeling of power and control was the same.

That Eve Duncan wanted his head as part of her price for going with Logan was flattering. It showed how well he'd done his job. The dead cat had been a masterstroke. Death of pets always hit the nerve. He'd learned that when he'd killed the dog that had belonged to his fifth-grade teacher. The bitch had come to school with swollen eyes for a week.

He'd done his job; it wasn't his fault that Timwick's orders had backfired. Fiske had told him he needed a deeper strike, but Timwick had said it was premature, that it might not be needed.

Chicken bastard.

"Your front porch light is out," Logan said when Eve opened the door. "Do you have a bulb? I'll change it."

"I think there's one in the kitchen cabinet." She turned and started down the hall. "Funny, I changed it just last week."

The porch light was on when she returned a few minutes later with the new bulb. "You got it on."

"It was just a little loose. Is your mother here?"

"She's in the kitchen." She wrinkled her nose. "She took my going away very well. She's already planning on repainting the lab."

"Could I meet her?"

"Of course. I'll go get—"

"Mr. Logan?" Sandra was coming toward them. "I'm Sandra Duncan. I'm so glad you're taking Eve away during this stressful period. She needs a little vacation."

"I'm afraid it won't be a vacation, but it will definitely be a change. I'll try not to work her too hard." Logan smiled. "She's lucky to have someone like you taking care of her."

Logan had turned on the charm and her mother was melting, Eve noticed.

"We take care of each other," Sandra said.

"Eve tells me you're going to paint her lab. That break-in was a terrible thing."

Sandra nodded. "But the cleaning crew has scrubbed it almost spotless. When she gets back, she'll never know anything bad happened there."

"Well, I feel guilty taking her away before they've caught whoever did it. Eve told you that I'd arranged for security?"

"Yes, but Joe will take—"

"I'll feel better adding my bit. If you don't mind, I'll have someone call and check in every night."

"I don't mind, but it's not necessary." She gave Eve a hug. "Don't work too hard. Get some rest."

"You'll be okay?"

"I'll be fine. I'm glad to get rid of you. Now maybe I'll be able to invite Ron here for dinner without worrying about you giving him the third degree."

"I wouldn't have—" She grinned. "Well, maybe I would have asked him a *few* questions."

"See?"

Eve picked up her briefcase. "Take care of yourself. I'll call as often as I can."

"A pleasure to meet you, Ms. Duncan." Logan shook her hand, then picked up Eve's suitcase. "I'll take good care of her and bring her back as soon as I can."

That charisma again, flowing out and enveloping Sandra.

"I'm sure you will. Good-bye, Mr. Logan."

He smiled. "John."

She smiled back. "John."

She stood at the front door, watching them as they went down the stairs and the front walk. She gave a final wave and closed the door.

"What was the purpose of that display?" Eve asked.

He opened the car door for her. "Display?"

"You sent so much honey flowing toward Mom that she couldn't move."

"I was merely being polite."

"You were being charming."

"I've found it greases a few wheels. You object?"

"It's all lies. I hate it."

"Why do—" He paused. "Fraser. I was told he was a Ted Bundy type. Dammit, I'm no Fraser, Eve."

She knew he wasn't. No one was like Fraser except Lucifer himself. "I can't help— It just reminds me of— It annoys me."

"Since we'll be working together, that's the last thing we need. I promise I'll be as blunt and rude as I know how."

"Good."

"Not so good. I've been known to be pretty ugly on occasion." He started the car. "Ask Margaret."

"From the way you describe her, I doubt if she'd put up with it."

"True. She can be much nastier than me. But I do try."

"Where are we going?"

"Where did you tell your mother we were going?"

"I didn't tell her. I said you're based on the West Coast and she assumed that's where we're headed. She and Joe Quinn have my digital number in case of an emergency." She repeated, "Where *are* we going?"

"Now? The airport. We're taking my plane to my place in Virginia."

"I'll need equipment. Most of my stuff was destroyed. He missed only a few instruments."

"No problem. I've already equipped a lab for you."

"What?"

"I knew you'd need a place to work."

"What if I'd turned you down?"

"I would have looked for second best." He smiled and added in a melodramatic growl, "Or kidnapped you and locked you up in the lab until you did my bidding."

He was joking. Or was he? she wondered suddenly.

"I'm sorry. Too light? Just testing your sense of humor. By the way, you failed miserably. Is that rude enough for you?"

"Yes, I have a sense of humor."

"I haven't seen it." He drove down the exit ramp onto the freeway. "But don't worry, it's not required for the job."

"I wasn't worried. I don't care what you think of me. I just want to get this job done. And I'm tired of going at this blind. When are we—"

"We'll talk about it when we get to Virginia."

"I want to talk about it now."

"Later." He glanced at the rearview mirror. "This is a rental car and not secured."

At first she didn't realize what he meant. "You mean it's bugged?"

"I don't know. I just don't want to take a chance."

She was silent a moment. "Are your cars usually . . . secured?"

"Yes, since I sometimes do business as I move from place to place. Leaks can be costly."

"I imagine they can be. Particularly when you play around with something like a buried skeleton."

"I'm not playing." He glanced at the rearview mirror again. "Believe me, Eve."

It was the second time in seconds he had checked the mirror, and the traffic wasn't that heavy. She glanced over her shoulder. "Are we being followed?"

"Maybe. Not as far as I can tell."

"Would you tell me if we were?"

"It depends on if I thought it would scare you off." He glanced at her. "Would it?"

"No. I gave you my terms and I'm committed. The only thing that would make me back away now would be if I thought you were lying to me. I won't stand for that, Logan."

"Point taken."

"I mean what I say. You hobnob with all those politicians who talk out of both sides of their mouths. I'm not like that."

"My, how sanctimonious you sound."

"Think what you like. I'm being up-front with you. I just don't want you to make any mistakes about me."

"Point taken. I assure you, no one could mistake you for either a politician or a diplomat," he said dryly.

"I take that as a compliment."

"And I take it you don't like politicians."

"Does anyone? These days we all seem to have to choose the lesser evil."

"There are some people out there who want to do a good job."

"Are you trying to convert me? Forget it. I don't like Republicans any more than I do Democrats."

"Who did you vote for in the last election?"

"Chadbourne. But not because he was a Democrat. He convinced me he'd be a decent president."

"And you think he has?"

She shrugged. "He got the aid to dependent children bill passed even though Congress had him gridlocked."

"A gridlock's like a logjam. Sometimes you have to toss in something explosive to break it up."

"Those fund-raisers you've been giving aren't exactly explosive."

"It depends on your viewpoint. I do what I can. I've always

believed a person has to take a stand. If you want to change things, you have to work with the system."

"I don't have to work with it. I don't have to have anything to do with it except on election day."

"No, you bury yourself in your lab with your bones."

"Why not?" She gave him a sly glance. "They're better company than most politicians."

To her surprise, he didn't take the bait. "My God, maybe you do have a sense of humor." He chuckled. "Suppose we agree to disagree. My dad always told me never to argue religion or politics with a woman."

"How sexist of him."

"He was a great guy, but he lived in a different world. He wouldn't have known how to deal with women like you or Margaret."

"Is he still alive?"

"No, he died when I was in college."

"Am I going to meet Margaret?"

He nodded. "I called her this afternoon and told her to be at the house."

"Wasn't that a little inconsiderate? She had to fly in from California, didn't she?"

"I needed her."

The bald statement said it all, she thought. He might pretend to be browbeaten by this Margaret, but he expected her to jump when he called.

"I asked her nicely. Nary a whip in sight."

"Sometimes they don't have to be in view to get the effect."

"Well, I promise I won't use coercion on you, visible or otherwise."

She met his gaze with a cool one of her own. "No, you won't. Don't even try, Logan."

"They're boarding now," Fiske said. "What do you want me to do? Find out his flight plan and follow him?"

"No, his secretary told her father she was going to the Virginia house. He's got that place loaded with more security than Fort Knox. We've got a surveillance team outside the gates, but we won't be able to touch him once he's inside."

"Then I should move before he gets there."

"I told you, he's too visible. We don't want to do anything to him unless it's absolutely necessary."

"Then I'll go back to the house. The mother is still—"

"No, she's not going anywhere. You can pick up that string later if we decide we need a distraction. We have something more urgent for you to do. Come back here."

FIVE

The jet landed at a small private field near Arlington, Virginia. Their luggage was immediately transferred into a stretch limousine parked by the hangar.

All the ease that money could buy, Eve thought wryly. No doubt the chauffeur would display the obsequious formality of a Wodehouse character.

The red-haired driver got out. "Hi, John. Good trip?" He was freckled, good-looking, not over thirty, and dressed in jeans and a checked shirt that reflected the blue of his eyes.

"Good enough. Gil Price, Eve Duncan."

Gil shook her hand. "The bone lady. I saw your picture on *60 Minutes*. You're prettier in person. They should have concentrated on you instead of on that skull."

"Thank you, but I had no desire to appear on national television. I've had enough of cameras in my life."

"John doesn't like cameras either. I had to break one

last year in Paris." He grimaced. "And then John had to settle out of court with the bastard who claimed I'd broken his head instead of his camera. I hate paparazzi."

"Well, the paparazzi don't usually trail me around, so you won't have that problem."

"I will if you hang around with John." He opened the back door. "Hop in and I'll get you to Barrett House PDQ."

"Barrett House? It sounds very Dickens."

"Nope, it used to be an inn during the Civil War. John bought it last year and had it completely remodeled."

"Has Margaret arrived?" Logan asked as he followed Eve into the car.

"Two hours ago and crabby as hell. I'm charging you hazard pay for that pickup." Gil jumped into the driver's seat. "I can't understand it. How can she not love me? Everyone loves me."

"It must be a flaw in her character," Logan said. "It certainly couldn't be because there's anything wrong with you."

"My thought exactly." Gil started the car and flicked on the CD player. The limo was immediately filled with the doleful strains of "Feed Jake."

"The window, Gil," Logan said.

"Oh, right." He grinned over his shoulder at Eve. "John used to have a Jeep, but he can't stand country music so he got this hearse so he could have a privacy window."

"I like country," Logan said. "I just can't stand those songs of woe you hug to your bosom. Bloodstained wedding gowns, dogs at grave sites . . ."

"That's because you're full of mush and you don't like to show it. Do you think I haven't seen your eyes water? Now, take 'Feed Jake.' It's a—"

"You take it. The window."

"Okay." The window glided up soundlessly and the music faded out.

"I hope you don't mind," Logan said.

"No, I have trouble with sad songs. But I can't imagine you crying in your beer over one."

He shrugged. "I'm human. Those country-song writers know exactly how to hit you."

Her gaze shifted to the back of Gil's head. "He's nice. Not exactly what I expected in one of your employees."

"Gil's not what anyone expects, but he's a good driver."

"And bodyguard?"

"That too. He used to be in the Air Force Military Police, but he doesn't respond well to discipline."

"Do you?"

"No, but I usually try to work my way around it instead of punching people out." He gestured out the side window. "We'll be on my land in a few minutes. It's pretty country with lots of woods and meadows."

"I suppose so." It was too dark to see more than shadowy trees. She was still absorbed with the comparison Logan had made between himself and Price. "And what do you do when you can't work around anyone who tries to discipline you?"

"Why, punch them out." He smiled. "That's why Gil and I get along. We're soul mates." They turned a curve in the road, and a twelve-foot-tall elaborate wrought iron fence loomed before them.

She watched Gil press a control on the dashboard, and the gates swung slowly open.

"Is the fence electrified too?" she asked.

He nodded. "And I have a security man monitoring the grounds by video camera from the carriage house."

She felt a sudden chill. "Very high-tech. I want my own remote to open those gates."

He looked at her.

"Gates that keep people out can also keep them in. I don't like the idea of being in a cage."

"I'm not trying to keep you prisoner, Eve."

"No, not if you can get what you want any other way. But what if you can't?"

"I can't force you to work."

"Couldn't you? You're a very clever man, Logan. I want my own remote to open those gates."

"Tomorrow. It will have to be programmed." He smiled sardonically. "I think it's safe to assume I won't try to bulldoze you in the next twenty-four hours."

"Tomorrow." She leaned forward as the house came into view. The moon had come out from behind the clouds and lit the place. Barrett House was a sprawling two-story stone building that looked like the nineteenth-century inn Gil had said it had once been. There was nothing pretentious about it, and the ivy covering the walls softened the stone. As Gil stopped the car in front of the front door, she asked, "Why buy an inn that you had to restore? Why not just build a new house?"

Logan climbed out of the car and held out his hand to help her. "It had a few unique features that appealed to me."

"Don't tell me. It had its own graveyard."

He grinned. "The Barrett family cemetery is just over the hill. But that wasn't why I bought the inn." He opened the tall mahogany front door. "There aren't any live-in servants. I have cleaning people come in from town twice a week. We'll have to fend for ourselves in the kitchen."

"It doesn't matter. I'm not accustomed to servants, and food isn't a high priority for me."

His gaze ran over her. "I can tell. You're lean as a greyhound."

"I like greyhounds," Gil said as he carried the luggage into the hall. "Graceful and those great, big wistful eyes. I had one once. Nearly killed me when he died. Where do you want her bags?"

"The first door at the head of the stairs," Logan said.

"Right." Gil started up the steps. "Pretty boring. My quarters are in the old carriage house, Eve. You should ask him to put you out there. More privacy."

"This will be more convenient to the lab," Logan said.

And more convenient for Logan to keep tabs on me, Eve thought.

"Margaret must have gone to bed. You'll meet her in the morning. I think you'll find everything you need in your room."

"I want to see my lab."

"Now?"

"Yes. You may not have equipped it properly. I may have to supplement it."

"Then by all means come with me. It's one of the added rooms in the back. I haven't seen it myself. I had Margaret get you everything she thought you'd need."

"The efficient Margaret again."

"Not only efficient. Exceptional."

She followed Logan across a huge living room with a fireplace large enough to walk into, plank floors covered by woven hemp carpets, and oversized leather furniture. It looked like a lodge, she decided.

He led her down a short hall and then opened a door. "Here you are."

Coldness. Sterility. Gleaming stainless steel and glass.

"Oops." Logan grimaced. "This must be Margaret's idea of scientific heaven. I'll try to warm it up for you."

"It doesn't matter. I won't be here that long." She strode over to the pedestal. It was sturdy and adjustable. The three video cameras on tripods next to it were top-notch, as were the computer, mixer, and VCR. She moved over to the workbench. The measuring instruments were high-grade, but she preferred the ones she had brought with her. She took the wooden box from the shelf above the bench, and sixteen sets of eyes stared up at her. All variations of hazel, gray, green, blue, brown. "Blue and brown would have been sufficient," she said. "Brown is the most prevalent eye color."

"I told her to get you everything you could possibly need."

"Well, she did that." She turned to look at him. "When can I start to work?"

"In a day or two. I'm waiting for word."

"And I'm supposed to sit here and twiddle my thumbs?"

"Would you like me to dig you up one of the Barretts to practice on?"

"No, I want to finish the job and go home."

"You gave me two weeks." He turned away. "Come on, you're tired. I'll show you to your room."

She *was* tired. She felt as if a thousand years had passed since she had walked to her lab that morning. She had a sudden pang of homesickness. What was she doing here? She didn't belong in this strange house with a man she didn't trust.

The Adam Fund. It didn't matter whether she belonged here or not. She had a job and a purpose. She came toward him. "I meant what I said. I won't do anything criminal."

"I know you meant it."

Which didn't mean he accepted it. She flicked off the overhead light and moved past him into the hall. "Are you going to tell me why you brought me here and why I should do what you want me to do?"

He smiled. "Why, it's your patriotic duty."

"Bull." Her gaze narrowed on his face. "Politics?"

"Why do you assume that?"

"You're known for your activities in public view and behind the scenes."

"I suppose I should be relieved that you no longer think I'm a mass murderer."

"I didn't say that. I'm exploring all options. Politics?"

"Possibly."

A sudden thought occurred to her. "My God, are you trying to smear someone?"

"I don't believe in smear campaigns. Let's say things aren't always what they seem, and I believe in bringing the truth to light."

"If it's to your advantage."

He nodded mockingly. "Of course."

"I don't want to be part of it."

"You're not part of it . . . unless I'm right. If I'm wrong, you go home and we forget you were ever here." He was preceding her up the stairs. "What could be more fair?"

Maybe his reason didn't involve politics. Maybe it was entirely personal. "We'll see."

"Yes, we will." He opened her door and stood aside. "Good night, Eve."

"Good night." She went inside and closed the door. The room was country comfortable with a canopy bed with a rust and cream quilt, simple pine furniture. The only thing in it that interested her was the telephone on the end table. She sat down on the bed and dialed Joe Quinn's number.

"Hello," he answered sleepily.

"Joe, Eve."

His voice lost all trace of drowsiness. "Is everything okay?"

"Fine. I'm sorry to wake you, but I just wanted to tell you where I am and give you my phone number here." She rattled off the number printed on the extension. "Got it?"

"Got it. Where the hell are you?"

"Barrett House. Logan's place in Virginia."

"And this couldn't wait until morning?"

"Probably. But I wanted you to know. I feel . . . disconnected."

"You sound uneasy as the devil. You took the job?"

"Why else would I be here?"

"And what's scaring you?"

"I'm not scared."

"The hell you're not. You haven't called me in the middle of the night since Bonnie—"

"I'm not afraid. I just wanted you to know." She had a thought. "Logan has a driver, Gil Price. He used to be in the Air Force Military Police."

"You want me to check him out?"

"I . . . think so."

"No problem."

"And you'll watch out for my mother while I'm gone?"

"Sure, you know I will. I'll ask Diane to go over and have coffee with her tomorrow afternoon."

"Thanks, Joe. Go back to sleep."

"Yeah, sure." He paused. "I don't like this. Be careful, Eve."

"There's nothing to be careful about. Bye."

She hung up the phone and stood. She'd take a shower, wash her hair, and then get to bed. She really shouldn't have woken up Joe, but hearing a familiar voice made her feel better. Everything about this place was low-key and unthreatening, including likable Gil Price, but she was still on edge. She couldn't tell how much was authentic and how much had been layered on to disarm her, and she didn't like being so isolated.

But now she had a link to the outside world.

Joe would be her safety net while she was walking this tightrope.

"Eve?" Diane Quinn rolled over in bed and propped her head on her hand. "Is everything all right?"

Joe nodded. "I think so. I don't know. She took a job that may not be— Forget it. Probably nothing to worry about."

But Joe would worry, Diane thought. He always worried about Eve.

He lay back down and pulled up the covers. "Go by and visit her mother tomorrow, will you?"

"Sure." She turned out the light and cuddled closer. "Whatever you say. Now go back to sleep."

"I will."

He wouldn't go back to sleep. He'd lie there in the darkness thinking and worrying about Eve. Smother the resentment. She had a good marriage. Joe had inherited enough money from his parents to give them a comfortable lifestyle even without his salary. He was thoughtful, generous, and great in bed. She'd known when she married him that he and Eve were a package deal. It hadn't taken her long to realize the bond between Joe and Eve was too strong to break. They were so close, sometimes they finished each other's sentences.

But that bond wasn't sexual. Not yet. Maybe never. That part of him was still hers.

So smother the envy and resentment. Be Eve's friend, be Joe's wife.

Because she was bitterly aware she couldn't be one without being the other.

• • •

"She called Joe Quinn thirty minutes ago." Gil set a sheet of paper on the desk in front of Logan. "Here's a transcript Mark made of the conversation."

Logan smiled faintly as he glanced through the text. "I don't believe she trusts us, Gil."

"Smart lady." Gil threw himself into the easy chair across the room and draped a leg over the arm. "Now, I'm not surprised she doesn't trust you. You're pretty transparent, but it takes someone ultraperceptive to suspect me."

"It's not your acting ability, it's those damn freckles." He frowned. "I've been trying to contact Scott Maren in Jordan. Any calls?"

"No calls." Then he snapped his fingers. "Except from your lawyer, Novak."

"He can wait."

"Do you want Mark to foul up the connection if she tries to call again?"

He shook his head. "She'd only use her digital. She still might if she knows the phone in her room is bugged."

"Whatever you say." He paused. "When do we go for it?"

"Soon."

He lifted a brow. "You wouldn't be holding out on me, would you?"

"I have to make sure everything's right. Timwick's been too close on my tail."

"You can trust me, John."

"I said I'm waiting."

"All right, you closemouthed bastard." Gil stood up and strolled toward the door. "But I don't like going in blind."

"You won't."

"I'll take that as a promise. Get some sleep."

"I will."

When the door closed behind Gil, Logan glanced down at the transcript again and then tossed it to one side. Joe Quinn. He couldn't afford to underestimate the detective. Eve had inspired intense loyalty in Quinn. Loyalty and friendship and what else? he wondered. Quinn was married, but that didn't matter.

Hell, it wasn't any of his business if it didn't interfere with what he needed Eve to do. Besides, he had enough to worry about.

Scott Maren was wandering around Jordan and might be taken down at any minute.

Timwick might have seen through Logan and drawn conclusions. Those conclusions would frighten him enough to give the order to secure his position.

Logan couldn't wait to get hold of Maren.

He pulled out his personal phone book and flipped it open to the back page. There were only three names and telephone numbers on the page.

Dora Bentz.

James Cadro.

Scott Maren.

Bentz's and Cadro's telephones might be bugged, but he should still call and verify they were all right. Then he'd send someone to pick them up.

He reached for the telephone and dialed the first phone number.

Dora Bentz.

The phone was ringing.

Fiske finished tying the woman's legs to the bedposts and pushed her nightgown up above her waist.

She was in her fifties, but she had damn nice legs. Too bad about that pouchy belly. She should have worked out, he thought. Situps would have taken care of that pouch. He did two hundred situps a day and his own belly was iron hard.

He got a broom out of the kitchen closet and came back to the bed.

The phone was still ringing. Persistent.

He shoved the broom up the woman. The killing had to look

like a sex crime, but he wouldn't risk ejaculating inside her. Semen was evidence. Many serial killers had trouble ejaculating anyway, and the broom was a nice touch. It spelled out woman hatred and home desecration.

Anything else?

Six deep, savage wounds on her breasts, duct tape over her mouth, the open window . . .

No, it was a clean job.

He'd have liked to stay awhile and admire his handiwork, but the phone hadn't stopped ringing. Whoever was on the other end might get worried and call the police.

One more check. He walked to the head of the bed and gazed down at her.

She stared back at him, her eyes as wide open, her expression as terrified as when he'd plunged the knife into her heart.

He took out the envelope with the photographs and the typewritten list Timwick had given him at the airport. He liked lists; they kept the world in order.

Three photographs. Three names. Three addresses.

He crossed Dora Bentz's name off the list.

The phone was still ringing as he left her apartment.

No answer.

It was three-thirty in the morning. There should have been an answer.

Logan slowly replaced the receiver.

It didn't have to mean anything. Dora Bentz had married children who lived in Buffalo, New York. She could be visiting them. She could be on vacation anywhere.

Or she could be dead.

Timwick could be moving quickly to tie up all the loose ends.

Shit, Logan had thought he had time.

Maybe he was jumping to conclusions.

Hell, so what? He'd always trusted his instincts, and they were shouting at him now.

But sending Gil to check on Dora Bentz would be a tip-off. Timwick would know what he only suspected now. Logan could try to save Dora Bentz or he could remain safe for a few more days.

Shit.

He picked up the phone and dialed Gil's number in the carriage house.

Lights. Moving lights.

Eve stopped drying her hair, slowly got up, and went to the window.

The black limousine that had picked them up at the airport was gliding down the driveway toward the gates.

Logan?

Gil Price?

It was almost four o'clock in the morning. Where would anyone be going at this hour?

She doubted if she'd be told if she asked tomorrow morning.

But she'd damn well do it anyway.

SIX

Eve didn't fall asleep until five, and then her slumber was restless. She woke at nine but forced herself to stay in bed until almost ten, when a thunderous knock sounded on the door.

The door opened before she could answer, and a small, plump woman strode into the room. "Hi, I'm Margaret Wilson. Here's the gate control you wanted." She set the remote on the nightstand. "Sorry if I woke you, but John says I screwed up on the lab. How the hell was I to know you wanted pretty? What do I need to get? Pillows? Rugs?"

"Nothing." Eve sat up in bed and gazed curiously at Margaret Wilson. The woman was probably in her early forties. The gray gabardine pantsuit she wore slimmed her plump figure and complemented her dark, sleek hair and hazel eyes. "I told him that I wasn't going to be here long enough for it to matter."

"It matters. John likes things right. So do I. What's your favorite color?"

"Green, I guess."

"I should have known. Redheads are pretty predictable."

"I'm not a redhead."

"Well, almost." She looked around the room. "This kind of thing okay?"

Eve nodded as she threw back the covers and got out of bed.

"Good, then I'll get on the phone and order some stuff. It should be— Oh, my God, you're a giant."

"What?"

Margaret was glowering at her. "How the hell tall are you?"

"Five nine."

"A giant. You'll make me feel like a midget. I hate tall, skinny women. They do something to my psyche and I become overaggressive."

"You're not that small."

"You're patronizing me." She grimaced. "And I'm being defensive. Oh, well, I'll have to fight it. I'll just keep telling myself that I'm much smarter than you. Get dressed and come on down to the kitchen. We'll grab some cereal and then I'll take you for a walk around the grounds."

"That's not necessary."

"Sure it is. John wants you kept happy and he says you don't have anything to do right away. If you're anything like me, you'll go crazy." She headed for the door. "But we'll take care of it. Fifteen minutes?"

"Fine." She wondered what the response would have been if she had said otherwise. Margaret's tactics made a steamroller look subtle.

But it was hard not to like her. She hadn't smiled once, but she exuded a vibrant energy and cheerfulness. She was blunt, bold, and like no one Eve had ever met. She was a breath of fresh air after the dark tension she sensed in Logan.

"The Barrett family graveyard." Margaret waved a hand at the small iron-fenced cemetery. "There's no grave later than 1922. Do you want to go in?"

Eve shook her head.

"Thank God. Cemeteries depress me, but I thought you might be interested."

"Why?"

"I don't know. All those bones and stuff you work with."

"I don't hang around graveyards like some kind of ghoul, but they don't bother me." Particularly family cemeteries. No lost ones here, and it was extremely well kept. All the graves were even covered with pallets of fresh carnations. "Where did all the flowers come from? Are there Barretts still in the neighborhood?"

"No, the direct line died out about twenty years ago." She pointed at a gravestone. "Randolph Barrett. The family scattered over the years and Randolph Barrett was the last to be buried here back in 1922. The graveyard was in pretty sad shape when John bought the property. He gave orders for it to be cleaned up and fresh flowers brought in every week."

"I'm surprised. I wouldn't think Logan would be that sentimental."

"Well, you never know what John is going to do. But I'm glad he brought in a landscaper for this job. Like I said, cemeteries depress me."

Eve turned and started down the hill. "They don't depress me. Sadden me, maybe. Particularly the babies' graves. Before modern medicine, so many children didn't live to grow up. Do you have any children?"

Margaret shook her head. "I was married once, but we both had careers and were too busy to think about kids."

"Your job must be very demanding."

"Yep."

"And varied." She paused. "Like this one. You can't say that skeleton hunting is in many people's job description."

"I don't hunt, I just do what I'm told."

"That could be dangerous."

"John will keep me clear of trouble. He always has before."

"He's done this before?"

"Bones? No, but he's been known to walk some mighty thin lines."

"But you trust him?"

"Hell, yes."

"Even if you don't know what he's looking for? Or do you?"

Margaret grinned. "Stop pumping me. I don't know anything about anything and I wouldn't tell you if I did."

"You won't even tell me if it was Logan who left in the middle of the night?"

"Sure. John's still here. I saw him before he disappeared into his study this morning. It was Gil who left."

"Why?"

Margaret shrugged. "Ask John." She added bluntly, "You came here because John made it worth your while. I handled the transfer to the Adam Fund. He'll tell you everything when he thinks it's time. Trust him."

"I don't have your faith in him." She glanced at the carriage house. "Is that where the gates are monitored?"

Margaret nodded. "It's a pretty elaborate system with video cameras all over the place. Mark Slater does all the monitoring."

"I haven't met him yet."

"He doesn't come up to the house much."

"Does Logan's house on the West Coast have security like this?"

"Sure, there are lots of nuts out there. Men in John's position are prime targets." Her pace quickened. "I have some work to do. Will you be okay if I leave you alone this afternoon?"

"Yes. You don't have to baby-sit me, Margaret."

"Actually, I enjoyed it. You're not what I expected from a bone lady."

Bone lady. That's what Gil had called her. "The correct term is forensic sculptor."

"Whatever. Like I said, I expected someone very cool and professional. Hence the mistake I made with the lab. Not that I'd admit to John that I made a mistake. I told him it was all his fault because he didn't let me know what I had to contend with. It's not good for him to know that I'm not perfect. It would make him feel insecure."

Eve smiled. "I can't imagine that."

"Everyone has insecure moments, even me." She added gloomily, "But only when I stand next to giants like you. It comes from growing up a shrimp with four six-foot brothers. Is your mother tall?"

"No, only medium height."

"Okay, then you're a freak and I'll magnanimously forgive you. I won't mention it again."

"Thank you. I appreciate the—"

"I was wondering where you were." Logan had come out of the house and was walking toward them. "Did you have a good night?" he asked Eve.

"No."

"I have those reports to finish," Margaret said quickly. "See you later, Eve."

Eve nodded, her gaze on Logan. Dressed in black jeans and sweatshirt, he looked very different from the man she had met that first day. Not only because of the clothes, but because he seemed to have stripped off the sleek image and completely discarded it.

"Strange bed?"

"Partly. Why did Gil Price leave right after we got here last night?"

"I had an errand for him to run."

"At four in the morning?"

He nodded. "It was a rather urgent errand. He should be back tonight." He paused. "I was hoping you'd have a day or two to become acclimated to the situation, but we may have to pick up the pace."

"Good, I don't need to become acclimated. Just bring me the bones and let me get to work."

"We may have to go to them."

She stiffened. "What?"

"You may have to do a cursory examination right after we excavate and determine if it's worthwhile to bring the skeleton here. My source could have lied, and the skull might be damaged too badly for a face to be reconstructed."

"You want me to be there when you dig it up?"

"Maybe."

"Forget it. I'm not a grave robber."

"It may be necessary for you to be there. That could be the only—"

"Forget it."

"We'll talk about it later. It may not be necessary. Did you enjoy the graveyard?"

"Why does everyone assume I enjoy grave—" Her gaze narrowed on his face. "How did you know I was at the cemetery?" She glanced at the carriage house. "Of course, your video cameras. I don't like being spied on, Logan."

"The cameras scan the ground continuously. They just happened to catch you and Margaret at the cemetery."

It could be true, but she doubted if anything just "happened" in Logan's life. "I liked the fresh flowers."

"Well, I'm living in the Barretts' house. I figured that was the least I could do."

"It's your house now."

"Is it? The Barretts built the inn, they lived and worked here for over a hundred and sixty years and saw a lot of history troop by. Did you know Abraham Lincoln stayed here right before the end of the Civil War?"

"Another Republican. No wonder you bought the place."

"Some of the places Lincoln stayed in I wouldn't have touched on a bet. I value my comfort too much." He opened the front door for her. "Have you called your mother?"

"No, I'll do that this evening when she gets home from work." She smiled. "Providing she's not out on the town. She's keeping company with a lawyer from the D.A.'s office."

"He's lucky. She seemed very nice."

"Yes, and she's smart too. After Bonnie was born, she finished high school and then went to technical school to learn court reporting."

"She finished school after your daughter—" He stopped. "Sorry, I'm sure you don't want to talk about your daughter."

"I don't mind talking about Bonnie. Why should I? I'm very proud of her. She came into our lives and made everything different." She added simply, "Love can do that, you know."

"So I've heard."

"It's true. I'd tried to get my mother off crack, but couldn't. Maybe I was too bitter and resentful. God knows, sometimes I thought I hated her. But Bonnie came and I changed. Somehow all the bitterness was gone. And my mother changed too. I don't know whether it was just the right time and point in her life or it was because she knew she had to get off the crack in order to help me raise Bonnie. My God, how she loved Bonnie. No one could help but love her."

"I can understand that. I saw her picture."

"Wasn't she beautiful?" She smiled luminously. "So happy. She was always so happy. She loved every waking hour that she—" She had to swallow to ease the tightness in her throat and then said brusquely, "I'm sorry, I have to stop talking now. I can go only so far, and then it starts to hurt. But I'm getting better all the time."

"Christ, stop apologizing," he said roughly. "I'm sorry I made you talk about her."

"You didn't make me do anything. It's important that I keep her with me, that I never let myself forget her. She existed. She became a part of me, maybe the best part." She turned away from him. "And now I think I'll go to my lab and see if I can do a little work on Mandy."

He looked at her in surprise. "You brought those fragments with you?"

"Of course. There's probably not much I can do with them, but I couldn't give up without trying."

He smiled. "No, I can see you couldn't."

She felt his eyes on her as she walked away. She probably shouldn't have shown him how vulnerable she could be, but the conversation had seemed to flow from one subject to another. Logan had listened intently and sympathetically and made her feel as if he really cared. Maybe he did care. Maybe he wasn't the manipulator she suspected him of being.

And maybe he was. What the hell difference did it make? She wasn't ashamed of how she felt about Bonnie, and there was no way he could twist anything she had said and use it against her. The only advantage he might have gained was that she felt a little closer to him now; the very act of talking to him about Bonnie had caused the most tentative of bonds to be formed. But a connection that tentative was easy to break and wouldn't influence her in any way.

She opened the door of the lab and went directly to the briefcase she had left on the desk. She unlocked it and began taking the skull fragments out of the case. Putting them together would be like working on a jigsaw puzzle with some pieces the size of tiny splinters. What was she thinking? she wondered in despair. It was crazy, probably impossible.

The task would be impossible if she took that attitude, she thought impatiently. Reconstructing Mandy was her job, and she'd find a way to do it. The connection with Mandy was one she could trust, a bond she could afford to hold on to.

"Hello, Mandy." She sat down at the desk and picked up a nasal bone, the largest left intact. "I guess we'll start here. Don't worry. It may take a long time, but we'll get there."

"Dora Bentz is dead," Gil said baldly when Logan picked up the phone.

"Shit." His hand tightened on the receiver.

"Stabbed to death and apparently raped. She was found by her sister in her apartment about ten this morning. They were planning on going to an aerobics class together. The sister had a key and let herself in after she kept knocking and didn't get an answer. The window was open and the police think it's a simple rape-murder."

"Simple, hell."

"If it's not, it was done very well," Gil said. "Extremely well."

Like the vandalism of Eve's lab in Atlanta. "Were you followed?"

"No doubt about it. You knew I would be."

"Can you find out from one of your old buddies who Timwick might be using?"

"Maybe. I'll put out some feelers. Do you want me to come back there?"

"No. I've been trying to contact James Cadro all morning. According to his office, he's camping with his wife in the Adirondacks." He paused. "Hurry. I wasn't the first one to inquire about him."

"Do we know where in the Adirondacks?"

"Somewhere near Jonesburg."

"Great. That's what I like. Precise directions. I'm on my way."

Logan replaced the phone. Dora Bentz dead. He could have saved her if he'd acted yesterday. But, dammit, he'd thought they'd all be safer if he didn't display any interest in them, if he seemed to ignore their existence.

He was wrong. Dora Bentz was dead.

It was too late for her but maybe not for the others. A distraction could possibly save lives and give him the witnesses he desperately needed.

But he couldn't move fast without Eve Duncan. She was the key. He had to be patient and let her begin to trust him.

Trust building would be a slow process with someone as wary as Eve. She was smart and somewhere along the way she would find out that there was more danger to her and her family than an act of vandalism.

Scratch trust.

Then find a way to overcome her resistance and catapult her into his camp.

He leaned back in his chair and began to go over the possibilities.

• • •

"Hi." Margaret stuck her head into the lab. "The decorators in charge of warming up the lab are here. Can you vacate the place for an hour and let them do their thing?"

Eve frowned. "I told you it wasn't necessary."

"The lab isn't perfect, therefore it's necessary. I don't do my job halfway."

"Only an hour?"

"I told them you didn't want to be bothered and they'd lose the sale if they took longer. And you do have to eat." She checked her watch. "It's almost seven. How about having soup and a sandwich with me while we wait?"

"Just a minute." She carefully moved the board with Mandy's bones to the bottom drawer of the desk. "Tell them not to touch the desk or they'll lose more than a sale. I'll murder them."

"Right." Margaret turned and disappeared.

Eve took off her glasses and rubbed her eyes. A break would probably be good. She had made only a little progress in several hours and her frustration was growing. But a little progress was better than none. She'd tackle the work again after eating.

She encountered six men and two women in the hallway, bearing accent pillows, chairs, and carpets, and had to press back against the wall to avoid the stampede.

"This way." Margaret took her arm, maneuvered her around two men carrying a rolled carpet, and led her toward the kitchen. "It's not as massive an undertaking as it looks. One hour, I promise."

"I'm not timing you. A few minutes either way isn't going to matter."

"Not going too well?" Margaret asked sympathetically. "Too bad." They entered the kitchen and Margaret gestured to the two places set at the kitchen table. "I made tomato soup and cheese sandwiches. Is that okay?"

"Fine." Eve sat down, picked up her napkin, and spread it on her lap. "I'm not that hungry."

"I'm starved, but I'm on a diet and trying to be good." She sat down opposite Eve and looked at her accusingly. "You've obviously never been on a diet in your life."

Eve smiled. "Sorry."

"You should be." She reached for the TV remote on the counter. "Mind if I turn on the set? The President's having a press conference. John has me tape and listen to all of them and report to him if there's anything interesting."

"I don't mind." She began to eat. "If you don't mind my not paying any attention to it. Politics isn't my cup of tea."

"Nor mine. But John is fairly obsessed with it."

"I heard about the fund-raisers. Do you think he wants to go into politics himself?"

She shook her head. "He couldn't stand the bullshit." She watched the TV for a moment. "Chadbourne's damn good. He's practically oozing warmth. Did you know they're calling him the most charismatic president since Reagan?"

"No. It's a big job and charisma doesn't get the work done."

"But it can get you elected." She nodded at the TV. "Look at him. Everyone says he might carry Congress this time."

Eve looked. Ben Chadbourne was a big man in his late forties with a handsome face and gray eyes that sparkled with life and humor. He answered one of the reporters' questions with a good-natured jab. The room erupted into laughter.

"Impressive," Margaret said. "And Lisa Chadbourne's not chopped liver. Did you see her suit? Valentino, I bet."

"I wouldn't know."

"Or care." Margaret grimaced. "Well, I care. She always attends every press conference, and the only kick I get from watching them is seeing what she wears. Someday I'm going to be skinny enough to wear suits like that."

"She's very attractive," Eve agreed. "And she's doing wonderful work raising money for abused children."

"Is she?" Margaret's tone was absent. "That suit's got to be Valentino."

Eve smiled with amusement. She would never have dreamed a dynamo like Margaret would be so interested in clothes.

The suit in question was precisely cut to enhance Lisa Chadbourne's slim, athletic body. The soft beige color made her olive skin and sleek dark brown hair gleam in contrast. The President's wife was smiling at him from the sidelines, and she appeared both proud and loving. "Very nice."

"Do you think she's had a face-lift? She's supposed to be forty-five but she doesn't look a day over thirty."

"Maybe." Eve finished her soup. "Or maybe she's just aging well."

"I should be so lucky. I saw two new lines in my forehead this week. I stay out of the sun. I use moisturizer. I do everything right and I'm still going downhill." Margaret flicked off the television set. "Looking at her depresses me. Chadbourne's just saying the same old things. Lower taxes. More jobs. Aid to children."

"Nothing wrong with that."

"Tell that to John. Hell, Chadbourne says and does everything right and his wife smiles sweetly, has as many charities as Evita Peron, and bakes her own cookies. It's not going to be easy for John's party to oust an administration that everyone's calling the second Camelot."

Unless he could find a way to smear the other party. The more Eve thought about it, the more likely that explanation seemed, and she didn't like it one bit. "Where is Logan?"

"He's been in the study all afternoon making phone calls." Margaret stood up. "Coffee?"

"No, I had some in the lab an hour ago."

"Well, evidently I did something right by providing the coffeemaker."

"You did a great job. I have everything I need."

"Lucky woman." She poured coffee into her own cup. "Not many people can say that. Most of us aren't as fortunate. We have to compromise and—" She looked up, stricken. "God, I'm sorry. I didn't mean that you—"

"Forget it." She stood up. "Now I believe I have about twenty minutes more until your decorators finish with my lab. I think I'll go to my room and make a few phone calls too."

"Have I chased you off?"

"Don't be ridiculous. I'm not that sensitive."

Margaret's gaze raked her face. "I think you are. But you handle it damn well." She paused and then added awkwardly, "I admire you. In your place, I don't think I could—" She shrugged. "Anyway, I didn't mean to hurt you."

"You didn't hurt me," Eve said gently. "Truly. I do have phone calls to make."

"Then go make them. I'll finish my coffee and then go nag those decorators and get them out of your way."

"Thank you." Eve left the kitchen and strode quickly to her room. What she had told Margaret had been partly true. Time had formed scars on the wounds and, in many ways, she *was* lucky. She had a worthwhile profession, a parent she loved, and good friends.

And she'd better check in with one of those friends, see if Joe had dug up anything more on Logan. She didn't like how the situation was shaping up, she thought grimly.

No, she'd call Mom first.

It took six rings before Sandra picked up, but when she did she was laughing. "Hello."

"I guess I don't have to ask if you're okay," Eve said. "What's so funny?"

"Ron just spilled paint on his—" She broke off, giggling. "You'd have to be here."

"You're painting?"

"I told you I wanted to paint your lab. Ron offered to help me."

"What color?" Eve asked warily.

"Blue and white. It's going to look like sky and clouds. We're trying one of those new finishes that you do with garbage bags."

"Garbage bags?"

"I saw it on TV." The receiver was suddenly covered. "Don't do that, Ron. You're messing up the clouds. The corners have to be done differently." She came back on the line. "How are you?"

"Fine. I've been working on—"

"That's nice." She was laughing again. "No cherubs, Ron. Eve would have a cow."

"Cherubs?"

"I promise, just clouds."

Good God, cherubs, clouds. "You're busy. I'll call you again in a few days."

"I'm glad you're having a good time. Getting away is good for you."

And it was obviously not causing her mother any problem. "No more trouble?"

"Trouble? Oh, you mean the break-in. Not a bit. Joe dropped by after work with Chinese food but left right after Ron got here. It turns out they know each other. I guess it's not so strange, Ron being in the D.A.'s office and Joe—Ron, you need more white in that blue paint. Eve, I have to go. He's going to ruin my clouds."

"We wouldn't want that. Good-bye, Mom. Take care of yourself."

"You too."

Eve was smiling as she hung up. Sandra sounded younger than she had ever heard her, and everything was Ron and how everything and everyone related to Ron. Nothing wrong with being young. Kids grew up quick in the slums and maybe Sandra would be able to snatch some of that childhood magic now.

Why did that thought make Eve feel a thousand years old?

Because she was stupid and selfish and maybe a little envious.

Joe.

She reached for the telephone again and then stopped.

Logan had known she had gone to the cemetery.

She didn't like the idea of that electronic beehive in the carriage house.

She was being paranoid. Video cameras didn't necessarily equate to bugged telephones.

But they might. Ever since she'd arrived there she'd had the vague sensation of being caught in a web.

So she was paranoid.

She stood up, dug her digital out of her shoulder bag, and punched in Joe's number.

"I was just going to call you. How are things going?"

"They're not going. I'm treading water. He wants to involve

me more than I'm comfortable with. I need to know what I'm looking at. Did you dig up anything?"

"Maybe. But it's pretty weird."

"What's not weird about all this?"

"It seems he's lately acquired an obsession about John F. Kennedy."

"Kennedy," she repeated, startled.

"Yeah. And Logan's a Republican, so that by itself is already weird. He paid a visit to the Kennedy Library. He ordered copies of the Warren Commission Report on Kennedy's assassination. He went to the book depository in Dallas and then to Bethesda." Joe paused. "He even talked to Oliver Stone about the research he did for his movie *JFK*. All done very casual and quiet. No urgency. You'd never even make the connection between his actions unless you were looking for a pattern, like I was."

"Kennedy." It was bizarre. "That can't have anything to do with why I'm here. Is there anything else?"

"Not so far. You asked for out of the ordinary."

"Well, you certainly gave it to me."

"I'll keep looking." He changed the subject. "I ran into your mom's current flame tonight. Ron's a nice guy."

"She thinks so. Thanks for keeping an eye on her for me."

"I don't think I'm going to have to do much more of it. Ron seemed pretty protective himself."

"I haven't met him yet. Mom's afraid I'll scare him off."

"You might."

"What do you mean? You know I want whatever's best for Mom."

"Yep, and you'll kick ass until you get it for her."

"Am I that bad?"

Joe's voice softened. "No, you're that good. Look, I've got to go. Diane wants to catch a nine o'clock movie. I'll call you when I know anything more."

"Thanks, Joe."

"Forget it. I probably didn't help you much."

He probably hadn't, Eve thought as she hung up. Logan's

interest in JFK might be just coincidence. What possible connection could there be between the ex-president and her present situation?

Coincidence? She doubted if anything Logan did was coincidental. He was too sharp, too much in control. His search for information about Kennedy was too recent not to be suspicious, and if he'd tried to keep his interest in Kennedy under wraps, it was for a reason.

What reason? It couldn't be of—

She stiffened with shock.

"Oh, my God."

SEVEN

The library was unoccupied when she entered a few minutes later.

She slammed the door closed, flicked on the light, and strode toward the desk. She opened the right-hand drawer. Just papers and telephone books. She slammed it shut and opened the left-hand drawer.

Books. She pulled them out and set them on the desk.

The Warren Commission Report was on top. Beneath it was the Crenshaw book on the Kennedy autopsy and then a well-thumbed book titled *The Kennedy Conspiracy: Questions and Answers.*

"May I help you?" Logan stood in the doorway.

"Are you crazy, Logan?" She glared at him. "Kennedy? You've got to be out of your mind."

He crossed the room and sat down at the desk. "You appear to be a little upset."

"Why should I be upset? Just because you've

brought me here on the wildest goose chase ever conceived by man. Kennedy?" she repeated. "What the hell kind of crackpot are you?"

"Why don't you sit down and take a deep breath." He smiled. "You scare me when you loom over me like that."

"Bullshit. This isn't funny, Logan."

His smile vanished. "No, it's not funny. I was hoping it wouldn't come to this. I tried to be so careful. I take it you didn't just decide to ransack my office out of curiosity. Joe Quinn?"

"Yes."

"I heard he was very smart." He shook his head. "But you're the one who sicced him on me. Why couldn't you have just left it alone?"

"You expected me to wander around in the dark?"

He was silent a moment. "No, I guess I didn't expect it. But I hoped. I wanted you to go into this unprejudiced."

"I'd be unprejudiced no matter what I suspected. You have to be when you do my kind of work. But I can't believe you want me to help you dig up Kennedy."

"No manual labor is required. I just need you to verify—"

"And get shot in the process. For God's sake, Kennedy is buried at Arlington Cemetery."

"Is he?"

She went still. "What the devil are you saying?"

"Sit down."

"I don't want to sit down. I want you to talk to me."

"Okay." He paused. "What if it isn't Kennedy buried at Arlington?"

"Heaven help me, not another conspiracy theory?"

"Conspiracy? Yes, I guess that about covers it. But with a slight twist. What if it were one of Kennedy's doubles who was shot in Dallas? What if Kennedy died before the Dallas trip?"

She stared at him in disbelief. "Kennedy's doubles?"

"Most public figures have doubles to protect both their lives and their privacy. It's estimated Saddam Hussein has at least six."

"He's a dictator of a third-world country. No one could get away with that here."

"Not without help."

"Whose help?" she asked sarcastically. "Little John-John? Maybe brother Bobby?" Her hands clenched into fists at her sides. "You're nuts. It's the most outrageous thing I've ever heard. Who the hell are you accusing?"

"I'm not accusing anyone. I'm just looking at possibilities. I've no idea how the man died. He had all kinds of health problems that weren't public knowledge. His death could have been by natural causes."

"Could? My God, are you suggesting the cause might not have been natural?"

"You're not listening. Dammit, I don't *know*. The only thing I do know is that a deception that extensive would have involved more than one person."

"A White House conspiracy. A cover-up." She smiled mockingly. "And isn't it convenient for you that Kennedy was a Democrat? You can paint the opposition as a bunch of unscrupulous connivers not worthy of winning the election this year. What a coincidence that a massive smear like this might translate to a victory for your party."

"It might."

"You bastard. I don't like smear campaigns. And I don't like being used, Logan."

"Understandable. Now, if you're through venting your displeasure, will you listen to me for a moment?" He leaned forward in his chair. "Eight months ago I got a call from a man named Bernard Donnelli, a mortician who owns a small funeral home outside Baltimore. He asked me to meet him. He told me just enough to intrigue me, so I flew to Baltimore the next day. He was scared and met me in a parking garage at five in the morning." He shrugged. "No imagination. He must have thought he was Deep Throat or something. Anyway, he was more greedy than he was scared and offered to sell me information." He paused. "And an object that he thought I might find valuable. A skull."

"Only a skull?"

"The rest of the body was cremated by Donnelli's father. It seems that the Donnelli Funeral Home has been used for decades by the Mafia and Cosa Nostra to dispose of bodies. The Donnellis became known to the mob as being very discreet and reliable. However, one particular disposal made Donnelli Senior very uneasy. Two men appeared one night at Donnelli's home with a man's body and, though the money they paid him was extraordinary, he was uneasy. They weren't his regular customers and couldn't be counted on to play by the rules. They tried to keep him from seeing the corpse's face, but he caught one glimpse and it was enough to scare him shitless. He was afraid they'd come back and cut his throat to eliminate him as a witness. So he rescued the skull and hid it away to use as a weapon and an insurance policy."

"Rescued it?"

"Not many people know that it takes a temperature of twenty-five hundred degrees and a burning time of at least eighteen hours to completely destroy a skeleton. Donnelli managed to position the body so that the skull would partially avoid the flames. When the two men left after forty-five minutes, Donnelli retrieved the skull and burned the rest. Donnelli used the skull as a tool for blackmail, and before he died he told his son, Bernard, where he'd buried the skull. A rather macabre legacy but profitable, very profitable."

"Donnelli died?"

"Oh, he wasn't murdered. He was an old man and had a bad heart."

"And who was he blackmailing?"

Logan shrugged. "I don't know. Donnelli Junior wouldn't tell me. The deal was for the skull."

"And you're saying you didn't press him?"

"Why would I tell you that? Of course, I tried to get it out of him. All he'd tell me was what I've told you. He wasn't as gutsy as his father and he didn't like living on the edge. He offered me the location of the skull and the story in exchange for enough money to set him up in Italy with a new face and identity papers."

"And you took the deal?"

"I took it. I've paid more for prospects with less potential."

"And now you want me to bring that potential to fruition."

"If what Donnelli told me was the truth."

"It isn't. The entire story is crazy."

"Then why not go along with me? What's the harm? If it's not true, then you'll come out with your pocket full of my money and I'll come out with egg on my face." He smiled. "Both prospects should bring you extreme pleasure."

"It's a waste of my time."

"You're being well paid to waste it."

"And if there's any truth at all to the story, it's not smart for me to go around digging up—"

"But you said there wasn't any truth to it."

"It's too wild to think it's Kennedy, but it could be Jimmy Hoffa or some Mafia goon."

"Providing I haven't paid through the nose for a fairy tale."

"Which you've probably done."

"Then come with me and we'll find out." He paused. "Unless you think you couldn't do the job with an unprejudiced mind. There's no way I want you putting Jimmy Hoffa's face on this skull."

"You know damn well I'm too good to do that. Don't try to manipulate me, Logan."

"Why not? I'm good at it. We all do what we're good at. Aren't you even a little bit curious to find out if Donnelli's telling the truth?"

"No, it's just another wild-goose chase."

"Not so wild if they tried to scare you off. Or perhaps you'd rather forgive and forget what happened to your lab?"

Manipulation again. Strike where it hurts. She turned away. "I'm not forgetting anything, but I'm not sure I believe—"

"I'll double the contribution to the Adam Fund."

She slowly turned back to him. "Dammit, you're paying too much for too little. Even if it's true, it all happened a long time ago. What if nobody cares that the Democrats did a massive cover-up?"

"What if they do? The climate is right. The public is sick to death of being manipulated by politicians."

"Just what are you up to, Logan?"

"I thought you had me figured out. I'm just your run-of-the-mill low-life tycoon trying to stack the deck."

She wasn't close to figuring him out and there was no way she would accept one word he had spoken as truth.

"Will you think about it?"

"No."

"Yes, you will. You can't help yourself. Give me your decision in the morning."

"And what if I say no?"

"Why do you think I bought a property with a cemetery?"

She stiffened.

"Just joking." He smiled. "I'll send you home, of course."

She started for the door.

"And I won't ask for the Adam Fund money back. Even if you don't complete your part of the bargain. Which makes me appear a good deal more honorable than you, doesn't it?"

"I told you I wouldn't do anything illegal."

"I'm not trying to involve you in anything really illegal. No raid on Arlington or digging up a graveyard. Just a brief visit to a cornfield in Maryland."

"Which is probably still illegal."

"But if I'm right, our little transgression will come out smelling like the proverbial rose." He shrugged. "Think. Sleep on it. You're a reasonable woman and I think you'll agree that I'm not asking you to do anything that would betray your code of ethics."

"If you're telling me the truth."

He nodded. "If I'm telling you the truth. I've no intention of trying to convince you that I am. I know it wouldn't do any good. You'll have to make up your own mind." He opened the top desk drawer and pulled out a leather address book. "Good night. Let me know your decision as soon as you make it."

She was dismissed, she realized. No persuasion. No protestations. The ball was in her court.

Or was it?

"Good night." She left the library and swiftly climbed up the stairs to her bedroom.

Kennedy.

Impossible. Kennedy was lying at Arlington, not in some hole in a Maryland cornfield. Logan had been suckered into paying for nothing.

But Logan was anything but a sucker. If he thought there was any truth to Donnelli's story, that might be enough reason for her to look deeper into it.

And to give credence to any plan Logan might have for a smear campaign. He could be lying, digging desperately for a way to get what he wanted.

She had made a deal with him and he had kept his end of it.

Oh, what the hell. She was too tired to make a decision now. She would go to bed and hope she would see things more clearly in the morning. It would be the sensible thing to—

The window.

She stiffened and inhaled sharply. Imagination. She wouldn't let herself be tricked by her own mind. She was tired and discouraged and prey to her own imagination. She wouldn't let herself be—

The window.

She moved slowly across the room to the window and stood looking out into the darkness.

Darkness. Mosquitoes. Bugs. Snakes.

His Italian designer loafers were being ruined by the damp, rotting foliage on the trail, Fiske realized with annoyance.

He had never liked the woods. He remembered one time when he was a kid, he'd been sent to some fucking camp in Maine and been forced to stay there for two weeks. His parents were always sending him somewhere to get rid of him.

Bastards.

But he'd fixed them. He'd made sure the camp would never accept him back after that summer. They hadn't been able to prove anything, but the counselor had known. Oh, yes, he had known. It had shown in the prick's scared face, the way his eyes slid away from him.

That summer had taught him a few lessons he'd been able to apply to his chosen vocation. Camping nuts almost always needed reservations for a camping site at a national park, and each reservation was tidily documented by the forest rangers.

There was a glimmer of fire up ahead.

Target.

Approach directly or wait until they were asleep?

Adrenaline was starting to pump through him.

Direct approach. Let them see him, feel it coming.

He ruffled his hair and smeared a streak of dirt on his cheek.

The gray-haired old man was sitting staring into the fire. His wife came out of their tent, and she laughed and said something to him. There was an air of intimacy and affection between them that Fiske found vaguely annoying. But then, he found everything about this kill annoying. He didn't like being forced into practicing his skills in the middle of the wilds, and he would make sure the old man and woman realized it.

He paused, drew a deep breath, then burst into the clearing. "Thank God. Can you help me? My wife is hurt. We were setting up camp down the road and she fell and broke—"

"I know where they're camped," Gil said. "I'm on my way. But I'm two hours behind. The ranger said there was another inquiry earlier this evening."

Logan's hand tightened on the receiver. "Be careful."

"Am I stupid? Of course I'll be careful. Particularly if it's Fiske."

"Fiske?"

"I called my contact in the Treasury Department and the word is that Timwick's been known to use Albert Fiske on occasion. Fiske was a hit man for the CIA and a damn good one. He always wanted the toughest jobs, the most prestigious hits. He takes inordinate pride in his efficiency and ability to do jobs no one else can do. In the last five years he's severed his ties with the Company and struck out on his own, and he's done very well. He moves fast, knows the system well enough to make it work for him." He paused. "And he likes it, Logan. He really likes it."

"Shit."

"I'll call you back when I find them."

Logan slowly replaced the receiver.

"He moves fast."

How fast?

And in what direction?

The house phone on the desk buzzed.

"Ms. Duncan left the house three minutes ago," Mark said.

"Is she heading for the front gate?"

"No, she's going up the hill."

"I'll be right there."

Logan came into the carriage house a few minutes later.

"She's at the graveyard," Mark said.

Logan walked over to the bank of monitors. "What's she doing?"

"It's dark and she's in the shadow of that tree. She's not doing anything as far as I can tell. Just standing there."

Standing just outside a graveyard in the middle of the night.

"Zero in closer."

Mark made an adjustment on the control board and Eve's face was suddenly on the screen before him.

It told him nothing. She was looking at the flower-covered graves, her face totally without expression. What had he expected? Strain? Torment?

"Pretty weird, huh?" Mark asked. "What a nutcase."

"Damn you, she's not a nut—" He broke off, as surprised as

Mark at the sudden burst of fury. "Sorry, but she's not crazy. She's just carrying around a lot of baggage."

"Okay, okay," Mark said. "I just thought it was all kind of weird. I wouldn't be trekking up to a graveyard at night. I guess she—" He suddenly started to laugh. "Shit. You're right, she's normal as hell."

Eve was looking up into the trees, and the middle finger of her right hand was lifted in an obscene gesture.

"She's giving us the bird." Mark was still chuckling. "I think I like her, John."

Logan found himself smiling. He liked her too, dammit. He liked her strength and intelligence and resilience. Even her stubbornness and unpredictability intrigued him. In other circumstances he would have liked having her for a friend . . . or even a lover.

Lover. He hadn't realized he was regarding her in a sexual light until that moment. She was attractive, but he'd been more aware of her mind and personality than her tall, graceful body.

Yeah, sure. Who was he kidding? Hell, sex was always important and, if he was honest with himself, Eve's very breakability aroused him.

Which made him pretty much of a scumbag.

So forget it. Concentrate on what was important, the reason he'd brought her there.

And why the hell she was still in that damn graveyard.

The warm wind stirred the carnations on the graves and carried the faintest scent to where Eve was standing outside the fence.

She had told Margaret she wasn't a ghoul who hung around graveyards, so why was she there? Why hadn't she gone to bed as she'd intended instead of obeying the crazy impulse that had brought her there?

And it *was* impulse.

To believe something had called her there was insane, and she was not insane. She had fought that fight after Fraser had been executed and she had to be very careful not to let herself go down the path toward madness. It would be so easy. Dreaming of Bonnie at night was permissible, but she mustn't imagine Bonnie was there when she was wide awake.

Besides, Bonnie couldn't be here. She had never been in this place.

Logan had talked of death and graves and her mind had done the rest. No one had called her.

It was only an impulse.

She wasn't surprised to see Logan waiting for her when she entered the house an hour later.

"I'm tired. I don't want to talk, Logan." She walked past him and started up the stairs.

He smiled. "I gathered that from your extremely rude gesture."

"You shouldn't have been watching me. I don't like being spied on."

"A graveyard isn't the most pleasant place for a stroll. Why there?"

"What does it matter?"

"I'm curious."

Her hand tightened on the banister. "Stop trying to read some significance into everything I say or do. I went there because it was night and I knew the way. I didn't want to get lost."

"That's all?"

"What did you expect? I was up there having a séance?"

"Don't bite my head off. I was just curious. I was actually hoping the walk had cleared your head and you'd come to a decision about the—"

"It didn't." She started up the stairs again. "I'll talk to you in the morning."

"I'll be working most of the night, if you come to any—"

"Back off, Logan."

"Whatever you say." He added, "Since you obviously know I'm keeping an eye on you, I thought it only fair to keep you informed about my own whereabouts."

"Sure you did." She slammed her bedroom door behind her and headed for the bathroom. A hot shower would get rid of this tension. Then maybe she'd go back down to the lab and work on Mandy. She knew she wasn't going to sleep well tonight, and she might as well be productive.

It wasn't as if she were afraid of going to sleep and dreaming of Bonnie. Bonnie was never a threat. How could a loving dream be a danger?

And it had been pure impulse, not Bonnie calling her, that had led her to the graveyard that night.

The two bodies were lying in one sleeping bag, their arms draped around each other in a final embrace. They were naked and their eyes were wide open, staring into each other's face with terror.

A long tent stake was driven through both their bodies.

"Son of a bitch." Killing them was bad enough, but Gil felt there was something obscene about the way the old couple had been posed. It robbed their death of all dignity.

He looked around the campsite. No footprints. No visible evidence. Fiske had taken time to clean up.

Gil flipped open his phone and called Logan. "Too late."

"Both of them?"

"Yeah, nasty." More than nasty. Twisted. "What do you want me to do?"

"Come back. I haven't been able to contact Maren. He's in the desert somewhere. But that may be good. If we can't reach him, I doubt Fiske will be able to. We may have a reprieve."

"Don't count on it." He glanced at the two bodies. "Fiske isn't going to be twiddling his thumbs."

"I'm not counting on anything, but there's no way I want you heading for Jordan. I may need you."

Gil went still. "The skull?"

"I can't wait any longer. Everything's moving too fast. Come back."

"I'm on my way."

Very satisfactory.

Everything neat and he'd even been able to add a little whimsy.

Fiske was humming softly to himself as he unlocked his car and got in. He quickly dialed Timwick. "Cadro's done. I'm heading for Jordan on the next plane. Anything else?"

"Forget Maren for the moment. Go join the surveillance team at Barrett House."

Fiske frowned. "I don't like surveillance."

"You'll do this one. If Logan and the Duncan woman sneeze, I want to know about it and I want you on the spot."

"I don't like jumping all over the place until I finish the job. I still have Maren to—"

"We followed Gil Price when he left Barrett House yesterday morning. He went directly to Dora Bentz's apartment."

"So? I left it clean."

"You don't get the point. He knew about Dora Bentz and that means Logan knows. We can't—" Timwick drew a deep breath. "We need Logan, Price, and the Duncan woman dead."

"You said it was too risky."

"That was before we were sure Logan was on the right track. There's no question we can leave them alive now."

At last Timwick was showing some balls. "When?"

"I'll let you know."

Fiske pressed the end button of the phone. Things were definitely looking up. Both the challenge and monetary opportunities were escalating. He started humming again as he opened the glove compartment and took out Timwick's list. He drew a neat line through the second name and below Maren's name carefully wrote in block letters John Logan, Gil Price, and Eve Duncan.

Might as well keep things orderly.

He started the car, then grinned as he suddenly realized the song he was still humming.

Making a list, checking it twice.

Gonna find out who's naughty or nice . . .

EIGHT

"Wake up," Margaret said. "For God's sake, do you even have to sleep with those bones, Eve?"

Eve groggily lifted her head. "What?" She shook her head to clear it of sleep. "What time is it?"

Margaret was standing in front of the desk. "It's almost nine in the morning. John told me you weren't going to work anymore last night."

"I changed my mind." She looked down at Mandy on the desk in front of her. "I fit a few more pieces to the puzzle."

"And fell asleep working on it."

"I was going to close my eyes for just a minute." Her mouth felt nasty. "I guess I was tired." She pushed back her chair. "I need to go brush my teeth and shower."

"Not until you tell me what a good job I did on this lab."

She smiled. "Sorry, it's wonderful."

"Your enthusiasm is truly astonishing." Margaret

sighed. "I knew I should have told them to do it in sackcloth and ashes."

"I told you it didn't matter." She stood up and moved toward the door. "But I appreciate your effort."

"John wants to see you. He sent me to find you."

"I'll see him after I shower and change."

"Could you hurry? He's been pretty edgy since Gil got back."

Eve turned at the door. "He's back?"

Margaret nodded. "About an hour and a half ago. They're waiting for you in the office."

Waiting for her decision. Waiting to see if she'd go along on Logan's wild-goose chase.

Kennedy.

My God, in the clear light of day the idea was even more bizarre than it had been the previous night.

"And John authorized me to shift that other payment you agreed on to the Adam Fund," Margaret said. "I called the bank and you should be able to verify the transfer within another hour."

She hadn't agreed to that other payment. Logan was applying pressure, bribing her without insisting on a return favor. Well, let him give the money. It wouldn't influence her decision and the kids would benefit. "I trust you."

"Verify," Margaret said. "John insists."

Logan could insist until he was blue in the face. She'd do exactly what she wanted to do. Working on Mandy last night had been good for her. She felt much more in control of the situation that morning. "I'll see you later, Margaret."

"You took enough time." Logan scowled at her as she walked into the study. "We've been waiting."

"I had to wash and blow-dry my hair."

"And very nice it looks," Gil said from the corner of the room. "Worth every minute of the delay."

She smiled at him. "I don't believe Logan thinks so."

"I don't," Logan said. "It's rude to keep people waiting."

"It depends on whether you have an appointment or a summons."

Gil chuckled. "You shouldn't have sent Margaret, Logan."

"Dammit, I didn't want to appear pushy."

Her brow lifted. "Oh, yes?"

"Well, not obviously pushy." Logan gestured to the chair. "Sit down, Eve."

She shook her head. "This won't take long."

Logan tensed. "Look, I don't want you to—"

"Shut up, Logan. I'll do it. I'll go to your damn cornfield to get this skull. We'll bring it back here and I'll do the work you want me to do." She gazed directly into his eyes. "But we do it right away. I want this over with."

"Tonight."

"Fine." She started to leave.

"Why?" Logan asked suddenly. "Why are you doing it?"

"Because you're wrong and the only way I can prove you're wrong is to do the work. I want to be done with it and get back to what's important to me." She added coolly, "And, yes, I do want to see you with egg on your face. I want it so much that I might even volunteer to work on Chadbourne's reelection campaign."

"And that's all?"

She carefully kept her face without expression. Don't let him see anything. Don't let him know the panic she'd had to overcome last night. Don't give him a weapon to use against her. "That's all. When do we leave?"

"After midnight." He smiled crookedly. "As is proper for such a nefarious enterprise. We'll take the limo. It's only about an hour's drive from here."

She glanced at Gil. "Are you coming too?"

"I wouldn't miss it. I can't remember the last time I dug up a skull. Particularly one that promises to be this interesting." He winked. " 'Alas, poor Yorick, I knew him, Horatio.' "

She headed for the door. "Actually, that quote is closer to the mark than anything Logan's told me. That skull has a hell of a lot better chance of belonging to Shakespeare's Yorick than to Kennedy."

"They're on the move, Timwick," Fiske said into the phone. "Price, Logan, and the Duncan woman. They just drove out the gates."

"Be careful. You'll blow everything if they realize you're following them."

"No problem. We don't have to get close until there's need. Kenner planted a signal device in the limo when Price was at the Bentz apartment. We'll wait until they're on a deserted road and then overtake them and—"

"No, you'll let them get where they're going before you act."

"That may not be the ideal situation. I should—"

"Screw the ideal situation. You'll let them get where they're going. Do you hear me, Fiske? You let Kenner handle it. I've given him exact instructions and you'll do what he says."

Fiske hung up the phone. Son of a bitch. It was bad enough having to give in to Timwick without knuckling under to Kenner. He'd had a bellyful of the prick in the past twenty-four hours.

"I told you I was in charge," Kenner said from the driver's seat. "You're just along for the ride until I give the word." He jerked his head at the two men in the backseat. "Just like them."

Fiske gazed straight ahead at the limo's taillights in the distance. He drew a deep breath and tried to relax. It would be all right. He would manage to do his job in spite of Kenner's interference. He'd kill the three in the limo up ahead and cross their names off the list.

And then he'd start his own list with Kenner's name at the very top.

The cornfield should have reminded Eve of something as all-American as a state fair but all she could think about was a horror movie she'd seen about a group of ghoulish children living in a cornfield.

No children here.

Only death.

And a skull buried beneath the rich brown earth.

Waiting.

She slowly got out of the car. "It's there?"

Logan nodded.

"The field looks well tended. Where's the farmhouse?"

"About five miles to the north."

"It's a big field. I hope Donnelli gave you good directions."

"He did. I have them memorized." He got out of the car. "I know exactly where it's located."

"Those directions had better be good." Gil had opened the trunk and was taking out two shovels and a large lantern flashlight. "Digging's not my favorite pastime. I spent a summer on a road crew when I was working my way through college, and I swore I'd never do it again."

"Serves you right." Logan took the lantern and one of the shovels. "Never say never." He strode into the cornfield.

"Coming?" Gil asked Eve as he started after Logan.

She didn't move.

She could smell the earth where death waited.

She could hear the breeze as it rustled through the rows of tall corn.

She felt her chest tighten at the thought of sinking, drowning into that swaying sea of corn.

"Eve?" Gil was standing at the edge of the field, waiting. "John wants you with us."

She moistened her lips. "Why?"

He shrugged. "Ask him."

"It's stupid for me even to be here. I'm not going to be able to tell anything until I get back to the lab."

"Sorry, he wants you there when he digs it up."

Stop arguing. Do it. Get it over with. Get out of this place.

She followed Gil into the cornfield.

Darkness.

She could hear the rustling sound Gil was making ahead of her, but she couldn't see him. She could see nothing but the tall stalks all around her. It was like being buried. Even with a map and directions, how could Logan manage to find anything?

"I see a light ahead." Gil's voice drifted back to her.

It was more than she could see, but her pace increased.

Get it over with. Get out of here.

She could see the light now. Logan had set the flashlight on the ground and was already digging, his shovel spiking into the earth and tearing at the roots of the cornstalks.

"Here?" Gil asked.

Logan glanced up at them and nodded. "Quick. It's buried pretty deep so the farmer wouldn't dig it up when he was planting. You don't have to be careful. It's supposed to be in a lead-lined box."

Gil started digging.

She wished they'd given her a shovel, she thought after five minutes. Being busy would have been better than standing there, watching. Her tension was growing with every second.

This was stupid. There was probably nothing buried there and they were all behaving like people out of a Stephen King novel.

"I've hit something," Gil said.

Logan glanced at Gil. "Hallelujah." He began digging faster.

Eve moved closer to the hole and saw rusted metal through the loosened dirt. "Jesus . . ."

Why was she feeling so shaken? Just because Donnelli hadn't lied about the location didn't mean the rest of the story was true. There might not even be a skull in the box and the chances of it being Kennedy were out of sight.

Logan was prying open the lock on the box.

Only it wasn't a box, she suddenly realized. It was a coffin.

A baby's coffin.

"Stop it."

Logan looked at her. "What the hell?"

"It's a coffin. A baby . . ."

"I know that. Donnelli was an undertaker. How else do you think he got a lead-lined box?"

"What if it's not a skull?"

Logan's face hardened. "It's the skull. We're wasting time." He broke the lock on the coffin.

She hoped he was right. The idea of a little baby buried out here alone and lost was too heartbreaking to bear.

Logan was throwing open the coffin.

No baby.

Even through the heavy plastic wrapping she could make out the skull.

"Jackpot," Logan murmured. He brought the lantern closer. "I knew it was—"

"I hear something." Gil had raised his head.

Eve heard it too.

The wind?

Not the wind.

More purposeful. The same sound they had made as they had moved through the cornfield.

And the rustling was heading toward them.

"Shit," Logan muttered. He slammed shut the coffin, grabbed it, and jumped to his feet. "Let's get out of here."

Eve looked over her shoulder. Nothing. Just that menacing rustling. "It could be the farmer, couldn't it?"

"It's not the farmer. There's more than one." Logan was already running. "Don't lose her, Gil. We'll circle back through the field and come out on the road where we parked the car."

Gil grabbed her arm. "Hurry."

They shouldn't be talking. Someone would hear them. But that was crazy. What difference did it make? They were making as much noise crashing through the corn as whoever was pursuing them.

Logan was zigzagging through the field and they were following.

Running.

Suffocating darkness.

Rustling.

Her lungs were hurting.

Were they closer?

She couldn't tell. They were making too much noise themselves for her to figure it out.

"To the left," someone shouted behind them.

Logan tore through the corn at a right angle.

"I think I see something." A different voice.

Oh, God, it sounded as if the man were in the row next to them.

Logan was turning, heading back the way they came.

Gil and Eve were on his heels.

Faster.

Eve was completely disoriented. How could Logan tell where he was going?

Maybe he couldn't. They might run into whoever was pursuing them at any minute. Maybe they should—

Logan was turning again. To the left.

And they were out of the field and running toward the road.

The limo.

But over fifty yards away.

And a Mercedes was parked beside it. She couldn't see if there was anyone in it.

She glanced over her shoulder toward the field.

No one.

They were almost at the limo.

And the Mercedes door swung open.

Gil dropped her arm. "Get the coffin inside the limo, John." He turned, pulled out his gun, and darted toward the man who was getting out of the Mercedes.

Too late.

A shot.

She watched in horror as Gil fell forward. He struggled to his knees and tried to raise his gun.

Oh, God, the man was pointing his gun at Gil again.

She didn't even realize she was moving until her hand grasped the gun and jerked it aside. The man turned toward her and her hand chopped down on the carotid artery in his neck. He grunted. His eyes glazed over. He was falling.

"I'll drive. Get in the backseat with Gil." Logan was dragging Gil the few feet toward the limo. "Try to stop the bleeding. We've got to get out of here. They've got to have heard the shot."

Eve held the door for Logan and then dove into the seat beside Gil.

Jesus, he was pale. She tore open his shirt. Some blood, high up on the shoulder. What if he—

"They're coming!" Logan shouted as the limo jumped forward.

She glanced out the window and saw three men pouring out of the cornfield.

Gravel flew as the limo tore down the road.

Logan glanced in the rearview mirror. "How is he?"

"It's a shoulder wound. Not much bleeding. He's conscious again." She glanced out the window once more. "They've reached the road. Can you go any faster?"

"I'm trying," he said through his teeth. "It's like driving a damned yacht."

He had reached the paved road leading to the freeway, but the Mercedes was too fast. Its headlights were only yards behind them.

Then the Mercedes hit the side of the limo.

It was trying to force them off the road into the ditch.

It struck them again.

This time Logan barely managed to keep the car on the road.

"Pull ahead," she said. "We'll be dead in the water if we end up in that ditch."

"What do you think I'm trying to do?"

Thank God, the freeway was just up ahead.

The Mercedes hit the limo again and it spun toward the ditch.

Logan turned the wheel frantically and managed to keep the car from plunging down the incline.

"That last hit caused them to skid to the other side of the road. That's our chance," Eve said. "Hit it!"

He stomped on the accelerator.

"They're too close." Logan was looking in the rearview mirror. "They'll catch us before we reach the freeway."

"The . . . coffin," Gil murmured. "Give them—"

"No!" Logan said.

Eve looked down at the coffin at her feet.

"Give them the—"

Eve reached for the door handle.

"What are you doing?" Logan asked.

"Shut up," Eve said fiercely. "Gil's right. They want this damn coffin. They're going to get it. It's not worth our lives."

"What if they don't stop? You've given it up for nothing."

"I don't give a damn. Gil's already been shot over this skull. No one else is going to be hurt. Slow down and keep the car in this lane. No matter what happens."

The car slowed, but it was still a struggle for her to open the door against the force of the wind.

"They're gaining."

"Just keep the car in this lane." She dragged and pushed the coffin toward the door. "And as far ahead as you can."

"I don't think I—"

"Try." The wind had flung the door open and she shoved the coffin out. It bounced twice and skidded into the other lane.

"Now, we'll see." Eve's gaze was fixed on the oncoming Mercedes. "We've just got to hope they— *Yes.*"

The Mercedes had gone past the coffin. At first it seemed as if they were going to ignore it and continue the pursuit. But then it slowed, suddenly made a U-turn, and started back.

"The freeway's just ahead," Logan said. The limo flew down the road and up the ramp to the freeway.

Cars. Trucks. People.

Relief flooded Eve as Logan merged with the traffic. "Are we safe now?"

"No." Logan pulled over to the side of freeway. "Close that door." He turned to Gil. "How are you doing?"

"Just a scratch. Not even bleeding anymore."

"I'm not sure it's safe to stop. I'll call Margaret and have her get you some medical help. You're sure you're not bleeding? Can you hold on until we get back to Barrett House?"

"Sure." Gil's voice was weak. "If I survived your driving, I can survive anything."

Thank God, he was well enough to joke, Eve thought with relief.

"You couldn't have done any better," Logan said. "And for that nasty remark I should dump you out and let you walk."

"I'll shut up." He closed his eyes. "And since that's so difficult for me, I'll think I'll take a little nap."

"Bad idea," Logan said as he pulled back into the traffic. "Stay awake. I have to know if you lose consciousness."

"Sure. Anything to oblige. I'll just rest my eyes."

Logan met Eve's gaze in the rearview mirror.

She nodded and his foot pressed harder on the accelerator.

"What the hell are you doing?" Fiske screeched. "You're losing them."

"Shut up," Kenner said. "I know what I'm doing. The box is more important."

"You idiot. Nothing's more important. We went to all this trouble and now you're letting them get—"

"Timwick said that if it came to a choice between retrieving what they went after or getting them, we should go for the retrieval."

"We can go back for it later. They're just trying to divert us."

"Do you think that didn't occur to me? I can't take the chance. It's in the middle of the road. It could be damaged or found."

"In the middle of the night?"

"Timwick wants what's in that box."

Fury jolted through Fiske. There was no way they could catch up with Logan now. All because of Timwick's obsession with that damn box.

And Kenner was just like Timwick, so concerned with the small stuff that he couldn't see what was really important. You took one objective at a time and never let yourself be distracted.

Certainly not by a fucking box.

Two men in white uniforms streamed out of Barrett House as soon as Logan stopped the limo. Gil was transferred to a stretcher and whisked inside.

Eve got out of the car. Her knees were so weak, she had to lean against the fender.

"You okay?" Logan asked.

She nodded.

"I'll tell Margaret to get you a cup of coffee," he said over his shoulder as he headed toward the house. "I have to make sure Gil is going to be all right."

Dazed, she watched him disappear. Too much had happened in too short a time for her to comprehend that it was really over. Or even that it had actually happened.

But the crushed side of the limo was mute testimony to that terrifying chase.

And Gil Price's wound was not a figment of her imagination. He could have been killed. They all could have been killed if she hadn't tossed the coffin out of the limo.

"Coffee." Margaret was thrusting a mug into her hand. "Come into the house and sit down."

"In a minute. My legs don't seem to be working right now." She took a sip of the coffee. "How's Gil?"

"Conscious and flippant as hell. The doctor's ready to muzzle him."

The coffee was strong and the caffeine was beginning to kick in. "How did you get a doctor out here at this time of night?"

"Money moves mountains." Margaret leaned against the limo. "You scared?"

"Hell, yes. Shouldn't I be? Maybe you're used to people shooting each other, but I'm not."

"I'm scared too. I never thought—" She drew a shaky breath. "I never expected this. I thought— I don't know what I thought."

"But you still trust Logan enough to keep working for him?"

"Sure." She straightened. "But I'm damn well going to ask him for a raise and hazard pay. You ready to go inside now?"

Eve nodded.

Hazard pay. Logan's generosity was making sense to her now. This wasn't about dead cats and vicious vandalism. This was about murder. They had tried to murder Gil. They might have killed all of them if the limo had ended up in that ditch.

"Better?" Logan had come down the stairs. "You have more color."

"Do I?" She took another sip of coffee. "How's Gil?"

"Flesh wound. Braden says he'll be okay." He turned to Margaret. "We don't want the police report filed yet. Talk Braden into a delay."

"Yeah, sure, and let them accuse me of suppressing—" She sighed and headed for the stairs. "I'll take care of it."

Margaret had reached the top before Logan turned back to Eve. "We need to talk."

"I'd say that's an understatement." She moved toward the kitchen. "But, right now, I have an empty cup and I need more coffee."

He followed her and dropped down into a chair at the table. "I'm sorry you were frightened."

"Is that supposed to make me feel all warm and fuzzy?" Her hand was shaking as she poured the coffee. "It doesn't. Right now I'm scared, but when I get over it, I'm going to be mad as hell."

"I know. I can't expect anything else." He paused. "You were pretty amazing tonight. You probably saved Gil's life. Where did you learn karate?"

"Joe. After Bonnie was— I told you I'd never be a victim again. Joe taught me how to take care of myself."

He smiled. "And everyone else too, evidently."

"Somebody had to help him. You obviously thought more of

that damn coffin than of your friend. My God, you're obsessed. I'm surprised you agreed to slow down so I could toss that thing out."

His smile faded. "Gil's been trained to take care of himself too. He had his job. I had mine."

"And I have mine." She stared into his eyes. "But I never bargained for anyone shooting at me."

"I told you they'd try to stop us."

"You didn't tell me they'd try to murder us."

"No, I guess I didn't."

"You know damn well you didn't." Her voice rose with anger. "The whole thing was a disaster. You risked your life on a wild-goose chase and dragged me along with you. You almost got me killed, you son of a bitch."

"Yes."

"And there was no reason for it. I didn't have to be there."

"Yes, you did."

"What was I supposed to do? Work on the skull in the damn cornfield?"

"No."

"Then, why did—"

"Dr. Braden's leaving." Margaret was at the entryway. "I believe things will go smoother if you clap him on the shoulder and see him on his way, John."

"Right." Logan stood up. "Will you come with me, Eve? We're not finished."

"You bet we're not." She followed him into the foyer and watched him with the doctor. Smooth as honey. Persuasive as Lucifer. It took only a few minutes for him to send the man happily on his way.

She stood in the doorway as he escorted the doctor to his car.

"He's good, huh?" Margaret murmured.

"Too good." Suddenly the rage was gone, replaced by weariness. What the hell difference did it make? Let him weave all his little webs and plots. None of it concerned her any longer.

Logan waved at the doctor, and then turned back to face her.

His gaze narrowed warily. "You're not angry anymore. That could be bad or good."

"Or neither. Why should I get upset? It's all water under the bridge. I'm going upstairs to pack. It's over and I'm out of here."

"It's not over."

She stiffened. "The hell it's not."

Margaret hurriedly said, "I think I'll go check on Gil," and left them.

Logan's gaze never left Eve's face. He repeated, "It's not over, Eve."

"I agreed to one job and one job only. Even if I weren't ready to cut your throat for putting me in the spot you did tonight, that job ended when I tossed that skull out of the limo. If you think I'm going to hang around here while you try to retrieve it, you're crazy."

"I don't have to try to retrieve it."

Her eyes widened. "What the hell do you mean?"

"Come with me."

"What?"

"You heard me."

He turned and walked away from her.

NINE

The cemetery.

He was already past the wrought iron gate when she caught up with him. He moved purposefully down the row of graves.

She didn't follow. "What are you doing?"

"Retrieving the skull." He stopped before Randolph Barrett's grave, lifted the pallet of carnations, and moved it aside. He picked up the shovel that had been hidden beneath it and began to dig. The earth was soft, recently turned, and the task went quickly. "Since you called my hand, I have to supply you with a skull."

She stared at him in disbelief. "Are you completely crazy? Digging up any old corpse to—" She inhaled sharply as a sudden thought occurred to her. "Good God."

He glanced up at her and answered her unspoken question. "Yes, I retrieved the skull from that cornfield two months ago."

"And you buried it again here. That's why you

covered all these graves with flowers. You wanted to erase any sign the grave had been disturbed."

He nodded as he kept on digging. "There's an old saying that the best place to hide anything is in plain sight, but I admit I'm too anal to just leave it at that. I had Mark install an alarm that would go off if the box is touched, and I had him turn it off when I was in the house just now."

"And you must have substituted another skull in that coffin in the cornfield." She glanced at the name on the tombstone. "Was it Randolph Barrett's?"

"No, Barrett's only temporarily sharing his quarters. He died when he was sixty-four. I wanted a younger skull, so I bought one from a medical school in Germany."

Her head was whirling. "Wait a minute. Why? Why have you gone to all this trouble?"

"I knew they'd tumble to what I was doing eventually and that I might need a diversion. I hoped I wouldn't have to use it. I tried every way I could not to tip my hand, but something must have gone wrong. You hadn't even started the project. Things were moving too fast and I had to throw them off the track."

"What do you mean, moving too fast? I don't know what the hell you're talking about."

"You don't have to know. It's safer for you if you don't." He threw down his shovel, bent, and picked up the square lead box he'd uncovered. "All you have to do is the job I paid you for."

"I don't have to know?" Shock reverberated through her as all the implications of his deception hit home. "Why, you son of a bitch."

"Maybe." He set the box aside and began shoveling the dirt back into the grave. "But it doesn't change anything."

"It changes everything." Her voice was shaking with anger. "You took me out there to that damn cornfield, knowing it was for nothing."

"It wasn't for nothing. They knew you were on the job and I needed you there for window dressing to make the trip more convincing."

"And almost got me killed."

"Sorry. I cut it a little close."

"Sorry? Is that all you've got to say? What about Gil Price? He was shot. He was trying to save that skull for you and it wasn't even the right one."

"I hate to disappoint you. I know you want to pile all the guilt you can on my shoulders, but Gil knew exactly what he was doing. He arranged for the purchase of the skull for me."

"He knew? I'm the only one who was left in the dark?"

"Yes." He put the shovel down and drew the pallet of carnations over it and the grave. "I wouldn't have let him walk into something like that without warning him."

"But you let me walk into it."

"You were supposed to be a bystander. Gil was going to participate. I didn't know you'd be forced to—"

"Bystander." She was growing more furious by the second. "You set me up. I wondered why you wanted me there, but I didn't think it was to use me as bait."

"The skull was the bait. As I said, you were there to make it all credible. I needed to make sure that they'd think our trip had enough significance for them to follow us."

"You wanted them to chase us. You wanted them to get close enough so there would be a valid excuse for shoving that coffin out the limo."

He nodded. "They had to believe that only desperation would force me to give up the skull. I was planning on being the one to toss out the coffin, but then Gil was hurt and I had to drive."

"And Gil told me to do it. Christ, you even argued with me."

"I figured it was the quickest way to get you to do it. You were angry enough with me to do anything I didn't want you to do."

"And you would have risked letting Gil and me die to fool them."

"I was in that car too."

"If you want to commit suicide, that's your business. You had no right to endanger anyone else."

"I thought it was the only solution."

"Solution? My God, you're so obsessed with your damn politics, you were willing to stage a charade that could have killed all of us."

"I needed to buy you some time."

"Well, then, you did it for nothing." Her eyes blazed at him. "If you think I'd touch this job now, you're crazy. I'd like to strangle you and bury you here beside Randolph Barrett." She whirled away from him. "No, I'd like to bury you somewhere no one would ever find you. You deserve it, you callous bastard."

"Eve."

She ignored him as she started down the hill.

"You have a perfect right to be angry with me, but there are things for you to consider. Will you let me clarify the situation so that you—"

She continued to ignore him and speeded up her pace. Manipulative son of a bitch. Crazy, conniving bastard.

She met Margaret on the stairs as she headed for her room. "Gil's asleep. I think—"

"Arrange a car and a flight for me," she said curtly. "I'm out of here."

"Oops. I gather John wasn't very persuasive." She grimaced. "Can't say I blame you, but you really can trust John to—"

"Forget it. Make that flight the next one out."

"I'll have to check with John."

"Get me out of here or I'll walk to Atlanta." She slammed the door of her room, flipped on the light, and moved toward the closet. She dragged her suitcase out, tossed it on the bed, and headed for the bureau.

"You do have to listen to me," Logan said quietly from the doorway. "I know it's difficult to see things clearly when you're this upset, but I can't let you leave until you know what you're facing."

"I'm not interested in anything you have to say." She threw an armful of underthings into the suitcase. "Why should I? They'd probably be lies. Your credibility with me is the pits. You deceived me and you nearly got me killed."

"But you weren't killed. Getting you killed is the last thing I want."

She went back to the bureau and opened another drawer.

"Okay, let's explore the situation. You didn't think what I wanted you to do was dangerous enough to cause anyone serious problems. It seems you were wrong. They wanted the skull enough to kill for it. Therefore, they think it's as important as I do."

She dumped the contents of the second drawer into the suitcase. "It's not Kennedy."

"Then prove it to them. Prove it to both of us."

"Screw you. I don't have to prove anything to anyone."

"I'm afraid you do."

She whirled to face him. "The hell I do."

"You do if you want to keep alive." He paused. "And keep your mother alive."

She stiffened. "Are you threatening me?"

"Me? No way. I'm just telling you how it is. The situation's escalated to the point where you have only two options. Prove I'm right and let me go after the bastards with evidence. Prove me wrong and you can go to the media and get everyone off your back." He looked directly into her eyes. "Because the alternative is to have them go after you and put you down. They won't care if Donnelli's story is true or not. They won't want to take the chance."

"I can get police protection."

"That might help for a while. But it's not a permanent solution."

"I can have Joe drag your ass in for questioning. I can tell them everything."

"And I'll find a way to walk out, smelling like a rose. That's what lawyers are for." He added soberly, "I don't want to fight you, Eve. I want to keep you alive."

"Bull. You want exactly what you've wanted from the beginning."

"Yes, but one doesn't rule out the other. What happened at your lab was a warning, but what happened tonight showed they've pulled the gloves off."

"Maybe."

"Listen, think about it." He studied her face and then shook his head. "I'm not getting through to you, am I? Okay, I didn't want to tell you, but other witnesses are already being eliminated. Three people have been killed in the last few days."

"Witnesses?"

"My God, the case has been riddled with unexplained deaths since the assassination. You must have read about it." He paused. "And now it's started again. That's why I wanted to cause a diversion tonight. I hoped the killing would stop if they had another focus."

"Why should I believe you?"

"I can give you the names and addresses of the victims. You can check with the local police. As God is my witness, I'm telling you the truth."

She believed him. She wished she didn't because his words shook her. "There's no reason for anyone to hurt my mother."

"Not if they can get at you. If they can't, they might decide to use her as a threat or an example like that cat in your lab."

Blood. Her terror and horror at the first sight of the wreckage surged back. He had probably meant the reminder to do just that, but it wasn't necessary. The memory was vivid and knife-sharp and couldn't be pushed away. "You keep saying 'they.' I'm tired of walking around in the dark. Who were those men following us tonight? Who's doing this?"

He didn't answer for a moment. "The man who's calling the shots right now is James Timwick. Do you recognize the name?"

She shook her head.

"He's very high in the Treasury Department."

"And he was there tonight?"

"No, I'm not sure who those men were. They probably don't have any official status. Timwick wouldn't want any direct connection to him. In a conspiracy like this the fewer people who know, the safer he'd be. It would be much easier for him if he could use the full force of the government. But I'd bet they're hired guns."

Hired guns. It sounded like something out of a bad western. "And who did that to my lab?"

"Gil says it could be Albert Fiske. He's worked for Timwick before."

Fiske. That blood and horror now had a name. "I want Joe to know. He can track the bastard down."

"Do you really want to involve Quinn before you have proof? Timwick is a heavyweight. With one phone call he could make your friend's life very difficult." His voice lowered persuasively, "Go for that proof, Eve. Do your job. You'll make things easier for Quinn and safer for yourself."

"And do what you want."

"There's a downside to everything. But don't cut off your nose to spite your face . . . or me. You think I'm wrong. Wouldn't proving it punish me for all the problems I've forced on you?"

"Attempted murder can hardly be called a problem."

"I've leveled with you. And I've warned you. It's your decision now."

"It always has been."

"Then make the right one." He turned to leave. "It will take a little time to arrange security to take you home. I'll tell Margaret to make reservations for you on the afternoon flight out of Washington National."

"What if I want to leave now?"

He shook his head. "I've made you a target and I'm going to protect you as best I can. I'll also double the security surrounding your mother and the house in Atlanta." He looked back at her. "Change your mind, Eve. Forget how angry you are at me and do what's best for you and your mother."

The door closed behind him before she could answer. Hit and run. Manipulative bastard.

"Keep your mother alive."

She tried to smother the panic rising inside her. He had cleverly chosen the words that would strike deepest. She should ignore everything he'd said and get the hell out of there. She'd never have come if she'd known it could lead to this. He'd deliberately deceived her and embroiled her in a situation that—

Slow down. Forget the fact that she wanted to wring Logan's neck. The situation existed. Now what could she do about it?

Prove me wrong.

Tempting bait. If she worked hard, in a couple days she could have the proof.

And give in to Logan after all the hell he'd put her through?

No way. Not if there was any other path she could take.

Do what's best for you and your mother.

She slowly moved to the window. It was beginning to get light. By afternoon she could be on her way home. God, how she wanted to be back where everything was safe and familiar.

But it might no longer be safe there. Just the decision to take Logan's job might have destroyed the peace and safety she'd so carefully cultivated through the years since Fraser's execution. She was being drawn back into that nightmarish quagmire in which she'd almost drowned after Bonnie died.

She would *not* drown. If she survived Bonnie's death, she could survive anything.

BARRETT HOUSE
TUESDAY AFTERNOON

Logan was standing in the foyer when she came down the stairs just after one o'clock.

A slow smile lit his face. "You don't have your suitcase."

"It's still packed. I'm going to get out of here the minute I'm finished. But I decided that doing the job is the best way to cut all ties to this mess." She moved down the hall toward the lab. "Where's the skull?"

"You're heading right toward it. The box is on your desk." He followed her. "But don't you think you'd better get some sleep first?"

"I've already slept. I took a shower and a nap after I made my decision to get on with it."

"You could have sent me word and relieved my mind."

"I have no desire to relieve your mind."

"I can see your point. But you're doing the intelligent thing."

"If I didn't think that, I'd be heading for the front door instead of the lab." She gave him a cool glance. "And let's be clear. The minute I prove that skull doesn't belong to Kennedy, I'm going to call the newspapers and let them know what an ass you are."

"Fair enough."

"And I won't be held incommunicado. I'm calling Mom and Joe every day I'm here."

"Have I ever tried to stop you? You're no prisoner. I hope we can work together."

"Not likely." She threw open the door of the lab. The lead box occupied the center of the desk, and she moved brusquely toward it. "I work alone."

"May I ask how long it's going to take you?"

"It depends on the condition of the skull. If it's not a jigsaw puzzle, two, maybe three days."

"It looked pretty intact to me." He paused. "Try to make it two, Eve."

"Don't push me, Logan."

"I have to push you. I don't know how much time I bought. Timwick won't assume the skull he has is the right one. He'll have it examined by one of your forensic counterparts. He's bound to find out he's got the wrong one."

"According to you, he wouldn't want to take the chance of having the skull identified."

"He'd have to. He wouldn't risk tapping DNA or dental records, but he'd do this. There are always ways to dispose of people who know too much. So if the sculptor's good . . . two days?"

"It depends if he works on a cast of the skull or the skull itself. And if he's willing to push himself."

"He won't have to push himself, Timwick will be doing it for him. Who's good enough?"

"There are only four or five top forensic sculptors in the country."

"So I found out when I was searching for one. My attorney had an easy job gathering the shortlist."

She opened the lead box. "I wish to hell you'd picked someone else."

"But you're the best. I had to have the best. Who's second best?"

"Simon Doprel. He has the touch."

"Touch?"

She shrugged. "You do the measuring and the judgment calls, but when you get down to the final stages of the sculpting, it's pretty much instinct. It's as if you *feel* what's right and wrong. Some of us have it, some don't."

"Interesting." He grimaced. "And maybe a little eerie."

"Don't be stupid," she said coldly. "It's a talent, not some kind of paranormal idiocy."

"And Doprel has it too?"

"Yes." She carefully lifted the scorched skull out of the box. Caucasian. Male. Facial bones almost entirely intact. A good portion of the back of the skull was missing.

"Not very pretty, is he?" Logan said.

"You wouldn't be pretty either if you'd gone through what he did. Donnelli was lucky. The brain could have blown forward instead of backward and then there wouldn't have been any blackmail . . . or any reconstruction."

"The fire caused the brain to explode?"

She nodded. "It happens almost all the time with fire victims."

He went back to the previous conversation. "So Doprel would be a reasonable first choice?"

"If Timwick could get him. Most of his work is done for the NYPD."

"Timwick can get him." He looked at the skull. "Two days, Eve. Please."

"It will get done when it gets done. Don't worry, I'm not going to waste time. I want this over." She moved over to the pedestal and placed the skull in the center. "Now, get out of here. I've got measuring to do and I have to concentrate."

"Yes, ma'am." A few moments later the door closed.

She hadn't taken her eyes away from the skull. Shut Logan out. Don't let anything get in the way. Every measurement had to be exact.

But not yet. First she had to establish a link, just as she usually did. It was probably going to be harder since this was an adult and not a child. She had to remember that he was also a lost one. She measured different parts of the cranium and wrote the numbers down on her pad. "You're not who he says you are, but that doesn't matter. You're important in your own right, Jimmy."

Jimmy? Where had that come from?

It could be Jimmy Hoffa or some Mafia goon.

Grinning, she remembered the reasons she had told Logan she shouldn't take the job.

But here she was doing it.

And Jimmy was as good a name as any.

"I'm going to do all kinds of undignified things to you, but it's all for a good cause, Jimmy," she murmured. "Just hang in there with me, okay?"

CHEVY CHASE, MARYLAND
TUESDAY EVENING

"I've no time for this, Timwick," Simon Doprel said. "You've pulled me away from an important case that's going to trial next month. Find someone else."

"It's only a few days. You agreed to do it."

"I didn't agree to leave New York and come down here to the country. Your men practically kidnapped me. Why couldn't you bring the skull to me?"

"It had to be kept confidential. Don't back out now. Finding out if this is the terrorist we've been looking for is more important than a murder case."

"What's the Treasury Department doing chasing terrorists?" Simon asked sourly.

"We always get involved if the threat concerns the White House. If you need anything, just ask Fiske. He'll be closer than your shadow until you finish the job." Timwick smiled. "We want to make you as comfortable as we can while you're with us." He walked out of the room and closed the door.

It was just as well Doprel was so reluctant to do the job, he thought grimly. He would work at top speed, and speed was what they needed.

When Timwick had been told how the skull had been tossed from the limo, he'd been immediately suspicious. The retrieval might have been a little too easy. Fear for their lives could have made Logan sacrifice the skull, but it might also have been a diversion. Why not take out the skull before throwing out the coffin? Panic?

Logan wasn't a man to panic, but he'd been driving. Kenner had said it was the woman who had thrown out the coffin. At any rate, they would know soon.

And the surveillance would go on at Barrett House until they did.

"You're awake." Logan came into the room and dropped down in the chair beside Gil's bed. "How are you feeling?"

"A hell of a lot better if that doctor hadn't doped me up," Gil growled. "My shoulder's fine, but I've got a jumbo headache."

"You needed the rest."

"Not twelve hours." He struggled to sit up. "What's happening?"

Logan leaned forward and adjusted the pillows against the headboard. "Eve's working on the skull now."

"I'm surprised. I thought your decision to take her along was a mistake. You could have scared her off."

"Or made her mad enough to dig in her heels. It could have gone either way. But I didn't have a choice. I needed to make them think that what we were doing was important. I wasn't expecting them to get that close."

"You mean you were hoping they wouldn't." He smiled sardonically. "Don't bullshit me. You would have done it anyway."

"Probably." He added soberly, "That doesn't stop me from being sorry about letting you take the heat."

"That's why I was there. We agreed that I'd run interference while you took care of the red herring." Gil made a face. "But I was clumsy. I would have been toast if it hadn't been for our bone lady. She was damn good."

"Yes, very good. It seems Quinn thought she should know how to protect herself from the Frasers of the world."

"Quinn again?"

Logan nodded. "He always seems to be in the background, doesn't he?" He stood up. "I'm going to go down and take Eve a sandwich. She hasn't left the lab yet."

"I'm sure she'll be grateful you're going to allow her to eat."

"Drop the sarcasm."

"I wasn't being sarcastic. I meant it. Now that you've got her on the job, I imagine you'll crack the whip until you get what you want."

"She wouldn't let me. Anything I can get you?"

"My CD player and discs." He grinned. "How thick are these walls? I was thinking about tormenting you with Loretta Lynn's 'Coal Miner's Daughter.'"

"If you do, I'll ask Margaret to come in and play Florence Nightingale."

"You wouldn't dare, I'm a sick man." His smile disappeared. "How much time do you think we have?"

"Three days maximum. Once they find out they've got the wrong skull, they'll launch an all-out war. We've got to be out of here by that time." He headed for the door. "So get well and on your feet."

"Tomorrow. I'll be up and functioning and back at the carriage house. I'm tempted to loll in bed with Loretta and Garth Brooks, but it's not worth the chance of Margaret nursing me."

Logan closed the door and went downstairs to the kitchen. Fifteen minutes later he was knocking on the lab door, a ham sandwich and bowl of vegetable soup on a tray in his hand.

No answer.

"May I come in?"

"Go away. I'm busy."

"I have food. You've got to stop and eat sometime."

"Put it down and I'll get to it later."

Logan hesitated and then set the tray on the table beside the door. "Try to make it soon. The soup will get cold."

Christ, he sounded like a nagging wife. How far the mighty had fallen. It's a good thing Margaret wasn't nearby to hear that curt rejection. It would have amused the hell out of her.

TEN

"You didn't eat your dinner. You can't work if you don't eat, Mama."

Eve slowly raised her head from the desk.

Bonnie was sitting on the floor by the door, her arms linked around her knees. "And it's dumb to fall asleep at your desk when you have a bed to go to."

"I was going to close my eyes for only a minute," she said defensively. "I have work to do."

"I know." Bonnie looked at the skull on the pedestal. "Good work."

"Good?"

"I think so." Bonnie's forehead was creased in a puzzled frown. "I'm not sure. I think it's important. That's why I called you up to the cemetery."

"You didn't call me. It was an impulse."

Bonnie smiled. "Was it?"

"Or maybe all those flowers on the graves stirred

some kind of subliminal message. I knew Logan was devious and maybe I suspected he was— Stop smiling."

"I'm sorry. I'm actually very proud of you. It's nice to have a mom who's so smart. Wrong, but still very smart." She looked back at the skull. "You're getting along pretty well with Jimmy, aren't you?"

"Fair. There are some problems."

"You'll solve them. I'll help you."

"What?"

"I always try to help you in whatever you do."

"Oh, now you're my guardian angel? And I suppose you were looking out for me when I was in that limo the other night."

"No, I couldn't do anything. It scared me. I want to be with you but not yet. It's not your time and it would upset the balance."

"Bull. If there was any sense or balance in the universe, you would never have been taken from me."

"I don't know how it works. Sometimes things go terribly wrong. But I don't want it to go wrong for you too, Mama. That's why you have to be very careful now."

"I'm being careful and trying my darnedest to get out of this mess. That's why I'm working on Jimmy."

"Yes, Jimmy is important." Bonnie sighed. "I wish he weren't. It would be easier." She leaned back against the wall. "I can see you're going to push yourself to exhaustion in the next few days. If you won't go to bed, lay your head back down on the desk and go to sleep."

"I am asleep."

"Of course you are. Sometimes I forget I'm only a dream. Well, will you do me a favor and lay your head back down on the desk? It's a little weird sleeping sitting upright in that chair."

"You're the one who's weird." She laid her head on her arms on the desk. After a moment she asked in a low voice, "Are you leaving now?"

"Not yet. I'll stay awhile. I like to watch you when you're sleeping. All the kinks and worries kind of flow away. It's nice to see you that way."

Eve could feel the tears burn her eyes even as her lids closed. "Weird kid . . ."

BARRETT HOUSE
WEDNESDAY MORNING

"You didn't eat anything last night." Logan opened the door and strode into the lab carrying a breakfast tray. "I hate to have my labor wasted. I'm going to stay and watch you polish off this meal."

Eve looked up from the skull. "Your concern is touching." She went to the sink and washed her hands. "Except I know you just don't want me to keel over and waste time."

"Exactly." He settled himself in the visitor's chair. "So humor me."

"The hell I will." She sat down at the desk and took the napkin off the tray. "I'll eat because I'm hungry and it's sensible. Period."

"That's putting me in my place. I don't care as long as you eat." He was studying her face. "You look surprisingly rested but your bed hasn't been slept in."

"I took a nap here." She drank the glass of orange juice. "And stay out of my bedroom, Logan. You've invaded too many parts of my life as it is."

"I feel a sense of responsibility. I want to help."

"To speed up the work?"

"Only partly. I'm not a complete bastard."

She took a bite of omelette.

He chuckled. "That was a weighted silence. Well, at least you're not openly attacking me. That nap was good for you. I sense a slight mellowing."

"Then you sense wrong. I just don't have time to try to analyze your good and bad points. I'm busy."

"Even that's a concession." His gaze went to the pedestal. "I see you've gotten to the voodoo doll stage. Did you name him too?"

"Jimmy."

"Why did—" He chuckled again as he understood. "It's not Hoffa, Eve."

"We'll see." To her surprise, she found herself smiling. After the tension of the hours of work it was good to relax for a few moments . . . even with Logan. "Though I don't think you'd be this involved with a labor leader."

"Well, let's just say I wouldn't regard resurrecting him of paramount importance." His gaze returned to the pedestal. "Interesting. It seems impossible you can rebuild a face with that little to go on. How do you do it?"

"What do you care? As long as it gets done."

"I'm cursed with an inquiring mind. Is that so odd?"

She shrugged. "I guess not."

"What are those little sticks called?"

"Tissue-depth markers. They're usually made of ordinary pencil erasers, the kind you use in a mechanical pencil. I cut each marker to the proper measurement and glue it onto its specific point on the face. There are more than twenty points of the skull for which there are known tissue depths. Facial tissue depth has been found to be fairly consistent in people the same age, race, sex, and weight. There are anthropological charts that give a specific measurement for each point. For instance, in a Caucasian male of average weight, the tissue-depth thickness at the mid-philtrum point is—"

"What?"

"Sorry. I mean the space between the nose and top lip is ten millimeters. The architecture of the bone beneath the tissue determines whether someone has a jutting chin or bulging eyes or whatever."

"And what do you do next?"

"I take strips of plasticine and apply them between the markers, then build up to all of the tissue-depth points."

"It sounds like a connect the dots game."

"Sort of, only in three-dimension and it's a hell of a lot more difficult. I have to concentrate on the scientific elements of building the face, like keeping true to the tissue-depth measurements as I fill in between the plasticine strips and considering where the facial muscles are located and how they affect the contours of the face."

"But what about the size of the nose? Old Jimmy doesn't have one."

"That's a toughie. The width and length is determined again by measurements. For a Caucasian like Jimmy, I measure the nasal opening at the widest point and add five millimeters on each side for the nostrils. That gives me the width. The length, or projection, depends on the measurement of the little bone at the base of the nasal opening, called the nasal spine. It's very simple. I multiply the spine measurement by three and add the mid-philtrum tissue-depth measurement."

"Ah, the dreaded mid-philtrum again."

"Do you want to know this or not?"

"Yes, I always joke when I'm faced with something a little out of my depth." He made a face. "Honest, I didn't mean it. Go on."

"The nasal spine also determines the angle of the nose. It will show me if the nose is turned up, angled down, or very straight. Once you've got the nose, the ears are easier. They're usually as long as the nose."

"It sounds very precise."

She shrugged. "I wish it were. Even with all the formulas and measurements and scientific data about what makes up a nose, there's no way I can be sure I'm reconstructing the original nose. I've just got to do my best and hope I come close."

"And the mouth?"

"Measurements again. The height of the lips is determined by measuring the distance between the top and bottom gum line. The width is generally the distance between the canine teeth, which usually coincides with the distance between the centers of the eyes. Thickness of the lips comes from the anthropological charts for tissue depth. Like the nose, I have no clues about the unique shape, so I have to use instinct and judgment to—" She pushed the tray away and stood up. "I don't have time to talk anymore. I have to get back to work."

"Then I assume I'm dismissed again." He rose to his feet and picked up the tray. "Would it be all right if I come in and watch you sometime, or would that be invading your space?"

"Why? Do you think I'm really going to make him look like Jimmy Hoffa?"

"No. But could it happen?"

She shook her head. "Haven't you been listening? The bone structure tells the tale."

"What about the smoothing and filling-in process and the judgment calls on the nose and mouth and—"

"Okay, if you have a preconceived idea of identity, it might influence what you do. That's why I never look at photos until I'm finished. During this period I don't allow myself any creativity. Pure science has to guide the basic foundation for the face. When the technical development is complete, then I can consider the face as a whole and give artistic judgment full rein until it's finished. If I didn't do it that way, the product would just be a sculpture and not a facial reconstruction." Her lips tightened. "You can bet I wouldn't let that happen. Jimmy's not going to look like Hoffa unless he's Hoffa. So you don't have to keep an eye on me, Logan."

"That wasn't my intention." He grimaced. "If I admit I'm tense and maybe a little worried, would you please let me come?"

"Doubts? I thought you were so sure it was Kennedy."

"I want to see that skull come to life, Eve," he said simply. "I know that I don't deserve any consideration, but will you let me?"

She hesitated. She was still annoyed and resentful. After all he had done, she should tell him to go jump in the lake. On the other hand, a truce might be necessary for getting out of this predicament safely. She lifted one shoulder in a half shrug. "I don't care if you don't talk to me. I probably wouldn't know you're in the room. If you open your mouth, you're out."

"Not a word." He headed for the door. "You won't even know

I'm here. I'll bring you food and coffee and then curl up in the corner like a docile pussycat."

"I don't know any cats that are docile." She moved toward the pedestal and was already closing him out. "Just be quiet . . ."

CHEVY CHASE
WEDNESDAY AFTERNOON

"You don't seem to be progressing very fast, Doprel," Fiske said. "And you're not even working on the skull."

"I never work on the skull," Doprel said. "I'm making a cast and I'll do the work on that."

"Does everyone? It seems like a waste of time."

"No, but I prefer to do it that way," Doprel said with irritation. "It's safer. I don't have to be so careful of the skull."

"Timwick wants the work done quickly. This cast is—"

"I work the way I work," Doprel said coldly. "I find it goes even faster when I don't have to be cautious."

"Timwick doesn't care if the skull is damaged. We don't have time for the cast." He paused. "I'd think you'd want to get this done fast so you can go home."

"It's not the way I—" He hesitated. "Screw it. What the hell do I care if the damn thing gets broken? I'll work on the skull. Now leave me alone, Fiske. You're supposed to bring me meals and get me what I need, not criticize my methods."

Arrogant prick. He was treating Fiske like a lousy servant. Fiske had seen those scientific types before. They thought they were better and smarter than everyone else. Doprel with all his training and brains couldn't do what Fiske did in a million years. He wouldn't have either the cunning or the guts.

But maybe Doprel would learn his mistake before this was over. Timwick said it depended on the results. Fiske smiled. "I didn't mean to offend." He started to leave. "Let me go make a pot of coffee for you."

BARRETT HOUSE
WEDNESDAY
10:50 P.M.

Done.

Eve stepped back, took off her glasses, and wiped her stinging eyes with the back of her hands. The meticulous work of laying the clay strips was finished, and her eyes were strained badly. She didn't dare do anything else right now; she couldn't risk making a mistake. She'd sit down, rest for an hour or so, and then begin again.

She crossed to the desk, dropped down in the chair, leaned back, and closed her eyes.

"Are you okay?" Logan asked.

She jumped, and her gaze flew to the far corner of the lab. Jesus, she had forgotten he was in the room. In the past twenty-four hours, he had moved in and out of the lab like a ghost, and she couldn't remember him even speaking to her.

Maybe he had. She had been so absorbed with Jimmy that she didn't remember much of those hours. She vaguely recalled she had called her mother once but had no idea what she had said.

"Okay?" Logan repeated.

"Of course I'm okay. I was just resting. I don't have the best vision in the world and my eyes are strained."

"With good reason. I've never seen anyone work with that much intensity. Michelangelo probably was less tense when he was sculpting *David*."

"He had more time."

"How's it coming?"

"I don't know. I never know until it's done. I'm through with the donkey work. Now comes the hard part."

"A little rest might help." He was sitting with apparent ease, but she was suddenly aware of the tension in him.

"I *was* trying to rest," she said dryly.

"Sorry. And I was trying to help." He smiled crookedly. "I've been expecting you to collapse any minute."

"But you didn't stop me."

"I can't. The clock's ticking." He paused. "How long?"

"Twelve hours. Maybe a little longer." She wearily leaned back in the chair again. "I don't know. As long as it takes. Don't nag me, dammit."

"Right." He rose jerkily to his feet. "I'll leave you alone to rest. Why don't you lie down on the couch? When do you want me to wake you?"

"I don't want to sleep. I just have to rest my eyes."

"Then I'll come back later." He added as he moved toward the door, "If you don't mind."

"It doesn't matter." She closed her eyes again. "Tell me, Logan, doesn't all this subservience and courtesy stick in your throat?"

"A little. But I can live with it. I learned a long time ago that if you're not the most important chip in a computer, you grease the wheels and don't get in the way."

"I believe that's the worst mix of metaphors I've heard."

"How would you know? Your mind's probably too blurry for you to think straight."

"I don't have to think. From now on it's pure instinct. I just have to be able to see."

"I can feed you, but I can't help you there."

"At this point, no one can help me."

The door closed behind him.

"No one," she murmured. "It's just between you and me, isn't it, Jimmy?"

CHEVY CHASE
WEDNESDAY EVENING
11:45 P.M.

"He's nearly finished, Timwick," Fiske said. "He said the job was easier than he thought. Maybe another twelve hours."

"Have you seen the skull?"

"I can't make anything of it. It doesn't even have a nose or eyes yet. I think you're wasting your time."

"I'll be the judge of that. Call me when he's done and I'll come right down."

Fiske replaced the receiver. Twelve more hours and he'd know if Doprel or Logan and Duncan were the targets. He almost hoped it was Doprel. Logan and Duncan were more of a challenge, but Doprel was beginning to annoy him beyond belief.

BARRETT HOUSE
THURSDAY
6:45 A.M.

Smooth the clay.

Delicacy.

Sensitivity.

Let the tips of your fingers move of their own volition.

Don't think.

Help me, Jimmy.

The clay was cool, but her fingertips felt warm, almost hot, as they molded and smoothed.

Generic ears. She had no idea whether they'd stuck out or had longer lobes.

A longer, thinner nose.

Mouth?

Generic again. She knew the width but not the shape. She made the lips closed, without expression.

Eyes.

So important. So difficult. No measurements and very few scientific indicators. Okay, don't be in a rush. Study the shape and angle of the orbits. The size of eyeballs were all pretty much the same and grew only a little from infancy to adulthood. Should she make Jimmy's eyes protruding, deep-set, or somewhere in between? The angle of the orbits and the bony ridge above would help her decide.

But not yet. Eyes were always a clincher. Most forensic sculptors worked from top to bottom and the eyes went in close to the beginning. She had never been able to do that. She'd found that she had an even greater tendency to hurry if the eyes were looking at her.

Bring me home.

More smoothing along the cheekbone. Not too deep.

Don't look at the face as a whole. Take each section and feature separately.

Smooth.

Fill in.

Slow down. You can't let go yet. Don't let your mind totally guide your hands. Don't visualize. Build. Measurements are still critical. Check them again.

Nose width, 32 mm. Okay.

Nose projection, 19 mm. Okay.

Lip height, 14 mm. No, it should be 12. Bring the top lip down, it's usually thinner than the bottom lip.

Build up more around the mouth, there's a major muscle under there.

More shaping to the nostrils.

A little creasing on each side of the nose. How deep?

What's the difference? Nobody ever identified anyone by a skin crease.

Deepen the area around the lower lip.

Why? It didn't matter. Do it.

Smooth.

Mold.

Fill in.

Sun lines around the eye cavities. Lines around the mouth.

She was working feverishly now. Her hands flew over Jimmy's face.

Almost finished.

Who are you, Jimmy? Help me. We're almost done. We'll take a photo and circulate it and someone will take you home.

Smooth.

Mold.

Stop. Don't gild the lily.

She stepped back and drew a deep breath. She'd done all she could do.

Except the eyes.

What color? Logan would probably prefer she use blue. Kennedy's blue eyes were as famous as his smile. Screw Logan. This couldn't be Kennedy and why should she indulge Logan. She took another step back and allowed herself to look at the full face for the first time. She would use the brown she usually—

"Oh, my God."

She stood frozen, staring at the face she'd created. She felt as if she had been kicked in the stomach.

No.

It was a lie.

She moved slowly, heavily, over to the table, where the small eye case lay open. The eyeballs glittered up at her—blue, brown, gray, hazel, green.

She took the case and carried it to the pedestal.

She was exhausted; her mind could be playing tricks on her. The eyes would make a difference. Brown. Put in brown eyes.

Her hand was shaking as she took out the first brown eyeball and inserted it in the left cavity. Then she took the second eyeball and fitted it to the right.

"You've put in the wrong eyes," Logan said from the corner. "You know it, Eve."

She stared straight into the brown eyes before her, her back rigid. "I don't know it."

"Put in the right eyes."

"It's a mistake. I made a mistake somewhere along the way."

"You don't allow yourself to make mistakes. Put in the eyes that you know belong with the face."

She took out the brown eyes and put them back in the case. She stood staring blindly down at the eyes in the case.

"You know which ones to use, Eve."

"All *right*." She reached down, picked up the eyeballs, and jammed them in the sockets.

"Now step back and look at him."

She moved back from the pedestal. Incredible. God in heaven, it couldn't be true.

But there couldn't be any doubt.

"You bastard." Her voice was shaking as she stared into the gray eyes. *She* was shaking. She felt as if the entire globe was trembling on its axis. "It's Ben Chadbourne. It's the President."

CHEVY CHASE

"Well?" Doprel asked sourly. "Is it your terrorist?"

Timwick gazed at the skull. "You're sure this is a correct representation?"

"I'm sure. May I go home now?"

"Yes, thank you for your hard work. I'll have you driven back to New York immediately. Naturally, you'll keep this quiet. We wouldn't want a security leak."

"I've no desire to talk about this job. It hasn't been a highlight of my career. I'll go pack." Doprel strode out of the room.

"Shall I take him back?" Fiske asked from where he stood behind Timwick.

"No." Timwick turned away from the bust. "The skull's a ringer. Doprel's not important anymore. I'll send him home with someone else. I have other work for you and we'll have to move fast." He moved toward the phone. "Leave me alone. I have some phone calls to make."

He waited until Fiske was out the door before he punched in the secure line at the White House. "It's not him. Same age. Same general facial structure. But it's not him."

BARRETT HOUSE

"You lied to me," Eve whispered. She whirled on Logan. "You *lied.*"

"Yes. It's the last lie I'll tell you, Eve."

"You expect me to believe that? Every way I turn I find out you've lied to me again. You never thought it was Kennedy. My God, you even put all those books and reports about him in your desk just to make me believe what you wanted me to believe. It was all some kind of wild red herring."

"There wasn't anything wild about it. I worked very hard to make that lie plausible. I had to have a cover to hide the fact that I was having Donnelli's claim investigated. That's why I laid the false trail to Kennedy. So they couldn't be sure if I suspected something or I was just a crackpot. I had also begun a discreet search for a forensic sculptor, the one person who could reveal if there's any truth to Donnelli's story."

"Me."

"Yes, you were the key player I needed."

Her gaze went back to Jimmy's skull. No, not Jimmy anymore. Ben Chadbourne, President of the United States. She shook her head. "It's all crazy. When you told me what had happened at Donnelli's funeral home, I assumed it had taken place decades ago. That's what you meant me to think."

"Yes. It was only two years ago."

"Lies."

"You had to be entirely uninfluenced, with no preconceived ideas. That was the only way to guarantee that you would reconstruct the face that belonged on that skull." His gaze followed hers to Chadbourne's face. "It was something of a miracle watching you work, bringing him to life. I was almost sure it was him, but every touch seemed to—"

"How did he die? Murder?"

"Probably. It would make sense."

"And that man in the White House is one of his doubles?"

He nodded.

She shook her head. "It's too bizarre. It couldn't be pulled off with Chadbourne anymore than with Kennedy. The office is too public."

"But they did it."

"Timwick?"

"He's the front man."

"Fronting for who?"

"Chadbourne's wife. She has to be the one pulling the strings. She's the only one who has the power to protect any double and coach him."

Lisa Chadbourne. Eve remembered her at the press conference; she had stood on the sidelines, her gaze fixed lovingly on her husband. "And she's supposed to be a murderer?"

"Maybe. We can't be sure until we find out what happened to Ben Chadbourne."

"What motive could she possibly have?"

"I don't know. Ambition, possibly. She's smart and savvy and knows how to manipulate a situation. She worked her way through law school and became a partner in a prestigious law firm. After she married Chadbourne she pushed him until he made it to the White House. Once there, she did everything right." He smiled sardonically. "She's the perfect first lady."

"I don't believe it could be her."

"I didn't think you would. I had a few problems believing it myself. I'd met her a few times and I liked her. That combination of charm and intelligence can be very disarming."

Eve shook her head.

"I'm throwing too much at you. I wish I could let you have longer to absorb it all, but I can't. We're almost out of time." He stood up. "All right, don't believe it's Lisa Chadbourne. Believe someone else is behind it. But you'll grant that she has to be in on any conspiracy for it to work?"

"That's . . . reasonable." She glanced back at the skull. "But what if this isn't Chadbourne? What if this is the double?"

"It's Chadbourne."

"Because you want it to be?"

"Because it is. It's the only thing that makes sense." He paused. "Because it was James Timwick who delivered that body to Donnelli."

"How can you be sure? Donnelli's father could have lied."

"I'm sure he could have. He appears to have been pretty much of a scumball. But he wasn't a dumb scumball. He dealt with some pretty lethal characters and he had to protect himself. He'd equipped his crematorium with an audiotaping setup. He got Timwick on audiotape." He smiled crookedly. "It was part of his legacy to his son and the bait that hooked me. Because of that tape, I had Gil check into the story."

"If you had a tape that incriminating, you wouldn't need any more proof. You could take it to the authorities or the media and let them—"

He was shaking his head. "It wasn't incriminating enough. No detail. No 'Hey, I'm James Timwick and I'm burning up the President of the United States.' It was just general conversation while they were in the crematorium. Timwick ordered one of his men to help him with the body. Once, he asked Donnelli for a chair so he could sit down. Evidently the poor man had a taxing evening and he was tired. Comments like that."

"Then how do you know it was Timwick?"

"I'd met him before. He's director of the Secret Service and attended a good many of Chadbourne's functions and he—"

"Secret Service. You said he was high up in the Treasury Department." Her lips tightened. "Oh, yes, the Secret Service is part of the Treasury Department. Just another little evasion."

"Sorry." He continued. "Timwick had a very distinguished career and was a key player in getting Chadbourne elected. His voice is very distinctive. He's from Massachusetts and the accent is pretty unmistakable. I had a hunch it was him, and when Donnelli Junior sent me the cassette, I ran some of the videotapes I made of Chadbourne on the campaign trail and did a comparison. It wasn't difficult. Timwick isn't a man who likes to stay in the background. I think he was disappointed Chadbourne didn't give him a cabinet post."

"I can't believe they let Donnelli live to blackmail them. Why didn't they just force him to give up the tape and the skull?"

"He told them he put a copy of the tape and an explanation in the hands of a lawyer, who would send it immediately to the media if he disappeared or died of unnatural causes."

"Then he died of a heart attack, and his son did disappear."

"But they weren't responsible, so they had to assume Donnelli Junior had made a better deal. I imagine the hunt for him was pretty intense. I was careful, but there might have been something that led them to believe Donnelli might have made contact with me." He shrugged. "Maybe not. It could be they were looking for anything or anyone suspicious and I set off the alarm bell."

"It's incredible. Why would they do away with Chadbourne?"

"I have no idea. I can only guess." He shrugged. "Lisa Chadbourne's a unique woman. Some people say that she would have made a better president than her husband. But the consensus is that the country isn't ready to accept a woman president yet, so she has to work behind the scenes. It must have grated on her to always stay in the background. And Ben Chadbourne was a strong man himself. Maybe she wanted more control over him. More control of the country."

"That's a lot of maybes."

"They're all I have to give you. All I can tell you is that I believe it happened. Will you do me a favor? Go to the library and pop in the videotapes in the top desk drawer. There are three of them with recent Chadbourne speeches and press conferences. I've edited them for comparison. I'd appreciate it if you'd try to watch with an open mind."

"And what do you expect me to see?"

"Just watch them."

"It's crazy. Like some kind of—"

"What can it hurt?"

She was silent and then jerkily nodded her head. "Okay." She headed for the door. "I'll watch them."

As soon as she left, Logan crossed to the desk and dialed Gil at the carriage house. "She's finished. The skull is Chadbourne."

Gil cursed softly. "I don't know why it comes as a shock. We knew it probably would be."

"Hell, I watched her doing it and I felt the same way when I saw it."

"How is she taking it?"

"Multiply your reaction by about a million and you'd come close. She's not sure she believes me. Can't blame her. I wouldn't after all the deceptions I've laid on her. At least she agreed to look at the tapes. After she finishes, I'll have another go at her."

"Do we have time?"

"God knows. But the ID on the skull is just the first crack in the door. We still need her and we need her to believe he's Chadbourne. After that, everything will fall in line. Are you ready to go?"

"Yep."

"Tell Mark and Margaret to pack up everything. Get them out of here as soon as possible."

"Done."

Logan replaced the receiver and moved to stand before Chadbourne's skull. Poor bastard. He didn't deserve this fate. Logan had never agreed with his politics, but he had liked the man. No one could help but like Ben Chadbourne. He had dreamed dreams and tried to turn them into reality. He lacked practicality and probably would have increased the national debt astronomically, but there weren't many men who dreamed at all these days.

And those who did usually ended like this man staring back at him with bright glass eyes.

ELEVEN

It couldn't be true.

Chadbourne . . .

Eve's gaze was fastened on the TV screen. The last tape was almost over. The face was the same, the mannerisms the same, even the voice and intonations seemed identical.

Lisa Chadbourne was present at almost every public function starting after November two years before, and Eve had begun to focus on her during the last tape.

Always charming, never losing her loving smile, her gaze always fastened on Chadbourne. Chadbourne glancing frequently at her with affection and respect even in the midst—

Eve suddenly sat upright in her chair.

She watched the tape for a few more minutes, jumped to her feet, and hurried across the room to rerun the tape from the beginning.

. . .

"She's signaling him," Eve said flatly when she walked back into the lab ten minutes later. "A whole set of signals. When she smooths the front of her skirt, he cracks a joke. When she folds her hands on her lap, he gives a negative response. When she straightens the collar of her suit, it's a yes. I don't know what the rest means, but those are pretty obvious. Whenever he's uncertain, she gives him the answer."

"Yes."

"You knew it. Why didn't you tell me to watch out for it?"

"I hoped you'd find out for yourself."

"She's controlling him like a puppet," she said slowly.

Logan's gaze narrowed on her face. "And do you really believe the Ben Chadbourne who was elected to the presidency would let anyone else pull the strings?"

She was silent a moment. "No."

"Then is it reasonable that man is not Ben Chadbourne?"

"It's not reasonable, it's crazy." She paused. "But it could be the truth."

"Thank God." His sigh of relief came from deep in his chest. He moved toward the door. "Pack up the skull. There's a leather carrying case in the closet. We've got to get out of here."

"Not until we talk. You haven't told me everything, have you?"

"No, we'll talk later. I don't know how much time we have right now. The only reason I risked staying this long is that I had to have your cooperation."

"We do have time. For God's sake, do you expect someone to break through those electric gates?"

"Maybe." His lips tightened grimly. "It could happen. Anything could happen. Think about the power of the presidency. There isn't much that couldn't be covered up if you have enough clout. As long as they think they have Chadbourne's skull, they'll go slowly, eliminate us one by one at their leisure. But as soon as they find out they have the wrong skull, they're going to assume we have the right one. The gloves will come off. And they'll do anything to get the skull back and erase every witness."

A bolt of panic jolted through Eve. If she believed that skull on the pedestal was Ben Chadbourne, then she had to believe the threat was as deadly as Logan said.

After all the lies he had told her, there was no way she could trust him, but she had created Chadbourne's face with her own hands and mind. If she trusted her own skill and integrity, then she had to believe the skull was Ben Chadbourne.

She strode quickly across the room toward the pedestal. "Get moving. I'll pack up the skull."

CHEVY CHASE

"Kenner and six of his men will be here in ten minutes in a chopper," Timwick told Fiske as he strode out of the lab. "You're going to Barrett House."

Fiske stiffened. "I won't knuckle under to that prick Kenner again."

"You won't have to knuckle to anyone. It's your game now. Kenner's only instructions are to assist and clean up after you."

It was about time. "Logan and Duncan?"

"And everyone else in the place. Margaret Wilson and the electronics man went to the airport earlier today. We'll have to track them down later. They're relatively unimportant, or Logan wouldn't have permitted them to leave. But Price, Duncan, and Logan are still at Barrett House. They're your targets. Handle it any way you have to. We can't have anyone left alive who knows what they were doing there."

This was more like it. Clean and neat. Whoever Timwick had phoned clearly had more intelligence than he did. "No witnesses?"

"No witnesses."

"What the hell are you doing?" Logan asked as he strode back into the lab carrying a duffel bag. "That skull was supposed to be packed."

Eve repositioned the cameras. "Taking some more shots of the head. I may need them."

"Get them later."

"Are you going to guarantee we'll be somewhere with technical equipment?"

He hesitated. "No."

"Then, shut up." She took two more shots. "I'm hurrying as fast as I can."

"We have to get out of here, Eve."

She took three shots of the left profile. "That should be enough. Where are those photographs you said you had of Ben Chadbourne?"

He reached into his duffel and brought out a brown envelope.

"Are they current?"

"None taken more than four years ago. May we go now?"

She stuffed the envelope in her purse, placed the skull in the leather box beside the pedestal, and fastened the latches. She pointed to the small metal box beside the cameras. "Stuff that in your duffel. I may need it."

"What is it?"

"It's the mixer. I can probably jerry-rig cameras, VCRs, and monitors, but a mixer is sometimes specialized and more difficult. I may not—"

"Never mind. Forget I asked." He picked up the mixer and put it in his duffel. "Anything else?"

She shook her head. "Just grab Ben's case. I'll get Mandy."

"Mandy?"

"You have your priorities. I have mine. Mandy's just as important to me as Ben Chadbourne."

"Take whatever you like. Just get out of here."

Gil met them at the front entrance. "Sorry, I've got only one bag for you, Eve. With this shoulder, I can't manage anything else."

"It doesn't matter." She started for the front door. "Let's go."

"Wait. There's another— Shit."

She heard it too. A low throbbing, becoming louder by the second. Helicopter rotors.

Logan went to the window. "They'll be landing in a few minutes." He ran toward the kitchen.

Eve followed him. "Where's Margaret? We've got to—"

"She and Mark left over an hour ago," Gil said. "They should be at the airport by now. In three hours they'll be at a safe house in Sanibel, Florida."

"Where are we going? Shouldn't we try to get to the limo?"

"No time. And there's bound to be someone watching outside the gate." Logan was opening the door of the walk-in pantry. "Come on." He reached under one of the bottom shelves, lifted up a trapdoor, and tossed his duffel bag into the darkness. "Don't ask questions. Just climb down the ladder."

She scrambled down the ladder and found herself in some kind of cellar with an earthen floor. Logan followed. "Close the pantry door, Gil."

"Done. They're in the house, John. I heard them at the front door."

"Then get the hell down here and close the trapdoor," John ordered.

"Stand aside. I'm tossing down the suitcase." A moment later the light was blocked as Gil closed the trapdoor and bolted it.

Running footsteps on the wood floor above them.

Shouts.

"Where are we?" she whispered. "A cellar?"

"Yes, with a tunnel." Logan's voice was almost inaudible as he set off down the passageway. "You asked why I bought this particular house. It was used by the Underground Railroad to smuggle slaves out of the South before the Civil War. I had the beams reinforced. The tunnel leads a half mile north and underneath the fence to the woods. Stay close. I can't risk a flashlight until we get around the next curve."

He was walking so rapidly, she and Gil were almost running to keep up with him.

They must be away from the house. She could no longer hear steps above them, she realized with relief.

Logan's penlight suddenly illuminated the darkness in front of them. "Run. They'll be searching the house, and it won't be long before they find the trapdoor."

She *was* running, dammit.

Her breath was coming in labored pants.

She heard Gil cursing softly behind her.

He was wounded. How much longer could he keep up this pace?

Up ahead Logan was opening a door. Thank God.

Up the ladder.

Daylight.

A thick screen of shrubs hid the door, but light filtered through them.

Fresh air.

Outside.

"Quick," Logan said. "Just a little farther . . ."

They followed Logan around the shrubs and deeper into the woods. Behind another screen of bushes, a car, an older model Ford with the blue paint beginning to chip.

"Get in back." Logan placed Chadbourne's case on the floor of the passenger seat and climbed in the driver's seat.

Eve sank into the backseat beside Gil and set Mandy's case on the floor at her feet. She barely had the door shut, when Logan started the car and it began moving over the bumpy terrain. Jesus, what if they got a flat tire? "Where are we going?"

"There's a back road three miles away. Once we reach it, we'll circle the woods and head for the freeway." The car hit another bump. "That should buy us a little time. They'll probably use the helicopter to try to spot us, but even if they do, the license plates on this car couldn't be traced to me."

If they even reached the road, Eve thought as they plowed over one more shrub.

"It's okay." Gil's gaze was fixed on her face. "I had heavy-duty tires and a new engine put on this baby. It's not as decrepit as it looks."

"How's your shoulder?" she asked.

"Okay." He smiled slyly. "But my spirits would be a hell of a lot better if it wasn't John doing the driving again."

"No one in the tunnel." Kenner was climbing back up the ladder into the pantry. "It leads to the woods. I've sent two men to reconnoiter."

"If Logan arranged a bolt hole, he would have arranged transport." Fiske moved out of the pantry. "I'll scout the area from above in the helicopter. Stay here and burn the place to the ground. Nothing's cleaner than fire."

Kenner shrugged. "Okay. Then I'll set an explosion."

Idiot. It was a good thing Fiske was in charge now. "No explosion. That's not clean. Set a fire. No gasoline. Make it look like bad wiring."

"That will take time."

"Taking time is worth it to keep a job clean." He headed toward the helicopter. "See to it."

He had been in the air ten minutes when he flipped open his cell phone and dialed Timwick. "No one was at the house. We're scouting the area, but no progress so far."

"Son of a bitch."

"We may still find him. If we don't, I'm going to need a list of locations Logan might go to."

"You'll get them."

"And I've ordered the place burned to the ground to destroy any evidence."

"Good. Actually, I was going to tell you to do that anyway. It was part of the contingency plan I was given." Timwick paused. "One more thing. I need a body in those ruins."

"What?"

"A man's body burned beyond recognition."

"Who?"

"Anyone. As long as the height is close to Logan's. Get back to me when it's done."

Fiske pressed the end button and put his cellular away. It was the first time Timwick had indicated he was actually taking orders and not just consulting with his cohorts. Interesting that they wanted Logan to appear dead. He wondered just what—

He suddenly grinned, then turned to the pilot. "Get back to the house right away."

The adrenaline and pleasure were pumping through him as he thought of Timwick's words.

Anyone. As long as the height is close to Logan's.

Kenner.

"We're going south," Eve said. "Is it too much to hope you're taking me home to Atlanta?"

"Yes. We're going to North Carolina, to a house on the shore there." Logan glanced over his shoulder from the driver's seat. "If you think this through, you'll realize you don't want to bring trouble down on your mother by going home."

No, she didn't want to do that, she thought wearily. She was caught in a whirlpool of deceit and death and Mom had to be kept clear. "And just what are we going to do in North Carolina?"

"We have to have a base," Gil said. "The house in North Carolina is right by the beach, in a prime tourist area. Our neighbors will be people on vacation, and they won't care about newcomers."

"You have it all planned out." Eve smiled crookedly. "You were that sure it was Chadbourne?"

"Pretty sure. You can see I had to make plans based on the assumption."

"I can't see much of anything right now except that you've used me without a scrap of conscience. You deliberately caught me in a trap so that I would have no choice but to try to expose Chadbourne's death."

"Yes." Logan met her gaze in the rearview mirror. "Deliberately."

She looked out the window at the flowing traffic. "Bastard."

"Right."

"Could you dial one of my country stations on the radio, John?" Gil asked plaintively. "I need soothing. I'm a sick man and all this tension isn't good for me."

"In your dreams," Logan said.

Eve turned to Gil. "And you're not a good ol' country boy turned chauffeur, are you?"

"Sure I am." He shrugged. "But I also did a stint with the Secret Service under the last administration and another six months with the Chadbourne administration. I was pretty sick of dealing with Timwick's little regime and wanted to get as far away as I could from Washington. I thought a nice, peaceful job on the Seventeen Mile Drive was just the ticket." He grimaced. "It didn't work out as I'd planned, but you might say that my few contacts in convenient places have increased my value to John."

"And Margaret?"

Gil made a face. "She's just what she appears to be. A top sergeant of the business world."

"She doesn't know about Chadbourne?"

Logan shook his head. "I tried to keep her as clear as I could. She doesn't even know about the beach house. I made the arrangements myself."

"How kind."

"I'm not a complete son of a bitch," he said roughly. "I don't want anyone risked unnecessarily."

"But I was a necessary risk. Who made you God, Logan?"

"I did what I had to do."

"For your damn politics."

"No, more than that. The man in the White House may be acting like Ben Chadbourne, but he doesn't have either his ethical standard or his training. I don't want that man able to press a button that could start World War III."

"So now you're not a political opportunist, you're a patriot?"

"Patriot, hell. I just want to protect my ass."

"Now, that I can believe."

"It's not necessary that you believe me. It's necessary that you know we're on the same side."

"Oh, yes, we're on the same side. You've seen to that. You've tossed me right into the middle of this mess." She leaned back against the seat and closed her eyes. "And do you know who that man in the White House is?"

"We believe he's Kevin Detwil. He's one of three doubles who were used during Chadbourne's first year in office," Gil said. "Detwil was used only twice at brief public appearances and then resigned. He said he had to go home to Indiana on personal business, but he actually went to South America and had more plastic surgery done."

"*More* plastic surgery?"

"He had some done in Washington before he got the job. When he was drawn into the plot, he had to look exactly like Chadbourne, including scars on the lower back. He also had to be coached in depth about gestures, voice intonations, and so on. And he had to be briefed on policy, politics, the day-to-day living at the White House. Lisa Chadbourne would have been able to help him, but he couldn't just be thrown into the role."

"This is all supposition, I assume."

Gil shrugged. "The other two doubles are alive and well and doing occasional appearances. Detwil never showed up in Indiana. However, I managed to track him to a private clinic near Brasilia and a Dr. Hernandez, who had the reputation of supplying new faces to embezzlers, murderers, and terrorists. Detwil entered the clinic under the name Herbert Schwartz. A short time after Mr. Schwartz was discharged, the unfortunate Dr. Hernandez fell off the terrace of his penthouse."

"Kevin Detwil," Eve repeated slowly. "He has to be unbalanced to do something like this. Yet the government must have had a profile on him. A security check?"

"Of course, but there aren't that many men in the world who

could pass as the President, so the choice is limited. The security check in these cases is mainly to determine if the subject is discreet enough to keep his silence and wouldn't shoot anybody and embarrass the administration." Gil added, "Detwil's background shows a stable, ordinary child of moderate intelligence, who became a rather dull, ordinary man. He's unmarried, was raised by his mother, and lived with her until her death five years ago."

"What about his father?"

"Split when Detwil was a kid. Evidently he was pretty well under his mother's thumb."

"Which set him up beautifully for Lisa Chadbourne," Logan said. "A man with that background would allow himself to be molded by another dominant woman."

"But would he take a chance like this? You said he was dull and ordinary."

"But you saw the tapes. He loves it. He sparkles," Logan said. "Suppose you had a lifetime of being a wallflower. Then suddenly you become the most powerful man in the world. Everyone defers, everyone listens. He's a male Cinderella and Lisa Chadbourne has handed him the glass slipper."

"With strings," Eve pointed out.

"He probably wouldn't have it any other way. He's used to strings and they can make some men feel secure."

"Then I gather he's not a weak link for her."

"He might be nervous at times but not when she's anywhere near him, and she's not about to let him out of her sight. She's probably made herself the most important thing in his life."

"Important enough to kill Chadbourne for her?"

Logan shrugged. "She probably wouldn't risk involving him in the actual crime. He wouldn't have the backbone."

"If she did kill him. You have no proof he was murdered."

"I was hoping you might help us there."

She had known that was his intention, but she wasn't about to commit to any more right now. She needed time to digest everything she had been told and decide if it could be the truth. "I bet you are."

"You have little choice."

"Bullshit."

"Well, not any other decent ones."

"Don't talk to me about decency."

"I believe it's time to turn on the radio," Logan murmured. "Why don't you try to nap for a while? I'll wake you when we get to North Carolina."

He switched on the radio, and strains of Grieg's *Peer Gynt Suite* filled the car.

"Oh, my God." Gil huddled in the corner. "Eve, tell him to turn it off and save me. I think I'm having a relapse."

"Save yourself." The music was soothing her raw nerves. "I haven't noticed you being particularly solicitous regarding my needs. Not if they got in the way of what Logan wanted."

"Ouch." Gil grimaced. "Forget I asked. I can get used to classical. In fact, by the time we get to the beach house, I'll probably like old Grieg better than Reba McIntyre."

TWELVE

"You're sure it's been done, James?" Lisa Chadbourne asked Timwick. "For God's sake, it took you long enough. I can't have any more mistakes."

"Barrett House is in flames right now. The delay was only because it took a while to make sure the cause looked like faulty wiring."

"And you have a team on the way to retrieve the body? I don't want the fire department paramedics to get there first."

"I'm not a fool, Lisa. They'll whisk it away and take it to Bethesda."

He sounded pissed. She had obviously been too authoritative. Everyone else was easy, but it was always more difficult to strike a good balance with Timwick. In public he was properly respectful and subservient, but in private he never let her forget they were partners. She softened her voice. "I'm sorry, I know you're doing everything you can. I'm just frightened. I feel a little helpless."

"As a king cobra."

She felt a ripple of shock. It was the first time Timwick had ever used sarcasm with her. Not a good sign. She'd been noticing how nervous and on edge he'd been lately, and now he was taking it out on her. "Do I deserve that, James? We agreed it had to be done, and I've always been honest with you."

A silence. "I didn't expect this to happen. You told me everything would go smoothly."

Don't get angry. Look at the big picture. She needed Timwick. He had his job just as she had hers. She kept the irritation from her voice. "I'm doing my best." She reminded him gently, "It was you who didn't wait long enough at the funeral home. There wouldn't have been a problem if you'd made sure Donnelli had done his job."

"I sat there and watched him burn. I thought it was safe to leave. How was I to know it took so damn long to burn a body?"

She would have known. She would have researched and found out all she needed to know. She had been a fool to trust Timwick to do the same. "I know. It's not your fault. But now we have to cope with it . . . and Logan. You found no trace of the skull?"

"There were signs that the Duncan woman had been working, but no skull. If she's as good as reported, we have to assume she's completed the work."

Lisa felt the muscles of her stomach tighten. "It will be fine. Her work alone proves nothing. We just have to make sure they're discredited in the media before they get more proof. We took the first step today. Your job is to find them and make sure that no other damage is done."

"I know my job. You just keep Detwil in line. He was a little too boisterous at the last press conference."

She was handling Kevin perfectly. Timwick had deliberately added that dig to get back at her for criticizing his handling of Donnelli. "You think so? I'll watch it, James. You know how I rely on your judgment." She paused. "What about the Duncan woman? So far we've aimed most of our efforts against Logan. She may prove as difficult."

"I'm keeping my eye on her, but Logan is the power player. He's calling the shots."

"Whatever you say. But could you give me a more complete report on Duncan?"

"It is complete. What else could you want to know?"

"More about her professional background. They'll try for a DNA match and she's bound to have contacts."

"After tomorrow they'll know how dangerous it is to surface. With any luck we'll catch them before they can get anything else done."

"We'd be foolish to rely on luck, wouldn't we?"

"For God's sake, how much DNA could be left after it's been through a fire?"

"I've no idea, but we can't take the chance."

"And, like I said, Logan will be calling the shots. They can't just walk into a DNA lab with that skull. We know where they'll be going for help. I've already got Ralph Crawford at Duke staked out. If we don't get them right away, they'll walk right into our—"

"Please, James," she said gently.

"Okay." She could hear the impatience in his voice. "I'll get it."

"Good. And let me know as soon as the body arrives at Bethesda." She hung up the phone, got up, and strode toward the bedroom.

Logan will be calling the shots.

She wasn't so sure. Her file on Eve Duncan reported a strong, intelligent woman who wouldn't walk behind any man. Who should know better than Lisa how a strong woman could shape situations to suit herself? Timwick, as usual, was underestimating the opposition. She would have to be the one to keep an eye on Eve Duncan.

"Lisa?"

Kevin was standing in the bathroom doorway wearing Ben's red paisley robe. It was one of the few garments of Ben's that Kevin liked. He had a fondness for bright colors that she'd had to curb. Ben rarely wore anything but navy or black.

He was frowning. "Is something wrong?"

She forced a smile. "A little problem with Timwick."

"Can I help?"

"Not in this. Let me handle it." She went to him and slipped her arms around his neck. He smelled of Ben's specially blended lemon cologne. Fragrances were important. Even when you didn't realize it, it was a subtle reminder of who a person was. Sometimes when she woke suddenly in the middle of the night she thought Ben was still lying next to her. She whispered in Kevin's ear, "You were superb today at that AARP meeting. You had them in the palm of your hand."

"Really?" he asked eagerly. "I thought I did pretty well."

"Brilliant. Better than Ben could ever have done." She kissed him gently. "You're doing such a good job. We could be in the middle of a war now if you hadn't taken over."

"He was that unstable?"

She had drummed Ben's supposed instability into Kevin's head a hundred times, but he always wanted reinforcement. Guilt? No, he just liked the idea he was saving the world. For an intelligent man, Kevin could be incredibly vain and naive. "Do you think I'd be doing what we're doing now if I hadn't been afraid of what he'd do?"

He shook his head.

"And you've been magnificent. I think we'll get the health bill passed this year. Have I told you how proud I am?"

"I couldn't do it without you."

"Maybe I helped you in the beginning, but you're surpassing anything—" She threw back her head and grinned impishly at him. "My God, you're getting hard as a rock. I've got to remember what praise does to you. It keeps me a happy woman." She backed away from him and slipped off her robe. "Now, come to bed and I'll tell you how marvelously you handled the Japanese ambassador."

He chuckled and moved toward her, eager as a kid for the romp to come. She kept the teasing, bold smile as she slipped into bed.

She and Ben had shared a bed, and bringing Kevin immediately into hers was a necessary part of the plan. He had been hesitant, even shy at first, and she'd had to use her every skill to draw him in without appearing too aggressive. She could have found other ways to manage him, but this was best. It was her job to make sure Kevin was controlled.

And sex was the greatest controller of all.

Arrogant bitch.

Timwick leaned back in his chair and rubbed his eyes. It was all very well for Lisa to order him around and then go to bed and let him do the work. She was there in the White House, acting like royalty, and he was in this crummy office, working his ass off. She wanted results, but she didn't want to dirty her hands, and she turned a blind eye to what she didn't want to see. He was the one who kept things running and protected them from disaster. Where would she be now if he hadn't stepped in?

Eve Duncan. She was Logan's tool, nothing more. It was stupid to make her a priority. If Lisa hadn't been such a feminist, she would have admitted that Logan was the prime threat.

Jesus, it seemed as if there were threats closing in all around him.

His hands clenched the arms of the chair. Keep calm. He was doing everything he could to save the situation. He *would* save it. He had too much at stake to take off and run. If he stuck it out, he'd have everything he'd ever wanted.

He reached for the telephone. Do what she said—for now. He needed her to help stop the exposure of the cover-up and he needed her to push Detwil into the White House for another term. After that he'd find a way to gain control. Let Lisa think she was running the show.

He'd give her enough information on Eve Duncan to choke her.

• • •

"Wake up, we're here."

Eve opened her eyes to see Logan getting out of the driver's seat.

She yawned. "What time is it?"

"After midnight." Gil reached for the door latch. "You slept most of the way."

It seemed impossible that she could have fallen asleep. Her nerves had been taut as wires.

"You've had a rough couple of days." Gil answered her unspoken question. "I dozed a little myself. But I admit I'll be glad to stretch out."

She was so stiff, she had to catch hold of the door when she got out of the car. She watched Logan climb the steps and unlock the front door. He was carrying the leather case with Chadbourne's skull. Trust Logan to keep his priorities in order, she thought dryly.

"Ready?" Gil asked as he grabbed her suitcase.

"I'll take that."

"I can manage. Take Mandy's box." He was already following Logan up the steps.

She didn't want to go inside. The air was cool and wet in her nostrils, and the sound of the sea against the shore was like a blessing. She hadn't been to the shore in a long time. Joe had taken her to Cumberland Island after she'd left the hellhole but she had no memory of what the island looked like. All she could remember was Joe holding her, Joe talking, Joe holding back the night.

Joe. She had to call Joe. She hadn't spoken to him since before the night they'd gone to the cornfield. She had deliberately avoided calling him and pulling him deeper into this morass. But if she didn't call him soon, he'd be storming Barrett House with a SWAT team.

The wind was coming up and blowing the surf into whitecaps before they reached the shore.

Bonnie had liked the ocean. Eve and Sandra had taken her to

Pensacola a few times and she had streaked up and down the shore, laughing and chattering and looking for seashells.

She closed the car door and walked down to the pier.

"Eve."

She didn't turn around at Logan's call. She didn't want to go into the house. She didn't want to face him or anything else just then. She needed time for herself.

She pulled off her sandals, sat down on the low pier, and dangled her feet. The water was cool and silken as it flowed against her skin.

She leaned her head against the post, listening to the rush of the sea.

And remembering Bonnie . . .

"Are you going after her?" Gil said. "She's been out there almost an hour, John."

"Soon." God, she looked lonely. "I don't think she wants company."

"You don't want her to think too much. Thinking can be a dangerous thing. She's already resentful."

"I'm tired of driving her, dammit. Let her have some peace."

"I doubt if she allows herself to be driven in a direction she doesn't want to go."

"But it's possible to block out every other path so she's forced to take the only one left." Logan had done that since the moment he had met her. He was doing it now.

So was he going to stop because he was having a few twinges of conscience?

Not likely.

So repair her broken trust and use her again. "I'll go get her." He went down the porch steps and strode across the sand to the pier.

She didn't look at him as he approached. "Go away, Logan."

"It's time you came in. It's getting chilly."

"I'll come in when I'm ready."

He hesitated and then sat down beside her. "I'll wait for you." He took off his shoes and socks and dangled his feet in the water.

"I don't want you here."

"You know, I haven't done anything like this since I was in Japan." He gazed out at the ocean. "There doesn't seem to be time enough in the day to relax."

"Are you trying to bond with me, Logan?"

"Maybe."

"Well, you're not doing it."

"No? Too bad. Then, I guess I might as well just sit here and relax."

Silence.

"What are you thinking about?" he asked.

"Not Chadbourne."

"Your daughter?"

She stiffened. "Don't use Bonnie to try to get close to me, Logan. It won't work."

"Just curious. I guess I don't understand your obsession with identifying skulls. Oh, I know your daughter was never found, but you can't expect to—"

"I don't want to talk about it."

"I watched you with Mandy and then with Ben Chadbourne. There's almost a . . . tenderness."

"So I'm a little crazy. Everyone's a little bonkers on some subject or other," she said jerkily. "I assure you I don't think their souls are hanging around those bones."

"Do you believe in an everlasting soul?"

"Sometimes."

"Only sometimes?"

"Okay, most of the time."

He was silent, waiting.

"When Bonnie was born, she wasn't like me or Mom or anyone. She was just . . . herself. All complete . . . and wonderful. How could that be if you're not born with a soul?"

"And that soul is eternal?"

"How do I know? I . . . think so. I hope so."

"Then why are you so passionate about returning those bones to their families? It shouldn't make any difference."

"It makes a difference to me."

"Why?"

"Life is important. Life should be treated with respect, not tossed away like some useless bit of trash. There should be a . . . home for everyone. I never had a real home when I was a kid. We moved from tenement to tenement. Motel to motel. Mom was— It wasn't her fault. But everyone should have a place, a permanent place in the scheme of things. I tried to give Bonnie a home, the best home I could manage, where I could love her and take care of her. When Fraser killed her, I had nightmares about her lying in the forest for the animals to—" She was silent a moment and her voice was uneven when she spoke again. "I wanted her home, where I could take care of her as I always had. He'd taken her life, I didn't want him to take that last bit of caring away from either of us."

"I see." Christ, he was seeing more than he wanted to see. "Do you still have nightmares?"

She was silent again and then she said, "No, not nightmares." She swung her legs out of the water and onto the pier. "I'm going inside." She picked up her sandals and rose to her feet. "If your curiosity is satisfied, Logan."

"Not entirely. But you're evidently not going to confide anything else to me."

"You've got that right." She looked down at him. "And don't think you've made any headway with this cozy chat. I haven't told you anything I wouldn't tell anyone else. Joe and I agreed that it was healthiest for me to talk about Bonnie."

"We need to talk about Chadbourne."

"No, we don't. Not tonight."

She walked away from him.

Tough lady. Exceptional lady.

He watched her start up the steps of the beach house. The

light pouring through the windows shimmered on her red-brown hair and silhouetted her slim, strong body.

Strong but vulnerable. That body could be hurt and broken and destroyed.

And he could very well be responsible for just that happening.

Maybe trying to reconnect with her hadn't been such a good idea. She had walked away as strong and independent as ever, and he was the one feeling uncertain.

And, yes, perhaps even a little vulnerable.

"I've been thinking, Lisa," Kevin murmured in her ear. "Maybe we should— What do you think about—a baby."

Oh, good God. "A child?"

He got up on one elbow and gazed down at her. "A child would be very popular. Everyone loves kids. If we started now, it would be born right after my next term starts." He hesitated. "And I'd . . . like it."

She reached up and stroked his cheek. "Do you think I wouldn't?" she asked softly. "Nothing would please me more. I've always wanted a child. But it's not possible."

"Why? You said Chadbourne couldn't have children, but we can take care of that now."

"I'm forty-five years old, Kevin."

"But there are all those fertility drugs now."

For a moment she was actually tempted. She had spoken the truth; she had always wanted a child. She and Ben had tried so hard to conceive. She remembered him joking and saying what an advantage kids were to any politician, but that was one time she hadn't cared about political advantage. She'd wanted someone of her own, someone to belong to her.

Forget it. Impossible. The tears that filled her eyes weren't totally for Kevin's benefit. "Don't talk about it. It hurts me that we can't do it."

"Why can't we?"

"It would be too difficult. There could be all kinds of problems for a woman my age. What if the doctor decided I had to have complete bed rest for the last months of pregnancy? That happens sometimes, and I wouldn't be able to travel with you during the campaign. That could be dangerous for us."

"But you're so strong and healthy, Lisa."

He must have been brooding about this for a long time to be this persistent. "It would be a risk we shouldn't take." She pushed the one button she knew would stop him cold. "Of course, we could give up our plans for another term. But you're such a wonderful president, everyone admires and respects you. Do you want to give all that up?"

He was silent. "You're sure it would be that risky?"

He was already relinquishing the idea, as she'd known he would. No way would he go back to anonymity after the power and respect he'd become accustomed to. "Right now is just the wrong time. I'm not saying we couldn't consider it later." She stroked his lower lip with a forefinger. "But do you know how touched I am that you think so much of me? I'd love nothing better than to—"

The phone on the bedside table rang, and she reached over to pick it up.

"The body's arrived at Bethesda," Timwick said.

The body. Cold. Impersonal. That's how she should view it too. That's how she had to view it. "Excellent."

"Have you managed to contact Maren?"

"He's somewhere out in the desert. I'll have to try again."

"We don't have much time."

"I said I'll take care of it."

"The media is crawling all over the hospital. Should we start it in motion?"

"No, let them speculate and then pop the story on them in the morning. We want them hungry enough to jump on any tidbit of information." She hung up.

"Timwick?" Kevin asked.

She nodded absently, her mind still on Bethesda.

"I don't like the bastard. Do we still need him?"

"Be a little grateful," she said teasingly. "He's the one who discovered you."

"He always treats me like a stupid ass."

"Not in public?"

He shook his head.

"Well, maybe you won't have to see much of him. I've been thinking you should give him an ambassador's post. Maybe in Zaire. After all, you are the president."

He laughed delightedly. "Zaire."

She got up and slipped on her robe. "Or Moscow. It's supposed to be very uncomfortable in Moscow."

"But you promised him the vice presidency next term. We'll have to name him as my running mate at the convention." He grimaced. "He's not going to give that up."

No, the vice presidency was the only carrot that had drawn Timwick into the plan. He'd been bitterly disappointed that Ben had not given him a cabinet post, and Lisa had never seen a more ambitious man. A hunger that intense could pose future problems for her, but she couldn't worry about Timwick now. "Maybe we can think of a way of getting around it."

"It would really be better if we can keep Chet Mobry as vice president. He hasn't caused us any trouble."

"He could have caused us big trouble if we hadn't kept him on the road with nonstop goodwill missions. He never agreed with our policies. We could do the same with Timwick."

"I guess so, but he's been— Where are you going?"

"I have a little work to take care of. Go to sleep."

"Is that why Timwick called you?" He frowned. "You never tell me what you're doing."

"Because it's only small, unimportant details. You take care of the big picture, I do the little stuff."

His frown disappeared. "You'll come back when you're finished?"

She nodded. "I'm only going into the next room to look at a

dossier. I want to be prepared for your next meeting with Tony Blair."

He lay back down on the pillows. "He'll be a piece of cake after the Japanese."

He was getting cocky. But it was better than the intimidation he'd shown when he'd first slipped into Ben's place. "We'll see." She blew him a kiss. "Go to sleep. I'll wake you when I come back."

She closed the door and walked to the desk across the room. It took her ten minutes to get through to Scott Maren and another five to explain the situation and its urgency.

"Christ, Lisa, it's not that easy. What excuse am I going to give for cutting my stay here short?"

"You're clever. You'll come up with something." She added quietly, "I need you, Scott."

Silence. "It will be all right. Hang tough, Lisa. I'll call the hospital and tell them to hold off the autopsy. I'll be there as soon as I can."

She hung up the phone. God, she was lucky to have Scott. He was going to be essential with damage control.

She turned on the computer, entered her password, and opened the file on Eve Duncan. Everything was moving smoothly toward a salvage of the situation, and yet she was uneasy.

Eve Duncan's image on the screen stared back at her. Kinky tousled curls, only a minimum of makeup, large brown eyes behind round wire-rimmed glasses. There was a world of character in that face, more than enough to make her fascinating-looking instead of just attractive. But the woman ignored the basic rules of power; she didn't use the assets she was given. She reminded Lisa of herself during her first few years of college, when she'd thought brains and determination would do it all. God, that seemed a long time ago. She'd probably had the same intensity she saw in Eve's expression. It hadn't taken her long to learn that intensity scared people. It was better to hide your passions behind a sweet smile.

Yet Eve's background showed she was a survivor, and Lisa respected survivors. She was one herself, or she would never have been able to make it through these last years. Smiling sadly, she gently touched Eve's image.

Sisters. Opposite sides of the same coin. Survivors.

Too bad.

She started reading Eve's dossier, looking for a weakness, a way to topple her.

She was only two-thirds through the report when she found it.

Gil and Logan were sitting in front of the television set when Eve came into the living room the next morning.

"Shit," Gil murmured. "They really gutted it. I liked that old house."

"What happened?" she asked. "Barrett House?"

Gil nodded. "It seems John got cheap on the wiring."

The picture on the screen showed a smoking ruin with only two chimneys still intact.

Gil added, "But you'll be glad to know he was punished for his miserliness. John died in the fire."

"What?"

"Burned beyond recognition. But they're comparing dental and DNA records now. Such a fine man. Detwil just issued a statement about how John was loved and respected by everyone in both parties. He even said John had invited him to Barrett House for the weekend to talk about their policies."

"Why would he say that?"

"How do I know? I thought it was overkill myself." He switched off the television set. "I can't bear any more. John and I were so close. Practically brothers." He went over to the kitchen bar. "Anyone for breakfast?"

Eve turned to Logan. "This is crazy. You're not exactly unknown. Do they think they can get away with this?"

"For a while. They'll see that the DNA and dental records will match. They've taken the body to Bethesda."

"So what does that mean?"

"It means they can control things at Bethesda. They have an

inside man there. He'll see that everything is handled to their liking. It will buy them time."

"What are you going to do?"

"Well, I'm not going to show myself and try to prove they're wrong. I'd find myself in a maximum security cell as an imposter and suffer an unfortunate accident." He stood up. "Besides, I have things to do."

"Who do you suppose— Who was that man who died?"

Logan shrugged.

She shivered. It had started. A man had died, a life thrown away.

"Coffee?" Gil asked. "There's danish."

She shook her head.

"Can we talk about Chadbourne now?" Logan asked politely. "I believe the situation is escalating."

"You're damn right we'll talk," she answered. "I want my mother safe. I don't want my house going up in flames with her in it."

"I'll call Margaret, tell her I'm still of this world, and to find a hiding place for your mother."

"Now."

"She's being very well guarded. Can I finish my coffee first?" He gazed at her over the rim of the cup. "Are you going to help me, Eve?"

"Maybe. If I don't think you're keeping me wandering around blind." She turned to Gil. "I want to know about this Timwick you think is pulling the strings. You worked under him?"

Gil nodded. "Not close. As a humble Secret Service man, I was not privy to the great man's confidence."

"What's he like? You have to have made judgments."

"He's smart, ambitious, and knows how to pull strings to get what he wants. Personally, I wouldn't have wanted him to back me up in a tight situation. I've seen him explode too often. I don't think he reacts well under pressure." He paused. "Is he dangerous? Hell, yes. Volatility translates too often to unreasonable violence."

"What about Fiske?"

"He's only a hired man. Calculated, efficient, and likes what he does. Anyone else?"

"You tell me. There could be a dozen people lurking in the wings you haven't told me about."

"As I mentioned before, they would need to keep down the number of people involved," Logan said. "And we'd be stupid to try to keep you in the dark now. You know what we know. Everything is out on the table. Will you help us?"

"If my mother is safe." She stared directly into his eyes. "And I'm going to help myself, not you. I'd be an idiot not to know what a target you've made me. And the only way I can help myself is to prove Ben Chadbourne is really dead. DNA and dental records are the only legally acceptable proof. So we have to go after them."

"And your suggestion?"

"I'm not a DNA expert or a forensic anthropologist with the additional qualifications necessary to do the extraction. So we take the skull to one of the most respected anthropologists in the profession, see if he can get enough DNA to make a match."

"The skull went through a fire."

"It's still a possibility." She added deliberately, "As I think you know. I was just the first shot in your arsenal. I'll bet you've even chosen the forensic anthropologist to do the work."

"Dr. Ralph Crawford. Duke University. He has the qualifications we need."

She shook her head. "Gary Kessler. Emory."

"He's better?"

"At least as good and I know him."

"Another Quincy?" Gil asked.

"That TV show drives Gary crazy. Besides the fact that it's inaccurate, people are always confusing pathologists with forensic anthropologists."

"Well, what is the difference?"

"Pathologists have medical degrees and residence training in pathology. Anthropologists don't have medical degrees, they have doctorates in anthropology and some of them specialize in the human skeletal system and its changes during a lifetime. Like Gary Kessler. He's worked with several Atlanta pathologists and is well respected. Besides, since you were researching Crawford, it's very likely that they won't think we'd go to anyone else."

"They've probably been looking at your background with a magnifying glass too."

"And they'll find out I've worked with ten to twelve anthropologists in L.A., New York, and New Orleans and that I've been bombarded with requests since that *60 Minutes* story. It will take time for them to check out everyone's specialty and they would consider Gary a long shot since I haven't worked with him in over two years."

Logan slowly nodded. "You're making sense. And, under the circumstances, it may be easier to convince someone you know to help."

Since those circumstances involved probable trouble with the law, she could see the problem. "What about dental records?"

"That may be more difficult. Chadbourne's dentist was a woman named Dr. Dora Bentz." He paused. "She was one of the people Fiske murdered after you came to Barrett House. You can bet every dental file Chadbourne ever had has been switched."

"You said it was a witness who was murdered." She held up her hand as he started to speak. "Never mind. Why should I expect truth from you?"

"I'm not going to defend myself. It was a different situation."

She noticed he didn't apologize or claim he'd do anything else. "Then we're left with the DNA. What if we don't have enough for a test? Could we find a way to force Detwil to take a test to prove *his* identity?"

"No way," Logan said flatly. "He's now the president. We bear the burden of proof. Besides, his medical records could be switched like mine."

"Couldn't we try? He's got to have relatives."

"Other than his mother, who died seven years ago, he had one older half brother."

"Had?"

"John Cadro. He and his wife were killed the day after Dora Bentz."

Jesus. "It doesn't have to be a close relative. They proved the Anastasia impostor wasn't genuine by comparing her DNA to Prince Philip of England's. Isn't there anyone else?"

"Not that we can readily trace. They chose Detwil very carefully."

"What about the mother? They could exhume—"

"I don't mean to make a morbid pun, but we don't have time to dig deeper. Once we go public, we have to have full proof."

"Why don't we have time?"

"Because we'll be dead within twelve hours after we show ourselves," Gil said bluntly. "According to the news, John is already dead. That leaves only you and me, and they have the power of the presidency behind them. I'm sure the scenario is already in place. Quick, logical, and thorough. Timwick was always thorough."

Eve shivered. "There has to be another lead . . . someone else."

"Yes, there is. Scott Maren."

"Another relative?" She grimaced. "And is he dead too?"

"No. He's Chadbourne's personal physician, and he's been out of the country, which probably saved his life." He paused. "But I'm not sure we'll be able to use him. I believe he's probably involved in the actual murder."

"How?"

"Opportunity. Two years ago, on the morning of November second, Ben Chadbourne checked into Bethesda for his annual checkup. The body appeared at Donnelli's funeral home after midnight on November third."

"You think that's when the switch was made?"

Logan nodded. "It had to have been choreographed perfectly, with one Ben Chadbourne checking in and another checking out. Maren probably gave the real Chadbourne a lethal shot claiming it was vitamin B or something."

"So he's their inside man at Bethesda," Eve said slowly. It was possible and diabolically clever, she thought. A physician was in a position of trust and yet dealt with the means for taking life every day. "This has to be supposition. Maren would have had to go through all kinds of security checks before he became Chadbourne's physician."

"I'm sure he did," Gil said. "But he's highly respected and also a close friend of the President's. Maren, Chadbourne, and Lisa Chadbourne all went to college together. Either Chadbourne or his wife was probably instrumental in getting him his position at Bethesda."

"Why would he do it? Why would he take that chance?"

Logan shrugged. "I don't know, but I'd bet he did. That's why I've been trying to contact him. We might be able to persuade him to implicate Timwick and Lisa Chadbourne."

"I can't see that Maren is a lead. There's no way he'd admit he was involved if it's true. He'd be a fool."

"Maybe." Logan paused. "Unless we could convince him that he's a dead man if they're not taken out. When I made up my list of their possible targets for elimination, Maren ranked high on it."

Eve thought about it. "He's the only witness who can link Lisa Chadbourne and Timwick to her husband's death."

"Right. If there's no such witness and the death is discovered, they could set up a patsy, claim it was a terrorist plot or some other conspiracy. But Maren is real, and if he goes down for the murder, they couldn't be sure he wouldn't talk and bring them down with him. I haven't any doubt that from the moment the plan was conceived, they were already planning on killing him."

"But will he believe that?"

"We can try. We don't have much choice. He's our only hope right now."

"You said he was out of the country. Where is he?"

"Detwil sent him on a goodwill mission to Jordan to inspect the hospitals there. It was high-profile and he was supposedly requested by the king of Jordan. On the surface it's an honor that would increase Maren's prestige."

"And below the surface?"

"Possibly a setup. Fiske would have found it easy to kill him there and shift the blame to a foreign dissident group. I think Bentz and Cadro were killed because they suspected I might be getting too close, but Maren was always a target."

"He won't cooperate. For God's sake, if he killed the President, he's a dead man either way."

"Not if we offer him a deal."

"You don't have authority to offer him—" She studied his face. "What are you thinking?"

"That I want Detwil and Lisa Chadbourne out of the White House, and I don't care how I do it." He paused. "Even if it means helping Maren set himself up somewhere with a fat bank account."

"Make a deal with a murderer?"

"What if we can't get DNA proof? Can you suggest anything else?"

She was too confused to think clearly about anything at the moment. "What's to stop Fiske from still going to Jordan after Maren?"

"The situation has changed. They need Maren, and they won't kill him until his usefulness is ended." He smiled. "Remember, they took my body to Bethesda. They're going to want Maren there to cover up. He was supposed to come back day after tomorrow, but now he'll be winging his way home at warp speed. While we go to Emory to see Kessler, Gil's going to Bethesda and try to gather Maren in."

"How is Gil going to keep from being gathered in himself? They're bound to be on watch for us."

"Through the magic of disguise," Gil said. "I'm going to dress up as a female nurse." He tilted his head. "A blonde, I think. With great boobs."

"What?"

"Just joking. Don't worry, I'll handle it."

She was already worried. She didn't want any harm to come to him. Gil might have been involved in the plot to deceive her, but he was a likable rascal.

And, dear Christ, there had been too many deaths already. People she had never met were dying. She seemed to be in the middle of a circle of ever-widening ripples of destruction. Thank God, those ripples hadn't touched anyone close to her yet.

And they mustn't touch them.

"You're talking as if you can move around without any problems," she pointed out. "What about money? What about ID? Credit cards can be traced and—"

"Logan took care of that. He had me buy a few handy-dandy phony driver's licenses on the black market. You're Bridget Reilly. I thought your red hair looked like you might be of Irish descent. The picture is very satisfactorily blurred and—"

"*My* picture?" She turned to Logan. "You got a phony driver's license for me?"

He shrugged. "I had to be prepared. I had Gil get IDs for everyone who was at Barrett House. I thought it might come down to this."

Damn him. He had not only known the trouble he was involving her in, he had planned on it. "And I suppose you had Gil set up phony credit cards for all of us too?"

He nodded. "But I brought enough cash to see us through most situations."

"You're absolutely incredible."

"I had to be prepared," he repeated.

She had to get out of the room, or she'd do something violent.

"Call Margaret." She headed for the bedroom. "I'm going to phone my mother and tell her to be ready to go."

"Her phone will be monitored, you know."

"I'm not an idiot. I know they'll be watching my mother. I'll be careful, but I've got to warn her. I'll use my digital phone and call her on hers."

"She has a digital too?"

"Of course. Joe got them for us. He says there are all kinds of creeps out there listening in on cellulars. Digitals are almost foolproof."

"I should have known it was the ubiquitous Mr. Quinn," Logan murmured. "Is there anything he doesn't think of?"

"No, he's a good friend and he keeps us safe." She gave him a cool glance over her shoulder. "I can guess why you wouldn't understand that concept."

THIRTEEN

Sandra had seen the morning news, and it took Eve ten minutes to get past her exclamations of relief and deflect her barrage of questions to tell her that Margaret was coming.

"What do you mean, I have to leave?" Sandra said. "What's going on, Eve?"

"Nothing good. I can't talk about it."

"Is John Logan really dead?"

"No. Look, Mom, it's going to be nasty, and until I get it cleaned up, I want you somewhere safe and out of public view."

"Safe? I'm safe here. Joe stops by every other day, and that black and white is parked out in front every night."

"Mom . . ." She had to find a way of convincing her. "Do what I ask. Please. It's bad. Trust me. I'm scared of what may happen."

"Scared?" Sandra was silent. "I believe you are

scared. I haven't seen you act like this since Fraser—" She broke off and then said, "I want to see you."

"I can't come there. It would only endanger you."

"What are you mixed up in, Eve?"

"I can't tell you that either. Will you do this for me?"

"I have a job. I just can't run off—"

"They'll kill you," she said baldly. "Or they'll use you to kill me. Is that what you want? For God's sake, tell the office you have a family emergency. Believe me, it's true."

"Kill you," Sandra repeated, and for the first time Eve heard fear in her voice. "I'm going to call Joe."

"I'm going to call him myself. But he may not be able to help you. Don't leave the house and don't open the door to anyone but the person I send after you."

"And who is that?"

Christ, what if they found a way to monitor the conversation? She couldn't have Margaret a target. "They'll have ID. I'll fax a picture—" No, her fax machine had been destroyed along with almost everything else in the lab, and besides, a fax might not be safe. "I'll get a photo and information to you somehow." She paused. "And, Mom, don't go anywhere with anyone else, no matter what kind of ID they show you. Not the police, not the FBI or Secret Service. No one."

"When will this person be here?"

"I don't know. Soon. I don't even know how they'll contact you. They may not want to come to the house. Just do what they say. Okay?"

"I'm an adult, Eve. I don't go blindly where I'm led. God knows, I did enough of that when I was growing up." She sighed. "Okay, okay, I'll go along with this. But I wish to hell you'd never heard of John Logan."

"Me too, Mom. Me too."

"And you take care of yourself."

"I will." She paused and then said impulsively, "I love you."

"My God, now I am scared. You don't get sappy very often." She said awkwardly, "I love you too, Eve." She quickly hung up the phone.

Eve pressed the end button on her phone. Expressing affection was still never easy for either of them. There had been too many years of noncommunication during Eve's childhood.

But Sandra knew she loved her. She didn't have to say it.

She braced herself. Now Joe.

She quickly dialed Joe's private digital phone number.

He picked up immediately.

"Joe?"

A silence, and then his voice came low, hard. "What the *hell* are you up to?"

"Can you talk? Is there anyone around?"

"I'm walking out to the parking lot. Why didn't you call me? Why the hell didn't you return—"

"I was busy. Stop yelling at me."

"I'm not yelling." It was true, but every word was laden with anger. "I could strangle you."

"You may have to stand in line."

"Is that supposed to be funny?"

"No. I'm in trouble, Joe."

"That's pretty clear. Did you kill Logan?"

Her hand tightened on the receiver. "What?"

"Did you kill him?"

"Are you nuts?"

"Answer me. Look, if you did it, I know it was self-defense, but I have to know so I can fix it."

"Why would you think— Of course I didn't kill him. He's not dead. It's all a lie."

Silence. "Then I'd say you're in very deep shit. Have you seen CNN?"

"About Barrett House burning? Yes, I know about that."

"No, the latest bulletin. The one that mentions you as a suspect."

"Me?"

"Novak, that hotshot lawyer of Logan's, was interviewed, and he said you were staying with Logan at Barrett House." He paused. "He said you were Logan's lover and he had been concerned about the relationship because you were unbalanced."

"Son of a bitch."

"They know about Lakewood, Eve."

She stiffened. "How could they know? How could anyone know? You buried the records. You promised me that I—"

"I don't know how they found out. I thought I had it covered."

"You should have been more—" Christ, she was blaming Joe for something that wasn't even his responsibility. "They mentioned Lakewood?"

"Yes." He paused. "I told you that there was no reason to hide it. There's nothing wrong about—"

"It seems there is reason."

Joe cursed softly. "Tell me where you are. I'll come to you."

She tried to gather her wits. "I shouldn't see you. As long as you're not involved you'll be—"

"Tell me. I am involved. Tell me or I'll hunt you down. I'm damn good at hunting."

She knew better than anyone else how determined Joe could be. "I'm coming to Atlanta. I need to see Kessler. I'll meet you at the Hardee's parking lot out in Dekalb at ten tomorrow morning. That's about six blocks from Emory."

"Right." He didn't speak for several seconds. "How bad is it, Eve?"

"Big-time. It couldn't be any worse."

"Sure it could. You couldn't have me to help fix it."

She smiled shakily. "That's true. That would make it worse." She thought of something. "Will you dig up a picture of Logan's assistant, Margaret Wilson, and run it over to my mother? Tell her that Margaret is the one who's going to help her."

"Help her do what?"

"She's going to see that Mom gets to somewhere safe."

"*I'm* taking care of her." There was an edge to his tone. "You don't need any other help."

"Don't do this to me, Joe. I need all the help I can get. Will you get the picture to her?"

"Of course I'll do it. But you'd better have a damn good reason for not trusting me."

"I do trust—" Maybe he'd understand when she explained

everything to him. She thought of something else. "And will you find a picture of James Timwick and a man called Albert Fiske, who works for him? Bring it with you tomorrow."

"Timwick should be no problem. He's on the news fairly frequently, but who's Albert Fiske?"

"A name I need to put a face to. Good-bye, Joe."She pressed the end button.

Lakewood. My God, Lakewood.

She put her phone back in her purse and stood up. She could hear the television in the next room. Logan and Gil would be hearing about Lakewood.

But Logan must already know. The lawyer was his snoop and it was Logan's money that had dug up all the facts about her past.

Logan again. Damn him.

Gil and Logan both looked up when she walked into the room.

"The plot thickens," Logan said as he switched off the TV.

"Yes, I'm crazy and you're dead," she said jerkily. "They want to make it hard for us to make any move at all."

"Not hard. Impossible," Gil corrected her. "Were you really at Lakewood?"

"Ask Logan."

Logan shook his head. "I didn't get that morsel of information. I guess Novak was saving that to sell to Timwick."

"You knew he was dealing with them?"

"I suspected the possibility. Novak's ambitious." He paused. "But the question is how valuable is that piece of information to them. How long were you at Lakewood?"

"Three weeks."

"Who committed you?"

"Joe."

"Christ. The authorities. Not a good image."

"It wasn't the authorities," she said fiercely. "It was Joe."

"Quinn was with the FBI at the time."

"They didn't know about it. Nobody knew about it. Not even my mother."

"She's next of kin. She would have had to know."

Eve shook her head. "Lakewood isn't a public institution. It's a small private hospital in South Georgia. Joe admitted me under another name. Anna Quinn. He told them I was his wife."

"And you went in voluntarily?"

She smiled crookedly. "No, Joe can be a powerhouse when he chooses. He bulldozed me into it."

"Why?"

She didn't answer.

"Why, Eve?"

What the hell. He'd find out anyway. "The night Fraser was executed, I took an overdose of sedatives. I was staying at a motel near the prison and Joe came to check and found me." She shrugged. "He made me throw up several times and walked me around that damn room until I was out of danger. Then he took me to Lakewood. He stayed there with me for three weeks. At first they wanted to sedate me, but he told them that wasn't why he brought me there. He made me talk to every shrink in the place. He made me talk about Bonnie. He made me talk about Fraser. He made me talk about my mother. Hell, he even made me talk about my father, and I hadn't seen him since I was a baby." She grimaced. "But he didn't think I was opening up enough with the good doctors, so after three weeks he checked me out and took me to Cumberland Island and kept me there for another week."

"Cumberland Island?"

"It's a wild island off the coast. One hotel, but Joe didn't check us in there. We camped out and Joe administered his own brand of therapy."

"And did you open up with him?"

"Joe didn't give me any choice." Her lips twisted ruefully. "I told you, he can be a powerhouse. He wasn't about to let me go crazy or kill myself. He wouldn't have it. So I had to cope."

"Quinn must be pretty impressive," Gil said.

"Oh, yes. No doubt about it. There's nobody like him." She walked over to the window and looked out at the surf. "I fought him like a tiger. He wouldn't let me go."

"I wish he'd buried the Lakewood records deeper."

"So do I. In the neighborhood where I grew up there were a lot of crazies, but you were really bonkers if you had to go to an asylum. But Joe doesn't think like we do. He's very direct. If something's broken, you get an expert to fix it. He didn't see any stigma about staying at a mental hospital. That didn't scare him."

"Did it scare you?" Logan asked.

She was silent a moment. "Yes."

"Why?"

She said haltingly, "I was afraid I belonged there."

"Ridiculous. You had enough stress to give anyone a nervous breakdown."

"And how close is a nervous breakdown to going over the edge? You never realize what a tightrope we all walk until you almost slip into the chasm."

"But you fought back."

"Joe jerked me back." She crossed her arms over her chest. "And then I got mad as hell and disgusted with myself. I wasn't about to let Fraser take anything else from me. Not my life and not my sanity. I wasn't going to let him win." She turned to face Logan. "And I'm not going to let Timwick and her win either. The question is how are we going to keep them from making everyone think I'm nuts."

"We can't. Not now. We're on the defensive," Logan said. "We can't do anything until we have a weapon to launch an offensive."

She had known that, but she'd hoped for good news, not reality. "Did you call Margaret?"

He nodded. "She's on her way."

"Where will she take my mother?"

"She's consulting with the security service who's guarding your mother now. Wherever they decide to stash her, I told Margaret I wanted them to take at least one guard. Did you tell Sandra to expect her?"

"Yes, and I told Joe to meet us tomorrow in Atlanta." She saw an expression flit across Logan's face and demanded, "What?"

"Nothing. It just might not have been wise to involve him. The fewer people who—"

"Crap." She ignored the fact that that had been her own initial thought. "I trust him more than I trust you or Gil."

"I can see why." Gil rose to his feet. "I'm eager to meet the interesting Mr. Quinn. I think I'll go for a walk. Care to join me, John?"

Logan nodded. "I can use some air." He moved toward the door. "We'll be back soon. Keep an eye on the news, will you, Eve?"

They wanted to talk over the situation alone. They'd weigh the recent developments and try to plan an offensive. Well, let them. They'd learn soon enough that she wouldn't be shut out of decisions any longer.

On the other hand, she just might want to shut them out. Tomorrow she'd be with Joe again. Logan had used her and she had no confidence he wouldn't do it again, but she could trust Joe. They'd been a team for a long time, and together they could work their way through anything, including Timwick and Lisa Chadbourne.

Lisa Chadbourne. Did the fact that her name had come so easily to Eve mean she'd accepted Lisa Chadbourne as the prime conspirator? The signals she had used with Detwil indicated complicity but didn't necessarily mark her as the kingpin.

But the woman she'd studied in the videotapes was not the type to accept second place. She exuded confidence and charisma.

And Gil's description of Timwick had not been of a man who would be able to pull off a deception of this magnitude. It would take nerves of steel and the ability to think on your feet. According to Gil, Timwick was a man who might crumble under pressure.

If Lisa Chadbourne was the prime player, then Eve had better study her very carefully.

She went to her handbag and pulled out the tapes she had stuffed in it before leaving Barrett House. She popped one in the VCR and settled on the sofa in front of the television.

Lisa Chadbourne's smiling face appeared on the screen. Beautiful, intelligent, and, yes, fascinating. Eve felt tension ripple through her, and she leaned forward, her gaze never leaving Lisa Chadbourne.

"What are you doing?" Logan asked when he walked in on her two hours later. "Lisa Chadbourne?"

Eve flipped off the VCR. "Nothing. I was just studying her."

"Her signals to Detwil?"

"Some. Mainly body language. Expressions. They tell a hell of a lot."

"Do they?" Logan's gaze narrowed on her face. "I wouldn't think they'd tell you anything. I'm sure she's very good at disguising her emotions."

She shrugged. "I'm an artist and I've made it my business to learn a lot about facial expressions. When I first became a forensic sculptor, I even took a course in expressions and body language and how they relate to psychology. Expressions can make all the difference in identification. A face without expression is like an empty slate."

"And what did you learn about Lisa Chadbourne?"

"She's a little arrogant, bold, but wary too. Perhaps a little vain." She frowned. "No, not vain. She's too confident to be vain. She just knows who she is and she likes herself."

"Smug?"

Eve shook her head. "No." She hesitated. "She's . . . intensely focused . . . and maybe a little lonely."

"Quite a crystal ball you have," Gil said.

"Some of it's guesswork. Maybe a lot of it. People can usually control most of the muscles of the face. Except the ones around the eyes. They're very difficult to manage. But even a lack of expression can sometimes tell a story." She returned to Lisa Chadbourne. "I'd bet she has a very small circle of friends and she'd keep everyone but those few at a distance."

Logan raised his brows. "That wasn't my impression when I met her. I assure you no one could be warmer or more gregarious, and she handles people better than anyone I know."

"And she's good enough to fool you. She turned on the charm and focused the full force on you. Men still rule the world, and she's made it her business to get along with them. It's probably second nature to her now."

"But she's not good enough to fool you?"

"Maybe, if you hadn't provided me with the tapes that spotlight her every move and expression. She's quite wonderful and almost never steps out of character. When it happens it's for only a split second and then she's back in character again." She shrugged. "Thank God for freeze-frame. It can be very illuminating."

"So you've decided she's just a lonely, misunderstood woman who became innocently involved?" he asked mockingly.

"No, I think she could kill a man. She projects determination and intensity as strong as an atomic blast. I think she could do anything she needed to do and there's no way she'd be a pawn. It would be her way all the way." She switched the television set back on. "I'm afraid I was too busy to watch the news for you. You can catch up on it yourself."

"You're assuming a lot from just looking at those videotapes."

"Believe me or not. I couldn't care less."

"Oh, I believe that body language and facial expressions can be a dead giveaway. Studying them is one of the key courses in the negotiating seminars I send all my corporate executives to. It's just that we have to be very careful about assuming anything about Lisa Chadbourne."

"We have to be careful about everything connected with her." She headed for the front door. "I'm going down to the pier."

"May I go with you?" Logan asked.

"No, I don't remember being invited when you and Gil wanted to talk."

"Ouch," Gil said.

She ran down the porch steps. The beach was deserted except for a few children playing volleyball several hundred yards from the pier. She supposed she should be worried about being recognized. CNN had probably shown a photograph of the crazy pyromaniac who had killed Logan.

Crazy. She flinched from the word. Damn Lisa Chadbourne. She'd had to use the part of Eve's life that could still bring pain. She could almost see her going over the possibilities and then striking like a black widow spider at the heart of—

Why was she so sure it was Lisa Chadbourne who was responsible for the attack on her? She could be wrong. It could be Timwick.

She wasn't wrong. Lisa Chadbourne would never underestimate another woman. She had too much respect for herself.

She sat down on the pier and looked down into the water.

"You're assuming a lot just from looking at those videotapes."

She *was* assuming a lot. She could be imagining the subtle nuances she thought she'd caught while watching Lisa Chadbourne.

The hell she could. She had trained herself to recognize and portray expression.

And her observations were more than clinical. She had felt the same gut instinct she experienced in the last stages of sculpting.

She *knew* Lisa Chadbourne.

Fraser.

She shivered as she looked down into the water. Lisa Chadbourne and Fraser were nothing alike. So why was she thinking of them as one?

Because the fear was back a second time. It had returned the day her lab had been destroyed so violently and she had thought of Fraser. Lisa Chadbourne had been the guiding hand then, just as she was now.

Fraser had been tainted with a madness that Eve had not seen in Lisa Chadbourne, but they both possessed the assurance that came with power.

The pleasure derived from power was a strong motivator. Fraser's power had come from killing. Lisa Chadbourne's motivation was obviously more complicated . . . and possibly even more deadly. The thirst for power on a global scale could be far more damaging than on a smaller personal scale.

To hell with global scale. Nothing could be more damaging than what had happened to Bonnie. The world was made up of personal stories, personal tragedies, and the brutal acts that Fraser had committed were every bit as evil as the killing done by Lisa Chadbourne.

Murder was murder. They had taken a life and life was sacred. She wasn't sure that Detwil was the danger Logan saw him to be. She didn't know about politics or plots or diplomatic implications, but she knew about murder. She had lived and eaten and slept with it.

And, God, how she hated it.

"Keep watching the mother, James." Lisa's brow knit as she gazed at the Duncan dossier in the computer. "Duncan obviously has a soft spot for her. I think we can find a way to use her."

"I am watching her," Timwick said. "I've never stopped. We believe Duncan placed a call to her mother this morning. She was on a digital phone, but we had stationed a man with an amplifier outside the house. We got only snippets of the conversation, but I'd bet she's trying to remove her mother from the equation."

Smart. Just exactly what Lisa would have done. Erase every weak point. "That mustn't happen. Deal with it."

"Permanently?"

Christ, violence was Timwick's solution for everything. "No, we may need her."

"She's being watched by Madden Security, Logan's team, as well as the Atlanta P.D. It may be difficult to make a clean move."

"Do your best. Send Fiske. He handled the Barrett House matter exceptionally well. What about the forensic anthropologist?"

"We're watching Crawford at Duke University."

"What about the people Eve Duncan worked with?"

"We're working our way through the list. That takes time."

"We don't have time. It shouldn't be that difficult. He'd have to have qualifications and experience working in DNA."

"There are more people with the DNA qualification than you'd think. It's the wave of the future."

"We've got to cut the list down. Send it to me and I'll do it." She checked her wristwatch. "I have to go. I'm scheduled for a meeting. I'll get back to you."

She hung up and started to close Eve Duncan's file. Then she hesitated, gazing at Eve's image.

Eve was moving swiftly to prevent any more damage. Lisa had had a hunch that Eve would try to save the mother even though Sandra seemed to have done precious little for her. She'd let her daughter grow up on the streets and had done nothing to keep her from becoming pregnant and having that illegitimate child.

Yet Eve had obviously forgiven her mother and was loyal to her. Loyalty was a rare and valuable quality. The more Lisa studied the woman's file, the more she was coming to admire her . . . and know her. She kept seeing similarities between them. Lisa's own parents had been loving and supportive but she, too, had worked her way out of the tenements and fought the system against all odds.

What was she thinking? she wondered impatiently. She mustn't be swayed just because she was beginning to feel a certain empathy with Eve Duncan. She had set her feet on a particular path, and she must follow it to the end.

No matter who got in the way.

FOURTEEN

"Well, you made it," Joe said sourly as he walked over to the car. "I'm surprised. This baby looks like it's seen some miles."

"It attracts less attention." Logan climbed out of the driver's seat and faced him. "Would you have preferred I drove Eve around in a red Lamborghini?"

"I'd prefer you didn't drive her around at all." He stared at Logan. "I'd prefer that you'd never set eyes on her, you son of a bitch."

Christ, he was uptight, Eve thought. Joe looked more menacing than she'd ever seen him, and Logan was bristling like a guard dog. She hurriedly got out of the car. "Get in the backseat with me, Joe. Logan, you drive us to Emory."

Neither man moved.

"Dammit, you're drawing too much attention. Get in, Joe."

He finally climbed into the car.

She drew a breath of relief, said, "Drive, Logan," and climbed in.

Logan returned to the driver's seat and started the car.

"Did you get the picture of Margaret to my mother?" she asked Joe.

"Last night." His gaze was fixed on the back of Logan's head. "I scouted the area myself and ran across his security team. I almost threw them in the lockup before I got them to identify themselves."

"Anyone else?" Logan asked.

"Not that I could tell. No obvious stakeout."

"They wouldn't be obvious and they'd be good. Very good. With the most sophisticated surveillance equipment in the business."

"Why?" Joe turned to Eve. "What the hell's going on? Talk to me."

"Did you bring me the pictures of Timwick and Fiske?"

He reached into his jacket pocket and brought out an envelope. "And that's another thing. I checked into Mr. Fiske and he's real nasty. You shouldn't even be within shouting distance of the bastard."

"I'll try not to be." He didn't look nasty, she thought absently, more like a stereotypical butler. Hazel eyes gazed mildly out of the picture. His nose was long and aristocratic, and his gray-flecked, carefully trimmed mustache was the epitome of neatness. Though he appeared to be only in his late thirties, his barbered brown hair was slightly gray at the temples and receded sharply from a broad forehead.

There was nothing aristocratic about James Timwick. His face was broad, almost Slavic, and his eyes were a pale blue. He was younger than she'd thought he'd be, perhaps in his early forties, and his hair was jet black.

"Now tell me why you had me bring those to you," Joe said.

Because I needed to see the face of the enemy, the men who might try to kill me. Not an explanation she could give Joe, who was already near meltdown. "I thought it might help." She tucked the pictures in her handbag. "Thank you, Joe."

"Don't thank me. Tell me what I need to know."

She had to make one last try. "You don't need to know. I'd rather you opted out of this."

"Tell me."

He wasn't going to be dissuaded, she realized resignedly. "Okay, but let me tell it my way. Don't try interrogating me, Joe."

They had arrived at Emory and were parked in the lot for a good ten minutes before Eve stopped speaking.

He was silent a moment, gazing down at the leather case at her feet. "Is that him?"

"Yes."

"It's damn hard to believe."

"I agree," Eve said. "But it's Ben Chadbourne, Joe."

"You're sure?"

She nodded. "And that's why I want you out of it. I don't know what will happen."

"I do." Joe's lips tightened grimly. "And so does Logan. He knew what he was getting you into from the beginning."

"Yes, I did," Logan said calmly. "But that doesn't change the present scenario. We have to do that ourselves."

Joe gave him an icy glance and then turned back to Eve. "You can't trust him. It would be better if I got rid of him for you."

"Got rid of him?"

"It would be easy enough. Everyone thinks it happened already anyway."

Her eyes widened. "Joe."

He shrugged. "I didn't think you'd go for it." He opened the car door. "Stay here. I'll reconnoiter the area and feel out Kessler for you. What makes you think he'll want to become involved?"

"He has integrity plus curiosity and an obsessive nature. It's why he's in the profession."

"Well, you should know about obsessions." He slammed the door shut and moved quickly across the parking lot.

"A very violent man for an officer of the law," Logan murmured.

"He's not violent. He's just angry. He wouldn't really have—"

"Oh, I think he would. For a few minutes my neck was definitely on the line. I think I'd better step very carefully around Quinn."

"Joe believes in the law," she said fiercely. "Dammit, he's a good cop."

"I'm sure he is, but I'm equally sure his SEAL training gets in the way occasionally. Particularly when the law doesn't seem to be working and his friends are involved."

"Joe doesn't kill."

"Now. Did you ever ask him how many men he killed when he was a SEAL?"

"Of course I didn't. We were at peace when he was in the service."

"But SEALs have missions even in peacetime."

"Why are you doing this? Why are you trying to make me distrust Joe?"

"Maybe self-preservation." He smiled grimly. "And because I want you to admit that one nod of your head and I would have been a dead man a few minutes ago."

"I won't admit any—"

"Be honest."

She didn't want to be honest, not if it meant admitting she didn't know Joe as well as she thought she did. Joe was one of the bedrocks of her life. He was everything stable and trustworthy. When everything else had been falling apart around her, Joe had always been there. She would not think of him as a killer because that would be comparing him to Fraser. No. Never.

"Has he ever talked to you about his time in the SEALs?"

"No."

"Did you know he's killed three men in the line of duty since he's been in Atlanta?"

Her gaze flew to his face.

"I didn't think so. Quinn's smart and he knows you well. He'd keep that part of his life separate from you."

"He's no murderer."

"I didn't say he is. There's no question that those deaths were self-defense and that the scum he killed deserved to die. I'm just saying that Quinn is multifaceted and very dangerous."

"You're trying to take away my trust in him."

"And he's trying to take away any trust you might have in me. I'm just defending myself."

"I have no trust in you."

"You have a little. At least, you know we're on the same side. I won't have Quinn stealing that away." His gaze went to Joe, who was now climbing the steps of the geoscience building. "And I don't want to have to fight Quinn along with everyone else."

Eve followed his glance. It was as if she were looking at Joe in a different light. He was always confident, always moved with a springy grace, but now she could see the relentless efficiency in his entire attitude. Powerhouse, she had called him, and powerhouse she knew him to be, but not deadly.

She could sense the deadliness now.

"Damn you."

"We're all savages," Logan said quietly. "We all kill when it means enough to us. Food, revenge, self-preservation . . . But Quinn knew you couldn't take it, so he made sure you didn't see that side of him."

"And would you kill too, Logan?" she asked bitterly.

"If the circumstances warranted it. And so would you, Eve."

She shook her head. "Life is too precious. There's no excuse for murder."

He shrugged. "Excuse no, but reason is—"

"I don't want to talk about it." She leaned back and stared out the window, shutting him out. "I don't want to talk to you at all, Logan. Just leave me alone, okay?"

"Sure."

Of course he'd agree. He'd turned loose a serpent and now was willing to watch it work its poison.

She wouldn't let him. She wouldn't let him destroy the trust she had in Joe. Logan was the outsider, not Joe. She wouldn't brood and wonder and let his words eat at her.

Logan said softly, "But it's true, you know."

• • •

"It's okay." Joe opened the car door for Eve and helped her out. "The coast is clear. Kessler's alone. His assistant, Bob Spencer, was there, but I had Kessler get rid of him."

She picked up the case containing the skull. "What did you tell Gary?"

"Not what was in the surprise package, but I filled him in on everything else. You're right, he's curious." He took the case from her and his hand closed on her elbow. "Let's get him started on it."

"I'm beginning to feel a little de trop." Logan got out of the car. "I trust you won't mind if I tag along?"

"I do mind," Joe said. "But I'll put up with you as long as you don't get in the way." His pace quickened as he guided Eve across the parking lot. "How long will this take?"

"Kessler's part won't take long if he can find a good source of DNA to extract. It's the lab work I'm concerned about. DNA testing can take months."

"You worry about getting a good sample, I'll take care of getting the DNA testing pushed through." Joe held the door to the building open for her. "No problem. I'm good at pushing. It's one of my—" His gaze suddenly narrowed on her face. "Why are you looking at me like that?"

She glanced away from him quickly. "I don't know what you mean."

"The hell you don't."

She shook off his hand and kept walking. "Stop probing, Joe. There's nothing wrong."

"Maybe." His glance shifted to Logan. "Maybe not."

She opened the door of the lab and saw Kessler sitting at his desk, eating a sandwich.

He looked up and glowered at her. "I hear you're trying to get me tossed in the cooler. Thanks a lot, Duncan."

"There's mustard on your mustache." She took the case from Joe and went to stand before Kessler. She picked up the paper napkin on the desk and wiped his mouth and bristly gray mustache. "Christ, you have to be the messiest eater on the planet, Gary."

"Eating should be a pleasurable function when a man's alone. I shouldn't have to worry about a woman coming in and criticizing me. Particularly one who's come begging." He took another bite of his sandwich. "What have you got yourself into, Duncan?"

"I need a little help."

"If the news reports are right, you need help from a lawyer, not me." He looked behind her. "You're Logan?"

Logan nodded.

Kessler smiled slyly. "I understand you've got a potload of money?"

"Enough."

"Care to part with some? Things aren't the same as when I was a young man. It's a sad fact that we brilliant scientists need patrons these days."

"Maybe we could come to an arrangement," Logan said.

"Back off, Gary." Eve unfastened Ben's case. "You know very well that if you're interested enough, you'll do the job for nothing."

"You have a loud mouth, Duncan," Kessler said. "There's nothing wrong with a little greed. And, besides, I might have become more of a philistine since we last worked together." His tone was absent, his gaze fixed on the case. In spite of his words, she could sense his excitement. He reminded Eve of a kid waiting to see what was in a Christmas package. "And sending Quinn in ahead to try to rouse my curiosity is a pretty obvious ploy. I would have thought you'd be a little more subtle."

She grinned. "If something works, I don't fuss with it."

"It must have been something pretty interesting that pulled you into a mess like this." His gaze never left the case. "You're not usually stupid."

"Thank you."

She waited.

He finally said impatiently, "So who is it?"

She opened the lid and carefully lifted out the skull. "You tell me."

"Oh, shit," he whispered.

Eve nodded. "Yes."

He took the skull from her and put it on his desk. "It's no joke?"

"Would I be on the run if it was a joke?"

He stared at the face. "My God. Chadbourne." He looked at her. "If it is Chadbourne. Did you know who you were working on?"

She shook her head. "I went at it blind. I had no idea until I finished."

"And what do you want from me?"

"Proof."

"DNA." He frowned. "And what have I got to work on? I suppose you worked on the actual skull again? Why can't you make casts? There's no telling what you destroyed."

"It was already clean. The body had been through a fire."

His gaze narrowed. "Then what do you think I'm supposed to do?"

"I thought . . . the teeth. The DNA would have been protected by the enamel. You could split a tooth and extract the DNA. Is that possible?"

"Possible. It's been done before." Kessler added, "But it's not a sure thing."

"Will you try?"

"Why should I? This isn't any of my concern, and it could be big trouble."

Joe spoke up. "I'll be here to guard you while you're working." He glanced at Logan. "And I'm sure Mr. Logan would be glad to make it worth your while."

"Within boundaries," Logan said.

They were going about this all wrong, Eve thought impatiently. They'd had Gary from the moment he'd seen the face. He just needed a little push over the line. "Don't you want to know if it's really Chadbourne, Gary? Don't you want to be the one to prove it?"

Kessler was silent a moment. "Maybe."

He wanted it all right. She could see the excitement he was trying to hide.

"It would be megadifficult," she said. "Hell, you'll probably have enough for a book."

"Not so difficult." He scowled. "Unless you screwed up the teeth too."

"I didn't touch them any more than I could help." She smiled. "And you know my work doesn't interfere with yours. It's all there, waiting for you."

He glanced up from the skull. "I know exactly what you're doing, you know."

"Of course you do. Now, are you going to do it, or do we take the skull to Crawford at Duke?"

"Appealing to my competitiveness won't work either. I know I'm the best in the business." He sat back down in the chair. "But I may do you the favor. I've always liked you, Duncan."

"You'd do it even if you hated my guts." Her smile faded. "But I'm not going to lie. The situation is more dangerous than getting in trouble with the law."

"I gathered that." He shrugged. "I'm an old man. I need a little something to keep the adrenaline pumping. Can I use my own lab?"

"We'd rather you don't. We think we're safe, but we don't want to take any chances. Is there someplace else you can work?"

"You do make things hard for me." He thought for a minute. "My lab at home?"

She shook her head.

"I've a friend who's a professor at Kennesaw State, which is about forty minutes from here. He'll let me use his lab."

"Fine."

"What about my assistant?"

She shook her head. "Let him take over your classes. I'll help you."

"I probably won't need it." He added testily, "But you can clean off all this damned clay. I want a nice, clean surface."

"Okay." She braced herself. "But I need to do a superimposition first."

"And I'm supposed to twiddle my thumbs and wait?"

"I'll hurry. We need it, Gary. You know the teeth are important with superimposition and we don't know how many teeth you're going to have to take. We can't verify the dental records, so we need every bit of evidence we can get our hands on."

"Maybe," he granted reluctantly. "But my DNA will carry the day."

"I know. But will you use your pull to borrow video equipment from the audio-visual department? I already have the mixer."

"You don't want much," Gary said sourly. "Taking valuable equipment off campus? They'll yell bloody murder."

"Don't tell them you're taking it off campus."

"They'll still kick up a fuss."

"Charm them."

"Yeah, sure. Then they really will suspect I've gone around the bend. I'll threaten and blackmail them instead."

"You're right, we wouldn't want you to act out of character."

"But you'll work your skinny butt off and get your stuff done pronto."

"I'm not arguing."

"Amazing," Kessler murmured. "How long to clean up the skull?"

"An hour, maybe two. I want to be very careful."

"Then I'll get your equipment and then run down my assistant and tell him I'll be gone for a couple of days." Kessler moved toward the door. "Pack up our presidential friend. I'll be back as soon as possible."

She said quietly, "Thanks, Gary. I owe you."

"Yes, you do, and I'll make sure you pay me."

"You played him very well," Logan said as the door closed behind Kessler.

"We understand each other." She glanced at Joe. "Will you follow him and make sure he's safe? I didn't want to make an issue of it, but I don't want him running around the campus all by himself."

"You said yourself that you didn't think they'd figure out the connection."

"I don't want to take any chances. I persuaded him to help us. I feel responsible."

"And I feel responsible for you."

"Please, Joe."

"I don't want to—" He broke off as he saw her expression. He turned away abruptly. "Stay with her, Logan. If you let anything happen to her, I'll break your neck." The door closed behind him with a decisive click.

Violence again. She gazed blindly down at the skull.

"Are you ready to go?" Logan asked.

"Not yet. I'm going to pack up Ben and then rifle through Gary's equipment for something to chip this clay off." She crossed to the table and opened the cabinet. "You can contact Margaret and find out when my mother will be safe."

"I can phone from here."

"I don't want you underfoot. Go outside and do it."

"I'd like to oblige, but Quinn gave me orders. I really would like to keep my skin intact."

"*I'm* giving you orders. You're not doing any good here. Get out of my way and see that Mom's safe or I'll go home and do it myself. It's what I want to do anyway."

He held up his hand in surrender. "I'm on my way."

He was gone.

She drew a breath of relief. She didn't want any of them around her right now. She was too unsettled and needed to get things back in perspective. Work was the only thing that would do that. The sooner they got to that lab at Kennesaw State, the better she'd be.

She found three wood instruments that looked sharp enough to be effective but not too sharp to do crucial damage if her hand slipped. She dropped them in her handbag and then carefully repacked Ben's skull in the case. "Okay, Ben. Sorry to put you through this, but I've got to take all that clay off you. Put it on, take it off. All this running around and fussing doesn't seem fair, does it?" She fastened the case. "But here we go again."

"Mrs. Duncan? Open the door. Margaret Wilson."

Sandra studied the plump woman through the peephole and compared her to the photograph in her hand.

"Mrs. Duncan?"

"I heard you." Sandra unlocked the door. "Come in."

Margaret shook her head. "No, I have the van at the curb. We have to leave now. Are you ready?"

"As soon as I get my suitcase." She went to the living room and came back with the case. "Where are we going?"

"We can't talk here." Margaret preceded her down the porch steps. "Don't worry, you'll be safe."

"Why can't we talk here. I'm not—" Sandra made the connection. "Bugged? You think my house is bugged?"

"That's what I was told. Hurry."

"Bugged." Sandra locked the front door. "What the hell is going on?"

"I hoped you'd know." Margaret moved briskly down the walk. "I thought we'd compare notes and come up with some answers. Usually, I don't mind traveling blind for John, but I'm a little uneasy about all this." She opened the passenger door. "Get in." She indicated the short, burly man in the driver's seat. "This is Brad Pilton. He's with Madden Security and he's one of the crew who's been watching over you the past several days. He's supposed to be our bodyguard."

"I *am* your bodyguard," Pilton said, pained. He nodded politely at Sandra. "Ma'am."

"Well, you're not very big." Margaret climbed into the backseat. "Not that that's a hindrance in most cases. I approve of small. Still, I think I'd have chosen someone else for the job if I'd seen you first. There are uses for big and brawny. Not that you don't have excellent credentials."

"Thank you." He started the van and edged away from the curb.

"Where are we going?" Sandra repeated. "Or can't we talk?"

"The van's safe. It belongs to the security company, but I insisted Pilton check it out for bugs anyway. We're going to the mall."

"The mall?"

"North Lake Mall." She smiled at Sandra. "We need to do a car switch in case we're followed. We'll go in one door and out another."

"And from there?"

"Lake Lanier. I've rented a small cottage. You'll be safe and cozy."

Lake Lanier. She and Ron had talked about going up there over Labor Day, Sandra remembered wistfully. But he'd said they'd stay at the hotel on Pine Island. He wasn't much on rustic. Well, neither was she. In spite of their differences, they had a lot in common.

"Something wrong?" Margaret's gaze was on her.

"I guess not. All this seems like a bad dream to me."

"Me too." Margaret leaned forward and squeezed Sandra's shoulder. "Don't worry. We'll get through it together."

"I think we're being followed," Pilton said.

Sandra tensed and glanced over her shoulder. "Where?"

"The dark blue Mercury."

"Are you sure?"

Pilton nodded. "Don't worry. We expected it. We'll lose him at the mall."

Someone was following them. Someone who might want to hurt her, Sandra thought with a shiver.

For the first time, the threat became real to her.

Fiske watched the van pull into a parking space at North Lake Mall and the three passengers hurry through the doors of the south entrance. He didn't bother to park. He'd cruise around the mall and see if he could spot the three as they came out another door.

It was doubtful. There were too many lots and too many exits.

It didn't really matter. His favorite listening device had paid off again. He knew where they were going, though he wished Margaret Wilson had been a little more explicit. Lanier was a huge resort area with thousands of rental properties.

Which meant he should start the ball rolling on locating the right one immediately.

He took out his electronic earpiece and punched in Timwick's number on his phone. "Duncan's mother is being taken to a cottage on Lake Lanier. The place was probably rented yesterday or today by Margaret Wilson. I need to know where it is."

"I'll get on it." Timwick hung up the phone.

Fiske decided that in the meantime he'd check into a hotel and wait. Things were proceeding very well. He'd been upset about leaving Atlanta before everything was tidily brought to completion.

But now he was back.

"Everything's fine," Margaret told Logan on the phone. "We've changed cars and we're on our way to Lake Lanier."

"Call me when you get there."

"I told you, everything's fine. Pilton is sure we're not being followed any longer."

"Pilton?"

"The bodyguard. Though his body isn't much bigger than mine."

"No big deal. I'd bet on you over Goliath any day."

"Me too. That's why I'm reassuring myself about Pilton. Okay, I'll call you when we get to the cottage. Anything else?"

"Just stay out of sight." He ended the call.

Everything's fine.

Maybe it was fine, but he was still uneasy. He'd expected getting Sandra Duncan away from the house to be more difficult.

Unless they wanted her out of sight as much as he did. It would be easier to dispose of someone who was hiding from the world.

But only if they found her.

"I told you to stay with Eve." Joe Quinn was walking up the steps toward him.

"And she told you to stay with Kessler."

"He's right behind me."

"And I'm a hundred yards from the lab."

"That's a hundred yards too far."

"I had phone calls to make and I think she wanted me out of her hair."

"She has good taste."

Time to try to bridge the gulf. "You're absolutely right. She's perfectly right to resent me. So are you." He gazed into Quinn's eyes. "But don't give me orders. We're on the same team and I'll do everything I can, but I'll work with you, not for you, Quinn."

Joe's lips twisted. "And not against me? Just what did you tell her about me?"

"What I had to tell her to protect my position. I assure you that it was nothing but the truth."

"As defined by John Logan."

Logan nodded. "I think you know what I told her. I imagine it's what you've been carefully hiding for years."

"Damn you."

"I believe I was entitled to protect myself. You were becoming a little too lethal. Suppose we come to an agreement. You agree to work with me willingly, if not amicably, and I'll stop bringing up your alter ego to Eve."

Quinn stared at him a moment. "Screw you." He passed him and went into the building.

Logan let out the breath he hadn't known he was holding. He had confronted many dangerous men in his time, but Quinn was definitely in a class by himself. It astonished him that Eve hadn't picked up on it.

Maybe not so strange. To her Quinn was the protector, the man who had saved her and sustained her.

It was difficult to equate a savior with a terminator.

FIFTEEN

KENNESAW STATE UNIVERSITY
1:05 A.M.

"How's it going?" Logan squatted beside Eve's chair. "Have you got a minute?"

"No, I haven't got a minute. It took me forever to jerry-rig this equipment and set it up." She adjusted the TV monitor. "And I've just started."

"Margaret called from Lanier. I have the phone number. I thought you'd want to talk to your mother."

"Why didn't you tell me? Of course I want to talk to her."

Logan dialed the number and handed his phone to Eve. "How are you, Mom?"

"Tired. Worried about you," Sandra said. "Hell, worried about me. Other than that, I'm in great shape. When is this going to be over, Eve?"

"I wish I knew." She changed the subject. "How's the cottage?"

"Nice. It's on the water. Great view."

But Sandra didn't sound as if she appreciated either

the cottage or the view. Who could blame her? Eve had disrupted her life and yanked her away from the pleasant, comfortable niche she'd made for herself. "Try to enjoy it and relax. Do you have any books to read?"

"Margaret brought a few suspense novels, but you know I don't read much. There's a big TV set." A pause. "Do you suppose I could call Ron? I wouldn't tell him where I was."

"No, don't do it. Honest, I'll try to have you out of there in a few days."

"Okay." Sandra's tone was despondent. "I guess I'm kind of lonely. I'll be fine. You just take care of yourself."

"I will. Good night, Mom. I'll call you every day." She handed Logan the phone. "Thanks. I feel a little better now."

"That was the intention. How is she?"

"Depressed. She wants her life back." She gazed blindly at the monitor. "She deserves a good life. She's had a hard time and now things are looking up for her. She's met someone she cares about. Mom's always needed people."

"And you haven't?"

She shrugged. "I guess I've never thought about it. There was always too much work to do."

"Always?"

"Not always. Not when Bonnie—" She turned to look at him. "You're probing again, Logan."

"Sorry, I'm just wondering what makes you tick." He gazed at the skull on the pedestal. "Besides an obsession with our friends who have passed over. It's interesting that you don't seem to have made any close friends after your daughter was killed."

"I've been busy."

"And perhaps you don't want to come close to anyone again and risk being hurt."

"Do you expect me to be awed by your perceptiveness? I'm well aware I'm avoiding new relationships and the reason for it."

"Of course you are. You're a brilliant woman. So why don't you do something about it?"

"Maybe I don't want to do anything about it."

"Not even to live a fuller, richer life?"

"You don't know how full and rich my life is compared to what it was before. I was lost and now I'm found." She said haltingly, "I was drowning in pain and I've managed to climb to dry land. That's enough, Logan."

"It's not enough. It's time to go on."

She shook her head. "You don't understand."

"I'm trying."

"Why?"

"I like you," he said simply.

She stared at him. "What are you up to, Logan?"

"I don't have an agenda. I do make new friends . . . even if there's a risk of losing them. I like you and I admire you. I just thought I'd tell you."

"Before you start using me again."

"Yes."

"You're totally incredible." She looked back at the monitor. "Do you expect me to say all is forgiven and let's go play in the sandbox?"

"No, I told you, no agenda. We're past all that now. I just wanted to be honest with you for a change. Sorry I disconcerted you." He rose to his feet. "I'd better let you get back to work."

"Yes, you had."

"I thought you'd have more done by now."

She was relieved that odd moment of revelation and intimacy was over and that Logan's usual demanding self was back. He was right. He had disconcerted her. "It took me longer than I thought to clean up Ben." She glanced at Kessler, who was seated at the table at the far end of the lab. "Gary wasn't pleased. He's been chomping at the bit to get to work and I still need the skull for verification."

"Why did you take those photographs at Barrett House?"

"Insurance."

"How long is the superimposition going to take? This place is a little too public. I want to get out of here."

"I'm hurrying as fast as I can." She adjusted the camera

aimed at the skull on the pedestal, and then made a minor adjustment on the second camera aimed at one of the photographs of Ben Chadbourne Logan had given her at Barrett House.

"How long is this going to take?" he repeated.

"It depends. Setting up sometimes takes the longest, and I haven't used this equipment before. I think I've got it right."

"How does it work?"

"Haven't you got something else to do?"

"Just interested. Am I bothering you?"

"I suppose not." She made another adjustment. "As you can see, the one camera is focused on the skull, the other on the photograph. The angle on the skull and the photograph both have to be the same. Then both cameras are connected to a mixer, an editing machine that I've connected to a VCR. The VCR plays the images on the monitor. The mixer can create a split screen where a line runs vertically and horizontally between the images at the same time or half of each image. The line can be moved to show less of one image and more of the other. That's called a wipe. But what I need to do is cause a fade."

"And what's that?"

"It's sort of like a dream sequence in a movie. You know, when one image blurs and then suddenly becomes another? One image is superimposed on another and then I equalize the fade so that you can see the photograph and the skull both as if the person's skin is transparent."

"Can you show me now?"

"Here it comes." She brought the two images up on the monitor and started to work.

"Why did you pick the—"

"Be quiet. I'm busy."

"Sorry."

She was only vaguely aware of him beside her during the next period of painstaking adjustment.

Move.

Too much.

Backtrack.

Adjust.

Again.

Again.

And still again.

"Christ." Logan leaned forward, his gaze on the ghostly merged image. "It's almost spooky."

"Nothing spooky about it. It's just a tool."

"May I talk now?"

"You appear to be doing it." She made another adjustment.

"Why did you choose the photograph with Chadbourne smiling?"

"The teeth. Teeth are rarely perfect and each set has its own irregularities. If the teeth are a match, we hit the jackpot. That's why I had to have the skull before Gary started pulling the teeth."

"And do these teeth match?"

"Oh, yes," she said with satisfaction. "Definite match. Perfect match. Can't you see?"

"They look good to me, but I'm no expert. And I'm being distracted by that ghostly effect."

"It *all* matches." She pointed. "See how the bite line on the skull is even with the lip line on the photograph." She tapped the nasal opening. "And this is the same size and shape as the nose. The eyeballs are centered in the orbits of the skull. There are several other checkpoints and they all match."

"So what happens now?"

"I print out several copies of this picture on the screen and go to the next photograph."

"But you told me this was a definite match."

"For an ordinary person. Not for the President of the United States. Every feature has to be verified. I need a better side shot of the ear canal and the muscle attachment at the side of the—"

"I get your point." Logan held up his hand to stop the flow of words. "Can I help?"

"You can go talk to Gary and pacify him until I finish. He'll be pouncing on me any minute."

"I hear. I obey." He rose to his feet. "Pacifying seems to be all

I'm good for these days. It's annoying not to be able to take action myself."

"I prefer you in passive mode," she said dryly. "Every time you take action, I sink deeper into this quicksand."

"No comment." He strode across the lab toward Kessler.

She looked back at the screen. She had known the superimposition would validate the work she'd done on the skull, but it still sent a ripple of excitement through her. One more block in the wall of evidence she had to build. "We're getting there, Ben," she whispered.

She hit the print button on the Sony video printer.

3:35 A.M.

It was raining.

She hadn't realized that when she was working in the lab. Now she leaned against the open doorway of the front entrance, looking out over the manicured lawns of the campus. The cool, humid air felt good in her lungs as she took a deep breath.

She should be tired, but she was still pumped from working on the match.

"You shouldn't be out here." Joe was leaning against the brick wall a few yards from the door. "Go back inside."

"I need some air."

"Did you finish?"

"I finished the superimposition. Gary's barely started on extracting the DNA." She looked at his clothes. "You're wet."

"Not much. The overhead ledge protects me. It kind of feels good." He grimaced. "I guess I'm a little hot under the collar."

"I noticed. But you shouldn't blame Logan. It was my decision to do the job. I knew there was a risk. The fee was just too good."

"I'll bet he didn't let you know how risky before he drew you in."

"It was still my decision." Why was she defending Logan? Joe was right to condemn Logan's methods and she had been as angry as Joe when she found out how she had been used. She changed the subject. "It's late. You shouldn't be here. Diane will be worried."

"I called her."

"If you told her you were with me, then that wouldn't stop her from worrying. She had to have seen CNN."

"I didn't tell her."

"You *lied* to her?"

"No, I just told her I was working late."

"That's almost a lie. I'd be furious if you weren't honest with me."

"You're not Diane. She prefers to be kept in the dark when something unpleasant raises its head. She's never become accustomed to being married to a cop. She'd much rather I quit the force and find something with a little more prestige to do."

"Well, I can't argue the situation isn't as unpleasant as it comes, but I'd still want to brain you. Marriage should be a partnership."

"There are all kinds of marriages."

"I don't suppose I should be surprised. You don't tell me everything either." She glanced away from him, staring into the distance. "For instance, you never mentioned you'd killed anyone in the line of duty."

"You've had enough violence in your life. You didn't need any more."

"Was that your decision? Just like the one you made to protect Diane? Keep the delicate females away from any hint of unpleasantness."

"Did I want to protect you?" he asked roughly. "Hell, yes. But I also wanted to protect myself. I knew you'd be like this. I didn't want you to look at me and see Fraser."

"I'd never do that. I know you. I'm sure you did only what you had to do."

"Then turn around and let me see your face."

She braced herself, turned, and looked at him.

"Shit," he said through his teeth.

"I just have to become accustomed to the idea. I feel as if I don't really know you."

"You know me better than anyone on this earth, just as I know you better than anyone else does."

"Then why didn't you tell me about—"

"All right, I'll tell you." His hands clenched into fists at his sides. "You want a body count? Three. Two of them were into drug running. The third just liked killing and reminded me of Fraser. I've often wondered if that one really was self-defense. Maybe I didn't want to take the chance of him walking." His voice lowered. "And I never lost a minute's sleep over any of them. Does that make you feel like you know me any better?"

"Joe, I don't—"

"Do you want me to talk about my stint in the SEALs? No, I can see you don't. Three is enough for you. You don't want the grim reaper's shadow anywhere near you. I knew that and accepted it."

"Why didn't I hear about those deaths?"

"Because I saw that you didn't want to know about them. Figuring that out was easy. You never watched or read local news after Bonnie. I just had to make sure no one in the department talked." He gazed into her eyes. "And I'd do it again. You weren't ready to face the idea that I wasn't Andy Griffith ambling around Mayberry. You may never be ready." His glance shifted past her to the hall leading to the lab. "And I'm not pleased with our Mr. Logan for stirring up this hornet's nest."

"Then you shouldn't have threatened him."

"Do you think I don't know that? I was stupid. I was angry and I let you see it." He smiled recklessly. "Or maybe I'm lying to myself. Maybe I meant to do it. It could be I was sick and tired of— But how the hell long do you think I can keep everything inside without—" He took a long breath. "Don't blow what we've got, Eve. We've been together a long time. Like you said, you know me."

"Do I?" she whispered.

"Okay, we'll start over. I'll be honest with you even if it tears you apart. Satisfied? " He turned away from her. "Because I'm not. But then, I'm used to that. It's become a way of life to me."

"What do—"

"This isn't getting us anywhere. I've got to go check out the perimeter." He started down the steps. "But don't worry, if I find any bad guys, I'll handle them with kid gloves. We wouldn't want any more blood on my hands, would we?"

He was angry with her. Maybe he had a right. He was her friend, closer than a brother, and she had pushed him away and closed him out. Joe knew her too well not to be aware of everything she was feeling.

But she didn't know him that well. She had thought she did, but she'd had no idea of all that he'd hidden from her.

Face it, she hadn't wanted to know. Policemen dealt with violence every day and, if she had let herself think about it, she would have known it would touch Joe.

"I didn't want you to look at me and see Fraser."

She had denied it, but hadn't that been her first thought when Logan told her about the deaths in Joe's past? It wasn't rational, it wasn't fair, but the thought had been there.

Another ripple Logan had set in motion to disturb her life. Only this time it was more like a tidal wave.

Block it out. She had enough to worry about just then. Easy to say. The idea of angering Joe wasn't easy to block out.

And what if it wasn't only anger? What if she had hurt him? Joe was tough, but he could be hurt. God, she didn't want to hurt him.

She couldn't dismiss the idea, but she had to put it on the back burner and consider all the ramifications later. Joe was too important to her. If she began to worry about him, she wouldn't be able to do anything else.

So go back in and see if you can help Gary. Get this business over with so you can go back to living a normal life with normal problems.

She turned and strode down the hall toward the lab.

• • • •

Kessler glanced up as she reached him. "You okay?"

"Sure. I just needed some air. How are you doing?"

"Not good." He looked back down at the molar he was cutting. "The poor bastard may be toothless before I get enough for a sample. This is the third one I've cut into."

"Do you need me to help?"

"And share the credit?"

She smiled. "I promise I'll never tell."

"Sure. I've heard that before. Go away."

"Whatever you say." But she didn't move, watching as he carefully cut through the enamel on the tooth. "I've been thinking. After we get the sample, it might be a good idea if you went away for a while. Maybe to your place on the shore."

"Ah, are you trying to save my neck, Duncan? Maybe feeling a little stirring of guilt?"

"Yes."

"Good. A little guilt is good for the soul." His gaze was narrowed on the tooth. "But don't flatter yourself that I'm doing this for you. This job is going to make me a star. I've always wanted to be the center of attention."

"Yeah, sure, that's why you work like a demon and live like a hermit."

"It takes one to know one. Another fifty years and you'll probably be living in your lab, eating cold Domino's pizza."

"And lying about wanting to become famous? Admit it, you're just curious."

"Partly." He carefully started opening the tooth.

"And what's the rest of it?"

"Did you know I spent my early childhood in Munich during the thirties?"

She shook her head, gazing at him in surprise. "You've never talked about it."

"No, we talk only about our jobs, don't we? The bones, the dead . . ." He adjusted his glasses on his nose. "My mother was

Jewish but my father was of good Aryan stock with high government connections. The Nazis put pressure on him to divorce her, but he refused. He owned a small bakery and for two months he had to replace the windows that were broken every day. He held out and still refused. Then one night he didn't come home from the shop and we were told he'd been run over by a truck. He lost a leg and spent nine months in a hospital. By the time he was up and about, it was all over. The shop was out of business and the Nazis had begun to round up the Jews. We managed to get to Switzerland and then later to America."

"Oh, God, that's terrible, Gary. I'm sorry."

"I wasn't sorry. I was mad. I watched those sons of bitches striding around the neighborhood, running over everyone who got in their way. Bullies. Taking away everything that made life worth living. God, I hate bullies." He nodded at the skull. "And the people who did this are like those damn Nazis, running over the whole damn world. They make me sick. I'll be damned if they get away with it this time."

She swallowed to ease the sudden tightness in her throat. "Why, Gary, you sound downright noble."

"Hell, yes. Besides, this may be my swan song, and I want it sung loud and clear."

"Swan song? Are you planning on retiring?"

"Maybe. I'm past retirement age. I'm an old man, Eve."

Eve shook her head. "Not you, Gary."

He chuckled. "You're right, I'm not old. Whenever I look in the mirror, I see the young stud I was at twenty. Maybe a few more wrinkles, but I don't often notice them. It's like that superimposition you do. No matter what's on the top layer, that young man is underneath and I know he's there. Do you suppose every old geezer is as self-deluding as me?"

"You're not self-deluding. We all see what we want to see. We all have a vision of ourselves." She tried to smile. "And, dammit, you're not old and you're not going to retire. I need you."

"True. It takes a benevolent and exceptional man to deal with someone of your headstrong nature and many faults. I may have to stick around just to keep you in— Shit." He pushed the tooth aside. "Another blank. Go away. You're bringing me bad luck."

"Well, that's a profoundly scientific notion." She turned away. "Call me if you need me."

"Not likely." He bent over the skull again as she walked away.

"Any progress?" Logan straightened in his chair across the room.

"Not yet."

"I saw a cot in the back room. Why don't you try to take a nap?"

She shook her head. "I need to be here in case he changes his mind about not needing help." She sat down beside him and leaned her head back against the wall. "It's my responsibility. I brought him into this."

"He seems to be enjoying himself." Logan's gaze was fixed on Kessler. "In a cerebral way."

"Cerebral? Hell, he thinks he's Schwarzkopf or Eliot Ness or Lancelot or some other—" She drew a deep breath and said fiercely, "And you'd better see that nothing happens to him, Logan. I should have gone to your man at Duke. All I thought about was who was best for the job. I didn't think about how dangerous this could be for Gary."

"As soon as we get the DNA sample and an affidavit, we'll whisk him away out of the limelight."

"Like you whisked my mother?"

"I told you she was safe, Eve. You talked to her."

"She's not safe. She won't be safe until this is over." None of them would be safe. Joe and Gary and her mother had been drawn into the net, and Eve had done it.

"All right, she's not as safe as I'd like her to be," Logan said. "But it's the best I can do right now." He paused. "Kessler appears to have upset you. What did he say?"

Nazis and swan songs and a young man in the mirror. "Nothing much. Nothing important."

It was a lie. Gary's life was important. The fact that she had never scratched more than the surface of Gary Kessler's past was important. It was a night of revelations, she thought wearily.

Logan, Joe, and now Gary. She closed her eyes. "Just keep him safe, okay?"

THE WHITE HOUSE

7:20 A.M.

"Kessler," Lisa said as soon as Timwick picked up the phone. "Check out Kessler at Emory."

"I know my job, Lisa. I'm checking out Kessler. He's on my list."

"Then put him higher on your list. Duncan's worked with Kessler several times. It was in the stuff on the disc you messengered over."

"She's worked with other people too." She heard him rustling papers. "And she hasn't worked with him in over two years."

"But he was the first anthropologist she ever worked with. They have a history. It would mean something to her."

"Then why hasn't she worked with him lately? Logan researched Crawford at—"

"Have they shown up at Duke?"

"No, but it's early days yet."

"Early? You should have caught them by now. Time's running out. Put Kessler at the top of the shortlist." She hung up the phone.

She shouldn't have been so sharp; it wasn't smart. The more desperate Timwick became, the more resentful he grew and the more domineering he tried to be. But, Christ, how could an intelligent man have so little imagination? Couldn't he see that it was Duncan and not Logan who was the key?

She drew a deep breath and tried to compose herself. She mustn't panic. She mustn't lose control. Okay, the problem was two-pronged. One, Ben's skull must be recovered; any evidence was moot without the skull. Two, Logan and Duncan must be eliminated and any other possible evidence destroyed. Dammit, Timwick was doing neither. She had known he was a weak link since that mistake with Donnelli and had made alternate plans to enact whenever necessary.

It was necessary. The more time passed, the more dangerous everything became. She had to take the reins completely in her own hands.

How had she come to this point? She had never wanted any of this. It wasn't fair.

Well, the world wasn't fair. You just had to do whatever you had to do. There wasn't any way she could reverse what she'd done that day, so she just had to protect herself and all she'd gained.

She opened her phone book to the name and number she had gotten from Timwick three weeks earlier.

She quickly dialed the number. It rang three times before it was answered.

"Mr. Fiske? We've never talked before, but I believe it's time we did."

SIXTEEN

KENNESAW STATE UNIVERSITY

11:50 A.M.

"Got it." Eve's hand tightened on the thermal case that contained the vial with the DNA sample. "Now let's get out of here. We can't afford any deterioration."

"Is there enough?" Logan asked.

"Just enough." She turned to Kessler. "Where do you suggest we take it, Gary?"

"I assume you don't want to take a chance on any of the obvious or well-known testing centers?"

She shook her head.

"But you want a place with excellent credentials."

She nodded.

"Duncan, you're an incredibly demanding woman. And you're fortunate that I'm incredible enough myself to meet your absurd demands." He lowered his voice dramatically. "I know a man."

"I don't want a man. I want a lab."

"You'll have to settle for Chris Teller."

"And who is Chris Teller?"

"A student of mine who went on to become a MacArthur Fellow. Brilliant man. He's been doing research on the medical side of DNA, but he needed to put food on the table, so he opened a small lab in Bainbridge, Georgia, last year. It's a three-man operation and they intend to keep it that way. The lab is listed as a medical research lab, not a forensic testing center."

"It sounds good."

"Of course it's good. It's perfect. You'd think I'd been dabbling in conspiracies all my life. Chris takes DNA profile jobs only when he needs to pay the bills, but he's absolutely accurate. We can't risk bungling. I'm not sure I can get another sample."

She nodded slowly. "Bainbridge, okay. I'll take it down myself and—"

Gary was shaking his head. "I'll do it. You said you need speed. I'll appeal to him as a fellow scientist."

"Look, I'll take Joe. Surely Teller will cooperate with the police."

"Not if he's deep in research and doesn't want to stop. He'll just tell Quinn to go somewhere else. We'll get better cooperation if I handle it."

"Your job is done," Eve said. "It's time for you to go somewhere and loll on the beach for a while. I can't ask you to do anything more, Gary."

"I didn't hear you ask," Gary said. "And I'll decide when my job is done. Are you trying to cheat me out of my book contract?"

"I'm trying to keep you alive."

Gary took the thermal case from her and headed for the door. "I have to stop by my house and pick up clothes and an overnight bag."

"Gary, this is crazy. Let me—"

"You want to be helpful? Go get me samples for Teller to compare this one to." He opened the door. "If you want to follow me down to Bainbridge, come ahead. But I'm in charge of this sample, Eve."

"Gary, listen to—" He'd already left the laboratory, and Eve hurriedly followed him down the hall and out the front door.

"What's going on?" Joe came toward her. "Where's he going?"

"A DNA lab in Bainbridge. He's got the sample. I told him I'd take it, but he wanted to go himself."

"Stubborn bastard." Joe started down the steps. "I'll handle it, Eve."

"No." Logan had come out of the building. "Eve and I will follow Kessler to Bainbridge. You go see Chadbourne's sister, Millicent Babcock."

"I suppose you want a DNA sample from her?"

"Yes, but even if that's a match, it will be only an indication, not proof accepted in a courtroom. We also need direct DNA from Ben Chadbourne. He and his sister were very close. He stayed with her several times during the campaign and he must have sent her birthday cards or notes that still have saliva traces on the envelopes. Or if he left any clothes at her house, there might still be hair or—"

"And how am I supposed to get those little mementoes?"

"That's up to you."

"And where's Chadbourne's sister?"

"Richmond, Virginia."

"And, of course, you're not trying to get me out of the picture?"

"Not this time. We need those comparison samples. The sooner we get them, the sooner this will be over."

Joe hesitated and then said, "Okay. Chadbourne's DNA and a sample from his sister. What do you need from her? Blood?"

"Saliva will do for now," Eve said. "But the sample should be refrigerated and expressed immediately."

"I'll bring it myself." He looked at Logan. "I don't suppose you know if she smokes?"

Logan shook his head. "Sorry."

Joe shrugged. "Saliva's no problem. If she doesn't smoke, she probably drinks coffee. It's the national addiction these days. It's Chadbourne's DNA that's going to be a headache. Letters will be the most likely source but how the hell am I going to get . . ." He started down the steps. "I'll find a way to do it. I'll be on your heels before you know it. You just take care of Eve until I get down there, Logan."

"Will you do me a favor and follow Gary to his house and stay with him until we get there?" Eve asked. "I have to pack up Ben's skull and my papers, and I don't want him to be alone." Eve's gaze was on Gary, who was now getting into his car. "Take care of him, Joe."

"And try to persuade him to stop at a lawyer's office and get an affidavit," Logan added.

Eve turned to face him.

He shrugged. "Sorry to be callous, but it's smart to have back-up evidence in case anything happens."

He meant in case Gary was killed, Eve thought, suddenly feeling sick.

"I'll get the affidavit and the damned DNA samples." Joe was hurrying after Gary. "You just get Eve away from here and out of sight, Logan."

"It's done." Logan took her elbow and nudged her back inside the building. "That's one order of Quinn's I won't have a problem obeying."

In the lab he packed up the skull while Eve gathered the photographs and printouts and stuffed them in her briefcase. "There's no air service to Bainbridge. We'll have to drive."

"It's safer than taking a plane anyway. Particularly out of your home city." He started for the door. "Ready?"

It would have been too bad if she wasn't ready, she thought ruefully. Logan was on the move and she either had to follow him or be left behind.

And she wasn't about to be left behind.

"Why don't you try to get some sleep?" Logan said. "You worked all last night. I promise I won't land us in a ditch."

"I don't want to sleep. We've been driving a long time. It's almost dark. Aren't we almost there?"

"Another hour or so."

An hour was too long when Eve was this restless. "Have you heard from Gil?"

"Last night. No progress yet. It may take time to approach Maren on a confidential basis. I'm sure he's very busy overseeing the work on my corpse."

"That's not funny."

"I didn't think so either, but it's better if you laugh."

"Is it?"

"I've always thought so. It keeps you sane."

"Then I'll vote for that." She gazed at the taillights of Gary's car on the road ahead of them. "Are you speaking from experience? How close have you come to the edge, Logan?"

"Close enough."

"No." She turned to face him. "Don't give me that evasive bull. It's not fair. Tell me. You know everything about me."

"I doubt it. You're a multifaceted woman. It wouldn't surprise me if you had a few secrets."

"Tell me."

"What do you want to know?"

"The edge."

"Ah, you want to see my scars."

"You've seen mine."

He was silent a moment. "I was married once when I was pretty young. It was during the time I lived in Japan. She was Eurasian and the most beautiful woman I'd ever seen. Her name was Chen Li."

"You're divorced?"

"She died of leukemia." He smiled crookedly. "It wasn't like your loss. No violence. Except on my part. I wanted to tear the world apart when I couldn't find a way to help her. I was a cocky bastard and sure that there wasn't a mountain I couldn't climb. Well, I couldn't climb that one. It took over a year for her to die, and I had to watch it. Is that a deep enough scar for you?"

She looked away from him into the darkness. "Yes, that's deep enough."

"And do you know me better now?"

She didn't answer. "Did you love her?"

"Oh, yes. I loved her." He glanced at her. "You know, you

really shouldn't have asked. You have a soft heart and it would have been easier for you to dislike me if you hadn't seen I'm human, like everyone else."

It was true. Understanding always made antagonism more difficult. His very restraint underscored the pain he'd undergone. "I've never doubted you were human."

"Maybe. Maybe not." He changed the subject. "Teller's lab may not be open when we reach Bainbridge. We'll probably have to check into a motel and wait until tomorrow morning."

"Can't we call him or something? Maybe Gary could—"

"Kessler's going to arouse enough suspicion by the pressure he's going to apply on Teller. It would be a little over the top to ask him to stay open until we got there."

No doubt he was right but, dear God, she wanted to move more quickly. "You don't understand. It sometimes takes weeks to get a definitive report on a DNA sample. Gary's going to ask Teller to do it in a few days. Private labs have the capability to be faster because they're not as backlogged, but every minute is going to count."

"Will some of my filthy lucre help urge him to do a little overtime?"

She shook her head. "I don't think so. He sounds like a dedicated professional."

"He still has to pay the mortgage. Kessler seemed to think Teller might need money."

True. Maybe she was wrong. Money could move the world. She herself had been tempted by the bait he had dangled before her. "Let Gary try his way first."

"No offense. Just trying to help."

"I know you were. Why should I take offense? There's nothing wrong with money."

He stared at her in surprise.

"I just don't like it used as a club."

"But bribery is okay?"

"In certain cases."

He smiled. "Like the Adam Fund?"

"Hell, yes."

"Even when I used it to deceive you?"

"No, that wasn't right." She looked into his eyes. "But I let you do it. I'm not stupid. I knew there was something wrong, but I still took the chance. I wasn't like you—I wasn't afraid someone was going to make a mistake and blow us all up. I wanted the money. I thought it would help and I was willing to run the risk. If I hadn't gone with you, none of this would have happened. I wouldn't be in trouble and Mom would be safe." She shrugged. "I'd like to keep blaming you, but we all have to accept responsibility for our own actions."

"That wasn't the impression I got," he said dryly. "You wanted to cut my throat."

"There are moments when I still do. You were wrong. But I was wrong too, and I have to live with it." She gazed out the window. "I just don't want anyone else hurt because I was wrong."

"You're being very generous."

"I'm not generous," she said wearily. "But I try to see things clearly. I learned a long time ago that it's easy to blame everyone else when it hurts to blame yourself. But in the end you have to face it."

He went still. "Bonnie?"

"We were at a school picnic at a neighborhood park. She wanted to go to the ice cream stand and get a cone. I was talking to her teacher and I let her go alone. There were kids and parents all around and the stand was only a short distance from the picnic table. I thought it was safe. It wasn't safe."

"For God's sake, how could that be your fault?" he asked roughly.

"I should have gone with her. Fraser killed her but I didn't care for her well enough."

"And have you been wearing that hair shirt all these years?"

"It's hard not to second-guess yourself when you make a mistake as big as that."

He didn't speak for a moment. "Why did you tell me?"

Why had she told him? She usually avoided talking about that day; the memory was still a hideous raw wound. "I don't know. I made you tell me about your wife. I . . . think it hurt you. I suppose I thought it was only fair to even the ground."

"And you have an obsession about being fair."

"I have to try. Sometimes it doesn't work. Sometimes I find myself closing my eyes and hiding away in the dark."

"Like you did with Quinn?"

"I didn't hide—" She was lying. Admit it, she had tried not to see everything about Joe's life clearly. The image she had of him was too important to her. "Maybe I did. But not usually. Not if I can help it."

"I believe you."

She was silent a moment. "What about Millicent Babcock? Will she be in danger if they find out Joe got a sample from her?"

"Harming her wouldn't be much use to them. Chadbourne has an aunt and three first cousins living. It would be pretty obvious if they're all taken down. Besides, it's Ben Chadbourne's DNA that's the conclusive proof. She's probably safe."

Probably.

Probably her mother was safe. Probably Gary would not be hurt. Probably Millicent Babcock would not be killed.

Probably wasn't good enough.

She leaned her head back on the seat and closed her eyes.

Let it be good enough. No more deaths. Please, no more deaths.

WASHINGTON
11:05 P.M.

"Mr. Fiske?" Lisa Chadbourne leaned closer to the car window and smiled. "May I get in? It's a little public out here."

Fiske glanced around the street and then shrugged. "It looks pretty deserted to me."

"That's why I chose it. All the federal offices close at five in this neighborhood." She got in the passenger seat and shut the door. "But I'm sure you'll understand that I can't take any chances. I'm fairly recognizable these days."

True. The velvet-trimmed hood of her brown cape was pulled forward to shadow her features, but the minute she pushed it back, Fiske instantly recognized her. "It really is you. I wasn't sure. . . ."

"You were sure enough to hop a plane and come to Washington to meet me."

"I was curious, and you said you'd make me an offer that would intrigue me. I'm always interested in advancing myself."

"And you were flattered that I would go over Timwick's head and speak to you directly?"

"No." The conceited bitch thought he should fall all over himself just because she was the President's wife. "You don't mean anything more to me than anyone else. I don't need you, you need me. Or you wouldn't be here."

She smiled. "You're right. You have a unique talent and an efficiency I appreciate. I told Timwick the way you handled the problem at Barrett House was admirable." She paused. "But, unfortunately, Timwick is not as efficient and he's become nervous and irrational. He's begun to disappoint me. You do realize that he's merely been channeling orders from me?"

"Not the President?"

"Definitely not the President. He's not involved."

He was disappointed. It would have been a feather in his cap to have done this job for the most important man in the free world. "Then I should be charging more money, shouldn't I?"

"Should you?"

"If he doesn't know about what you're doing, then he's a potential threat. If he was involved, he could protect me. You can't do shit."

"Do you want to be protected, Fiske? I don't think so. I've read your dossier and I don't believe that's one of your priorities. You're not a man who relies on anyone but himself."

His gaze narrowed on her face with sudden interest. Smart. "Money is protection."

"Your fees are exorbitant. You probably have enough in a bank in Switzerland to live like a king."

"I'm worth my fee."

"Of course you are. I'm just pointing out that you could have retired in safety a long time ago. So why are you risking your neck doing this?"

"There's never too much money."

She shook her head. "You like it. You like the risk. You like the game. It gives you immense satisfaction, and the harder the game, the greater the risk, the better you like it. You love the idea of doing something no one else can do." She paused. "The most difficult thing on earth is getting away with murder, isn't it? That's the supreme challenge, the most interesting game."

Christ. Maybe too smart. "Perhaps."

"Don't be so wary. We all have our own agendas. I find your philosophy perfectly reasonable, and it happens to coincide perfectly with my needs. That's why I chose you."

"*You* chose me? Timwick chose me."

"Timwick gave me a number of dossiers and he thinks we chose you together. I chose you, Fiske. I knew you were the one I needed." She smiled. "And I knew you were the man who needed me."

"I don't need anyone."

"Of course you do. I'm the one who can increase the difficulty of the game. I can give you a challenge that you've never been faced with before. Don't you find that idea exciting?"

He didn't answer.

She chuckled. "You do. I knew you would. You're probably sick of working under Timwick. You like bold strokes—decisive, clean thinking. You won't have any problem with waffling from me."

He'd bet he wouldn't. "You're cutting Timwick out of the picture?"

"I'm saying that you go back to Atlanta and check on Kessler. You pay lip service to Timwick, but you obey my orders and answer directly to me."

"It would help me decide if I knew what all this is about."

She studied him. "No, it wouldn't. You don't care. You think all of our complicated machinations are stupid. You're just trying for a power hold. You appreciate power. It's part of the game."

His lips twisted. "You think you know me that well?"

She shook her head. "But I know you well enough to survive you."

"Do you?" He put his hands around her throat. "Did you ever realize how difficult it would be to kill the first lady and get away with it? Think what a kick it would be for me to show those bastards how stupid they are."

"I thought about it." She stared directly into his eyes. "But then you'd be on the run and the game would be over. What a disappointment. I can stretch out the game for a long time."

His hands tightened until he knew there would be bruising. Hurt her, make her back down.

She didn't flinch. "I have a list for you." Her voice was hoarse. "Or, rather, an addendum to the list you were given before."

His grasp didn't loosen.

"I knew you'd like lists. I told Timwick so. That's why he gave you—" She drew a deep breath as his hands fell away from her. "Thank you." She rubbed her throat. "Timwick told you to check out Kessler?"

"Yes, but he didn't seem to think it was important. He's more concerned with Sandra Duncan."

"She's also important. I may have to make a decision about her shortly, but I don't want Kessler overlooked. Unless you reach him immediately, Kessler will be making DNA tests, probably not at the university. Find him. Don't let him have time to get the results."

"DNA?"

"On the skull. You know about the skull."

He smiled. "No, you tell me about it. What's so important about that skull?"

"You know all you're going to know. Except that I want the skull and you're going to get it for me."

"Am I?"

"I hope you are. I'm not Timwick, I'll never take you for granted."

He tilted his head. "Now, I wonder who you killed? A lover? A blackmailer?"

"I need that skull."

"You're an amateur, or you wouldn't be in all this hot water. You should have let an expert handle it."

"I realize my mistake. That's why I'm having an expert handle the matter now." She reached into her pocket and pulled out a folded piece of paper. "Here. My private digital phone number is on the back. Unless it's an emergency, please try not to call me before seven in the evening."

He looked down at the folded paper in his hand. "You're taking a chance. Your fingerprints must be all over—" Gloves. She was wearing leather gloves. "Then I assume it's also not handwritten?"

"Computer, and you won't find any prints on that sheet but your own. My phone is under another name and the paperwork is buried so deep that it would take years to unearth it." She reached for the door handle. "I'm very efficient too, Fiske. That's why you and I will work so well together."

"I'm not saying I'm agreeing."

"Think about it." She got out of the car. "Read the list and think about it."

"Wait."

"I have to get back. You can understand how difficult it is for me to get away unnoticed."

"But you did it. How?" he asked, curious.

"I explored those possibilities the first week I moved in. I wasn't about to become a prisoner. It's not too difficult."

"And you're not going to tell me." He thought about it. "There was a rumor about a subterranean tunnel linking the White House to the Treasury Department. Supposedly Kennedy used it when he wanted to meet Marilyn Monroe. Is that how—"

"Would I tell you? You'd regard getting into the White House as a plum in your list of accomplishments. The difficulty factor might just make killing me too tempting to resist, and I want you focused elsewhere."

Shake the bitch. He suddenly leaned forward. "There are at least thirty-five secret agents and over a hundred uniformed guards at the White House at any given time. It's good to know there are ways to avoid them."

Her face was without expression. "You have the numbers down pat."

"As you say, it's a challenging scenario. The possibilities have always intrigued me."

"But you have to remember that I have Timwick schedule those Secret Service men at times and places that make it easy for me to avoid them. Timwick's not going to help you."

"Not even if I tell him that you asked me to meet you tonight?"

"You won't do that. It would be against your interests."

He was silent a moment. "You don't fool me. You were scared like all the rest. I could feel your heart jump under my thumbs. You're scared now."

"I am. Some things are worth being scared about. Call me." She walked away from him and down the street.

Tough woman. Tough and smart and gutsy. A hell of a lot more guts than Timwick.

But maybe she was too smart. She had come very close in her assessment of him, and it made him uneasy. He didn't like the idea of anyone predicting how he would react in any given situation. He wasn't sure he liked the idea of working with a woman.

"Read the list."

She had guessed how a man of his temperament would appreciate a list. But why had she thought reading her list would make him favor her?

He unfolded the paper and bent closer to the lights of the dashboard.

He started to laugh.

• • •

The phone rang as Lisa was walking into her bedroom.

"Okay," Fiske said. He hung up the phone.

A man of quick decision and few words, she thought dryly as she returned her phone to her handbag. Not to mention a certain lethal impulsiveness for which she had not been prepared. She would have to hide the bruises from Kevin tonight and wear a scarf tomorrow.

"Lisa?" Kevin called from the bedroom. "Where have you been?"

"Just for a walk in the garden. I needed some air." She hung her cape in the closet and grabbed a bathrobe with a cowl neck. "Now I need a hot shower. I'll be in soon, Kevin."

"Hurry. I want to talk."

Talk. God, she wished it was only sex. Listening to Kevin ramble and inserting the appropriate praise and encouragement was a strain she didn't need. For a moment, when Fiske had put his hands on her throat, she had thought she was going to die. Handling Fiske was going to be very difficult.

But she could do it. She had to do it. Don't think about how frightened she'd been. She had done good work tonight. Fiske was hers.

She stepped beneath the hot spray of the shower and let the water run over her. God, she felt dirty. Just being in the same car with that filthy murderer had made her feel contaminated.

But she was a murderer too.

Not like him. She would *not* see herself in the same light as that beast.

Don't think about him. She closed her eyes and commanded her muscles to relax. This was her moment. Enjoy it. She had very little time to herself. She almost wished she were free like Eve Duncan.

What are you doing now, Eve Duncan? Is it as hard for you as it is for me? She leaned her head against the wall of the shower and whispered, "Where are you, Eve?"

Fiske would find her. Fiske would kill her and Lisa would be safe. Why was there no comfort in that thought?

"Lisa?" Kevin was outside the bathroom door.

Dammit, couldn't they let her have one moment alone? "Coming." She stepped out of the shower and dried her tears. Christ, what was wrong with her? Fiske must have shaken her more than she could have believed. She slipped on her robe, zipping it up to the chin, then ran a brush through her hair.

Smile. Be warm and sympathetic. Don't let him see, don't let any of them see. She swung open the door and kissed Kevin on the cheek. "Now, what's so important that you couldn't wait to tell me?"

"This isn't a very nice motel. I think there are bugs," Bonnie said.

Eve turned over in bed. "We had to find a place that was unobtrusive. Bugs shouldn't make any difference to you. You're ectoplasm, remember?"

Bonnie smiled. "Anything that makes a difference to you makes a difference to me. You always hated bugs." She settled herself in the chair next to the bed. "I remember how you yelled at the exterminator when he didn't do a good job getting rid of the roaches in my room."

That had been the summer before Bonnie had disappeared.

Bonnie's smile faded. "Oh, dear, I didn't mean to remind you of anything sad."

"Did it ever occur to you that your coming to me automatically reminds me of something sad?"

"Yes, but I'm hoping someday you'll realize that I'm always with you."

"You're not with me."

"Why are you trying to hurt yourself? Just accept me, Mama." She changed the subject. "You did a good job on Ben but, then, I knew you would."

"So now you knew who it was all the time?"

"No, I keep telling you that I don't know everything. Just sometimes I get a feeling."

"Like about the bugs in this crummy motel room? That's pretty safe."

Bonnie giggled. "It is, isn't it?"

Eve found herself smiling. "It was my first thought when I came into the room."

"And you think I'm using that?" Bonnie clucked reprovingly. "How suspicious you are, Mama."

"Then tell me something I don't know. Tell me where you are."

Bonnie tucked one leg beneath her. "I like Mr. Logan. I wasn't sure at first, but I think he's a good man."

"Whoever said ghosts have good judgment."

Bonnie smiled slyly. "Progress. That's the first time you admitted I might not be your imagination."

"The judgment of figments of imagination are questionable too."

"Well, your judgment is pretty shaky too. You shouldn't be so hard on Joe."

"I'm not condemning Joe."

"Yes, you are. Because of me. But he's a good man too, and he cares about you. Don't push him away."

"I'm very tired, Bonnie."

"And you want me to go away."

Never. Never go away. "I want you to stop preaching at me."

"Okay, I just don't want you to be left alone." Her smile faded. "It's dangerous for you to be alone now. I'm afraid of all the bad things that are coming."

"What bad things?"

Bonnie shook her head.

"I can handle them."

"You think you can handle anything because of what you went through with me. Maybe you can. But maybe you can't."

"And maybe I don't want to handle them," she said wearily. "Maybe I just want to let things happen. God, I'm so tired of it all."

"And I'm tired of you mourning me."

"Then go away and forget me."

"That's not an option, Mama. The remembering goes on forever, just like the love does. I just want you to be happy again."

"I'm . . . content."

Bonnie sighed. "Go to sleep. I guess there's no talking to you until you're ready."

Eve closed her eyes. "Where are you, baby?" she whispered. "I want to bring you home."

"I am home, Mama. Whenever I'm with you, I'm home."

"No, I need you to—"

"Hush, go to sleep. That's what you need right now."

"Don't tell me what I need. What I need is to find out where you are so that I can bring you home. Maybe then I wouldn't have these crazy dreams about you."

"They're not crazy and you're not crazy. You're just stubborn."

"And you're not?"

"Sure, I'm your daughter. I'm entitled. Go on to sleep, and I'll just stay here and keep you company for a while."

"So I won't be alone?"

"Yes, so you won't be alone."

SEVENTEEN

NAVAL MEDICAL CENTER
BETHESDA, MARYLAND
7:45 A.M.

"I *am* hurrying, Lisa." Scott Maren's hand tightened on the phone. "For God's sake, I have to be careful. You've got media crawling all over this place. I've switched the teeth X rays, but it's not going to be as easy to switch the DNA samples."

"But you can do it?" Lisa asked. "You've got to do it, Scott."

"I'll do it," he said wearily. "I told you I'd take care of you."

"Do you think I'm worried only about myself? It's you. I feel so guilty that I let you help me. No one must know."

"It's not your fault. I bought into it." He had bought into it over twenty years ago, when Lisa had come to his apartment and they'd become lovers. She hadn't been married to Ben then, and their affair had lasted only a year, but the short duration hadn't mattered. He'd loved Lisa since they'd met that first year at Stanford. In spite of the nightmare she'd brought into his life, he loved her still. The pattern was set and couldn't be broken. "It will be all right."

"I know it will. You've never failed me."

"And I never will."

"Let me know when it's finished." She paused. "I'm very grateful, Scott. I don't know how to repay you."

"I didn't ask to be repaid." But Lisa had made sure that he had benefited after Ben's death. Honor, fame, money. But they weren't enough. When she left the White House he would see that she came to him as she should have all those years before. She didn't realize that they were bound closer now than they had ever been before.

"I don't know what I would have done without you, Scott."

Lisa in bed. Lisa laughing at his jokes. Lisa with tears in her eyes as she told him she was going to marry Ben. "I'll let you know when I have news for you."

"Good-bye, Scott." She hung up.

"Dr. Maren?"

He turned around to see a red-haired young man in an orderly's uniform standing in the doorway. "Yes? Am I wanted?"

"Not that I know about." The young man came into the office and closed the door. "My name is Gil Price. I'd like to talk to you."

BAINBRIDGE

8:40 A.M.

Chris Teller's laboratory was located in a small building on the outskirts of Bainbridge. Its clapboard walls were covered with ivy and it looked more like a Yale fraternity house than a science lab. Even the sign on the lab was so small, Eve would have missed the building entirely if she hadn't been closely following Gary.

TELLER LABORATORIES.

"This is the home of state-of-the-art science?" Logan murmured.

"Everything isn't the way it appears on the surface. Gary trusts him, so I do too." She parked beside Gary's Volvo in the parking lot and waited. When Gary got out of his car and came toward her, she asked, "Do you want us to go in with you, Gary?"

"If you want to blow any chance I have," he said dryly. "This may be a small southern town, but they do have television sets and newspapers. Stay here. I may be a while."

She watched him walk briskly into the building. His step was eager, vigorous . . . young. Ivanhoe going into the fray against the Black Knight, she thought apprehensively.

"Easy." Logan gently pried her clenched fingers from the steering wheel. "He's not going to face anything more than rejection in there."

"Right now. We should never have let him come."

"I doubt if we could have stopped him." He leaned back in the seat. "What's the process? You said it might take days even if Kessler can persuade him to accelerate. Why does DNA identification take so long?"

"It's the radioactive probe."

"Probe?"

She raised a brow. "Are you trying to distract me, Logan?"

"Yes, but I really don't know the process." He shrugged. "Except what I learned in the O. J. Simpson trial. And that courtroom hardly provided a definitive, unbiased course on DNA."

"The DNA strand we took from Ben will be dissolved in a solution of enzymes that target specific points on the strand and cut it into fragments. A small amount of DNA is put in a tray with a special gel, then a current of electricity is sent through the gel. The current pulls the fragments along and arranges them by length and weight."

"And where does the probe come in?"

"The technician transfers the fragments to a nylon membrane and the radioactive probe is applied to it. The probe seeks out and marks specific points on the DNA. X-ray film is placed over it for several days to develop. When that's done, the DNA will appear as dark bands on the X-ray film."

"And that's the DNA print?"

She nodded. "That's the DNA profile and there's only a

one-in-a-million chance that anyone else might have the same profile."

"And there's no way of accelerating the probe?"

"There's one method I've been hearing about lately, but it's been slow to catch on in the laboratories. It's called chemiluminescence. The radioactive probe is replaced by a chemically activated probe that interacts with chemical reagents that then release light in the form of photons."

"What are photons?"

"Particles of light. Whichever area of the X-ray film they strike will be exposed, and the result is the same dark bands of DNA you'd see with the radioactive probe method. Most of the big labs have started using chemiluminescence, but I don't know if this small lab has. Gary will tell us. Keep your fingers crossed."

"I hoped—"

"I told you it might not be overnight."

"Several days . . ."

"Stop repeating that," she said sharply. "I know we don't have that much time. Maybe Gary will have good news."

"I hope so." He paused. "You're clenching again."

She deliberately loosened her grip on the steering wheel. "And you're not helping."

"I'm trying," he said quietly. "I'll do anything I can. Do you want me to go into the lab and send Kessler away? I'll do it. Hell, I'm aching to do something, anything. I'm tired of standing aside and letting everyone else take the risks."

Oh, God, another Ivanhoe. She would never have thought it of Logan. But maybe she should have, considering that year of agonized frustration he'd spent with his dying wife. He was not a man who would easily accept or recognize defeat.

"Well?"

He was trying to hide his eagerness, but it was there. Beneath that cool, tough exterior lay a desire to smash something.

Jesus, men were idiots.

"Don't you dare. I've no desire to end up in jail or some loony bin because you're bored and want to loose all your Neanderthal instincts."

She could see he was disappointed, but he shrugged philosophically. "I don't believe Neanderthals were ever bored. Their brains were too undeveloped, their life span too short, and they spent most of their time just keeping alive."

"The comparison is close enough to be apt."

He made a face. "Ouch. Which part?"

He was no Neanderthal. He was smart and charismatic and she was learning that the code guiding his life was as inflexible as the one that guided hers. She looked away from him. "You were telling me the truth, weren't you? It really wasn't politics. You're doing this because you think you're saving the world."

"Hell, no. I'm doing it because I'm afraid not to do it. Because there's a chance that the sky could fall and I don't want to look back and know I stood aside and let it happen." He took her chin in his hand and turned her head to look into her eyes. "I'd feel responsible. Like you, Eve."

"Hair shirt?" she whispered.

"I don't believe in them. You do what you can and then you go on."

His touch was disturbing. His words, the way he thought . . . *He* was disturbing. She turned her head and gazed out the window. "Or you learn to live with your hair shirt."

"That option is unacceptable," he said harshly. "Choosing a career like yours was probably the worst possible thing you could have done. Why didn't someone stop you? Why didn't Quinn keep you on that island until you healed, until the memory dimmed a little?"

She looked at him in wonder. He was so wrong. Why couldn't he understand? "Because he knew it was the only way I'd survive."

"Is this surviving? You're a workaholic, you have no personal life, you're the most driven woman I've ever met. You need—"

"Back off, Logan."

"Why the hell should—" He drew a deep breath. "Okay, I'll drop it. It's none of my business, right?"

"Right."

"Then, dammit, why does it *feel* like my business?"

"You're used to running things."

"Yeah, that's it." He pulled his phone out of his pocket. "My organizational instincts. When I see waste, I dive in and try to get rid of it." He stabbed savagely at the numbers on the keypad. "And, Christ, am I seeing a wasteland in you."

"My life isn't a waste. Far from it. Who are you phoning?"

"Gil."

"Now? Why?"

"It's past time I heard from him." He pressed the send button. "And I need a distraction at the moment. Big-time."

So did she, she thought, relieved. The past few minutes had been too intense and upsetting, and her present life was already in such chaos.

"What's happening?" Logan said into the phone. "Why the hell haven't you contacted me, Gil? Yes, I am surly, dammit."

He listened. "Don't be stupid. It could be a trap. Maren's already killed one man."

Eve stiffened.

"Don't do it." He listened again. "Yes, she's here. No, I won't let you talk to her. Talk to me."

Eve held out a hand.

He muttered a curse and handed her the phone. "He's an idiot."

"I heard that," Gil said. "John's a little testy, isn't he? That's why I wanted to talk to you. I really don't need to be yelled at in my present state."

"What state is that?"

"I'm walking a tight line. Maren is one cool customer."

"You spoke to him about the deal?"

"He denied everything and pretended he didn't know what I was talking about."

"That's a logical reaction. I didn't think it would work."

"But I think it did work. I could see I was hitting the bull's-eye. Maren didn't call the hospital security guards. That's a good sign. I told him to think about it and meet me at a designated place on the Potomac near the C and O canal. Tonight at eleven."

"He won't come. He'll talk to Lisa Chadbourne and they'll set a trap for you."

"Maybe."

"No maybe." Her hand clenched on the telephone. "You and Logan told me she probably persuaded him to kill for her. Do you think he's going to believe she'd betray him?"

"He's a very smart man. It's not easy to fool him. It's hard for me to believe he'd let her talk him into killing Chadbourne in the first place. I think I can make him see that he has to cut his losses and get out before he's history."

"Don't meet him, Gil."

"I have to meet him. If I wrap up Maren, we've got Lisa Chadbourne. I'll let you know how it goes." Gil hung up.

She handed the phone back to Logan. "He's going to do it."

"He's an idiot," Logan said between his teeth.

"You said he was a professional and knew what he was doing."

"I never said his judgment was infallible. The meeting tonight is a mistake."

She thought it was a mistake too. Unless Lisa Chadbourne's hold on Maren had weakened, there was no way he'd betray her. And she would never allow that hold to be broken.

Until she broke it herself.

"She's going to be angry."

"What?"

"Lisa Chadbourne. I think she probably regards Maren as her property. She's going to be angry that we're trying to take him away from her."

"It's hardly reasonable she'd feel possessive of a man she intends to dispose of."

"Who's to say she's always reasonable? She has emotions like everyone else. She's going to be on edge and maybe a little panicky when she finds out we're close to Maren. It will be a surprise. She won't have realized we'd made that connection."

"Gil could be right. Maren might not tell her."

"You don't believe that."

He shook his head.

"Then what are we going to do?"

"You're going to wait here with Kessler. I'm going to fly up to Washington and go with Gil to that meeting."

"You could be recognized."

"Screw it."

"Or caught in the same trap."

"Ditto." He got out of the car and went around to the driver's side. "I'll need the car. I'll drive to Savannah and hop a plane from there. You drive back to the motel with Gary."

She slowly got out, then reached into the backseat and retrieved Ben's case. "What about the test results?"

"You get them. You said it might be days." He slipped behind the wheel. "I'm no help here anyway."

And Ivanhoe had action to be taken and a castle to be won.

She wanted to hit him.

"Phone and let me know what happens." She opened the passenger door of Gary's Volvo. "Providing you're alive to do it."

"I'll be alive." He started the car. "I'll be back tomorrow. You should be safe." He frowned. "Should isn't good enough. I can't take the chance. I'll call Kessler from the airport and get him to pay one of Teller's security guards to go to the motel and keep watch until I get back."

"And what excuse is he going to give Teller?"

"Kessler's been pretty innovative so far. Let him worry about it."

"Timwick's probably still camped out at Duke, and it'll take time for anyone to track us here. This is definitely off the beaten path as far as forensic labs are concerned."

But she was no longer certain that the Duke diversion had worked. Lisa Chadbourne wouldn't focus totally on Logan; she had too much respect for women.

"A security guard parked out front at the motel won't hurt. Be sure and lock your door," Logan said. "And call me if you notice anything suspicious. Anything."

"I'll be careful."

He hesitated. "I have to go, Eve. Gil is my friend and I brought him into this."

She got into the Volvo and put Ben's case on the floor. "So go." She gave him a cool glance. "I don't need you, Logan. I've never needed you. I'll handle this myself."

"Keep Ben's skull with you."

"Have you ever seen me leave him anywhere?" She smiled bitterly. "I know who's important in the scheme of things."

"That's not true. It's just that—"

"Go on." She waved her hand dismissingly. "Go help Gil. Go do what you have to do."

"Why the hell are you— I thought you liked Gil."

"I do and I want him safe." But she didn't want Logan dead, and the more she thought about Lisa Chadbourne, the more frightened she became. "I'm not arguing. I know it wouldn't do any good. Good-bye, Logan."

He still hesitated.

"Good-bye, Logan."

He muttered an oath beneath his breath and backed out of the parking space. In another minute he was gone.

Alone.

It's not good for you to be alone, Mama.

She was accustomed to being alone. When the door was shut and the world closed out, wasn't everybody alone?

Yet it was strange that she was feeling more alone now than ever before.

"Where's Logan?"

She turned and saw Gary had walked up to the car. "Winging his way north. Gil Price needed him," Eve said. "What did you find out?"

"Well, there's some bad news and some good news. The good news is that Chris has converted their method over to chemiluminescence. They could work up a DNA profile for me today."

"And the bad news?"

"He said he won't do it. He's too busy." He held up his hand. "I know. I know. You don't have to say it. He'll do it. I just have to be a little more persistent. It won't be today, but I may be able to get the initial profile tomorrow. I just thought I'd come out and give you a report." He tossed her his keys and started back toward the lab. "Go back to the motel. I'll probably be here until after midnight. I'll take a taxi."

She didn't want to go back to the motel. She wanted to go into the lab and help. She wanted to do something.

Yes, sure, and blow everything Gary was trying to do.

Forget it. Her irrational impulse was only due to the fact that she had nothing to do, sitting there waiting was getting on her nerves. She could almost sympathize with Gary and Logan, who had seized the opportunity to take action, any action, even if it held an element of recklessness.

What was she thinking? Recklessness had nothing to do with her life. She needed steadiness and serenity. Taking chances was not for her.

She mustn't begin to think about Lisa Chadbourne as if she were some kind of superwoman. Logan was probably right about Gary and her being safe for the time being. Accept it. Relax. After the tension and pace of the last days, she should be glad for a boring few days in Bainbridge.

"I've narrowed the possibility of the safe house at Lanier down to four," Timwick said as soon as Fiske picked up the phone. "They were all booked day before yesterday."

"By Wilson?"

"How the hell would I know?" Timwick asked sourly. "Do you think she'd use her real name?"

"She'd have to make a deposit. That means a credit card."

"And who's to say that she doesn't have a phony? Do you think Logan wouldn't have made provisions for that? Got a pen?" He rattled off the four addresses. "Get on it right away."

"As soon as I can."

"What the hell do you mean?"

"You told me to check out Kessler. I'm at Emory now and he left on an unexpected trip yesterday morning."

"Where?"

"I've no idea. I'm on my way to talk to his assistant and see if I can find out."

"The mother is more important. Kessler is just a long shot. Logan will be going to Duke if he wants an expert."

"Now that I'm here, I might as well check it out."

"I told you to drop it. Go to Lanier."

"What do you want me to do if I find her?"

"Just stake her out. I'll let you know."

"I told you I don't like stakeouts. I'll find her, but you assign someone else for the donkey work, Timwick."

The silence at the other end of the phone was frigid. The chicken bastard didn't like being told what to do. Well, he'd better get used to it. Timwick didn't know it, but the game had changed and the queen was controlling the board.

"You realize that you can be replaced, Fiske."

"But it would be difficult at this stage of the game. Why not let me do what I do best?"

Another silence, colder than the last. "Very well, report to me as soon as you've located the women."

"Right." Fiske hung up the phone and moved quickly toward the dorm where Kessler's assistant, Bob Spencer, lived. He'd tell Spencer he was an old friend of Kessler's, maybe take him out to dinner and pump him. Even if he didn't know Kessler's location, Fiske might be able to find out the lab where Kessler generally did his tests. Find out where the tests are being done, Lisa Chadbourne had said.

No problem.

"He *knew*?" Lisa murmured. "My God, he knew, Scott?"

"Not for sure. My take is that Logan made an educated guess."

"And then sent Price to lay the cards on the table. Why?"

Scott didn't answer for a moment. "A deal. He wants you more than he wants me, Lisa."

"What kind of deal?"

"I'm out of the country, out of the picture, somewhere with a new identity, if I furnish evidence against you."

Panic rushed through her and she fought to quell it. She had known Logan was smart and that he might suspect her, but she'd hoped he wouldn't make the connection with Scott. "He's lying. They'd never let you off."

"Perhaps."

Her stomach clenched. "And were you tempted, Scott? Just a little?"

"For God's sake, I'm calling you, aren't I? Does that sound like I want to strike a deal?"

"No, I'm sorry. I'm scared. I never thought they'd guess it was you." Jesus, it was all falling apart.

No, it wasn't. She just had to think, to make adjustments. "We can work our way out of this. We may be lucky that they thought you might make a deal. They could have gone to the media."

"But we've blocked that route for them."

"Did you finish substituting the records?"

"Right after Price left me."

The panic subsided a little. It was going to be all right. She could see her way clear now. "Thank God. Then I'll talk to Kevin right away and start the ball rolling. It's going to be fine, Scott."

"Is it?"

"Of course it is. I promise you."

"You've promised me a lot of things, Lisa," he said wearily.

"And haven't I given you everything I promised? You've lived the sweet life all these years."

"You think I couldn't have done it without you?"

"I didn't say that, Scott."

He was silent a moment. "Sorry."

He sounded odd, and she knew better than to overlook any change in him. The situation was too delicate. "What's wrong?"

"Price said something else. He told me about three people who'd been murdered quite recently and that the murders conveniently erased problems for you. He asked if I wasn't afraid that I'd be killed too."

"And are you afraid, Scott? After all these years, are you afraid I'd hurt you?"

Silence. "No, I guess not."

"That's not good enough. Don't guess, *know*."

He didn't say anything.

She closed her eyes. Christ, not now. Don't let him doubt now. "We'll talk. I'll prove it to you. But now we have to deal with Price as cleanly as possible to save you."

"Not to mention you."

"All right, save both of us. Go ahead and meet Price. I'll have Timwick there before you."

"And?"

"We'll take Price and try to use him as a bargaining tool for the skull. We have to have that skull back."

"You think Logan will deal?"

"We've got to try." She paused. "Trust me, Scott. I won't let Logan take you down. Not after all you've done for me." She hung up.

Her heart was beating too hard. Breathe deeply, steadily. It was only another challenge.

But it was a challenge she shouldn't have had to meet. If Timwick had done his job with Donnelli, no one would ever have suspected Scott and she would not have had to make this decision. Panic was turning to rage. Logan and Duncan were coming too close and she was losing control.

So gain control. She had a way out. She'd call Timwick and tell him the problem.

But first she had to talk to Kevin and guide him on the path he had to take.

. . .

Joe called Eve at eight that evening. "I've managed to get a letter Chadbourne wrote to his sister when their mother died a few months before he took office. I don't think there's any doubt that he licked that particular envelope himself."

"Great. How did you get it?"

"You don't want to know. That would make you an accessory. But I haven't gotten the sample from Millicent Babcock yet, and I thought that would be the easiest. I'm following her and her husband to the country club this evening and see if I can get my hands on a glass." He paused. "How are you?"

"Fine. Gary is going to be able to get the DNA right away."

"Good." Another silence. "Is Logan taking good care of you?"

She avoided answering. He would go ballistic if he knew Logan wasn't here. "I take care of myself, Joe."

"I should be there. I should have told Logan to come here and follow that Babcock woman around. I didn't trust him to get the job done, but I'm spinning my damn wheels."

"You'll get it tonight."

"I'd better or I'll mug the damn woman and get a blood sample instead. You're not laughing. I was joking, dammit."

"Sorry, nothing seems very funny to me right now."

"Me neither. I'll try to be there tomorrow. Take care of yourself."

"Joe." She stopped him before he could hang up. "Have you called Diane?"

"Before I left Atlanta."

"She'll be worried about you. I'm feeling guilty enough about involving you. I don't want to send her off the deep end too."

"I'll call her."

"Now?"

"Now, dammit." He ended the call.

She put the phone back on the table. At least Joe was safe and behaving with his usual protectiveness. Tomorrow he'd be here and she'd once more feel that sense of homecoming that was always present when she was with Joe.

Now she had only to wait for Logan to call and tell her he and Gil were okay.

Call her, Joe thought. You promised Eve you'd call Diane. Now do it.

He dialed his home number and Diane picked up immediately.

"Hi, babe, just thought I'd check in. How are you doing?"

"Where are you, Joe?"

"I told you, out of town on a case. I should be able to wrap it up pretty soon."

"What case?"

"Nothing you'd be interested in."

"Oh, I think I'd be interested." Her tone was hard. "Do you think I'm stupid, Joe? I'm tired of pretending I'm blind. All this stuff on television. It's Eve, isn't it?"

He was silent. He knew she wasn't stupid, but he'd hoped she'd pretend the problem didn't exist, as she usually did with issues that made her uncomfortable.

"Isn't it?"

"Yes."

"It's gone too far, Joe." Her voice was shaking. "How long do you think I can put up with this? We have a good life and you're risking everything we have for her. Is she worth it?"

"You know I can't turn my back on her."

"Oh, I know that. Nobody knows it better. I thought I could take it, but she dominates your goddamned life. Just why the hell did you marry me, Joe?"

"You're upset. We'll talk about this when I come home."

"If you come home. If she doesn't get you killed." Diane slammed down the phone.

Jesus, he'd made a mess of it. Why had he thought the marriage would work? He'd given her everything he could, everything he'd thought she wanted. He'd tried to balance honesty with kindness, but Diane had pride, and no matter how he tried to avoid inflicting pain, it was inevitable. Everything Diane had said was true. She had every right to wonder why he had married her.

He hoped she never found out.

EIGHTEEN

The scent of the damp, mossy riverbank hit Logan as soon as he got out of the car. The smell of earth reminded him of the cornfield in Maryland.

Not a particularly happy memory, Logan thought. A successful diversion, but he still remembered Eve's face when she found out he'd used her as bait.

"Smells good, doesn't it?" Gil breathed deeply as he started to walk toward the river. "Reminds me of home."

The area appeared deserted and, at least, Gil had chosen a meeting place with no trees or cover. "The gulf? You're from Mobile, aren't you?"

"A little town outside Mobile."

"*Deep* South."

"Where else did you think I learned to love Garth Brooks?"

Logan's gaze raked the bank. It should be there . . . God, he wished there were moonlight. "But you tell me country is universal."

"But every universe has to have a home planet." He glanced at Logan. "Relax. It's going to be okay. No one can approach us without us seeing them. If anyone but Maren shows we can take off."

"And if we're cut off from the car?"

"We can always swim."

"I've got a better idea." He breathed a sigh of relief as the moon came out from behind the clouds and he saw the gleam of stainless steel. "I rented a speedboat and arranged to have it brought downriver and staked out over there."

Gil started to laugh. "I knew you would. God, you're anal, John."

"It's better than swimming."

"Do you think I wouldn't have done it myself if I hadn't known you'd provide?"

"How the hell do I know what you'd do? You arranged this damn-fool meeting. Why couldn't you just have him call you?"

"Because he may need more persuading. It's too easy to hang up a telephone."

"And you have a death wish."

"*I* have a death wish? The risk isn't as great for me as for you. I've already taken one bullet this month. I figure that puts the odds on my side. You should have stayed in Georgia and let me handle it."

Logan didn't answer.

"Of course, I realize that you were afraid something might happen to me." Gil gave him a sly glance. "Naturally, you didn't want anything to happen to a man of my brilliance and charisma."

"No?"

"And besides, you don't have that many friends who are willing to put up with your lack of appreciation for the finer things of life. Yes, I should have known you'd hop on a plane for purely selfish reasons."

"Purely selfish."

"Ah, you admit it."

"You bet I do. I couldn't stand another day at Bainbridge. The only thing I could get on the radio was Hank Williams Jr. and that damn song 'Feed Jake.'"

Gil chuckled. "God, really? That's got to be my kind of town."

"I agree. I've got an airline ticket in my pocket for you." His lips tightened grimly. "If you survive tonight."

Gil's smile faded. "This is worth the chance, John. I managed to shake Maren. I could see it."

"Then, where is he?"

"We're early. I think he'll be here."

Only forty minutes early. But there was no sign of movement on the bank of the canal or the river. If there was a trap, he couldn't see it.

Maybe Gil had succeeded in convincing Maren. It was possible. Perhaps in a hour all this would be over and their work on Ben's skull would be of secondary importance.

Lord, he hoped so.

But where the hell was Maren?

The security guard looked up from talking to the clerk at the information desk. "Good night, Dr. Maren," he said, smiling. "Late night."

"Paperwork. It's the bane of my existence. Good night, Paul." He went out the glass doors and headed for his reserved space, where his classic 1957 Corvette was parked. The timing was right. Thirty minutes and he'd be at the canal.

He pulled out of the lot and turned left. With any luck, it would be over before he got there. Timwick didn't really need him to act as bait to catch Price.

So why was he going? Was it truly Price who was to be caught in the trap?

The poison Price had injected was eating into him. Lisa. Death.

Stop it. It wasn't true. Price had given him supposition, not proof. Lisa and he were bound together. She knew it as well as he did.

A red traffic light flashed on the cross street ahead.

Symbolic?

It wouldn't hurt to be cautious. He wouldn't go to the meeting with Price. He'd go to his house and wait for Lisa to call him and tell him what had happened. The tension immediately left him with the decision. He'd turn right at the next intersection and in ten minutes he'd be home and safe.

He braked as he neared the red light.

Nothing.

He pumped frantically.

The Corvette moved toward the intersection.

It was late. Maybe the traffic—

A garbage truck was heading for the intersection. Huge. Fast Oh, God, it was moving too fast to stop.

The truck hit the driver's side of the Corvette like a tank, driving the small car sideways into the streetlight on the corner. It tore through the fiberglass, through flesh and bone and muscle.

Lisa.

The man coming toward them had Maren's tall build and he was alone.

"I told you I got to him," Gil murmured.

A low throbbing to the south.

Logan's heart jumped. "The hell you did."

The air.

Why hadn't he thought about the air? Logan thought, even as the brilliant blue lights of the helicopter speared down at them out of the darkness.

"Run for the boat! Keep low."

Gil was already streaking for the speedboat.

The man they'd thought was Maren was running toward them.

A bullet whistled by Logan's ear.

"Son of a *bitch.*"

Gil was in the boat, untying the line from the stake.

The damn helicopter was almost on top of them, flooding the boat with cold blue light.

Logan jumped in the boat and turned on the throttle.

The water ahead of them was sprayed with bullets from above.

"Stay low." Logan started zigzagging the boat across the water, trying to avoid the cone of light. "If we can make it to that inlet, we're home free. There's a thick tree cover, and there are too many residences for them to keep shooting. We'll ditch the boat and—"

Another spray of bullets, closer.

Too close.

Christ, that beam was like a spotlight. How could they miss?

Unless they wanted to miss.

Unless they were more valuable alive than dead.

The skull. Jesus, they needed the skull.

The speedboat tore into the inlet and was engulfed in shadows from the overhanging trees.

Not safe yet. Not as long as they remained in the boat. He pulled the boat close to the bank and cut the motor. He jumped out and grabbed the lead.

He could hear the helicopter overhead. "Come on, we'll go up to the house and see what kind of transport we can—"

Gil was staring at him, his eyes glittering.

"Gil?"

Why hadn't Logan called?

Eve rolled over in bed and looked at the illuminated face of the alarm clock on the nightstand. It was almost three in the morning. Surely he could have picked up the damn phone and let her know he and Gil were safe.

If they *were* safe. If the trap hadn't been sprung.

Go to sleep. They were hundreds of miles away. She couldn't help by lying there, staring into the darkness.

And wishing she hadn't been so curt to Logan before he'd left.

My God, she was having all these morbid regrets, as if he weren't on his way back to her.

Back to her? Back to Ben and the forensic testing, back to their joint purpose.

Never back to her.

Kessler knocked on her door at seven-thirty the next morning. "There's something you should see." He came into the motel room and switched on the television set. "The President's press secretary just issued a statement. CNN is repeating it now." When a picture of Kevin Detwil appeared on the screen, Kessler murmured, "Look at him. Even knowing it's not Chadbourne, I still can't—"

The shot immediately switched to the group of reporters firing questions at Jim Douglas, Chadbourne's press secretary.

"It wasn't John Logan in the fire?"

"So I've been told. The man who burned to death at Barrett House was Abdul Jamal."

"And you think an assassination conspiracy is a possibility?"

"I wish I could say it wasn't. I assure you the President doesn't like the idea of being a target. But since the fire occurred at the time President Chadbourne was invited to visit Barrett House, Mr. Timwick tells me he has to consider the possibility and increase his security."

"And Logan is suspected of instigating this conspiracy?"

"We sincerely hope not. Even though they're on the opposite ends of the political spectrum, the President has always held him in respect. It's his sincere wish that Logan will come forward and explain all this." He paused. "Until that time, we must consider Logan a threat to both the President and the country. Jamal was a known terrorist and assassin and the Secret Service believes that the President's visit to Barrett House would have been a disastrous mistake."

"We were told the body was almost entirely destroyed. How did you manage to match the DNA to Jamal?"

"Mr. Timwick asked that a check be made."

"Then you already suspected that Jamal was at Barrett House."

"When the President goes anywhere, we have to make sure the situation is secure. You all know how fanatically determined Logan has been to see that the President is not elected to a second term. When Mr. Timwick discovered that Mr. Logan may have had contact with Jamal on his last visit to Japan, he asked Bethesda to run a check on Jamal." He held up his hand. "No more questions. The President wishes me to assure you that under no circumstances will this threat interfere with his attendance at the funeral of his good friend, nor with the execution of his duties as president." Jim Douglas turned and walked out of the room.

There was a final shot of the President in the Rose Garden, which must have been taken at some other time. He was smiling down at Lisa Chadbourne and she was smiling back with just the right amount of support and concern.

"My God." Eve turned off the set and turned to Kessler. "How hard are they looking for Logan?"

"They've pulled out all the stops. He's a prime suspect." Kessler added, "And you too."

She crossed her arms over her chest to keep from trembling. "Now I'm a terrorist as well as a murderer?"

"You've been downgraded. You're just an accessory. Logan is the murderer. They believe he had a falling-out with Jamal about the terms of the assassination and killed him."

"And burned down the house to hide it."

"Correct."

"It's completely preposterous. No one could believe a story like that. Logan is a respectable businessman. Why would he become involved with terrorists?"

"I'm not so sure they won't believe it," Gary said slowly. "The average person sitting before a television set has a tendency to accept what the authorities tell him, and people in general have no liking for big business. Haven't you heard that the only way to get someone to accept a big lie is to tell some little truths along with it? You'll notice that Douglas stressed two points. Logan's political 'fanaticism,' and his visits out of the country. They've started with basic provable facts and layered in DNA science and the average American's fear of foreign terrorists. It's a pretty complete package."

Complete enough to make it impossible for Logan to surface without danger of being shot on sight. "She had it all planned." Eve still found it hard to believe. "That was why, when that body was found in Barrett House, Detwil issued a statement praising Logan and revealing that he'd planned to go there that weekend. We thought she was trying to have Maren switch the DNA to prove the body was Logan's. Instead, she was setting this up."

He nodded. "Identifying that body as Jamal makes your situation a hell of a lot more difficult."

Difficult. It made it a nightmare. "Logan will be a target of every law enforcement body in the country."

Maybe he was already dead. Why hadn't he called her?

No, the media would have picked up on Logan's capture or death. She suddenly remembered the press secretary's last words. "What funeral? What was he talking about?"

"Scott Maren. He was killed in an automobile accident last night. They just announced that the funeral would be two days from now."

The words struck her like a blow. "What?"

"A truck broadsided his Corvette."

"Where? Near where Gil was supposed to meet him?"

"No, only a few blocks from the hospital. They think something was wrong with his brakes."

"Murder."

Gary shook his head. "Not as far as the officials are concerned. They're investigating, but they think it's just an accident. Respected doctor, liked by everyone. No motive."

"It was murder." It was too coincidental. Lisa had gotten rid of Maren because she'd been afraid he'd become a liability. Which meant Maren had told her about Gil approaching him.

"They set a trap for Gil." And Logan had walked into the trap with him.

"It's possible. But we don't know. We have to wait and see. In the meantime, I think it would be a good idea if you stayed away from the testing lab," Kessler said. "Logan would like you to stay here with Teller's security guard."

"No, I'll go with you."

"To protect me?" He made a face. "What can you do sitting in a car in the parking lot? I appreciate the effort, but I can care for myself. Besides, it's only ten minutes from here. I promise I'll phone if I need you."

"I'll go, dammit."

"What about Logan? Have you heard from him?"

"No."

He touched the circles beneath her eyes. "And you're worried. Shouldn't you stay here and wait for him? He's the one who is in danger."

"I can't help him. I don't even know where he is."

"He's a bright young man. He'll come back." He turned to leave. "I have to get to the lab. Chris promised me those results late today, but he works better with a little subtle browbeating."

She tried to smile. "There's nothing subtle about you, Gary."

"Perhaps not, but I'm effective." He paused at the door. "You stay here. You have no car and I won't let you in my Volvo."

"I'd feel better going with you."

"Since I'm in control of the transport, I get my way. I'll see you for dinner. Come to my room at eight. I saw a menu flyer from Bubba Blue's Barbecue." He shook his head. "What a name. Thank God they deliver. I have a vision of sawdust on the floor, a rattlesnake in a glass case, and a moaning country singer. I shudder at the chance we're taking."

The door closed behind him.

She was shuddering too, but for a different reason. She closed her eyes, but she could still see Lisa Chadbourne's face as she looked up at Detwil. The loyal wife protecting her husband in his hour of need.

But it was Logan who was in need. Logan and Gil who were on the run.

Where the hell were they?

"Sweet Jesus," Sandra murmured, her gaze on the television screen. "What's happening to her, Margaret?"

"Nothing. They haven't been caught and they won't be. John's too smart to let that happen. This is just upsetting you." Margaret turned off the set. "Hell, it's upsetting me too."

"Why hasn't she called me?"

"She called you yesterday."

"But she must know I'd see— What should we do?"

"What we're doing. Sit tight until John gets everything straightened out."

"Yeah, sure." She nibbled at her lower lip. "Maybe we should do something."

"Like what?"

"I have a friend in the D.A.'s office."

"No," Margaret said sharply, then she tempered her tone. "He couldn't help and he'd lead anyone interested right to us."

"Maybe not. Ron would be careful."

"Sandra, no."

"I can't just sit here." She looked Margaret in the eye. "I know you think I'm some kind of lightweight, but I've been around the block a couple of times. Give me a chance to do something."

"I don't think you're a lightweight," Margaret said gently. "I think you're smart and kind and under normal conditions you'd be taking care of me. These aren't normal conditions. Just be patient, okay?"

Sandra shook her head.

"Okay, then try to get your mind off it. How about a game of blackjack?"

"Again? You always beat me. You must spend half your time in Las Vegas."

"Well . . ." Margaret grinned. "One of my brothers *is* a dealer."

"I knew it."

"Okay, no blackjack. I'll make the supreme sacrifice and let you cook me another one of those wonderful meals. You do realize I'm going to be a blimp before we get out of here."

"I'm a lousy cook, and you know it. Stop trying to distract me."

"Well, the casserole last night was better than the chili for lunch. Maybe you're getting better."

"And maybe cows can fly." She might as well go along with her, Sandra thought resignedly. Margaret could be relentless, and besides, cooking did keep her occupied. She rose to her feet. "I'll make a pot roast. But you have to make the salad and do the dishes."

"I'm just a drudge," Margaret groaned. "Okay, let's get at it."

Third time lucky.

Fiske watched the two women bustling around the kitchen. The scent of meat and peppers drifted to him and reminded him he hadn't had breakfast that morning. The smell evidently had attracted Pilton too, because he had come in from the porch and was standing in the kitchen, talking to Margaret Wilson.

Fiske backed away from the window into the shrubbery and set off through the woods. He reached his car, which was parked in the driveway of an empty rental cottage. Now that Sandra Duncan had been located, he could call and pacify Timwick. Then he'd contact Lisa Chadbourne and tell her of his progress. Though from what he'd seen on the news that morning, she'd been a little too busy to worry about Sandra Duncan.

Too bad about Scott Maren. The doctor had been on the list Timwick had given him and he felt a little cheated that the job had been given to someone else.

He opened the glove box, took out the list, and drew a line

through Maren's name. He couldn't take credit, but he could keep the list accurate.

He had another name to add to the list. He carefully wrote in the name Joe Quinn. Kessler's assistant had been very helpful last night.

He took out the pictures of Quinn and Kessler that Timwick had faxed him and studied them. Kessler was old and would probably pose no challenge, but Quinn was young, fit, and a cop. He might prove interesting.

He glanced down at the road atlas open on the passenger seat. Kessler's assistant had known nothing about Kessler's recent activities but he knew his pattern, his methods, his friends, his modus operandi.

He knew about the work done by Chris Teller's research center in Bainbridge.

So now Lisa Chadbourne had a choice of targets.

"How did I do?" Kevin asked. "Was the statement right? Do you think I should have told Douglas to be a little more stern?"

"You were great," Lisa said patiently. "The statement to the media was just right. You made yourself seem regretful and Logan appear dangerous enough for us to have a reason to go after him."

"Self-defense." He nodded. "It should work."

"It will work." She handed him the paper she'd just printed out. "You need to memorize this. I want you to sound completely extemporaneous."

"What is it?"

"The eulogy you're giving for Scott Maren."

He glanced over the text. "Touching."

"A little tearing wouldn't be remiss. He was one of Ben's best friends."

"And yours." Kevin was staring down at the speech and his next words came haltingly, "Wasn't he?"

She tensed. She didn't like his tone. She'd become accustomed to taking Kevin's willful blindness for granted. "Yes, he was my good friend. He did a great deal for me . . . and for you."

"Yes." He didn't look up from the speech. "It's strange. The accident, I mean."

"He always insisted on driving that little Corvette. Everyone told him that he should switch to a bigger car."

"No, I mean right now."

"What are you trying to say, Kevin?" She took the speech away from him. "Look at me."

He flushed. "I'm confused. Everything's happening too fast. First, this business with Logan and now Scott dying."

"Do you think I had anything to do with Scott's death?" She let tears fill her eyes. "How could you? He was our friend. He was helping us."

"I didn't say that," he said quickly.

"You might just as well have said it."

"No, I didn't mean—" He gazed at her helplessly. "Don't cry. You never cry."

"You've never accused me of— Do you think I'm some kind of monster? You know why Ben died. Do you think I'd ever do that again?"

"With Logan."

"To save you. Logan should never have interfered with what you're doing."

He reached out and awkwardly touched her shoulder. "Forget it. I didn't mean—"

"I can't forget it." She stepped back and thrust the speech at him. "Go on to your office and learn that eulogy. And, while you're at it, decide whether I could have written those words about Scott if I'd ever meant harm to him."

"I know you didn't— I just wondered why it happened."

She turned her back on him and walked over to the window.

She could feel his gaze on her and then heard the sound of the door closing behind him.

Thank God. She didn't think she could have held on another minute. The entire night and morning had been a nightmare.

Damn him. Damn him. Damn him.

Tears were still running down her cheeks as she reached for her phone and dialed Timwick.

"Why?" she asked hoarsely. "Damn you, why?"

"Maren was a threat. He's always been a threat. I told you he needed to be eliminated when Logan started probing."

"And I told you not to do it. Scott was never a threat. He helped us."

"He was a loose thread, Lisa. And Logan was too close to unraveling him. You were too soft to do it, so I did it myself."

She closed her eyes. "He would never have betrayed me."

"You're not the only one in this." She could hear the panic in his voice. "I couldn't take the chance." He changed the subject. "The press conference went well. It gives us the firepower we need. We found the speedboat. But we haven't gotten a lead on Price and Logan yet. I'll keep you informed." He hung up.

He had dismissed the killing of Scott as if it were unimportant.

Just another death . . .

How many more? she wondered. How much more blood . . .

She sank down in her desk chair and covered her eyes.

Oh, God, Scott, forgive me. I never thought— I can't seem to stop it now. It goes on and on and I have to go with it.

Think. Was there any way out? She had to have the skull. The scenario she had set up gave Timwick the ability to make sure Logan could be killed on sight.

More killing. And after him, Fiske's list would kick in and the deaths would go on.

She couldn't stand it.

A deal?

No, Logan was a stubborn man and would not give up even if sense and practicality told him that he should. Men were always too—

But Eve Duncan knew where the skull was and she had no male ego to stop her from thinking clearly. Duncan was a clever woman who would recognize that all their options were gradually disappearing.

Lisa straightened and wiped her eyes. She turned and switched on the computer.

Eve Duncan.

NINETEEN

The phone rang.

Logan?

Eve snatched her phone from the table where she'd put it in readiness. "Hello."

"Hello, Eve. I hope you don't mind my calling you by your given name. Please do the same. I believe events have established a certain intimacy between us."

Eve straightened in shock.

"You do know who this is?"

"Lisa Chadbourne."

"You recognize my voice. Good."

"How did you get my number?"

"I've had it since the first dossier on you was given to me. It didn't seem prudent to contact you under the circumstances."

"Since you were trying to kill me?"

"Please believe I never meant to harm you until you

interfered. You should never have accepted Logan's offer." She paused. "And you should never have permitted Logan to try to persuade Scott to betray me."

"I don't control Logan. Nobody does."

"You should have tried. You're intelligent and you're strong. All it would have taken was a little effort. Maybe all this could have been—" She stopped to steady her voice. "I didn't mean to get emotional on you. I don't expect you to understand, but it's been a bad day for me."

"I don't understand." The shock had dissipated a little and the sheer outlandishness of the conversation hit Eve abruptly. "And I don't care."

"Of course you don't care." She paused. "But it's necessary that you try to understand. I have to see it through. It's like being on a roller coaster. You can't get off until you reach the end. I've fought too hard, I've given up too much. I can't lose all I've gained."

"Through murder."

Silence. "I want it to end. Let me find a way to end it, Eve."

"Why did you call me?"

"Is Logan there?"

Relief rushed over her. If Lisa didn't know where Logan was, it meant that he and Gil could be safe. "Not right now."

"Good. He'd get in the way. For a brilliant man, he's not at all reasonable. You're not like him. You can see the advantages of compromise." She paused. "As you did when you begged them not to execute Fraser."

Eve's hand tightened on the phone. She hadn't expected her to touch that wound.

"Eve?"

"I'm here."

"You wanted Fraser to die, but you wanted something else more. You were reasonable enough to deal for what you wanted."

"I don't want to talk about Fraser."

"I can see why you don't want to remember him. I mentioned him only because you have to be reasonable now."

"What do you want from me?"

"The skull and any other evidence you and Logan have gathered."

"And what do I get for handing over those things to you?"

"The same deal you offered Scott. You disappear and turn up somewhere with enough money to keep you for the rest of your life."

"And what about Logan?"

"I'm sorry, it's too late for Logan. We had to act publicly to make sure he's no threat to us. You can just fade away, but I can't call off the hunt for Logan. He's on his own."

"And my mother?"

"You can take her with you. Can we deal?"

"No."

"Why? What else do you want?"

"I want my life back. I don't want to spend the next fifty years hiding out for something I didn't do. I don't consider that option viable."

"It's all I can offer. I can't have you here. It's too dangerous for me." For the first time, Eve could hear an edge of steel to Lisa Chadbourne's voice, and something else—panic. "Give me that skull, Eve."

"No."

"I'll find it anyway. It will just be easier if you give it to me."

"Even if you find it you're afraid the truth will come to light in an awkward and public manner. That's the only reason you're offering me a deal."

"God, no." Both the hardness and fear were gone from her voice now. It reflected only weariness and sadness. "You refuse?"

"I've told you that."

"Would it be so bad to let me stay in the White House? Look what I've done through Kevin. The new bill to save Medicare. Tougher laws on animal and child abuse. There's a good chance I can get the National Health Bill passed before the election. Do you know what a miracle that is when we don't control Congress?" Her voice hardened with desperation. "But I've only started.

There's so much more that I've planned for next term. Let me do it, Eve."

"And seize immortality for yourself? I don't regard murder as a permissible method for pushing bills through Congress."

"Please. Reconsider."

"No deal."

Silence. "I'm sorry. I wanted to make it easy for you. No, that's not true. I wanted to make it easier for me. I wanted it to stop." Lisa cleared the thickness from her voice. "You've misjudged your position, Eve. It's not as strong as you think, and there are always two sides of a coin. I hope I'll be able to give you another chance later, but I doubt it. I'll have to move forward. You will remember it was your choice?" She hung up.

Eve had thought she had grasped the woman's personality and motivations, but she hadn't gone deep enough. She wondered if anyone could go deep enough with Lisa Chadbourne. She had been thinking about her as a ruthless monster like Fraser, but the woman she had just spoken to was very human.

But not vulnerable. She might not be a monster, but her determination would never waver.

Eve's hand was shaking as she put down the phone on the table. Christ, she was scared. She had believed she had a slight advantage because she had studied and felt she knew Lisa Chadbourne.

The advantage was gone. Not only did she not know Lisa Chadbourne, but the woman had also been studying her. Lisa Chadbourne also knew Eve.

Two sides of a coin.

Bribery on one side. Death on the other. It couldn't be clearer. She had refused Lisa's offer and now she had to face the consequences.

Why the hell couldn't she stop shaking? It was as if Lisa had been in the room with her and—

A knock on the door.

Her gaze flew across the room.

Don't answer the door, Logan had said.

Two sides of a coin.

For God's sake, Lisa Chadbourne wasn't some supernatural being who had transported herself to this motel. Eve rose to her feet and strode to the door. And assassins didn't knock politely.

The second knock wasn't polite though. It was hard, impatient, and demanding.

"Who is it?"

"Logan."

She gave a quick glance through the peephole. Thank God. She unfastened the chain bolt and unlocked the door.

Logan strode into the room. "Pack your clothes. You're getting out of here."

"Where have you been?"

"On my way here." He opened her closet, took out her bag, blazer, and windbreaker and threw them on the bed. "I took a taxi to Baltimore-Washington airport, rented a car, and drove here."

"Why didn't you call me?"

He didn't answer.

"Dammit, why didn't you call me? Didn't you know I'd be worried?"

"I didn't want to talk to—" He unzipped her bag. "Will you pack? I want you out of here."

"The DNA profile isn't done yet. Gary found out the lab could escalate the process, but Joe hasn't come with the comparison samples and Gary says it won't—"

"I don't give a damn," he said harshly. "You're out of it."

"That's going to be hard to do. Did you hear about Abdul Jamal?"

"On the radio coming down."

She watched him take an armful of underthings out of the bureau drawer and drop them into the bag. His clothes were rumpled and grass-stained and there was a scratch on his forearm. "I'm not going anywhere until you talk to me."

"Then I'll pack for you and dump you in the car with the rest of the luggage."

"Stop mishandling my property and look at me, dammit."

He slowly turned to look at her.

She stiffened when she saw his face. “Jesus,” she whispered. “What happened, Logan?”

“Gil’s dead.” His movement was jerky, uncoordinated, as he flung more clothes from a drawer onto the bed. “Shot. I don’t think they even meant to kill him. They were just firing warning shots. But now he’s dead.” He threw clothes into the duffel. “I left him in a boathouse near the river. I’m sure you won’t approve, considering how you feel. No home for Gil. I just left him and took off running.”

“Gil,” she repeated numbly.

“He was born near Mobile. I think he has a brother. Maybe later we can—”

“Shut up.” She grabbed his arms. “Shut up, Logan.”

“He was joking before it happened. He said he was safe because he’d taken his bullet for the month. He was wrong. He wasn’t safe. He didn’t know what hit him. He just—”

“I’m sorry. God, I’m so sorry.” Without thinking she stepped closer and wrapped her arms around him. His body felt stiff and unrelenting, his muscles locked against her. “I know he was your friend.”

“That’s more than I know. If he was my friend, would I have let him run the risks he did?”

“You tried to persuade him not to meet with Maren. We both tried. He wouldn’t listen.”

“I could have stopped him. But I knew there was a chance he was right about Maren. I could have knocked him on the head or gone by myself. I didn’t have to let him go.”

Dear heaven, he was hurting and she couldn’t reach him. “It wasn’t your fault. It was Gil’s decision. You couldn’t know that—”

“Bullshit.” He pushed her away. “Finish packing. I’m getting you out of here.”

“And where am I supposed to be going?”

“Anywhere away from here. I’ll put you on a boat to Timbuktu.”

“No.” She crossed her arms over her chest. “Not now. You’re too upset to be reasonable. We need to talk about this.”

“Pack. There’s nothing to talk about.”

"We're going to talk. Let's get out of here." She headed for the door. The emotion in the room was so thick, she felt as if she was suffocating. And, it would be better if she could get him away from that damn packing he was obsessing about. "I've been cooped up in here all day. Take me for a drive."

"I'm not going—"

"Yes, you are." She grabbed Ben's case, threw open the door, and glanced over her shoulder. "Which car?"

He was silent.

"Which car, Logan?"

"The beige Taurus."

She moved toward the car parked across the lot. He reached it before she did. She waited for him to unlock the door.

His lips curved in a sardonic smile as he reached for Ben's case. "And everywhere that Eve goes, the skull is sure to follow," he murmured, then put the case in the backseat. "But then I told you to never leave it alone, didn't I? Even though it makes you an automatic target."

"Do you think I'd pay any attention to what you said if I didn't think it was the right thing to do? Not likely, Logan."

As soon as they got into the car, she said, "Drive."

"Where?"

"I don't care." She leaned back in the seat. "As long as it's nowhere you can put me on a boat to Timbuktu."

"I'm not going to change my mind."

"And I'm not going to try to argue with you when you've probably been planning this all the way from Washington. Just drive."

He drove. He didn't speak for the next thirty minutes. "May I go back now?"

"No." His body was still rigid with tension. How the hell could she break through to him? Shock? She could tell him about Lisa Chadbourne's call. Definitely not. That would only reinforce his determination. Give him some more time.

• • •

Lisa stared down at the phone.

Pick it up. Make the call. You've waited too long already.

No deal, Eve Duncan had said.

All right, accept it.

It had to go on.

Do what you have to do.

Lisa picked up the phone.

It was over an hour later and the rays of the sun were casting long shadows when Logan pulled off the highway into a dirt lay-by. "I'm not going any farther. Get it over with."

"Will you listen to me?" Eve asked.

"I'm listening."

And stubbornly determined not to hear. Or maybe not stubborn, she thought wearily. Maybe he was afraid to hear.

It was odd to think of confident and decisive Logan as being afraid. "Remember what you told me? Do the best you can and then go on? You're full of hot air, Logan."

"So I don't practice what I preach."

"You're not responsible for Gil's death. He was a grown man and he made his own decision. You even tried to talk him out of it."

"We've already gone over this."

"And you're not responsible for me. I'd have to yield you that right, and I won't do that. I'm the only one who guides my life. So don't give me that bullshit about putting me on a boat and sending me to Outer Mongolia."

"Timbuktu."

"Wherever. I'm not going anywhere. I've gone through too much. I've too much invested in my life to throw it away. Do you understand?"

He didn't look at her. "I understand."

"Then I guess we can go back to the motel."

He started the car. "But it doesn't make any difference. I warn you, I'll find a way to get you on that boat."

She shook her head. "I get seasick. I remember when we

came back on the ferry from Cumberland Island, I was sick as a dog."

"I'm surprised you noticed."

"I didn't understand it either. I felt as if my life had ended and it didn't seem fair that my body was punishing me too."

"But Quinn took care of you."

"Yes, Joe always takes care of me."

"Have you heard from him?"

"Last night. He's found a letter that's almost certain to contain Chadbourne's saliva, but he's having trouble getting the sample from Millicent Babcock. He was going to follow her and her husband to the country club and try to swipe a drink glass."

"Your stalwart policeman is going to steal?"

Talking was helping him. The muscles on Logan's forearms were a little less rigid.

"That's not like stealing." She decided not to confide the fact that Joe had gotten the letter through dubious means.

"Did you ever read *Les Misérables*?"

"Yes, and I can see Joe stealing bread to feed a hungry child."

He smiled lopsidedly. "Your hero."

"My friend," she corrected him.

His smile disappeared. "Sorry, I don't have the right to criticize Quinn. I've failed pretty miserably in the friend sweepstakes."

"Stop beating yourself up. Your thinking is blurred. When did you last sleep?"

He shrugged.

"You'll feel better after you have a good night's sleep."

"Will I?"

She hesitated and then said bluntly, "Probably not. But you'll be able to think clearer."

He smiled faintly. "Have I ever mentioned how much I like that brutal honesty of yours?"

"It wouldn't do any good to give you a sugar-coated pill. You'd only laugh at me. You've been through pain before. You know there's no quick fix. You just have to ride with it."

"Yes, that's the only way to handle it." He paused. "But I

wouldn't laugh at you, Eve. No way." He took his hand from the wheel and covered her hand that lay on the seat between them. "Thank . . . you."

"For what?" She tried to smile lightly. "Saving myself a trip to Timbuktu?"

"No, that's still on the agenda if I can work it in." He squeezed her hand and then slowly released it. "I believe I envy Quinn."

"Why?"

"Many things." His lips tightened grimly. "But it's much more desirable for a man to be protector and comforter than the other way around. Crying on your shoulder like this displays a certain lack of strength."

"You didn't cry on my shoulder."And no one could ever say Logan lacked strength. "You yelled at me and threw my clothes around."

"Same thing. Sorry, I lost control. It won't happen again."

She hoped it wouldn't happen again. Her response to his pain had startled her. It had been an almost maternal reaction. She had taken him in her arms and had wanted to rock him until the agony disappeared. She had wanted to comfort and heal, to hold and caress. His vulnerability had broken through barriers that his strength would never have breached. "No problem. Just hang my clothes back up and we'll call it even."

She looked out the window. The need was over. Shut him out. He was coming too close.

She could feel his gaze on her, but she didn't look at him. She kept her eyes on the sun setting behind the trees.

He didn't speak again until he pulled into the parking space near her motel room. "I have to talk to Kessler. When do you expect him back from the lab?"

She checked her wristwatch. Seven forty-five. "He might be in his room now. I was supposed to go to his room at eight and we were going to order dinner to be delivered." She made a face. "Bubba Blue's Barbecue. Gary said he could imagine the place probably had a rattlesnake in a glass case, sawdust on the floor, and a country singer yodeling— Oh, shit." Her eyes filled with tears. She had been so busy comforting Logan that Gil's death had not hit home until that moment. Would she ever listen to a country song again without remembering Gil Price?

"Yeah." Logan's eyes were glittering. "I told him he'd love this place. That all they had on the radio was country music like—" He abruptly opened the door and got out of the car. "I have to go to my room and shower and change clothes." He reached in the backseat and pulled out the case. "I'll take custody of Ben for a while. I'll meet you in Kessler's room in twenty minutes."

She nodded numbly as she moved toward her door. Gil Price, humor and gentleness and a zestful love of life. All that gone. Death. Creeping close, striking down Gil. Who was next? Logan could have died with Gil.

The other side of a coin.

She went into the room and shook her head as she saw the clothes scattered on the bed. She'd clean up this mess and try to—

Screw it.

She was scared and worried and chillingly aware of the shadows drawing near. She hadn't talked to Mom since last night and she needed to make contact. She reached for the telephone in her bag.

No answer.

What the hell?

She dialed the number again.

No answer.

The other side of a coin.

Your position isn't as strong as you think.

Mom.

Her hand was trembling as she dialed Logan's room number. "I can't reach Mom. She's not answering her phone."

"Don't panic. It may be—"

"Don't *tell* me not to panic. I can't reach her."

"It may be nothing. Let me call Pilton and check."

"What's the chance of that hap—"

"I'm going to call Pilton," he interrupted. "I'll get back to you." He hung up the phone.

Nothing was wrong.

Fiske hadn't found her.

Nothing was wrong.

The phone rang.

She jumped to answer it.

"She's fine," Logan said. "I talked to her. She and Margaret were just sitting down to dinner. The battery on her phone was down."

Safe. The relief was so intense, she felt almost sick. "She's okay?"

"She's worried about you. She'd like to break my neck. But she's okay."

She couldn't talk for a moment. "You know that boat to Timbuktu, Logan?"

"Yes."

"I want my mother on it."

"We'll work on it right away. Will you go with her?"

Hell, yes. Get me out of here. "No, I'll see you in Kessler's room in fifteen minutes."

"I have a copy of the DNA report," Gary said as soon as he opened the door. "Where's Quinn with those comparison samples?"

"He should be here soon." She looked beyond him to Logan, who was sitting in the chair across the room. "Logan told you about Gil Price?"

Gary nodded. "Not good."

"Very bad. You've done everything you can, Gary. You've got the report for us. For God's sake, will you leave now?"

"When I finish. When I have Quinn's samples."

"That's not good enough. We don't need you anymore. Joe can go to the lab and get—"

"No, Duncan." Gary's voice was gentle but firm. "I finish what I start."

"That's stupid. You'll end up like Gil Price." She whirled on Logan. "Tell him."

"I've tried," Logan said. "He won't listen."

"Like Gil. Gil wouldn't listen either." She drew a deep breath. "But you have to listen. She's going to— Two sides of a coin."

"What?"

"Lisa Chadbourne. She phoned me this afternoon."

Logan sat up straight in his chair. "What the hell?"

"She wanted to make a deal with me for the skull."

"Why didn't you tell me she called?" Logan asked grimly.

"Think about it. Were you in a mood to listen? You wouldn't have been reasonable."

"I don't feel reasonable now either. Did she threaten you?"

"In a way."

"What kind of way?"

"She was . . . sad. What difference does it make?" she asked impatiently. "I just want Gary and my mother out of this. Okay?"

"Did she say anything to lead you to believe that she knows anything about Bainbridge or your mother?"

"Of course she didn't. She's too smart. She'd never give anything away." She turned to Gary. "But you have to—"

"The only thing I have to do is call Bubba Blue's Barbecue," Gary said. "Do you want ribs or steak?"

"I want you to leave."

"Or maybe a pork sandwich?"

"Gary . . ."

He reached for the phone and started dialing. "Give me your order or you'll get the ribs."

She gazed at him helplessly. Dammit. "Steak."

"Good choice."

Joe Quinn arrived at the door thirty minutes after the delivery man from Bubba's brought the food.

"Got it." Joe held up the two black thermal bags. "How fast can you get a comparison?"

She eagerly turned to Gary. "Tonight?"

He shrugged. "Maybe. I'll call Chris and see if I can persuade him to go back to the lab tonight." He wiped the barbecue off his fingers and reached for the telephone. "Get out of here. It's going to take some talking. He worked most of last night for me and he's not going to like this."

Joe opened the door. "When you're ready to go, I'll drive you to the lab, Gary."

Gary waved an acknowledging hand.

"You okay?" Joe asked Eve as they walked out.

"As good as can be expected. Gil Price was killed."

Joe glanced at Logan. "Your friend?"

Logan nodded.

"I heard about the press conference. Everything's going to hell, isn't it?"

"That's pretty accurate."

"What are you planning to do with the DNA evidence once you get it?"

"I have a few friends in Washington who would go to bat as long as the proof is there."

Joe shook his head. "Too chancy."

"Not with Andrew Bennett in my corner. He's chief justice of the Supreme Court."

"Better than a politician but still risky."

"You have a better idea?"

"The media."

"Lisa Chadbourne's an expert at manipulating the media."

"Maybe, but name me a reporter who's not ready to blow up an entire administration if it sells newspapers."

"The story's too bizarre," Eve said. "And they've laid too many obstacles for us to even get near a newspaper."

"I could do it."

Eve shook her head.

"I know a man with the *Atlanta Journal and Constitution.* Peter Brown. Won a Pulitzer five years ago."

"For God's sake, you'd get arrested yourself for harboring criminals, Joe."

"Peter will keep his mouth shut."

"Maybe," Logan said.

"Definitely." He met Logan's eyes. "I've already called him and he's interested. Hell, he's salivating. He's only waiting for the DNA."

"Son of a bitch. Without consulting us?"

"I had to do something while I was spinning my wheels in Richmond. It's better than trusting a politician."

Eve held up her hand. "Why don't we wait until we get the results before we start arguing about what to do?"

"I want this over," Joe said. "I want you out of it."

"No more than I do," she said wearily. "It's getting—"

"He'll do it," Kessler announced as he came out of the room. "He's meeting me at the lab in twenty minutes."

"Let's go." Joe moved toward a black Chevrolet a few yards away. "How long will this take, Gary?"

"Six, eight hours."

"Pack your bag, Eve." Joe slipped into the driver's seat and started the car. "I'll be back as soon as I get the report. We'll go pick up your mother and I'll find a safe place for you until we can wrap this up."

Before she could say anything he was pulling out of the lot.

"Well, we agree on one thing," Logan murmured. "We both want you out of here and somewhere safe."

"The media wasn't a bad idea."

"No, it's solid. We may go that route. But we need Washington too."

"Then why did you argue with him?"

He shrugged. "I'm afraid it's becoming a habit." He turned away. "I'll go pack and make a few calls to my friends in Washington. I can't let Quinn get ahead of me."

Teller's research lab was dark except for lights shining in one area of the lower floor.

Burning the midnight oil, Fiske thought. The center was supposed to close at six; now, why would anyone be there at one in the morning? Two cars in the parking lot. One Chevrolet with a rental tag.

He had a hunch he'd struck pay dirt.

He popped the lid of his trunk and got out of the car. He opened the lid of his electronic equipment case and took out his listening device.

A few minutes later he was back in the driver's seat. He settled himself more comfortably and waited for them to come out of the building.

TWENTY

4:05 A.M.

Eve was waiting at the window when Joe and Gary pulled up into the motel parking lot. "They're here," she tossed over her shoulder to Logan. She threw open the door. "Done?"

"Done." Gary handed her the briefcase. "Millicent Babcock's sample strongly indicated a relationship." A brilliant smile lit his face. "Chadbourne's saliva was a definite match, of course."

"Of course. I know that." Eve smiled shakily. "You'd be scowling and calling me names if it wasn't."

"And rightly so. For wasting my valuable time."

"I've called and arranged a condo in Fort Lauderdale for you." Logan gave him a card. "It's booked under the name Ray Wallins. Stay there until we call you and let you know it's safe."

Kessler smiled slyly. "A luxury condo? With maid service?"

Logan grinned. "Maybe. Don't push your luck."

"A man of my skills and intellect deserves luxury. It shouldn't be wasted on philistines like you, Logan."

Logan handed him an envelope. "Cash. It should keep you content for a few months."

"Ah, that's better." Kessler tucked the envelope in his jacket pocket. "It will do until the first advance on my best-selling book comes in." He looked at Eve. "I may need an assistant, my spelling is atrocious. I might be persuaded to give you a room in my condo if you ask me nicely, Duncan."

"I can't spell either."

"I guess that means no. Oh, well, you'd have tried to hog the credit anyway."

Joe came out of the hotel room carrying Eve's bag. "We're out of here, Eve. If we start now, we can be at Lanier by nine."

She nodded, still looking at Gary. "Thank you. You've been wonderful."

He nodded. "Magnificent."

"You'll leave now?"

"I'll throw my clothes into my suitcase, put the case in my Volvo, and I'm on my way to Fort Lauderdale. Five minutes."

"We'll wait."

"Duncan, it's not—" He shrugged. "What a stubborn woman." He disappeared into his room and came out a few minutes later. He put his suitcase in his car and turned to face her. "Satisfied?"

"Yes." She stepped closer and gave him a hug. "Thank you," she whispered in his ear.

"You're really becoming boring, Duncan." Gary got into his car and turned on the engine.

"Are you ready to go?" Logan asked Eve. "I assume you're going with Quinn, since he's done everything but toss you in the car. I'll follow you to Lanier."

"We're leaving now." Joe got into the driver's seat. "Are you packed?"

"Everything's in my car." Logan crossed the parking lot toward the brown Taurus.

"Eve?" Joe said.

She nodded quickly and opened the passenger door. The first

obstacle, proof, was overcome. She had the DNA reports in the briefcase in her hand. Gary would be safe and so would her mother when they reached her in a few hours.

Thank God.

4:10 A.M.

Fiske took the listening device out of his ear and dialed Lisa Chadbourne.

"They were staying at the Roadway Stop in Bainbridge," Fiske said. "I followed Kessler and Joe Quinn back from the DNA Testing Center. Logan and Duncan are here too. But none of them are staying. Quinn just put Duncan's suitcase in his car. Duncan said good-bye to Kessler. He's not going with them. Kessler's driving out of the parking lot now."

"What about Logan?" Lisa Chadbourne asked.

"He's getting in another car. A brown Taurus."

"Does she have the skull with her?"

"How do I know? She's not going to be carrying a skull under her arm like a purse. I guess she could have stuffed it in her bag. Or maybe Logan has it."

"Or maybe they've hidden it somewhere. I'm not asking for your guesses. You haven't seen it?"

The bitch was beginning to annoy him. "No way."

"Then don't let them out of your sight. I *need* that skull."

"You've told me that. Logan's following Quinn out of the parking lot."

"Then go after them, dammit."

"No problem. I know where they're going. They're heading north to pick up Duncan's mother at Lanier."

"You're sure?"

"I just heard Quinn say it."

A silence. "You're positive you won't lose them."

"I won't lose them."

"Then I have something else for you to do."

. . .

Eve's digital phone rang when they were forty miles outside Bainbridge.

"Duncan. Don't—"

She could barely hear the words.

"What?"

"Dun-can . . ."

Her heart jumped. "Gary?"

Another voice. "He wanted to say good-bye."

"Who is this?" she whispered.

"Fiske. She wants the skull, Eve."

"Where are you?"

"Back at the motel. I ran our good Dr. Kessler off the road and then persuaded him to come back to his room for a little discussion."

"I want to talk to Gary."

"He's not able to talk anymore. She said to tell you it won't be the last. Give her the skull, Eve." He hung up.

"Oh, God."

"What is it?" Joe's gaze was fixed on her face.

Her stomach was clenching. She couldn't breathe. "Turn around. We have to go back to the motel."

"What?"

"Fiske . . . and Gary. I know it was Gary."

"You can't be sure. It might not be him. It could be a trick."

"Dammit, I know it was Gary. He called me Duncan."

"It's a trap, Eve."

"I don't *care*. We have to go back." Dear Jesus, that whisper. "Turn around, Joe."

"The next place I can. I'll put on my emergency lights to signal Logan."

"Hurry." She tried to think. She had the briefcase with the DNA reports, but Logan had the skull. If it was a trap, she had to make sure— "No, stop. I have to give him the briefcase."

They pulled off the highway, and Logan stopped beside them.

Joe got out of the car and shoved the briefcase at him. "We're going back to the motel. Kessler called Eve. It's Fiske."

"Get in the car with me, Quinn," Logan said. "Eve, you wait here."

"Screw you. Let's go, Joe."

Joe started the car.

"I'll follow you," Logan said.

"Don't you dare," Eve said fiercely. "She wants the skull. If I have to bargain with it to save Gary, I'll do it. But I won't have any bargaining power if Fiske takes it away from you."

"Fiske won't—"

Joe was already streaking down the highway toward the motel.

She wants the skull, Eve.

Give her the skull.

Gary.

The door of Kessler's room was cracked open, and light streamed through the narrow opening.

"Stay here." Joe got out of the car.

"I'm going to—"

"Don't argue with me. Hey, this is what I do." He drew his gun from his shoulder holster. "It will be okay." He pressed against the wall to one side of the door and kicked the door open.

No barrage of shots.

No one barreling through the door.

Nothing.

Joe waited a moment and then crouched low and ran into the room.

She couldn't *stand* it. She jumped out of the car and ran toward the door.

Joe was suddenly standing in front of her, barring the way. "No, Eve."

"What do you— *No.*" She pushed him aside and ran into the room.

Gary was lying on the floor in a pool of blood, a knife protruding from his throat.

She fell to her knees beside him. "Gary."

"Come on." Joe tried to lift her to her feet, but she shrugged him off. "We have to get you out of here."

"We can't leave him." She noticed for the first time the two other knives pinning Gary's palms to the floor. "Oh, Joe, look what he did to him."

"It's over, Eve. I have to get you out of here."

Tears were running down her cheeks. "He hurt him. He did it on purpose. He wanted me to know he hurt him. *She* wanted me to know."

"He's not hurting anymore."

She was rocking back and forth as pain seared through her. "It's not fair. He wanted to fight them. He wanted to—"

"Eve, look at me."

She gazed blindly up at Joe's face.

His eyes . . .

He reached down and touched her hair with the most exquisite tenderness. "I'm sorry," he said gently.

His fist lashed out and struck her chin.

Darkness.

"Is she hurt?" Logan was getting out of his car when Joe carried Eve out of the motel.

"No, get the car door for me."

Logan opened the passenger door of Joe's car. "What happened to her? Fiske?"

"Me." He put her in the seat and closed the door. "She wouldn't leave Kessler."

Logan's gaze flew to the open door. "What—"

"Dead."

"Fiske?"

"Not there." Joe went around the car and got into the driver's seat. "Get in your car and get out of here. She told you not to come back."

"But it appears Fiske didn't want to bargain after all."

"He wanted to shake her. It wasn't pretty." He reached into

the glove compartment and took out a paper towel. “Blood.” He began to wipe the stains from Eve’s hands. “Lots of blood.”

“Shit.” Logan’s gaze was fastened on Eve’s pale face. “What did you do to her?”

“I knocked her out.” Joe started the car. “Kneeling there in Kessler’s blood was bad for her. Fiske might as well have been standing over her with another butcher knife.”

“A knife?”

“I told you it wasn’t pretty.”

“She’s not going to be pleased that you manhandled her.”

“I did what I had to do. Do you have a gun?”

“Yes.”

“But you didn’t tell Eve.” Joe smiled sardonically. “You knew how she’d react. You served me up for barbecue but you protected your ass. Well, keep that gun handy and stay close behind me. If you get hijacked, I might stop and help you.” He backed up the car. “If you’re lucky.”

Blood.

Knives.

Pinned.

Oh, God, he’d crucified Gary.

She opened her mouth to scream.

“Wake up.” She was being shaken. “Wake up, Eve.”

Her lids flew open.

Joe. Joe in the driver’s seat next to her. Darkness all around her.

A dream. It had all been a dream.

“A dream . . .”

He shook his head.

“Gary . . .” Tears began to pour down her cheeks. “Dead?”

Joe nodded.

She huddled in the seat, trying to get away from the nightmare. But it came at her. Blood. Gary. Joe’s hand on her hair. Darkness.

“You hit me,” she said dully.

“I had to do it,” he said quietly.

"You thought I couldn't stand it."

"Maybe. But I knew I couldn't stand it."

"She wants the skull. The other side of a coin . . . She didn't even try to bargain. She said she had to move forward. She wanted to show me she had the power to reach out and kill someone close to me."

"That seems to be the picture."

"Gary wasn't even really involved," she said numbly. "He was out of it. Fort Lauderdale— We shouldn't have let him go alone."

"We thought it was safe. We had no idea Fiske knew we were in Bainbridge."

"She wants the skull, Eve."

"Where's Logan?" she asked.

"A few miles behind us."

"He still has the skull?"

Joe nodded.

"Give her the skull."

"She said to tell you it won't be the last."

Fear jolted through her. "My mother."

"We're on our way to her right now."

"She warned me Gary wouldn't be the only one. How far away are we?"

"Another three hours."

"Go faster."

"Easy."

"Don't tell me that. She knows I care about my mother. It's only logical that she'd choose Mom as another target."

"Or that she'd make sure you'd think that and draw you to her. It isn't a fact that they know where your mother is."

"We didn't realize that Fiske found out about Bainbridge." Her nails dug into her palms as her hands clenched into fists. "But he did. He did."

"Yes."

"And he could be on his way to Lanier now. He could be ahead of us."

"But not necessarily to kill your mother. It's more likely that he'd want to get there ahead and set a trap. After all, the skull is the objective."

She took out her phone. "I'm going to warn them."

"Fine. Good idea. But don't panic them into running. They could be safer where they are until we get there. Just tell Pilton to be on the alert."

They could be safer?

Who the hell knew if anything she did would make them safer with Fiske out there?

Her hand was shaking as she dialed the number.

Fiske got back in the car he'd parked in the driveway of the deserted cottage. Daylight was breaking in the east and filtering through the mist-shrouded tops of the pine trees.

He figured he had at least an hour's lead. He had scouted the Duncan cottage and it was clear the Duncan woman had been busy on the phone. Lights were burning and he had watched Pilton go back into the cottage and shut the door after reconnoitering the perimeter. They were waiting for him.

Well, wasn't that what he had wanted? A challenge.

He dialed Lisa Chadbourne. "She warned them."

"But they're still there?"

"I think they're waiting for her. Pilton came out fifteen minutes ago and threw some bags into the van, but no one's come out since."

"Don't let them leave." She paused. "And don't touch them. Not until you get me that skull."

"The mother would be a good goad. Better than Kessler." He paused and then insinuated a goad himself. "Though I handled Kessler exceptionally well. Do you want the details?"

A silence. "I told you the results I needed. I don't need the details."

Squeamish. "I kept Kessler alive long enough for him to call her. It wasn't easy with knives in—"

"I said I don't need to know. Now remember that Eve Duncan can only be pushed so far. Don't foul this up, Fiske."

"You're beginning to sound like Timwick."

Another silence. "Sorry. I'll leave it in your hands. I know you won't fail me." She hung up the phone.

That damn skull again, tying his hands, keeping him from doing his job.

He leaned forward and opened the glove box. He had plenty of time to update his list. With one bold, satisfying stroke, he crossed out Gary Kessler's name.

8:35 A.M.

Eve jumped out of the car as soon as it stopped at her mother's cottage.

"Hold it." Joe was beside her, pushing her to one side. "I go in first."

He had gone in first at the motel and found Gary. "No. Mom!"

No answer.

Then Sandra called out, "It's okay, Eve. Pilton won't let me come out, but everything's fine."

Relief almost made Eve ill. "We're coming in."

Logan had pulled in behind Joe's car. "It's okay?"

"Apparently." Joe was scanning the surrounding woods. "Maybe. Go in and make sure they're ready to go. I'll stay out here."

Logan followed Eve toward the porch.

"Wait." Joe asked, "Where's the skull, Logan?"

"Front passenger seat. Keep an eye on it."

"I'll do that." Joe's gaze never left the woods. "Hurry and get everyone into the cars."

He was out there.

Christ, he could almost smell him, Joe thought.

Smell the blood. Smell the hunger.

His nerves were screaming Fiske's presence. It was as if he'd been catapulted back into his past of targets and sanctioned killings. Fiske would understand that world. He was out there now, primed, ready. To do what?

Throw a stick of dynamite into the cottage?

Launch a sniper attack as they came out on the porch?

If that were true, Joe would be the first target. The sentry was always the first put down.

But Fiske was acting at a disadvantage. His orders would not have been solely assassination.

The skull.

Joe smiled grimly. So let's end it now. Let's make the hunter the hunted.

Are you watching, Fiske?

He took off his jacket, reached into Logan's car, and pulled out the leather case containing the skull.

Bait, Fiske.

He deliberately held up the case above his head.

See it?

He started running, zigzagging through the brush toward the woods.

Come and get it, bastard.

Fiske's eyes opened wide in shock.

The son of a bitch was taunting him. And he was doing it with that leather case, which had to contain the skull.

He watched Quinn run across the rough terrain. He knew what he was doing and he was good. He'd be no easy target.

Pleasure and eagerness suddenly surged through him. The Chadbourne bitch had said to get the skull. First priority. He'd had no idea the priority would offer him such an interesting challenge.

He set off in a diagonal path to intercept Quinn.

. . .

"Margaret, you go in the van with Pilton," Logan said as he came down the steps. "We'll take Sandra with us."

"I'm to go back to Sanibel?" Margaret asked. "When will you contact me?"

"When it's safe," Logan said. "I'm going to let Quinn set up a meeting with that reporter with the—"

"Where's Joe?" Eve had stopped on the top step.

"He's got to be around here." Logan swiftly scanned the area.

Eve's gaze went to the car.

No Joe.

Her heart was beating so hard it hurt. "Fiske."

"I doubt if Fiske could surprise him," Logan said. "Quinn's tough."

"He surprised Gary."

"Quinn's not Gary. He's not a victim. He'd be more likely to—" Logan strode over to his car. "Son of a *bitch*."

"What?"

"The case. Quinn took the case."

"Why?" Oh, Jesus, stupid question. She knew why. Joe wanted it over and, as usual, he'd taken the matter in his own hands. "He thinks Fiske is here."

"And I'd bet on his instincts," Logan said. He turned to Pilton. "You stay here. I'm going after him. If I'm not back in— Where the hell are you going, Eve?"

She was running toward the woods. "I'm not going to let Fiske hurt him. I won't let that happen."

She heard Logan curse. He was following her, running right behind her. "What the hell do you think you're going to do? You're not some kind of commando."

"Joe's out there because of me," she said fiercely. "Do you think I'd let him go alone?"

"And how do you intend—"

She was no longer paying any attention to him. She had

entered the woods and stopped, breathing hard. Don't call him, that would alert Fiske. Then how was she going to find Joe before Fiske found him?

Don't think of that. Walk softly. Look at the shadows.

Logan was beside her. "For God's sake, go back. I'll find him."

"Be quiet. I'm listening. He has to be—"

Logan had a gun in his hand.

He followed her gaze. "You may be damned glad I have it."

She was glad, she realized with shock. If that gun could save Joe, then she would use it herself. Gary had died because he was helpless.

Joe must not die.

The leaves of the bushes moved gently behind him and Joe darted to the left behind a gnarled tree.

"Are you here?" he asked softly. "Come and get me, Fiske."

The bushes stirred like the breath of a whisper.

"You want the skull? It's right here." He slipped deeper into the woods. God, it was all coming back. Hunt, find, kill. The only difference was the light. Most operations took place at night. "Take it from me."

Fiske was close. Joe could smell the faintest odor of garlic and toothpaste.

Where was the scent coming from? Right and a little to the rear. Too little. Too close. Move faster.

Distance.

Silence.

Speed.

The scent was weaker now. He had a little time.

Come on, Fiske. Step into my parlor.

Where the hell was the bastard? Fiske wondered in irritation. It was like following a ghost.

He stopped behind some shrubs, listening, his gaze traveling around the circle of trees.

No sound.

Dammit, Quinn had made no sound since ten minutes before.

"Over here."

Fiske's gaze flew to the left.

The leather skull case, sitting beneath an oak tree fifty feet away.

A trap.

Did Quinn think he was an idiot? The minute he showed himself, Quinn would put a bullet in him.

But where was Quinn? Fiske scanned the area around the case. Quinn's voice had sounded as if it had come from there, but Fiske couldn't be sure.

The faintest movement.

Shrubbery to the left.

Wait. Be sure. Move closer.

If he shot, he'd give away his own position.

The leaves *were* stirring.

He caught a glimpse of pale blue denim.

Then it was gone.

But the bushes were moving.

Quinn was coming nearer.

He moved another step closer. He raised his gun, waiting for the next rustle to the right.

But the next rustle came from the left, far to the left.

He whirled and pointed his gun.

Logan. And the Duncan woman.

His finger tightened on the trigger.

"*No.*" The yell came from above him. He looked up and saw that Quinn had catapulted himself from the branches of a tree.

Fiske swiveled and got off a shot even as Quinn landed on him and dropped him to the ground.

Another shot.

Bastard. Quinn had been waiting up there, lining him up for the kill. Christ, Quinn might have won if not for Logan and Duncan.

But he hadn't won. Fiske had won, as he always did. He could feel Quinn's warm blood on his chest and the body pinning him was limp.

Another name to cross off his list.

But first he had to get the body off him. Logan was running toward them and Fiske had to free the hand holding his gun.

Why couldn't he move?

Pain. Chest.

Not only Quinn's blood, but his own.

The second shot.

He had failed, he had failed, he had failed, he had failed.

Darkness coming. Horror coming.

He screamed.

Fiske was dead when Logan pulled him off Joe's body.

Mother of God.

Eve fell to her knees beside Joe. His chest . . . blood.

"Is he alive?" Logan asked.

She could see the faintest throbbing in his temple. "Yes. Call 911. Quick."

She was barely aware of Logan reaching for his phone and moving away. Her gaze was fixed on Joe's face.

"Don't you dare die. Do you hear me, Joe? I won't have it." She pulled up his T-shirt. Where was the denim shirt he'd been wearing? she wondered vaguely. Pressure. You were supposed to apply pressure.

His lids opened. "Fiske?"

"Dead." She placed her hand on his chest above the wound and pressed hard. "You shouldn't have done it."

"Had—to kill him."

"I don't care that you killed him. You shouldn't have risked— Who asked you to do that? You're all the same. Gary and Logan and you. Think you can save— Don't close your eyes. You're not going anywhere."

He tried to smile. "I . . . hope not."

"How is he?" Logan was kneeling beside her. He handed her a blue shirt, Joe's shirt. "Can you use this? I found it over there in the bushes. Quinn must have tossed it there."

She quickly tore the shirt and used a piece of it as a pressure bandage. "Did you call 911?"

"Yes, they should be here soon. We shouldn't be here when they do. I didn't mention this was a shooting, but the medics will notify the police the minute they see Quinn and Fiske."

"Get out—" Joe stopped. "Can't help, Eve."

"I'm not going to leave you." She glared down at him. "And you don't have the strength to sock me this time."

"Stay . . . background. Let Pilton . . ." He slumped sideways, unconscious.

"God in heaven." She closed her eyes. "He's bad, Logan."

"He's not dead yet." He rose to his feet, turned, and knelt beside Fiske. "I'm going back to the cottage and tell Pilton to talk to the medics. When we hear the sirens I'll have Margaret come out here and stay with Quinn and get you out of sight. That's the best course." Logan was going through Fiske's pockets.

"Why are you doing that?"

"I'm removing identification. The harder we make it for the authorities to identify Fiske, the longer we'll have before Lisa Chadbourne finds out she has to replace him." He pulled out keys dangling from a National rental car key chain, and a wallet. He glanced at the driver's license and credit cards. "Though he's done a pretty good job himself. Roy Smythe . . ." He stuffed the wallet in his back pocket. "After we leave, I'll have Margaret and Pilton find his rental car and clean it out before they hit the road."

She couldn't think about damage control just then. "I'm going with Joe to the hospital."

"No, we'll follow him." He held up a hand to stop her protest. "Don't argue. Unless you stay in the background, you'll be picked up and shoved in jail—if you're not shot on sight." He rose to his feet, adding sarcastically, "Either way, you won't be able to hang over Quinn's bed and offer tea and sympathy."

"He saved your life, you son of a bitch," she said.

"Who asked him to save my life? I'm tired of the great Quinn dispensing—" He snatched up the skull case and strode back toward the cottage.

What was wrong with him? He had no right to be angry with Joe. He spoke as if he—

The wound was bleeding more heavily.

She pressed harder.

Don't you die, Joe.

Joe was taken to the emergency room at Gwinnett General Hospital, twenty miles from the lake. Logan, Sandra, and Eve followed the ambulance in Logan's car.

"I'll go in and check on him." Sandra hopped out of the car. "Park in the lot somewhere out of sight. I'll come out when I have some news."

"I can do—"

"Shut up, Eve," Sandra said firmly. "I've allowed myself to be pushed and prodded and stashed for days. Joe's my friend too, and I'm worried about him. Besides, he wouldn't thank me if I let you go in and be recognized." She strode quickly through the glass doors of the emergency room.

"That seems to be that." Logan drove away and parked between two trucks that obscured any vision of the interior of the Taurus. "I guess we wait."

Eve nodded wearily. "But I have to do one more thing." She took out her phone and dialed Joe's home phone number. "Diane, this is Eve. I have to tell you something. Joe is—" The words stuck in her throat. Get it over with. "Joe's been hurt."

"My God."

"It's . . . bad. He's at Gwinnett General. You'd better come."

"How bad?"

"I don't know. He's been shot. He's in the emergency room."

"God damn you." Diane slammed down the phone in Eve's ear.

She flinched.

"Telling bad news is never pleasant," Logan said quietly.

"She sounded as if she hates me." She moistened her lips. "And who can blame her? It's my fault. I should never have let Joe—"

"I've never noticed him asking permission. I doubt if you could have stopped him."

"I *know* him. I saw his face before we went into the cottage. I should have realized that he thought something was wrong."

"May I point out that you were a little upset?"

"No." She leaned her head against the window. "He's dying, Logan."

"We don't know that."

"I know it." She whispered, "I . . . love him, you know."

He looked away from her. "Do you?"

"Yes. He's like the father and brother I never had. I don't know what life would be like without Joe. Funny, I never thought about it before. He was just always there and I thought he always would be."

"He's not dead yet."

If Joe died, would he be with Bonnie?

"Stop crying," Logan said hoarsely. He pulled her into his arms. "Shh, it's going to be all right." He was rocking her. "Let me help."

He was helping. Comfort and warmth were flowing from him, surrounding her. He couldn't heal the wound, but he was touching her, keeping away the loneliness. For the moment that was enough.

TWENTY-ONE

Sandra was frowning when she came back to the car two hours later.

Eve tensed. "Joe?"

"Not good. They don't know if he'll make it." Sandra got into the backseat. "They've operated and taken him to intensive care."

"I want to see him."

"No chance. Only close family members are allowed."

"It's not fair. He'd want me there. I need to—" She drew a deep breath. It wasn't what she needed but what Joe needed that mattered. "Is Diane there?"

"She got here just as they were wheeling him out of the operating room." Sandra made a face. "She was cold as ice to me. You'd think I'd shot him."

"It's not you. She's really angry with me. You're my mother. She probably blames you for bringing me into the world."

"I guess so. But I thought she liked me. I had coffee with her only a few weeks ago. I thought she liked both of us."

"She's just upset. It'll be different when Joe gets better." If he got better. If he didn't die. "When will they know?"

"Perhaps tomorrow." Sandra hesitated. "But I can't go back in there, Eve. A policeman came into the ICU right before I left. He was checking on Joe."

Of course. Joe was a cop, and cops took care of their own. The hospital would soon be crawling with officers.

Logan was already starting the car. "Then we've got to get out of here. Pronto."

"And where are we going?" Sandra asked.

"I told Margaret and Pilton to meet us at that Hardee's near Emory where we met Quinn." Logan drove out of the parking lot. "She'll take you to Sanibel and then arrange to get you out of the country."

"No," Sandra said.

Eve stiffened. "It's the only safe thing, Mom. You've got to do it."

"I don't have to do anything." Her lips thinned. "And who says it's the safest thing? You? Logan? Neither of you has done such a good job of keeping yourself safe, and Joe's lying in that hospital. Why should I believe you'd do any better at seeing that I don't get killed?"

Panic iced through Eve. "Mom, please. You have to do as I say."

"Bullshit." Sandra looked her in the eye. "I've done everything you and Margaret told me to do. You've all treated me as if I were some half-wit child. It's finished, Eve."

"I want to keep you safe."

"I intend to be safe." She turned to Logan. "Drive me to the Peachtree Arms Apartments. It's right off Piedmont."

Eve recognized the address. "You're going to Ron's place?"

"You bet I am. It's what I've wanted to do all along."

"Do you really think he'll take you in and hide you?"

"I'll find out, won't I? Or maybe we'll discuss it and decide I should turn myself in as a material witness to Joe's shooting. I'll ask them to put me in jail for protective custody. Whatever I do, it will be my decision." She looked back at Logan. "Drive or let me out of the car."

Logan hesitated and then pressed on the accelerator. "This may be a mistake, Sandra."

"If it is, it won't be my first. Hell, I've made every one in the book at one time or another." She said to Eve, "I won't be able to go to the hospital, but I'll call them several times a day and let you know how Joe's doing."

"Mom, don't take this chance. I could never forgive myself if anything happened to you."

"Don't you dare say that. You're my daughter, not my mother. You take care of yourself, I'll take care of myself. No guilt, dammit. I won't be another Bonnie."

Eve's eyes widened.

"Oh, shit, don't look at me like that." Sandra leaned forward and squeezed Eve's shoulder. "Just let me go, Eve. Let *her* go."

"We're not talking about Bonnie."

"Oh, yes, she's here every minute of every day. She's behind your every word and gesture."

"That's not true."

Sandra shook her head. "You don't have to forget her to let her go, baby. Just let a little light come into your life. God, it's dark where you are."

"I'm—fine. Everything will be okay once this is all over."

"Will it?"

"Mom, I can't take this right now."

"I'll be quiet. I know you're hurting. But don't try to run my life, Eve. It's taken me too long to learn how to do it myself."

"Piedmont is right ahead," Logan said.

"The Arms is around the corner."

"What if Ron's not home?" Eve asked.

"I have a key." Sandra smiled. "I've had it since our third date. That I never told you says something about the way you intimidated me, doesn't it?"

"I never tried to—"

"I know." Logan had stopped before the apartment building and Sandra got out of the car and grabbed her suitcase. "I'll check every three hours with the hospital. If you don't hear from me, you'll know his condition hasn't changed."

"Be careful. I *hate* your taking a chance like this."

"And I'm relieved that I'm doing something on my own. I've felt like some kind of pawn, moved back and forth by you and Logan and even this Fiske person. It's time I took control."

Stunned, Eve watched her mother walk into the apartment building.

"Phoenix rising from the flames?" Logan murmured.

"She's doing the wrong thing. I'm scared to death."

"Maybe not. Ron could be a good guy who'll do everything he can to protect her."

"Against Lisa Chadbourne? Against Timwick?"

"Well, Fiske is out of the picture. Our first lady will have to hire another hit man and that may take a little time. Particularly if she doesn't find out right away that Quinn put him down."

"Not enough—"

"You can't do anything about it," Logan said. "Your mother has made her choice, Eve. You can't protect her if she won't accept your protection."

"She doesn't understand. Gary and Joe— She doesn't understand what can happen."

"I believe she understands very well. She saw Joe taken away in that ambulance. She's not stupid."

"I didn't say she was stupid."

"Then why do you treat her as if she were?"

"I just want to protect her. I don't want to lose her."

"Like you lost Bonnie?"

"Shut up, Logan."

"I'll shut up. Sandra already said it all." He got on the I-85 entrance ramp. "But I'd think about what she said. She's a smart lady. I had no idea how smart."

"Where are we going?"

"To meet Margaret and tell her to get out of town. I don't suppose I could persuade you to go with her?"

Anger was suddenly replacing fear. "And will you go? How about you boarding that boat for Timbuktu, Logan? Why don't you forget about Gil?" The words were tumbling out, exploding with fury that was building every second. "Why don't you forget about Ben Chadbourne? Just run away and say screw the world."

He pursed his lips in a soundless whistle. "You don't have to bite my head off. It was just a suggestion. I didn't think you'd—"

"It was a lousy suggestion. I won't leave Joe and Mom. I'm tired of running and hiding and being afraid. I'm tired of people I care about getting hurt and I'm tired of feeling helpless. I swore a long time ago I'd never be a victim again, and it's happening. *She's* making it happen." Her voice was shaking with intensity. "I won't *tolerate* it any longer. Do you hear me? I'll never let her—"

"I hear you," Logan said. "I get the picture loud and clear, but I'm fuzzy about how the hell we're going to stop her."

So was Eve. Then she remembered her mother's last words to her, the words that had struck a deep chord and triggered her rage.

It's time I took control.

Lisa Chadbourne had been the one in control, the one on the attack. She had killed Gary. She might have killed Joe.

But her mother was alive. Eve was alive, so was Logan. And they were going to stay alive.

No more deaths, she had prayed.

She wasn't praying now.

She was taking control.

Margaret got out of the van, leaving Pilton in the passenger seat. "How's Quinn?"

"We don't know," Logan said. "Intensive care."

"I'm sorry," Margaret told Eve. "You okay?"

Eve nodded.

"How's Sandra? She was pretty fond of him, wasn't she?"

"Yes." Her eyes were stinging. Change the subject. Don't think about Joe. "She won't be going with you. She's staying here."

Margaret frowned. "Do you think that's a good idea?"

"No, but she does. She won't listen to me."

"Perhaps I could talk to—"

"She's through listening," Logan said. "Now, you and Pilton take off."

"Pilton deserves a bonus, you know," Margaret pointed out. "He never figured he'd be a fugitive when he took the job. The police will be looking for him."

"Then give him a bonus."

"A big bonus. He's been a good—"

"Where's Fiske's car?" Eve asked suddenly. "Did you find it?"

"Pilton found it. It was parked in the driveway of an empty rental property about two miles from our cottage."

"Did you clean it out?"

"Clean as a whistle. We dumped everything from the glove compartment and the trunk into garbage bags. Then I drove the car to the airport and left it in the long-term lot."

"Where are the bags?"

"In the back of the van."

Eve moved toward the van. "Let's get them, Logan."

Margaret watched them toss the garbage bags into the backseat of their car. "You think he had something important?"

"I don't know," Eve said. "Probably not, since he was a professional. But we don't have any other leads."

"Be careful with that bigger bag. There was enough firepower in Fiske's trunk to start a small war," Margaret said as she climbed back in the van. "A rifle, two handguns, shells, a few boxes that contained some kind of electronic bugging equipment. He didn't believe in traveling light." She smiled grimly at them. "Good luck. Be sure you keep alive, John. The bonus I'm going to charge you for my part in this mess is going to make Pilton's look sick."

Eve was already crawling into the backseat as Pilton's van left the parking lot. "I'll look through the bags. You drive." She opened the bigger bag first. What did she know about weapons? That she didn't like them, that they frightened her, that to her they represented only violence and horror.

But they hadn't frightened Fiske. He had used these weapons. They wouldn't frighten Lisa Chadbourne. She had ordered their use.

Eve put her forefinger on the barrel of the rifle. The metal was warm, smooth, almost pleasing to the touch. Somehow she had expected it to be cold.

"Find anything?" Logan asked.

Nothing she had wanted to find. "Not yet."

"I bet there won't be any way to trace those guns to Lisa Chadbourne."

"I know." Lisa would leave no trail that could lead back to her. Eve's search was probably hopeless.

To lose hope was to admit defeat. She'd be damned if she'd lose hope.

She pushed the first bag aside and started on the second. Rental car papers in a green folder, a first-class ticket to Washington on Delta Airlines, an airline schedule, a few receipts from restaurants, two in Atlanta, one in Bainbridge.

Bainbridge.

Don't think about Bainbridge. Don't think about the motel room where Gary had died.

A folded piece of paper. Another receipt?

She unfolded the paper.

She went rigid.

A list of several names. Some typewritten, some inked in.

Her own name, Logan's, Joe's, her mother's—

And two other names that caused her eyes to widen in shock.

My God.

She forced herself to continue down the list.

Gary Kessler. Neatly crossed off.

She stared down blindly at Gary's name.

Just another name on the list.

Gil had said Fiske was obsessed with neatness and efficiency. So kill a man and cross him off the list.

"What is it?" Logan was looking at her face in the rearview mirror.

"A list. Gary's name." She folded the paper and stuffed it into her purse. She'd look at it again later and think about it harder. It hurt too much just then. She went through the other papers. Nothing else of interest. "Find us a place to stop."

"A motel?"

"No, they'll be looking for us in this area. She'll wonder why she hasn't heard from Fiske and there will be discreet inquiries. They'll find out about Joe."

Joe.

She quickly shied away from the thought of him. When she remembered Joe in that hospital, she couldn't focus on anything else.

"You know we should leave this vicinity."

"No, Joe may need me."

"You're not being reasonable. You can't even go to—"

"I don't care." She couldn't leave Joe, not when she didn't know whether he was going to live or die. "Just find us a place to stop for a while. I need to think."

"I've already been thinking. I believe we should contact Peter Brown, the reporter on that Atlanta newspaper."

"Maybe." She rubbed her aching temple. "But he's Joe's friend. We really need Joe to—"

Joe again. They needed Joe. *She* needed Joe.

The memories came flooding back. Joe stopping by her lab to nag her for working too hard. Joe joking with her, talking quietly and—

"Just relax," Logan said. "We don't have to decide anything this minute. I'll drive for a while and see if I can find somewhere unobtrusive to park."

• • •

Logan stopped at a McDonald's ten miles south of Gainesville and bought burgers and Cokes to go. He pulled off the highway and drove on a bumpy dirt road for another five miles, then stopped several yards from a large pond.

"This should be private enough." Logan turned off the engine. "Though there's probably a farmhouse over that next hill. It's not easy finding a spot of wilderness in this day and age."

"How far are we from the hospital?"

"Driving fast, forty minutes." He got out of the car, grabbed Ben's case, and came around and opened her door. "Come on, let's walk down by that pond. I think we both need some exercise."

Anything to release a little of this tension. She picked up her handbag and joined him.

The pond was muddy and the bank slippery. It must have rained recently. The sun was starting to go down, casting glittering bars of light on the water's surface.

After thirty minutes Logan asked, "Better?"

"No. Yes." She stopped beside a tree and leaned her cheek against the trunk. "I don't know, Logan."

"I want to help you. Dammit, tell me how to help you."

Make Gary rise from the dead. Tell me Joe's going to get well.

She shook her head.

"Quinn's not the only one who can help you. Let me try."

She sank down on the ground. "I'll be okay, Logan. I just have to think. I know there's a way to end it, but it has to come clear and I'm not thinking clearly."

"Are you hungry?"

"No."

"You should be. You haven't eaten in nearly twenty-four hours."

Bubba Blue's Barbecue. Gary had ordered food delivered . . .

"You stay here." He set Ben's case down beside her. "I'll go bring the food to you."

She watched him stride up the slope. Get a grip, she thought in disgust. She was behaving like a wimp and he was worried about her. The cold calculation of Gary's name on that list had thrown her into a tailspin, and it was taking her a little time to rec—

Her phone was ringing.

Mom?

She dug frantically in her purse for the phone.

"Eve?"

Lisa Chadbourne.

Eve started to shake. "Damn you. Damn you to hell."

"You gave me no choice. I tried to give you a way out."

"And then you killed Gary."

"Fiske killed— No, I won't deny it. I told him I wanted it done."

"And did you tell him to kill Joe too?"

"No, that wasn't in the immediate plan."

But she wasn't denying it might be on her agenda. "He's dying."

"And I assume the dead man who was found with him was Fiske?"

"He tried to kill Joe."

"Evidently he didn't succeed. I understand Quinn may still live."

"He'd better."

"Are you threatening me? I can understand your bitterness, but haven't you realized that you can't win? How many more people have to die, Eve?"

"You don't have Fiske anymore."

"Timwick will find a substitute. Quinn is very vulnerable now. He's on life support, isn't he?"

A bolt of sheer rage shot through Eve. "Don't you even think about it."

"I don't want to think about it," Lisa said wearily. "The idea sickens me, but I *will* have it done, Eve. Just as I had Kessler killed. Just as I'll have everyone you care about killed. You have to give me the skull and that DNA report."

"Go to hell."

"Listen to me, Eve. Think about it. Is it worth it?"

"You're saying if I give you the skull that Joe will live?"

"Yes."

"Liar. Joe wouldn't be safe. My God, you even killed Scott Maren, and he was supposed to be your friend."

Silence. "That wasn't my decision. I didn't know about it until it had been done. Timwick is in a panic and striking out. I'll see that Quinn's safe. Believe me."

"I don't believe you."

"Then, what do you want, Eve? What can I give you?"

"I want you brought down." She closed her eyes and said the words she'd never thought she'd say to anyone. "I want you dead."

"I'm afraid that's not one of your choices."

"That's all I'll ever want."

"That's not true." Lisa paused. "I was afraid that Fiske would fail, so I've been sitting here wondering what I could offer you. And then it came to me. So simple. I know what you want even more than you want me crushed down."

"There isn't anything."

"Oh, but there is, Eve."

Eve was still staring down at the phone when Logan came back.

He stopped a few feet away, his gaze narrowed on her face. "Was it your mother? How's Quinn?"

She shook her head. "It was Lisa Chadbourne."

He stiffened. "And?"

"She wants the skull."

"So what's new? Is that enough to send you into shock?"

"Yes." She put the phone back into her handbag. "It's enough."

"Did she threaten you?"

"She threatened Joe and Mom."

"Sweet."

"But I'm not sure she can guarantee their safety even if I

make the deal. She said Timwick is in a panic and she lost control of him when he killed Maren. She might lose control of him again."

"And she might never have lost control and given the order herself."

"Maybe. I don't know. I can't think right now."

If I make the deal . . .

The phrasing abruptly hit home to him. "My God, you're actually thinking about it. What the hell did she say to you?"

She didn't answer.

He fell to his knees beside her. "Tell me."

She shook her head. "My head's messed up. Maybe later."

"Maybe?"

She changed the subject. "I want you to call the hospital."

"To check on Quinn? Your mother said she—"

"No, I want you to call the nurses' station. I want you to tell her that you intend to kill Joe."

"What?"

"I want you to be obscene and ugly and explicit. I want you to tell her how you're going to pretend you're hospital personnel and slip into his room and cut off his life support. Or maybe give him a shot he'd never wake up from. I want you to sound crazy and homicidal."

He slowly nodded. "They'll report the anonymous call to the cops hanging around the hospital and they'll be on the lookout."

"I'd do it myself, but a man is usually perceived as more lethal."

"Perception can be faulty as hell. I'll call right away." He frowned. "What are you doing?"

She was on her knees, reaching for Ben's case on the ground beside her. "I just want to hold Ben's skull case."

"Why?"

"I'm not going to run away with it. I just want to have it in my hands."

He didn't like that any more than he liked the way Eve was

acting. "Maybe we should think about leaving here. We need to find somewhere to sleep."

"Okay, we'll go back to Gainesville later tonight." She looked away from him and down at the case on her lap. "Make the call."

Sandra called Eve at eleven that night. "Joe's vital signs have stabilized. He's still critical but it's looking better."

Hope surged through Eve. "When will they know for sure?"

"I don't know. Tomorrow morning, maybe. How are you?"

"Okay."

"You don't sound okay."

"I'm fine, Mom. Are you with Ron?"

"Yes, he's right here. He says he's not going to move two feet from me until this is over. He thinks you should come in and talk to the police. So do I. You've got to get this mess straightened out."

It sounded so easy, she thought tiredly. Deposit everything in the arms of the police and let them take care of it. "Call me back when you find out more about Joe. Take care of yourself, Mom."

"Quinn's better?" Logan asked.

She nodded. "But not out of the woods." She opened the car door. "I'm going to walk down to the pond. You don't have to go with me."

"In other words, my company's not wanted." He glanced at Ben's case in her hand. "But evidently our skeletal friend is. You haven't set it down all evening. Are you going to tell me why you're toting that thing around?"

She wasn't sure herself. Maybe she thought it would give her the answer. God, she needed an answer. "I just want it with me."

"Weird."

"Yes, haven't you heard? I don't have all my marbles."

"Crap. You're one of the sanest people I know."

"But look at the company you keep." She moved down the

moonlit slope. The leather of the case was smooth beneath her touch.

Help me, Ben. I'm lost and I need someone to find me.

Eve had been sitting underneath that tree for over two hours.

And she was hugging that leather case like it was a baby.

He couldn't stand it any longer. Logan got out of the car and stalked down the slope.

"I'm sick of being patient and understanding. You tell me what's happening. Do you hear me? I want to know what the hell Lisa Chadbourne told you."

She didn't speak for a moment, and then she whispered, "Bonnie."

"What?"

"She offered me Bonnie. She offered to find Bonnie for me."

"How could she do that?"

"She said that she'd have the cases reopened, that she'd send an army of police and military to question and search. She said she'd been thinking about it. The search couldn't be obviously for Bonnie. It would look too suspicious for her. They'd choose one of the other children to publicly focus on, but the searchers would have their orders. It would be Bonnie they'd be looking for."

"My God."

"She said that they'd spend years if they had to. She promised to bring Bonnie home to me."

"And all you have to do is give her the skull and the DNA report? It's a trick. She'd never follow through."

"Just the skull. She said I could leave the country and keep the DNA report until she delivers Bonnie."

"A pretty weak hold."

She closed her eyes. "Bonnie."

"She wouldn't keep her word."

"Maybe she would."

"I won't let you do it."

Her eyes flicked open and she said fiercely, "Listen to me, Logan. If I decide to do this, neither you nor anyone else is going to stop me. I'll run right over you. If anyone can find Bonnie, Lisa Chadbourne has the power to do it. Do you know what that means to me?"

"Yes," he said harshly. "And so does she. Don't let her use you like this."

She shook her head. "You don't understand."

He did understand and he ached for her. Lisa Chadbourne had used the one lure that was irresistible to Eve. "When do you have to let her know?"

"She's going to call me at seven in the morning."

"It would be a terrible mistake."

"She said Joe and Mom would be safe, that all the killing would be over. She'll even try to get Timwick to stop looking for you."

"Fat chance. You'd be crazy to believe her."

"I believe she doesn't want any more killing. I don't know if she can stop it, but I think she wants it over."

"When she calls, let me talk to her."

She shook her head.

"I thought we were in this together."

"Together? You've already said you'd try to keep me from doing it."

"Because I know it's a mistake."

"It's a mistake to leave Bonnie alone out there."

"Eve, the stakes are too high to let—"

"Shut up, Logan." Her voice was tight. "Just leave me alone to think. You're not going to convince me. I already know every argument against it."

But every cell in her mind and body was telling her to do it, Logan thought. He wanted to strangle Lisa Chadbourne.

"Okay, I won't try to persuade you right now. Just think about it." He rose to his feet. "And remember Kessler and Joe Quinn."

"I haven't been thinking about anything else."

"That's not true. I don't believe you can think of anyone but Bonnie. Just weigh—"

She wasn't listening to him anymore. She was looking down at the skull case but he didn't think she was seeing that either.

She was only hearing the siren call that Lisa Chadbourne had sung.

And she was seeing only Bonnie.

TWENTY-TWO

Lisa Chadbourne called at seven on the dot the next morning. "Well?"

Eve drew a deep breath. "I'll do it."

"I'm glad. Believe me, it's best for everyone."

"I don't care about everyone. If I did, I wouldn't be dealing with you. Listen to me. I want you to set me and my mother up somewhere out of the country, as you promised. I want you to call off your dogs after Logan and I want you to leave Joe Quinn alone."

"And you want Bonnie."

"Oh, yes." Her voice was shaking. "You have to find her and bring her to me. That's absolutely nonnegotiable."

"I'll find her. I promise you, Eve. I'll arrange for Timwick to pick up the skull and then—"

"No. I don't know if your promise is good enough. I'm taking a big chance. Who's to say you won't go back on your word once you have the skull?"

"You'll still have the DNA records. You know they could cause me a great deal of trouble."

"Perhaps not enough without the skull."

"Then, what are you asking?"

"I'm not asking, I'm demanding. I want to see you. I want you to pick up the skull."

"That's not possible."

"It's the only way I'll deal."

"Look, a woman in my position can't move around freely. What you're asking is impossible."

"Don't lie to me. A woman who can kill her husband and get away with it can find a way to meet me. I'm putting my life on the line and I've got to use what I can to survive. I don't have many weapons, but I'm an artist. I've made a study of facial expressions and I've also studied you. I think I'll be able to tell if you intend to keep your word."

A pause. "You'll bring the skull with you?"

"It will be hidden close by. But I guarantee you won't be able to find it if you decide to set a trap for me."

"And what if this is a trap for me?"

"Take what precautions you like as long as they don't pose a threat to me."

"And where do you suggest we meet?"

"Somewhere near Camp David. It would be easiest for you to go there for the weekend. Particularly since you've supposedly suffered the loss of your friend Scott Maren. Just state Camp David as your destination and have the pilot set down before you reach there."

"It seems to be a reasonable plan. What about Logan?"

"He's out of it. I took the skull and papers and left him during the night. He told me I was crazy. He thinks you'll betray me."

"But you're not listening to him?"

"I'm listening. He may be right." Her hand tightened on the phone. "I have to do it anyway. You knew I would, didn't you?"

A silence on the other end of the line. "This meeting isn't a good idea. It would be safer if you drop the skull off where Timwick can pick it up."

"Safer for you."

"Safer for both of us."

"No, I have to see your face when you tell me you're going to find Bonnie. You've told too many lies. I have to do whatever I can to make sure you're not deceiving me."

"Believe me, it's not a good idea."

"Take it or leave it."

"Give me a moment to think about it." Another silence. "Very well. I'll meet you. But you can understand that I'm going to bring Timwick."

"No."

"Timwick can fly a helicopter and he's Secret Service. That means I'll be able to eliminate both my guard and the pilot without suspicion." Lisa paused. "And he has equipment that will be able to tell me if either you or the area is wired. I do have to protect myself."

"And who's going to protect me from him?"

"I'll send Timwick away once I'm assured you haven't set a trap for me. I won't come without him, Eve."

She gave in. "Okay. No one else. If I see any sign of anyone else, I won't meet you."

"Fair enough. Now tell me where you want to meet."

"I'll call you when you're in the air and near Camp David."

"Caution. When do you want me to leave?"

"Tomorrow. Eight A.M."

"Very well. Remember, it takes thirty minutes to reach Camp David from the White House." She paused. "If I can't talk you into a drop. It would really be safer for both of us."

"I said no."

"Then tomorrow." Lisa hung up.

Eve pressed the end button. It was done. Logan had called it a terrible mistake, but she'd rolled the dice anyway.

She needed transportation to get to Washington today, and there was one more thing she had to do before she left. She dialed her mother. "How's Joe?"

"I just finished talking to the hospital. He's out of intensive care."

Eve closed her eyes as waves of relief washed over her. "He's better? He's going to live?"

"He regained consciousness during the night. The doctors are being cautious, but all the signs are promising."

"I want to see him."

"Don't be crazy. You know that's not possible."

But it didn't stop the desperation she was feeling. Who could guess what was going to happen at Camp David? She needed to see Joe. "Okay. I need some help. Will you rent a car for me and pick me up?"

"What happened to the car Logan had?"

"We've parted company. They're searching for him harder than they are for me, and there's probably an order to shoot on sight."

"I'm glad you're not together. I didn't like the idea of the two of you—"

"Mom, I don't have much time. I'm in a women's rest room at the Gainesville Recreational Park. It's deserted at this hour, but I can't stay here very long. I hate to ask it of you, but will you pick me up?"

"I'm on my way."

Mom was on her way. Eve would drop Sandra off back at the condo and then she would be on her way too. She sat down on the floor, put down her handbag next to Ben's case, and leaned back against the concrete block wall. Breathe deep. Try to relax. She was doing what she had to do.

Tomorrow: eight A.M.

Tomorrow: eight A.M.

Lisa stood up and moved over to the window.

Tomorrow she would have Ben's skull and the primary threat would be over.

It could be a trap, but Lisa's gut instinct told her she had played the one card that Eve Duncan couldn't resist. The woman was obsessed with finding her daughter, and Lisa had played on her torment and brought the woman to her knees. She supposed she should feel triumphant.

She didn't feel triumphant.

She wished she'd been able to convince Eve that a meeting wasn't necessary. She had honestly planned on keeping her part of the bargain.

Or had she? she wondered wearily. She'd thought she knew herself, but she'd never dreamed she would do the things she had already done.

She just wished Eve hadn't set up the meeting.

NEAR CATOCTIN MOUNTAIN PARK
THE NEXT DAY
8:20 A.M.

The helicopter was approaching from the north.

Eve made the call.

"I'm in a glade one mile from route 77 by Hunting Creek. Set down in the glade. I'll come to meet you."

"As soon as we do a sweep of the area and make sure it's secure," Lisa Chadbourne said. "Timwick likes to be cautious."

It was Lisa who liked to be cautious, Eve thought. But Eve had been cautious too. She'd made very sure the surrounding area was all clear before she'd made the call.

Hands nervously clenching and unclenching she watched the helicopter circle the clearing.

"One person." Timwick pointed at the infrared blur on the LCD screen. "The nearest other heat source is at the diner on route 77, three miles away."

"Electronics?"

Timwick checked another screen. "Nothing in the area anywhere near Duncan."

"You're sure?"

"Of course I'm sure. It's my ass too."

Lisa felt a tinge of sadness as she looked at the solitary blur on the screen and realized Eve was down there alone and unprotected. "Then let's go down and see if we can save it, James."

Lisa Chadbourne was getting out of the helicopter.

Eve had made the deal. She had set the time and place and yet it still seemed bizarre that Lisa was really there.

Eve watched her as she jumped to the ground. She looked just as she had on the videos—beautiful, serene, glowing. Well, what had she expected? Some marks of dissipation or cruelty? Lisa had killed her husband and still appeared the same as in those videos. Why would any other death make a difference?

Gary. Blood. Daggers. The hideous scene in that motel room flashed before Eve's eyes.

It should make a difference. It should.

Don't think about it. Be calm.

She moved toward the helicopter.

Lisa Chadbourne said crisply, "Hello, Eve. James called security at Camp David just now and said we'd landed to check out a light on our control panel. We have ten minutes tops. Either we're back in the air by then or they'll become alarmed and send someone to this area."

"Ten minutes should be enough time."

"Don't say anything, Lisa." Timwick got out of the helicopter and came toward Eve.

She instinctively took a step back.

He was holding an instrument that looked like one of those metal detector wands used at airport security. "Hold out your arms."

"You said the entire area was clean, James," Lisa said.

"It doesn't hurt to be careful." He ran the wand over Eve's body. "Turn around."

"Don't touch me."

He went behind her and ran the wand from shoulder to feet. "She's okay. No weapons. No wire."

"Forgive James," Lisa said. "He's been extremely nervous lately. It's yours and Logan's fault, I'm afraid. Go away and let us talk, James."

Timwick started to move toward the trees.

"No," Eve said sharply. "I notice nobody gave me a chance to go over him with that damn wand. I don't want him out of my sight." She pointed at a spot beside the helicopter. "Sit down."

"What?"

"You heard me. I want you sitting with your legs crossed. It would take you longer to attack from that position."

Timwick's lips thinned. "This is humiliating, Lisa."

"Do it." Lisa was smiling faintly. "You're not quite as helpless as I thought, Eve."

Timwick dropped to the ground and crossed his legs. "Satisfied?"

"No, reach into your jacket and remove your gun. Put the safety on and toss it out of reach."

"I don't have a gun."

"Remove your gun," Eve repeated.

Lisa nodded. "Let's get this over with, James."

Timwick muttered a curse, pulled out his gun, put on the safety, and tossed his gun across the glade.

Eve turned to Lisa. "Now I'm satisfied."

"You've used up valuable time." Lisa glanced at her watch. "Two minutes to be exact."

"It was worth it. I don't trust him."

"I suppose you have a right to be suspicious." She paused. "Now give me Ben's skull, Eve."

"Not yet."

"You want me to tell you that you'll get your Bonnie back?" She looked her straight in the eye. "There's no way of being sure, but I'll do everything in my power to find her." Her voice vibrated with sincerity. "I promise you, Eve."

Oh, God, she was telling the truth. Bonnie could come home.

"The skull, Eve. I don't have much time. I've papers and money for you in the helicopter and James has arranged a plane to fly you and your mother out of the country. Give me the skull, and James and I will get back in that helicopter and disappear from your life."

Would there ever be a moment when Lisa Chadbourne wasn't a part of her memory and life?

"The skull."

"It's over there beneath the trees." Eve glanced warily at Timwick as she moved toward the edge of the glade. "I'm watching you, Timwick."

"James isn't going to interfere." Lisa followed her. "He wants that skull as much as I do."

"But what about after I give you the skull?"

Lisa didn't answer. Her forehead was creased in a frown. "Where is it? Did you bury it?"

"No." She stopped and pointed at the leather case, which was half obscured by a bush. "There it is."

"In plain sight? You said we wouldn't be able to find it."

"A bluff. Would it have done me any good to bury or hide it? You'd have gotten all kinds of detectors in here."

"In this case, it seems I overestimated you." She laughed. "My God, I thought you'd worked out something brilliant." Her smile faded. "If it is Ben. You threw a ringer at us before."

Eve shook her head. "It's Ben Chadbourne. Look for yourself."

Lisa picked up the case. "I hear you do wonderful sculpting work. Will I really be able to see the resemblance?"

"Open it."

Lisa stared down at the case. "I don't think I want to."

Eve shrugged. "Whatever you like. But I'm surprised you'd take the chance of not doing it."

"I can't take a chance." Lisa braced herself and slowly opened the latches. "Let's see if you're as good as your reput— Dear

God." She reeled back against the tree, staring down at the scorched skull. "What is—"

"Sorry it's not as handsome as you expected. Gary Kessler always liked to work on a clean skull, so he made me break down what I'd done. You remember Gary. You told Fiske to kill him, didn't you?"

Lisa couldn't take her gaze off the skull. She whispered, "Ben?"

"That's what a man looks like when you burn him. All the skin melts away and—"

"Shut up." Tears were suddenly flowing down Lisa's cheeks.

"And you see the jagged hole in the back of the skull? That's what happened when his brain exploded. When you're in a fire, your brain boils and eventually—"

"Shut up, you bitch."

"But Gary's death was different. You told Fiske that he had to show me that I had to give you the skull. You told him you wanted him crucified."

"I didn't tell him that. I just told him he had to shock you into realizing you had to give in. I had to show you. It was your fault. I wanted it all to stop. I told you it would stop if you'd give me Ben's skull, but you wouldn't do it." She looked down at the skull. "Ben . . ."

"How did you kill him?"

"Scott Maren gave him a shot. It was very quick, very merciful. He didn't suffer." She drew a deep breath and struggled for control. "Making me look at this skull was very cruel, Eve."

"Don't talk to me about cruelty. You had Gary and Gil killed. Joe almost died."

"Are you satisfied now?" Lisa asked. "Christ, you're hard. I was actually feeling sorry for you."

"You mean because you intended to kill me? Because you never expected to let me leave here?"

"I told you to arrange a drop. I knew I couldn't let you stay alive if you gave me the opportunity— It's my *job*." She jerkily turned toward Timwick. "We're leaving, James. Take care of her."

Timwick slowly rose to his feet. "You want me to kill her?"

"No, I don't want it, but it has to be done. So do it."

Timwick looked at Eve. Then he turned and walked toward the helicopter.

"James!"

"Screw you."

Lisa went rigid. "We agreed it had to be done."

He opened the helicopter door. "And did we agree that Fiske would take me out too? When was it going to be, Lisa?"

"I don't know what you mean."

"The list. You gave Fiske another list. I saw it. He combined your list and mine. I know his handwriting."

"How could you see something that doesn't exist." She moistened her lips. "If there was a list, it certainly didn't come from me. You know he often had his own agenda."

"He wouldn't kill the hand that was feeding him. Not unless another one was feeding him too. You thought you didn't need me any longer."

"Nothing can be proved. Fiske is dead."

"You'd find someone else to put me down."

"You're making a mistake." She started toward the helicopter. "Listen to me, James."

"I'm through listening. I'm out of here."

"They'll catch you."

"Not if I have a head start. That was part of the deal. I'll call Camp David and tell them we're on the way. That should give me enough time." He got into the helicopter. "Burn in hell, bitch."

"Timwick!" She reached for the door. "It's a trick. It's a lie. Don't give up all we've worked for. Kevin will appoint you—"

The helicopter lifted off and Lisa fell to the ground.

Eve watched her struggle to her knees.

Lisa Chadbourne gazed at Eve across the clearing. "*You* did this."

"Actually, you did it. You're the one who told me Timwick was in a panic. A man in a panic will snatch at any straw."

"You set me up." There was still a thread of disbelief in her voice.

"It was my plan. But it was Logan who approached Timwick with the list."

"But when I suggested bringing Timwick with me, you objected."

"I knew you'd want to bring Timwick. It was the smart move and you're a very smart woman. If you hadn't suggested it, Timwick would have persuaded you it was the thing to do." She smiled without mirth. "But he didn't have to convince you, did he?"

"All this won't do you any good. I can work around having Timwick—" She froze. "Oh, my God, you're wired, aren't you?"

"Yes."

"And you showed me Ben's skull to deliberately shake me up."

"I hoped it would. Most people find skeletons frightening. Particularly their victims."

Lisa was silent, obviously thinking back over their conversation. "Very bad but not completely damning. In court any transcript can be interpreted to mean any—"

"Logan also arranged for three witnesses to hear the transmission. Peter Brown, a reporter on the *Atlanta Journal and Constitution*, Andrew Bennett of the Supreme Court, and Senator Dennis Lathrop. All highly respected men. After we made the decision, Logan got moving. He had almost a full day to convince Timwick that he was your next victim."

Lisa turned pale and suddenly looked twice her age. She sank back on her heels. "How . . . clever. I told Timwick in the beginning we had to be careful of you. The electronic monitoring was obviously bogus, but I saw the infrared so I assume we have a little time before Logan gets here."

Eve nodded.

"Good. I need a few minutes to pull myself together. It seems impossible it's all gone down—" She swallowed. "I thought I had you. I thought your Bonnie was the key."

"She was the key."

"But you gave up the chance to—"

"The stakes were too high. You hurt people I cared about."

"I was going to do it, you know. I was going to keep my promise about finding Bonnie. Keeping my word about her would have made me feel better."

"I believe you."

Eve tensed as Lisa rose to her feet.

Lisa shook her head. "I'm not going to try to hurt you. I'm the one who's the walking wounded. You've—destroyed me."

"You destroyed yourself. Where are you going?"

"I dropped Ben's skull when I ran for the helicopter." She fell to her knees beside the skull. "It's so . . . small. It surprises me. He was such a big man. In every way, Ben was larger than life. . . ."

"Until you killed him."

Lisa acted as if she hadn't heard her. "He was so smart. He had such dreams. And he would have made them all come true." She stroked the left cheekbone. She whispered, "What an incredible man you were, Ben Chadbourne."

Lisa's touch was almost loving, Eve realized with shock. All the horror, all the terror was gone.

Lisa's eyes were glistening with tears when she glanced up at Eve. "The tabloids are going to want photographs of him. They always like the shots that are the most morbid and ugly. Don't let them take a picture of Ben like this. I want everyone to remember him as he was. Fight them. Promise me."

"I promise. No pictures except the ones entered as evidence at the trial. After that, I'll see that he goes home."

"Home." She was silent a moment, and when she spoke again there was wonder in her tone. "It actually matters to me. But it wouldn't matter to Ben. He always said it's what we leave behind that matters, not what we become or where we go after we die." She stared down at the scorched skull and tears welled in her eyes again. "God, this *hurts* me, Ben. I didn't think I'd have to see you. You told me I wouldn't have to see you."

Eve froze. "What did you say?"

Lisa looked at her. "I loved him," she said simply. "I've always loved him. I always will. He was kind and caring and extraordinary. Did you really think I could kill a man like that?"

"You *did* kill him. Or had Maren kill him for you."

"I persuaded Scott to prepare the shot." She lowered her eyes to the skull. "But Ben took the hypodermic from Scott and injected himself. He didn't want Scott to have the responsibility. That was the kind of man he was."

"Why?"

"Ben was dying of cancer. He found out a month after he was inaugurated."

It was a moment before Eve recovered enough to ask, "Suicide?"

"No, suicides are cowardly. There was nothing cowardly about Ben. He just wanted to spare—" She stopped for a moment to steady her voice. "He planned it all. He knew that all his dreams were going down the tube. We'd worked for fifteen years to get him into the White House. What a team we were. . . . He had to choose Mobry as vice president because we needed the South, but he always said I was the one who should have been on the ticket. I didn't care. I knew I'd be there to help him. Then to find out that he was going to die before he could accomplish what he needed to . . . It wasn't fair. He couldn't stand it."

"*He* planned it all."

"He chose Kevin Detwil. He told me how to handle him, what to tell him to make him most effective. He knew I'd need Timwick. He told me what bait to use to get him to cooperate."

"Timwick knew about his illness?"

"No, Timwick thought it was murder. Ben believed he'd be more controllable if he thought he was an accomplice to the murder of the President. He was right." She smiled bitterly. "He was right about everything. Everything was going well. We all had our jobs to do. Mine was to control Kevin and work behind the scenes to make sure that Ben's bills passed. I managed to get seven through Congress this term. Do you realize how hard I worked?"

"And what was Timwick's job?" Eve asked grimly.

"It wasn't meant to be killing. He was just there for protection and to make it easier to deceive everyone. He got scared. He panicked and I couldn't control him."

"Then your Ben evidently wasn't right about him."

"He would have been right if everything had gone as planned. If Donnelli had done what he was supposed to do. If Logan had never entered the picture." She looked at Eve. "If you'd decided to mind your own business."

"If no one else became suspicious."

"What were the odds of that happening? Ben's plan was almost foolproof. Do you realize what you've destroyed? We wanted to bring compassion and order to government. We wanted only to help people. It wasn't fair that we weren't going to get the chance."

"You committed murder. Even if you didn't kill your husband, you ordered Fiske to kill."

"I didn't want— I didn't mean— It all went crazy, I don't know how. But I promised Ben I'd see it through. It was my job. I had to do it. Don't you understand? One thing just flowed into the other, and suddenly I was caught up in—" She stopped. "I'm behaving very badly. I should have a little dignity. Particularly since this is probably all still being taped." She straightened, threw back her shoulders, and suddenly a brilliant smile lit her face. "You see, I can get through this. I can get through anything. I'll smile and be sincere and they won't believe those tapes."

"Oh, I think they will. It's over, Lisa."

She lifted her chin. "Not until I've fought the last fight."

"Would Ben want you to fight? A scandal of this magnitude will disrupt the government for months and tarnish everything you've done for him."

"I'll know the moment to quit and step aside . . . just as Ben did." She was silent a moment and then shook her head. "It's rather ironic that you set up our meeting at Camp David. Did you know that FDR called Camp David Shangri-La?"

"No."

"Shangri-La. A lost dream . . ." Her gaze shifted to the edge of the trees. "They're coming. I believe I'll go to meet them. Boldness is always best."

Eve watched her move gracefully across the glade toward the place where Logan and three other cars had pulled to a stop.

The gun.

Lisa had stopped beside the gun that Timwick had tossed away and was looking down at it.

"No!"

"You've destroyed everything Ben and I have worked for. You think I'm a murderer. I could pick that gun up and prove you right. I don't think I'm in range of your friends over there. Are you afraid of dying, Eve?"

"No, I don't think so."

"I don't believe you are either. I think you're afraid of living." She glanced over her shoulder. "I would have found your Bonnie. You'll have to live with that knowledge. Now you may never find her. I hope you don't." She gave the gun a little kick to one side. "You see how nonviolent I am? Rejecting the opportunity for revenge, going forward to meet justice." She smiled. "Good-bye, Eve. Maybe I'll see you in court." She started back across the glade. "And then again, maybe I won't."

"She thinks she can get out of it," Eve told Logan as she watched Lisa get into the back of the car with FBI agents. "She just might do it."

"Not if we keep her separated from Kevin Detwil. They're going to try to isolate her for the next twenty-four hours. It's going to be difficult as hell considering who she is. Chief Justice Bennett is going directly to Detwil and play him the tape."

"You think he'll fall apart?"

"Probably. He's always needed her to bolster him. If he doesn't crumble immediately, there's always the list. That should do it."

"But why was Detwil's name on the list too? I can understand

Timwick. He was becoming unstable and threatening her plans. But she needed Detwil for another term."

"I doubt if he was an immediate target. She probably put his name on the list to intrigue Fiske. What more difficult target than the President?"

"But she would have done it eventually."

"Oh, yes, Detwil was living proof. I imagine she would have had Fiske set up some DNA-destroying accident. Maybe the explosion of *Air Force One*."

"There are a lot of people who travel with the President on *Air Force One*."

"Do you think that would matter to her?"

"Yes. No." She shook her head. "God, I don't know. Maybe."

He took her arm. "Come on, let's get out of here."

"Where are we going?"

"You're letting me choose? How refreshing. After bulldozing me into trapping Lisa Chadbourne, I was sure you'd have some plan."

She was all out of plans. She was all out of energy. She felt drained. "I want to go home."

"Not yet, I'm afraid. We're going to Senator Lathrop's house and stay there until the first uproar is over and we're officially cleared of suspicion. They don't want some gun-happy government man shooting us by mistake."

"How kind," she said ironically.

"Not kind. We're very valuable material witnesses. We'll be under strict guard until this is over."

"When can I go home?"

"A week."

She shook her head. "Three days tops."

"We'll try." His brow lifted. "But remember, we are, after all, dealing with the overturning of a presidency."

"You deal with it, Logan." She got into the car. "Three days. Then I'm going home and see Joe and Mom."

TWENTY-THREE

WASHINGTON, D.C.

"It's a madhouse." Eve turned away from the lace-curtained window. "There must be hundreds of reporters out there. Why the hell don't they go bother someone else?"

"We're a big story," Logan said. "Bigger than O.J. Bigger than Whitewater. Bigger than Clinton's peccadilloes. Get used to it."

"I don't want to get used to it." She was prowling back and forth across the senator's library like a restless tiger. "It's been five days. I need to get home. I need to see Joe."

"You told me your mom said Joe was getting better every day."

"But they won't let me talk to him."

"Why not?"

"How the hell do I know? I'm not *there*." She stopped before his chair, hands clenched. "I'm cooped up here in this . . . this place. I can't go out without getting mobbed. We couldn't even go to Gil's or Gary's funerals. And it's not going to stop, is it?"

Logan shook his head. "I tried to tell you. The minute Detwil broke down and confessed, it triggered a frenzy."

And they had been in the center of that frenzy, Eve thought. They'd been kept virtual prisoners in the senator's house, watching the explosion of events on television. Kevin Detwil confesses, Chet Mobry sworn in as president, Lisa Chadbourne imprisoned.

"It's going to go on and on," she said. "It's like living in a fishbowl. How will I work? How will I live? I can't *stand* it."

"The media will lose interest eventually. After the court case is over, we'll be yesterday's news."

"That may take years. I think I may strangle you, Logan."

"No, you won't." He smiled. "Then you wouldn't have anyone to share your misery with. Company is important at a time like this."

"I don't want your company. I want Mom and Joe."

"The minute you go home to them, they'll be targets too. They won't be able to move without a camera fixed on them. They won't have a life either. Do you think your mother's relationship with her new beau will withstand that kind of stress? What about Joe Quinn? How will the Atlanta P.D. react to a detective who can't take two steps without being on TV? How about his marriage? Will his wife like—"

"Shut up, Logan."

"I'm trying to give it to you straight. You're the one who told me always to be honest with you."

"You knew it would be like this."

"I didn't think of the media repercussions. I suppose I should have considered them, but I just wanted her brought down. That seemed the only important thing."

He was telling the truth. She wished he weren't. She was so frustrated, she needed to blame someone, anyone.

He added quietly, "And I believe in the end that was the only thing important to you too."

"Yes." She went back to the window. "But it shouldn't be like this. We brought her down and now we're drowning with her."

"I won't let you drown." He was suddenly standing behind her, his hands lightly resting on her shoulders. "Not if you let me help you, Eve."

"Can you give me my life back?"

"I intend to do that. It just may take a while." He was massaging the taut muscles in her shoulders. He bent and whispered in her ear, "You're too tense. I believe you need a vacation."

"I need to work."

"Maybe we can combine the two. Did you know I have a house on an island just south of Tahiti? It's very secluded besides having excellent security. I go there when I need to escape for one reason or another."

"What are you saying?"

"I'm saying that you need to escape, and so do I. It would take a very enterprising reporter to follow us that far." He added roughly, "And look at you. You've been through hell and I'm to blame for most of it. Let me try to make amends. You need to rest and heal. It's boring as the devil on the island. Nothing to do but walk on the beach, read, and listen to music."

It didn't sound boring. It sounded like salvation. She slowly turned to look at him. "I could work?"

He made a face. "I should have known that was coming. I'll have a lab built for you. Margaret will do it right this time."

"Will they let us go?"

"The judicial powers that be? I don't anticipate any problem as long as they know where we are and that we aren't going to disappear permanently. The last thing they want are leaks or testimony compromised by the media."

"When could we leave?"

"I'll check and make sure, but possibly early next week."

"I could stay there until I'm needed?"

"As long as you like."

She gazed out the window at the horde of reporters across the street. They looked hungry, but she knew they'd never get enough. Some of them were probably kind, but after Bonnie had disappeared she could remember an occasional reporter saying something deliberately hurtful so they could catch the pain in her expression. She couldn't go through that again.

"You'll do it?" Logan asked.

She slowly nodded.

"Good. And you won't mind if I'm there too? You're not the only one who needs to escape. It's a big plantation house and I promise I won't get in your way."

"I don't mind." Peace. Sunlight. Work. She wouldn't mind anything if it meant getting away from all this uproar. "Once I begin working, I probably won't know you're around."

"Oh, I think you will. You have to surface sometime and we'll be fairly isolated." He moved toward the door. "I'll be pretty hard to miss."

"Ten minutes." The head nurse frowned as she stared over Eve's head at the crowd of reporters being held back by hospital security. "We can't tolerate this disruption. We've had enough trouble keeping the media away from Mr. Quinn. He's a sick man."

"I won't disturb him. I just want to see him."

"I'll run interference with the reporters," Logan said. "Take as long as you need."

"Thanks, Logan."

"And do you suppose since we're going to go to a desert island together you might call me John?"

"It's not a desert island, it's a tropical island, and I don't think I could get used to another name now."

"Ten minutes," the head nurse repeated. "Room 402."

Joe was sitting up in bed and she stopped inside the door just to look at him.

"I didn't expect— You look . . . wonderful. How long have you been sitting up?"

He scowled. "You'd know if you'd bothered to call."

"I did call. Every day. There was some foul-up. They wouldn't let me talk to you."

A flicker of undefinable expression crossed his face. "You called?"

"Of course I called. Do you think I'd lie to you?"

"No." He smiled. "Then I suppose I'll have to permit you to come over here and give me a hug. Gently, of course. They just let me off my back yesterday and I'm not going to make waves. These nurses are tough."

"I've noticed. I've got only ten minutes." She walked over to the bed and hugged him. "But that should be long enough, since you're being so surly." She sniffed. "And you stink of antiseptic."

"Always complaining. I give my life's blood for you, and do I get any appreciation?"

"No." She sat down on the bed. "You were stupid and I'd have never forgiven you if you'd died, Joe."

"I know. That's why I didn't."

She took his hand. It felt warm and strong and . . . Joe. Thank you, God. "I sent Mom a copy of the tape from the wire and told her to play it for you. I hope she got through that army of nurses. Logan had to promise the Justice Department the moon to get a copy of it."

"She got through. You seem to be the only one having trouble getting through to me." He laced his hand through hers. "And that tape nearly gave me a heart attack. Why the hell did Logan let you do it?"

"He couldn't stop me."

His lips tightened. "I would have stopped you."

"Bullshit."

"Did you have to go rushing in? Couldn't you have waited?"

"She killed Gary." She whispered, "And I thought she might still kill you."

"So I'm to blame."

"You bet you are. So stop yelling at me. I couldn't wait for you to rise from the dead and help me. I had to do it myself."

"With Logan's help." He scowled. "But not enough help, damn him."

"Lisa held out an opportunity, but it was for me, not him. Logan helped big-time. He set up the scenario to reel in Timwick. He had your friend at the newspaper contact Timwick and show him the list, and then arrange for Logan to see him. Do you know how dangerous that could have been? What if Timwick hadn't been as desperate and frightened as we hoped?"

"Have they caught Timwick yet?"

"No, he seems to have dropped off the face of the earth."

"No one can disappear without leaving traces." His brow was creased in thought. "He has to be caught. He's an end that has to be tied up or it will bug you for—"

"Not you, Joe."

"Did I say I intended to go after him? I'm only a wounded crock of a man. Why are you worried? Timwick fell apart. He's no threat."

"You corner a rat and you get bitten."

"Then why did you set up that meeting with Lisa Chadbourne and Timwick? You pushed her to the limit. There was no telling what her reaction was going to be. Someone should have been there to back you up."

"It wouldn't have been logical for Logan to be at the meeting."

"Screw logic."

"You know I'm right. Lisa Chadbourne would have known Logan would never agree to my giving up that skull for Bonnie. In order to ring true, I had to pretend I'd taken the skull and run."

He was silent a moment. "And did it ring true? Just how close did you come to going along with her?"

"You know the answer to that."

"Tell me. How close?"

"Close."

"Why not all the way?"

She shrugged. "Maybe I didn't trust her. Maybe I doubted she could do it. Maybe I was too angry about what she'd done to you and Gary."

"And maybe it's the first step."

"What?"

"Nothing." He squeezed her hand. "But no more of this shit until I'm up and strong enough to keep you in line. Logan's doing a lousy job."

"He's smart enough not to try." She paused. "And actually he's being very kind. He's going to take me away to some island he owns in the South Pacific until all this media frenzy is over."

"Oh?"

She didn't like the sound of that. "It's a good idea. I can work there. You know how impossible it would be for me here. It's almost worse than— It's really a good idea, Joe."

He was silent.

"Joe?"

"I think you're right. You need the rest and you need to get away. I think you should go with him."

"You do?"

He grinned. "Don't look so stunned. You told me yourself what a good idea it is. I'm just agreeing."

"Good," she said uncertainly.

"Is Logan here with you?"

She nodded. "We're leaving for Tahiti as soon as I say good-bye to Mom."

"When you leave, will you tell him to come in and see me for a minute?"

"Why?"

"Why do you think? I'm going to tell him to take good care of you or I'll toss him into a volcano. Does Tahiti have volcanoes?"

She chuckled, relieved. "His island is actually south of Tahiti."

"Whatever." His hand tightened on hers. "Now, shut up. I figure I have five minutes left and I want to spend it looking at you, not listening to you gush about Tahiti."

"I don't gush."

But she didn't want to talk either. She just wanted to sit there and feel the peace and well-being she always felt when she was with Joe. In a world where everything was turned upside down, he really hadn't changed. He was alive and strong and would get stronger every day.

It was good to know that when she came back, everything would be exactly the same.

"You wanted to see me?" Logan asked warily.

Joe gestured to the chair next to the bed. "Sit down."

"Why do I feel as if I've been summoned to the principal's office?"

"Guilt?"

Logan shook his head. "Don't play that game with me, Quinn. I'm not buying it."

"You accused me of deceiving Eve and you're doing it yourself. She thinks you're being kind to her."

"I will be kind."

"You'd better be. She needs it now." He added deliberately, "And if she so much as calls and tells me she's broken a fingernail on that island, I'll be there."

"You're not invited." He smiled faintly. "And, for your information, there are no volcanoes on the island."

"She told you?"

"She was amused. She was relieved that you didn't give her any arguments. I was a little relieved myself, but, after I thought about it, I realized that it would have been a wrong move on your part. You don't make many wrong moves, Quinn."

"Neither do you. You handled Eve very smoothly. She honestly thinks you only want to make amends and help her get her life together."

"I do want to help her."

"And you also want her in your bed."

"Absolutely." He paused. "But I also want her in my life for as long as I can keep her there." He smiled. "That shook you. You don't mind the idea of a sexual interlude, but you don't want me to become committed. It's too late. I am committed and I'm going to make a damn good stab at making sure she becomes committed too."

Joe looked away. "It won't be easy."

"I have time and solitude on my side. She's a remarkable woman. I don't intend to let her go. No matter what you do."

"But I've no intention of doing anything." Joe's gaze shifted back to him. "Right now. I want her to go away with you. I want her to go to bed with you. If you can, I want you to make her love you."

Logan lifted a brow. "How generous. May I ask why?"

"It will be the best possible thing for her. She needs it to come back to life. She made a breakthrough when she gave up the chance to get Bonnie back. You can help her take another step."

"So you're prescribing me as therapy?"

"Call it what you like."

Logan's gaze narrowed on Joe's face. "But, God, you hate it, don't you?"

Joe didn't answer the question. "It's the best thing to do. You can help her right now. I can't." He added, "But if this experience doesn't prove as good for her as I hope, believe me, I can always find a volcano."

Logan believed him. Quinn was lying wounded in that bed and should have looked helpless. He didn't look helpless. He looked strong and contained and enduring. Logan remembered when he had judged Quinn one of the most intimidating men he'd ever met. Now he realized the protective side of Quinn was even more dangerous. "I'll be very good for her." He couldn't resist a tiny goad as he moved toward the door. "Of course, you may not be able to judge. We may be too busy to see much of you in the future."

"Don't try to stand between us. It won't work. We have too much history." He stared straight into Logan's eyes. "And all I have to do is tell her that I have a new skull and need her and she'll come."

"The hell she will. What kind of bastard are you? You want her to heal, but you're ready to pull her back into that world."

"You've never understood," Quinn said wearily. "She needs it. And as long as she needs it, I'll give it to her. I'll give her anything in the whole damn world she needs. Including you, Logan." He turned his head away. "Now, get out of here. She's waiting."

Logan wanted to tell him to go to hell. He did understand Eve and he was going to be good for her. All he needed was the chance, and Quinn was giving him that chance.

Quinn? What the hell? He was acting as if Quinn was some powerful figure standing behind the scenes, pulling all the strings.

Bullshit.

"Eve is waiting." He opened the door. "She's waiting for *me*, Quinn. In three hours we'll be on board that flight that will take us a world away from you. Have a nice day."

He was grinning as he sauntered down the hall toward Eve.

Damn, that last jab felt good.

"She was here." Diane stood in the doorway. "The nurses are all talking about it at the desk. Why did Eve come?"

"Why not? She wanted to see me." Joe's gaze narrowed on her face. "She was worried because she couldn't reach me by phone. The hospital wouldn't put her through."

An almost indiscernible emotion flickered across her face. "Really?"

Guilt, he recognized wearily. He'd been hoping it wasn't true. Or maybe he'd been hoping she had done it. It would give him an excuse to do what he should do.

"You know, don't you?" Diane said bitterly. "I broke the rules. I interfered." Her hands clenched at her sides. "Well, dammit, I had a right to do it. I'm your wife. I thought I could go on watching the two of you together, but she's interfering with our life and I won't have it. Do you know what people are saying about the way she drew you into this mess? It's not fair. It's bad enough for me to know how little I count. You've shown the whole world that you don't give a damn about—"

"It's true," he said gently. "Everything you say is absolutely true, Diane. I've not been fair and you've been very patient. I'm sorry I got you into this. I was hoping it would work."

She didn't speak for a moment. "It can still work." She moistened her lips. "You just have to— Maybe I lost my temper and said some things I didn't mean. We just have to talk this out and come to a fair compromise."

But she was asking for the one compromise he couldn't make. He had disappointed and hurt her enough. He wasn't going to keep on doing it. "Shut the door and come and sit down," he said quietly. "You're right, we do have to talk."

. . .

"Are you okay?" Logan stood beside Eve, who was looking out the window from her airplane seat. "Your hands are clutching the arms of that chair as if it were going to take off without you."

She released her grip. "I'm fine. It just seems strange leaving home and going so far away. I've never been out of the country."

"Really?" He sat down beside her. "I didn't know that. But then, there are a lot of things I don't know about you. It's a long flight. Maybe we could talk?"

"You want me to confide all my girlhood dreams, Logan?"

"Why not?"

"Because I don't remember having any girlhood dreams. I've always thought they were sappy fairy tales made up by Madison Avenue."

"Adult dreams?"

"No way."

"God, you're a difficult woman." His gaze went to the metal case on the floor beside her. "Is that what I think it is?"

"Mandy."

"It's a good thing we have a private charter. You would have scared airport security if that had passed through X ray." His gaze was still on the case. "I'm afraid I'd forgotten about her. But, of course, you wouldn't have forgotten."

"No, I don't forget."

"That's both promising and terrifying. I hope you're not planning on working on her during the flight?"

She shook her head. "It wouldn't be safe. Turbulence."

"What a relief. I could see bones flying about like shrapnel. I'm glad you're waiting until you get to the island. Okay, since you're not working and you won't tell me your innermost secrets, maybe we could play cards?"

He was smiling at her and trying to make her feel at ease. A little of her loneliness and tension ebbed away, and she felt warmth ripple through her. He was right. The flight was going to be long. The time they'd spend together before she would have to come back to the real world was going to be even longer. So make it as easy for him as he was trying to make it for her. "Maybe we could."

"A first break in the armor," he murmured. "If I'm lucky, you'll even smile at me by the time we reach Tahiti."

"Only if you're *really* lucky, Logan."

She smiled at him.

EPILOGUE

"This beach isn't like the one near Pensacola," Bonnie said. "It's nice but I think I like the water better there. This surf is too smooth."

Eve turned her head to see Bonnie building a sand castle a few yards away. "It's been a long time. I thought maybe I wasn't going to dream about you again."

"I decided to stay away awhile and give you a chance to let me fade away." Bonnie put a finger into the side of her castle and began to make a window. "It was the least I could do when Joe was making such an effort."

"Joe?"

"And Logan too. They both want the best for you." She made another window. "You've been having a good time here, haven't you? You're much more relaxed than when you came."

Eve looked out at the light shimmering on the blue ocean. "I like the sun."

"And Logan has been real nice to you."

"Yes, he has." What an understatement. During these

months she had tried to keep Logan at a distance, but he wouldn't have it. He had drawn closer and closer both mentally and physically until he had become firmly entrenched in her life. The development filled her with a mixture of comfort and uneasiness.

"You're worried about him. You don't have to be. Everything shifts and changes with time. Sometimes things start out one way and become something else down the road."

"Don't be ridiculous. I'm not worried about him. Logan can take care of himself."

"Then, why are you so restless?"

"I guess I feel as if I'm marking time." She made a face. "And I have to go back next month and give my testimony against Lisa Chadbourne in court. I'm dreading that. Detwil has made a deal to testify against her, but she's still fighting."

"I don't think you'll have to testify."

"Of course I will."

Bonnie shook her head. "I think she's already decided it's time to give up. She's done all she could for Ben. She won't want it all to come out in court."

"She's going to confess?"

Bonnie shook her head. "But it will be over."

I'll know the moment to quit and step aside . . . just like Ben did, *Lisa had said.*

"Don't think about it," Bonnie said. "It makes you sad."

"It shouldn't. She did terrible things."

"You're having a hard time because she wasn't like Fraser. It frightens you to know that the best of intentions can spawn evil. And what she did was evil, Mama."

"I think she would have found you, baby. I think she would have kept her promise."

"And killed you."

"Maybe not. Maybe I could have found a way . . . I'm sorry, Bonnie. Maybe if I hadn't wanted so badly to trap her, I could have done something to—"

"Will you stop it? I keep telling you that's important only to you. It doesn't matter."

"It does matter." She swallowed. "I thought when you didn't come to— I mean when I didn't dream of you that you might be angry. Because I hadn't chosen to bring you home when I had the chance."

"For goodness' sake, I was glad you didn't knuckle under to her. But all that agonizing you did afterward was a great disappointment to me. Joe's right, you've taken your first step. You chose life instead of a pile of bones, but you still have a long way to go."

Eve frowned. "I haven't heard from Joe lately."

"You will soon. I think he's located Timwick."

"Another court case."

Bonnie shook her head.

"What do you mean?"

"He's not going to want you upset, Mama. Timwick will probably just disappear." She tilted her head and studied her. "You're taking that very well. You've accepted that side of Joe."

"I don't like it, but it's better than blinding myself to it."

"I think you'd accept almost anything if it means keeping Joe in your life. Everyone else could slip away, but Joe has to be there. Have you ever asked yourself why?"

"He's my friend."

Bonnie laughed. "Good heavens, you're stubborn. Well, I think your 'friend' will soon be here."

She smothered the leap of excitement. "And how do you know? You heard it on the wind, I suppose. Or maybe it came to you in a clash of thunder in that storm we had last night."

"You know, Joe is a little like a storm. Full of lightning . . . He kind of swoops sometimes and then he quiets down again. Interesting. Aren't you glad he's coming?"

Glad? Oh, God, to see Joe again . . . "How can I be glad about something I don't know is true? I'm probably just doing guesswork about why I haven't heard from Joe."

"It's true." She frowned down at her castle. "I wish I had a flag for the battlements. Remember that tiny flag you made for my castle in Pensacola? You tore a piece off the red beach towel."

"I remember."

"Oh, well, I guess it's fine as it is."

"It's a wonderful castle," she said unevenly.

"Now, don't get soppy."

"I'm not getting soppy. Actually, your castle could use at least one more turret. And where's your drawbridge?"

Bonnie threw back her head and laughed. "I'll do better next time. I promise, Mama."

"You're going to stay here?"

"As long as you stay. But you're already getting bored."

"I am not. I'm perfectly content."

"Have it your own way." She jumped to her feet. "Come on, I'll walk partway back to the house with you. Logan's planning a wonderful evening for the two of you." Her eyes were twinkling. "It should make you very . . . content."

"If I'm napping beneath this palm tree, how am I going to stroll back to the house with you?"

"You can do anything in a dream. I'm sure you'll rationalize it as sleepwalking or something dumb like that. Come on, get up, Mama."

Eve got to her feet, brushed the sand off her shorts, and started down the beach. "You are a dream, baby. I know it."

"Do you? Tomorrow when you come back here the tide will have washed away my sand castle." She smiled at Eve. "But you won't risk coming back tonight before that happens, will you?"

"I might."

Bonnie shook her head. "You're not ready. But I'm beginning to have hope for you."

"Is that supposed to thrill me? I'd really be bad off if—"

"Look at that sea gull." Bonnie's head was lifted to the sky; a radiant smile lit her face, and her red hair shone in the sunlight. "Have you ever noticed how their wings seem to move as if they're hearing music? What song do you think he's hearing?"

"I don't know. Rachmaninoff? Count Basie?"

"Isn't he beautiful, Mama?"

"Beautiful."

Bonnie picked up a seashell and hurled it far out into the water. "Okay, ask me the question so we can get it over and enjoy ourselves."

"I don't know what you mean."

"Mama."

"It's not right. I have to bring you home."

"You know what my answer will be. Someday you'll not ask me and I'll know you're healed." She tossed another shell into the sea before turning to smile lovingly at Eve. "But I realize you have to do it now, so ask me, Mama."

Yes, ask the question.

Ask a ghost. Ask a dream.

Ask of love.

"Where are you, Bonnie?"

Dear Reader:

As I came close to the end of *The Face of Deception*, I knew there had to be another Eve Duncan Book.

When I first created Eve, she was just a forensic sculptor with no personal history. But she quickly took on a life of her own, a life of sadness and triumph, and emerged one tough lady. She learned to endure every parent's worst nightmare: the loss of a child. Because I'm also a mother, I can imagine Eve's torment. It's too wrenching for me to leave her behind right now, not with her search for Bonnie just barely begun.

So I'm creating another story. In her quest to bring Bonnie home, Eve faces a challenge that is both intimate and terrifying. A killer will test her endurance, bring her to the edge of sanity. And Eve will wonder what she's willing to do to survive.

I hope you're looking forward to finding out the answer.

Warmest wishes,

Iris Johansen

Iris Johansen

BOOK TWO

THE KILLING GAME

IRIS JOHANSEN

BANTAM BOOKS

NEW YORK TORONTO LONDON SYDNEY AUCKLAND

My sincere appreciation once again to N. Eileen Barrow with the FACES Laboratory at Louisiana State University. She always meets my bizarre questions with courtesy, warmth, and a sense of humor.

Also my deepest thanks to Engineer Jarod Carson with the Cobb County Fire and Emergency Services for giving so generously of his time and help.

THE KILLING GAME

CHAPTER ONE

Talladega Falls, Georgia
January 20
6:35 A.M.

THE SKELETON HAD been in the ground for a long time. Joe Quinn had seen enough of them to recognize that. But how long?

He turned to Sheriff Bosworth. "Who found it?"

"Two hikers. They stumbled on it late last night. Those rains the past few days washed it out of the ground. Hell, that storm slid half the mountain into the falls. A real gully washer." His gaze narrowed on Joe's face. "You must have hotfooted up here from Atlanta as soon as you heard about it."

"Yes."

"You think it's connected to one of the Atlanta PD's cases?"

"Maybe." He paused. "No. This is an adult."

"You're looking for a kid?"

"Yes." Every day. Every night. Always. He shrugged. "The initial report didn't say whether it was an adult or a child."

Bosworth bristled. "So? I never have to make reports like this. We're pretty crime free here. Not like Atlanta."

"You knew enough to recognize possible knife wounds to the skeleton's rib cage. But I do admit our problems are a little different. What's your population?"

"Don't come up here and slam me, Quinn. We've got a strong law enforcement body. We don't need any city cops messing around our jurisdiction."

He'd made a mistake, Joe thought wearily. He hadn't slept in nearly twenty-four hours, but that was no excuse. It was always an error to criticize local police even when they were taking potshots at you. Bosworth was probably a good cop, and he'd been polite until Joe cast aspersions on how he did his job. "I'm sorry. No offense."

"I do take offense. You have no idea what our problems are here. Do you know how many tourists we have every year? And how many get lost or hurt in these mountains? We may not have murderers or drug dealers, but we take care of every one of our citizens besides those tenderfeet who come up from Atlanta and camp in our parks and fall down in gorges and mess up—"

"Okay, okay." Joe held up his hand in surrender. "I said I was sorry. I didn't mean to downplay your problems. I guess I'm a little jealous." His gaze wandered out over the mountains and the falls. Even with Bosworth's men climbing all over, taping and scouring the area, it was still unbelievably beautiful. "I'd like to live here. It would be nice to wake up every morning to all this peace."

Bosworth was slightly appeased. "It's God's country. The Indians used to call the falls 'the place of tumbling moonlight.' " He scowled. "And we don't find skeletons like this. This must be one of yours. Our people don't kill each other and toss the bodies into the ground."

"Perhaps. It's a long way to transport a body. But in this wilderness, it would be quite a while before a corpse is discovered."

Bosworth nodded. "Hell, if it hadn't been for the rains and the mud slide, we might not have found it for twenty, thirty years."

"Who knows? It might be that long already. I'll get out of your way. I'm sure your medical examiner will want to get at the bones and examine them."

"We have a coroner. He's the local undertaker." Bosworth added quickly, "But Pauley's always willing to ask for help when he needs it."

"He'll need it. If I were you, I'd make a formal request to our pathology department. They're usually willing to cooperate."

"Could you do it for us?"

"I can't. I'll be glad to put in a word, but I'm here in an unofficial capacity."

Bosworth frowned. "You didn't say that. You just flashed your badge and started asking me questions." His eyes suddenly widened. "My God, you're Quinn."

"It's no secret. I told you that."

"But I didn't make the connection. I've been hearing about you for years. The skeleton man. Three years ago you were over in Coweta County checking out two skeletons found there. Then there was that body found in the swamps near Valdosta. You were down there too. And that skeleton up near Chattanooga that you—"

"Word does get around, doesn't it?" Joe smiled sardonically. "I'd think you'd have better things to talk about. So? Do the stories make me some kind of urban legend?"

"No, just a curiosity. You're looking for those kids, aren't you? The ones Fraser killed and then refused to tell where he'd buried them." He frowned. "That was almost ten years ago. I'd think you'd give up."

"Their parents haven't given up. They want their children home for proper burial." He looked down at the skeleton. "Most victims belong to someone somewhere."

"Yeah." Bosworth shook his head. "Kids. I never understand why anyone would kill a kid. It makes me sick."

"Me too."

"I've got three kids. I guess I'd feel the same way those parents do. God, I hope I never find out." Bosworth was silent a moment. "Those cases must have been closed when Fraser was executed. It's mighty decent of you to keep trying to find those children on your own time."

One child. Eve's child. "It's not decent. It's just something I've got to do." He turned away. "Thanks for putting up with me, Sheriff. Call me if I can act as liaison between your coroner and the Atlanta PD."

"I'd appreciate that."

He started down the cliff and then stopped. To hell with not offending another law officer. The sheriff was clearly out of his depth, and by the time someone knowledgeable came on the scene, it might be too late to save the evidence. "Could I make a couple of suggestions?"

Bosworth stared at him warily.

"Get someone out here to photograph the body and entire crime scene."

"I was going to do that."

"Do it now. I know your guys are doing their best to locate evidence, but they're probably destroying more than they're finding. A metal detector should be used in case there's any evidence covered by the mud. And get a forensic archaeologist to excavate the skeleton and an entomologist to examine any dead insects or larvae. It's probably too late for the entomologist, but you can never tell."

"We don't have any of those people on our staff."

"You can hire them from a university. It may save you from having egg on your face later."

Bosworth thought about it and then said slowly, "Maybe I'll do that."

"It's up to you." Joe continued down the hill toward his car parked on the gravel road below.

Another blank; it had been a long shot anyway. But he'd had to check it out. He had to check them all out. Someday he'd get lucky and find Bonnie. He had to find her. He had no choice.

BOSWORTH STARED AFTER Quinn as he walked down the hill. Not a bad guy. A little too cool and contained, but maybe that went with dealing with those scumbags in the city. Thank God, he didn't have any weirdos out here. Just good people trying to lead a good life.

The skeleton man. He hadn't told the truth. Quinn was more of a legend than a curiosity. He had once been an FBI agent but had quit the Bureau after Fraser was executed. He was now a detective with the Atlanta PD and supposedly a good cop. Tough as nails and squeaky clean. These days it was hard for city cops not to give in to temptation. That was one of the reasons Bosworth stayed in Rabun County. He never wanted to experience the cynicism and disillusionment he had seen in Quinn's face. He couldn't be forty yet, but he looked as if he had gone to hell and back.

Bosworth glanced down at the skeleton. This was the kind of thing Quinn faced on a daily basis. Hell, he even went looking for it. Well, let him have it. Bosworth would be glad to get rid of the skeleton. It wasn't fair for his people to be drawn into this nasty—

His walkie-talkie buzzed and he pressed the button. "Bosworth."

"QUINN!"

Joe looked over his shoulder at Bosworth at the top of the cliff. "What?"

"Come back up here. My deputy just radioed me that my men on the far ridge have found more bodies." He paused. "Well, skeletons."

Joe tensed. "How many?"

Bosworth's plump face had paled in the early morning light, and he looked dazed. "Eight, so far. He thinks one of them is a little kid."

THEY HAD FOUND the Talladega bodies.

Dom turned off the television set and leaned back in his chair to consider the ramifications.

As far as he knew, this was the first time any of his kills had been discovered. He had always been very careful and methodical, always going the extra mile. In this case many extra miles. Those had all been Atlanta kills and he had transported the bodies to what had been his favorite graveyard then.

Now they had been found, not through diligent search but by an accident of nature.

Or an act of God?

Any religious fanatic would say that God's hand had uncovered those bodies to bring him to justice.

He smiled. Screw all those holier-than-thou fanatics. If there was a God, he looked forward to taking him on. It might be the challenge he needed just then.

The Talladega skeletons were little threat. By the time of those murders, he had learned enough not to leave a hint of evidence. If there had been any mistakes, the rain and mud had probably erased them.

He hadn't been as careful in the early days. The thrill had been too intense, the fear too vivid. He'd even picked his victims at random to make the kill more uncertain. He was long past such foolishness. But he'd been so methodical lately that the excitement was dwindling. If the excitement went away, then so did his reason for living.

He quickly blocked the thought. He'd gone through this before. He just had to remember that the satisfaction came from the kill itself. Everything else was a plus. If he needed a challenge he'd choose someone harder, someone with ties, someone who was loved and would be missed.

As for the discovery at Talladega, he must look on it only as an interesting development, something to watch with amusement and curiosity as the law struggled to put together the pieces.

Who had been the kills at Talladega? He vaguely remembered a blond prostitute, a homeless black man, a teenager selling his body on the streets . . . and the little girl.

Funny, but until that moment he'd completely forgotten about the little girl.

Pathology Department
Atlanta
Five days later

"The child was seven or eight, female, and probably Caucasian." Ned Basil, the medical examiner, read from the report on his desk, which had come from Dr. Phil Comden, a forensic anthropologist at Georgia State. "That's all we know, Quinn."

"How long had she been in the ground?"

"Uncertain. Possibly between eight and twelve years."

"Then we have to find out more."

"Look, it's not our problem. The skeletons were found in Rabun County. The chief stretched a point to even get a forensic anthropologist to examine these bones."

"I want you to recommend facial reconstruction."

Basil had known that was coming. The moment they'd brought in the kid's skeleton, it was a given. "It's not our problem."

"I'm making it our problem. Nine bodies were found in Talladega. I'm asking for reconstruction on only one."

"Look, Chief Maxwell doesn't want to be drawn into this mess.

She'd only turn me down. She allowed you to bring the child's body here because she knew that all the missing-children groups would be on her ass if she didn't make the token effort."

"I need more than a token effort. I need to know who this child is."

"Didn't you hear me? It's not going to happen. Why don't you give up?"

"I need to know who she is."

Jesus, Quinn was relentless. Basil had run into him a few times before, and the detective had always interested him. On the surface he appeared quiet, easy, almost lazy, but Basil had always been aware of his razor-sharp intelligence and alertness. He'd heard somewhere that Quinn was an ex-SEAL, and he could believe it. "No recommendation, Quinn."

"Change your mind."

He shook his head.

"Have you ever done anything wrong, Basil?" Quinn asked softly. "Something you wouldn't want anyone to know?"

"What are you getting at?"

"If you have, I'll dig until I find it."

"Are you threatening me?"

"Yes. I'd offer you money, but I don't think you'd take it. You're pretty honest . . . as far as I know. But everyone has something to hide. I'll find it and I'll use it."

"You son of a bitch."

"Just make the recommendation, Basil."

"I haven't done anything that—"

"Lied on your income tax? Let an important report slide by because you were overworked?"

Dammit, everyone lied on their income tax form. But municipal employees could be booted out on their ass for that. How could Quinn find out about—

He'd find out. Basil's lips tightened. "I suppose you want me to recommend the forensic sculptor too?"

"Yes."

"Eve Duncan."

"You bet."

"There's no betting about it. Everyone in the department knows it's her kid you've been looking for all these years. The chief won't go for that either. Duncan's too high-profile after that political cover-up case she worked on. Reporters would be climbing all over the place if she was brought in."

"It's been over a year. That makes Eve old news. I'd work it out."

"Isn't she somewhere in the South Pacific now?"

"She'd come back."

Basil knew Eve Duncan would come back. Everyone at the Atlanta PD was familiar with her story. A young girl who had borne an illegitimate child and then fought her way out of the slums against enormous odds. She was nearly finished with college and was on her way to a decent life, when she had been struck by the cruelest blow. Her daughter, Bonnie, had been murdered by a serial killer and her body had never been found. Fraser, her killer, had been executed without revealing the location of any of the bodies of the twelve children he'd confessed to killing. Since that time Eve had dedicated herself to finding other lost children, alive and dead. She had gone back to school, gotten a degree in fine arts from Georgia State, and become a top forensic sculptor. She had qualified in age progression and superimposition, earning a superior reputation in both.

"Why are you hesitating?" Quinn asked. "You know damn well she's the best."

Basil couldn't deny that. She had helped the department out on many occasions. "She carries a hell of a lot of baggage. The media will go—"

"I said I'd take care of it. Recommend her."

"I'll think about it."

Quinn shook his head. "Now."

"The department won't pay to fly her back."

"I'll do it. Just put through the recommendation."

"You're pushing, Quinn."

"It's one of my finest talents." His lips lifted in a sardonic smile. "But you won't even feel the bruise."

He wasn't so sure. "It's a waste of my time. Chief Maxwell will never go for it."

"She'll go for it. I'll tell her that I'll release your recommendation to the press if she doesn't. It will be a question of letting Eve work on the skull in privacy or have the media asking the chief why she's not doing everything possible to solve the little girl's murder."

"She'll can your ass."

"I'll risk it."

It was clear he'd risk anything to get his way in this matter. Basil shrugged. "Okay, I'll do it. It will be a pleasure to see you kicked out on your ear."

"Good." Quinn headed for the door. "I'll be back in an hour to pick up the recommendation."

"I'm going to lunch. Make it two hours." A minor victory, but he'd take anything he could get. "You think it's the Duncan kid, don't you?"

"I don't know. Maybe."

"And you want her mother to work on the skull? You bastard. What if it is Bonnie Duncan? What the hell do you think that will do to her mother?"

The only answer was the door closing behind Quinn.

An island south of Tahiti
Three days later

He was coming.

Her heart was beating hard, fast. She was too excited. Eve Duncan drew a deep breath as she watched the helicopter settle on the tarmac. Good heavens, you'd think she was waiting for the angel Gabriel. It was only Joe.

Only? Her friend, her companion through the nightmare that had almost torn her apart, one of the anchors of her life. And she hadn't seen him in over a year. Dammit, she had a right to be excited.

The door was opening and he was getting out of the aircraft. God, he looked tired. His face was almost always without expression and, to anyone unfamiliar with it, impossible to read. But she knew that face. From a thousand different situations she had memorized every glance, every tightening of the mouth, the little secret signs that told so much. There were new deep lines graven on either side of his mouth, and his square face was a little pale.

Yet his eyes were the same.

And the smile that lit his face when he saw her . . .

"Joe . . ." She ran into his arms. Safety. Familiarity. Togetherness. All was right with the world.

He held her tightly for a minute and then pushed her back and dusted a kiss over the bridge of her nose. "You have a few freckles. Have you been using your sunscreen?"

Protective. Bossy. Caring. Two minutes, and they were back where they were when she'd left him all those months before. She grinned up at him as she adjusted her wire-rimmed glasses. "Of course, but it's hard not to get a little sun here."

He studied her up and down. "You look like a beachcomber in those shorts." He tilted his head. "And relaxed. Not totally relaxed but not wound up tight as you were the last time I saw you. Logan's been taking good care of you."

She nodded. "He's been very kind to me."

"And what else?"

"Don't be so nosy. It's none of your business."

"That means you're sleeping with him."

"I didn't say that. But what if I am?"

He shrugged. "Nothing. You were in pretty bad shape after what you went through with that last reconstruction. It's entirely natural for you to have drawn close to Logan. A billionaire who whisked you away from the media to his own island in the South Pacific? I'd be surprised if you hadn't fallen into his bed and even more surprised if he hadn't made sure you would."

"I don't fall into anyone's bed. I make a choice." She shook her head. "Now, stop picking on Logan. You always were like pit bulls with each other." She led him toward the Jeep. "And he's going to be your host while you're here, so you might as well be civil."

"Maybe."

"Joe."

He smiled. "I'll try."

She breathed a sigh of relief. "Did you see Mom before you left?"

"Yes, she sent you her best. She misses you."

Eve wrinkled her nose. "Not much. She's too involved with Ron. Did she tell you they're going to be married in a few months?"

He nodded. "How do you feel about that?"

"How do you expect me to feel? I couldn't be happier for her. Ron's a nice guy and Mom deserves a good relationship. She's had a rough life." That was an understatement. Her mother had grown up in the slums, been addicted to crack for years, and when she was fifteen had brought Eve into the same nightmare world. "It's good she has someone. She's always needed people, and I've always been too busy to give her the attention she should have."

"You did your best. You were always more like a mother than a daughter to her."

"For a long time I was too bitter to do her much good. It was only after Bonnie came that we managed to bridge the gulf." Bonnie. When her daughter had been born, she had changed everything, transformed Eve's whole world and everyone in it. "It will be better for Mom now."

"And what about you? She's all you have."

Eve started the Jeep. "I have my work." She smiled at him. "And I have you, when you're not yelling at me."

"I notice you didn't say Logan. Good."

"Were you trying to trap me? I care very much for Logan."

"But he hasn't got you sealed and delivered." Joe nodded with satisfaction. "I didn't think he could do it."

"If you don't stop talking about Logan, I'll dump you beside the road and let you hitchhike back to Tahiti."

"I'd have a tough time. No boats land on this island."

"Exactly."

"Okay. Since you have me at a disadvantage."

Yeah, sure. Joe at a disadvantage was a rare phenomenon. "How's Diane?"

"Fine." He paused. "I haven't seen much of her lately."

"A cop's wife has a hell of a life. Another rough case?"

"The roughest." He gazed out at the sea. "But I wouldn't have seen her anyway. Our divorce was final three months ago."

"What?" Shock rippled through Eve. "Why didn't you tell me?"

"There wasn't much to tell. Diane never really became accustomed to being a cop's wife. She'll be happier now."

"Why didn't Mom say anything to me?"

"I asked her not to worry you. You were supposed to be relaxing."

"Oh, God, I'm sorry, Joe." She was silent a moment. "Was it my fault?"

"How could it be your fault?"

"You were my friend, you helped me. For God's sake, I got you shot. You were almost killed. I know she was angry with me."

He didn't deny it. "It would have happened anyway. We should never have gotten married. It was a mistake." He changed the subject. "What kind of work have you been doing since you've been here?"

She looked at him in frustration. The divorce must have hurt him, and she wanted to help. But he had always edged away from talking about his marriage. Maybe she could get something out of him later. "I haven't had much work. Principally superimpositions and age progressions. A few reconstruction cases the LAPD sent me." She made a face. "I soon discovered that most agencies prefer a forensic sculptor on the same continent. I'm pretty inaccessible here. I've actually done some regular sculpting to keep myself busy."

"Satisfying?"

"In a way."

"Not a good way?"

"It feels . . . strange."

"Most people would say that working on skulls is a little strange. What does Logan say?"

"Logan thinks regular sculpting is healthy for me. He's probably right."

"Does it feel healthy?"

"No, there's something . . . missing."

"Purpose."

She was not surprised Joe understood. He understood everything about her. "It's the lost ones. I could be doing more to help the lost ones come home. Logan says I need to distance myself. He thinks I should walk away, that it's the worst possible career for me to have."

"And what do you say to him?"

"To mind his own business." She grimaced. "Just like I tell you. I wish you'd both realize I'm going to do what I want to do regardless of what either of you think."

Joe laughed. "I never had any doubt about that. I don't think Logan does either. Are you going to let me see your work? I've never seen you sculpt anything but skulls."

"Later maybe." She gave him a hard stare. "If you're decent to Logan." She turned into the driveway leading up to the large white plantation house. "He's been terrific to me. I won't have you abusing his hospitality."

"Nice house. Where do you work?"

"Logan had a lab built for me on the beach beside the house. Stop trying to change the subject. Are you going to be nice to Logan?"

"You're very defensive. As I remember, Logan can take care of himself."

"I always defend my friends."

"Just friends?" His gaze narrowed on her face. "Not lovers?"

She looked away from him. "Lovers can be friends. Stop probing, Joe."

"Does it make you uneasy? Or are you already uneasy? Is he pushing too hard?"

"No, *you're* pushing too hard." She parked in front of the house and jumped out. "Back off."

"No problem. I think I've got my answer." He took his suitcase out of the backseat. "I'll be much less abrasive once I have a shower. Do you want me to face Logan now, or do you want to show me where to lay my weary head?"

Less abrasive was definitely better. "You can join us later for dinner."

"If I'm supposed to dress for dinner, you'll have to send me to the kitchen. I brought only this one suitcase."

"Are you nuts? You know I don't live like that. I change a couple of times a day only because it's so hot here."

"You never know. You're running in fast company these days."

"Logan isn't fast company. Well, not here on the island. We live as casually as I did in Atlanta."

"Very smart of Logan."

"He works hard too. He does as much here as he did when he was in the States. He likes to relax when he gets the chance." She stopped at the front door. "Why have you come, Joe? Are you on vacation?"

"No, not exactly."

"What do you mean?"

"Well, the department does owe me a few weeks. I've worked a lot of overtime while you've been here basking in tropical bliss."

"Then why do you say you're not 'exactly' here on vacation? Why did you come, Joe?"

"To see you."

"No, why now?"

He smiled. "To bring you home, Eve."

LOGAN TURNED AWAY from the window as she came into the study. "Where is he?"

"I showed him to his room. You'll see him at dinner." She wrinkled her nose. "I know you can hardly wait."

"Bastard."

She sighed. Having to strike a balance between these two men she cared about was irritating. "I could have met him in Tahiti. You promised you'd be nice to him."

"As nice as he is to me." Logan held out his hand to her. "Come here, I need to touch you."

She moved across the room and took his hand. "Why?"

He didn't answer. "We both know why he's here. Has he talked to you yet?"

"He said only that he came to bring me home."

He cursed. "And what did you answer?"

"I didn't."

"You can't go, dammit. You'll just fall back into that dark hole where I found you."

"It wasn't so dark. I had work. I had purpose. You never understood that, Logan."

"I understand that I'm going to lose you." His hand tightened on hers. "You've been happy here, haven't you? Happy with me?"

"Yes."

"Then don't let it happen. Don't listen to that damn Pied Piper."

She stared at him helplessly. Dear heaven, she didn't want to hurt him. Tough, smart, charismatic John Logan, corporate giant and businessman extraordinaire. She'd never dreamed he'd be this vulnerable. "My staying here wasn't supposed to be a permanent arrangement."

"I want it permanent. I never intended anything else."

"You never told me."

"Because I had to walk on eggshells or you'd have run away. I'm telling you now."

She wished he hadn't. It made her decision more difficult. "We'll talk about it later."

"You've already made up your mind."

"No." She had grown accustomed to this lovely, tranquil place. She had grown used to Logan. These had been days of tenderness, affection, and peace. If she also felt restlessness, wouldn't it eventually go away? "I'm not sure."

"He's going to try to make you sure."

"I make my own decisions. He won't pressure me."

"No, he's too smart. He knows you too well. That doesn't mean he won't use everything he can to make you go back. Don't listen to him."

"I have to listen to him. He's my best friend."

"Is he?" He gently touched her cheek. "Then why is he drawing you into a world that could destroy you? How long can you deal with skulls and murder without having a breakdown?"

"Someone has to do it. I can bring closure to a lot of parents who are still searching for their children."

"Then let someone else do it. You're too close."

"Because of Bonnie? She only makes me better at what I do. She makes me work harder for those other parents who also want to bring their children home."

"It makes you a damn workaholic."

She grimaced. "Not on this island. I don't have enough to do."

"Is that the problem? We can go back to the States. We'll go to my place in Monterey."

"We'll talk about it later," she repeated.

"Okay." He kissed her hard and sweet. "I just wanted to get in my innings before Quinn. You have options. If you don't like the ones I've given you, we'll find others."

She hugged him. "I'll see you at dinner."

"Think about it, Eve."

She nodded and left the room. How could she not think about it? She cared about Logan. Did she love him? What was love? she wondered. She didn't know much about man-woman love. Eve had thought she loved Bonnie's father, but she'd been only fifteen; later she'd recognized her feelings for him as passion and a need for comfort in a rough world. She'd had a few other encounters, but they'd been unimportant, fading immediately into the shadow of her work. Logan was not unimportant, and he'd fight being overshadowed by anyone or anything. He could rouse her to passion and he was kind and caring. She would be sad if he disappeared from her life. Surely that could be love.

She didn't want to analyze anything now. After she talked to Joe would be soon enough. She'd go down to her lab and work for a while on that age-progression photo of Libby Crandall, who'd been kidnapped at age eight by her father.

Eve moved down the hallway toward the French doors that led to her lab. Sunny. Everything was sunny and bright and clean on this island. That's how Logan wanted to keep her life, always in sunlight, away from the darkness. Why not let him? Let the pain fade. Let the memory of Bonnie slip away. Let someone else help all the other children who were lost out there.

Not possible. Never. Bonnie and the lost ones were woven into the fabric of her life and her dreams. They were a big part of who she was, maybe the best part.

Logan knew her so well, it seemed impossible he'd never accepted the truth about her.

That she belonged in the darkness.

Phoenix, Arizona

Darkness.

Dom had always liked the night. Not because it was concealing but because of the excitement of the unknown. Nothing appeared the same at night, and yet for him everything became so much clearer. Wasn't there something by Saint-Exupéry about that?

Oh, yes, he remembered. . . .

When the destructive analysis of day is done, and all that is truly important becomes whole and sound again. When man reassembles his fragmentary self and grows with the calm of a tree.

He was never fragmented, but night did make him feel calm and strong. Soon the calmness would be gone, but the strength would sing through him like a thousand-voice choir.

Choir. He smiled as he realized how one thought led to another.

He straightened in the driver's seat. She was coming out of the house. He had chosen her carefully for difficulty; he was sure she would be more stimulating than his last kill. Debby Jordan, blond, thirty-one, married, mother of two. She was treasurer of the PTA, had a nice soprano voice, and belonged to the Hill Street Methodist Church choir. She was going to choir practice now.

She would never get there.

CHAPTER
TWO

JOE AND LOGAN were polite during dinner, but Eve could sense the antagonism between them.

She *hated* it. She liked everything honest and clear. Watching them was like watching two icebergs drift toward each other and never knowing when they would collide because there was so much hidden beneath the surface.

She couldn't stand it. To hell with dessert.

She jumped to her feet. "Come on, Joe. Let's go for a walk."

"I'm not invited?" Logan murmured. "How rude, and we haven't finished dinner."

"I'm finished." Joe stood up and threw down his napkin. "And, no, you're not invited."

"Oh, well, I'd only be bored. I think I've guessed what you're going to say to Eve." He leaned back in his chair. "Go ahead. Do what you came to do. I'll talk to her when she gets back."

"You wouldn't be bored." Joe strode toward the door. "Hell, you're scared shitless."

Eve hurried after him into the hall. "Dammit, did you have to say that?"

"Yes." He smiled. "It had to come out. I've been too nice all evening. It was giving me indigestion."

"You're in his house."

"That gives me a bellyache too." He headed for the French doors. "Let's go walk on the beach."

She would be glad to get out of the house too. The tension was so thick, she couldn't breathe.

She kicked off her shoes as soon as they reached the terrace and watched Joe take off his shoes and socks and roll up his pant legs. It reminded her of the last time she'd seen him on his speedboat, bare-chested, khakis rolled up to his calves, laughing over his shoulder at Eve and Diane as he weaved the boat across the lake. "Do you still have the lake cottage?"

He nodded. "But I gave the Buckhead house to Diane as part of the settlement."

"Where do you live now?"

"An apartment near the precinct." He followed her down the path toward the beach. "It's fine. I'm not there much anyway."

"I can tell." Her feet sank into the cool, soft sand. This was better. The sound of the surf was calming, and being alone with Joe was soothing too. They knew each other so well, it was almost like being by herself. Well, not really. Joe never let her forget who and what he was. It was just that they . . . meshed. "You're not taking care of yourself. You look tired."

"It's been a rough week." He fell into step with her and walked in silence for a few moments. "Did your mother tell you about Talladega?"

"What?"

"I didn't think she would. It's all over the newspapers but she wouldn't want to tell you anything that might jar you away from here."

She stiffened. "What's happened?"

"Nine skeletons were found on the bluff near the falls. One of them is a little girl. Caucasian."

"How . . . little?"

"Seven or eight."

She drew a deep breath. "How long has she been buried?"

"The first estimate is between eight and twelve years." He paused. "It may not be Bonnie, Eve. The other skeletons are adults, and as far as we know, Fraser killed only children."

"As far as we know. He wouldn't tell us anything." Her voice was uneven. "The bastard only smiled and wouldn't tell us anything. He told us he buried her and then wouldn't tell us a damn—"

"Easy." Joe took her hand and gently squeezed it. "Take it easy, Eve."

"Don't tell me to take it easy. Bonnie might have been found and you expect me to be calm about it?"

"I don't want you to get your hopes up. The kid might be older. The time she was in the ground might be longer or shorter."

"It might be her."

"It's a possibility."

She closed her eyes. Bonnie.

"And it might not."

"I could bring her home," she whispered. "I could bring my baby home."

"Eve, you're not listening. It's far from a sure thing."

"I'm listening. I know that." But she was closer than she'd come all these years. It could be Bonnie. "Can we check dental records?"

He shook his head. "No teeth in any of the skulls."

"What?"

"We think the killer pulled the teeth to prevent identification."

She flinched. Smart move. Brutal but smart. Fraser had been smart. "There's still DNA. Could you get enough samples for tests?"

"We got some from the bone marrow. The lab's processing it. But you know the results could take a while."

"What about using the same private lab we used last time?"

"Teller's not doing DNA profiling any longer. He wasn't pleased with all the publicity his lab got on the job he did for us."

"Then how long?"

"Four weeks minimum."

"No. I'd go crazy. I have to know." She drew a deep breath. "Will they let me reconstruct her face?"

"Are you sure you want to?"

"Of course I want to." Seeing Bonnie's face come to life beneath her hands . . .

"It's going to be traumatic for you."

"I don't care."

"I do," he said roughly. "I don't like to see you bleed."

"I won't bleed."

"The hell you won't. You're bleeding now."

"I have to do it, Joe."

"I know." He looked out at the sea. "That's why I came."

"Can you get them to let me do it?"

"I've already set it up."

"Thank God."

"It could be the biggest mistake I've ever made."

"No, it's the right thing, the kind thing."

"Bullshit." He started back for the house. "It's probably the single most selfish thing I've done in my life."

"What do you know about the killings?"

"I'll fill you in on the details on the plane. I have tickets for both of us on a flight tomorrow afternoon from Tahiti. Is that too soon?"

"No." Logan. She had to tell Logan. "I'll pack tonight."

"After you tell Logan."

"Yes."

"I could tell him."

"Don't be stupid. Logan deserves to hear it from me."

"Sorry. You're a little overwrought. I only meant to—"

"What a puny word. Southern belles are overwrought. Scarlett O'Hara might be overwrought. *I'm* not overwrought."

He smiled. "Well, you're better than you were a few minutes ago."

Was she? The dread of facing Logan and telling him she was leaving had superseded other emotions, but as soon as the job was done and she was alone, the pain would come flooding back.

Then face it. Let the pain come. She had faced it for years. She could face it again. She could face anything now.

She had a chance to bring Bonnie home.

Phoenix, Arizona

Dom placed the candle in Debby Jordan's hand and rolled her into the grave he'd dug for her.

He had hurt her. He'd thought he'd evolved beyond the primitive need for the victim's pain. But in the middle of the kill he'd suddenly realized he wasn't feeling enough and he'd panicked. He'd pierced and torn in a frenzy of frustration. If the pleasure of the kill disappeared, what was left for him? How could he go on living?

Smother the panic. It would be all right. He had always known this day would come, and the problem was not unsolvable. He just had to find a way to bring freshness and challenge back to the kill.

Debby Jordan was not a portent of the ultimate boredom and deadness he feared most. It didn't matter that he had hurt her.

. . .

DAMMIT, SHE HAD hurt him.

Eve gazed out at the surf gently rushing against the shore. She'd run out to the beach after she'd spoken to Logan hours ago, and she'd been sitting there ever since, trying to regain her composure.

There was already so much pain inflicted by strangers in this world; why did she have to hurt someone she cared about?

"You told him?"

She turned her head to see Joe standing a few yards away. "Yes."

"What did he say?"

"Not much. Not after I told him it might be Bonnie." She smiled sadly. "He said you'd played the one card he couldn't top."

"He's right." Joe sat down beside her. "Bonnie's always the indisputable factor in all our lives."

"Only in mine. You never knew her, Joe."

"I know her. You've told me so much about her that I feel as if she's my child."

"Really? Did I tell you how much she loved life? Every morning she'd come and jump on my bed and ask me what we were going to do, what we were going to see that day. She radiated love. I grew up choking on bitterness and poverty and I used to wonder why I was given a child like Bonnie. I didn't deserve her."

"You deserved her."

"After she came I tried to deserve her." Eve forced a smile. "I'm sorry, you're right. I shouldn't burden you with this."

"It's no burden."

"Sure it is. It should be only my albatross."

"Not possible. When you're hurting, everyone around you feels it." He picked up a handful of sand and let it slowly sift through his fingers. "Bonnie's still here. For all of us."

"You, Joe?"

"Sure, could it be any different? You and I have been together for a long time."

Since that nightmare time after Bonnie had disappeared. He had been an agent with the FBI then, younger, less cynical, capable of being shocked and horrified. He had tried to comfort her, but there had been no comfort in the world during that hideous period. Yet he had somehow managed to pull her back single-handedly from a nearly fatal depression until she could function on her own. She grimaced. "I don't know why you stick around. I'm a lousy friend. I never think about anything but my work. I'm selfish as hell or I would have known you and Diane were having trouble. Why do you put up with me?"

"I wonder sometimes." He tilted his head, as if considering. "I suppose I'm used to you. It's too much trouble to make new friends, so I guess I'll have to keep you."

"Thank God." She drew up her knees and linked her arms around them. "I hurt him, Joe."

"Logan's tough. He'll get over it. He knew you weren't going to be a sure thing when he lured you here."

"He didn't lure me here. He was trying to help."

Joe shrugged. "Maybe." He stood up and pulled her to her feet. "Come on, I'll walk you back to the house. You've been out here long enough."

"How do you know?"

"I saw you run out. I've been waiting on the terrace."

"All this time?"

He smiled. "I didn't have any other pressing engagements. I figured you needed the time alone, but now you should go to bed."

He had stood there in the darkness, silent, strong, waiting patiently until he could help her. She suddenly felt stronger herself, more optimistic. "I'm not going back to the house but you can walk me back to the lab. I have some work to do and then I have to pack."

"Do you need help?"

She shook her head. "I can manage." She headed toward the small house a hundred yards away. "I've just been putting it off."

"Second thoughts?"

"You know better." She opened the door of the lab and turned on the light. "But sad thoughts. Regretful thoughts." She moved toward the computer on the desk. "Go away. I have to finish this age progression. It's been a long time for Libby's mother. She's almost given up hope."

"Nice place." Joe's gaze was wandering around the room, from the beige couch heaped with orange and gold pillows to the framed pictures on the bookcase. "You've made it yours. Where's the sculpture you've been working on?"

She nodded at the pedestal beside the large picture window. "Your bust is a work in progress. But there's a finished one of Mom in the armoire beside the door."

"My bust?" He stared at it. "Good God, it *is* me."

"Don't be flattered. I didn't have any models, and I know your face almost as well as I do my own."

"Jesus, I can see you do." He touched the bridge of the nose. "I never realized anyone noticed that little bump. I broke it playing football."

"You should have had it taken care of at the time."

He grinned. "But then I would have been too perfect." He paused. "I'd have thought you'd do one of Bonnie."

"I tried. I couldn't do it. I just found myself staring at the clay." She adjusted her glasses and brought up the picture of Libby on the monitor. "Maybe later."

"But you think you can reconstruct the little girl's skull?"

He was being very careful not to refer to it as Bonnie's skull, she noticed. "I have to do it. I can do whatever I have to do. Go away, Joe. I have to work now."

He strolled toward the door. "Try to get some sleep."

"After I finish the progression." She pulled up the photographs of Libby's mother and maternal grandmother. Study them. Don't think about Bonnie. Don't think about Logan. Libby deserved her entire attention. She had to age the eight-year-old girl to fifteen. It wasn't going to be easy. Block everything else out.

Don't think about Bonnie.

"TOO BAD YOU don't have time to finish Joe," Bonnie said.

Eve turned over on the couch and saw Bonnie standing staring up at Joe's bust. She looked as she always did when she came to Eve: blue jeans, T-shirt, red hair a riot of curls. But she appeared smaller than usual next to the pedestal.

"I have more important work to do now."

Bonnie wrinkled her nose as she glanced at Eve over her shoulder. "Yeah, you think you've found me. I keep telling you I'm not there anymore. It's just a bunch of bones."

"Your bones?"

"How do I know? I don't remember any of that anymore. You wouldn't want me to remember."

"God, no." She paused. "But I think you know where he buried you. Why won't you tell me? I just want to bring you home."

"Because I want you to forget the way I died." Bonnie moved over to the window and gazed out at the sea. "I only want you to remember me when I was with you and how I am now."

"A dream."

"A ghost," Bonnie corrected. "Someday I'm going to convince you."

"And then they'll lock me up in the nuthouse."

Bonnie giggled. "No way. Joe wouldn't let them."

Eve smiled and nodded. "He'd cause a ruckus. I'd rather avoid the entire scenario if you don't mind."

"I don't mind. It's probably better that you don't tell anyone about me." She tilted her head. "It's kinda nice having these times all to ourselves. Like a very special secret. Remember the secrets we used to have? The time we surprised Grandma on her birthday with that trip

to Callaway Gardens. We made her get in the car and then we took off. The flowers were so pretty that spring. Have you gone there since?"

Bonnie running around Callaway Gardens, her face alight with joy and excitement . . . "No."

"Stop that." Bonnie frowned. "The flowers are still beautiful, the sky is still blue. Enjoy them."

"Yes, ma'am."

"You say it, but you don't mean it." She gazed back out at the sea. "You're glad to be leaving the island, aren't you?"

"I have a job to do."

"You'd have left the island soon anyway."

"Not necessarily. It's been very peaceful here. I like the sunlight and the tranquillity."

"And you like Logan and didn't want to hurt him."

"I did hurt him."

"He'll be sorry to see you go, but he'll be okay." She paused. "I knew Joe would come for you, but I didn't know— I don't like this, Mama."

"You've never liked the idea of me searching for you."

"No, I mean . . . I have a feeling . . . there's a darkness."

"You're afraid I won't be able to survive working on your skull."

"It's going to be bad for you, but that's not what . . ." She shrugged. "You'll go anyway. You're so stubborn." She leaned against the wall. "Go back to sleep. You have all that packing to do. You did the age progression very well, by the way."

"Thank you," she said mockingly. "Talk about self-praise."

"I can't compliment you about anything," Bonnie said plaintively. "You think you're doing it yourself."

"Since you're a dream, that's the logical conclusion." She was silent a moment. "Libby's father was supposed to be a violent man. He took her as a revenge kidnapping. Is Libby still alive? She's not with you?"

Bonnie lifted her brows. "In your dreams or the other side? You can't have it both ways, Mama."

"Forget it."

A smile illuminated Bonnie's face. "She's not here with me. You have a chance of bringing her home."

"I knew that." Eve turned over on her side and closed her eyes. "I wouldn't have done all that work if I hadn't known there was a good chance."

"A logical supposition?"

"Exactly."

"Not instinct?"

"Sorry, I hate to pop your bubble, but these dreams of you are the only foolishness I'll lay claim to." She paused. "Are you coming with me?"

"I'm always with you." A silence and then haltingly, "But it may be difficult for me to get through. The darkness . . ."

"Is that skeleton you, baby?" Eve whispered. "Please. Tell me."

"I'm not sure. I can't tell if the darkness is for you or for me. . . ."

WHEN EVE WOKE, the palest glimmer lightened the horizon. She stayed in bed for another twenty minutes, watching the dawn creep over the ocean. Strange, she didn't feel as rested as she usually did after dreaming of Bonnie. She was a little uneasy. A psychiatrist would say the dreams were a catharsis, a way of handling her loss without going insane—and he'd probably be right. The dreams had started about a year after Fraser was executed, and their effect was positive. So she'd be damned if she'd go to some shrink to try to rid herself of them. A memory of love never did anyone any harm.

She swung her legs to the floor. Time to stop brooding and get moving. She had to pack and meet Joe at the house at eight.

And say a final good-bye to Logan.

. . .

"YOU LOOK LIKE you're visiting a dying friend." Logan was coming down the stairs when she reached the hall. "Are you ready to go?"

She braced herself. "Yes."

"Where's Quinn?"

"Waiting in the Jeep. Logan, I never—"

"I know." He waved dismissively. "Come on, let's get going."

"You're coming with us?"

"Don't look so wary. Only as far as the heliport." He took her elbow and nudged her toward the door. "I won't be left here like a forlorn lover. That's bullshit. I'm hereby kicking you off my island. Don't ever come back." He smiled crookedly. "Unless it's tomorrow, or next month or next year. Come to think of it, I might accept you if you hurry back in the next decade. Otherwise, forget it."

She smiled with relief. "Thanks, Logan."

"For making it easy for you? Hell, there's no way I'd taint your memory of our time here. We were too good together." He opened the front door. "You're a special woman, Eve. I don't want to lose you. If you don't want me as a lover, I'll be your friend. It will take a little while for me to adjust, but it will happen. I'll make it happen."

She reached up and kissed his cheek. "You're already my friend. I was a mess when I came here with you. No one could have been more generous or done more for me than you during this last year."

He looked down at her and smiled. "I haven't given up, you know. I want a hell of a lot more. This is just the first stage of a sneak attack."

"You never give up. That's one of the things that's so wonderful about you."

"See, you're already appreciative of my sterling qualities. I intend to capitalize on that and move forward." He pushed her toward the Jeep, where Joe waited. "Come on, you'll miss your helicopter."

. . .

THE HELICOPTER WAS already sitting on the tarmac when Joe pulled into the heliport.

"May I speak to you a moment, Quinn?" Logan asked politely.

Joe had been expecting it. "Get on board and buckle up, Eve. I'll be right with you."

She gave them both a wary glance but didn't interfere.

When she was in the helicopter Logan asked, "It's not Bonnie, is it?"

"It could be."

"You son of a *bitch*."

Joe didn't respond.

"Do you know how much this is going to hurt her?"

"Yes."

"But you don't care. You wanted her to come back and you used Bonnie to do it."

"She wouldn't have thanked me if I hadn't told her about the skeleton."

"I could break your neck."

"I know. But it wouldn't be the intelligent thing to do. You've done a good job of making Eve grateful as well as sad. The last thing you want is for her to leave on a sour note. That would make it much more difficult to draw her back."

Logan drew a deep breath. "I'll be coming back to my office in Monterey next week."

"I thought that would be the next move."

"I'm keeping an eye on you. You won't be able to blink without me knowing it. If this reconstruction does any damage to Eve, I'll decimate you."

"Fine. Are you finished now?"

He started the Jeep. "I'm just beginning."

Joe watched him drive away. Logan was a tough bastard, but he genuinely cared about Eve. He had many qualities Joe admired—intelligence, fairness, loyalty. If things were different, if he weren't an obstacle, Joe might have liked him.

Too bad.

He was an obstacle and Joe had learned when he was in the SEALs that there were three things you could do about an obstacle. You could jump over it. You could go around it.

Or you could pound it into the ground until it didn't exist.

THE PLANE FROM Tahiti had scarcely reached optimum altitude when Eve asked Joe about Talladega. "I want to know everything." She grimaced. "And don't tell me I'm overwrought again, or I'll sock you."

"No, I believe I'll avoid that word in the future," Joe murmured.

"You said she was the only child?"

"Unless they've found more bodies while I've been gone. But I doubt it. They scoured the area pretty thoroughly."

She shuddered. Nine lives gone. Nine human beings buried in the earth and abandoned. "Have you been able to identify any of them?"

"Not yet. We don't even know if they're native to Rabun County. We're combing missing persons records statewide. Then we'll see if any of the DNA profiles on our possibles match our skeletons. It's doubtful that they were all buried at the same time. It looks like someone was using the bluff as his own private cemetery."

"Fraser," she whispered.

"Eight adults, one child," he reminded her. "Fraser confessed to killing twelve children. He never mentioned any adults, and he had nothing to lose after he was convicted."

"That doesn't mean anything. Who the hell knows what he did? He would never tell us anything that might help the parents find those children. He wanted us to suffer. He wanted the whole world to suffer."

"It's a long shot. You've got to be prepared to find out this is another killer."

"I'm prepared. No clues?"

"The rib cages of three victims showed signs the deaths were probably caused by knife wounds. We're not sure about the others. But the killer might have left a signature. There was wax residue in the right hands of all the skeletons."

"Wax? What kind of wax?"

He shrugged. "They're analyzing it."

"They should be done by now. Why are they moving so slowly?"

"Politics. The mayor doesn't want another serial killer to make Atlanta look bad and Chief Maxwell doesn't want to take the flak. The city's already had Wayne Williams and Fraser. The chief would just as soon keep this case in Rabun County. Unfortunately, Rabun doesn't have our facilities and she's having to offer limited assistance. The FBI Behavioral Science Unit is also lending a hand. They're already at Talladega to examine the site and the skeletons."

"Then how did you get permission for me to do the reconstruction?"

"Well, actually, I had to twist a few arms. The chief's afraid there'll be a media circus if they find out you've been brought in."

"God, I hope not." She had fled thousands of miles to escape the publicity, and now she was confronted with it again.

"We'll keep them away. I've set up a lab for you at the lake house."

"They'll still find us. There are always leaks."

He smiled. "I have a few ideas on how to circumvent them. Trust me."

She couldn't do anything else. She leaned back in the seat and tried to relax. It was going to be a long flight, and she had to rest to be ready for the work that lay ahead.

A child's skull to bring to life.

Bonnie?

. . .

"COME ON." JOE grabbed her arm after they'd cleared Customs. "We can't go out in the waiting area. There's a mob of reporters out there." He smiled at the red-coated customer service representative beside him. "Right, Don?"

"Enough to cause you a big problem. This way." He led them toward an emergency exit. "A skycap will bring the bags."

"Where are we going?" Eve asked as they went down a stairway.

"Employees entrance leading outside the North Terminal," Joe answered. "I thought there would be a leak and called Don to help us." Don ushered them through a long hall and out into the street in front of the terminal. "Thanks, Don."

"No problem." Don waved over the skycap who had just come out the door. "I owed you a favor, Joe."

Eve watched Don disappear back into the terminal. "Okay, now that we're away from— What are you doing?"

Joe was in the middle of the street. "Hailing your own personal cab."

A gray Oldsmobile pulled to a stop beside them. A woman was at the wheel.

"Mom?"

Sandra Duncan smiled. "I feel like an undercover agent or something. Were there reporters at Customs?"

"So I was told," Joe said as he and the skycap loaded the luggage into the trunk.

"I thought there would be when I saw the newspaper this morning."

Joe tipped the skycap. Eve jumped in the front seat and Joe got in the back. A few seconds later her mother was driving down the street toward the airport exit.

"Joe called you?" Eve asked.

"Somebody had to do it." Sandra grinned at her. "Since my own daughter didn't see fit to let me know."

"I would have called you once we were settled."

"But now I have you to myself until we get to Joe's place." She gave her an appraising glance. "You look good. You may have put on a pound or two."

"Maybe."

"And you have freckles."

"That's what Joe said."

"You should have worn your sunscreen."

"Joe said that too."

"Joe has good sense."

"You look wonderful." It was true. Her mother looked young, chic, and glowing with health and vitality. "How's Ron?"

"As good as can be expected." Her eyes were twinkling. "He says I exhaust him. I do lead him a pretty strenuous dance. But what the hell. Life's too short not to enjoy it."

"How's your job?"

"Fine."

"This is a weekday. Am I making you miss work?"

"Yep, but they were glad I didn't come in. After the story in the paper this morning, they knew reporters would be all over the courthouse if I showed up."

"I'm sorry, Mom."

"It doesn't matter. I'm the best court reporter they have, and they know it. All this uproar will die down again just like it did the last time." She glanced over her shoulder at Joe. "I'm heading up north toward your cottage. Do you want to stop anywhere?"

Joe shook his head. "No, but I want you to drive around the city a little to make sure we're not followed."

"Right." Sandra glanced at Eve, her expression sobering. "Joe says the chances aren't good, Eve. It may not be Bonnie."

"A lousy chance is better than none at all." She smiled. "And stop fretting, Mom. It's going to be okay. Whatever happens, I can handle it."

"You know I don't approve of this. You've got to let her go before you tear yourself apart. I loved Bonnie too, but I had to come to terms with reality."

What Sandra had done was come to terms with her view of reality, and it was obviously bringing her happiness. Well, more power to her. Eve ignored the tiny flicker of envy and said, "I'm not avoiding reality. I'm just trying to find my daughter and put her to rest."

Sandra sighed. "Okay, do what you have to do. Call me if I can help."

"You know I will." Sandra was frowning, so Eve reached over and affectionately squeezed her arm. "It's not going to be that bad. The reconstruction will take only a few days, and then I'll know."

Sandra grimaced. "A few days can sometimes seem like a century."

EVE DUNCAN.

Dom studied her photograph in the newspaper. Curly red-brown hair framed a face that was more fascinating than pretty. Hazel eyes gazed at the world from behind round gold-rimmed glasses. He remembered seeing this picture in the paper last year and thinking how she had changed from that desperate woman at the Fraser trial. The older Eve Duncan looked stronger, more confident. A woman whose determination could move mountains and topple governments.

And now she was turning that determination in his direction. Of course, she didn't know it was his direction. She wanted only to find her child—which made her just as vulnerable as she had been all those years before.

He had actually considered her as a kill back then but had dismissed the idea almost immediately because of the notoriety of the

Fraser trial. She had been too visible and there were enough satisfying, less risky kills.

But the satisfaction was waning.

He could correct that problem now, he thought with relief. Eve Duncan was strong enough to challenge and purge him. He would tread carefully with her, inject each moment with every possible drop of emotion, build slowly so the final explosion would be strong enough to clear away all the deadness and debris inside him.

He had a strong belief in fate and was beginning to think Eve Duncan had been put at this place and time just for him. It was lucky he had ignored temptation when she first passed through his life. Then she would have been only an ordinary kill, no more important than any other.

Now she could be his salvation.

CHAPTER THREE

"NICE." SANDRA'S GAZE traveled over the cottage and then down to the boat dock. "I like this, Joe."

"Then why didn't you come here all the times I invited you?" Joe started unloading luggage from the trunk.

"You know I'm city born and bred." Sandra drew a deep breath. "But I could tolerate this. Eve should have told me about that beautiful view of the lake."

"I did," Eve said. "You wouldn't have any of it."

"Well, it is pretty isolated. Aren't there any other houses on the lake?"

"No, Joe bought the lake and surrounding acreage and won't sell any of it."

Sandra grinned at Joe. "How unfriendly of you."

"I like privacy when I'm up here." He closed the trunk. "I get enough of people when I'm in the city. I kept the title in the name of my trust and no one knows I own this place. Not even the department." He smiled at Eve. "Except a few chosen friends."

"Well, at least the cottage looks nice and friendly," Sandra said.

Eve had always liked the A-frame. It was small and cozy and had plenty of windows that welcomed the sun and the outdoors. "Come on in and see the inside."

"I have to get back to the city. Ron worries when I don't show up for dinner."

"You could call him."

Sandra shook her head. "Hey, I'm not stupid. I don't want him getting used to eating alone. I'll call you tomorrow and we'll talk then." She gave Eve a long hug. "Welcome home, baby. I've missed you." She stepped back and looked at Joe. "Do you need a lift back to town?"

"I have a Jeep up here. I'll use that. Thanks, Sandra."

"No problem." Sandra got back in the driver's seat and started the car. "See you soon."

Eve watched the car disappear down the gravel road, then helped Joe carry the luggage up the porch steps.

"You know, I don't get it." He shook his head. "You two haven't seen each other for over a year, and she goes off to dinner with her boyfriend and it's okay with you?"

"You don't have to get it. We understand each other." No one who had not been there during her hellish childhood would be able to empathize. The scars were still there and they would never go away, but she and Sandra had built on them and forged a bond they could live with. "Mom has never had a stable relationship before. She has a right to protect it. She's really hooked, isn't she?"

"Yep." He unlocked the door. "But she doesn't appear to mind."

"No." Eve paused. "It will seem strange not to have Diane here."

"Why? You came here before I was married. Diane never really liked this place. She preferred civilization."

She glanced around and remembered how Joe's retriever had always bounded up to greet her. "Where's George? Is he in the city apartment?"

"No, Diane has him. I'm never home. He's better off with her."

"That must have been hard."

"Yeah, it was. I love that dog." He opened the door and gestured to a corner of the room.

"Good God." Video cameras, a computer, a worktable and pedestal. "Where did you get all this?"

"I raided your lab in town and brought out all the equipment the insurance company replaced after it was trashed last year. I think I got everything."

"I think you did too." She went inside. "You seem to have met all my needs."

"My goal in life," he said lightly. "I stocked the house with food too. It's chilly in here." He crossed to the fireplace and knelt before the logs. "I'll light the fire before I leave."

"You're not staying?"

He shook his head. "Reporters are looking for you. It will be hard to trace the cabin but not impossible. I have to find a way to cast out a few red herrings." He paused. "And I'm going to tell Sandra not to come up here until you've finished the job. She might be followed. If you want to catch up on everything, do it on the telephone. Okay?"

"Okay." He had mentioned everything except what was most important. "And when do I get the skull?"

"Tomorrow. It's still at Georgia State with Dr. Comden, the anthropologist who did the report. I'll get a release from the department, pick it up tomorrow morning, and bring the skull with me in the afternoon. If there's any change of plan, I'll call you." He moved toward the door. "In the meantime, try to get some sleep. You didn't doze more than an hour on the flight over."

"Okay." She added deliberately, "But first I'm going to call Logan and tell him we've arrived safely."

"He won't expect it."

"But he'll appreciate it. I'm not going to shut him out of my life just because we're not together anymore. He deserves more than that."

Joe shrugged. "I'm not going to argue with you. Just don't let him upset you. You need to rest."

"I'll rest."

"I mean it. Neither one of us knows how you're going to react when you see that kid's skull. Exhaustion won't help. I don't want you going to pieces."

"I won't go to pieces."

"Get some sleep," he repeated. The door shut behind him.

She went to the window and watched him stride around the cottage toward the garage, where he kept the Jeep. A few minutes later it appeared in the driveway and then disappeared from view down the road.

She was alone.

The sunlight suddenly seemed weaker, colder, as it touched the lake. On the far bank, pine trees cast shadows that blended and formed a dark blanket. She shivered, then moved over to the blazing fire and held out her hands. The warmth was welcome, chasing away the chill that had attacked her.

Imagination. Everything was as it was before Mom and Joe had left. Eve just wasn't accustomed to being alone any longer. On the island she had seldom been by herself. Even when she was working, Logan was never more than five minutes away.

Face it. The chill hadn't come from loneliness but from dread and nervousness. She was no more sure than Joe of how she would react to having that skull in her hands. If she would be able to close out the horror and be totally professional.

Of course she would. She owed it to Bonnie.

Or whoever the little girl might be. She mustn't think of her as Bonnie, or her hands and mind might play tricks on her. She had to view the skull with total detachment.

But when had she ever been able to do that? she wondered ruefully. Every reconstruction concerning a lost child was heart-wrenching, leaving her emotionally drained by the time she finished. But she had to control all emotion this time. It was absolutely necessary not to let herself fall into that dark pit.

Keep busy. Don't think about what awaited her. She reached for the telephone and dialed Logan's digital number. No answer. The call went to his voice mail.

"Hi, Logan, just calling to tell you that I'm at Joe's cottage. I'm fine and I'm going to get the skull tomorrow. I hope everything's well with you. Take care." She hung up.

Not being able to touch base with Logan made her feel even more isolated. That safe, sane life with Logan seemed so far away already and was growing more distant with every second.

For God's sake, snap out of it. She'd go for a walk along the lake and tire herself so that she'd sleep.

All the clothes in her suitcases were tropical, so she went into Joe's bedroom and found jeans and a flannel shirt. She put on her own tennis shoes and grabbed Joe's windbreaker. A moment later she was out the door and going down the steps.

SHE WAS ALONE.

Dom watched Eve Duncan stride briskly down the path to the lake. Her hands were in the jacket pockets and there was a faint frown on her face.

She was taller than he remembered but appeared very fragile in the oversize jacket. She wasn't fragile. He could see that in the way she moved, the set of her chin. Strength was often more of the spirit than the body. He'd had kills that should have succumbed immediately but had fought ferociously. She would be such a one.

All that subterfuge at the airport had been interesting, but he had been a stalker too long to be taken in by it. He had learned a long time ago that you had to keep one step ahead if you were going to reap your reward.

And that reward was almost in his grasp. Now that he knew Eve Duncan's whereabouts, he could put the game in play.

Georgia State University

"Good morning, Joe. Could I talk to you a minute?"

Joe stiffened as he recognized the tall man straightening away from a wall of the Science Building. "I'm not answering any questions, Mark."

Mark Grunard smiled engagingly. "I said talk, not question. Though if you really feel you need to open up and—"

"What are you doing here?"

"It wasn't difficult to figure out that you'd come here to pick up the skull. I'm only glad my fellow journalists are too busy trying to track down Eve Duncan. Now I have you all to myself."

Joe silently cursed the Atlanta PD for releasing the whereabouts of the skeleton. "The hell you do. No story, Mark."

"Do you mind if I walk you down the hall to Dr. Comden's office? I'll take off the minute we reach the lab. I have a proposition for you."

"What are you up to, Mark?"

"Something beneficial to both of us." He fell into step with Joe. "Will you listen?"

Joe studied him. Mark Grunard had always impressed him as being both honest and smart. "I'll listen."

. . .

"YOU CAME FOR the kid?" Dr. Phil Comden rose to his feet and shook Joe's hand. "Sorry I didn't have much on my report." He moved toward the door at the end of the corridor. "I read that Eve Duncan is doing the reconstruction."

"Yes."

"You know facial reconstruction won't stand up in a court of law. You should wait for the DNA."

"It's going to take too long."

"I guess so." He led Joe into the lab toward a bank of drawers similar to ones used in morgues. "You just want the skull?"

"Yes, you can return the rest of the skeleton to the Pathology Department."

"She thinks this is her kid?"

"She thinks there's a possibility."

"Bummer." He reached for the drawer handle and pulled it open. "You know when you're working on one of these kids you can't help but think about how they—shit!"

Joe pushed him aside and looked down into the drawer.

EVE ANSWERED THE phone on the first ring.

"It's gone," Joe said harshly.

"What?"

"The skeleton's gone."

She went rigid with shock. "How could that be?"

"How the hell do I know? Dr. Comden says the skeleton was in the drawer last night when he left the lab. It wasn't there at noon today."

She tried to think. "Could the Pathology Department have picked it up?"

"Dr. Comden would have had to sign the release."

"Maybe there was some foul-up and they picked it up without getting—"

"I called Basil. No one was authorized to pick up the skeleton."

She was dazed. "Someone has to—"

"I'm trying to find out where the snafu is. I just didn't want you to wait around for me to bring it to you. I'll call you when I know something."

"She's . . . lost again?"

"I'll find her." He paused. "It could be a macabre joke. You know how college kids can be."

"You think one of the students stole the skeleton?"

"That's what Dr. Comden's guessing."

She closed her eyes. "Oh, my God."

"We'll get it back, Eve. I'm questioning everyone who was near the lab last night and today."

"Okay," she said numbly.

"I'll call you when I know something," he repeated, then hung up.

Eve put down the receiver. She mustn't get upset. Joe would find the skeleton. Dr. Comden was probably right. It must be some kid who thought it hilarious to pull such a prank and—

The phone rang. Joe again?

"Hello."

"She was a pretty little girl, wasn't she?"

"What?"

"You must have been very proud of your Bonnie."

She froze. "Who is this?"

"I had trouble remembering her. There have been so many. But I should have remembered her. She was special. She fought for her life. Do you know that children very seldom struggle? They just accept. That's why I seldom choose them anymore. It's like killing a bird."

"Who is this?"

"They flutter and then go quiet. Bonnie wasn't like that."

"You lying son of a bitch," she said hoarsely. "What kind of sicko are you?"

"Not the usual kind, I assure you. Not like Fraser. Though I do have an ego, I never take credit for someone else's kills."

She felt as if she'd been punched in the stomach. "Fraser did kill my daughter."

"Did he? Then why didn't he tell you where her body was? Where all the bodies were?"

"Because he was cruel."

"Because he didn't know."

"He knew. He just wanted to make us suffer."

"That's true. But he also wanted to increase his notoriety by confessing to kills he had no business claiming. At first I was irritated, and then amused. I even spoke to him in jail. I'd left a message saying I was a newspaper reporter and he wasn't going to let that chance go by. When he called me back, I gave him a few more details to feed the police."

"He was caught in the act of killing Teddy Simes."

"I didn't say he was totally blameless. Actually, he had legitimate claim to the Simes boy and four others. But the rest were mine." He paused. "Including little Bonnie Duncan."

Eve was shaking so badly, she could scarcely hold the receiver. She had to control herself. It was a crank call. Some pervert who wanted to hurt her. She'd gotten a few similar calls during Fraser's trial. But this man sounded so calm, so sure, almost indifferent. Make him talk. Make him prove he was lying. "You said you don't like to kill children."

"I was experimenting at that point. I was trying to see if they were worthwhile pursuing on a regular basis. Bonnie almost convinced me of it, but the next two were a terrible disappointment."

"Why—are you—calling me?"

"Because we have a bond, don't we? We have Bonnie."

"You lying bastard."

"Or, rather, I have Bonnie. I'm looking at her right now. She was much prettier when I put her in the ground. It's sad that we all end up as a collection of bones."

"You're . . . looking at her?"

"I remember her walking toward me across the park at the school picnic. She was eating a strawberry ice-cream cone and her red hair was shining in the sunlight. There was so much life in her. I couldn't resist."

Darkness. Don't faint.

"You have that same spark. I can tell. Only you're so much stronger."

"I'm going to hang up now."

"Yes, you sound a bit under the weather. Shock can do that. But I'm sure you'll recover soon. I'll be in touch."

"Damn you. *Why?*"

He was silent for a moment. "Because it's necessary, Eve. After this little chat, I'm even more convinced than I was before. I need you. I can feel your emotion like a tidal wave. It's . . . exhilarating."

"I won't answer the phone."

"Yes, you will. Because there's always a chance you might get her back."

"You're lying. If you killed those other children, why did you bury only Bonnie with all those adults?"

"I'm sure I must have buried more than they found. I vaguely recall at least two other children. Let's see . . . two boys. Older than Bonnie. Ten or twelve."

"Only one child's skeleton was found."

"Then they missed the others. Tell them to try in the gorge itself. The mud slide must have washed them over."

The line went dead.

Eve slid down the wall to the floor. Cold. Ice cold.

Oh, God. Oh, God.

She had to do something. She couldn't just sit there in horror.

Joe. She could call Joe.

She dialed his digital number with a shaking hand.

"Come back," she said when he answered. "Come back."

"Eve?"

"Come—back, Joe."

"What the hell's wrong?"

There was something else she should tell him. "Talladega. Tell them—to look in the gorge—itself. Two—little boys." She hung up and leaned against the wall. Don't think about it. Wrap the numbness around you until Joe gets here.

Don't faint. Don't let out the scream building inside you.

Just wait until Joe comes.

SHE WAS STILL sitting on the floor when Joe arrived an hour later.

He was across the room in four strides, kneeling beside her. "Are you hurt?"

"No."

"Then why the hell did you scare me to death?" he said roughly. He carried her to the couch. "I nearly had a heart attack. Christ, you're cold."

"Shock. He said— I was in shock."

He was rubbing her left hand, warming it. "Who said you were in shock?"

"Phone call. I thought it was a crank. Like one of those calls I got after Bonnie—" She had to stop for a minute. "But it wasn't a crank. Did you call Talladega?"

"Yes." He took her other hand and began massaging it. "Talk to me."

"He said he had Bonnie's bones." The numbness was wearing off and she was beginning to shake. "He said she wasn't as pretty as when he—"

"Take it easy." Joe grabbed the throw from a chair and tucked it around her. He crossed to the kitchenette and began making instant coffee. "Just take deep breaths. Okay?"

"Okay." She closed her eyes. Breathe deep. Ride out the pain. Ride out the horror. In. Out. Let it go or it will rip you open.

"Open your eyes." Joe was sitting on the couch beside her. "Drink this."

Coffee. Hot. Too sweet.

He watched her drink half the cup. "Better?"

She nodded jerkily.

"Now talk to me. Slowly. Don't force it. If you have to stop, do it."

She had to stop three times before she finished. When she finally fell silent, he just sat there for a moment. "Is that all? Have you told me everything?"

"Isn't that enough?" she asked unevenly.

"Hell, yes." He nodded at the cup. "Drink the rest."

"It's cold."

"I'll get you another." He got up and strode back to the kitchenette.

"He killed Bonnie, Joe."

"It could have been a crank call."

She shook her head. "He killed her."

"You're not yourself. Give yourself some time to think it over."

"I don't need time. He knew about the ice cream."

He looked up at her. "The ice cream?"

"He said she was eating a strawberry ice-cream cone that day in the park."

"That detail has never been released to the press," Joe murmured.

"Fraser knew it. He told the police that Bonnie had been eating a strawberry ice-cream cone."

"He also described what she was wearing."

"He could have found that out by reading the papers."

"He knew about the birthmark on her back."

Eve rubbed her aching temples. Joe was right. That was why they had been so sure that Fraser had killed her. Why had she been so sure? "He said he tricked Fraser into calling him back by saying he was a newspaper reporter and then fed him details. Is that possible?"

Joe thought about it. "It's possible. Fraser was giving interviews to anyone who would listen. It drove his defense attorney crazy. And no one would have known the substance of their conversation since Georgia has a law against taping without permission. Why would they have even tried to tape it? Fraser had already confessed to the murders. It was going to be an open-and-shut case."

"None of the bodies he'd said he'd buried had been found."

"That wasn't as important to them as it was to you."

God, she knew that. It had been like beating her head against a wall to get them to keep on searching after the confession. "It should have been."

Joe nodded. "But they had enough to send Fraser to the electric chair. Open and shut."

"And the ice cream . . ."

"A lot of time has passed. The vendor might have told any number of people."

"The police told him not to discuss it."

Joe shrugged. "For some people the case was closed when Fraser was executed."

"Okay, the vendor could have told someone. But what if he didn't? What if Fraser didn't kill her?"

"Eve . . ."

"What if that bastard who called me killed her? He stole her from the lab. Why would he do that, unless he—"

"Shh." Joe brought her the fresh cup of coffee and sat down

beside her again. "I don't know the answer to any of those questions. I'm just playing devil's advocate so we can strike a sane balance."

"Why should we be sane? That son of a bitch who killed her can't be sane. You should have heard him. He loved hurting me. He kept hammering away at me until he drew blood."

"Okay, let's talk about him. What about his voice? Young? Old?"

"I couldn't tell. He sounded like he was talking from the bottom of a well."

"Mechanical distorter," Joe said. "What about phrasing? Accent? Vocabulary? Slang?"

She tried to remember. It was difficult to separate the manner from the words that had caused her so much pain. "No accent. He seemed . . . well spoken. I think he's educated." She shook her head wearily. "I don't know. I wasn't trying to analyze anything from the moment he mentioned Bonnie. I'll try to do better next time."

"If there is a next time."

"There will be. He was exhilarated. He said so. Why would he call me once and just leave it at that?" She started to take a sip of coffee, then stopped. "You have an unlisted number here. How did he get it?"

Joe shook his head. "I'm more concerned that he found you."

"Guesswork?"

"Possibly." He paused. "We have to consider that he still may be some kid at the university playing a nasty joke on you."

She shook her head.

"Okay, then there's the possibility that he was the murderer of those people at Talladega. But he didn't kill Bonnie and wants to take credit for it as he accused Fraser of doing."

"He knew about the ice cream."

"Or he's one of those people who confess to every murder and had nothing to do with any of them."

"We'll know soon enough about that one," Eve whispered. "If they find those boys at Talladega."

"They're searching now. I called Robert Spiro the minute I hung up with you."

"Who's Robert Spiro?"

"An agent with the FBI Behavioral Science Unit. He's part of the team handling Talladega. Good man."

"You know him?"

"He was at the Bureau when I was there. He moved to the Profiling Unit a year after I resigned. He'll call me if they find anything."

"No." She set down her cup and tossed the throw aside. "I need to go to Talladega."

"You need to rest."

"Bullshit. If they missed those bodies before, I'm not going to let them make the mistake again." She stood up. Jesus, her legs felt weak. They'd get better. Walk. "Can I take the Jeep?"

"If you take me with it." Joe put on his jacket. "And if you wait until I make enough coffee to fill a thermos. It's cold outside. This isn't Tahiti."

"And you're afraid I'm still in shock."

He headed for the kitchenette. "No, you're almost back to normal."

She didn't feel normal. She was still shaking inside and felt as if her every nerve was exposed and raw. Joe probably knew it and was tactfully ignoring it. She had to ignore it too. Just do one thing at a time. First, find out if that bastard had told her lies about Talladega. If he had lied about Talladega, then he could have lied about Bonnie.

But what if he was telling the truth?

THEY REACHED TALLADEGA Falls after midnight, but the searchlights and lanterns dotting the surrounding cliffs made it seem like day.

"Want to wait here?" Joe asked as he got out of the Jeep.

She was staring up at a cliff. "Is that where they found them?"

"The first skeleton was discovered on the next ridge, the rest up there. The child was found nearest the gorge." He didn't look at her. "It's just a hole in the ground. There's nothing there now."

But a little girl had been buried at that spot all these years. A little girl who might be Bonnie. "I have to see it."

"I thought you would."

"Then why did you ask if I wanted to wait here?" She got out of the car and started walking.

"My protective instinct." He turned on his flashlight and followed her. "I should know better."

"Yes." There had been a frost earlier in the evening, and the earth crunched beneath her feet. Was she walking in the footsteps of the murderer as he carried his victims to their graves?

She could hear the roar of the falls. Then, as she reached the top, she saw it pouring in a long, silver stream across the gorge. Brace yourself. Don't turn your head. Not yet.

"To your left," Joe said quietly.

She drew a deep breath and tore her gaze from the falls. She saw yellow tape and then . . . the grave.

Small. So small.

"Okay?" Joe was holding her elbow.

No, she wasn't okay. "She was buried here?"

"We think so. This is where she was found, and we're pretty certain the mud slide just uncovered her."

"She was here all along. All this time . . ."

"It may not be Bonnie."

"I know that," she said dully. "Stop reminding me, Joe."

"I have to remind you. You have to remind yourself."

The pain was too strong. Block it out. "It's beautiful here."

"Very beautiful. The sheriff says the Indians called the falls 'the place of tumbling moonlight.' "

"But he didn't bury them in this place because it's beautiful," she said shakily. "He wanted to hide them where they'd never be found and brought home to the people who loved them."

"Don't you think you've been here long enough?"

"Give me a minute more."

"Whatever you need."

"God, I hope he didn't hurt her," she whispered. "I hope it was over quickly."

"That's enough." Joe turned her away from the grave. "Sorry, I thought I could stand it, but I can't. I've got to take you away from—"

"Stop right where you are and don't move a muscle."

A tall, thin man was walking toward them along the edge of the cliff. He was holding a flashlight in one hand and a revolver in the other. "Identify yourself."

"Spiro?" Joe stepped in front of Eve. "Joe Quinn."

"What are you doing up here?" Robert Spiro demanded. "It's a good way to get shot. We've got this area staked out."

"The FBI? I thought you were here in an advisory capacity."

"We were, but we've taken over the investigation. Sheriff Bosworth didn't argue. He wanted out."

"You think the murderer is going to come back? Is that why you're staking out the graves?" Eve asked.

Spiro glanced at her. "And who are you?"

"Eve Duncan, this is Agent Robert Spiro," Joe said.

"Oh, how do you do, Ms. Duncan." Spiro shoved the gun in his underarm holster and lifted the lantern higher to look at her. "Sorry to scare you, but Quinn should have let me know you were coming."

Spiro was in his late forties with deep-set dark eyes and brown hair that sharply receded from a broad forehead. Lines bracketed both sides of his mouth, and the expression on his face was more world-weary than anything Eve had ever seen. She repeated, "You think he's going to come back? I know it's not uncommon for a serial murderer to return to the graves of his victims."

"Yeah, even the very smart ones can't resist that last thrill." He turned to Joe. "We haven't found anything yet. You're sure this is a solid tip?"

"It's solid," Joe said. "Are you stopping to wait until daylight?"

"No. Sheriff Bosworth said his men know the gorge like the backs of their hands." He looked at Eve. "It's cold near these falls. You need to get out of here."

"I'll wait until you find the boys."

He shrugged. "Suit yourself. It may be a long time." To Joe he said, "I need to talk to you about that 'solid' tip. Care to take a walk?"

"I won't leave Eve alone."

"Charlie!" Spiro called over his shoulder, and a man with a flashlight appeared. "Joe Quinn, Eve Duncan, this is Agent Charles Cather. Take Ms. Duncan to her car and stay with her until Quinn comes back, Charlie."

Charles Cather nodded. "Come with me, Ms. Duncan."

"I won't be long, Eve." Joe turned to Spiro. "If we're going to walk, let's go to the command center."

"Whatever." Spiro started back along the cliff edge.

Eve watched them. They were closing her out and she was tempted to go after them.

"Ms. Duncan?" Charles Cather said politely. "You'll be more comfortable in your car. You must be cold."

She looked down at the grave. Yes, she was cold. Cold and tired and empty. The sight of that grave had nearly torn her apart, and she needed a little time to recover. Besides, Joe would not let her be closed out for long. She started down the cliff. "Come on, I have some hot coffee in the Jeep."

. . .

"COULD I HAVE another cup?" Charlie Cather leaned back in the passenger seat. "I'm really feeling this cold. Spiro says I need to toughen up, but I tell him it's from living in South Georgia all my life."

She poured him more coffee. "Where in South Georgia?"

"Valdosta. Do you know it?"

"I've never been through there, but I've heard about the university. Have you ever gone to Pensacola? I used to take my daughter there on vacation."

"Every spring break. Nice beach."

"Yes. Where's Agent Spiro from?"

"New Jersey, I think. He doesn't talk much." He grimaced. "Well, not to me. I'm new at the Bureau, and Spiro's been there forever."

"Joe seems to respect him."

"Oh, so do I. Spiro's a great agent."

"But you don't like him?"

"I didn't say that." He hesitated. "Spiro's done profiling for nearly a decade. It does something to a man."

"What?"

"It . . . burns him out. Profilers usually socialize only with other profilers. I guess when you're a man who stares at monsters every day, it's hard to talk to someone who doesn't do that too."

"You're not a profiler?"

He shook his head. "Not yet. They just accepted me into the unit and I'm still training. I'm here to tote and fetch for Spiro." He took a sip of coffee and then said quietly, "I've seen your picture in the paper."

"Have you?"

"I'm sorry if that's your little girl they found up there."

"I've known for a long time that there was no hope. I just want to bring Bonnie home so I can lay her to rest."

He nodded. "My dad was MIA in Vietnam and they've never found the body. Even when I was a kid I used to worry about where he was. It didn't seem right that he was lost there."

"No, it doesn't." She glanced away from him. "And my daughter wasn't in a war."

"No? Seems like there are wars everywhere. You can't even send a kid to school without worrying if one of his classmates has an attack rifle. Somebody has to stop it. That's why I joined the FBI."

She smiled. "Charlie, I do believe you're one of the good guys."

He made a face. "I sounded pretty hokey, didn't I? Sorry. I know I'm green as grass compared to Spiro. Sometimes I get the feeling he thinks I'm still in kindergarten. Demoralizing as hell."

Eve could see how it would be. She supposed a person aged quickly in a job like Spiro's. "Are you married, Charlie?"

He nodded. "Last year. Martha Ann." A sudden smile illuminated his face. "She's pregnant."

"Congratulations."

"We should have been sensible and waited. But we both wanted kids. We'll make out."

"I'm sure you will." She was feeling better. Life wasn't all graves and monsters. There were people like Charlie and Martha Ann and the baby on its way. "Want some more coffee?"

"I've almost emptied your thermos. I'd better not—"

"Open the window." It was Joe, his face pressed against the fogged glass.

She rolled down the window.

"They found them," Joe said. "At least they found bones. They're bringing them up to the command center now."

She got out of the Jeep. "Children?"

"I don't know."

"Two?"

"There are two skulls."

"Intact?"

Joe nodded.

"Then I'll be able to tell. Take me there."

"Can I talk you out of it?"

She was already climbing the cliff. "Take me there."

THE STRETCHER WAS rigged on a pulley and Eve watched as it was hoisted up slowly. On the stretcher were two blanket-wrapped bundles.

"You're trying to keep the bodies separated?" she asked Spiro.

"As best as we can. I wouldn't bet on the bones not being mixed up. It looked like the mud slide washed them down."

The stretcher reached the top of the cliff and was settled on the ground. Spiro knelt beside it and opened one blanket. "What do you think?"

"Give me some more light." She knelt next to him. So many bones. Splintered. Broken. Like the bones of an animal after carnivores had—

Get a grip. Do your job. The skull.

She took it in her hands and examined it. No teeth. Joe had told her the other skulls didn't have teeth. Ignore the horrifying image of the murderer pulling them. Concentrate. "It's a child. Preteen male. Caucasian."

"You're sure?" Spiro asked.

"No. Anthropology isn't my specialty, but I'd bet on it. I've done hundreds of reconstructions on children this age." She gently put the skull down and opened the other blanket. It held fewer bones and the skull was staring up at her.

Bring me home.

Lost. So many lost ones.

"Anything wrong?" Spiro asked.

"Leave her alone, Spiro," Joe said.

Could anything be more wrong than a world that could destroy children? "No, nothing's wrong. I was just studying it." She picked up the skull. "Another male. Preteen Caucasian. Maybe a little older than the other." She put the skull down and got to her feet. "You'll have to get a forensic anthropologist to confirm." She turned to Joe. "I'm ready to leave now."

"Hallelujah."

"Wait," Spiro said. "Joe told me about the telephone call. I need to talk to you."

"Then come to my cottage to see her." Joe was already pushing Eve down the cliff. "We're out of here."

"I want to see her now."

Joe looked back over his shoulder. "Don't push it," he said softly. "I won't have it, Spiro."

Spiro hesitated and then shrugged. "I guess it can wait. God knows, I have enough to do here."

EVE SETTLED INTO the passenger seat. "You didn't have to make an issue of it. I could have talked to him."

"Yeah, I know." He stomped on the accelerator. "And you could have stayed up on that ridge, staring at those bones. Or gone back to look at that little girl's grave. How about leaping over tall buildings in a single bound? You don't need any more punishment to prove you're Superwoman."

She leaned back on the headrest. God, she felt tired. "I'm not trying to prove anything."

He was silent a moment. "I know. It would be easier if you were."

"He told me the truth. There were two other children up there. He could have been telling the truth about Bonnie."

"One truth doesn't guarantee another."

"But it makes what he told me more plausible."

Another silence. "Yes."

"And if it's true, then he's been out there all along. Walking, breathing, enjoying life. When Fraser was executed, at least I had the comfort of knowing Bonnie's murderer had been punished. But it was all a lie."

"You're jumping to conclusions."

But she had a terrible feeling she wasn't. "There were two preteen boys Fraser admitted to killing. John Devon and Billy Thompkins."

"Yes, I remember."

"We have to identify only one of them to form a link between Fraser and the caller. I want you to persuade Spiro to give me one of those skulls to reconstruct."

"There may be some red tape. The FBI has their own way of doing things."

"You know Spiro. You were in the FBI. You can get him to cut through the tape."

"I'll try."

"Do it." She smiled mirthlessly. "Or you'll find another skeleton missing. If I can't have Bonnie, I *will* have one of those boys."

"You're already thinking of her as Bonnie."

"I have to call her something."

"There was another missing girl of about the same age on Fraser's kill list."

"Doreen Parker." She closed her eyes. "Damn you, Joe."

"You want it too much. I won't have you taking that kind of fall if it's not true."

"Just get me a skull."

He muttered a frustrated curse. "I'll get it for you. Spiro should be grateful for any help on this case."

"Then let him be grateful. We're going to need him. He knows about monsters."

"So do you."

Only one monster. The one who had dominated her life since

Bonnie had disappeared. She had called the monster Fraser and now she found that might not even be its name. "I don't know enough. But I'm going to have to learn."

"You're so sure he's going to contact you again?"

"He'll call me." Eve smiled bitterly. "As he said, we have a bond."

CHAPTER FOUR

"GO TO BED," Joe said as they stepped inside the cottage. "I'll call Spiro and put in a request for a skull."

Eve glanced at her watch. It was almost four in the morning. "He won't be in a very accommodating mood if you wake him up."

"I doubt he's asleep. He doesn't sleep much when he's on a case. He's pretty driven."

"Good." She headed for her bedroom. "I believe in driven."

"Tell me something I don't know." He reached for the phone on the table. "Go on, get some rest. I'll get your skull for you."

"Thanks, Joe." She closed the door behind her and moved toward the bathroom. Shower and go to bed. Don't think of Bonnie. Don't think of those two little boys. Don't try to draw conclusions. All that could wait until she was rested and able to conquer the horror and the shock. Tomorrow when she woke she would try to put the pieces together.

"YOU LOOK LIKE hell," Joe told Eve. "Couldn't you sleep?"

"A few hours. My mind wouldn't turn off. Is Spiro going to give me a skull?"

"He wouldn't commit. He said he'd discuss it when he finished talking to you."

"He's coming here?"

"He'll be here by three this afternoon." He checked his watch. "Another thirty minutes. You have time for breakfast or lunch. Which do you want?"

"Just a sandwich." She headed for the refrigerator. "I can't seem to get warm. I borrowed another one of your flannel shirts."

"I noticed. It looks better on you." He sat down at the bar and watched her build a ham and cheese sandwich. "I don't mind sharing with you. I've become accustomed to it over the years. It's kind of comfortable."

She nodded in perfect understanding. Being with Joe was as comfortable as feeling his soft shirt against her body.

"I have something to tell you." Joe shook his head when she looked up in alarm. "It's not that bad, but you have to know."

"Know what?"

"Mark Grunard's found out where you are."

She frowned. "Mark Grunard?"

"TV journalist. He must have spent days digging into records to find this cottage. I had to make a deal. You've heard of him?"

She nodded slowly. "He's on Channel Three. Investigative reporting. I remember him from Fraser's trial." She grimaced. "As well as I can remember anyone or anything except Fraser."

"I told you I had to find a way to draw reporters away from here. I couldn't do it by myself, so I had to make a deal."

"What kind of deal?"

"Mark Grunard's spot on the six o'clock news last night was about the search for you. He showed a shot of this cottage and expressed his disappointment that this wasn't the hideaway. However, he had been given a tip about a houseboat off the coast of Florida. After the broadcast he hopped a plane to Jacksonville, and I'd bet half the reporters in the city did too."

"And what did you have to promise him?"

"An exclusive. He keeps quiet until we're ready to release. But you'll have to meet with him here a couple of times."

"When?"

"The first one fairly soon. He's already paid his first installment on the deal. He'll want something in return. Do you have an objection to Grunard?"

She tried to remember Mark Grunard more clearly. Older, graying at the temples, with Peter Jennings's warmth. "No, I guess not." She smiled. "What would you have done if I'd told you I couldn't stand him?"

"Ditched him." He grinned. "But it makes my life easier that I don't have to go back on my word. Finish your sandwich."

"I'm eating." She took another bite. "What made you choose Grunard? Do you know him well?"

"Well enough. We have an occasional drink together at Manuel's. But he really chose me. He was camped out at Georgia State yesterday morning when I went to pick up the skull and made me an offer I couldn't refuse."

"And you can trust him?"

"We don't have to trust him. As long as he thinks he's going to get a payoff, I guarantee he'll lay those red herrings all over the South."

"I guess we can't expect more than—"

A knock on the door.

"Spiro." Joe started across the room. "You should have finished your sandwich, dammit."

"Dictator." She pushed the plate away as Joe let Robert Spiro in.

He nodded politely. "Ms. Duncan." He turned to Joe. "I've been fending off the media all morning. They want to know how I knew there were two more skeletons in that gorge."

"And what did you tell them?"

"That it was profiler instinct," he said sourly. "Why not? After all we've done to debunk it, they still believe there's something spooky about our unit anyway." Spiro turned to Eve. "Is there anything you have to add to what Joe told me?"

Eve looked at Joe.

He shook his head. "I told him everything."

"Then there's nothing else," Eve said. "Except that he's going to call again."

"Maybe."

"He'll call. And I want you to be ready for him. Can you bug the phone?"

"Hasn't Joe arranged that yet?"

"I was a little busy last night," Joe said dryly. "Besides, getting my department to do the bug will require finesse, because the Atlanta PD is fighting becoming involved."

"Then they're fighting a losing battle if those two boys are who you think they are."

"Let me find out," Eve said. "Give me a skull."

Spiro was silent.

"Give it to me."

"It could be dangerous to involve you any more."

"I couldn't be more involved."

"Yes, you could be, if this man who called you is really the murderer of those people at Talladega. Right now he's looking at you as a passive victim and feeling a wonderful sense of power. That might even be enough for him. But the minute you take aggressive action, he could become angry and desperate to reassert himself."

"It won't be enough for him." She stared him in the eye. "And I won't be a passive victim. That son of a bitch has Bonn—that little girl's bones. He killed her."

"Possibly."

"Probably. He knew about those boys. Can you get enough DNA for an analysis?"

"We're trying. The bones are pretty shattered and—"

"And then there will be another delay while the samples are analyzed. Give me a skull."

Spiro raised his brows and glanced at Joe. "Obstinate."

"You don't know the half of it. Better give her a skull."

"Are you going to be responsible, Quinn? I'm not kidding about any initiative raising the ante."

"I'm the only one responsible for me," Eve said. "Give me a skull."

He smiled faintly. "I'd be tempted to do it if I didn't know what a—"

The phone rang.

Joe started toward the phone by the door.

"Wait." Spiro nodded at Eve. "Pick it up. Is there another extension?"

The phone rang again.

"Kitchen," Joe said.

Spiro ran to the kitchen, and Eve picked up the receiver at his signal. "Hello."

"Listen carefully." The voice was unmistakable. "I know you probably have this phone bugged by now, and I'm not going to stay on the line long. From now on I'll call you on your digital phone." He chuckled. "Did you enjoy your trip to Talladega? Cold night, wasn't it?"

He hung up.

She slowly hung up and turned to Spiro.

"He's using a mechanical voice distorter," Spiro said. "Is that how he sounded before?"

"Yes."

"Interesting."

"He knew about my trip to Talladega. He must have followed us."

"Or he's bluffing."

She shivered. "I don't think he's bluffing."

"Neither do I." He shrugged. "I'll give you your skull. It's not going to make any difference. He's going to play out his scenario no matter what we do."

"How can you tell?" Joe asked.

"There are two kinds of serial killers. The disorganized and the organized. A disorganized killer is spontaneous, random, and sloppy. Talladega has some of the marks of an organized killer. Bodies hidden and transported. Weapon and evidence absent. We'll probably find other signs as we go along. Your caller's being very careful not to be recognized. There's nothing sloppy about this man, which fits the usual pattern."

"What's the usual pattern?" Eve asked.

"Average to above-average intelligence, aware of police procedures and may even associate with the police. Owns a car in good condition, travels frequently, usually commits crimes out of his area of residence. He's socially adept, has verbal skills that he uses to—"

"That's enough." Eve shook her head. "You argued with me but you believed this man is the Talladega monster all along, didn't you?"

"My job is to take the supposed truth apart and look at it every way possible." He headed for the door. "When he calls again, write down everything he says the moment you hang up. Digital calls are tough to trace, but I'll arrange for a bug on the house phone. He might decide to call on that line if he can't reach you on your digital."

"How does he even know I have a digital? How will he get my number? It's private. For that matter, Joe's number here is unlisted too."

"There are ways if you're determined enough and smart enough. As I said, one of the characteristics of the organized serial killer is average to above-average intelligence. But you're right. One of the first things I'll do is run a check on the phone companies and see if there's been any detected infiltration into their computer banks." He stopped at the door. "I have a skull in my car. Come out and get it, Joe."

"And what are you going to tell Joe that you don't want me to hear?"

He hesitated and then shrugged. "That I'm sending Charlie down to guard the cottage while you're working on the skull. I have to go back to Talladega to meet with Spalding from the Child Abduction Serial Killer Unit and explain why I'm stepping on his toes by giving you a skull. CASKU might have their own forensic sculptor on tap."

"I don't need Charlie. Joe is here."

"A little more protection won't hurt. A hell of a lot more protection wouldn't be bad. I'll try to arrange it as soon as possible. One of the other marks of the organized killer is that he targets his victim." He frowned. "Though the victim is almost always a stranger. It makes me uneasy that he wants to establish an intimate link with you."

"I'm sure he's sorry to upset your profile," she said ironically. "It could be he's not going to play by your rules."

Spiro's lips tightened grimly. "You'd better hope he does. It may be our only way of catching him."

"When will Charlie be here?"

"A couple of hours. Why?"

"I want Joe to go back to Atlanta and get me photographs of those boys. I'll need to verify after I do the reconstruction."

"Joe should stay here," Spiro said. "I'll have the Bureau fax me the photographs to Talladega and I'll bring them to you myself."

"Thank you."

"Don't thank me. I should tell you to leave this place and go to the city. You're too isolated here."

"I need the isolation to work on that skull."

"And I need to get my hands on that killer." He shrugged. "So I guess I'm willing to risk your neck to get him."

"Nice," Joe said.

"Don't give me that." Spiro suddenly whirled on him. "I warned you both of the danger of working on a skull, and you wouldn't listen. Well, don't blame me for doing anything I can to get that asshole. I've just spent a week staring at those nine graves. God knows how many more he's killed. Can you guess how many serial killers are out there? We probably catch only one in thirty. The dumb ones. The ones who make mistakes. The smart ones walk away and kill and kill again. This is one of the smart ones. But this time we have a chance. I don't know why, but he's giving us a shot at him, and I'm damn well going to take it."

"Okay. Okay." Joe lifted his hands in surrender. "But don't expect me to let you use Eve as bait."

"Sorry." Spiro struggled for control. "I didn't mean to— Maybe I need a vacation."

"It wouldn't surprise me," Joe said.

"Hell, I'm in good shape. Half the profilers in my department need therapy. Just be careful. I don't like this. There's something . . ." He shook his head. "Come on and get your damned skull."

Eve crossed to the window and watched Spiro open his trunk, pull out a small cloth-wrapped bundle, and give it to Joe. He lifted his head as if feeling her gaze on him and smiled sardonically at her. He raised his hand in farewell and slammed the trunk shut.

What had Charlie said about him?

A man who stares at monsters.

She knew how close to the edge that could push you. She'd been there.

Joe came into the cottage and shut the door. "Well, you've got it. I suppose you're going to want to start right away?"

She nodded. "Put it on the pedestal. Be careful. I don't know how much damage it's already sustained."

He unwrapped the cloth and placed the skull on the pedestal.

"It's the younger boy," she said. "What's his name?"

"John Devon. *If* he is one of Fraser's vic—"

"Don't give me ifs right now, Joe. I know what you're trying to do, but it's just getting in my way." She stepped closer to the pedestal and stared at the small, fragile skull. Poor child. Lost child. "John Devon," she whispered.

Bring me home.

God, I'll try, John.

She straightened her glasses and turned to the worktable. "It's getting dark. Will you turn on the lights? I've got to start measuring."

SPIRO CAME TO the cottage the next morning shortly before noon. He waved the manila envelope in his hand. "Got the photos. Do you want to see them?"

"No." Eve wiped her hands on a towel. "I never look at the photos until I'm finished. They might influence me."

He studied the skull. "Neither of those kids looked like that. Those little sticks sticking out all over make him look like a torture victim from the Spanish Inquisition. What are they?"

"Tissue-depth markers. I measure the skull and cut each marker to the proper depth and then glue it on its specific point on the face. There are more than twenty points of the skull for which there are known tissue depths."

"Then what?"

"I take strips of plasticine and apply them between the markers and build up to all of the tissue-depth points. When that's done, I start the smoothing and filling-in process."

"It's incredible that you can come as close as you do with just measurements."

"Measurements go only so far. Then technique and instinct have to take over."

He smiled. "I'm sure they do." He turned to her. "Have you gotten any more calls?"

"No."

He glanced around the cottage. "Where's Quinn?"

"Outside somewhere."

"He shouldn't have left you alone."

"He hasn't left me alone more than five minutes in the past twenty-four hours. I told him to go take a walk."

"He shouldn't have listened to you. It's not—"

"Where's Charlie?" she interrupted. "Joe's been trying to reach him since last night. He called Talladega and was told he'd left there, but he didn't show up here."

"Sorry if you were nervous. I knew Quinn was guarding you and I had a car patrolling the area. I sent Charlie to take a report on Talladega to Quantico. He'll be here tonight."

"I was too busy to be nervous. It was Joe who was anxious. But I'd think you'd make the reports yourself."

"There are some advantages to being a senior agent. I try to avoid Quantico. I'd rather be in the field." He smiled. "And Quinn is usually more than adequate. The Bureau was very sorry to lose him." His gaze shifted back to the skull. "When will you be finished?"

"Tomorrow, maybe. I don't know."

"You look tired."

"I'm okay." She took off her glasses and rubbed her eyes. "My eyes sting a little. That's always the worst of it."

"It won't be before tomorrow?"

She looked at him in surprise. "What difference does it make? I had to persuade you to even let me do the reconstruction."

"I want to know. If it is John Devon, it will give me somewhere to start. That's more than I have now." He paused. "This is a real nasty can of worms," he muttered. "And I've got a feeling . . ."

She smiled. "One of those 'spooky' profiler instincts?"

"So I get hunches occasionally. Nothing spooky about that."

"I guess not."

He walked over to the window and gazed out. "I'm worried about this killer. Those bodies were buried years ago and he was very careful even then. What's he been doing since that time? What did he do before Talladega? How long has it gone on?"

She shook her head.

"You know, I've often wondered what killers become if they're permitted to go on for a long time. Do they change? How often can you kill before you change from monster to super monster?"

"Super monster? It sounds like something out of a comic book."

"I don't think you'll find him funny if you ever have to confront him."

"You mean a killer becomes smarter over the years."

"Smarter, more experienced, more arrogant, more determined, more calloused."

"Have you ever dealt with one of these super monsters?"

"Not that I know about." He turned to look at her. "But then, wouldn't a super monster take on the coloration of everything around him? You'd pass him on the street and never suspect him. If he'd been allowed to go on long enough, Bundy might have become a super monster. He had the fundamentals but he was too reckless."

"How can you be this clinical?"

"If you let in emotion, you're at an immediate disadvantage. The man who called you wouldn't allow himself to become emotional if it got in his way. But he'd prey on *your* every emotion. It's part of the power trip." He shook his head. "Don't let him feel your fear. He'll feed on it."

"I'm not afraid of him."

He studied her. "I believe you're telling the truth. Why aren't you afraid? You should be. Everyone's afraid to die."

She didn't answer.

"But maybe you're not," he said slowly.

"I have the same sense of self-preservation everyone does."

"I hope you do." His lips tightened. "Listen to me, don't underestimate this man. He knows too much. He could be anyone. He could be a clerk who works for the phone company or the cop who stops you for speeding or a lawyer with access to court records. Remember, he's been at this a long time."

"How could I forget?" Her gaze shifted to the skull. "I have to go back to work now."

"I guess that's my exit cue." Spiro headed for the door. "Let me know when you finish."

"I will." She had already closed him out as she began to join the markers.

JOE QUINN WAS waiting beside Spiro's car. "Come on, I want to show you something."

"I didn't think you'd go very far." Spiro followed him around the house. "You shouldn't have left her alone."

"I didn't leave her alone. I was never out of sight of the cottage." He left the driveway and moved into the shrubs. He knelt down. "See these marks? Someone was here."

"That's not a foot imprint."

"No, he cleaned the area. But the grass is bent. He tried to comb it, but he was in a hurry."

"Very good." Spiro should have known Quinn would pick up on any anomaly. He was sharp, and his SEAL training made him particularly formidable. "You think it was our man?"

"I don't know anyone else who would try to disguise his being here."

"He's watching her?"

Quinn raised his head, his gaze on the woods. "Not now. No one's out there."

"You'd sense it?" Spiro said mockingly. "ESP?"

"Something like that." He smiled crookedly. "Maybe it's my Cherokee blood. My grandfather was a half-breed."

And maybe it was that SEAL training again. Search and destroy. "You must have expected to find this or you wouldn't have gone looking."

"He was ugly to her. He wanted to hurt her. I thought he might want to see her pain." He stood up and moved back a step. "Or maybe he wanted to make sure he knew where she was. Either way, he'd come. Get a forensic team out here to see if they can collect any evidence."

"Listen, we've got our hands full at Talladega. Get your own people to do it."

"They won't do anything until they're sure they have to be involved, and they won't know that until Eve finishes the reconstruction. They won't dare not jump in at that point because of Eve's reputation."

"But until then I guess you have to rely on me. In which case, it would behoove you to ask instead of order."

"Please," Joe bit out.

Spiro smiled. "You gave in too easily. I would have had a team out here anyway."

"Bastard."

"You needed taking down a notch." He turned away. "Charlie will be here by dark. I understand you've been worried."

Joe's gaze narrowed on his face. "You wanted me to worry. When I couldn't reach Cather, I called you. When you didn't answer your digital, I phoned the command site and Sheriff Bosworth said you were too busy to take the call."

"He was right. It turned out that no aerial shots had been taken of the grave sites to determine if there's a pattern. It kept me pretty busy coordinating the photography."

"Too busy for a two-minute phone call? You wanted to make me sweat."

"Worry keeps a man sharp. You're going to need to be sharp."

"And I'm not sure Cather's the agent to guard Eve. He doesn't impress me."

"He's not standard FBI, if that's what you mean. He's not cynical and he's eager instead of methodical. I had a hell of a time getting him approved for the unit, but that doesn't mean he's not fully qualified. And a fresh eye sees things a jaded one doesn't. He'll do a good job. Besides, I've given orders for three other agents to do sentry duty and patrol the woods around the cottage. They'll report to Charlie. Satisfied?"

"Hell, no."

"No, you want a battalion."

"The fewer the guards, the more likely that maniac will come calling."

Spiro looked him directly in the eye. "That's right. I'll supply enough men to keep her safe, but I don't want to discourage him."

"You'd rather she run the risk?"

"Don't be ridiculous. She's valuable. She may be our only lead."

"Answer me."

"I have to catch this one, Quinn. I can't take a chance on him slipping away. You can laugh, but after these days at Talladega, staring at those graves, I sometimes feel—" He stopped and then shrugged. "He's mine."

"And Eve?"

"She's only one woman. There's no telling how many more people he'll kill if we don't get him now."

"You bastard."

"Yes, but if you want that killer, I'm your best bet. I'll keep on going until I have him." He started to walk away but stopped. "You know, I don't like Eve Duncan's attitude."

"Too bad. She's working her butt off to get an identification on that skull."

"No, that's not what I—" A frown creased Spiro's forehead. "She's not afraid of him. He's not going to like that. It will make him angry and more determined to break her. If he can't reach her, he'll try for someone close to her."

"I twisted a few arms over the phone last night and got a twenty-four-hour guard on her mother."

"Good."

"But I didn't tell Eve and I'm not going to tell her about anyone watching the cottage. So make sure your forensic guys don't plod around here like elephants. She's working so hard, I doubt she'd notice if they did, but she's got enough to worry about."

"You're very protective."

"You'd better believe it. You might think about that, Spiro. Because if that asshole gets to her and it's your fault, she won't be the only victim."

CHARLIE CATHER ARRIVED at the cottage four hours later. "Sorry to be late." He grimaced. "I meant to get here an hour ago, but I got a late start from Quantico. I hoped I'd get the analysis before I left, but they hadn't finished."

Eve glanced up from the skull. "What analysis?"

"From VICAP. Violent Criminal Apprehension Program. It's a nationwide database that allows us to type in all the facts of a violent crime and then does a search for similar modi operandi on reported crimes during a given period."

"I didn't know Spiro had authorized one," Joe said.

"Oh, he did, and we've been giving VICAP the reports on the bodies to narrow their search. They've been waiting for the last report, but it got lost in a damn paper shuffle. I found it only right before I left Talladega, so I took it myself to Quantico."

"And what given period did you tell the computer?" Eve asked.

"Thirty years. Just to be safe."

She stared at him, stunned. Thirty years?

Charlie turned to Joe. "I told them to call me here with the results. I'll be outside in my car. Will you tell me when it comes?"

"Why not wait here?" Eve asked.

Charlie shook his head. "Spiro told me to be on guard duty outside. He wouldn't appreciate having me warming my tush inside." He grinned. "I could have told them to call me on my digital, but I thought it wouldn't hurt to use the phone call to get me inside to defrost." He walked over to the pedestal. "You've made a lot of progress, haven't you? How much longer?"

She shrugged. "It depends on how it goes."

"They do a lot of computer imaging and stuff at Quantico, but this is kind of . . . personal."

"Yes."

"He looks so fragile. Poor little kid. God, it makes me sad. I don't know how you take it."

"The same way you stand what you do. It's my job."

"It makes you scared to bring a kid into this world, doesn't it? You know, some of the guys at the unit won't let their kids out of their sight. They've seen too much of what goes on to ever feel safe. I'll probably feel the same way after my baby is—"

"I'll let you know when you get your call," Joe interrupted. "Eve has to get back to work now."

The dismissal was pointed. Charlie's words had been thoughtless and Joe was stepping between her and possible hurt, Eve realized.

"Yeah, sure." Charlie headed out the door. "I'd appreciate it. See you later."

"You didn't have to toss him out," Eve told Joe. "He didn't mean any harm."

"He talks too much."

"He's just young. I like him." She turned back to the pedestal. "They probably won't find anything through the VICAP search. They haven't caught the bastard in over ten years."

"Then it's time they did."

Joe sat on the couch and picked up his book. "I'll give you another hour and then you stop to eat. No arguments."

"We'll see."

"No arguments."

She glanced at him. He was giving off the aura of the quintessential immovable object.

What the hell. An immovable object could be very comforting in this volatile world. "Okay. No arguments."

LOGAN CALLED WHILE Eve was at dinner. "I got your two messages. I was running around the island, closing up shop. I'm flying out to Monterey tomorrow."

"You didn't tell me you were leaving the island."

"It's not the same now. Time to get back to the real world." He paused. "Are you working on the skull?"

"Not the little girl. A boy we found."

"You said you were going to work on— Why the hell are you still there?"

"Things happened."

"You're not telling me everything. Hell, you're not telling me anything."

She knew darn well if she told him what had been happening he would be on his way immediately. "I'm going to get the little girl's skull. I have to work on this one first."

Silence.

"I don't like it. There's too much you're not saying. I'm going to fly out to Monterey tonight instead of tomorrow. I'll call you as soon as I arrive."

"Logan, it's wonderful of you to want to help, but you can't do anything this time."

"We'll see." He hung up.

"He's coming here?" Joe asked.

"Not if I can help it. I don't want him near that killer."

He frowned. "You're being a little more protective than I'd like."

"Too bad. Logan's a great guy and my friend. You feel protective toward your friends." She deliberately met his gaze. "Don't you, Joe?"

He grimaced. "Okay, you got me." He changed the subject. "Want some dessert? We've got Rocky Road ice cream."

ANOTHER CALL CAME on Eve's digital phone at eight that evening.

Eve tensed. Her phone, not the cottage phone. It could be her mother. It could be Logan again. It didn't have to be that monster.

Joe picked up her phone, which she'd laid on the coffee table after she'd talked to Logan. "Do you want me to answer?"

She shook her head. "Give it to me." She punched the button. "Hello."

"Bonnie's waiting for you to come and get her."

Her hand tightened on the phone. "Bullshit."

"After all these years of searching for her, you've come so close. It's a pity you're going to fail now. Have you finished with the boy's skull yet?"

"How do you know I'm doing—"

"Oh, I'm keeping close watch over you. After all, I do have a vested interest. Haven't you sensed me standing behind you, looking over your shoulder as you work on the skull?"

"No."

"You should. You will. Which boy is it?"

"Why should I tell you?"

"It doesn't really matter. I only vaguely remember them. They were just two of those frightened little birds. Not like your Bonnie. She was never—"

"You bastard. You probably don't have the guts to kill anyone. You creep around, making anonymous phone calls, threatening and trying to—"

"Anonymous? Is that annoying you? You can call me Dom if you like. But what's in a name? A rose by any other name would smell as—"

"The only thing that annoys me is that you think you can terrify me with these pitiful tricks."

"And now you're trying to annoy me." He laughed in delight. "And I believe you're succeeding. How refreshing. It only proves how right I was to choose you."

"Did you harass those other poor people at Talladega before you killed them?"

"No, that would have been reckless, and I wasn't at that point yet."

"But you are now?"

"I'm at the point where I'm willing to take a few chances to make life interesting. It was bound to happen sometime."

"Why me?"

"Because I need something to cleanse me. The moment I saw your photograph in the paper I knew you were the one. I looked at your face and I could see all the emotion and torment that's building inside you. It's only a question of making that emotion soar until it breaks through." He paused. "Can you imagine what an explosion that will be for both of us?"

"You're insane."

"Quite possibly. By your standards. Science has made such a study of the mind of the murderer. The causes, the early signs, the way we justify killing."

"How do you justify it?"

"I don't. Pleasure is justification enough. I recently heard that recreational homicide went up twenty-five percent in the last ten years. I started long before that. It seems that society is finally catching up to me, doesn't it? Maybe you're all going mad too, Eve."

"Bullshit."

"Then why let me go on killing? Have you ever considered that perhaps we've never really lost our cave instincts? The bloodlust, the search for power through that final act of violence. Perhaps in your heart of hearts you all wish you could be like me. Haven't you ever wanted to hunt, to prey?"

"No."

"You will. Ask Quinn how it feels. He's a hunter. He has the instinct. Ask him if his heart beats faster when he nears the kill."

"Joe's not like you. No one is like you."

"Thank you. I regard that as a compliment. I believe it's time to hang up now. I just wanted to touch base with you. It's important that we get to know each other. You're not one to fear the unknown."

"I'm not afraid of you."

"You will be. But it's clear I'll have to work at it a little harder. No problem. I wouldn't have it any other way." He paused. "Bonnie misses you. You should really be together." He hung up.

Pain tore through her. Damn him. He'd had to throw that last jab. She pressed the off button and looked at Joe. "He just wanted to touch base with me. The bastard wants me to be afraid of him."

"Then pretend to be afraid. Don't challenge him."

"Screw that."

Joe smiled faintly. "I thought I'd try. Did you find out anything we can use?"

"He said his name is Dom. He's been killing for more than ten years and does it purely for pleasure. He's analytical about himself and the world in general. He's as smart as we thought he was." She turned back to the pedestal. "Will you write all that down and call it in to Spiro? I have to get back to work."

"It wouldn't hurt for you to take a break."

"Yes, it would," she said fiercely. "I won't let that bastard disturb my concentration. He wants to control me, and I'll be damned if I let him. I won't give him anything he wants."

She stood before the skull. Her hands were shaking a little. Steady them. It was time for the final stage. Nothing must interfere with the sculpting. She had to be cool and detached.

Haven't you sensed me standing behind you, looking over your shoulder as you work on the skull?

She restrained the impulse to turn her head. No one was staring at her back or over her shoulder. No one was behind her but Joe.

If she let Dom influence her by sparking her imagination, then it would be a victory for him. Close him out. Think of the little boy, not of the monster who had killed him.

Bring him home.

With slow, certain strokes she began to mold the child's face.

SHE WAS STRONGER than Dom had thought.

A surge of excitement tingled through him. She was going to

stretch him, make him work for every ounce of emotion he drew from her.

It was no real surprise. He had been prepared for it. He welcomed it. It would force him to dig deep to find a way to jar her.

He already had an idea how to do it.

He started the car, backed out of the convenience store parking lot, and headed back to Atlanta.

CHAPTER FIVE

5:40 A.M.

FINISHED. EXCEPT FOR the eyes.

She reached for her eye case on the worktable.

Brown was the most prevalent eye color, and she almost always used brown eyes when reconstructing. She placed the glass eyeballs in the sockets and stepped back.

Is it you, John Devon? Did I do a good enough job to bring you home?

"Do you want the photo now?" Joe asked quietly.

She'd been vaguely aware that he'd been sitting on the couch all through the night, waiting. "Yes."

He stood up and opened the large envelope on the coffee table. He discarded one photo and carried the other to her. "I think this is the one you want."

She stared at the photo without touching it. He was wrong, she didn't want it.

Take it. Bring him home.

She reached out and took the photo. She should have put in blue eyes, she realized dully. Everything else was a match. "It's him. It's John Devon."

"Yes." He took the photo and tossed it on the workbench. "I'll call Spiro right after I get you to bed."

"*I'll* call him."

"Shut up." He was pulling her across the room and down the hall. "I said I'd do it. You've done your part."

Yes, she'd done her part. John Devon had been found and that meant—

"Stop thinking," Joe said roughly as he pushed her down on the bed. "I knew it would start eating at you the minute you finished. But, dammit, you've got to rest now." He disappeared into the bathroom and came back with a damp washcloth. He sat down beside her and began wiping the clay from her hands.

"I should take a shower."

"When you wake up." He tossed the washcloth on the nightstand, made her lie down, and covered her with a quilt.

"I was afraid it was going to be him," she whispered. "Half of me wanted it to be John Devon, but I was afraid too."

"I know." He turned out the bathroom light, sat down beside her, and took both her hands in his. "But you wouldn't give up, would you?"

"I couldn't. You know I couldn't."

The slight tightening of his grasp was his only answer.

"Since it was John Devon, that means that monster might have been telling the truth. Fraser might not have killed Bonnie."

"He could still have been the one who killed her. Because Dom killed one of the children Fraser confessed to murdering doesn't mean he killed all of them."

"But the chances are better now that Dom killed her."

"I don't know, Eve," he said wearily. "I just don't know."

"And he might still have her. That little girl could be my Bonnie. It wasn't enough that he killed her; he's keeping her like some kind of trophy."

"He's keeping her as bait."

"I hate the idea of that monster with her. I *hate* it."

"Shh. Don't think about it."

"And how am I supposed to stop?"

"Hell, how do I know? Just do it." He paused. "This is what he wants from you. Control. Wouldn't he love the idea of you lying here suffering because of something he'd done? Go to sleep and cheat the son of a bitch."

He was right, she was doing exactly what Dom wanted her to do. "I'm sorry. I didn't mean to fall apart. I must be tired."

"Now, I wonder why?"

"I'm confused. It's difficult not to— I wanted to bring her home but not like—"

"Face it after you've slept for a while."

"You have to call Spiro."

"It will wait. I'll stay here until you go to sleep."

"You haven't slept either."

"How do you know? I doubt you were aware I was on the planet while you were working on that boy."

"That's not true."

"Isn't it?"

"I always know you're there. It's like—" It was hard to explain. "It's like having an old oak tree in your garden. Even if you don't pay attention to it, you never really forget it's there."

"I believe I've been insulted. A tree? Are you trying to call me a knothead?"

No, if he was like a tree, it was because he gave shelter and strength and endurance. "Smart man. I should have known I couldn't fool you."

"And I'm not *that* old."

"Old enough." She was smiling, she realized. A moment before she had been in pain, but she felt better now. Joe always made it better. "I'm okay. You don't have to stay with me."

"I'll stick around. You've got to be hysterical if you're calling me an oak tree. The only way you'll get rid of me is by going to sleep."

She was already getting drowsy. It was safe to let everything go for now. Joe was there, holding back the darkness. "This reminds me of when we were on Cumberland Island after Fraser was executed. Remember? You held my hands like this and made me talk and talk. . . ."

"Now I'm trying to shut you up. Go to sleep."

She was silent a moment. "He's beginning to scare me, Joe."

"There's nothing to be scared about. I won't let anything happen to you."

"I didn't think I'd be afraid. I was only angry at first, but he's smart, and killing me isn't his main priority. He has to make me feel . . . he has to hurt me. He needs it."

"Yes."

A sudden thought exploded through her. "Mom."

"She's under guard. I made sure he can't touch her."

Relief surged through her. "You did?"

"It was the logical move. Not bad for a knothead."

"Not too bad." If Mom was safe, a prime weapon was taken away from Dom. He couldn't hurt Eve through someone she loved.

The hell he couldn't. He still had Bonnie.

But Bonnie was dead. Eve might be sick with horror at the thought of him having Bonnie, but he could no longer hurt her daughter. Eve was the only one who could be hurt, and she would hide that hurt from him.

"It's okay. I told you, your mom's safe," Joe said. "There's no reason to be uneasy."

She *was* uneasy. Trust Joe to sense it. Not about her mother. If Joe said she was safe, she was safe. She was just . . .

Forget about it. Go to sleep and when she woke they would find a way to catch the bastard and bring Bonnie home. He wasn't invincible. He had made a mistake when he contacted Eve. There wasn't any way he could really hurt her.

She had no reason to be uneasy.

HER NAME WAS Jane MacGuire and she was ten years old.

Dom had seen her a few days before when he was cruising the public housing developments on the south side. He had first been attracted by her red hair and then by her air of independence and defiance. She walked down the street as if daring the world to get in her way. No docile little bird here.

Too defiant to appeal to Eve Duncan? Her own daughter had been completely different. But then, Bonnie Duncan had not been brought up in four foster homes like Jane MacGuire. She'd had no need to learn to be streetwise.

He cruised slowly behind the kid. She was going somewhere. She had a purpose.

She suddenly darted into an alley. Should he go after her and risk having her see him? The danger wasn't that great. As usual when he was on the hunt, he'd taken the precaution of a disguise.

He parked the car and got out. She was too good a prospect. He had to make sure.

SON OF A bitch. The creep was following her again.

Well, let him, Jane thought crossly. He was just another dirty old man like the ones who hung out at the school yard and drove away fast if Jane screamed for the teacher. She knew this alley and could run faster than him if she needed to get away. She had noticed him following her yesterday and kept to the public streets.

She couldn't do that today.

"I'm here, Jane."

She saw Mike crouched inside a big cardboard box against the brick wall. He looked cold. He'd probably slept in the box last night. He usually did when his father came home. Bad luck the bastard had decided to wander back in January, when it was so cold.

She reached into a jacket pocket and handed him the sandwich she'd stolen from Fay's refrigerator that morning. "Breakfast. It's pretty stale. I couldn't get anything else."

She watched him gobble down the food, then shot a glance behind her.

The creep had ducked into the shadows of a garbage dump. Good place for him.

"Come on. Time to go to school," she told Mike.

"I ain't going."

"Sure you are. You want to grow up stupid like your father?"

"I ain't going."

She played her trump card. "It's warm there."

Mike thought about it and then got to his feet. "Maybe I'll go just today."

She'd thought he would. The cold and an empty belly were enemies. She'd spent a lot of nights in alleys herself when she'd been staying with the Carbonis. That was the foster home before Fay's and it was there she'd learned that if she caused enough trouble, not even the welfare money would make foster parents keep her. Welfare was always ready to give them another kid if one didn't work out.

Fay was much better. She was always tired and often crabby, but sometimes Jane thought she might grow to like her . . . if she stayed long enough.

She glanced back at the creep. Still hiding behind the dump. "I think maybe you should find another place to sleep tonight. There's a place near the Union Mission. I'll show you."

"Okay. You goin' to school now?" Mike asked. "Maybe I could walk along with you."

He was lonely. He was only six and hadn't learned how to ignore the emptiness yet. "Sure. Why not?"

She smiled at him.

DOM HADN'T BEEN sure until he'd seen her smile.

The smile was warm and sweet. All the more appealing because of the kid's usual air of wariness and toughness. Without that streak of softness he wouldn't have been sure. But now he was convinced.

Little Jane MacGuire was perfect.

"YOU'RE SURE HE'S the Devon boy?" Spiro asked when Joe opened the door later that afternoon.

"It's close enough." Joe gestured to the pedestal. "The picture's on the worktable. See for yourself."

"I'll do that." He crossed the room. "Where's Ms. Duncan?"

"Still sleeping."

"Wake her up. I need to talk to her."

"Screw you. She's exhausted. Talk to me."

"I have to—" He gave a low whistle as he compared the reconstruction with the photo. "Damn, she's good."

"Yes."

He tossed the photo back on the worktable. "I almost wish it wasn't him. You realize what this means?"

"Yes, and so does Eve."

"I'm going to have to use her, Quinn."

"No one uses Eve."

"Unless she wants to be used," Eve said from the doorway. She came toward them. She'd obviously just gotten out of bed; her hair was tousled, her clothing rumpled. "And the fact that he's John Devon doesn't make that much difference to you, Spiro. You would have tried to use me anyway."

Spiro glanced back at the skull. "He could be telling the truth about Fraser taking credit for his kills."

"Some of his kills," Joe corrected Spiro. "All we have are the two boys."

"Aren't they enough?" Spiro turned to Eve. "Are you going to help me?"

"No, I'm going to help *me*. You and Joe keep my mom safe and I'll let you use me as bait."

"The hell you will," Joe said.

She ignored him and asked Spiro, "He's been watching me, hasn't he?"

"Quinn told you?"

"No, but Dom knew about our trip to Talladega." She glanced at Joe. "What else?"

"Someone's been keeping an eye on the cottage. I had Spiro send a forensic team yesterday to go through the bushes where he'd been standing, watching."

"Thanks for telling me."

"I'm telling you now. You were a little busy before." He smiled. "I don't think he'll be back with Charlie and those other guards patrolling outside and me inside."

"Don't be too sure. He's bored or he wouldn't have taken these many chances."

His smile faded. "You think he's that unbalanced?"

"I believe he's desperate for some reason. But I don't think he'll try to kill me yet. Not until he gets what he wants."

"And when he does, we'll be here," Spiro said.

"Will you?" she said wearily. "Why would he attack if he knows there's a chance he'll be caught? If he's as smart as you believe, he'd find a way to get to me and elude you. Did your team find any evidence in the stuff they collected yesterday?"

"We're still sifting through—" Spiro shook his head. "We don't think so."

She shrugged. "I rest my case."

"And what do you suggest?"

"That we go after him, not wait for him to come after me."

"It's much safer for you to—"

A knock on the door.

Charlie smiled apologetically. "Sorry to bother you, but I wondered if my call had come through. It's taken a lot longer than I thought it would."

"No call," Joe said.

"Why not ask me?" Spiro said dryly. "Did it occur to you that as your superior, I'm the one they would contact?"

Charlie eyed him warily. "Did they?"

"Last night. They're faxing the full report to me at Talladega. They were surprised I knew nothing about your request that they call you directly."

Charlie grimaced. "Sorry. I guess I was being a hot dog."

"Well, eagerness is better than apathy."

"Did they find any cases that matched?" Joe asked.

"Two possibles. Two skeletons were found three months ago in San Luz, a suburb of Phoenix. No teeth. Wax sediment in the right hands."

"Children?" Eve asked.

Spiro shook his head. "Adults. One man. One woman."

"Arizona," Joe repeated. "That's a long way."

"Who says Dom is a local boy?" Spiro said.

"He was here ten years ago," Eve said. "He's here now."

"It's a mobile society, and organized serial killers are known to be particularly mobile." Spiro turned toward the door. "At any rate, I'll send a man to Phoenix to see if he can find out anything more from the local PD. We'll probably have to organize an interstate task force now."

"Could I go?" Charlie asked.

"No, you may not," Spiro said. "You stay here and guard Ms. Duncan. I don't want you out of sight of the cabin, and you make sure those other perimeter guards are on their toes."

"Eve," she said dryly. "Formality is pretty silly under the circumstances."

"Eve." Spiro smiled. "I suppose you're right. We all may become more intimate than we'd like before this is over. Good-bye. I'll let you know if I find out anything else." He paused at the door. "Stay inside, Eve. I evidently have more faith in my guys and your friend Quinn than you do."

As soon as the door closed behind Spiro, Charlie grinned. "I'd better get outside. I could see Spiro wasn't pleased with me for going over his head. It will take a little groveling and strict obedience for me to redeem myself."

She smiled back, then returned to her bedroom to shower.

Phoenix, Arizona. Two bodies.

Eleven at Talladega. Two in Phoenix. How many more had Dom killed? How could a man murder that many people and remain human?

Was he human? How much evil could he commit without his soul becoming twisted and—

She was cold and starting to shake. Stop it. It didn't matter what manner of monster Dom had become. All that was important was that they catch him and keep him from murdering again.

The hot water poured out of the showerhead onto her body.

But it didn't banish the chill.

• • •

"FOR HEAVEN'S SAKE, stop prowling, Joe," Eve said. "It's after midnight. Why don't you go to bed?"

"You go to bed. I'm a little tense, okay?"

"You don't have to bite my head off."

"Yes, I do. It's one of the few things that I'm allowed. There's damn few of them that I can—" He stopped. "Sorry. Maybe I'm getting cabin fever waiting for something to happen."

So was she, and she didn't feel like being sweet and generous about Joe's nerves. "If you won't go to bed, make yourself useful and go out and give Charlie a cup of coffee."

"Maybe I will."

She drew a deep breath as the front door shut behind him a few minutes later. She had never seen Joe this explosive. Ever since that afternoon he'd been—

Her phone rang.

"Did I wake you?" Dom asked.

Her heart was pounding. "No, I wasn't asleep."

"Oh, yes, you must have slept after you finished working on little Johnny Devon. It was him, wasn't it?"

"I told you I wouldn't tell you anything."

"Defiant. That means I guessed right. I knew you'd do a fine job. You take great pride in your work."

"Why are you calling me?"

"It's important that I stay in touch with you, that we get to know each other better. I'm sure that's what Agent Spiro told you. Draw the bastard out. Find out everything you can for the FBI profile. Isn't that right?"

"Something like that."

"I'll cooperate. But you have to give me something too. I want a profile on you, Eve."

"You already seem to know a great deal about me."

"Not enough. For instance, do you believe in reincarnation?"

"What?"

"Reincarnation. Millions of people do, you know. Such a comforting belief." He chuckled. "As long as you don't come back as a cockroach."

"What are you talking about?"

"But I don't think God would let your Bonnie come back as a cockroach, do you?"

"Shut up."

"That hurt, didn't it? I could almost feel it myself. Pretty little Bonnie . . ."

It *had* hurt. The bizarre idea had stabbed her. Stupid to let him hurt her. Even stupider to let him know he'd hurt her. "It didn't bother me. Why should it? I don't believe in reincarnation."

"You should consider it. As I said, it could be very comforting. I've been thinking a lot about it lately. Are you familiar with the Bible?"

"Some."

"It's not my favorite tome, but there are some unique ideas in it. I found one particularly amusing. Genesis 2:22."

"I don't know what that is."

"I'll tell you. But first go to the front door and get my present."

"Present?"

"It's on the left edge of the porch. I couldn't just come up to the front door and leave it with that FBI agent watching you so closely."

She moistened her lips. "What kind of present?"

"Go get it, Eve. I'll hang on."

"I'd be dumb to go outside just because you tell me to. You could be waiting for me."

"You know better. You know I'm not going to hurt you yet." He paused. "But I won't promise not to hurt Quinn if you call him. This is just between us. Go get the present."

She moved toward the door.

"Are you doing it?"

"Yes."

"Good. Now, let's see. They say that the souls of victims of violence are troubled and return to earth as soon as possible. So Bonnie would have been reincarnated immediately."

"Bull."

"I killed her ten years ago, didn't I? That means we're looking for a ten-year-old child. Either a boy or a girl." He chuckled. "Since we've ruled out cockroaches. Are you at the front door yet?"

"Yes."

"Check the window and you'll probably see your stalwart guard sitting in his car by the lake. That's where he was when I left your package a few hours ago."

She glanced out the window. Charlie wasn't in the car, he was standing by the front fender, talking to Joe.

"Are you on the porch yet?"

"No."

"Are you afraid of me, Eve? Don't you want to know what's in the package?"

"I'm not afraid of you." She opened the door. She was wearing only an old T-shirt, and the cold wind struck her bare legs. "I'm on the porch. Where's the damn package?"

"You'll see it."

She did see it, a small brown cardboard box on the very left edge of the porch.

"Quinn would say you're foolish to go near it. It might be a bomb or maybe I put some kind of gas or poison in the box. But you know I don't want you injured or dead."

She did know it. She moved toward the box.

"Or maybe I do. I could be waiting in the shadow of the porch right now. Do you see any suspicious shadows, Eve?"

"No, where are you?"

"But it's so dark on the porch you can't see shadows, can you?"

She stopped in front of the box.

"Eve?" Joe had turned away from Charlie and had seen her.

"Or I might be in my car, miles away. Which do you think is true?"

She knelt beside the box.

"Eve!"

She opened the box.

Something hard and white gleamed inside.

Dom's voice was soft in her ear. " 'And the rib, which the Lord God had taken from the man, made he a woman, and brought her unto the man.' Genesis 2:22."

"What the hell are you doing?" Joe was beside her, trying to draw her away from the box.

She shoved him. "Leave me alone."

"God and I have a lot in common. If you believe in reincarnation, then by killing your Bonnie I, like God, created a brand-new human being. Though I didn't actually create her from Bonnie's rib, I thought you'd appreciate the symbolism." He paused. "By the way, her name is Jane." He hung up.

The phone dropped from her hand. She stared down into the box.

"Don't touch it," Joe said.

"I'll call Spiro and get a team down here to check it out." Charlie ran down the steps toward his car.

"Dom?" Joe asked.

She nodded.

"Did he tell you what this is?"

She nodded again.

So small . . .

She reached down and touched it with one finger. Smooth . . .

Tears began to run down her cheeks.

"Eve."

"It's Bonnie. It's Bonnie's rib."

"*Shit.*" Joe picked her up and carried her inside. "Son of a bitch. Bastard."

"Bonnie."

"Shh." He sat down on the couch and rocked her. "Dammit, why didn't you call me?"

"Bonnie's rib."

"It could be an animal bone. He could have lied to you."

She shook her head. "Bonnie."

"Listen to me. He wanted to hurt you."

And he had succeeded. God, how he had succeeded. Pain was searing through her. She had told herself only last night that he had no real weapon against her, that she could control— Dammit, she couldn't stop crying.

And she couldn't stop thinking of that little fragment of Bonnie in that box.

"Go bring it in."

"What?"

"It's . . . cold out there."

"Eve," Joe said gently. "It's evidence. We can't move—"

"Do you think he'd leave any evidence? Go get it."

"Even if it's Bonnie, she can't feel—"

"I know I'm not being reasonable. I just don't want her out in the cold if I can help it. It . . . hurts me. Bring her in."

Joe muttered a curse and got to his feet. A moment later he came back with the box. "You're not looking at it again." He crossed the room and slid the box into a drawer of her worktable. "And it's going to the lab for analysis."

"Okay."

"And stop crying, dammit."

She nodded.

"Oh, shit." He dropped down beside her and gathered her in his arms. "You're killing me. Please. Stop crying."

"I'm sorry. I'm trying. It was the shock. I didn't expect—" She swallowed. "He got the response he wanted from me, didn't he?"

"What did he say?"

She shook her head. "Not now. Give me a minute."

His arms tightened around her. "Take all the time you need. I'll give you ten years if you need them. Why not? Hell, I've already given you one decade."

What was he talking about? She didn't have a decade. She might not have any time at all. She buried her head in his shoulder, trying to get past the horror of the box and face an even greater horror. "He said that—" She couldn't go on. Not yet.

Her name is Jane.

"IT'S ALL BULLSHIT," Joe said flatly. "Reincarnation?"

"Did he sound as if he believed in it?" Spiro asked Eve.

"Not really."

"Then he could have been manipulating you."

"He'd like me to believe it." She smiled bitterly. "That could make it very entertaining for him."

"He knows you're too intelligent to fall for that crap," Joe said.

"He also knows I care about children." Her hands clenched on her lap. "And bones aren't enough for him. What if he's chosen his next victim? What if he can make me a part of the kill, make me the cause of it?"

"Clever," Spiro murmured.

"It's nice to be so detached," Eve said unevenly. "I'm not finding much to admire in the bastard."

"I'm not admiring him, merely assessing his capabilities. And this is all supposition on your part."

"He went to a great deal of trouble to bring me that box."

"And it gave you a great deal of pain. He may regard that as enough return."

She shook her head. "It's just the opening gambit. He hit me with Bonnie. He hit me with the threat to another little girl. And he tried to tie the two together in my mind."

"And did he succeed?" Spiro asked.

"Of course not."

Spiro's gaze narrowed on her face. "Not even a little?"

She looked down. "I wouldn't let him do that to me."

"I hope not."

"We have to find her. We have to find that little girl."

"She may not even exist," Joe said.

"She exists."

"If she did exist, he may already have killed her."

She shook her head. She wouldn't believe that. "I don't think so."

Spiro said, "I'll rush the analysis of the contents of that box and get back to you." He turned to Joe. "I want to know how Dom got that close to the house."

"Don't you think I've asked myself the same question a million times? It shouldn't have happened. But it did. Eve needs more guards."

"This lake curves around like a snake. There's nothing to stop anyone from taking a canoe into one of the inlets and making his way to the cabin. I'd have to set up a two-mile chain of agents to monitor all that lakefront."

"At least get a truckload of equipment out here and trace his calls to Eve."

"I don't know how much good it will do," Spiro said. "But I agree that—"

"No," Eve said.

They both looked at her.

"If he finds out we're trying to trace the calls, he may not call again. I have to talk to him."

Joe muttered a curse.

"You know I have to do it, Joe."

"Oh, yes, he's got you, dammit."

"And what if he doesn't call you?" Spiro asked.

"He'll call again. Soon." She lifted her head. "He wants me to know who the girl is."

"You know who she is. He already told you her name and her age."

"That was just a tease. Enough to make me worry but not enough for me to find her. We *have* to find her."

"Then it's your responsibility to convince Dom to tell you more," Spiro said.

Her responsibility. That was what Dom wanted, for her to be responsible for the life of that child. For her to try to save a little girl she didn't even know.

Her name is Jane.

And she was only ten years old. Too young to know how to fight the monster stalking her.

Just a little girl. She'd be helpless. . . .

JANE'S FIST LANDED squarely on Chang's nose and blood spurted. "Give it back."

Chang screamed and clutched his nose. "Fay, Janie hit me. I didn't do nothing and Janie hit me."

"Jane, stop it," Fay called from the kitchen. "And, Chang, quit tattling."

"Give it back," Jane said through gritted teeth.

"Thief. Crook." Chang backed away. "I'm going to tell Fay and she'll have you put in jail."

"Give—it—back." She punched him in the stomach and then grabbed the apple that dropped from his hand. She was halfway across the room when Fay said, "Stop right there, Jane."

Sighing, she stopped in her tracks. Bad luck. A few seconds more and she would have been out the front door.

"She stole an apple from the fridge. She's been stealing stuff for the last two days." Chang smiled maliciously. "You gonna have her arrested, Fay?"

"What kind of stuff?" Fay asked.

"Food. I saw her put a sandwich in her schoolbag yesterday."

"Is that true, Jane?"

Jane didn't answer.

"And she punched me."

"Be quiet, Chang. For heaven's sake, you're two inches taller than she is."

"You said I shouldn't fight," he said, sulking.

"I also said you shouldn't tattle, but you do it." Fay dug into her pocket and handed him a tissue. "Go on. You'll be late for school."

Chang wiped his nose. "Jane was late yesterday."

"Jane's never late for school."

"She was late yest—" He met Jane's warning gaze and backed toward the door. "Ask her." He bolted out of the house.

Fay crossed her arms over her chest. "So I'm asking you."

"I was late."

"Why?"

"I had something to do."

"What?"

Jane was silent.

"Have you been stealing food?"

"Not much."

"You know I have a tough time stretching the food budget for the three of you."

"I won't eat tomorrow."

"You don't eat enough now. It's Chang and Raoul who are always hungry. Which brings me to ask why you stole food, when half the time I can't get you to eat my dinners."

Jane didn't answer.

"When I was in the fourth grade there was a bully who made me give him my lunch every day. I'd understand if you—"

"No one made me do it."

Fay smiled faintly. "And if they tried, you'd punch them in the nose."

Jane nodded.

"If you have a problem, it might help if you talk to me."

"I don't have a problem."

"And you wouldn't tell me if you did. Why do I even try?" Fay wearily brushed a strand of hair back from her forehead. "Go on. You'll be late."

Jane hesitated. It would be harder to get food now. Could she trust Fay? "May I keep the apple?"

"If you tell me why."

"Someone needs it."

"Who?"

"He can't go home right now. His father's there."

"Who?"

"Could I bring him here?"

"A child? Jane, you know I can't accept any more children. But if he's having trouble at home, we can call Family Services and see if they can intercede with his parents."

She should have known Fay wouldn't understand. "They won't help. They'll go see them and then they'll leave and make a report. It would make it worse for him."

"Who is this? Tell me."

Jane started for the door.

"Jane, I want to help you. Trust me. You're going to get into trouble."

"I'll be okay. I won't be late for school again."

"That's not what I mean." Fay was looking helplessly at her. "I want to be your friend. Why can't I get through to you? Why do you keep everything bottled up inside?"

"Could I have the apple?"

"I shouldn't let you— Oh, go ahead, take it. But I don't want you punching Chang again."

"Okay." Jane opened the door and ran down the steps. That she had made Fay unhappy made her feel bad. For a moment she had thought Fay would understand and help her, but she should have known better. You couldn't count on anyone to help you. You had to do it yourself.

At least Fay had not made her give up the apple the way some grown-ups would have. But there would be no more food for Mike from Fay's refrigerator. She would have to find it somewhere else.

Her forehead creased in a frown as she began to consider how she would do it.

CHAPTER SIX

DOM MADE EVE wait over forty-eight hours before he called again.

"Did you like my gift?" he asked.

"I hated it. You knew I would."

"But how could you hate your own flesh and blood? Oops, slip of the tongue. No flesh, no blood, just bone."

"Who is she?"

"I told you, it's your Bonnie."

"No, you know who I mean. Who is this Jane?"

"Well, she may be your Bonnie too. Have you thought about the possibility of—"

"What's her last name?"

"She's not as pretty but she has the same red hair. Unfortunately, she's had a rougher time this go-around than when she was your Bonnie. Four foster homes." He clucked regretfully. "So sad."

"Where is she?"

"You'd recognize the place."

She felt a sudden chill. A grave? "Is she alive?"

"Of course."

"Do you have her?"

"No, so far I've only been observing her. I find her very interesting. You will too, Eve."

"Tell me her last name. Dammit, I know you want me to know."

"But you have to earn it. It's part of the game. Don't try to bring the police into it or I'll be very unhappy. I'm sure your maternal instincts will lead you to little Jane. Find her, Eve. Before I become impatient." He hung up.

She punched the end button.

"No luck?" Joe asked.

She stood up. "We're going to Atlanta."

"What the hell?"

"He said I'd recognize the place where she can be found. I know Atlanta better than any other place. Do you have contacts with child welfare?"

He shook his head.

"Do you know anyone else who can help us? He said she'd been in four foster homes. There have to be records."

"We can try Mark Grunard. I don't know anyone who's better at digging out information, and he has contacts everywhere."

"Will you call him?"

"Look, the Atlanta PD will help now. They have no choice, not after the Devon ID."

"He doesn't want me to bring in the police. He wants me to find her. It's like some kind of game to him."

"Will you stay here and let me go and look for her?"

"I told you, that's not what he wants. He wants me to search for her. It has to be me."

"Then don't give the bastard what he wants."

"And have him send me her head in a box?" she asked unevenly. "I can't risk that. I have to find her and find her quick."

"Okay, but I'm going with you." He reached for the phone. "Go pack a toothbrush and a change of clothes. I'll call Mark and tell him what we need so he can get started on it."

"Set up a meeting with him. Dom's got to see me making the effort to find her. He'll be watching me."

"That's no problem. I told you I'd promised Mark you'd see him as soon as possible. I'll have him meet us at my apartment in the city."

JOE'S APARTMENT WAS in a luxury high-rise across the street from Piedmont Park. He drove down into the secured gated parking garage and they took the elevator to the seventh floor.

"It's about time, Joe. I've been waiting almost an hour." Mark Grunard grinned at them. "Don't you realize I'm an important man in this town?" He extended his hand to Eve. "I'm glad to see you again, Ms. Duncan. Though I'm sorry it's in these circumstances."

"So am I." She shook his hand. He appeared almost the same as she remembered him—tall, fit, with a charming smile. Perhaps in his early fifties, he showed the years with a few more laugh lines around his blue eyes. "But I'm glad you've agreed to help us."

"I'd be an idiot otherwise. This is big stuff. It's not often I get a chance at an exclusive that could net me an Emmy."

"What about your fellow reporters?" Joe asked. "Are we going to be safe here?"

"I think so. I laid a false trail to Daytona Beach in the newscast last night. Just don't be stupid." He frowned. "I contacted Barbara Eisley about our problem. She's head of Child and Family Services. It's not going to be easy. She says all files are private."

Red tape, Eve thought with frustration. A child could be murdered while they dithered about blasted rules. "Can't you persuade her?"

"Barbara Eisley's a tough nut. She'd make a great drill sergeant. Can you get a court order?"

Joe shook his head. "We can't go through the system. Eve's afraid Dom will move on the little girl if we do."

"Barbara Eisley has *got* to help," Eve said.

"I said it's not going to be easy, I didn't say impossible," Grunard said. "We just have to use a little persuasion."

"Could I see Ms. Eisley?"

Grunard nodded. "I thought you'd feel like that. We're taking her to dinner tonight." He held up his hand as Joe opened his mouth to protest. "I know, Eve can't go where she'll be recognized. I have a friend who owns an Italian restaurant on the Chattahoochee just outside the city. He'll give us good pasta and complete privacy. Okay?"

"Okay." Joe unlocked his apartment door. "Pick us up across the street, inside the park, at six."

"I'll be there."

Eve watched Grunard walk toward the elevators before she followed Joe into the apartment. "He appears very"—she searched for the word—"solid."

"That's why he's so popular." He locked the door and Eve looked around the apartment.

"Good God, you could have done better than this, Joe. It looks like a hotel room."

He shrugged. "I told you I didn't do much more than sleep here." He headed for the kitchen. "I'll make coffee and sandwiches. I doubt if we're going to eat much at that dinner with Barbara Eisley."

She followed him into the kitchen. She doubted she could eat much now either, but she'd have to. She needed all her strength. "I think I may have met Eisley before."

"When?"

"Years ago. When I was a kid. There was one caseworker . . ." She shook her head. "Maybe not."

"You don't remember?"

"I've blocked a lot of that time out of my memory." She made a face. "It wasn't a very pleasant period. Mom and I were moving from place to place and every month the welfare department was threatening to take me away from Mom and put me in a foster home if she didn't get off the crack." She opened the refrigerator door. "Everything in here is spoiled, Joe."

"Then I'll make toast."

"If the bread's not moldy."

"Don't be pessimistic." He opened the bread box. "It's just a little stale." He popped bread into the toaster on the counter. "Considering what you went through as a kid, you might have been better off in a foster home."

"Maybe. But I didn't want to go. Back then there were times I hated her, but she was my mother. To a child, family always seems better than strangers." She got the butter from the refrigerator. "That's why it's so difficult to take abused children from their parents. They want to believe everything's going to be all right."

"And sometimes it's not."

"Evidently, it wasn't for this Jane. Not if she's been in four foster homes." She went to the window and looked down into the street. "You don't realize how rough it is out there for kids, Joe."

"I realize. I'm a cop. I've seen it."

"But you haven't been there." She smiled at him over her shoulder. "Rich boy."

"Don't be snooty. I couldn't help it. I tried to get my parents to abandon me, but they wouldn't do it. They sent me to Harvard instead." He plugged in the coffeemaker. "It could have been worse; they were thinking about sending me to Oxford."

"Terrible fate." She looked back out the window. "You never talk about your parents. They died when you were in college, didn't they?"

He nodded. "Boating accident off Newport."

"Why don't you talk about them?"

"Nothing to talk about."

She turned to him. "Dammit, Joe, you didn't spring fully grown in Atlanta. I've tried dozens of times to get you to tell me about your folks and the way you grew up. Why do you keep dodging?"

"It's not important."

"It's as important as the way I grew up."

He smiled. "Not to me."

"You're only fifty percent of this friendship. You know everything about me. Stop shutting me out."

"I don't believe in living in the past."

"How the hell can I really know you if you won't talk to me?"

"Don't be crazy. You know me." He chuckled. "For God's sake, we've been together more than ten years."

He was dodging again. "Joe."

He shrugged. "You want to know about my parents? I didn't know them very well. They stopped being interested in me about the time I stopped being a cute little tyke." He got down cups from the cabinet. "Can't blame them. I was never an easy kid. Too demanding."

"I can't imagine you demanding anything. You're too self-reliant."

"Imagine it. Accept it." He poured coffee into the cups. "I'm still demanding as hell. I've just learned ways of camouflaging it. Sit down and eat your toast."

"You never demand anything of me."

"I demand your friendship. I demand your company. Most of all, I demand that you stay alive."

"Those are the most unselfish demands I've ever heard."

"Don't you believe it. I'm probably the most selfish man you've ever met."

She smiled as she shook her head. "No way."

"I'm glad I've got you fooled. But someday you'll find out how I've deceived you all these years. You slum brats just can't trust us rich kids."

"You've switched the conversation around to me again. Why do you keep doing that?"

"I'm bored with me." He yawned. "In case you haven't noticed, I'm a very dull fellow."

"The hell you are."

"Well, I have to agree that I'm witty and supremely intelligent, but my background's pretty mundane." He sat down opposite Eve. "Now, what about Barbara Eisley? What do you remember?"

Stubborn bastard, he'd told her as much as he was going to. She gave up as she had so many times before. "I told you, I'm not sure I knew her. There were so many caseworkers and, hey, they never stayed long in the job. Can't blame them. Techwood wasn't the safest neighborhood."

"Think."

"Bully." Okay, stop avoiding thinking about that hellhole where she had grown up. She let the memory flow back to her. Dirt. Hunger. Rats. The smell of fear and sex and drugs. "She might have been one of the caseworkers. I remember one woman in her late thirties. I thought she was old. She came to one of the houses on Market Street. I think I was nine or ten. . . ."

"Sympathetic?"

"I think so. Maybe. I was too defensive to judge. I was angry at Mom and the whole world."

"Then you may have trouble bonding with her tonight."

"I don't have to bond with her. I just have to convince her to open those files and help us find that child. There's no *time*."

"Easy." His hand covered hers on the table. "One way or the other, we'll get the records tonight."

She tried to smile. "I suppose if she won't help, you'll pull a Watergate at the welfare office?"

"Possibly."

He meant it. Her smile faded. "No, Joe. I don't want you to get into trouble."

"Hey, if you're good, you don't get caught. You don't get caught, you're not in trouble."

"Simplistic."

"The whole world should be so simple. I'd say the life of a kid is worth a little risk. If you're persuasive enough, it may not be necessary for me to turn burglar. Who knows, Barbara Eisley may not be as tough as Mark claims. She could be a pussycat."

"HELL, NO," BARBARA Eisley said. "I don't open those records for anyone. I'm up for my pension next year and I'm not taking any chances."

Barbara Eisley was definitely no pussycat, Eve thought in discouragement. From the moment Grunard had introduced them, she'd avoided talking about the files. When Joe finally pinned her down after dessert, she responded with the bluntness of a hammer blow.

"Now, Barbara." Grunard smiled at her. "You know that no one is going to jerk your pension for a little infringement involving a child's life. Besides, you've been with the department too long."

"Bull. I'm not diplomatic enough for the mayor or city council. They're just waiting for a reason to bounce me out of my job. The only reason I've lasted this long is that I know where a couple of political bodies are buried." She stared accusingly at Mark. "And you quoted me on that child abuse case two years ago. It made my department look negligent."

"But it caused extensive reform. That's what you wanted."

"And put my ass in hot water. I should have kept my mouth shut. I don't take risks like that anymore. I do everything by the book. I help you do this today, and tomorrow they find a way to use it against me. I'm not going to end up without a pension. I've visited too many old people in public housing trying to survive. That's not going to be me."

"Then why did you accept Mark's invitation?" Joe asked.

"Free dinner." She shrugged. "And I was curious." She turned to Eve. "I've read about you, but the media is sometimes full of hot air. I wanted to see for myself how you'd turned out. Do you remember me?"

"I think so. But you've changed."

"So have you." She studied Eve's face. "You were a tough little kid. I remember I tried to talk to you once and you just stared at me. I thought you'd be hooking or dealing by the time you were fourteen. I would have liked to have made another try with you, but I had too many cases." She added wearily, "There are always too many cases. Too many kids. And most of the time we can't help them. We take them away and the court gives them right back to their parents."

"But you try."

"Because I'm too stupid to give up hope. You'd think after all these years I'd learn, wouldn't you? You turned out all right, but it was nothing I did."

"You must make a difference sometimes."

"I guess so."

"You could make a difference this time. You could save a little girl."

"Get a court order. If it's that important, there should be no problem."

"We can't do that. I've told you I can't go through channels."

Barbara Eisley was silent.

"Okay, you won't give us the records, but maybe you remember something about this child," Joe said.

An undefinable expression crossed her face. "I don't handle casework any longer. I have too much paperwork."

Eve leaned forward. "But you do remember something."

Eisley was silent a moment. "I had to authorize taking a little girl out of a foster home two years ago. The couple who was caring for her claimed she was disruptive and disobedient. I had to bring the child in and interview her. She wouldn't talk to me, but she was covered with bruises. I checked her medical record and she'd been taken to Grady Hospital twice with broken bones during the last year. I gave permission for her to be removed from the home. I also removed the foster parents from our rolls." She smiled. "I remember thinking she must have been a gutsy little kid. She kept on giving those bastards hell."

"What's her name?"

She ignored Eve's question. "She was a smart kid. High IQ, did well in school. She probably figured they'd give her up as a meal ticket if she caused enough trouble."

"You placed her with another family?"

"We had no choice. Most of our foster parents aren't abusive. Sometimes we make mistakes. We can only do our best."

"Tell me her name."

Eisley shook her head. "Not without a court order. What if I was wrong?"

"What if you were right? She could die, dammit."

"I've spent my entire life trying to help kids. Now I've got to think of myself."

"Please."

She shook her head again. "I've worked too hard. I still work hard." She paused. "You'd think in my position I wouldn't have to take work home." She nodded at her briefcase beside her chair.

"But I had some old files on a computer disk to review, so here I go again."

Hope flared inside Eve. "That's too bad."

"It goes with the territory." She stood up. "It's been an interesting evening. Sorry I can't help you." She smiled. "I believe I have to go to the rest room. I suppose you'll be gone when I come back. I hope you find the little girl." Her gaze narrowed on Eve. "I just remembered, the kid reminded me a little of you. She stared at me with those big eyes and I thought she'd go on the attack any minute. Same tough little— Something wrong?"

Eve shook her head.

Barbara Eisley turned to Mark. "Thanks for dinner. But I still haven't forgiven you for quoting me in that story." She turned and made her way through the tables toward the rest room.

"Thank God." Eve reached for the briefcase. It was unlocked and there was only one disk in the leather pocket on the side. Bless Barbara Eisley. She tucked it in her purse. "She wants us to take it."

"You mean steal it," Joe murmured as he threw some bills down on the table.

"Which puts her in the clear." Eve turned to Mark. "Do you have a laptop with you?"

"In the trunk of my car. I always keep it there. We can check the disk as soon as we reach the parking lot."

"Good. You'll have to drop into Barbara Eisley's office tomorrow and leave the disk on her desk. I don't want to get her into trouble." She stood up. "Let's go. We need to be out of here before she comes back. She might change her mind."

"Not likely," Joe said. "It's pretty clear you impressed her when you were a kid."

"Or Jane did." She started for the door. "Or maybe she's just a woman trying to do the right thing in a wrong world."

. . .

THERE WERE TWENTY-SEVEN records on the disk. It took Mark twenty minutes to scan the first sixteen.

"Jane MacGuire," Mark read from the computer screen. "The age is right. Four foster homes. Physical description checks out. Red hair, hazel eyes."

"Can you print it out?"

Mark plugged a small Kodak printer into the laptop. "She's living right now with a Fay Sugarton who's also foster parent to two other children. Chang Ito, twelve, and Raoul Jones, thirteen."

"The address?"

"Twelve forty-eight Luther." He tore off the printout and handed it to her. "Do you want me to get out my street map?"

Eve shook her head. "I know where it is." Dom had said she would recognize the place. "It's in my old neighborhood. Let's go."

"You want to go see her tonight?" Joe asked. "It's almost midnight. I doubt if this Fay Sugarton will take kindly to being awakened by strangers."

"I don't care how she takes it. I don't want—"

"And what are you going to say when you do see her?"

"What do you think? I'm going to tell her about Dom and ask her to let us keep Jane until the danger is over."

"It will take some persuasion to make her do that if she cares anything about the kid."

"Then you'll have to help me. We can't leave her in a place where—"

"You're going to need Fay Sugarton's cooperation," Joe said quietly. "You don't want to get off on the wrong foot."

Okay, be sensible. Dom had set up the elaborate ploy because he wanted her to make contact with Jane MacGuire. He probably wouldn't make a move until she'd—

Probably? God, was she risking a child's life on probabilities? He could be at that house on Luther Street right then. "I want to go tonight."

"It would be better—" Mark began.

She cut him off. "I just want to make sure everything's okay there. I won't go inside and wake everyone up."

Mark shrugged and started the car. "Whatever you say."

THE HOUSE ON Luther Street was small and gray paint was peeling from the porch steps. But the rest of the house appeared neat and well cared for. Cheerful fake greenery hung from plastic baskets on the porch.

"Satisfied?" Mark asked.

The street was deserted. No cars cruising, no one stirring. Eve wasn't satisfied, but she felt a little better. "I guess so."

"Good. Then I'll drive you and Joe to his apartment and come back to watch the house."

"No. I'll stay here."

"I was expecting that." Joe reached for his phone. "I'll call for an unmarked car to park out here tonight and have the officer go in immediately if he sees anything out of the ordinary. Okay?"

"I'll stay here too," Mark said.

She looked at the two of them, undecided. And then she opened the car door. "Okay. If you hear or see anything, you call us."

"You're going to walk? Let me run you home."

"We'll get a taxi."

"In this neighborhood?"

"So we'll walk until we get to where we can find one. I don't want you leaving here."

Mark looked at Joe. "Will you please tell her she shouldn't be wandering this neighborhood? It's too dangerous."

"Jane MacGuire wanders around this neighborhood every day of her life," Eve pointed out. "She manages to survive." Just as

Eve had survived all those years ago. Jesus, it was all coming back to her.

"The car will be here in five minutes." Joe had finished his call and he and Eve got out of the car. "Don't worry, I'll take care of Eve," he told Mark. "Or maybe I'll let her take care of me. This is her turf."

"We'll be back at eight in the morning." Eve started down the street. Nothing really changed around here. The grass growing in the cracks in the sidewalk, the dirty words chalked on the pavement.

"And how do we get back to civilization from here?" Joe asked as he fell in beside her.

"This *is* civilization, rich boy," Eve said. "The real wilds are four blocks south. You'll notice I'm heading north."

"And where did you live?"

"South. You're a cop. You must be familiar with this area."

"Not on foot. They shoot at cops in this part of town . . . when they're not killing each other."

" 'They.' The mysterious 'they.' We're not all criminals down here. We have to live and survive just like anyone else. Why the hell do you—"

"Hold it. You know damn well who I was talking about. Why are you jumping on me?"

He was right. "Sorry. Forget it."

"I don't think we'd better forget it. You were talking as if you were still living in one of those houses on Luther Street."

"I was never lucky enough to live on Luther Street. I told you, this is uptown."

"You know what I mean."

She did know. "I haven't been down here since we moved out after Bonnie was born. I didn't think I'd react like this."

"Like what?"

"I was feeling like the kid I was all those years ago." She smiled ruefully. "I was on the attack."

"That's how Barbara Eisley described Jane MacGuire."

"Maybe she has a right to want to strike first."

"I don't doubt she has every right. I'm merely suggesting that you analyze what being back here has done to you. It's you against the world again." He added deliberately, "Or maybe you and Jane MacGuire against the world."

"Nonsense. I've never even met the child."

"Maybe you shouldn't meet her. Why don't you let me go see her alone in the morning."

She turned to face him. "What are you saying?"

"Why did Dom choose someone from this neighborhood? Why did he bring you back here? Think about it."

She walked in silence for a moment. "He wants me to identify with her," she whispered. Christ, she was already identifying with the little girl. She and Jane had walked the same streets, suffered abandonment and hardship, fought their way through loneliness and hurt. "He's setting me up. First talking to me about reincarnation and then choosing Jane MacGuire. He's not satisfied with killing a child and laying the guilt on my doorstep. He wants me emotionally involved with her."

"That's the way I figure it."

Bastard. "He wants me to feel as if he's killing my daughter all over again." Her hands clenched into fists at her sides. "He wants to kill Bonnie again."

"And that's why you shouldn't go near Jane MacGuire. You're already forming an attachment and you've not even met her."

"I can keep her at a distance."

"Sure."

"It won't be that difficult, Joe. Not if she's like me at that age. I wasn't exactly approachable."

"I would have approached you."

"And I would have spit in your eye."

"It's not a good idea for you to see her."

"I have to do it."

"I know," Joe said grimly. "He hasn't left you any way out."

No way out.

Of course there would be a way out. She had fought her way out of this neighborhood. She had fought her way back to sanity after Bonnie had been killed. She wouldn't let that son of a bitch trap her now. Joe was wrong. She loved kids, but she was no bleeding heart. She could save Jane MacGuire's life and beat that monster. All she had to do was keep at a distance a little girl she didn't even know.

But Dom wouldn't keep Jane at a distance. His shadow was already looming over her.

Don't think about it. Tomorrow she and Joe would talk to Fay Sugarton. Tonight Jane MacGuire was under guard and sleeping peacefully.

The little girl would be safe tonight.

Maybe.

"I'VE BEEN LOOKING for you, Mike. I told you to go to the alley near the mission." Jane sat down near the big cardboard box. "It's not good here."

"I like it," Mike said.

"It's safer where there are people."

"This is closer to home." Mike eagerly reached for the paper bag she held out to him. "Hamburgers?"

"Spaghetti."

"I like hamburgers better."

"I have to take what I can get." What she could steal, really. Well, it wasn't exactly stealing, was it? Cusanelli's gave its leftovers to Meals on Wheels or the Salvation Army instead of throwing them out. "Eat it and then go over to the mission."

He was already eating the spaghetti. "Why did you come so late?"

"I had to wait until the restaurant closed." She stood up. "I've got to get back."

"Now?" He was disappointed.

"If you'd been at the mission, I could have stayed a few minutes. It's too late now."

"You said Fay slept hard and wouldn't wake up."

Maybe. "I have to go climb in the kitchen window. Chang and Raoul have the room next door to the kitchen."

"I don't want to get you in trouble."

But he was lonely and wanted her to stay. She sighed and sat back down. "Just until you finish." She leaned against the brick wall. "But you got to go to the mission alley. It's not good to be alone. There are all kinds of creeps around who could hurt you."

"I always run away like you told me."

"But there's no one to hear you if you call out."

"I'm okay. I ain't scared."

She knew she couldn't make him understand. Fear was where his father lived. Everywhere else was safe in comparison. Maybe it would be okay tonight. She hadn't seen that creep for a couple of days. "How long does your father usually stay when he comes back?"

"A week, maybe two."

"It's already been a week. Maybe he's gone."

Mike shook his head. "I checked after school yesterday. He was on the porch with Mom. But he didn't see me."

"Did your mom?"

"I think so, but she looked away real quick." He stared down at the spaghetti. "It ain't her fault. She's scared too."

"Yeah."

"It will be just fine once he goes away again."

It wouldn't be fine. Mike's mom was one of the hookers who worked Peachtree, and she was gone more than she was home, but he still defended her. It always surprised Jane how kids could never see their parents the way they really were. "Are you finished with that spaghetti?"

"Not yet."

He had a bite left, but he wasn't eating because he wanted her to stay.

"Tell me about the stars again."

"You could find out for yourself if you learn to read. It's all in that book of legends in the school library. You got to learn to read, Mike, and you can't learn if you don't go to school."

"I only skipped once this week. Tell me about that guy on the horse."

She should go now. She would have only a few hours' sleep before Fay woke her to go to school. Mr. Brett had yelled at her for falling asleep in third period yesterday.

Mike nestled closer.

He was lonely and maybe more scared than he'd said. Oh, well, while she was there she could make sure no creep snuck up on him. "Just a little longer. If you promise me you won't come here anymore."

"I promise."

She tilted her head back. She liked the stars as much as Mike did. She had never noticed them until she'd gone to stay with the Carbonis. She could remember staring out the window and trying to close out the fear by seeing pictures in the sky. When she'd found the book in the library, it had helped even more. Books and stars. They had helped her; maybe they would help Mike.

Tonight was clear and the stars seemed brighter than usual. Bright and clean and far away from this alley off Luther Street.

"The guy on the horse is Sagittarius, but he's not really on a horse. He's half horse, half man. You see that string of stars? That's the string of his bow as he draws it back to . . ."

CHAPTER SEVEN

"I BEG YOUR pardon?" Fay Sugarton stared at her three visitors. "Jane?"

"She's in danger," Eve said, seated on the sofa with Joe and Mark. "Please believe me."

"Why? Because she's the right age, has red hair, and was in four foster homes before coming here? You admit you practically pulled her name from a hat."

"She matched the profile," Joe said.

"Did you check county records as well as city records?"

"We believe Dom would choose a child from this area."

"Maybe, maybe not. There could be other children in the county who match the profile. You didn't search in depth." Fay crossed her arms over her breasts. "And you don't even know if this guy who's calling you isn't some sicko practical joker."

"He knew about the two boys at Talladega," Eve said.

"That doesn't mean he's after Jane."

"Do you want to take the chance?"

"Of course I don't." She stared at Eve. "But I don't intend to let you jerk Jane away from me unless I'm convinced there's a need for it. She's been tossed from one home to another since she was two. I'm responsible for her now. I won't have her torn from another home and frightened out of her wits."

"We're not the ones who will frighten her."

"Bring me proof; show me how you'll protect her and I'll let her go."

Eve drew a deep breath. "Proof may come too late."

"You don't realize how damaged this child is. I want a chance at earning her trust." She turned to Mark Grunard. "And if you try to put me or any of this on TV, I'll sue the station."

He held up his hands. "I'm just an observer." He paused. "But I'd listen if I were you. No one is trying to victimize the child but this Dom. We're trying to save her, Ms. Sugarton."

Fay hesitated and then shook her head. "Bring me proof and I'll let you take her."

"You're putting the child at risk," Eve said.

Fay gave her a shrewd glance. "I don't imagine you'll let her become a victim. I'd bet you'll have a guard on her."

"That may not be enough. She needs to be hidden away."

"I don't see you hiding."

"That's my choice. A child has no choice."

Fay grimaced. "You don't know Jane."

"She's a *child*, dammit."

"A child who's been abused and neglected most of her life. She doesn't think much of grown-ups already, and you want me to tell her someone's trying to kill her just for the hell of it?"

"What kind of proof do you want?" Joe asked.

"It sounds like you found Jane too easily. I want the welfare people to go through *all* their records, both city and county, and make sure Jane is the only one who fits the profile. And have that FBI agent, Spiro, come by and talk to me. I trust the FBI." She glanced at Joe. "No offense, but my kids have had problems with the local police and I don't like you showing up with this TV man."

Eve looked at Joe. If Dom didn't want the police involved, he wouldn't be pleased at seeing the FBI there.

He shrugged. "I don't like it either, but we *have* located the little girl. He can't move on her without our knowing it now."

Eve turned back to Fay. "Then it's settled. You'll talk to Robert Spiro. Please listen to him. We've told you what a problem we're having with Family Services."

"I promise to listen. No more than that." She stood up. "Now, if you'll excuse me, I have housework to do and then I have to go to the grocery store." She said to Eve, "Sorry, but I have to be sure. Jane's a tough proposition. This may blow any chance I have of reaching her."

"For God's sake, help us."

"I'll do what I can. Right now she's at Crawford Middle School on Thirteenth Street." Fay walked to the chest across the room, rummaged through the top drawer, and handed a photograph to Eve. "That's her school picture from last year. She gets out at three and walks home. It's only four blocks. Keep an eye on her, but I don't want you talking to her." Her lips firmed. "If you scare her, I'll scalp you."

"Thank you." Eve thrust the photo into her purse. "But you're making a mistake."

Fay shrugged. "I've made a lot of them, but I can only do my best. I've had twelve foster children in the past six years and I think most of them are better for being with me." She moved to the door and opened it. "Good-bye. Give me proof and we'll work something out."

Mark Grunard said as they reached the street, "Tough lady. Evidently, she isn't easily impressed by my fame and sparkling personality."

"I like her." Eve scowled. "Though I'd like to break her neck. Why wouldn't she listen?"

"She believes she's doing what's best for the kid," Joe said. "And she's not about to take anyone's word without thinking it over first."

"So what do we do now?" Mark asked.

"You go home and get some sleep. You were up all night," Joe said. "As soon as we get to the car, we'll call Spiro and ask him to come down and talk to Fay Sugarton." He looked at Eve. "And then I assume this afternoon we watch the school and make sure the kid gets home all right?"

She started toward the car. "That's the plan."

"I'M TIED UP here. I can't come right now," Spiro said.

"It can't be that important. We need you," Eve told him.

"It's important enough." He paused. "We found another body on the bank across the falls. They're digging up the entire area to see if there are any more."

"God." That made twelve bodies. How many more?

"But I'll try to break away tonight and drive down. I won't be able to stay long."

"When can you get here?" Eve asked.

"I'll be there before nine, and we'll go to see the lady together," he said wearily. "Is that all right?"

"It will have to be if you can't get here before that."

Joe took the phone from her. "We're not going back to the cottage tonight. Send Charlie down here in case I have to leave Eve for any length of time." He listened. "No, we don't want Charlie to talk to Fay Sugarton. He has about as much presence and authority as one of her foster kids. We need you to impress her. What about Spalding from CASKU? Okay, if he's gone back to Quantico, you get down here yourself. I don't care if it sounds like an order. It *is* an order." He hung up.

"You didn't handle him very diplomatically," Eve said. "He's trying to help us."

"As long as it means catching Dom."

"It's his job to catch killers."

"Not quite. He's a profiler. He's supposed to analyze and report, not join in the chase." His lips tightened. "But now he wants that bastard almost as much as we do."

"We should be grateful for that."

"I'm grateful." Joe scowled. "Sometimes. When he doesn't put Bureau business in front of protecting—"

"Shut up, Joe."

He made a face. "Okay, Spiro's only doing his job. I suppose I'm a little uptight."

He wasn't the only one. Eve's nerves were strung taut.

Joe started the car. "Come on, I'll buy you a hamburger at the Varsity and then we'll go on to the school."

"MY GOD, I'D forgotten how fast kids can move when they get out of school." Joe chuckled. "They're like a herd of buffalo heading for water. Did you go to this school?"

"No, it wasn't here when I was growing up." Her gaze searched the crowd of children. "I don't see any redheads. Where is she?"

"You have a photograph." He paused. "I've been wondering why you haven't looked at it since you got it."

"I didn't think of it."

"Sure?"

She glanced at him. "Of course I'm sure. Stop reading significance into a simple oversight."

"There's nothing simple about you. It's time to look at the photograph, Eve."

"I was going to do that." She pulled the picture out of her purse. It's only a little girl. She has nothing to do with Bonnie.

Relief rushed through her. "Not very pretty, is she?" The child in the photo was not smiling and had short red hair curling around a thin, triangular face. The only attractive feature she could claim were large hazel eyes, and even they were glaring out of the photograph. "She obviously didn't want her picture taken."

"Then she must have character. I never wanted my picture taken either."

Joe's gaze shifted to her face. "You're relieved. You were afraid she'd look like Bonnie."

"It seems Dom has a bad eye. She and Bonnie are nothing alike. Hell, maybe he's lying about everything. Maybe he never saw Bonnie."

"If he was around here then, he would have seen at least a photo of her. The media plastered her face all over."

Because she was pretty and sweet and loved life so much, she touched everyone who saw her, Eve thought. Not like Jane MacGuire, who was prone to strike out. "That Dom thinks I'd identify with her only proves how crazy he is. You didn't need to worry, Joe."

"That's nice. Maybe." He straightened in the driver's seat. "There she is. She just came out of the front entrance."

Jane MacGuire was small for ten, dressed in jeans, T-shirt, and tennis shoes. She wore a green book bag on her back and strode straight ahead without looking to either side.

No dawdling. No stopping to talk with friends as Bonnie had done. Bonnie had so many friends . . .

She wasn't being fair. Bonnie had always been surrounded by love and trust. Jane MacGuire had a right to be wary. But, God, she was glad the child was nothing like Bonnie. "She's reached the street. Start the car."

• • •

THE CREEP HAD a different car. Bigger. Newer. Gray instead of blue.

Or it could be another creep, Jane thought. The world was full of them.

She broke into a trot and darted around the corner.

She waited.

The gray car coasted slowly around the corner.

She tensed. Was it following her?

A man and woman? Maybe they're not creeps.

Or maybe they were. Better not take any chances. She climbed over the chain-link fence, ran across the yard, then scrambled over the far fence.

Out the gate that led to the alley.

She glanced over her shoulder.

No car.

Keep running.

Her heart was beating too hard.

Stop it. Don't ever let the creeps scare you. That's what they wanted. Scare you. Hurt you. Don't let them do it.

It was going to be okay.

Two more blocks and she'd be at Fay's house. Maybe she'd tell Fay about the creeps. Fay was like the teachers at school. As long as she understood the danger, she'd do what she could to help. It was only when she didn't understand that she—

Jane ran out of the alley into the street. The house was right ahead. Half a block.

She looked back over her shoulder, and her heart leaped into her throat.

Gray car. Turning the corner.

She hadn't lost them.

She flew down the street toward Fay's house.

Fay would keep her safe. She would call the cops and maybe they would care enough to come.

If they didn't, at least she wouldn't be alone. Fay would be there.

She ran up the steps, threw open the door, and slammed it closed behind her.

Safe. She was safe.

Maybe she was stupid to be scared. Maybe she wouldn't tell Fay.

That would be really stupid. She'd tell her. "Fay!"

No answer.

The house was silent.

Fay must be in the kitchen. She always made sure she was home when Jane and the boys returned from school.

Yes, Fay was in the kitchen. Jane was sure she heard the loose board near the sink creak.

But why hadn't she answered?

She slowly started across the living room toward the kitchen. "Fay?"

"FAY SUGARTON ISN'T going to like this." Joe parked in front of the house. "She doesn't want us talking to the kid."

"Too bad. Dammit, we scared her. I'm not going to let her have nightmares about this." Eve opened the car door. "Fine tail you are. I told you not to let her know we were following."

"She's sharp." Joe got out of the car. "It's almost as if she was expecting it."

Eve glanced at him. "You think she knows she's being watched?"

"It seems we're going to have the opportunity to ask her." Joe climbed the steps and rang the doorbell. "If we can get Fay Sugarton to let us in the front door."

"She has no choice. She cares about the girl. It's not as if we're going to tell Jane about— Why isn't she answering the door?"

Joe rang the bell again. "She said she was going to the grocery store. Maybe she's not home and the kid's too scared to answer."

"She's had hours to get home from the store." She tried the door. "It's locked."

"The kid." He thought about it. "Then again, maybe not. What the hell." He put his shoulder against the door and broke through it. "Illegal is better than— Shit!" He crumpled to the floor as a baseball bat struck his kneecaps.

Jane whirled on Eve and struck her in the rib cage with the bat. Pain seared through Eve. She was barely able to dodge as the girl swung the bat at her head.

"Creep." Tears were running down her face. "Fucking creep." She swung the bat again. "I'll kill you, you dirty—"

Joe dove from his knees and brought Jane down.

"Don't hurt her," Eve gasped.

"Don't hurt her? I may have to have a knee replacement." He straddled the struggling child. "And she tried to knock your brains out."

"She's scared. We broke into the house. She thought—" Blood. The little girl was covered in blood. Her cheeks, lips, hands . . . "Oh, my God, she's hurt, Joe. He hurt her." She fell to her knees beside the girl and brushed the hair away from her cheek.

Jane sank her teeth into Eve's hand.

Joe pried her teeth apart and jerked Eve's hand away. "Careful." He cupped Jane's jaw and held it shut while he stared down into her eyes. "We're not going to hurt you, dammit. We're here to help. Now, where's Ms. Sugarton?"

Jane glared up at him.

"Police. Detective Quinn." He reached into his pocket and showed her his badge. He repeated, "We're here to help."

The child relaxed a little.

"Where are you hurt?" Eve asked.

Jane was still glaring at Joe. "Get off me."

"Get off her, Joe."

"This could be a mistake." Joe stood up and grabbed the bat.

Jane slowly sat up. "Lousy cop. Why weren't you here before?"

Tears were running down her cheeks again. "Never here when anyone needs you. Lousy cop. Lousy cop . . ."

"I'm here now. Where are you hurt?"

"Not hurt. *She's* hurt."

Eve stiffened. "Ms. Sugarton?"

"Fay." Jane looked toward the kitchen. "Fay."

"Jesus." Eve jumped to her feet and ran toward the kitchen.

BLOOD.

And more blood.

On the Formica table.

On the overturned kitchen chair.

On the tile floor where Fay Sugarton lay slumped, eyes staring at them across the room, throat gaping where it had been slashed.

"Don't move." Joe was standing beside her. "There could be tracks. We don't want to disturb them."

"She's dead," Eve said dully.

"Yes." He turned her around and gave her a push toward the living room. "Go back and take care of the kid while I call this in. See if she saw anyone."

She couldn't tear her gaze from those staring dead eyes. "Dom," she whispered. "It has to be Dom."

"Go."

She nodded and moved slowly from the kitchen.

Jane was sitting huddled against a wall, her knees drawn up to her chest. "She's dead, isn't she?"

"Yes." She dropped down on the floor beside her. "Did you see anyone?"

"I tried to help her. She was bleeding. I tried to stop the bleeding . . . but I couldn't. I couldn't stop it. My health teacher said if we ever have an accident, we should always stop the bleeding first. I couldn't do it. I couldn't stop it."

Eve wanted to reach out and draw Jane close, but she could almost see the wall the child had built around herself. "It wasn't your fault. I'm sure she was already dead."

"Maybe not. Maybe I could have helped her if I'd been smarter. I didn't pay much attention to what my teacher said. I didn't think—I didn't know—"

Eve couldn't stand it. She reached out and tentatively touched the child's shoulder.

Jane jerked away. "Who are you?" she said fiercely. "Are you a cop too? Why weren't you here? Why did you let this happen?"

"I'm not police, but I have to know what happened. Did you see—" To hell with it. The child was in no shape to answer questions. "What do you say we go on the porch and wait for the police to get here?"

At first she didn't think the girl would agree, but then Jane rose to her feet and strode out of the house. She sat down on the top porch step.

Eve sat down beside her. "My name is Eve Duncan. The detective inside is Joe Quinn."

The girl stared straight ahead.

"You're Jane MacGuire?"

The girl didn't answer.

"If you don't want to talk, that's fine. I know you must have cared very much for Ms. Sugarton."

"I didn't care anything about her. I just lived with her."

"I don't think that's true, but we won't talk about it now. We won't talk at all. I just thought it would make you feel better if we weren't strangers."

"Talking doesn't mean anything. You're still a stranger."

And the child was going to make sure she stayed that way, Eve thought. The tears were gone, but her back was straight and rigid and the wall of distrust was higher than ever. Who could blame her?

Any other child would have been in hysterics. It might have been a healthier reaction than withdrawal. "I don't feel much like talking either. We'll just sit here and wait. Okay?"

Jane didn't look at her. "Okay."

The child was still covered with blood, Eve realized suddenly. She should do something about it.

Not now. Neither of them was in any shape to do anything but sit there. She leaned her head against the newel post next to her. She couldn't get the memory of dead eyes out of her mind. Fay Sugarton had been a good woman, trying to do her best. She didn't deserve—

"I lied." Jane was still looking straight ahead. "I think . . . I liked her."

"So did I."

Jane fell silent again.

BARBARA EISLEY PULLED up at the curb at the same time as the first police squad car.

The officers poured into the house, but Barbara Eisley stopped before Jane. Her expression was amazingly gentle as she spoke to the child. "Do you remember me, Jane? I'm Ms. Eisley."

Jane stared at her without expression. "I remember you."

"You can't stay here any longer."

"I know."

"I've come to take you away. Where are Chang and Raoul?"

"School. Basketball practice."

"I'll send someone for them." She held out her hand. "Come with me. We'll get you cleaned up and then we'll talk."

"I don't want to talk." Jane stood and walked to the car at the curb.

"Where are you taking her?" Eve asked.

"The Child and Family Services holding facility."

"How safe is it?"

"It has security and she'll be surrounded by other children."

"I think you should let us take—"

"Bullshit." Barbara Eisley whirled on her, her tone as hard now as it had been gentle before. "She's my responsibility and none of you are going to touch her. I should never have become involved in this mess. The newspapers and politicians are going to come down on me like a ton of bricks."

"We have to keep her safe. Ms. Sugarton wasn't the target. She probably just got in the way."

"And you weren't able to help her, were you?" Barbara Eisley's eyes bored into her. "Fay Sugarton was a decent woman, an extraordinary woman who helped dozens of kids. She shouldn't have died. She might be alive now if I hadn't given you that—"

"And Jane might be dead."

"I should have kept out of it and that's what I'm doing from now on. Stay clear of me and stay away from Jane MacGuire." She turned on her heel and walked to the car.

Eve watched helplessly as it pulled away from the curb. Jane was sitting up straight in the passenger seat, but she looked terribly small and fragile.

"It was the only thing to do."

She turned to see Joe standing in the doorway. "I was hoping we could get her away before anyone showed up from Family Services."

He shook his head. "I called Eisley."

Her eyes widened. "What?"

"Child and Family Services always has to be involved in cases like this. They serve to protect the children from the media and police interrogation. They'll take the heat off Jane."

"We could have protected her."

"Would she have let us? We're strangers to her. At the welfare facility she'll be surrounded by kids and staff. She'll be much safer, and we can still keep an eye on her."

Eve was still uneasy. "I wish you hadn't . . ."

"She may be a material witness to a murder case, Eve. Did she talk to you?"

Eve shook her head.

"Then I'll have to see her later tonight."

"Can't you leave her—" Of course he couldn't leave Jane alone. She might have seen something. "Barbara Eisley may not let you talk to her. She's not pleased with us."

"Sometimes it helps to have a badge." He pulled her to her feet. "Come on. I'll drive you home. Forensics will be here any minute. I'll have to come back, but you don't need to be here."

"I'll wait for you."

"No, you won't. I may be here hours and the media will be right behind the forensic team." He nudged her down the steps. "I called Charlie. He's at the lobby of my apartment building now and will keep an eye on you until I get there." He opened the car door for her. "As soon as you're inside the apartment, call Spiro and Mark and tell them what happened."

She nodded. "And maybe I'll call Barbara Eisley and see if I can talk her into seeing me again."

"Give it a rest, Eve. Let her cool off."

She shook her head. She couldn't forget her last glimpse of Jane MacGuire, sitting ramrod straight, afraid she'd break if she lowered her defenses.

Dom could break her and butcher her. How close had Jane come to Dom in the kitchen?

Panic rose inside Eve at the thought. Smother it. The immediate danger to Jane was over.

The hell it was. "I'm calling Barbara Eisley as soon as I get to the apartment."

. . .

"NO," BARBARA EISLEY said coldly. "Don't make me repeat myself again, Ms. Duncan. Jane stays in our custody. Come near her and I'll have you tossed in jail."

"You don't understand. Dom killed Fay Sugarton in broad daylight. He managed to get inside her house and then he cut her throat right in her own kitchen. What's to stop him from doing the same thing to Jane at the welfare house?"

"The fact that every day we deal with abusive parents and mothers on crack and heroin who want their children back. We know what we're doing. The location of the holding facility is confidential. And even if he found out where it is, no one's going to get past our security."

"You've never had to deal with—"

"Good-bye, Ms. Duncan."

"Wait. How is she?"

"Not good. But she'll get better. I'll send her to the therapist tomorrow morning." She hung up.

Eve remembered those therapists. Sitting there probing with their questions and then trying to hide their resentment when they couldn't get through to her. Jane would chew them up and spit them out just as Eve had when she was a child.

"No luck?"

She turned to Charlie, who was sitting across the room. "No luck. I'll try again tomorrow morning."

"You're persistent."

"Persistence is the only weapon I have with Eisley. Sometimes it works. Sometimes it doesn't." Dear God, she hoped it worked this time. "Have you heard anything from the agent Spiro sent to Phoenix?"

"Not much, only that their PD is cooperating. I wish Spiro had let me go." He smiled. "Not that I'm not enjoying the company. It's just that I joined the FBI for more challenging work than guard duty. Although the subject does have me running all over Georgia to keep her under surveillance."

"Sorry. Coffee? I'm afraid there's no food in the refrigerator."

"I saw a Thai restaurant around the corner that delivers." Charlie pulled out his phone. "What do you want?"

She wasn't hungry, but she supposed she should eat something. "Anything with noodles, I guess. And get something to put in the refrigerator for Joe. He never stops to eat."

"Okay."

She picked up her purse and headed for the bedroom. "I need to call Spiro."

"No, you don't. I already did that after Joe phoned me. He swore like a trooper and said he's on his way."

She closed the bedroom door and leaned back against it.

She should call Mark, but she needed a little time to recover. She still felt sick about Fay Sugarton. Barbara Eisley couldn't be blamed for being angry.

She went to the window and looked down at the park across the street. It was dark now and the street lamps cast pools of light on the trees. The night shadows seemed threatening.

Are you down there, Dom? Are you watching, you bastard?

Her digital phone rang.

Joe? Spiro?

Her phone rang again.

She pulled it out of her purse. "Hello."

"How are you getting along with little Janie?"

"You son of a bitch."

"I was sorry I couldn't stay around to see your meeting, but the timing was a little tight. I didn't even get a chance to see the kid at close quarters."

"So you killed Fay Sugarton instead."

"You make me sound like a blunderer. There was no 'instead'

about it. I had no intention of killing the child yet. Fay Sugarton was the target."

"For God's sake, why?"

"You and Jane couldn't bond while Sugarton was around. So she had to be taken out of the way. How do you like our little girl?"

"I don't. She tried to brain me with a baseball bat."

"That wouldn't deter you. You probably admire her spirit. I don't think I could have chosen better."

"You made a lousy choice. She's nothing like Bonnie."

"She'll begin to grow on you."

"She won't have the chance. It won't work. She's not with me."

"I know. We'll have to take care of that, won't we? It's not what I had in mind at all. Go get her from welfare, Eve."

"It's impossible."

"She has to be with you. You'll have to find a way to make that happen."

"You're not listening. They'll toss me in jail if I even go near her."

A silence. "Perhaps I'm not making myself clear. Either get her out of that welfare house or I'll go in after her. I'll give you twenty-four hours."

Panic soared through Eve. "I don't even know where she is."

"Find out. Think about it. You have contacts. There's always a way. I'd find a way."

"There's security. You'd never get near her. They'd catch you."

"I'd get near her. All it would take is one careless moment, one bored or disgruntled employee."

"I don't care anything about that child. I could never feel the slightest affection for—"

"Yes, you could. You just have to get to know her. You've spent years trying to protect and find children you never knew. Now I've given you one of your own. The potential is mind-boggling."

"I'm calling the police as soon as I hang up."

"And seal Jane's fate? It would, you know. I'd never stop trying. If I can't find a way to do it right now, I'll wait. A week, a month, a year. It's amazing how the passing of time makes everything easier for me. People forget, people lower their guard . . . and you wouldn't be close enough to her to stop me. Twenty-four hours, Eve." He hung up.

He was crazy, Eve thought. Eisley had said no one could get into that welfare facility.

But Eve herself had doubted it.

All it would take is one careless moment, one bored or disgruntled employee.

Wasn't that what Eve had been afraid of all along? Wasn't that why she had been urging Eisley to let her take Jane?

Her throat tightened as fear raced through her. He would do it. Christ, he would find a way to kill Jane if she didn't get her out of the facility.

She only had twenty-four hours.

Joe. She had to call Joe.

She was halfway through his number when she hung up. What was she doing? Was she really going to ask him to compromise his job by kidnapping a child from under the nose of welfare?

But she *needed* him.

So what? Stop being a selfish bitch and do what has to be done yourself.

How? She didn't even know where Jane was.

You have contacts. There's always a way. I'd find a way.

She started punching a phone number.

Mark Grunard answered on the second ring. He wasn't pleased. "Nice of you to let me know about Fay Sugarton. I got to her house along with half the newsmen in the city."

"I meant to call you. Things happened."

"That wasn't our agreement."

"It won't happen again."

"You're damn right it won't. I'm bailing out. You and Joe should have—"

"I need your help. Dom called again."

Silence. "And?"

"Welfare is keeping the kid at their holding facility. He wants her with me. He gave me twenty-four hours to get her."

"What happens if you don't?"

"What do you think happens? She's dead, dammit."

"It would be difficult to get to her at—"

"He'll do it. I can't take a chance."

"What does Joe say?"

"Nothing. I'm not telling him. Joe's out of it."

He gave a low whistle. "He's not going to like that."

"He's done enough. I won't have Joe crucified for helping me."

"But since you're calling me, I take it you're willing to sacrifice my humble self?"

"You have less to lose and more to gain."

"What kind of help do you want from me?"

"I need to know where she is. Do you have any idea?"

"Maybe."

"What do you mean, maybe?"

"Look, the location of that facility is a bigger secret than Level 4 of the CDC."

"But you know where it is?"

"Well, I followed Eisley once when she took a kid there during a big court case."

Then Dom could have followed Eisley too.

"It's a big old house on Delaney Street that used to be a convalescent home. The location could have changed though. That was over two years ago."

"We'll try it. Eisley said there's a guard."

"A security guard who patrols the grounds. I suppose you want me to distract him."

"Yes."

"And then? Once you've got her where are you going to take her?"

"I don't know. I'll find a place. Will you help me?"

"You're putting my ass on the line."

"I'll make it worth your while."

"Yes, you will." His tone hardened. "Because I'm going to be with you every step of the way."

"I can't do—" She drew a deep breath. "Okay, we'll work something out. Come and get me. I'll meet you across the street at the park."

"Not before midnight."

"Mark, it's only five-thirty now. I want to get her out of there."

"Okay, eleven. But if you want to go any earlier, you'll have to go by yourself. It's bad enough we have to run the risk of the security guard. I want everyone in that house asleep before I go near it."

Five and a half hours. How could she wait that long? She was already a nervous wreck. Okay, chill out. Dom had given her twenty-four hours. "All right. I'll eat dinner and then tell Charlie I'm going to bed. The kitchen door leads to a laundry room that opens to the hall. I can slip out and meet you at the park at eleven."

"Right."

She hung up. Done. Mark Grunard had been tougher than she had thought. Not that she could blame him. She was asking a great deal and not many people would give without wanting something in return.

Except Joe.

Don't think about Joe. She couldn't have him with her.

"Come on out," Charlie called from outside the bedroom door. "Food's here."

She braced herself. Just get through dinner and hope to slip out before Joe comes home.

CHAPTER

EIGHT

"WOULD YOU LIKE to talk?"

"No." Jane stared straight ahead. Let her just go *away*. The house mother looked like a plump gray bird perched on the sofa and her cooing voice was driving Jane crazy. Maybe she was trying to be nice, but Jane had had enough. "I want to go to bed, Mrs.—" What was her name? "Mrs. Morse."

"You'll sleep better if you talk about it."

Talk about blood. Talk about Fay. Why did grown-ups always think it was better to talk everything over? She didn't want to think about Fay. She never wanted to think about Fay again. She just wanted to close the door to all the pain. No, there was one thing she had to know first. "Who killed her?"

"You're safe here, dear," Mrs. Morse said gently.

That wasn't what she had asked, and Mrs. Morse was lying. No one was safe anywhere. "Who killed Fay?"

"We're not sure."

"The cops have to have some idea. Fay never hurt anyone. Was it one of the gangs? Was anything stolen?"

"It's better if you don't think about it right now. We'll talk about it tomorrow." She reached out to stroke Jane's hair. "But we really should discuss how you're feeling."

She leaned away before the woman could touch her. "I don't feel anything. I don't care that Fay died. I wouldn't care if you died either. Just leave me alone."

"I understand."

Jane gritted her teeth. What could she say to make the woman leave her alone? She didn't understand. No one understood.

Except maybe Eve. Eve hadn't tried to talk. She had sat silently with Jane, but Jane had somehow felt—

Stupid. They had been together only a matter of minutes. If Jane got to know her, she'd see that Eve was the same as all the others.

"Is there anything I can do for you?" Mrs. Morse asked.

Let me out of here.

She knew better than to say it. She had been in this place before. She was being protected until they could find another home for her.

But Mike wasn't being protected. He was out there in the dark and he didn't know that there would be no food and no one to keep an eye on him.

And she was going to be locked up and not be able to help him.

Blood.

Fay's eyes staring up at her as she tried to stop the blood.

Bad. So much badness out there.

Mike.

"You're trembling," Mrs. Morse said. "My poor child, why won't you—"

"I'm not trembling," Jane said fiercely. She stood up. "I'm cold. You keep it too cold in this son-of-a-bitchin' place."

"We don't use language like that here, dear."

"Then throw me out, you old cow." She glared at her. "I hate it here. I hate you. I'm going to sneak into your room and cut your throat like that bastard cut Fay's."

The woman stood and backed away as Jane had known she would. These days threats of violence were treated cautiously by welfare personnel even when uttered by a kid like Jane.

"That wasn't necessary," Mrs. Morse said. "Go on to bed, dear. We'll discuss your problem in the morning."

Jane ran out of the living room, up the stairs, past the policeman posted outside her room, and slammed the door behind her. They'd given the tiny room to her alone this time, although she'd probably have to share once they decided she'd gotten over the shock of Fay's death. Most of the time each room was occupied by three, maybe four children.

And they'd never before posted a guard outside her door either. It must have something to do with what had happened to Fay.

She couldn't breathe. She moved over to the window and looked down at the yard below. Those rosebushes should be cut back. Fay had Jane prune her roses in the fall. She'd said that they'd come back fuller and more beautiful in the spring. Jane hadn't believed her, but she'd been willing to wait and see if—

Fay.

Don't think of her. She's gone. There's nothing you can do about her. Shut the door.

Think about Mike instead and the streets and the creeps who could hurt him. She could help Mike.

But not if she stayed here.

• • •

THE TWO-STORY BRICK building on Delaney Street was set back and surrounded by patchy lawns and poorly kept gardens. It had been built in the twenties and looked every one of its years.

"May I ask what you're going to do?" Mark asked politely as he parked the car on a side street. "It's almost midnight and I'm sure the place is locked up tight as a drum. Providing you can find her in the first place, I'd be interested to know how you're going to get inside and then get the kid out without being shot by the security guard. He makes regular rounds."

I'd be interested to know too, Eve thought. "Do you have any idea where they'd keep her?"

"Well, they kept the boy in that court case on the upper floor. A room on the south side. First window facing the back."

"By himself?"

Mark nodded. "He was a special case."

Would Jane also be a special case? She'd just have to cross her fingers and pray she'd get lucky.

"I'm going around back and see if there's any way I can get in from there." She got out of the car. "You cover the other side, and if you run into the guard, distract him."

"Piece of cake," Mark said sarcastically. "Why don't you give me something hard to do? It's not—"

"Duck." She dove back into the car and pulled Mark down on the seat. "Patrol car."

The Atlanta PD car cruised slowly by the welfare house, shining its lights on the front of the building and grounds as it passed.

Eve held her breath, half expecting the car to stop. Had they been seen?

The police car drove on and turned the corner.

"I think it's safe now." Mark raised his head. "I suppose we should have expected welfare to request additional security."

"We've got to hope the guard is still the only one on the grounds." Eve got out of the car. "And that the police car doesn't come back anytime soon. Hurry." She was already skirting the walk and crossing the grass. Don't think. Just move fast and pray.

She arrived at the back of the building and looked up at the second floor. First window on the south side.

The room was dark and the window closed.

Great.

A rusty drainpipe clung to the side of the building, but it was at least a yard from the window.

What the hell was she going—

What was that?

She looked over her shoulder.

A sound?

Someone standing in the shadows?

No, there was nothing. It must have been her imagination.

She turned back to the house. First she had to find a way to get up to the second floor. Then she'd have to get inside the room without scaring Jane. The more she considered the situation, the more helpless she felt. She'd do better figuring out how to get into the ground floor and then—

The window was opening.

Eve tensed.

Jane stuck her head out and looked down at her. Could she tell who Eve was? Yes, the moonlight was bright enough for recognition. But that didn't guarantee anything. Everyone must seem like a threat to Jane right now.

She stared at Eve for a long while. Then she touched her forefinger to her lips as if to hush her.

The gesture was conspiratorial; the two of them against the world. Eve didn't know why she'd gotten lucky, but she'd take it. God, yes, she'd take it.

Jane tossed a knotted sheet out the window. It ended twelve feet above Eve's head. Jane started climbing down it like a monkey; how was she supposed to—

"Catch me," Jane ordered.

"It's not that easy. If I miss, you'll break—"

"Don't miss." She let go of the sheet and fell into Eve's arms. The child's weight knocked them both to the ground.

"Get *off* me," Jane whispered.

Eve rolled to the left and managed to sit up. "Sorry. You nearly broke my ribs."

Jane was on her feet and racing around the building.

"Shit." Eve jumped up and ran after her.

"Lose something?" Mark was holding Jane in a hammerlock. She kicked backward and connected with his shin. "Ouch. Stop fighting me or I'll break your neck, you little demon."

"Don't hurt her." Eve knelt down in front of the child. "We're trying to help you, Jane. Don't be afraid."

"I'm not afraid. And I don't need your help."

"You needed me to catch you."

"It was a long drop. I didn't want to break my legs."

Eve made a face. "You'd rather break my ribs."

Jane stared calmly into her eyes. "Why not? I don't care anything about you."

"But you must not think I'm a danger to you, since you didn't scream when you saw me."

"I needed someone. I knew the sheet wouldn't reach the ground."

"But you do believe I'm no danger to you?"

"Maybe. I don't know." She scowled. "Why are you here?"

Eve hesitated. She didn't want to scare the kid, but she sensed that Jane would see through a lie. "I was afraid for you."

"Why?"

"I'll tell you later. We don't have time now."

Jane looked over her shoulder. "This isn't the cop."

"No, he's Mark Grunard, a reporter."

"He wants to write stories about Fay."

"Yes."

"We should get out of here, Eve." Mark's voice was impatient. "I didn't run into the guard, but he's bound to come around soon. And who knows when that patrol car will come back."

She was as eager to leave as he was, but she wasn't about to drag Jane kicking and screaming. "Will you come with us, Jane?" Eve asked. "Believe me, we just want you to be safe."

Jane didn't answer.

"You were leaving anyway. I promise we'll locate a place where they won't find you."

"Let me go."

Mark shook his head. "And have you run out on—"

"Let her go, Mark. It has to be her decision."

Mark's hold loosened and Jane quickly slipped out of his grip.

Jane gazed at Eve for a few seconds and then said, "I'll go with you. Where's your car?"

THEY HAD DRIVEN no more than four blocks when Jane said to Mark, "You're going the wrong way."

"Wrong way?"

"I want to go to Luther Street."

Fay's house. "You can't go back there," Eve said gently. "Fay's not there anymore, Jane."

"I know that. Do you think I'm stupid? She's dead. They'd take her to the morgue. I still have to go to Luther Street."

"Did you leave something there?"

"Yes."

"The police are at the house. They won't let you in and they'll take you back to welfare."

"Just take me to Luther Street. Okay?"

"Jane, listen to me. The house is under—"

"I don't want to go to the house. Just let me off at the alley two blocks away."

"The alley you ducked down this afternoon when you spotted our car?"

Jane nodded.

"Why?"

"I want to go."

"You left something in the alley?" Mark asked from the driver's seat.

"Why do you want to know? So you can put it on TV?" Jane asked fiercely. "It's none of your business."

"You are my business at the moment," Mark said. "Eve promised me a story if I helped her spring you. Do you know what the penalty is for kidnapping minors? I'll get thrown in jail and my career will go down the drain. I'm risking a hell of a lot and I don't need your sass, little girl."

Jane ignored him and turned to Eve. "Jail? Then why did you do it?"

"I was worried about you. I thought you might be in danger."

"Like Fay?"

Christ, what could she say now? The truth. "Like Fay."

"You know who did it?"

Eve nodded.

"Who?"

"I'm not sure of his real name. He calls himself Dom."

"Why did he do it? Fay never hurt anyone."

"He's not sane. He likes to hurt people. I know that's terrible, but there are people out there who don't care about anything but doing harm."

"I know that. The creeps. There are lots of them around."

Eve stiffened. "Are there?" She paused. "Have you seen any of them around lately?"

"Maybe." Jane glanced at Mark. "I watch the news on TV. They always show the creeps."

Mark shrugged. "It's my job."

"Have you seen anyone who scared you lately?" Eve persisted.

"He didn't scare me. He was just like those others who hang around the school yard."

"Did he follow you?"

"Sometimes."

"For God's sake, why didn't you tell someone?"

Jane looked out the window. "I want to go to Luther Street. Now."

"What did he look like?" Mark asked.

"Big. Quick. I didn't really see him. Just another creep. Take me to Luther Street or let me out of the car."

Mark glanced at Eve with raised brows. "Well?"

"Take us to the alley but use the Market Street entrance. We can't chance anyone seeing us from the house."

"You mean Quinn." Mark took a left at the next corner.

"Yes." Unless Joe had already gone back to the apartment and discovered she was gone.

"He's going to raise hell about this."

"I know." She leaned back in the seat. "I couldn't do anything else."

"I'm not complaining. If you weren't trying to protect Quinn, you wouldn't have felt it necessary to have my help. He's not above jettisoning me if he thought it better for you."

"Hurry," Jane said.

There was such tension in her voice that Eve glanced at her in surprise. Jane was sitting straight up in the seat, her hands clenched into fists at her sides. "We'll be there soon, Jane."

"Just what did you leave in that alley?" Mark asked softly.

Jane didn't answer, but Eve could see her fists tightening into her palms and felt a sudden chill. "Speed it up, Mark."

"I'm doing the limit."

"Then go over it."

"Considering what we've just done, it's not smart to risk—"

"Do it."

He shrugged and pressed the accelerator.

"Thanks." Jane didn't look at Eve as she spoke the word grudgingly.

"What's in that alley, Jane?"

"Mike," Jane whispered. "The creep saw him. I told him to go over by the Union Mission, but he's probably back on Luther. It's closer to his mom."

"Who's Mike?"

"He's too little. I tried to keep him— Kids are dumb when they're that little. They don't know . . ."

"About creeps, Jane?"

"His father's a creep but not like—" Jane drew a deep breath. "You think that creep who's been following me is this Dom, who killed Fay, don't you?"

"I'm not sure."

"But you think he did."

"I believe he might have done it."

"Son of a bitch." Jane's eyes were glittering with tears. "Dirty son of a bitch."

"Yes."

"I should have told her. I thought he was just one of those creeps who went after kids. There are lots of them around. I didn't know he'd hurt—"

"It wasn't your fault."

"I should have told her. She wanted me to tell her things. I should have—"

"Jane, it wasn't your fault."

She shook her head. "I should have told her."

"Okay, maybe you should have told her. We all do things we regret. But you couldn't know he'd hurt her."

Jane closed her eyes. "I should have told her."

Eve gave up arguing. She'd had her own share of guilt and regrets after Bonnie had been taken from her. But Jane was only ten. Children shouldn't have to bear such heavy burdens. But since when was life fair? "How old is Mike?"

"Six."

Eve felt sick. Jane was the target, not this little boy. But would Dom care? Another life would mean nothing to him.

"Fay wouldn't let me bring him home with me. She wanted to call the welfare people about him. But I knew they'd just send him back to his father. Mike's afraid of him. I couldn't let her call." Her eyes opened. "I tried to keep him safe."

"I'm sure you did."

"But the creep saw me with him. He knows Mike's alone."

"He may be safe." Eve touched her shoulder. Jane was stiff as a board, but at least she didn't move away. "We'll find him, Jane. I'm sure Dom isn't anywhere near Luther. There are police all over the neighborhood."

"You said he was crazy."

"Not about his own safety. I'm sure Mike will be all right until we get to him." She hoped she was telling the truth. "And after that I'll make sure he stays safe."

"He can't go back to his father."

"I'll make sure he's safe," Eve repeated.

"You promise?"

Good God, what was she getting herself into? One kidnapping wasn't enough? "I promise." She paused. "But you've got to promise me that you'll do as I tell you so I can keep *you* safe."

"I'm not like Mike. I can take care of myself."

"A promise for a promise, Jane."

She shrugged. "Okay, if you're not stupid about it."

Eve breathed a sigh of relief. "I'll try not to be stupid. I'm sure you'll tell me if I am."

"You bet I will."

Mark pulled off the street and stopped just inside the alley.

"Turn off your lights," Jane hissed. "Do you want to scare him?" She scrambled out of the car and ran down the alley.

"Jane!" Eve jumped out and followed her into the darkness.

The digital phone in her handbag rang.

She ignored it. She couldn't deal with either Joe or Dom just then.

But she might have to deal with Dom in the flesh, she thought suddenly. He might have known that Jane would come to the alley.

He might be waiting ahead in the darkness.

NO ANSWER.

Joe's stomach clenched as he hung up. She should have answered; she always had the digital phone on. If she were asleep, the ringing would have woken her up. But she'd been so upset, he doubted she'd fallen asleep.

And where the hell was Charlie Cather?

He called the apartment phone.

Charlie answered drowsily on the second ring.

"Everything okay?" Joe asked.

"Fine. Locked up tight. Ms. Duncan went to bed a couple of hours ago."

He still didn't like it. Why hadn't she answered her digital? "She's okay?"

"Fine. She was a little quiet, but that's not unusual, is it? She's concerned about the kid."

"Yes."

"Did Agent Spiro arrive?"

"He's at the crime scene. I'm back at the precinct, but I have these damn reports to type up."

"I hear you. God, I hate paperwork."

She should have answered the digital, Joe kept thinking. "Go check on her."

"What?"

"Dammit, go check on her."

"Wake her up?"

"If you have to wake her, do it. Check on her."

"She won't thank me if I— Okay, I'll check."

Joe waited.

She was probably fine. It was unlikely Dom would try to get to her at the apartment. Besides, that wasn't in his game plan. It would be too simple. He was using Jane MacGuire to bait the net.

And one woman had already been caught in that net. All afternoon and night Joe had been dealing with her murder. When he'd looked at Fay Sugarton, all he could think about was Eve. But when wasn't he thinking of Eve?

"She's gone."

Joe closed his eyes. God, he'd known it.

"I swear, no one got into the apartment, Joe. I've been here all the time, and I checked the doors after Eve went to bed."

"Did she get any phone calls?"

"Not on the apartment phone. And I didn't hear her digital ring."

"You might not have heard it if she was in another room."

"She didn't mention a call."

Dom had called her. Joe knew it in his gut. Dom had called and she had left the apartment.

To meet him?

She wouldn't have done that. It would have been stupid, and Eve was never stupid.

No, to lure her out of the apartment, Dom would have used a threat she couldn't ignore.

Jane MacGuire.

Shit.

He hung up and flipped his Rolodex for Barbara Eisley's pager. It was the only way he could get the address of the halfway house at this hour.

Eisley called back in less than a minute. But it took ten minutes for Joe to persuade her to give him the address.

Rage and fear were building inside him with every second. He wanted to *strangle* Eve. She had closed him out again. All the years of being together, and she had turned her back on him. He wished he'd never met the bitch. Who needed to have that kind of torment in their lives? Half the time he wanted to shake her and the other half he wanted to cradle her and take away her pain. She thought she was strong enough to take on anything, but she was no match for Dom.

Don't do it, Eve.

Don't run toward him.

Wait for me.

SHE WAS RUNNING.

The alley smelled of grease and garbage.

Darkness.

A sound to the left.

Her heart leaped to her throat.

Dom?

No, only a cat.

Where was Jane?

"Jane? Do you see her, Mark?"

"Here," Jane called out.

The big cardboard refrigerator box against the brick wall.

"Mike's okay." Jane crawled out of the box, dragging a small boy with her. "He's just scared. He said he kept hearing scratching tonight. Probably rats. He's hungry. You got anything in your purse?"

"I'm afraid not."

"Who are they?" Mike was staring at Eve and Mark warily. "Welfare?"

"I wouldn't do that to you," Jane said. "But you can't stay here any longer. There's some bad people hanging around."

"I'm okay."

"You'll be better where Eve will take you. Get your stuff."

Mike hesitated.

"There will be plenty of food."

"Okay." Mike ducked back into the box.

"Where are you going to take him?" Jane asked. "He's going to want to know."

So did Eve. "I've got to think about it."

"Not welfare."

"No."

"Not back to his father."

"Okay, Jane, I get the point."

"You promised."

She inhaled sharply. Something was gleaming wetly on the cardboard box. "I'll keep my promise."

Mike came out of the box carrying a duffel bag. "What kind of food? I like french fries."

"I'll see what I can do." She turned to Mark. "Take them back to the car, will you?"

Jane looked at her.

Mark raised his brows. "You're not coming?"

"In a minute."

He nodded and began to shepherd the children up the alley.

She reached out and gingerly touched the dark stain on the box. Not as wet as she'd thought, only a little came off on her fingertips. Her hand was trembling as she reached into her handbag and drew out a small flashlight.

The stain on her fingers was dark red, almost rusty.

Blood.

He kept hearing scratching tonight.

She shone the light on the box.

You've done well, Eve. A small reward . . .

She felt sick as she realized how close Dom had been to the little boy.

Reward?

Mike's life was her reward?

No.

The dots at the end of the sentence were leading downward.

Something white lay on the ground.

She slowly knelt down and shone the light on the small object.

A bone. Tiny, delicate. A child's finger bone.

Bonnie?

She felt faint and held on to the cardboard box to keep from falling to the ground.

Hold on. He wants you to hurt.

Oh, God, Bonnie . . .

Don't touch it. Don't touch anything. Maybe he's made a mistake this time.

See, she was getting better. She hadn't been able to leave the rib he'd left for her on the porch.

She could do it now. She could leave that fragile bone lying in the alley if it meant a chance at catching the bastard.

She struggled to her feet and turned off the flashlight.

Fight the pain. Walk.

Don't think of the bone. Don't think of Bonnie.

She couldn't save her daughter, but she might be able to save Jane and Mike.

Are you there, Dom? Go ahead, show me blood. Show me my daughter's bones. Everything you do is making me stronger.

I won't let you win this time.

CHAPTER NINE

THE MAN'S THROAT had been slashed.

"Son of a bitch."

Joe looked up to see Barbara Eisley standing a few feet away. She took a step closer and looked down at the body that had been rolled into the bushes bordering the house. "The security guard?"

"What are you doing here?"

"Why shouldn't I be here? You wake me up in the middle of the night and tell me that you're coming out here to disturb my people and you expect me to just go back to sleep?" She glanced back at the halfway house in which every light was blazing. "This is my responsibility. Where's Jane MacGuire?"

"I don't know."

"The house mother says she's not in her room. The guard's dead. Could she be dead too?"

"She could be." When Eisley flinched, he added, "But I don't believe so. There was a knotted sheet hanging from her window."

"So she climbed down—and dropped right into a murderer's hands."

"Maybe not."

Eisley's gaze raked his face. "Eve Duncan." She swore beneath her breath. "I told her to stay away from the kid."

"And she told you Jane was in danger. You wouldn't listen. You'd better pray Eve got to her before the man who killed your security guard did." He rose to his feet. "Don't let anyone touch anything or track around this area before the forensic team gets here."

"Where are you going?"

"To find Jane MacGuire."

"If Eve Duncan took her, it's kidnapping." She paused. "But since there are mitigating circumstances, if she returns the child within twenty-four hours, I might persuade the department not to press charges."

"I'll convey your generous offer to her. Providing she ever makes contact with me."

"You have to know where she is. That child has to be found." There was a hint of panic in her voice. "You're friends, aren't you?"

"I thought we were."

He could feel her gaze on him as he walked toward his car at the curb.

You're friends, aren't you?

Friends. Through all the years he'd forced himself to accept the relationship, and now she was even edging away from that.

At the worst possible time.

Screw friendship. Screw hope. I don't give a damn.

Just call and let me know that bastard hasn't gotten to you.

• • •

MARK PARKED THE car in front of the Peachtree apartment building. "Who lives here?"

"My mother and her fiancé," Eve answered. "She's the only one I could think of who'd be willing to take care of Mike."

Jane looked up at the thirteen-story high-rise. "Your mother?" she said doubtfully.

"She managed to raise me. I believe she can be trusted with Mike."

"Maybe."

Eve sighed with exasperation. Not only would she have to persuade Sandra to help, but her mother also had to win Jane's seal of approval. "He'll be safe here, Jane. The building has security, and my friend, Joe, arranged additional protection for my mother. He'll be fed and protected. What else can you ask for?"

Jane didn't answer as she headed for the front entrance with Mike trailing at her heels.

Eve looked at Mark. "Coming?"

"I don't think so. It's after one in the morning. I'd much rather face our serial killer than wake your mother and her boyfriend from a sound sleep and try to convince them to be instant parents. I'll wait here."

"Coward."

He smiled. "Yep."

She started after the children. She wasn't eager to face the task at hand either. She scarcely knew Ron Fitzgerald. She'd met him only once before she'd left for Tahiti. He'd seemed pleasant, smart, and genuinely devoted to her mother. But he owed Eve nothing.

Then she would tackle him first. Even though she hated imposing on Sandra, she didn't doubt her mother would help. She just didn't want to do anything that would mess up a relationship her mother obviously treasured. She'd ask her to take the kids into the kitchen and fix them something to eat, then explain the situation to Ron and appeal for his help.

. . .

"NO," RON SAID flatly. "I won't have Sandra involved in any illegal activities. Take the kids to the police."

"I can't do that. I told you—" Eve stopped and drew a deep breath. "I'm not asking you to accept Jane. That might put you both in danger. But Dom has no interest in Mike, or he would have killed him when he had the chance. I just need someone to take care of him until I can work my way through this mess."

"He's a runaway. There are serious repercussions for not returning him to his parents."

"For God's sake, according to Jane he's been on the street for days and no one's reported him missing. Do you think his parents care?"

"It's against the law."

And who should know better than a lawyer? "I need help, Ron."

"I can see you do, but Sandra is my concern. I'd like to help, but I can't afford to let her—"

"We'll do it." Her mother stood in the doorway. "Stop being a protective ass, Ron."

He turned to face her. "How long have you been standing there?"

"Long enough." She came toward them. "Do you think Eve would have come here if she'd had any other choice?"

"Let me take care of this, Sandra."

She shook her head. "That little boy is scared. We're not going to toss him back to his parents, and I'm not going to send Eve away when she needs me. I did that too many times when she was a kid." She paused. "But she's not your daughter. I can take Mike back to my own house."

He scowled. "The hell you will."

"Believe it." Her tone was quiet but firm. "We've been very happy, but there's more to my life than just you, Ron."

"Harboring a runaway is illegal, and I won't have you—"

"Did I ever tell you how many times Eve ran away when I was on crack?" She looked at Eve. "He doesn't mean to be hard. He's just never been there."

"I don't want to mess up anything for you, Mom."

"If taking a kid in from the cold can mess up what Ron and I have, then it's not worth keeping." She turned back to Ron. "Is it?"

He stared at her for a moment, and then he gave a faint smile. "Damn you, Sandra." He shrugged. "Okay, you win. We tell the neighbors he's my brother's kid visiting from Charlotte."

Relief surged through Eve. "Thank you."

Sandra shook her head. "You're so stubborn about standing alone and not letting anyone help you. It's nice to be able to do something for you."

Eve warily glanced at Ron.

"It's okay. I don't like it, but it's okay." He slipped his arm around Sandra's waist. "But you stay away from her until this bastard is behind bars. Do you hear me? I won't have Sandra in danger."

"I didn't intend anything else. Keep your digital phone on, Mom. I'll call periodically to make sure everything's okay." She stood up. "Now I'll go and find Jane and get out of here."

"I'm ready." Jane stood in the doorway. "Mike's having another pancake, Mrs. Duncan. You'd better stop him or he'll have a bellyache tonight."

"Another? Good heavens, he's already had six." Sandra hurried toward the kitchen.

Jane came forward. "We should leave now. I've explained things to Mike, but he may make a fuss if he starts thinking about me leaving." She looked at Ron. "You take good care of him. He may be scared of you at first. His father is big like you."

"I'll take care of him."

She studied him. "You don't want to do it." She turned to Eve. "Maybe we shouldn't—"

"I said I'll take care of him," Ron said testily. "I don't have to like it. I promised and I'll do it."

Jane was still frowning.

Christ, she had to get her out of there. "Come on, Jane." Eve pushed her toward the front door. "They'll be better off alone."

"I'm not sure that—"

Eve pulled her out into the hall and closed the door. "He'll be fine. Mom will take care of him."

"She doesn't cook very well. The pancakes were runny."

"Cooking isn't one of her talents. But she's a good person. You'd like her if you got to know her."

"I do like her. She's sort of like . . . Fay."

"And Fay was very protective, wasn't she?"

"Yes." Another silence. "That man."

"He's a nice guy. He won't hurt Mike."

"I don't like him."

Eve had liked him a lot better the first time she'd met him. But no one was perfect, and she should be glad he was protective of Sandra. "He's worried about my mother. Do you think I'd leave Mike if I wasn't certain?"

Jane stared at her with a frown and finally shook her head. "I guess not. Where are we going?"

"Someplace out of town where we can find a motel and get some sleep. I'm tired, aren't you?"

"Yes."

Eve could see Jane was exhausted. Her face was pinched and pale with strain and yet she had doggedly held on until Mike was settled.

Jane was silent until they got into the elevator. "Why?" she whispered. "Why is it happening?"

"I'll tell you, but not now. Trust me."

"Why should I?"

What could she say? After what Jane had gone through in the last twenty-four hours, why should she trust anyone? "I don't know. I'm not sure if I'd trust anyone either. I guess because I'm your best bet."

"That's not saying much."

Frustration made Eve speak sharply. "Well, it's all you'll get from me. It's all I can give you."

"You don't have to get nasty."

"Yes, I do. I feel nasty. I'm mad as hell and I don't need—" She bit her lower lip. "Sorry. Things are piling up on me."

Jane was silent until they reached the front entrance of the apartment building. "It's okay. I'd rather you be nasty and honest. I hate those soppy caseworkers who ooze all over me."

As a child, Eve had hated them too, but as an adult she felt bound to defend them. "They want only to do their—" Oh, what the devil. She was too tired for hypocrisy. "I promise I'll never ooze." She opened the back door of the car. "Jump in. We have to get out of here."

Mark looked over his shoulder at them. "I see we've lost one of our orphans."

"Mom will take care of him."

"So where to now?"

"Away from here. Fast. One of the first things the police will do to find me is talk to Mom. We're lucky we got here before they did. Go somewhere outside the city. A motel."

"Any preference?"

She shook her head. "Somewhere safe."

"Safe from Dom or safe from Joe Quinn?"

Joe.

Mark's narrowed gaze met hers in the rearview mirror. "Joe will find you, Eve."

She knew he would. It was only a matter of time. So she had to take advantage of that time. "I'll deal with Joe later."

He gave a low whistle. "Better you than me."

But no matter how much she dreaded it, she needed to call Joe at least one more time. She had to tell him about the scrawl on the cardboard box and the bone. Perhaps Dom had left some scrap of evidence.

He had made no detectable mistakes so far.

But wasn't he showing signs of recklessness? Mere hours after killing Fay Sugarton, he risked discovery by planting that bone only blocks from the crime scene.

Maybe he wasn't invulnerable. Maybe this time he'd left a clue to his identity.

So call Joe, take the flak, and tell him.

MARK GRUNARD DROVE them to a Motel 6 near Ellijay, Georgia. He arranged for a single room for himself and a double for Eve and Jane.

"As you ordered." He handed Eve a key. "I'll see you in the morning."

"Thanks, Mark."

"For what? I'd like to say I'm doing everything to save the kid, but I'm really interested only in the story."

"Thanks anyway."

She pushed Jane into the room and locked the door. "Bathroom. Wash up." Jesus, it was cold. She turned up the thermostat. "You can sleep in your underclothes tonight. I'll get you something else to wear tomorrow."

Jane yawned. "Okay."

She called Joe's digital number as soon as she was sure Jane was asleep in the twin bed next to her.

"Joe?"

"Where the *hell* are you?"

"I'm fine. And I have Jane MacGuire. She's safe."

"I've been hunting all over the city for you. Sandra wouldn't tell me a damn thing."

"Are the police bothering her?"

"Of course they are. What do you think?"

"Help her, Joe."

"As much as I can. She's not the one they want. Where are you?"

She didn't answer the question. "I just called to tell you there may be usable evidence in the alley off Luther Street. Dom left a message in blood on a cardboard box and a child's finger bone on the ground."

"Does the message say who the child is?"

"No."

Bonnie.

Close it out. Don't think about Bonnie.

"And I don't know who the blood belongs to."

"I do. The security guard at the welfare house you busted her out of."

"Christ." She shivered as she realized Dom might have already been preparing to go after Jane. "How long has he been dead?"

"We don't know yet. It was cold tonight. Time of death can be hard to determine when the body's been exposed to low temperatures. The last time anyone saw him was about eight-fifteen."

So his death could have occurred in the early evening, hours before she appeared on the scene. The eerie feeling she'd had as she had stood beneath Jane's window could have been imagination.

"Which makes you both a kidnapper and a suspect in a murder," Joe said.

"Murder?"

"You were at the scene. Though I don't believe anyone's going to seriously believe you're a murderer."

"That's comforting."

"But you'll be considered at least a material witness, and you'll be wanted for questioning. And then there's the kidnapping. There's an APB on you."

"You know why I had to get Jane out of there. Dom told me if I didn't, he'd go in after her."

"I thought as much." His voice was without expression. "It would have been nice if you'd called me and talked it over."

God, he was angry. "I had to do it myself."

"Did you? If I recall, I'm involved up to my neck. Why did you decide to cross me off your list?"

"You know why. I had to get Jane away even if I broke the law. You're a cop, Joe."

"You think that would have stopped me from helping? I'd have done it *for* you, dammit."

"I know." She swallowed to ease the tightness of her throat. "I couldn't allow it."

"You couldn't allow—" He had to stop to temper his tone. "Who the hell gave you the right to make my decisions for me?"

"I took the right."

"And you shut me out."

"I shut you out. Stay out, Joe."

"Oh, no. I've let you sweep me into the background too many times. I can take that but I won't have you walk away from me."

"I wouldn't be a good friend to you if I let you—"

"Screw friendship." His voice was hoarse with barely contained violence. "I'm sick to death of it. Just as I'm sick of standing on the sidelines and having you treat me like some old hound that needs nothing more than an occasional pat on the head."

Shock surged through her. "Joe."

"It's happened too often, Eve."

"The hell it has."

"The hell it hasn't. You're not even aware of it. You block everything out, and what you don't block out, you interpret to suit yourself.

You'll hang up the phone tonight and you won't look beyond what you want to see."

"I've never taken you for granted," she said in an uneven voice, "and I've never treated you as anything but my very dear friend."

"Then why didn't you tell me? Why don't you tell me where you are?" He took a deep breath and then his voice lowered persuasively. "Last chance. Let me come to you now. Afterward I'll step back. I'll let you bury your head and not—"

"I can't. You can't help me. Not this time."

He didn't speak for a moment, and she could sense his emotions seething in that silence. "Your choice. You know, I'm almost relieved. But I'll find you. I'm not going to let you close me out, and I'll be damned if I'm going to let that son of a bitch kill you."

"I don't want you to look for me. If you call me, I'll hang up. Do you understand?"

"I'll find you." He hung up.

She was shaking as she punched the off button. Joe was one of the bedrocks of her life, and she felt as if that rock had exploded beneath her feet. She had seen him angry before, but this was different. He had attacked her. He had said terrible, false things. She had never taken him for granted. She didn't know what life would be like without Joe. Why couldn't he understand she was doing only what was best for him?

Smother the hurt. Go to sleep. Try to forget.

She turned off the light on the nightstand.

I'll find you.

His words had sounded like a threat. The intimidating Joe she had spoken to tonight was the tough cop, the ex-SEAL. Relentless, unswerving, deadly.

Nonsense. Joe would never threaten her. Joe was closer than a brother, more protective than a father.

You treat me like some old hound that needs nothing more than an occasional pat on the head.

She couldn't think about Joe. She didn't need any more turmoil in her life.

You block everything out.

Hell, yes, she'd block out Joe for now and she'd be damned if she'd feel guilty.

She closed her eyes, ignoring the stinging behind her lids. Go to sleep. Tomorrow she would find a way to make sure Jane was safe from Dom. That was much more urgent than Joe's hurt feelings and lack of understanding. That could be solved later. It was Jane who was important now.

I'm sick of standing on the sidelines.

God, it wasn't that she thought Joe was less import—

Don't think of him. The message beneath those words was as disturbing as a volcano ready to erupt. She'd always known it was there but had chosen not to see it. And she couldn't permit herself to see it now.

She turned over, willing herself to go to sleep.

I'll find you. . . .

HER PHONE RANG, rousing her from sleep.

Joe? She wouldn't answer. She couldn't face any more arguments or—

It rang again.

Dammit, she had to answer or risk Jane being woken up.

She kept her voice to a whisper. "Hello."

"Did you go to the alley off Luther Street?"

Dom.

"Yes."

"Then you must have our sweet Jane. I thought she'd insist on going to help her little friend. She appears very fond of him. It's the kind of thing you would have done as a child, isn't it? Did I mention how much alike you are?"

"You killed the security guard."

"Just helping you a little. He would have gotten in your way. How did you get her out? The drainpipe? I had considered it, but—"

"Why are you calling?"

"I like to hear your voice. Do you realize how full of tension and emotion you are? I can hear every nuance of it. It's very exciting."

"I'm hanging up."

"Then I guess I'd better get down to the business of guiding you in the direction I want you to go. It's too dangerous for either of us to remain in Atlanta. They could arrest you for kidnapping, and that would spoil everything. You wouldn't be able to bond with Jane and I'd have to slit her throat. I'm sure you'd surround her with protection, so it would be a very difficult kill."

Her hand tightened on the phone. "If I were arrested, you would have no reason to kill Jane. Your little scenario would be spoiled."

"But I gave my word," he said gently. "I always keep my word. So you have to be careful not to get caught, don't you? That's why I want you to leave Atlanta."

"Are you afraid I might find you if I stayed?"

"On the contrary, I like raising your hopes. The idea of you searching for me is wonderfully stimulating. It's been a long time since I've felt this much excitement. I was always so concerned about making the kill perfect and undetectable, I never realized I needed a certain amount of interaction."

"You won't get it if I'm hiding away somewhere."

"I don't want you to hide away. I just want you out of Atlanta. I think it's time for you to take a trip to Phoenix."

"What?"

"I've always liked Phoenix."

"I know. You've killed there."

"You know that?"

"The FBI already has a fix on two murders you committed there years ago. So you're not as clever as you thought. We'll get you, Dom."

"Not from those kills. You won't find any evidence. I was very careful, and time will have erased what I didn't. It's only lately that I may have been bored enough to make a mistake. You have a small chance of catching me if you find a fresh kill."

"What are you talking about?"

"I think it fitting that you find the woman who brought us together. She wasn't very interesting, but that kill made me finally realize that there was something very wrong and eventually led me to you. She showed me the light, and then I showed *her* the light."

"In Phoenix?"

"Ah, you're beginning to sound eager."

"What was her name?"

"I don't remember. It didn't matter."

"When?"

"Five or six months perhaps. I can't remember. There was an earlier kill who gave me a hint of my problem, but she was the one who lit the way. It's important that the way be lighted for us, isn't it? Find her, Eve, and you may find me."

"Tell me where she is."

"You know better than that. You have to work for it." He paused. "She had a lovely voice, I understand. A soprano."

"She was a singer?"

"Go to Phoenix. Take Jane with you. Cling to her, nurture her . . . mother her. Did you find the bone?"

"Damn you."

He laughed. "You may have the complete set soon, and I'll have to start again. Doesn't Jane have an interesting bone structure?"

Don't lose your temper. He wanted to flay her with words so he would get a response. "Scatter all the bones you please. They're not Bonnie's."

"You did that very well. I could almost believe you meant it. Go to Phoenix, Eve."

"You bastard, why should I do anything you want me to do?"

"Phoenix. That's my last word on the subject." He hung up.

The last word. How many last words had the son of a bitch heard over the years? How many screams, how many pleas?

Had the woman in Phoenix pleaded with him before he killed her?

"It was him, wasn't it?" Jane asked out of the darkness.

Oh, shit.

"The man who killed Fay? Why did he call you?"

"It's a long story, Jane."

"I heard you say he wanted to kill me. Why? I didn't do anything to him. Neither did Fay."

"I told you he wasn't sane."

"But why does he want to kill me?" Jane's tone was fierce. "You *tell* me, Eve."

Eve hesitated. How much could she explain without terrifying the poor kid?

"Tell me."

Forget trying to be kind and soothing. Jane needed to know the threat and where it was coming from. If she'd made Bonnie more knowledgeable about the beasts out there, maybe she'd still be alive.

"Okay." She turned on the light. "I'll tell you, Jane."

"HE DIDN'T WRITE with his finger," Spiro told Joe, who waited by his car in the entrance to the alley. "That would have been too lucky. We found a stick with blood on one end behind the box. We'll probably find wood particles in the blood on the box. We'll examine the stick for fiber, since he probably wore gloves. What the hell was he doing here anyway?"

"I've no idea." Joe's gaze remained fastened on the four agents who were still swarming about the cardboard box. "Eve didn't confide in me. She just told me about the box and the bone."

"She must have been pretty shook up."

"No doubt." Joe got back in the car. "How fast can you process the tests?"

"Couple of days."

"Odds are the blood's the security guard's." He started the car. "Let me know as soon as you can."

"Where is she, Joe?"

"I don't know."

"Kidnapping's a serious offense."

"I know that." He lifted his gaze to meet Spiro's. "And you know why she took her."

"That's not my business. It's the court's. It's my job to catch her."

"Your job is to catch Dom. For God's sake, get your priorities straight."

Spiro smiled faintly. "My priorities *are* straight. I want Eve because she's my strongest lead to Dom." His gaze narrowed on Joe's face. "Where is she, Joe?"

"I told you, I don't know."

His brows lifted in surprise. "My God, maybe you don't."

"But I'm going to find out." He looked away from Spiro and said stiltedly, "I'd appreciate any information you can give me."

"My, that was hard for you, wasn't it? You must be desperate."

"I have to find her."

"I was wondering why you didn't try to talk your department out of issuing that APB on her. You want her found even if it means she gets tossed in jail."

"You didn't try to stop the APB either. You don't want her running around or hiding someplace where you can't contact her."

Spiro didn't answer.

"Will you tell me if you find out anything?"

"Maybe." Spiro shrugged. "Okay. Not that I have any faith that you'd return the favor."

Joe started the car. "Don't be too sure. Wherever Eve is, Dom is. I might need your help."

Spiro was still standing there as Joe drove off. He looked grimmer and more tired than ever in the harsh headlights. Would he call Joe if he got a lead on Eve? Joe wasn't sure. So don't trust Spiro to tell him.

All right, he had done all he could here.

Now it was time to stop feeling and start thinking.

And then go on the hunt.

"IT DOESN'T MAKE sense," Jane said. "I don't have anything to do with you. Neither did Fay."

"I know."

"I hate it. I hate you."

Eve flinched. She should have expected Jane's reaction. "I don't blame you. But the fact exists that Dom is a danger to you. You have to let me help protect you."

"I don't have to do anything."

"All right, you don't have to do anything. You can run away and maybe Dom won't find you. You can get yourself picked up by welfare and let the police protect you." She paused. "But you told me you don't trust the police."

Jane glared at her.

"Or you can go with me and work with me to keep yourself safe."

"I don't want to go anywhere with you." She was silent a moment. "You're going to Phoenix, aren't you? You're going to do what he wants."

"I don't think I have any choice, do you? He has to be caught, Jane."

"Yes." She lay as stiff as a stick in the bed. "He killed Fay. She never did anything to him and he killed her. I hate him. I hate the son of a bitch."

"So do I. We, at least, have that in common."

"He really thinks I'm your daughter? He's got to be crazy."

"I believe he just wants me to consider you my daughter."

She was silent a moment. "Was Bonnie much like me?"

Eve shook her head. "No. She was younger, softer, dreamier. You're more like what I was when I was growing up."

"I'm nothing like you."

"Have it your way."

"I will."

"But I believe you'll be safe as long as you stay with me. He wants us together. Will you come with me, Jane?"

Jane turned her back on Eve.

Don't push. Let her think. She's smart.

Eve turned out the light. "Let me know in the morning."

No answer.

What would she do if Jane refused to go with her? The question scared her to death.

She would face that possibility when it confronted her.

You bury your head.

And she wouldn't think about Joe or his unfair words. They stung too much.

Joe . . .

"What do you mean? Softer?"

"What?"

"Your daughter."

"I loved her very much. I wanted everything to be sweet and sunny for her. I've been thinking lately that maybe if I'd shown her— Never mind."

"You're saying you were stupid. Like I was about not talking to Fay."

"I guess that's what I'm saying."

Another silence. "I don't think you're stupid very often."

"Once is enough."

"Yeah."

Christ, she was saying all the wrong things. Jane was feeling guilty enough. "Fay's death had nothing to do with you, Jane. If there's someone besides Dom who was responsible, it's me. Let me try to make sure you don't get hurt too."

Minutes passed.

Go to sleep. She's not going to answer.

"I'll go with you," Jane said.

Eve breathed a profound sigh of relief. "Good."

"Not because I like you. I don't feel anything for you. I wouldn't care if he killed you. But I hate *him*. I hate what he did to Fay. I hate what he wants to do to me. I wish someone would slit his throat."

"I understand."

Yes, she understood the hatred and helplessness Jane was feeling as if the emotions were her own.

As if Jane were her own.

She instantly rejected the idea. It was what Dom wanted, the growing closeness and empathy, and she would not let him have it. Keep Jane at a distance. It should be easy. Jane was tough and wanted nothing to do with Eve.

She hadn't been very tough with Mike. When she had smiled at him, she had reminded Eve a little of Bonnie. The same luminous, loving quality . . .

Crazy.

Bonnie and Jane were nothing alike.

Thank God.

So stop thinking of either of them. Think instead of how to keep Jane safe in Phoenix.

And stop letting Dom call all the shots.

It was time to go on the hunt.

Her phone rang again.

What the hell?

"PHOENIX?" MARK'S TONE was thoughtful. "It is a long way from Atlanta. You might have a better chance of hiding the kid there." Standing outside McDonald's, Mark looked at Jane, who was inside, seated at a booth eating breakfast.

"Bull," Eve told him. "There's no place that's a long way from anywhere these days. You guys in the media have made sure of that."

"Technology has a little something to do with it." Mark took a drink of his coffee. "Going to Phoenix is a big risk, isn't it?"

"It's a bigger risk staying here."

"What about protection for the kid?"

"I have an idea what I can do."

"But you won't tell me?"

She shook her head.

"And that means you don't want me to go with you to Phoenix."

She shook her head again. "No one knows you're involved in my taking Jane. You've helped me enough."

"For a reason. I want the story, Eve. You *owe* it to me."

"I'll call you when I'm getting close."

"And I'm to trust you?"

"I won't turn my back on you."

He studied her. "I don't think you will." He shrugged. "Okay, I'll go back to work. I might run into something that'll help you. You'll let me know where you are?"

"I'll let you know."

"How are you going to get there?"

"I hope you'll let me borrow your car. I'll drive it to Birmingham and leave it at the airport."

"And how will you get on a plane without being recognized? You have to have an ID to go to the bathroom these days."

"I'll manage."

"I could drive you to Phoenix."

"You've done enough."

"Just thought I'd give it a shot." He glanced at Jane again. "She's not going to give you any trouble?"

"I didn't say that. She's wary of everyone, and that includes me. She hasn't said more than two sentences since we got up this morning. But at least I can reason with her." She held out her hand. "Thanks for everything, Mark."

He shook it and then dropped his car keys into her palm. "Remember, you owe me. I'm letting you off the hook right now, but I want that story."

"You'll get it." She started for the booth where Jane was sitting.

"Eve."

She looked back over her shoulder.

Mark's gaze narrowed on her face. "You're too damn confident this morning."

She made a face. "I wish I were."

"You're in better shape than you were last night."

"Things always look brighter in the morning."

"Not necessarily. I think you have an ace in the hole you're not telling me about."

She waved. "Good-bye, Mark. I'll be in touch."

He was wrong. She wasn't at all confident; she was scared and confused. What Mark had seen as confidence was only the faint glimmer of hope.

But she'd take it.

. . .

HE WAS WAITING at the parking lot at the Birmingham airport.

"You're an idiot." Logan drew Eve close and kissed her hard. "And Joe's a criminal idiot to allow you to get into a mess like this."

"Joe had nothing to do with it." She felt a deep sense of comfort as she stepped back and stared at him. He looked dear and strong and familiar. "He doesn't know anything about it."

"You made sure of that to protect the SOB."

"Let's not talk about Joe." She gestured for Jane to get out of the car. "Did you bring the ID?"

He handed her a leather pouch. "Cash, phony birth certificates, two credit cards, and a driver's license."

"Is he a crook?" Jane asked.

Logan glanced at her. "It depends on who you ask."

"On the streets they sell phony IDs to anyone who wants one."

"I don't sell, I buy. And you should be glad I was able to buy these at such short notice."

"This is John Logan, Jane. He's not a crook, he's a well-respected businessman."

"And he's the one you said would help us?"

"We couldn't board a flight without phony IDs."

"I've arranged a place for you to stay—it's on the outskirts of Phoenix. Two of my company's top security people will be there to keep an eye on you." He took Eve's elbow. "Come on, let's go."

"We say good-bye here." She hung back. "I don't want to be seen with you, Logan."

"You're not going to say good-bye to me until we reach Phoenix. I have a private jet waiting. That way you won't have to chance being recognized."

"No." She dug in her heels. "I know I agreed to let you help me when you called last night, but I don't want you to do anything more."

"Too late." He smiled. "I can handle the heat. Just watch me."

"I don't want to watch you. I don't want to be responsible for anyone else getting involved in this mess."

His smile faded. "Listen to me. I'm not backing away when you're in trouble. You should have called me instead of letting me hear secondhand from one of my associates in Atlanta."

"Associates? Are you having me watched, Logan?"

"Just keeping an eye on the situation." His lips tightened. "I couldn't be sure what Joe would do to keep you here."

"Joe's my friend, and he's done—"

"Okay." He held up a hand to stop her. "I'm just glad that you called on me instead of him. Too bad I won't see him. I'd like to rub his nose in it."

"He has more to lose than you. He's a cop and you're—"

"Just another philistine tycoon." Logan pushed her across the lot toward the exit. "With enough money to cover my tracks. So use me, dammit." He glanced at Jane, who had fallen into step with them. "Am I making sense, kid?"

She studied him. "Yes. Use him, Eve."

He looked a little surprised. "Very cool."

"I don't use people," Eve said. "Not if I can help it."

"Why not?" Jane asked. "He wants you to do it. We might need him."

"Very clear-thinking child." He tilted his head. "How about participating in my executive training program? I have a lot of employees who—"

"Is that supposed to make me feel good?" Jane gave him a disgusted glance. "Use him, Eve."

"The child's obviously of the opinion I'm not worth anything else," he murmured. "Use me, Eve."

"I'll let you take us to Phoenix," Eve said. "After that you get away from me, Logan."

"We'll discuss it in Phoenix."

CHAPTER TEN

IT WAS ALMOST dark when Logan drove up to the small red-tiled house near Scottsdale. She could catch just a glimpse of the house through the thick stand of trees and ornate Spanish-style gates.

Logan got out of the car, pressed a code into the panel by the gates, and the gates swung open. He returned to the car. "There are two remotes in a drawer in the hall," he told Eve. "Use them so you won't have to get out of the car. There are two security guards in a cottage to the north of the house. Herb Booker and Juan Lopez. They'll make the rounds regularly, but they won't bother you unless you press an alarm button."

"And where are the alarm buttons?"

"Kitchen, master bath, bedroom, living room beside the phones. You'll never be farther than a few feet from one."

"You seem to know the setup pretty well."

"I use this house when I come here for business. A little security never hurts."

"Are you sure he's not a crook?" Jane asked Eve.

"Charming," Logan said, amused.

"I'm sure." Eve got out of the car. "He's like a politician. They always have to have someone around to protect them."

"Ouch." Logan unlocked the front door. "Knowing the way you feel about them, I'd rather you think I'm like a crook. Why can't I convince you that there are honest, stalwart politicians out there?"

"We've always agreed to disagree." She pushed Jane in ahead of her and turned to face Logan. "Thank you. Go."

"There are two extra guest rooms."

"Go."

"I'm going to find the kitchen and make a sandwich." Jane moved down the hall away from them.

"See, she couldn't bear to see me cast out. I think she likes me. Smart girl."

"Only you could translate indifference into affection." Eve crossed her arms over her chest. "Go."

"She's not indifferent to me. We'd get along once we got used to each other. She reminds me a little of you when we first met."

"She's *nothing* like me."

He gave a low whistle. "Evidently, I said the wrong thing."

"Go, Logan. Please."

He smiled and stroked her cheek with a finger. "I'm going. I'm flattered you care so much about protecting me."

Joe had not been flattered. Joe had been angry and completely unreasonable, damn him.

"Is there anything else I can do for you?"

"I assume there's a computer and plenty of search software."

"Come on, I *manufacture* computers. The office also has an excellent library."

"Then, that's all I need."

"You'll find clothes for both of you in the two main bedrooms. I'm not sure Jane's will fit. She's kind of small for a ten-year-old."

"She's big enough to be a presence."

"I noticed." He leaned forward and kissed her. "Then I'm on my way. If you need me I'll be at the Camelback Inn."

"Dammit, Logan, I meant for you to go back to Monterey."

"I know you did." He started down the steps. "I'll leave you this rental car. I'll go to the cottage and get a lift to the hotel from one of the security guys."

"You listen to me, Logan. I've already taken more than I should from you. I'll feel guilty as hell if I get you in trouble."

"Good. Guilt can be useful in the hands of a clever man, and it shows you care about me."

"There was never any doubt about that, and you know it. After all we've been through together, I'd have to be a robot not to care about you."

He smiled back at her over his shoulder. "That's what I'm banking on."

"Logan."

He shook his head. "No, Eve. You can keep me from living in the same house with you, but you can't keep me from being nearby." He winked. "Besides, I'm anticipating the moment when Joe finds out that I'm the one who's been helping you."

Before she could answer he'd disappeared around the side of the house.

She should probably never have let him help her. Logan didn't know the meaning of a limited involvement.

No, that wasn't really true. He'd been very careful about observing the parameters she'd put on their relationship. He never moved too fast or too far for her. Considering his dominant nature, it must have been very difficult for him, and she valued him all the more for it.

At least, this time she had won a partial victory. With Logan, that was a major accomplishment. She'd worry later about convincing him to leave. For now she had work to do. But first, she needed to call Mom and check on her.

She crossed to the foyer table and dialed her mother's digital number. Sandra answered on the third ring.

"Everything okay?" Eve asked.

"Yes and no. Your killer hasn't shown up, but Ron was ready to strangle Mike himself. I don't think anyone ever made him take a bath before. He was ready to hit the streets again."

"Damn."

"Don't worry. They worked it out. Ron likes a challenge. He bribed him. He told him he'd bring home dinner from McDonald's each day he took a bath." Her mother chuckled. "He jumped at it. I think I'm insulted."

"All kids like McDonald's."

"Don't try to spare my feelings. We both know I'm a lousy cook. How are you?"

"Fine. I'll try to call you every other night. If there's any problem, even a suspicion of one, you call me."

"I will." Sandra paused. "Joe has no idea where you are or what you're doing."

"I thought it best."

"He's wound tight as a wire, Eve. I've never seen him that way before."

"Don't tell him anything."

"He's our friend. I'd feel better if he were with you. Why can't I—"

"No, Mom."

"Okay." She sighed. "But he's going to nag the hell out of me."

"You're tough. You can take it."

"He's tougher. But he likes me, so he won't run over me. Are you going to tell me where you are?"

"Phoenix."

"And I'm not to tell Joe."

"Please."

"It's a mistake."

"I've got to go, Mom. Take care."

"*You* take care."

Eve slowly hung up. Joe was doing what he did best, hunting. What would his next move—

"Want a sandwich?" Jane stood behind her. "It's turkey. I made two."

"Thanks." She wasn't hungry, but the overture was the first Jane had made since she'd agreed to come to Phoenix. "I'd like that." Eve followed her down the hall toward the kitchen. "I guess we're on our own as far as food is concerned. I'm afraid I'm not much of a cook."

"You've got to be better than your mother." She hopped up on a stool at the breakfast bar.

"You might change your mind. I haven't had much experience."

They ate in companionable silence.

"I can help," Jane suddenly offered. "I did most of the cooking in one foster home I was in."

"Was that at the Carbonis? Mrs. Eisley said you had a rough time with them."

"I did okay." Jane finished her sandwich. "You want me to help clean up?"

"There's not much to do. I can handle it." She had an idea. "Logan says there's a good library. I don't know if there's anything that you might want to read, but—"

"Books?" Her face lit up. "There are books here?"

"So Logan says."

Jane quickly covered the flicker of excitement. "I might take a look at them. There's probably nothing else to do." She got down from the stool, took her plate to the sink, and turned on the water. "Logan likes you. Do you sleep with him?"

Eve blinked. For God's sake, the kid was only ten. Ten but

no child, Eve reminded herself. She'd probably been through more in her short life than a woman of thirty. "That's none of your business."

Jane shrugged. "He's doing a lot for us. I just wondered if you have to pay him."

Sex for pay. Another aspect of life on the streets. Day-to-day contact with prostitutes had been a part of Eve's childhood, and, of course, Jane had been exposed to the same life. "No, Logan's my friend. Friends don't ask to be paid. He's a good guy." She added with a smile, "And he's *not* a crook."

"I didn't really think he was. I just wondered if I could piss him off."

"Jane."

"He didn't mind. He's pretty tough. Where's the library?"

"I have no idea."

She started for the door. "I'll find it."

"If you don't mind, take your books to another room after you choose them. I need to work at the computer."

"Why?"

"I need to see if I can access back issues of the local newspaper."

"Oh, to find that murdered woman?"

She nodded. "I don't have a lot to go on. Dom was very careful not to give me too much information. Just that the murder happened five or six months ago, she was a singer, and that her body hasn't been found. So I'm looking for a disappearance, not a murder."

"I'll stay out of your way." Jane vanished down the hall.

At least she didn't have to worry about keeping the child amused. It was clear Jane was an avid reader and eager to find the library. As for Eve, she'd grab a shower, change into jeans and a shirt, and hit the computer.

. . .

"YOU WANT ANY coffee?" Jane put the carafe and a cup down on the desk beside Eve. "It's pretty strong. I don't know how to make it any other way."

"That's fine." Eve leaned back in the chair and rubbed her eyes. "You didn't have to do this."

"If I'd had to, I wouldn't have." Jane curled up in a leather chair across the room. "You're not finding anything, are you?"

Eve shook her head. "I've gone back seven months. Maybe he was lying to me." She poured coffee. "It's after midnight. You should be in bed."

"Why?"

"Aren't you tired?"

Jane lifted her chin. "Aren't you?"

She was too tired for challenges at the moment. She made a face. "Yes, maybe I'll put you to work on this and go to bed."

"I'll try. But we work on Macs at school. What's that computer?"

"A Logan." Kids these days were so far ahead of where Eve had been at the same age.

"Logan?"

"John Logan makes computers."

"Like Bill Gates?"

"Sort of. But hardware, not software. And they're nothing alike. Did you find something to read?"

She nodded. "A book about some scientists who are trying to locate Troy. It's pretty cool." She paused. "And a book about forensic sculpting. You told me that's what you do for a living. Does it belong to you?"

"No, Logan hired me to work on a case and he believes in doing his research."

"The pictures are icky."

Eve nodded.

"Can you really do that?"

"I really can."

"Why?"

"It's my job. And sometimes I can help make parents feel a little better about losing someone."

"They should just go on and not think about them."

"Is that what you do?"

"Sure. Why not?" Jane stared at her defiantly. "I haven't thought about Fay since he killed her. She's dead. Why should I?"

Eve stared skeptically at her.

"It's true. I've thought about the creep who did it but not her." She got to her feet. "I'm going to bed." She strode out of the room.

So full of pain. What would it take to get such a damaged child to lower the walls she'd built around herself? Eve mustn't try to overcome that barrier. It would be the most dangerous course to follow just then.

The safest thing to do for both of them was to find the missing woman. Provided Dom had really killed that woman. As she'd told Jane, he might have lied to lure her out of Atlanta.

But why Phoenix?

He'd said he liked the city. Maybe there was something about the atmosphere here that triggered—

Stop analyzing and get to work. There had been nothing helpful in the paper during the five- to seven-month period Dom had specified. Maybe she should go back further. Or maybe not. Check the recent editions . . .

JANUARY 30. NOT even a month ago.

Debby Jordan was in her early thirties, married, the mother of two boys. She had disappeared on the way to choir practice.

I'm told she had a lovely voice. A soprano.

Eve scanned the initial story about the disappearance and then several follow-up stories.

Her husband had found her car in the church parking lot when she hadn't come home.

An investigation had turned up nothing.

The church had offered a two-thousand-dollar reward for any information.

Choir members had been interviewed and spoken of her kindness and the loveliness of her voice. "A soprano sweet as an angel's."

Several heartrending pictures of her husband and two little boys . . .

Debby Jordan.

Eve leaned back in her chair and closed her eyes. How Dom must have enjoyed throwing out lies and deceptive hints. You made it hard enough, but I've found her, Dom, you son of a bitch.

She felt too sick to feel any sense of accomplishment. A woman with everything to live for had died. Eve couldn't do anything about her death. But she could find the man who had killed her. The first step was to locate Debby Jordan's body.

Okay. Since Dom had wanted her to do just that, he would have given her some other clue. Think. Remember every word he'd spoken regarding Debby Jordan.

She showed me the light, and then I showed her *the light.*

She was the one who lit the way.

It's important that the way be lighted for us, isn't it?

She slowly straightened in her chair.

It was possible, if Dom wasn't making an ass of her.

The Indians called the falls "the place of tumbling moonlight."

Talladega Falls.

What had Charlie said about the two Phoenix killings?

Two skeletons were found three months ago in San Luz.

She jumped up and strode to the bookshelves. A dictionary. Pray that Logan had a Spanish-English dictionary. She found one and quickly rifled through it.

San—saint.

Her hands were shaking as she thumbed through the pages once more.

Luz—light.

Yes!

Light.

She drew a deep breath.

I've got it, you bastard. I've *got* it. Now give me a little more time and I'll find Debby Jordan.

She leaned forward and accessed the Internet search engine. Then she typed in one word.

Cadaver.

"WHERE ARE WE going?" Jane asked as she looked out the car window at the cactus-dotted terrain. "We're out in the desert."

"We'll be there soon."

"Where?"

"I told you I need help to find Debby Jordan. There's someone out here who may be able to give me that help."

Jane glanced over her shoulder. "There's someone following us."

"I know. It's one of Logan's security people."

"Oh." Jane looked back out the window. "It's ugly out here. Flat and brown. I like it better at home."

"Me too. But it's getting greener the closer we come to the mountains."

"A little."

Where was the turnoff? The directions in the Internet ad had been precise, but all she'd seen had been— There it was!

A wooden sign with an arrow and a single name painted on it.

PATRICK.

She turned left onto a bumpy dirt road. One more mile should bring her to the ranch.

"Patrick?"

"That's the name of the person who's going to help us. Sarah Patrick. She trains dogs for a living."

Jane's face lit with a smile. "Dogs?"

It was the first time she smiled since she'd left her friend Mike.

"These are working dogs, Jane. Not pets."

"What kind of work?"

"Obedience training. But I researched and found a few stories about her in the local newspapers. She belongs to a volunteer search and rescue team based in Tucson, and she's also affiliated with the ATF. She and her dog were at the Oklahoma City bombing a few years ago, in Tegucigalpa after Hurricane Mitch, and in Iran after the earthquake last year."

"What did they do there?"

"They tried to find survivors buried in the rubble." She paused. "And later they searched for the bodies of the dead. Evidently Ms. Patrick's dog has a very good nose."

"He smelled the bodies?"

"That's what search and rescue dogs are trained to do. They're pretty smart. The Atlanta PD uses special cadaver dogs occasionally."

"And that's what you want him to do? Find that woman Dom killed?"

Eve nodded. "Look, there's the ranch."

If it could be called a ranch. A log cabin, several spacious wire-pen enclosures, and a large corral that was equipped with apparatus that could have belonged in a child's playground. An old Jeep with faded, chipped green paint was parked on one side of the cabin.

"No dogs," Jane said, disappointed. "The pens are empty. She must not be a very good trainer if nobody wants to hire her."

Eve parked in front of the cabin. "Don't jump to conclusions. Maybe this is a slow time for her. Every business has its—"

The door swung open and a woman dressed in tan shorts and a plaid shirt came out of the cabin. "You lost?"

"Sarah Patrick?"

The woman nodded. "Don't tell me. You're from Publishers Clearing House. Where are my flowers and the six-foot check?"

Eve blinked.

"I guess you're not." Sarah Patrick sighed. "Too bad. The cash would probably have corrupted me, but I could have used the flowers. I can't grow anything out here. The soil's too sandy." Smiling, she stepped closer and looked in the window at Jane. "But kids are as good as flowers. My name's Sarah, what's yours?"

"Jane."

"It's a hot day. Come inside and have some lemonade, Jane." Her glance shifted to Eve. "You too, I suppose. Unless you're from the IRS. Then I'll sic my dog on you."

Eve smiled. "I'm Eve Duncan. You're safe. I came to offer you a job."

"No one's safe from the IRS. I make barely enough money to support myself and Monty, but I'm self-employed, so my tax returns always get noticed. They never understand when I claim Monty as a dependent."

Eve followed Sarah Patrick into the house. "Monty?"

"That's Monty." The woman nodded toward the fireplace.

A golden retriever lying full-length on the floor lifted his head, yawned, and wagged his tail.

"Lazy beast." Sarah went to the refrigerator. "We just came back from a five-mile run and *I'm* not in a state of collapse."

"You don't have all that hair," Jane said indignantly as she went down to her knees beside the dog. "He got hot."

Monty looked up at her with mournful eyes and then licked her hand.

Jane was melting, Eve saw in surprise. She turned to Sarah. "He's beautiful, but I can see how you'd have trouble with the IRS."

Sarah smiled. "It amused me to see if I could get away with it. Everything was fine until they audited me." She poured lemonade into two glasses. "I don't think Jane wants to be interrupted yet. Sit down." She went over to the sink and leaned against it. "I'll take pity and stay downwind of you. I haven't had a chance to shower yet."

She did have a gleam of perspiration on her tanned face and legs. Sarah Patrick was possibly in her late twenties, of medium height with short dark brown hair and a wiry, slim body. She wasn't a pretty woman, but her large, sparkling brown eyes and well-shaped mouth were appealing. What made her arresting was the forceful energy she exuded.

"She your kid?" Sarah's gaze was on Jane. "She's very loving. Loving's good."

Jane *was* being loving, Eve noticed. Who would have guessed that Jane would succumb to a retriever? "No, she's not mine."

"I like kids."

"You don't have any of your own?"

She shook her head. "I don't even have a husband." Her eyes twinkled. "Thank God. I have enough trouble."

"You're alone here?" Eve frowned. "You shouldn't advertise where you live."

"I get lonely. I can take care of myself." She looked at the retriever. "And I have a great guard dog. Didn't you notice?"

The guard dog had rolled over on his back in the most submissive position and caught Jane's hand playfully between his front paws. He made a *woo-woo* sound and stretched his neck to nibble at Jane's wrist.

"Yeah, sure," Eve said doubtfully.

Sarah chuckled. "I can see you aren't confident about my training program. Monty isn't a very good example. He has a few psychological problems. He's not sure which one of us is the dog."

"He's adorable."

Sarah's face softened. "You know it." She set the glass down on the sink. "Who recommended me as a trainer?"

"I found you on the Internet."

"I'd forgotten I'd posted an ad. That was years ago, and no one's ever answered it. I guess the directions out here are kind of discouraging." Her gaze narrowed on Eve's face. "Why weren't you discouraged?"

"I need you."

"There must be a dog trainer closer to where you live."

"I need a cadaver dog."

Sarah stiffened. "I should have known. Who are you with? ATF? Did Madden send you?"

"No ATF. No IRS. I don't know any Madden."

"I wish I didn't. That's one plus on your side." She shook her head. "I'm not interested. Are you with a police department? I can give you the names of several handlers who work with the police."

"I want you. According to the newspapers, you're the best in the business."

"I'm not the best. Monty's the best."

"Well, I don't believe he'll make a deal with me."

"Neither will I."

"Please. It should take only a few days."

Sarah shook her head.

"You don't appear too busy. I'll pay you more than your usual fee."

"I said no."

"Why not?"

"I don't like searching for cadavers."

"But you do it."

She glanced away. "Yes, I do it."

"Then do it for me."

"I think it's time you left."

Eve rose to her feet. "Please think about it. I need you."

"Well, I don't need this job." She turned toward Jane and the dog. "Come on, Monty. It's time you stopped making an idiot of yourself." She snapped her fingers.

What happened next was amazing. Monty rolled over, leaped to his feet, and was by Sarah's side in the space of seconds. His entire demeanor had changed. He was alert, charged with energy, and gazed at Sarah with total absorption.

"He's very obedient," Eve said. "I don't think there's any doubt who's the dog and who's the boss."

"I'm not his boss. We're partners. Monty obeys because he knows there are situations where we could both get killed if he didn't trust me." She moved toward the door and Monty was on her heels. "Please leave. You're not going to get what you want."

"I'm sorry you feel that way. Come on, Jane."

Jane frowned at Sarah. "Don't make him run when it's hot. It's bad for him."

"No, it's good for him. We run five miles twice a day, rain or shine. We have to keep in shape and tolerate every kind of temperature. It's important."

"He got tired." Jane reached out a hand to pet the dog. "You shouldn't—" Monty was backing away from her touch. "Why is he doing that? I thought he liked me."

"He does like you. He's just in work mode."

"Let's go, Jane." Eve headed for the car.

Jane reluctantly trailed her, gazing over her shoulder at Monty and Sarah Patrick. "I don't like him this way. He was different before."

They'd both been different before Eve had mentioned the cadaver search. The woman and the dog standing in the doorway were not the duo that had welcomed them into the cabin. No hint of humor or warmth showed in Sarah's face now. She looked tough as nails, and Monty reminded Eve of a witch's familiar, remote and clinging only to Sarah.

"It's very important," Eve called out to Sarah. "Think about it."

Sarah shook her head.

"Do you mind if I phone you and ask if you've changed your mind?"

"I won't change my mind."

Eve started the car.

"Wait." Sarah looked at Jane's disappointed face, and then she glanced down at the dog. "Go say good-bye, Monty." She snapped her fingers.

Metamorphosis. Monty bounded out of the cabin and stood up on the door of the passenger seat, trying to reach Jane through the open window.

Jane opened the door and Monty was on her, practically in her lap, whimpering and nuzzling her. She buried her face in his neck, her arms hugging him tightly.

"Enough," Sarah said.

Monty gave Jane a last slurp and backed away. He sat down, but his tail was pounding a drumroll on the ground.

"Thank you," Eve said.

Sarah shrugged. "What can I say? I'm a sucker for kids and dogs."

"Then listen to what I have to say. You could help—"

Sarah went into the cabin and closed the door.

Eve gritted her teeth in exasperation. Stubborn woman.

"She left Monty outside," Jane said. "What if he runs away and gets lost?"

"He won't get lost." She started to drive and glanced in the rearview mirror at Monty. No witch's familiar now, he was again the adorable dog who had melted Jane's reserve. He turned, padded to the door, and struck it with one paw. It was opened immediately and he entered the cabin. "She takes good care of him."

"She makes him run." Jane scowled. "I don't think I like her."

"I do. Sometimes if you're too soft, it does more harm than good."

"But he's a dog. He wouldn't understand."

Wouldn't he? Eve remembered her odd feeling when Sarah had looked into Monty's eyes and told him to say good-bye. It was as if they'd read each other's minds.

Witch's familiar . . .

Crazy. The golden retriever was not sinister. Even when he'd been in work mode, he'd been remote rather than intimidating.

"You like her even though she won't do what you want?" Jane asked.

"Maybe she'll change her mind."

Jane looked at her skeptically.

Eve felt skeptical herself. "I'll call her later." In the meantime she'd hit the Internet again and search for other options.

She had a hunch changing Sarah Patrick's mind would be almost impossible.

THE PHONE WAS ringing when Eve walked into the house.

"Did you get her?" Logan asked as soon as Eve answered.

"You had me followed."

"You wanted protection for the little girl."

"I take it they phoned back to tell you who I went to see?"

"Sarah Patrick. Cadaver dog. Smart move."

"She turned me down."

"Did you offer her enough money?"

"We didn't get that far. The minute I mentioned using Monty as a cadaver dog, she iced down. She accused me of being with the ATF and being sent by someone named Madden, whom she evidently doesn't like."

"Do you want me to help?"

"No, I want you to butt out. If I can't get Sarah, I'll get someone else to help me."

"But you want Sarah Patrick."

"Of course I do. She's the best in the business and she's a loner. She'd be less likely to turn me in to the police." She added dryly, "And she can't stand the IRS, which should prove she's the right stuff to you."

"Definitely."

"But if I can't have her, I'll find someone almost as good."

"I could try to—"

"No, stay out of it, Logan." She hung up.

"We're not going to see Monty again?" Jane asked.

My God, her voice was almost wistful. "Have you ever had a dog?"

Jane shook her head.

Eve felt sorry for her. She had fallen like a brick for Monty. Who wouldn't? He was utterly adorable. "I'll try again tomorrow."

"If you want to. He's kind of cute, but I don't really care." Jane headed down the hall. "I think I'll go read my book."

Sure she didn't care. She was just raising the walls again. An entirely natural response by a child who'd been betrayed too many times in her short life. Eve couldn't let the opportunity for Jane to have warmth and contact slip away.

She would try to get Sarah Patrick and Monty. If she couldn't, she'd find another handler with a dog as smart and appealing as Monty.

Fat chance.

Dammit.

She reached for the phone and dialed information for the number of the Camelback Inn.

CHAPTER ELEVEN

THE DESERT NIGHT was chill, the breeze sharp and cool on Sarah's face as she ran. Monty ran beside her, pacing her. She could feel the blood pumping through her veins, the muscles of her calves flexing with every step.

Monty was getting impatient. She could *feel* it. He wouldn't leave without permission, but he wanted to stretch out.

Halfway up the knoll, her pace faltered.

Monty looked back at her.

She chuckled. "Go on. Make me look bad. Beat it."

Monty flew.

She watched the moonlight brush a silver sheen on his golden coat as he ran straight up the incline. Beautiful . . . Scientists believed dogs were descended from wolves, but she never associated Monty with wild animals except in moments like these.

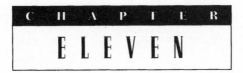

He was waiting for her on the top of the knoll.

She could almost see his satisfaction.

Weakling.

"I have two legs, not four." She stopped, trying to get her breath. "And I think you're part billy goat."

Excuses.

Monty loped over to lean companionably against her.

Silence. Wind. Night.

She closed her eyes, tasting them all. God, this was good.

Monty whimpered.

She opened her eyes and looked down at him. "What's wrong?"

He was staring down at the cabin miles below them.

"Monty?"

She moved closer to the edge, and then she could see it too. Lights. A car approaching the cabin.

She stiffened. Eve Duncan again? She had thought she'd made herself more than clear yesterday. But Eve had impressed her as being very determined. Maybe she'd decided to drive out and give it another try.

She was tempted to just stay up here until the woman got bored and went home.

Monty had other ideas.

He was already on the trail going down.

"Did I say we were going down?"

Child.

Monty loved kids, and he remembered the little girl Jane.

Okay. Face Eve Duncan, be brief, get rid of her.

Sarah started down the trail at a trot. "Wait for me, blast it."

Child . . .

It was not Eve Duncan's car.

Madden?

She stopped abruptly, her heart pounding. "Monty."

Monty stopped, tensing as he heard the note of panic in her voice. He looked back at her. *Fear?*

Damn right she was scared.

No child.

"I don't think so."

What should she do? Run? Face Madden?

Even if she and Monty stayed away from the cabin for days, Madden would still be there when she got back. She knew from experience he was totally relentless.

Okay, face him. She could always disappear later.

She strode forward, Monty trotting anxiously beside her.

Help?

"No. It's okay."

Monty whimpered.

"I said it's okay, dammit."

"Ms. Patrick?" A man was waiting by the cabin door. "I wonder if I can speak to you? My name is John Logan."

Not Madden.

Monty started to wag his tail as he sensed her relief.

"Always the optimist," she murmured. "He could be a bill collector, you know."

"Ms. Patrick?"

She strode toward him. "It's after nine at night, and Monty and I keep early hours. Call me in the morning."

"I've driven a long way, and I need to talk to you now." He smiled. "I assure you I'm very respectable."

His clothes and shoes were impeccable, but so were a lot of drug dealers'. "I don't like people dropping by late at night."

"Eve said you were difficult."

She should have known. "Eve Duncan? She asked you to come?"

"Not really. It was my idea, but she did ask for a little help." He gazed admiringly at Monty. "Beautiful animal."

He was a beautiful animal himself. Sleek like a cougar. Cougars could be dangerous. "Yes, he is." She opened the door. "And he's tired. Good night, Mr. Logan."

"Wait." His smile faded. "Could I come in? I'm expecting a telephone call."

"On my phone?"

"I took the liberty. It's from someone you know. Senator Todd Madden?"

She froze.

"May I come in?"

She went into the cabin and slammed the door.

He knocked. "It would really be better if I talk to you before he does. He strikes me as a man who could be very unpleasant when he's crossed."

Madden and everything connected to him was never pleasant. Calm down. Face the problem.

She opened the door. "Come in." She sat down in the rocking chair. "Get to the point and then get out."

"I'll be as quick as I can. Eve needs you to find a body buried somewhere in the area."

"Tell her to get someone else."

He shook his head. "She wants you. I can't blame her. I had my people do some research on you. You're quite remarkable."

"Am I?"

"Your work in Oklahoma City was incredible. And that earthquake in Iran last year that killed two thousand—you managed to save twenty-seven people buried in the rubble."

"And found sixty-eight dead."

"You remember the number?"

"I remember some of the numbers. I remember all the faces."

"Eve's not going to make you look at the face of this cadaver."

"I've always hated the word *cadaver*. It dehumanizes."

"All she wants you and Monty to do is locate the body. Then you can fade back into your little home in the desert."

"It's not that easy."

"You've worked with the police before on cadav—body searches. The Salt Lake City Police Department thinks very highly of you."

"Whoop-de-do."

He smiled. "Sergeant Levitz believes you can read that dog's mind. He said it's uncanny how you understand each other."

"Levitz isn't very bright. All dog owners will tell you their pet can almost talk. When you've been with someone as long as Monty and I, you learn to understand each other."

"Still, you'll admit it's an unusually strong bond." He gazed at Monty, who was lying at her feet. "Even I can see that."

She didn't answer.

"And you've been through a lot together."

"Yes. No body search."

He sighed. "We really need you. I'm afraid I'll have to insist."

"Screw you."

He checked his watch. "Is Madden very prompt? If so, he should be—"

The phone rang.

She picked up the receiver.

"Is he there?" Madden asked.

"He's here."

"He's a very important man, Sarah. He has a lot of political connections. I don't want to antagonize him, especially since pleasing him is such a simple matter."

"Simple for you."

"We've discussed this before. Logan assures me the task shouldn't take more than a day or two."

"That's too long. An hour is too long if it's not a case of life and death."

"I know you don't like cadaver searches, but it's necessary."

"How do you know it's not illegal?"

A pause. "Logan is a respectable businessman."

With political connections. Sarah's hand tightened on the receiver. "I don't want to do this, Madden."

"But you will do it." His voice lowered to a silky murmur. "Because you know the consequences if you don't, Sarah."

Son of a bitch.

"Two days. I'll give them two days."

"That's all I promised Logan. Good-bye, Sarah. Good hunting."

He hung up.

She turned to Logan. "Two days."

"Eve will be very happy."

"I don't give a damn if she's happy. I wish she'd never heard of me. I told her no and then she called you in to do her dirty work."

"Contacting Madden wasn't her idea. I didn't even tell her that Madden was the key. She wouldn't have used it. She just wanted me to find out if there was something she could offer you that would entice you to do the job."

"But you did use it."

"I'm more ruthless than Eve. I dug deeper and discovered a weapon in Madden. She wanted you, I got you." He glanced around the cabin. "You don't have a TV or a radio?"

"I don't need them."

"It keeps you a little uninformed."

"Blessedly uninformed."

"Eve mentioned she didn't see a TV." He held out the manila envelope he'd been carrying. "I believe you should know who you're dealing with. This is a dossier on Eve Duncan and newspaper articles about Talladega and the murder of a security guard. It won't tell you everything, but it gives you a good starting place."

"I'm not interested in Eve Duncan unless it will get me out of this job."

He shook his head. "But it may make you more willing to do it. Eve's trying to save a child's life."

"By forcing me to find a dead body?"

"Unfortunately." He moved toward the door. "By the way, if I were you, I wouldn't call the police and tell them where to find Eve. That would make me angry and I'd have to call Madden. My impression is that he doesn't give a damn about anything except his career. Am I right?"

"Police?"

"Read the file." He opened the door. "I'll tell Eve you're delighted to be of service."

She cursed.

"Eve will be in touch." His lips tightened. "Get the job done. I don't care if you like it or hate it."

Sarah watched the door close behind him. Her hands clenched into fists on the arms of the rocker. Keep your temper. Losing control won't do any good. It's only two days. Maybe there wasn't even a body.

But if there was, Monty would find it.

He whimpered and got to his feet, looking up at her.

She bent down, put her arms around him, and buried her face in his coat. "I'm sorry, boy," she whispered. She could feel tears sting her eyes. "We have to do it."

EVE RECEIVED A call from Sarah Patrick later that evening.

"Logan told me you'll help. That's very kind of you."

"I want it over as soon as possible," Sarah said. "We'll start the search tomorrow. Do you have a general area?"

"Maybe. I'm not sure. We may have to try a couple—"

"You have two days," Sarah said. "Try to get me a piece of the victim's clothing. Sometimes Monty responds more to the scent clinging to clothes than to a body."

"That may take a little while. I don't know if—"

"It's up to you. I told you what I need. I don't care if we find her or not. I'd rather we didn't. After you've got the clothing, call me and I'll meet you at the search site." She hung up.

Eve sat there a moment and then dialed Logan. "What the hell did you do to Sarah Patrick?"

"I got her to go to work for you."

"How? She was cold as ice."

"It's done. You have her for two days. Make use of her."

She should have known Logan would do whatever he had to do to make it happen. He'd been ruthless as hell in getting Eve to work for him. "I didn't want her hurt."

"She's not hurt. You're not hurt. And Jane isn't hurt. If you'll use Sarah instead of having qualms, you'll all stay alive and well. That's what's important, isn't it?"

He's right, she thought wearily. That's what's important. "She wants an article of Debby Jordan's clothing. Do you suppose you could get it without breaking into her house and scaring her family?"

"I'll manage. And no thanks are needed for my help with Sarah."

She felt ashamed. Why was she blaming Logan? She had made the call that had started him into action. Maybe she'd even subconsciously hoped that he'd go far beyond what she'd asked. "I'm sorry. I guess I'm a little discouraged. I don't know if Sarah will be able to find the body. I'm not sure where it's buried. I'm just taking my best shot."

"I'd like to go with you tomorrow. Any chance?"

"You've already done too much. I won't have you seen with me."

"There's no such thing as doing too much."

"Tell that to Sarah Patrick. She's giving me two days."

"Try to make it within her framework. I'd prefer not to have to squeeze again. As I dodged insults, I actually found myself liking her."

"I don't think she reciprocates. I got the impression she'd just as soon bury both of us as find Debby Jordan."

"Since you won't let me come with you, you'll just have to deal with her. I'll have your article of clothing by tomorrow morning."

IT WAS A white baseball jersey with the Arizona Diamondback logo on the front.

Sarah Patrick took the shirt without looking at it. "Has it been washed since she wore it?"

"No, Logan said she slept in it the night before she disappeared."

"Then how did he get it?"

"I didn't ask."

"He probably stole it from a bag for the homeless."

"He's not as bad as you think."

"No, he's probably worse."

"I was surprised you wanted the shirt. She's been buried for almost a month. The scent can't be—"

"I could have used a substance that simulates the decay smell, but that would have upset Monty. Not that the shirt may do any good anyway." She shrugged. "But we'll try." She glanced around the open field. "Why are we here?"

"This field is in back of the Desert Light subdivision."

"So?"

"Bodies have been located in two other places associated with light. Dom repeatedly mentioned light in our last conversation. I think he was trying to tell me something."

"Why didn't he just come right out and say where he buried her?"

"That wouldn't be as much fun for him. He wants to make me work."

"You mean he wants to make Monty and me work."

"He doesn't know about you." Eve wasn't sure that was true. Dom had not contacted her since she'd arrived in Phoenix, but that didn't mean he wasn't here, watching her.

"And you want me to search this field just because of the subdivision's name?"

"It's also close to the church where Debby Jordan disappeared."

Sarah gazed at her dubiously.

"Okay, it's not much to go on." Eve's lips tightened. "But it's all I've got."

"Whatever you say. I'll go on any wild-goose chase for two days. That's all you're getting from me." She took a canvas bag from her Jeep, then glanced at Jane, who was kneeling beside Monty. "Why bring her along?"

"Dom likes her with me and I can't chance leaving her alone. She won't get in the way."

"I didn't say she would. She seems a smart kid. But Monty's not going to be able to keep her company." She strode over to Jane and smiled down at her. "Sorry. It's time for Monty to work."

Jane got to her feet slowly. "May I go with you?"

Sarah looked at Eve.

Jane was already there. Was it any worse for her to search actively than sit in a car and wait? At least she'd be busy. She slowly nodded.

Sarah turned back to Jane. "We cover ground pretty fast and I usually take him over the terrain twice just to make sure we don't miss something."

"I'll keep up."

"Suit yourself." Sarah knelt down and opened the canvas bag. She pulled out a leash and fastened it to Monty's collar.

He went still.

"He knows something's happening?" Jane asked.

She nodded. "But he doesn't know what yet. I'm leashing him for my benefit, so I can better control our steps. I don't usually put a leash on him at all, only when we're in an unfamiliar environment or a leash makes people feel safer around him."

"Safer?"

"He's a big dog. Some people don't like big dogs."

"Then they're crazy," Jane said.

Sarah smiled. "I'm with you, kid." She reached into the canvas bag again and pulled out a denim belt that contained a multitude of pockets.

Monty stiffened.

"Now he knows we're on the job." Sarah fastened the pack around her waist. "It's his signal."

Monty lifted his head, his eyes bright and eager.

Sarah reached down and let him sniff the jersey. "Find her, Monty."

Eve leaned against the fender of her car and watched Sarah, Jane, and Monty walk the field. They moved fast, as Sarah had said they would, but the field was large and it took time to traverse every foot of it.

Monty held his head down, every muscle tensed as he moved over the terrain. Twice he stopped, hesitated, and then continued on. It was early afternoon before Sarah brought Monty back to the car. "Nothing."

"You're sure?" Eve asked, disappointed.

"Monty's sure. That's enough for me."

"How good is he?"

"He's damn incredible."

"Why did he stop those two times?"

"He sniffed something dead."

Eve stiffened. "What?"

"Nothing human. Monty knows the difference." She took off the dog's leash, then her own belt, and turned to Jane. "He's off duty now. Why don't you go play with him? He'd like that."

"Okay." Jane didn't have to be asked twice.

Sarah watched her run out into the field with Monty at her heels. "Monty likes her."

"She absolutely loves him."

"She's got good taste."

"Thanks for letting her trail along with you. She's had it pretty rough. Being with Monty is good for her."

"It's not her fault I've been railroaded into doing this." She looked pointedly at Eve. "It's yours."

Eve flinched. "You're right. So I might as well drive you as hard as I can while I've got you. You're not going to think any less of me."

"You have other sites in mind?"

"About eleven. They all have 'light' in their names."

"Eleven?"

Eve got out her city map and pointed to areas she'd circled. "Maybe twelve."

"You'll never make it in two days."

"We'll do the ones closest to Debby Jordan's church first. Is there any limit to how long Monty will be effective?"

"No, we worked for seventy-two hours straight in Tegucigalpa with only short rests. But you saw how long it took to rule out just this field."

"Then we'd better get moving." Eve folded the map. "Moonlight Creek is just fifteen minutes from here. We need to search both sides of the bank."

"That will take even longer than this field."

Eve got into her car. "Call Monty and Jane."

Sarah stared at her for a moment and then smiled grudgingly. "You don't know when you're beaten, do you?"

"Do you?"

Sarah turned and called, "Jane, bring my dog back. We've got work to do."

THEY SEARCHED UNTIL almost midnight but managed to rule out only four other sites. Seven left.

"That's it." Sarah took the leash off Monty. "We're calling it a day. I'm so tired, I can't see anymore."

"You don't have to see. Monty just has to smell."

Sarah shook her head. "God, you're one hard bitch."

"I have to be." Eve looked at Jane, who was asleep in the backseat.

Sarah's gaze followed hers. "He really kills kids?"

"He really does."

"Bastard."

"One more hour."

Sarah shook her head. "We can't see. I could get Monty hurt. I don't have that right."

"You said you worked longer in Honduras."

"We were trying to save lives, not find bodies." She gestured to Monty, and he jumped into the Jeep. "We're quitting for tonight."

"We didn't cover as many sites as I hoped."

"I told you we wouldn't."

"I know. I just wanted . . . you're not giving me enough time."

"Too bad."

"Yes, it is."

Sarah got into the Jeep. "We'll start at dawn tomorrow," she told Eve.

"Dawn?"

"Don't you want a full day?"

"Of course I do. But I thought that you—"

"Monty and I don't work banker's hours. I promised you two days. You'll get them."

Before Eve could reply, Sarah's Jeep was roaring down the road.

She got into her car and headed home.

Sarah was tough but not as tough as Eve had first thought. She had worked tirelessly, to the point of exhaustion, and would get only a few hours' sleep tonight before starting out again in the morning. Obviously, she had a soft spot for kids. Maybe Eve could persuade her to search more days and—

Her digital phone rang.

"You're keeping late hours," Dom said. "Are you becoming a little frantic, Eve?"

"Oh, God. You woke me up."

"Not unless you're asleep at the wheel."

Don't panic. It could have been a guess. "You haven't called in a while. I was hoping I was rid of you."

"It's been only a few days. I've enjoyed watching you scramble to find the lovely soprano."

"You're bluffing. You don't know where I am."

"I didn't for a little while. You slipped out of Atlanta very quietly. But I knew it was only a matter of time before you figured out the identity of my soprano. I only had to stake out Debby Jordan's home."

"I never went to her home."

"But one of John Logan's men did. It was easy to track him to Logan and Logan to you. Is he the one who helped you get out of Atlanta?"

"I don't know what you're talking about."

He chuckled. "You're trying to protect him. I'm not annoyed with Logan. He's just made the situation more interesting. Though I admit I was puzzled when you didn't show up on the grieving widower's doorstep and question him yourself. But I should have known you wouldn't do the obvious thing. Using Sarah Patrick is a stroke of genius. Too bad you went to the wrong places."

"I'll find her."

"I hope not too soon. I'm enjoying the hunt."

"Dammit, tell me where she is. You know you want me to find her."

"Not yet. Every day is making you more tired, more tense, more angry. I want it to go on."

"I'll find her tomorrow."

"That would disappoint me. I'd like the search to last at least a week."

"Then why don't you go dig her up and bury her somewhere else?"

"You know moving a body is a killer's worst mistake. I could be discovered, leave evidence. Anything. No, I think I'd do better to slow you down. Did I mention how much I liked the idea of you taking Jane wherever you go? She's with you now, isn't she?"

Eve didn't answer.

"You're growing closer, aren't you? Older children are smarter. You're able to talk to them. Bonnie was a little too young for you to—"

"Shut up."

"You see how tense you are? This hunt is terribly exciting. I'm beginning to wonder if little Jane is redundant. Killing her would slow you down, wouldn't it?"

"It would stop me in my tracks."

"No, I think you'd be angry enough with me to continue. Anger and sorrow are almost as good as fear."

Damn vampire. "I'm hanging up."

"Maybe I'll take the little girl tonight."

Her hand tightened on the receiver.

"Yes, that would slow you. Look in your rearview mirror."

Headlights.

"Do you see me?"

"It's not you. One of Logan's security men has been following us all day."

"He lost you at the last search site. But I felt bound to keep you company."

"You're lying."

"How long until you get home?"

She didn't answer.

"You'd better hurry."

She pressed on the accelerator.

"Yes, I think it's time I took Jane."

He was only bluffing.

Oh, God, the car behind her was going faster.

Her heart was pounding so hard it hurt.

Faster.

Ten blocks more to the house.

Were the lights closer?

Yes.

She went around the corner on two wheels.

Jane murmured something in the backseat as the car jerked.

"Did I ever tell you how I kill children? I do it slowly, since every emotion they emit is pure and singing. They're the only ones who deserve white. Fear and pain aren't clouded as they are in adults. Do you think Jane will be as brave as Bonnie?"

She wanted to kill him.

Four blocks.

"I hear you breathing. How frightened you are."

Headlights blinding her in the rearview mirror.

She dropped the phone on the seat.

And stomped on the gas.

Gates up ahead.

The remote. Open the gates.

They were moving too slowly. The car was right on top of her.

She almost tore through the gates.

Up the driveway.

The lights were still behind her. Coming through the gates.

She screeched to a halt in front of the house and leaned on the horn.

Come. Somebody come before he—

Knocking on the window. A face pressed against the glass.

"Ms. Duncan. Are you okay?"

Herb Booker.

She rolled down the window.

Headlights were still glaring in her rearview mirror from the car parked behind her. The driver's door was open.

"Eve?" Jane was sitting up sleepily.

"It's okay." Her hand tightened on the steering wheel. "Is that your car, Herb?"

"Sure. I've been behind you all day. Is something wrong? I got worried when you started speeding."

She slowly lifted the phone to her ear. "Damn you."

"Just kidding." He hung up.

"YOU LOOK BEAT." Sarah's gaze narrowed on Eve's face. "You okay?"

"I didn't sleep well. How are you?"

"Fine. Monty and I are used to getting by with a few hours' sleep."

Eve got out her map. "We hit the areas south of the church yesterday. I thought we'd go west today." She tapped a spot on the map. "This one first. Woodlight Reservoir."

"Are you sure? That will be a lot of ground to cover. You've got to pick your best shot," Sarah said. "I'll give you until midnight tonight."

"You won't change your mind?"

"No." Sarah turned and tossed Monty's leash to Jane. "Come on, kid, we've got to get this show on the road."

Eve looked at her in despair. After last night, the search seemed futile. Why were they doing it? Just to entertain that bastard?

No, they were doing it for the same reason Eve had in the beginning. The possibility that Dom might have made a mistake.

God, let him have made a mistake.

"WE HAVE TO stop now," Sarah said quietly. "Sorry."

Eve's hands clenched into fists. "It can't be midnight."

"It's one-thirty." She gestured, and Monty jumped into the Jeep.

"I suppose I should thank you for the extra time," Eve said dully. "You'd rather spit in my eye."

"That's not true." Eve was frustrated, but she couldn't fault Sarah's work. The woman had worked from dawn until then with only short breaks for Monty to drink and rest. "I only wish you'd give in and let me have one more day."

"I can't do that." Sarah didn't look at her. "I know you have good reason to search, but it's not my reason. My job is to protect Monty. I didn't want to do this job, and I've given you two days."

"It's not enough."

"I've given you all I can. And every hour of the past two days I've hoped we wouldn't find that woman." She shook her head. "So maybe it's just as well I'm out. Maybe I'm not working as hard as you want me to work."

"Bullshit. You'd never cheat."

"Find someone else."

"You know I can't afford a delay."

"I can't help you." She started the Jeep. "Sorry."

"If you were sorry, you'd help me. Finding bodies isn't pleasant, but I'd think you'd—"

"Pleasant?" Her voice was strained. "My God, you don't know what you're talking about."

"I know catching Dom and protecting Jane are more important than any objections you have to working another day or two."

"Your opinion. You have a right to it. I know only that I have to protect my world the way you're protecting yours." She paused. "Sorry."

Eve's eyes were stinging as she watched the taillights disappear. She would feel all right soon. She was just tired and discouraged. She'd go back to the house and hit the Internet and see if she could find another Sarah Patrick.

CHAPTER TWELVE

MONTY WHINED.

"Shut up." Sarah pressed the accelerator. "You don't know when you're better off."

Sad.

"I can't help it if she's sad. I have to take care of us."

Alone.

"We're all alone."

Not us.

She reached out and scratched his ears. "No, not us," she whispered.

He whined again.

"I said no."

Child.

That thought was tearing at Sarah too.

"It's not our business. Eve will take care of her."

Sad.

"Go to sleep. I'm tired of you nagging me. We're through. We got lucky and I'm not risking another day."

Monty settled down in the seat and laid his head down on his paws. *Child . . .*

"WHERE IS SHE, Mark?" Joe asked.

There was silence on the other end of the line. "How did you track me down?"

"It wasn't easy. The station was very cagey about giving me your new digital phone number. You changed it two days ago. Why, Mark?"

"I get a lot of nuisance calls. All media people do."

"And you took a two-week leave from the station."

"I was tired. I decided to come down here to Florida to bask in the sun."

"Or you knew I'd be searching for you."

"Really, Joe, I'd hardly go to all that trouble to avoid you."

"I think you would. Where is Eve, Mark?"

"How would I know?"

"She didn't have the address of the welfare house. It took me fifteen minutes to bully the information out of Eisley. Yet Eve was able to go there and take the kid away. I put two and two together and came up with you, Mark."

"Do you think Eisley would tell me where it's located?"

"I think you know where every body in the city is buried."

"That's an unfortunate turn of phrase."

"Where is she, Mark?"

"I've invested a lot of time and effort in this story. Eve doesn't want you to know where she is."

"I'm going to find her."

"Then you'll do it without my help."

"I don't think so. I'll find her or I'll find you. Believe me, you'll prefer that I find Eve."

"Is that a threat, Joe?"

"You'd better believe it. Where is she?"

"Let's just say that she's following Dom's lead."

"What lead?"

"That's for me to know and you to find out," Mark said silkily. "I don't like being threatened, Joe." He hung up.

Joe leaned back in his chair, chilled to the bone.

Christ.

Don't let fear get to you. Just find her. Keep at Mark until you've wrung every drop of information out of him.

He dialed Mark's number again.

Just find her.

MONTY WAS HOWLING.

Sarah sat upright in bed.

Monty almost never howled.

She turned on the bedside lamp and swung her feet to the floor.

He howled again and then broke off.

Oh, God.

She was through the front door in a heartbeat. "Monty?"

No answer.

She turned on the living-room light, then walked back outside, keeping the door open.

"Monty?"

No sound. Her hands clenched at her sides.

"Monty, where are—"

Something beside his water dish.

A large steak with bites taken out of it.

She never gave Monty red meat.

"No."

She ran out into the darkness. "Monty!"

She tripped over something furry. Something limp that—

Please. Please. No.

"Monty!"

SOMEONE WAS HONKING, lying on the horn until it ripped through the night.

What the hell?

Eve pushed away from the computer and stood up.

The phone on the desk rang.

"We have an intruder at the gates," Herb Booker said. "Please stay inside the house until we check it out."

"For God's sake, it has to be a drunk. I can't imagine anyone very menacing waking the entire neighborhood."

"Please stay inside."

"He'll wake Jane up, dammit." She headed for the front door.

The horn was still blaring as she walked down the driveway toward the gates. Juan Lopez was there before her.

Sarah Patrick's Jeep was stopped outside the gates. "Let me in, dammit."

"Open up," Eve told Lopez.

He pressed a remote and the gates swung open.

Sarah drove past Eve and up to the front door.

"It's okay," Eve told the security men.

Sarah was climbing out of the Jeep when Eve caught up with her. Eve took one look at her face and asked, "What's wrong?"

"What's not wrong?" Sarah said. "Son of a bitch. Dirty son of a bitch. I want to kill him."

"Dom?"

"Who else? No one else—"

Fear suddenly surged through Eve. "Sarah, where's Monty?"

"Dirty son of a bitch."

"Sarah."

"He tried to kill him." Tears were running down her face. "He tried to kill Monty."

"Tried?"

"He scared me to death. I thought he—"

"Sarah, what happened?"

"He threw a slab of beef next to Monty's water bowl. It was poisoned."

"You're sure?"

"A coyote got hold of it. He was dead when I found him."

"Thank God Monty didn't eat it."

"I didn't think he would. I've taught him not to eat anything I don't give him. But I didn't know—and then he wouldn't answer me." She wiped her damp cheeks with the backs of her hands. "Shit."

Eve nodded. "I know." She opened the door. "Come in."

"Just a minute. I've got to get Monty out of the back."

She couldn't see the dog. "Where is he?"

"On the floor."

"Why? Did he eat any poison at all?"

"No." She knelt beside the Jeep and her tone became soft and loving. "Come on, baby. Time to go."

Monty whined.

"I know. But we have to get out of the Jeep and go inside." She put the leash on him. "Come on, Monty."

He finally got to his feet and jumped down from the Jeep. His tail tucked between his legs, he moved slowly toward the front door.

"Are you sure he didn't get any poison?"

"I'm sure."

"Then what's wrong with him?"

"What do you think's wrong? He's sad. I had a devil of a time getting him away from that dead coyote. It must have been alive when

Monty found it. Monty has trouble dealing with death." She shrugged. "Don't we all?"

"You're saying he has psychological problems?"

Sarah glared at her. "What's odd about that?"

Eve held up a hand. "Not a thing." Looking at Monty, she could tell something was drastically wrong. His ears were pressed to the sides of his head, and his expression was terribly woebegone. "What can we do?"

"He'll be okay. He just needs a little time." She led Monty to the hall. "Is it okay if I take him to Jane's room?"

"She's asleep."

"He won't wake her."

"But what good would that do?"

"There's no one more alive than a child. It will help Monty to be near her."

"Therapy?"

Sarah stuck out her chin. "Jane won't mind. She's crazy about Monty."

Who wouldn't be crazy about Monty? Eve thought. Those big, soft eyes were so sad, it almost broke her heart. "Up the stairs. First door."

"Thanks."

Eve watched her lead Monty up the stairs, then went to the kitchen and started brewing a pot of coffee.

The coffee was almost done when Sarah appeared in the doorway.

"Get him settled?"

She nodded. "Sorry. Jane woke up."

"She'll go back to sleep."

Sarah said hesitantly, "He's in bed with her. But he's clean. I washed him off after I brought him home tonight."

"Do you take cream or sugar?"

Sarah shook her head.

Eve handed her a cup of coffee. "Stop looking so guilty. It's okay."

"No, it's not. Monty and I don't like to depend on other people."

"I don't think Monty minds as much as you do."

"You're right." She made a face. "He's probably better adjusted than I am."

"Why did you come here, Sarah? I don't think it's because Monty needed therapy."

"I was mad." Her lips tightened. "I wanted to kill the bastard. I still do."

"You're sure it was Dom?"

"Aren't you? I've no near neighbors who could be annoyed by Monty. He always stays close to me. No one ever tried to hurt him before he started to look for Debby Jordan. Someone wants to stop you from finding her."

Eve shook her head. "Just slow me down. Dom's having too much fun to stop me cold. He didn't realize that you'd refused to help me any longer."

"So he tried to kill Monty."

Eve nodded.

Sarah's grip on her cup tightened. "I won't stand for it. I'm going to get the bastard and hang him out to dry."

"I thought you were through."

"Don't be stupid. He tried to kill my dog. He might try again. The only way to protect Monty is to catch that son of a bitch." She took one more sip of coffee and set the cup down. "Time to get to bed. We have only a few hours to sleep. We'll set out at dawn."

"We will?"

"I'm staying here. It's safer for Monty. I'll need a room. Or if that's not possible, I can go get my sleeping bag. I'm used to roughing it."

"I can give you the bedroom across the hall from me."

"Thanks. I'll get my bag and Monty's things out of the Jeep." Sarah left the kitchen. "You go on to bed. I'll lock up."

Eve stared after her. An angry, protective Sarah Patrick was clearly a power to be reckoned with.

She turned out the light and started up the stairs. Well, this was what she'd wanted. She'd asked Sarah to continue to help. But she hadn't imagined the woman would barge in and take over.

Eve stopped at Jane's door and opened it. Jane was asleep again. Monty was in bed with her and she had an arm flung over the big dog.

What the hell. She could hold her own with Sarah Patrick. The dog was good for Jane, and the attack on him pointed out how close Dom was. He was getting tired of staying in the background and watching and waiting.

She shivered as she closed the door of Jane's room. It might not be bad having Sarah and Monty in the same house. She was feeling very much alone right now.

"Get to bed." It was Sarah passing her in the hall.

"Go to hell."

Sarah stopped at her bedroom door. "Sorry. I'm used to running things and I've been feeling pretty helpless lately. I'll try to watch it."

Eve smiled faintly. "Do that."

It was going to be all right. She and Sarah would adjust to each other. After all, they had a common goal now.

You made a mistake, Dom. You're not perfect. If you'd left it alone, Sarah would have stopped helping me. Now I have an ally.

Did you make another mistake with Debby Jordan?

"NOTHING?" EVE ASKED, disappointed.

Sarah shook her head. "Not a sign." She gestured to Monty, and he jumped into the car. "He thought there was something beneath that fallen tree, but then he changed his mind."

"Should we go back? Monty must be as tired as we are. Maybe he made a mistake."

"He doesn't make mistakes. He'll know it when he runs across it."

"It's been three days."

"She's not *there.*" Sarah paused and then tempered her tone. "Sorry. It's been a long day."

They had all been long days. From dawn to midnight and sometimes later. Sarah had a right to be annoyed. While she had sat in the car or stood watching, Sarah and Monty had hunted. It was a wonder they kept pushing.

Sarah was silent until they were almost back at the house. "How many sites are left?"

"Four."

"That's not many. Could he have lied to you?"

"He's capable of anything. But if we aren't on the right track, why did he try to kill Monty?"

"To make the scenario more believable?"

"It's possible," she said. "Maybe he likes seeing me run in circles."

"But you don't believe it."

"No, I think there has to be a payoff. He likes the excitement, the ups and downs. Hope and then disappointment. Tension and then release. If we found Debby Jordan, it would be a tremendous release for him."

"You sound like you know the bastard."

Sometimes Eve felt as if she did know him. He was always on her mind. And there were moments when she felt that if she turned around quickly, she would catch sight of him.

Imagination. Since that night he'd phoned her in the car, Juan Lopez and Herb Booker had been very much on guard and had assured her no one had been following her.

Maybe.

She turned the corner and saw the familiar gates of home. "We'll find her tomorrow," she told Sarah. "He didn't lie to me. I know that—"

"Watch out!"

Eve stomped on the brakes when she saw the man in the street. "Christ."

Lopez had stopped his car behind her and was running toward the man, gun drawn.

"No!"

Then Lopez was down, lying in the middle of the street.

My God, he was going to kill Lopez.

She jumped out of the car.

"Eve, are you crazy?" Sarah shouted.

"Stop it. Do you hear me? Dammit, stop it. You'll hurt him."

"I feel like hurting someone." Joe released his hold on Lopez's neck and stood up. "He was stupid to run at me."

"He was trying to protect me."

"He didn't do a good job. Logan's wasting his money."

"He does a very good job."

The gates were swinging open and Herb Booker was running out into the street.

Joe whirled, immediately on the offensive.

Eve stepped in front of him. "No, it's okay. I know him, Herb."

Herb looked at his partner, who was on the ground, slowly sitting up, and then at Joe. "It's not okay to me."

"He's a police detective."

"Since when do cops use Rambo tactics?"

"Joe's a little different." She turned to Joe. "Go on up to the house."

He smiled sardonically. "You're actually letting me in?"

"Shut up. I'm mad as hell at you. There was no call for hurting Juan."

"He had a gun."

"And you nearly killed him."

He shrugged. "Like I said, I was annoyed."

"Well, so am I." She got back in the car. "No one invited you here."

"Oh, I'm well aware of that." He turned and strode through the gates.

"*Who* is that?" Sarah asked Eve. "Herb was right. He reminded me of Rambo too."

"Joe Quinn." She drove up the driveway. "An old friend."

"Are you sure? The vibes he's giving off are more explosive than friendly."

"He's upset with me." Her lips tightened. "But no more upset than I am with him."

"He was at Fay's," Jane said from the backseat. "He jumped on me."

"You jumped on him first. With a baseball bat."

"You're defending him," Sarah noticed.

"It's habit." She parked and got out of the car. "You all go on to bed. I'll deal with him."

"He'll take some dealing," Sarah murmured. "But Monty and I are too tired to volunteer, and Jane doesn't have her baseball bat."

Jane chuckled. "Can Monty sleep with me tonight, Sarah?"

"Not tonight. You know that's only on special occasions." Sarah nodded at Joe, who was waiting by the door. "Be nice to Eve, or I'll sic my dog on you."

She didn't wait for an answer as she ushered Jane and Monty inside.

"Who is she?" Joe asked Eve.

"Sarah Patrick. Monty is her dog. If you knew where I was staying, I'm surprised you didn't know about Sarah. Didn't Logan tell you what was going on?"

"You've got to be kidding." He followed her into the house. "Logan told me no more than he had to, just that you were safe, he had two men guarding you, and that I should go jump in the lake."

"Then how did you find me?"

"Mark told me you were heading for Phoenix and that he thought you had an ace in the hole. I immediately thought of Logan. I started looking for him and learned that he'd left Monterey and was staying at the Camelback Inn. I'd also discovered that he owned this house, and I thought it logical that he'd provide you and Jane with a place to stay."

"How astute of you."

"I wouldn't be sarcastic if I were you." His tone was thick. "I've gone through hell trying to find you and not knowing if I'd get here before Dom did. I don't know how much control I have left."

"Not very much judging by that display you put on outside."

"Did it upset you? Too bad. But then, I've always known that violence upset you. You've had too much of it in your life. So I kept that part of me turned low. I'm tired of it, Eve. Accept me as I am." He looked around the foyer. "Very nice. Very cozy. Logan did you proud."

"He's been a great help."

His eyes narrowed. "Oh? How great a help? Lots of sympathy and intimate little chats?"

"Of course I talk to him. I call him whenever I get a chance, to tell him how things are going. Was I supposed to just drop him after he helped me get Sarah and all the other— Why am I defending myself? It's none of your—"

"There's only one thing I want to know. Has Dom contacted you since you've been here?"

"Yes."

He muttered a curse. "How does the bastard do it? He must be sticking as close as molasses to you."

"Why are you surprised? He's had decades of experience in stalking, and he must know every trick in the book. It wouldn't be any fun for him if he couldn't check my pulse." She walked into the living room and turned to face him. "I'm tired, Joe. Say what you've got to say to me and let me go to bed. We've got to get up at dawn and start searching again."

"Just like that?"

"Just like that." She lost patience with him. "Dammit, Joe, do you expect me to apologize to you for trying to save your job? I'd do it again. This is my concern, not yours."

"Your concerns have been mine since the day I first met you. They'll be mine until the day I—" He shook his head. "You're backing off, closing me out. I can feel it, dammit. How long do you think I can—" He took two steps forward and grasped her shoulders. "Look at me. For God's sake, look at me and see me as I am, not what you want me to be."

His eyes . . .

Her chest was so tight, she couldn't breathe.

"*Yes.*" His voice vibrated with intensity.

"Let me go." Her voice sounded faint even to her ears.

His grasp tightened and then he slowly released her. "I'm not stupid. After all these years, I'm not going to rush it. But you've kept me chained too long by pity. I can't take it anymore."

"Pity? I've never wanted your pity."

"How could I not feel pity? I ached with it. I ate and slept with it. It was dry as dust, but it was all I had. And every time I thought I couldn't take one more minute of it, you made me bleed again and I was caught." He held her gaze. "No more pity, Eve."

"I'm going to bed." She backed away from him. "We'll talk in the morning."

He shook his head. "No, we don't have to. I can wait now." He glanced at the couch. "I'll bunk down here."

"There's another spare bedroom."

"You can show me tomorrow. Go escape now."

She needed to escape. She was confused and panicky and there was a funny feeling in the pit of her stomach. And Joe, damn him, knew her so well, he was probably aware of exactly what she was feeling. "I'll see you tomorrow."

"It will be okay, Eve," he said quietly. For the first time, a faint smile lit his face. "Don't think about it. Ride with it, live with it for a while. I'm the same man you've known for the past ten years."

But he'd been almost a stranger during those moments when he was looking down at her.

When he was touching her . . .

How many times had he held her in the last ten years? In friendship, in sympathy, quieting the pain, helping her through nights of torment and loneliness.

Never like this.

"Good night," she murmured, then fled the room.

It was crazy, she thought as she took off her clothes and slipped into bed. It shouldn't be happening. Damn you, Joe. You shouldn't be feeling like this.

She shouldn't be feeling like this.

Her breasts were taut, aching against the coolness of the sheet, and there was an unmistakable tingling between her thighs.

Oh, shit.

Not for Joe. She didn't want to feel this animalistic lust for Joe. It didn't have any place in the compartment she'd given him in her life.

Compartment. Where had that thought come from? Because she couldn't bear to let him go, had she kept Joe in the one area of her mind and heart where she could accept closeness? How incredibly selfish.

It couldn't be true. She wouldn't let it be true. Yet that night at the motel in Ellijay, hadn't she known there was something else between them, something she wouldn't permit to come to the surface?

Perhaps tonight was only a temporary aberration on Joe's part. Maybe tomorrow he'd be back to normal.

But what about her? Could she ever look at Joe again in the same way? When he'd touched her and stared down at her with such intensity, he seemed to have changed before her eyes. She'd suddenly become *aware* of him. The physical, sexual Joe Quinn. The broadness of his shoulders, the slimness of his hips, his mouth . . .

She'd wanted to reach out and touch that mouth.

Heat. Tingling. Hunger.

Stop thinking of him that way. She had to regain her balance so she could convince Joe how destructive going in a new direction could be. Be logical, be cool. . . .

She was so upset, there wasn't any way she could be logical or cool.

Damn you, Joe.

JOE, DRESSED IN jeans and sweatshirt, his hair wet from the shower, met her in the hall when she came downstairs the following morning. "Coffee's made. Sarah, Jane, and Monty are in the kitchen. You're late." He smiled. "Didn't sleep well?"

She stiffened. "I slept fine."

"Liar." He started toward the kitchen. "Sarah filled me in on your progress, or lack of it."

His manner was casual, she noticed with relief. This was the Joe she knew. It was almost as if last night had never happened. "We still have a chance."

"If Dom didn't lie to you. Don't bank too much on there being evidence even if we find Debby Jordan. Spiro says nothing of value has been uncovered at the graves at Talladega."

"What about the cardboard box in the alley?"

"The same. The blood belonged to the security guard at the welfare house."

"And the two graves in Phoenix?"

"Spiro sent Charlie here to help look into that. Nothing yet."

"That doesn't mean we won't find something."

"He wouldn't have told you about Debby Jordan if it had a chance of incriminating him."

"Yes, he would. He's tired of being safe. He needs— I don't know what he needs, but I'm part of it. And he's made at least one mistake since I came here."

"Sarah's dog."

She nodded. "If he made one mistake, he may have made another."

"And if he didn't?"

"Then we'll find a way to get him. I can't let this go on indefinitely. I won't be made to hide and I won't be taunted by that bastard." She grimaced. "I can't *stand* it. He's feeding on me, Joe."

"Maybe you're right. Maybe Debby Jordan will be the key." He paused. "So let's get breakfast and hit the road."

"You're going with us?"

"You let the kid go. Why not me?"

"Jane has to stay with me."

He started to open the kitchen door, but she stopped him. "I don't want you to go with us, Joe."

"I'm going. You're not going to get rid of me again."

"Look, I've been careful. I've stayed out of sight. I've let Sarah handle the people who've come up and questioned us while we were searching, but there's always the possibility the police might find me. I don't want you to be with me if that happens."

He grinned. "Then I'd make a quick arrest myself. Did I forget to tell you that I persuaded my department chief that it was his idea to send me here as the Atlanta liaison on the interstate task force? So my job you're so worried about is safe."

"The hell it is. You're walking a tight line, and I don't want you to go with—"

"You're repeating yourself."

"And you're not listening. I don't need your help."

He looked at her pointedly. "You let Logan help you."

"I didn't want his help."

"But you still let him help you."

"That was different."

"Yes, it was different. I wanted to strangle you when you left me and went to him for help." He smiled. "But now I believe it's an encouraging sign. Think about it."

She didn't want to think about it. Suddenly she was feeling the same tightness in her chest, the same awareness she'd experienced the night before. Dammit, she didn't want to feel this way around Joe. He was her best friend, almost her brother. "It's all wrong. You're spoiling everything."

He went past her into the kitchen. "Adjust."

"EASY, BOY. YOU'RE going too fast." Sarah tightened her grip on the leash. Monty had been tense and moving at top speed since he'd reached this field at the rear of Dawn's Light Elementary School.

Instinct or impatience? He'd gone through days of search with nothing to show. God knows Sarah was tired and impatient.

It had to be nearly six. It was getting dark and the scraggly trees were casting longer shadows on the sparsely covered ground.

"How much longer?" Joe called from the car, which was parked at the edge of the field.

"Another fifteen minutes." She paused a moment, giving both herself and Monty a chance to catch their breath, her gaze fixed on Joe and Eve. It was odd watching them together. It was clear they were old friends; they had the comfortable habit of almost finishing each other's sentences. Yet there was something disquieting about the tension between them. People were too complicated. Dogs were much easier . . . most of the time.

"Are we almost done?" Jane asked.

"Soon." She started moving again. "Why don't you go to the car and get a sandwich? You must be hungry."

Jane shook her head. "I'll wait until you go back." She smiled eagerly. "Monty's going faster, isn't he? Why do you suppose he's doing that?"

"How should I know? I'm just along for the ride."

Jane frowned. "What's wrong with you?"

"Nothing." Her stride lengthened. "Go back to the car. You can't keep up."

"I always keep up."

"I told you to go back," she said sharply. "We don't need you."

Jane stopped, stared at her for a moment, and then turned on her heel and walked away.

She'd hurt the kid's feelings. But it couldn't be helped. She couldn't afford to concentrate on anything but Monty just then.

Faster.

To the left.

Faster.

Monty was straining at the leash.

Close.

Eagerness.

Hope.

Found!

Monty started to dig.

"No, Monty."

Found.

She didn't try to stop him again. He'd find out soon enough.

He froze into stillness.

Gone?

"Yes."

He backed away. *Gone.*

He was whimpering.

Christ, he was hurting.

She fell to her knees and put her arms around his neck.

Child?

"I don't think so."

But gone.

She felt tears sting her eyes as she rocked him gently. "Shh."

"What's wrong? Is he hurt?" Eve was standing beside her.

"Yes." And it was her fault. She had tried not to think about this moment, but she had known it would come. "He's hurt."

"Should we take him to a vet?"

Sarah shook her head. "It wouldn't do any good." Please stop whimpering. You're breaking my heart.

Gone.

"What happened?" Joe knelt beside the dog. "Does he need first aid? I've had training in—"

"He found her."

"Here? Debby Jordan?"

"I guess it's her," she said dully. "It's a human being and it's dead." She rose to her feet. "I'm taking Monty back to the car. He's done his job." She gently tugged on the leash. "Come on, baby."

Monty wouldn't move.

"You can't help, Monty. It's time to go."

He lay there, whimpering.

"Can I help?" Joe asked quietly.

"He won't leave her. He knows she's dead, but he won't accept it." She tried to steady her voice. "The damn idiot never accepts it."

"Then we'd better get him away from here." Joe picked up the retriever. "Easy, boy. I won't hurt you. Sarah wants you to go back to the car."

"Should I come with you?" Eve asked.

"Stay here." Sarah followed Joe. "There's no way I'm bringing Monty back if we lose the exact location."

Jane ran toward them when she saw Joe with Monty in his arms. "What's wrong? What happened to Monty?"

"He's okay." Joe set Monty carefully on the backseat. "He didn't want to come back to the car."

"Why not?"

Joe turned to Sarah. "I've got to get back to Eve and mark the site. Will you be okay?"

Sarah nodded, then she climbed into the backseat and lifted Monty's head onto her lap.

Jane stood watching her. "He looks sick."

"He's not sick, he's just sad."

"Why?" Her gaze flew to where Eve was standing. "He found her?"

"He found someone."

Jane shivered. "You know, I didn't really think it would happen. I knew it was right to search for her, but I—"

"I know." Sarah tried to smile. "I had mixed feelings about finding her too."

"Because you were afraid it would upset Monty?"

"I knew it would hurt him."

"He's been like this before?"

"Every time. When I brought him back from Tegucigalpa, he wouldn't leave the cabin for a month. He lost seven pounds. I had to coax him to eat."

"Will it be like that this time?"

"I hope not." She stroked Monty's head.

"You shouldn't have taken him there."

"He saved many, many lives. Was I to stop him from doing that?"

Jane frowned. "I guess not. But I don't like it."

"Neither do I."

"Are all dogs like him?"

"Golden retrievers are wonderful family and handicap dogs because of their gentleness. They're full of love, and Monty seems to have gotten a double dose."

Jane's hands knotted into fists at her sides. "I hate that he's hurting like this. Tell me what to do to help him."

Sarah knew from past experience that there was no quick fix. But the child was hurting almost as much as the dog, so she had to do something. "Climb in and sit with us. Pet him. Let him know you're here."

"He'd like that?"

"He likes children, and he particularly likes you, Jane. It could help."

Jane scrambled into the backseat and started stroking Monty. "He's still whimpering. You're sure this is helping?"

Sarah wasn't sure of anything but that love and a child's life force were miracles in themselves. She could use a little of that life force herself. "It couldn't hurt. Just stick with it."

There was silence in the car for several minutes. "Why do you do this?" Jane whispered. "You love Monty. You have to hate it."

"Not many other people are able to do what we do." She cleared her throat. "But I have to be careful how I use Monty. I'm responsible. I have to be the one who protects us."

"Why?"

"Because Monty is what he is and he loves me." Her hand moved caressingly on the dog's head. Come on, boy. Please don't hurt anymore. It's killing me. We have to get you over this. She whispered, "And he'll never, never tell me no."

DEBBY JORDAN WAS lying beneath this ground. Eve stared down at the area Sarah had indicated. It didn't look like a grave.

"Here?" Joe was standing beside her, carrying a red emergency flag he must have taken from the trunk of the car.

She gestured to the spot. "I can't believe Monty found her. I'd almost given up hope."

"Not you." He anchored the flag and stood up. "That should do it. Have you thought about what we should do now?"

"We can't excavate ourselves. We'd disturb any evidence. The local police?"

"We could go that route." He paused. "Or we could call Spiro."

"I'm wanted for kidnapping. I won't let him take Jane away from me."

"Then we'll have to work a deal, won't we?" His lips tightened. "One that won't make you the bait."

"We don't even know for sure it's Debby Jordan who's buried here."

"But you have a hunch it is, don't you?"

"Yes, I think it's her. He wanted me to find her, and we found her. But he wanted to stretch it out. This was probably too soon for him. We'll have to see what he does next."

CHAPTER THIRTEEN

"HOW'S MONTY?" JOE asked as Eve came down the stairs later that evening.

"Sarah's worried. He wouldn't eat his supper. Jane's hanging over him." She shook her head. "I thought he was going to be good for her, but I didn't foresee this."

"He probably *is* good for her. Caring never hurt anyone. There's not enough of it in this world."

Joe had cared. She remembered how tenderly he'd lifted the retriever and carried him back to the car. Strange how moving the gentleness of a tough man could be. "Did you reach Spiro?"

"Yes, he's on his way. He said he would have come anyway. Charlie's come across something pretty interesting about the other two cases."

"What?"

"He wouldn't talk about it."

"So much for sharing information."

"We'll get it out of him. Right now he thinks he's doing us a favor. We just have to convince him that we stand on equal ground."

The phone rang.

She tensed.

Joe looked at her. "Shall I get it?"

It wouldn't be Dom. Dom always called on her digital phone. "No, I'll answer it." She picked up the receiver.

"Good to hear your voice, Eve," Mark Grunard said. "Though I wish I'd heard it earlier. You promised you'd contact me."

"There wasn't any reason. I didn't know anything. How did you find out where I was?"

"Joe and I made a deal, and *he* keeps his word. Is he there?"

"Yes." She handed the phone to Joe. "Mark Grunard."

She sat and watched his face as he talked to Mark. No expression. The wariness and stillness were firmly back in place.

"He's coming." Joe hung up. "He wants to be on the spot in case anything interesting happens."

"He said you made a deal."

"It was the only way I could get him to tell me where you'd gone. I called him after I found out about this house."

"Without asking me?"

"Did you ask me before you flew the coop?" He added softly, "I'd have made a deal with the devil himself to find you, Eve. Shall I tell you what I'd do to keep you?"

The words came out of left field, surprising her, shaking her. "I don't want to—"

"I didn't think you'd want to know." He turned and moved toward the front door. "I'll drop it for now."

"Where are you going?"

"Back to the burial site. I don't like the idea of leaving it unattended."

Her eyes widened. "You think he'll come back to it?"

"If he's watching you, then he knows we found the grave."

"He won't try to move the body. He told me once that it would be stupid."

"Then I'll be guarding it for nothing. But it won't hurt."

"How long will you be there?"

"Until Spiro meets me there tomorrow morning. Don't expect me back until—"

"I'll go with you."

"Go to bed, you're not invited." He opened the door. "My job, Eve. You and Sarah have done yours."

"It's idiotic of you to go there tonight if you think he—"

She was talking to air. He was gone.

How dare he upset her and then terrify her by going back to Debby Jordan's grave? And how could he think that she'd be able to sleep? She'd be up all night, imagining him by himself in that field.

She *would* sleep. She wouldn't think of him. Let him risk Dom coming back and finding him. It would serve him right. He'd probably enjoy facing that son of a bitch. Joe'd karate-chop him as he had Lopez and walk away.

Her heart was pounding hard. Stop it. Don't think of him.

Go to bed and go to sleep.

JOE WAS SITTING several yards away from the grave site, and she could feel his gaze on her as she approached, but she couldn't see his expression in the darkness. There probably wasn't any expression. She usually had to watch for the faintest flicker of an eyelash or the movement of his mouth to know what he was feeling.

Though he'd made his feelings more than clear lately.

"I was expecting you." Joe patted the ground beside him. "Sit down."

"Well, I didn't expect to be here." She sat down and linked her arms around her knees. "I told you he wasn't coming."

"But you couldn't let me run the risk alone."

"You're my friend . . . sometimes."

"All the time. You shouldn't have come here by yourself."

"I'm never by myself. One of the security men followed me."

"Which is the only reason I feel the slightest gratitude to Logan."

"He's a good man."

"No comment."

She was silent as she gazed across the field at the red flag marking the grave. Are you there, Debby Jordan? I hope you are. God, I hope we can bring you home.

"She had two children?"

"Two little boys. According to the newspapers, she had everything. A good marriage, a family, friends. She was a good person trying to live a good life. Then one day she left home and never came back. No warning. No reason. Dom saw her and wanted her dead." She shook her head. "That's what's most frightening. You can live your life in the best way, the most moral way possible, and it doesn't make any difference. A madman chooses you at random and takes away everything. It's not fair."

"That's why we all have to live every moment as if it were our last and not close ourselves off."

He was no longer talking about Debby Jordan. "I don't close myself off. I just choose what I want in my life."

"Then you should widen your selection. It's pretty damn miserly."

"I'm content with the way things are."

"Bullshit."

"Dammit, why do you want to change everything?"

"Because I'm too selfish. I want more."

"I can't— I don't want—"

"Sex?"

Eve stiffened. It was the one subject she hadn't wanted to bring out in the open. God knows, she'd tried to push it away a hundred times while lying in bed last night.

"I think you do want it." He wasn't looking at her. "You've had a few sexual relationships since Bonnie died. Nothing serious. You wouldn't let them be serious. That would have interfered with your work."

Joe had never spoken to her before about those fleeting relationships. She hadn't known he'd even been aware of them. "It still would interfere."

"Then you'll have to learn to deal with it." His tone was almost offhand. "Because I'm here and I'm serious as hell. I've watched and I've waited. I learned to control jealousy and anger and desperation. I never tried to stop you from going to other men because I knew that every step would help you heal. But you needed something else from me. Well, you got it."

"Joe . . ."

"Everything I've done since I met you has been centered on you. You *became* my center. I don't know why. I never wanted it." He finally turned to look at her. "But if you can see beyond Bonnie and all those other lost kids, you'll find I'm pretty damn close to your center too."

"You're my friend, Joe."

"Forever. But I can be more. I can please your body." He paused. "And I can give you a child."

"No."

"That scared you. You're afraid to even think of it, but it would be the one act that might heal you. For God's sake, it wouldn't be a betrayal of Bonnie."

"No."

He shrugged. "I'm not pushing it. We have a long way to go before we get that far."

She stared at him in pain and bewilderment. "Joe, it wouldn't work."

"It *will* work. I'll make it work." He smiled. "My first goal is to get you to think of me as a sex object instead of as a brother. Shall I tell you how good I am in bed?"

He was joking. Or was he? She was so confused, she wasn't sure of anything about him anymore.

"No, I'd rather show you." His smile faded. "And I know this isn't the time or place. Though it seems as though we've spent most of our years together balanced on the edge of a grave." He reached over and touched her cheek. "You should think about the fact that a good portion of the time I'm looking at you I'm not seeing my friend. I'm seeing you in bed or on top of me or putting your hands on—" He threw back his head and laughed. "Your eyes are as wide as saucers."

"Damn you, Joe." She felt as if her face were on fire. "I won't think about it." But she would. She wouldn't be able to stop herself from remembering his words.

And he knew it.

"It's okay." He was still smiling as he pulled her into the crook of his arm. "Relax. I don't mind occasionally being just a shoulder to lean on. I'm only opening our relationship to more interesting possibilities."

She shouldn't take comfort from him. It wasn't fair. Besides, it confused the issues. And what the hell were the issues? Sex? Love? Friendship? Whatever they were, she should probably stay remote until she could think clearly.

Yet they had sat like this a hundred times, touched and shared thoughts and silences. How could she push him away? It would hurt too much. It would be like tearing out a part of herself.

"Stop fretting," Joe murmured. "This part will always stay the same. I'm not trying to take anything away from you. I'm just trying to give us both more."

"You must think I'm a selfish bitch," she said unevenly. "You've already given me so much. You saved my life and you saved my sanity. I'd give you anything you wanted if I wasn't afraid I'd end up hurting you. Sex is nothing. You'd ask for more and I don't know anything about a man-woman relationship. The boy who got me pregnant with Bonnie left as soon as I told him I wouldn't get an abortion. That wasn't exactly great training. I don't know if I could handle such a big commitment."

"You can handle it. You can handle anything."

"Yeah? I haven't handled any sexual relationship since with great skill."

"That's because it wasn't with me."

She suddenly chuckled. "You arrogant bastard."

He smiled. "Nothing but the truth." He pressed her head into the curve of his shoulder. "Go to sleep. You might get lucky and dream of me."

"I wouldn't give you the satisfaction. Your ego is too big as it is." She gradually relaxed. Weird, she thought drowsily, she shouldn't be able to fall back into the comfortable groove of years. But Joe seemed able to switch back and forth effortlessly and bring her along with him. "I shouldn't go to sleep. I came here in case Dom—"

"I know. The minute you showed up I knew I was safe."

"Shut up."

"Whatever you say."

"Yeah, sure. Catch me hurrying out to try to save your neck again."

"You'd do it."

Yes, she would. Without question and without thought. Because the concept of Joe hurt or killed was too frightening to contemplate.

To live without Joe . . .

SPIRO ARRIVED AT the field at ten-fifteen the following morning.

"Hello, Eve. You've been a very busy woman since I last saw you." His gaze went to the red flag. "That's it?"

Joe nodded. "That's it."

"We'd better hope that cadaver dog has a damn good nose. I'm going to look like an idiot if he's found a dead gopher."

"He has a good nose," Eve said. "Sarah says he can tell the difference."

"Sarah?"

"Sarah Patrick, his trainer."

"That's right, Joe told me about her." Spiro turned back to Joe. "And what if it's not Debby Jordan?"

"Then we start searching again."

"And I'm supposed to ignore the fact that I know Eve and the kid are here? You're asking a lot of me. I could lose my job. Besides possibly facing criminal charges for harboring a felon."

"Stop dancing around, Spiro. If you hadn't intended to deal, you wouldn't be here. You'd have sent a squad car of Phoenix's finest to pick us up."

"And tell me why I shouldn't do that?"

"We've given you one major lead. We may be able to get you more."

He was silent a moment. "The kid. Give her back to welfare and maybe we can—"

"No," Eve said flatly. "That's not negotiable."

Spiro turned to her. "Everything's negotiable."

"I'm not returning Jane." She paused. "But I'll make it easy for you. I'll give you what you want."

"No," Joe snapped.

"Be quiet, Joe. I knew it was going to come down to this." She stared directly into Spiro's eyes. "I'll give you my word to let you use me any way you want. But only if there's no other solution."

"And who's to decide if there's no other solution?"

"I will."

"That puts you in control. I don't like that."

"But you'll take it." She smiled wryly. "Because you're an obsessed man, Spiro. You want Dom almost as much as I do."

"More. Because I know what he is and what he can do. You're seeing him only from a personal point of view."

"You're right, my interest couldn't be more intensely personal. Deal?"

Spiro hesitated. "Deal."

"May I speak now?" Joe asked grimly. "I seem to have been left out in the cold again."

"We need him, Joe. It was the only way to get him."

"You could have let me give something else a shot first." He turned to Spiro. "You'd better try damn hard to catch that bastard, or I may declare your little deal null and void. In the most violent way possible."

Spiro acted as if he hadn't heard him. His gaze had shifted back to the grave site. "I'm calling the Phoenix PD to help excavate the site. That means I don't want either of you anywhere near this place. I'll tell them I received a tip about the grave from one of my informants." He looked at Eve. "I'm sending a man to your house with equipment for tracing and taping Dom's calls. I don't have much hope, but we've got to give it a try." He headed for the car. "I'm calling the Phoenix PD now. Get out of here."

"When will we know what you find?" Eve asked.

"I'll phone you tonight with a preliminary report." He smiled sardonically over his shoulder. "Just so you can be sure I'm working my ass off. Okay?"

"Okay." She looked at Joe. "I'll see you back at the house, Joe."

"I'll be a while," he said. "I believe I'll go down to the precinct, look at the files, and talk to Charlie Cather. I'm feeling uptight as hell. I need to *do* something."

THE CALL FROM Spiro came at eight forty-five that evening. "It's Debby Jordan."

"Positive?" Eve asked.

"Too early for DNA, but we got a match on the teeth."

"He didn't pull her teeth?"

"I was surprised too. Or maybe not. From what we could tell, he nearly carved her to pieces. He must have been in a frenzy."

"Enough to forget something as important as her teeth?"

"I'm just telling you what we found."

"Anything else?"

"Yes, there was a candle in her right hand. A taper. Pale pink."

She showed me the light and then I showed her *the light.*

"Can you trace the candle?"

"We'll give it a try. The problem is that candles have become so popular, everyone's manufacturing them these days."

That was true. Even Mom liked to light candles in the bathroom when she soaked in the tub. "When will you get the autopsy report?"

"Tomorrow at the earliest."

"Good-bye. Call me if you learn anything else, Spiro."

"Oh, you've decided you've wrung me dry and are throwing me away? I'll call you tomorrow." He hung up.

Candles.

Light.

I showed her *the light.*

What did it mean to him?

Frenzy. It was difficult to imagine Dom in a frenzy. He was too cool and deliberate. Yet he had said that Debby Jordan was a turning point for him.

"Eve."

She saw Jane standing in the doorway. "Hi. How's Monty doing?"

"I don't know." She shrugged. "Okay. I guess. I'm hungry. You want me to make you a sandwich too?"

Something was wrong. She was too indifferent. Why had she left Monty's side? "Sure. I'd like that."

"You don't have to come with me. I'll bring it here to the office for you." She disappeared down the hall.

Was she worried about Monty? Was she scared? It was always

difficult to know what Jane was feeling. But she was reaching out, and it was important that Eve be there for her.

She dropped down on the couch and rubbed her eyes. Too many things to think about. Too many needs to be met. Stop whining. At least things were moving forward.

"You asleep?"

She opened her eyes. Jane stood before her with a tray. "No, just resting my eyes. I didn't get much sleep last night."

Jane set the tray down on the coffee table. "I brought my sandwich too, but I guess you don't feel like company."

It was Jane who never admitted the need for companionship. "I was just thinking I was a little lonely. Sit down."

Jane curled up on the far end of the couch.

"Aren't you going to eat?" Eve asked.

"Yeah, sure." She picked up her sandwich and nibbled at it. "You're lonely a lot, aren't you?"

"It happens."

"But you've got your mother and Joe and Mr. Logan."

"That's true." She took a bite of her sandwich. "Are you lonely sometimes, Jane?"

She lifted her chin. "No, of course not."

"I just wondered. You haven't asked about Mike lately."

"You said that your mother was trying to get him taken away from his father. He'll be okay if they do that." She suddenly looked at Eve. "Why? Is something wrong? Did that lawyer toss him out and—"

"No, Mom says they're becoming buddies. Nothing's wrong." Not with Mike, but she was beginning to think something was wrong with Jane. "It's hard being far away from friends, and I know you like Mike. I've always found loneliness sometimes sort of ambushes you."

"Not me."

Try another road. "I'm surprised you're not with Monty. I'm sure he needs you."

A silence. "He doesn't need me. Sarah said I was helping, but he needs only her. He barely knows I'm there."

Ah, there was the pain. "I'm sure he does."

Jane shook her head. "He's her dog. He belongs to her." She didn't look at Eve. "I wanted him to belong to me. I thought if I loved him enough, he'd love me more than Sarah." She added defiantly, "I wanted to take him away from Sarah."

"I see."

"Aren't you going to tell me how bad that is?"

"No."

"It was bad. I . . . like Sarah. But I love Monty. I wanted him to belong to me." Her hands balled into fists. "I wanted *something* to belong to me."

"He does belong to you. He just belongs to Sarah more. It's natural. She was first in his life."

"Like Bonnie was first in yours?"

Shock rippled through her. "I thought we were talking about Monty. How did we get to Bonnie?"

"She belonged to you. That's why you're helping me, isn't it? It's for Bonnie, not me."

"Bonnie's dead, Jane."

"But she still belongs to you. She's still first." She took a bite of her sandwich. "Not that I care. Why should I care? It's nothing to me. I just thought it was funny."

My God, her eyes were glistening with tears. "Jane."

"I don't care. I really don't care."

"Well, I do." She slid across the couch and pulled Jane into her arms. "I'm helping you because you're a very special person and that's the only reason."

Jane's body was ramrod stiff in her arms. "And you like me?"

"Yes." Christ, she'd almost forgotten how small and dear a child's body felt. "I like you very much."

"I . . . like you too." Jane slowly relaxed against her. "It's okay. I know I can't be first, but maybe we can be friends. You don't belong to anyone like Monty does. I'd like to—" She stopped.

"Maybe we can," Eve said. Jane was breaking her heart. So defensive, so resistant, and yet so in need. "I don't see why not, do you?"

"No." Jane lay still against her for a moment, and then she pushed her away. "Okay. That's settled." She stood up and hurried to the door. "I'm going to get Monty some food and then I'm going to bed." The moment of softness was clearly over. Now Jane was eager to escape a situation that must have made her uneasy.

Well, wasn't Eve equally uneasy? The past few minutes had been as awkward for her as for Jane. They were quite a pair, she thought ruefully. "I thought you said Monty didn't need you."

"Well, he needs to eat. Sarah would have to leave him to get food, and that would make him sad." She added just before leaving the room, "He can't help it if he doesn't love me best."

Adjustments and compromises and acceptance. Jane's life had never been anything else, and she was afraid to ask for anything more, Eve thought as she rose to her feet. But there had been a breakthrough tonight. She was beginning to admit that she did need someone, and Eve had been chosen to fill the void.

Eve smiled in amusement as she started up the steps. Jane wasn't the only one who had to make compromises. Eve was playing second fiddle to a golden retriever.

It wasn't until she was in bed and had turned out the light that the significance of what had happened hit home.

Dom had gotten what he wanted.

Jane had crept beneath Eve's defenses and was becoming important to her.

Calm down. It's fine. Jane had not become Bonnie to Eve. What Eve felt for Jane was entirely different; Jane was more like a friend than a daughter.

But that might be close enough for Dom to make his move.

The thought sent a bolt of panic through her. It wasn't too late. She could push Jane away. She could pretend they'd never shared those moments in the office.

The hell she could. She could never hurt Jane that way.

Dom didn't know anything had changed. She could keep it from him. She'd just be careful to be distant with Jane whenever they were out of the house.

She could keep the truth from Dom.

"HI." JOE CAME into the kitchen and dropped down into a chair. "I could use some coffee."

"It's made. On the counter." Eve lifted her own cup to her lips. "You didn't come home last night."

"How do you know?" He got up and poured himself a cup. "Are you checking up on me? Good."

"I just knocked on your bedroom door and looked in when you didn't answer. You could have called."

"I hoped you were asleep." He grinned. "We sound like an old married couple."

"Why didn't you come back last night?"

"I went with Charlie to his hotel and had a few drinks." He made a face. "Well, more than a few."

"You tried to get him drunk?"

"Just mellow. Charlie's being very cagey. Spiro has him on a short leash since he went over Spiro's head about the VICAP report."

"I don't want to get him in trouble. You should have tried the Phoenix PD first."

"I did, but I ran into a stone wall. The local police are royally pissed at Spiro for not giving them the name of the informant who supposedly told him where Debby Jordan was buried."

"What's that got to do with you?"

"They think I'm a little too friendly with Charlie and Spiro. So I'm out in the cold unless I can find out information from either one of them."

"And did you?"

"It took me a long time before I could persuade him to tell me what he'd found out from the Phoenix police about the murders."

"Candles?"

"There were wax traces that turned out to be candles, but that's not it. The bodies had been buried much longer than the ones at Talladega."

"How long?"

"Between twenty-five and thirty years."

"My God." The time span staggered her. How many deaths, how many graves, Dom? "And no one's ever caught him. It seems impossible."

"As Spiro said, he was probably lucky in the beginning and then got smart." He paused. "But we may have gotten lucky ourselves. These two killings may have been a couple of the first he committed."

"What difference does that make? There can't be any evidence left after all this time."

"The bodies have been identified."

"How? The teeth had been pulled."

"DNA. Remember, the bodies were found almost three months ago. The lab reports came back two weeks ago." He lifted his cup to take a sip. "The police went through old records and came up with four possible missing persons cases. They visited surviving relatives and finally narrowed it down to Jason and Eliza Harding. Age fifteen and sixteen, brother and sister. Disappeared on September 4, 1970. Nice kids. Maybe a little wild. Jason played the guitar and was always talking about going to San Francisco someday. When they disappeared, their father told the police to check in Haight-Ashbury or L.A. There had been a young kid hanging around with Jason and Eliza, a likable kid, but Mr. Harding had begun to think maybe he was a bad influence. He and his two brothers had drifted into town a few weeks before. His brothers were quiet, almost moody, but Kevin was chatty, a ball of fire. He went on and on about different singing groups and musicians who were making a fortune in the coffeehouses on the West Coast. A regular pied piper."

"Dom?"

"His name was Kevin Baldridge. He and his brothers disappeared at the same time as Jason and Eliza."

"Could they trace him?"

Joe shook his head. "But there may be a picture of him."

"Oh, my God."

"Don't get excited. Mrs. Harding offered it to the police, but it wasn't in the file." He smiled. "Charlie's located the Hardings in Azora, a small town north of here. I don't think it's a photo that a mother would throw out, do you?"

"No." Joe was right. She shouldn't get excited, but, dear heaven, what a break. "Do they know their children's bodies have been found?"

"Not yet. Charlie's just located them. He's going to visit them tomorrow."

"I want to go with him."

"I thought you would. Sorry. It's not a good idea for him to be seen with a kidnapper. But I got him to promise to let you look at the photo as soon as it's logged in as evidence."

"A photograph."

"It might not be Dom."

"And it might be."

Tomorrow she might be able to see his face.

Joe set his cup down on the table. "I'm going to take a shower and get a little sleep." He stood up. "And then I'm taking you out to lunch."

"What?"

"It's going to drive you crazy marking time with nothing to do until we hear more from Spiro or Charlie. Unless you have another body you want to dig up." He headed for the door. "Be ready at noon."

Bossy bastard. "Maybe I don't want to go out to lunch. And maybe you shouldn't be seen with a kidnapper either."

"Then stand me up. I'll take Monty. He'd probably appreciate me more anyway. Though Sarah won't be pleased with me for giving him spicy Mexican." He left the room.

It was the second time in twelve hours she'd come second to that dog, she thought in amusement. It was enough to give a woman a complex.

But, at least, Joe's attitude had been light. She didn't need to deal with weightier personal matters just then. Not that she'd have a choice if Joe decided to— She wasn't going to worry about it. Joe was right. She'd go crazy if she didn't keep busy.

"Could I have some coffee?" Sarah stood in the doorway with Monty beside her. The woman looked as tired and shaky as the dog.

"Sure." Eve jumped to her feet. "Sit down. Would you like something to eat? You haven't had a bite since Monty found Debby Jordan."

"Is it her?" Sarah sat down at the table and Monty lay down at her feet. "Positive identification?"

Eve nodded.

"Thank God." She reached down and patted Monty on the head. "It's over, boy. No more."

"Eggs?"

"Just cereal. Please."

Eve put the cereal, a bowl, and milk before her. "Has Monty eaten?"

"A little last night. He's getting better." Sarah poured milk on the cereal. "Is it going to help? Are they going to find him?"

"There's one lead that looks promising." She told her about the photograph. "It's a lot more than we knew before."

"Yes." Sarah was silent. "I've been thinking about going back to my cabin tomorrow. The search is over. There's no reason for Dom to target Monty now."

He must have been in a frenzy.

"Dom doesn't have to have a reason. You found her body quicker than he wanted. Stay here."

"We can take care of ourselves. We were just caught without warning." Sarah rubbed Monty's ears. "And we like our own space."

"Please. Stay here. Just for a few more days. There's a chance that we may get a break soon." She paused. "And Jane will be worried about Monty. You know that."

"I know." Sarah shrugged. "Okay, a couple of days. But Monty will get well sooner at home."

And Monty's well-being was obviously the key to Sarah's existence. "Thanks."

Sarah finished the cereal and stood up. "I'm taking Monty for a run around the grounds. He needs the exercise." She made a face. "And so do I. Neither of us can stand being cooped up."

That seemed to be the consensus of opinion. Keep moving. Stop thinking of Dom. Mark time. "I'm going out to lunch with Joe. Will you and Monty keep an eye on Jane for me?"

"Sure. But she's more likely to be the one keeping an eye on Monty and me." Sarah grinned. "She's a nice kid. I'm going to miss her." Her smile faded. "It seems impossible that monster wants to kill her."

"But he does."

"Yeah, I know." She moved toward the door with Monty at her heels. "I learned a lot about monsters when I was at Oklahoma City."

"I don't know how you handled it."

"Yes, you do. You handle it one day at a time. One minute at a time. And try to find something in between to balance the craziness."

"You go take your dog for a run."

Sarah smiled faintly. "Or you go out to lunch with Joe. Whatever works."

Eve nodded. "Whatever works."

CHAPTER FOURTEEN

LOGAN CALLED EVE on her digital phone when she and Joe were on their way to lunch. "You found Debby Jordan."

"Yes."

"You could have called and told me and not let me read about it in the newspapers."

"I told you, I wanted you out of it." She'd wanted all of them out of it, but that didn't seem to be happening, she thought ruefully.

"Is Quinn still staying at the house?"

"Yes."

"Herb told me he was there. I didn't call you because I hoped you'd send him on his way, but I seem to be the one left out of the circle."

"I'm getting rid of Joe as soon as possible." She glanced at Joe. "But he's making that very difficult."

"Tell me about it. I should have known he'd find out about the house. Is he with you now?"

"Yes."

"Dammit, let me come and help you."

"No, Logan."

There was a silence. "You're closing me away from you. I can feel it."

"I have to do it."

Another silence. "That could mean a lot of things, couldn't it?"

"It means exactly what I said."

He muttered a curse and hung up.

She pressed the off button.

"He's pissed?" Joe asked.

"Yes."

"Good."

"Shut up." Tears stung her eyes. Maybe it would be better if Logan was angry with her. Perhaps she hadn't called him because she wanted him to be the one who walked away. Logan had pride and she had not wanted to hurt that pride.

You're closing me away from you.

It had struck a truthful note. My God, she had been pulling away from Logan, distancing herself? When had it started? Joe had come back into her life and turned everything upside down.

"Logan's done everything he could to make things easier for me, and yet he didn't interfere. Not like some people I know."

"That's his mistake. He always took the slow, civilized approach where you were concerned."

"The intelligent approach."

Joe just smiled.

She wanted to slap him.

"Sorry. Actually, I'm feeling fairly mellow toward Logan, and I shouldn't fault him. For years I made the same mistake. There's only one difference between us." His tone was suddenly no longer light. "He doesn't want you enough. You're not his center. He wouldn't do anything to get you. That's why he'll lose." Joe swung the wheel and the car coasted through the entrance gates of a pleasant little park. "And that's why I'll win." He parked at the side of the road. "Now, stop thinking and relax. We're here."

She looked at him in bewilderment. "Where?"

"Lunch." He nodded at a food cart parked by the playground a few yards ahead. "Galindo's. Herb says they make the best fajitas in Phoenix." He pulled a pair of sunglasses from the glove compartment and reached for a black straw hat from the backseat. "Put these on. You'll look like Madonna incognito."

"You've got to be crazy."

"Just hungry. I thought it would be nice to sit on one of those park benches, eat, and people-watch." He got out of the car. "It's too nice a day to be cooped up inside."

It *was* a nice day, and she didn't want to quarrel with him. She wanted to relax and try not to think of Logan or Dom. Tomorrow would be soon enough. Tomorrow they might have the photograph.

EVE AND JOE were sitting on a park bench, eating Mexican food, as if they hadn't a care in the world. She was smiling as she leaned toward Quinn and wiped a corner of his mouth.

Her entire attitude was subtly different today, Dom thought.

Hope?

Perhaps. She had found Debby Jordan.

Dom had no objection to hope. He had wanted to drag the search out a little longer, let the tension build and the relationship with Jane MacGuire grow, but he could deal with optimism. The fall was always greater when you'd climbed to the top. Perhaps it was even better that she'd found the woman so soon. Things were going to move fast from now on, and he'd be walking a tightrope. Excitement seared through him at the thought.

But pitting himself against Eve Duncan was more exhilarating still. She was evolving, toughening, changing just as he had changed. It was interesting to observe and know that he was responsible.

So hope was fine.

But there was something else going on with her. . . .

Watch her. Body language almost always told the story. If he studied her, it would come to him. He had begun to know her very well.

It would come to him.

SARAH AND JANE met Eve and Joe in the driveway.

Monty ran toward Eve, wagging his tail, when she opened the car door.

She gently patted his head. "He looks better."

"He is. Thank God." Sarah gestured and Monty ran back to her. "Nice lunch?"

"Very nice. Fajitas and chili," Joe answered. "I think Eve enjoyed it much more than your Monty would have. I was tempted to bring him a doggie bag, but Eve convinced me it wouldn't be wise."

"I would have murdered you. Monty gets gas."

"Have you been running all this time?"

"No, Jane and I had a picnic." She smiled at the little girl. "Jane said she couldn't remember the last time she had a picnic lunch."

Jane shrugged. "No big deal. Just a lot of ants and dirt in the sandwiches."

Sarah shook her head. "You're tough."

"Well, I guess Monty liked the picnic."

"Because you fed your roast beef to him."

"You told him to take it, and he needed it. He hasn't eaten much lately." Jane headed for the front door. "Come on, Monty. I'll give you some water."

Monty didn't move.

Sarah made another hand gesture and Monty bounded after Jane into the house.

"Thanks for keeping her company," Eve said.

"I enjoy her." Sarah was frowning slightly. "I wish I could— It's not easy for her."

"What?"

"I can't share Monty. She wants him to belong to her, and that can't happen. It's not safe for him to have a divided allegiance." She made a face. "Besides, we've been close too long. It kind of shuts everyone else out."

"She understands about compromises. She's made the adjustment."

"Compromises *suck*."

"I'll second that," Joe murmured. He headed for the front door. "I'm going to call Charlie Cather and then go down to the precinct. I'll see you tonight."

"Why are you calling Charlie? I thought you said he wouldn't let us go with him."

"Another try won't hurt."

Sarah's gaze followed Joe. "You were gone a long time. I was wondering whether Monty and I should come after you."

Eve smiled. "I don't need protection from Joe."

"No?"

"Time got away from us." She tilted her head. "You don't like Joe?"

"I didn't say that. I do like him. He was nice to Monty. I like most people who are nice to Monty. I just think he's a powerhouse and you have to be careful not to be run over by people like him. I've had a few experiences with powerhouses myself."

"For God's sake, we only had lunch. I won't be run over."

Sarah gave her a shrewd look. "Unless you want it to happen." She held up a hand as she strode toward the door. "It's none of my business. I think I'll go and see how Jane and Monty are doing."

Eve slowly followed her into the house. She could hear the sound of Jane's and Sarah's laughter in the kitchen. Joe must be in the office making his call.

Joe . . .

Unless you want it to happen.

Of course she didn't want it to happen. She wanted everything to go back to the way it was. It was too dangerous to let herself be swayed by the—

The house phone rang.

"There's a Mr. Grunard at the front gate," Herb Booker said when she picked up the receiver. "He said you're expecting him."

"Let him in, Herb." She felt a ripple of relief as she replaced the phone. The arrival of Mark Grunard brought her mind back to what was important.

She opened the front door before he could ring the bell.

"Well, this is more welcome than I've come to expect from you." Mark got out of the car. "I anticipated having to storm the gates."

She smiled. "I've never meant to close you out. I just didn't have anything important to share with you."

"I'm a journalist. I can make a story out of a trip to the grocery store."

"That's what I'm afraid of," she said dryly. "Come in and I'll fill you in on what's been happening. Off the record."

"Of course." He followed her into the living room. "Where's Quinn?"

"In the office, I think. He's going to the precinct later."

"Yeah, I heard how he finagled that job as liaison. Smart. And very convenient for me."

She turned to face him. "I want to cooperate with you, Mark. But I won't let you put Joe on the spot."

"Quinn can take care of himself."

Mark wasn't going to listen. Now that he was in the center of things, he was going to push until he got what he wanted. "I've been feeling a little guilty about you, Mark. I don't like the idea of breaking my word to anyone. But the minute you start making Joe's job awkward for him is the minute you'll be out of the loop."

Grunard smiled. "Now, why would I make Quinn's job difficult? We're all after the same thing. I'll go down to the precinct after I check into a hotel, but I won't get in Quinn's way." He was glancing around the room. "Nice place. Quinn told me Logan had set you up."

She gave him a blank stare. "I don't know what you mean."

He chuckled. "He also said you'd deny it."

"Logan has nothing to do with this. Leave him out—"

"I brought you a glass of milk, Eve." Jane was standing in the doorway. "Mrs. Carboni used to say that milk settled her stomach after she ate spicy food."

"I don't like being compared to Mrs. Carboni." She smiled as she took the milk. "But thanks anyway."

"No offense." Jane smiled back at her. "I used to sneak jalapeño juice into everything she ate. It's pretty hard to tell in spaghetti sauce. Sometimes the milk didn't help and she'd be up all night throwing up."

Eve laughed. "Good."

"This milk's safe. I wouldn't do that to you."

"My, my," Mark murmured. "I believe our little chickadee has mellowed."

Jane gave him a cool glance.

"Or maybe not." Mark smiled. "How are you, Jane?"

"I'm no chickadee." She left the room.

"Ouch." Mark wrinkled his nose. "It seems you're the only one she's tolerating these days."

"I'd have snubbed you too if you'd been that patronizing toward me. She's been holding up better than anyone could expect. She's been wonderful."

"Okay, okay." He held up his hands in surrender. "I see the two of you are presenting a united front. I think I'd better go find Quinn and get him to fill me in on what's been going on. It's safer. Where's the office?"

"Second door on your left," she said curtly.

He glanced back at her from the door. "Dom's done it, hasn't he? The kid's gotten to you."

"Don't be stupid. We're just used to each other, that's all. We live together."

He shook his head. "Then Dom had better never see you with her. He might make the same mistake I did."

Chill iced through her. Had the growing bond been that obvious? "He won't see her with me."

"Then that's okay." Mark left the room.

It wasn't okay. If Mark had made the connection so easily, maybe anyone would be able to see it also. She wouldn't let it happen. She would never take Jane from the house. Still she felt shaken and scared and a little sick. She needed warmth and life and—

Joe.

No, she couldn't go running to Joe.

Jane and Sarah were in the kitchen. She'd go there and sit down at the table and listen to them talk and laugh. She'd pet Monty and then maybe she'd call her mother. She'd keep busy and try not to think of the photograph or Dom or anything but the precious things in life.

And soon the chill would go away.

THE RED-HAIRED DOLL stared up at Eve with glassy brown eyes. Its porcelain throat was cut from ear to ear.

"It was in the driveway. Someone must have tossed it through the gate," Herb Booker said quietly. "The video camera at the gate went out and Juan found the doll when he went to check it. The camera lens had been shattered. Probably a shot from a long-range weapon, since the camera didn't pick up anything. I was going to call Mr. Logan, but I thought you should see this first."

"Yes," she said numbly.

"It wasn't there when Mr. Quinn or Mr. Grunard left earlier. I checked the gate myself." He hesitated. "It's a little girl doll."

"I can see that."

Bonnie.

Jane.

"It's nasty. I think we should call someone."

"I'll take care of it."

"No offense, ma'am, but it could mean the little girl is—"

"I'll take care of it, Herb." Her hand tightened on the doll. "Thank you for your concern."

"I think you should reconsider—"

"Go *away*." She stopped and tempered the sharpness of her tone. "I'm sorry. I'm upset. I need to be alone to think about this. I don't want you to call anyone, not even Mr. Logan. Do you understand?"

"I understand."

But he didn't say he wouldn't do it. Why should he? Logan paid his salary.

"Not even Mr. Logan," she repeated, and then gave him an out. "At least, not until tomorrow. Okay?"

He shrugged. "I guess so. Juan and I will both patrol the grounds tonight. You don't have to worry."

"Thank you."

Not worry? Dom had been close enough to toss this savaged doll practically on her front doorstep.

Booker still didn't move.

"Good-bye, Herb." She went into the living room and a moment later heard the front door close behind him.

She sat down on the couch, took out her digital phone, and laid it on the coffee table in front of her.

And waited for him to call her.

It was almost midnight when the phone rang.

"Just a reminder," Dom said.

"What's wrong? Did you get tired of sending me bones?"

There was a surprised silence. "You're angry."

"You bet I am."

"What an interesting development."

"Did you expect me to sit shivering in the dark, you son of a bitch?"

"I didn't really think about it. As I said, I only meant it to remind you of what was important in your life. I believe you may be forgetting."

"Important? You?"

"Yes. Right now there's no one more important to you than I am."

"Screw you." She hung up.

The phone rang again five minutes later.

She ignored it.

It rang four times more in the next hour.

She didn't answer.

IT WAS AFTER two in the morning when Joe came home.

She was still sitting on the couch, holding the doll, when he walked into the living room.

He took one look at the doll and then at her expression. "Shit. What the hell happened?"

"Dom tossed it onto the driveway. Herb didn't tell you?"

He shook his head. "I was wondering why they were both at the gate when I drove in. Did he call?"

"Yes."

He fell to his knees before her. "Bad?"

"The bastard's always bad. It's what he does." Her voice was shaking. "He thought I wasn't paying enough attention to him. He wanted to remind me that he was still around."

Joe gently stroked her hair back from her face. "You could hardly forget."

"That isn't enough for him. He wants to dominate my life. He wants to *be* my life." She looked down at the doll. "He tossed this ugliness at me so I'd remember Bonnie and Jane and all those other—"

"Shh."

"Don't shush me. I won't have it." She jumped to her feet. "You're treating me like the victim he wants me to be. I won't be a victim. I won't let him run my life."

"Easy." He rose to his feet. "I'm not the enemy here, Eve."

"I know." She took a step closer and buried her head in his shoulder. "Hold me."

He carefully slid his arms around her.

"No, dammit." She pressed against him. "*Hold* me."

He went still. "Are we talking about what I think we are?"

"I won't think of him. I won't think of death. That's what he wants me to do. I want to *live*."

"And you're equating sex with life?"

"Aren't they the same thing? If not, I don't know what the hell all the shouting is about."

"Sex can be a big part of life."

"I won't let him do this to me. I'm not going to sit around and wait for him to come knocking on the door or dictate to me. I'll do what I damn well please."

"Your declaration of tenderness is amazing."

"Do you think I don't know it's not fair to you? But you want it. You told me you wanted it. Have you changed your mind?"

"Hell, no." His lips firmed. "But this isn't what I had in mind."

"It's not what I had in mind either. But I won't have him—" Christ, what was she doing? This was *Joe*. Where were all her good intentions? Tears were suddenly running down her cheeks. "I'm sorry. Forget it. I don't know what I was thinking. Hell, I wasn't thinking. I was only feeling. Try to forgive me. I must have gone a little crazy. He made me so damn—"

The digital phone rang.

"Don't answer it. It's him. I hung up on him and he keeps calling back."

"Turn off the phone."

"Then he'd know he's won."

"Are you sure it's him?"

"It's Dom. I upset him. He wasn't getting what he wanted from me." She picked up the ringing phone and stuffed it in her purse. "He expected more of a payoff from that doll. You might as well give it to Spiro," she said, handing it to him. "See if he can get anything from it or trace it."

"I'll do that." His gaze narrowed on her face. "Are you okay?"

"Other than going temporarily insane, I'm in great shape," she said jerkily. She turned on her heel. "I'm going to bed. I'll see you in the morning."

"Yes."

The phone had stopped ringing by the time she had showered and gotten into bed. Maybe he'd given up. Thank God he didn't know the damage he'd almost done. No, that *she'd* almost done. She had to accept responsibility for her own actions. Anger and frustration were only excuses.

She reached over and turned out the light.

"You shouldn't have done that. I wanted to see you."

Joe was standing in the doorway, a dark figure silhouetted by the light in the hall.

An unmistakably naked figure.

"No," she whispered.

"Too late." He came toward her. "I've been invited."

"I told you I'd made a mistake. I said I was sorry."

"I'm not. You caught me off guard down there and hurt my ego. But once I had time to sort things out, I realized that opportunity was knocking."

"I didn't want to hurt your ego," she said unevenly. "I don't want to hurt you at all, Joe. That's why this can't happen."

"You want it to happen."

"No."

"Dom may have triggered it, but it must have been on your mind or it wouldn't have occurred to you."

"Of course I've been thinking about it. You made sure of that. I'm human, dammit."

"And I mean to make the most of it. It's been a night of revelations. You actually said you wanted to live. That's the first time I've ever heard you say that." He lifted the blanket. "Scoot over. I'm coming in."

His naked thigh touched hers.

She moved over. "It's a mistake, Joe."

His hand covered her breast. "Never."

She couldn't breathe. "Please."

His hand was between her thighs. "Do you know I've never really kissed you?"

She arched upward as his thumb found her. "You're not kissing me now."

"I'll get around to it. I'll get around to everyth— My God, you're ready for me. I thought I'd have to—"

Her digital phone rang.

Joe muttered a curse.

She whispered, "Turn it off."

He started to get off the bed and then stopped. "No." He moved back over her. "I promise you won't hear it soon."

She cried out as he plunged deep within her.

The phone was ringing.

He moved fast, hard.

The phone . . .

He lifted her, crushing her to him as he moved deeper, faster.

Was the phone still ringing?

She no longer heard anything but the beat of his heart against her ear.

"WHY DIDN'T YOU turn off the phone?" she asked drowsily.

"Why do you think?" He kissed her breast. "I was busy. Maybe I didn't want to take the time."

"Tell me."

"Ego. I wanted to be more important to you than Dom. I wanted to beat him." He kissed her nose. "You hurt my feelings a little."

"Not enough to stop you."

"It would have taken a major catastrophe to stop me. Dom doesn't qualify."

"He qualifies."

"He didn't win, did he? Therefore, he's out of the running."

For the time being.

"Stop thinking about him." He reached over, turned on the light, and switched off her phone. "I want to look at you."

She was blushing. "For heaven's sake, give me a blanket, Joe."

He shook his head. "I've wanted to see you like this for too long. Let me have my kicks."

Not when she felt as if she were melting wherever he looked at her. "Turn off the light. Please."

"Not until—" He saw her expression and turned off the light. "Maybe later?"

"Maybe."

"I forgot you're not all that experienced in this sport." He pulled her closer. "But you liked it? You like me?"

She didn't speak.

He was silent a moment. "After ten years I think I deserve the words."

Ten years. She felt tears sting her eyes. "If I weren't afraid you'd be completely impossible, I'd tell you that you were pretty good."

"*Pretty* good?"

"Very good."

"More."

"A stud, a stallion. Brad Pitt, Keanu Reeves, and Casanova rolled into one. I don't know why Diane ever let you go."

"She was a smart lady. She knew she deserved more than I could give her. It was a mistake from the beginning."

She raised herself on one elbow to look down at him. "Why did you marry her, Joe?"

"It will scare you if I tell you."

"The hell it will."

Silence.

"Why, Joe?"

"For you. I married her for you."

"What?"

"You were too isolated. I thought you needed a friend of your own sex."

"You're kidding."

"I told you it would scare you."

"Men don't get married to provide—"

"I did," he said simply.

She stared at him.

"You were my center. Everything revolved around you. It was a time in my life when I'd almost given up hope of being anything else to you. I thought I'd chosen someone who could give you the companionship you needed. Diane liked the nice things I could give her, and I honestly tried to make a go of our marriage." He shrugged. "It didn't turn out the way I hoped."

"That *is* scary."

"Obsessions always are." He put his finger on her lower lip. "As you should know, my love."

She stiffened.

"Love," he deliberately repeated. "Get used to it."

"I don't have to get used to anything."

"No, but you might as well. It will be more comfortable for both of us." He paused. "Don't be afraid to love me, Eve. I'm not a helpless child who can be taken from you. I'm tough and mean enough to survive for another fifty years or so."

"I'm not afraid."

"The hell you're not." He lowered his head, his lips barely touching her own. "But that's okay. You don't have to say you love me. I can wait."

"I don't love you. Not the way you want me to love you."

"I think you do." His lips moved back and forth in a gossamer caress. "But if you don't, that's okay too."

"It's not okay. It's all wrong. I'm damaged. No one should know that better than you. You should have someone who—"

"*You're* damaged? I'm the one who's been obsessed for the last ten years."

"It's not the same. I can't—"

"Shh." He moved over her again. "Don't think. Don't analyze. Let everything fall into place. Enjoy . . ."

HE WAS GONE when she woke.

Emptiness.

Loneliness.

It was stupid. She was acting as if she'd never slept with a man before. Sex, pleasure, departure—it was the way she liked her relationships. No lingering that might interfere with her work.

"Time to get up." Joe opened the door and came toward the bed.

"It's almost noon. I called Charlie and he's on his way back from Azora. He has the photograph."

She sat upright. "Are you sure I'll be able to see it?"

"You can ask Spiro yourself. He's on his way here."

"Why?"

"To pick up the doll."

Of course. "You called him this morning?"

"As soon as I got up. I told the security guys to let him in." He went to the closet. "Hit the shower. I'll get your clothes. What do you want to wear?"

"Anything. Jeans . . . a shirt." She ran into the bathroom and got in the shower. Joe could not have been more cool or businesslike. It was as if last night had never happened. Not that she objected. She would have felt awkward if he'd been any other way. Last night had been too— She shook her head. She didn't want to remember how erotic those hours with Joe had been.

"Come on. You need to eat before Spiro gets here." It was Joe standing outside the glass shower door. "Hurry."

"I *am* hurrying."

She opened the door, and he enveloped her in a huge bath towel and started patting her dry.

She reached for the towel. "For God's sake, I can do that."

His gaze dropped to her breasts. "I'm enjoying it."

Enjoy.

She felt heat move through her.

"I brought that blue plaid shirt. I like you in blue. Is that okay?"

"I guess so." She should stop him. The lazy movement of his hands beneath the soft towel was incredibly arousing. For some crazy reason the act seemed as intimate as sex. She moistened her lips. "You never told me you liked blue."

"I never told you a lot of things." He bent his head and kissed the hollow of her shoulder. "But I mean to make up for lost time. Want to go back to bed and hear the story of my life?"

Yes, she wanted to go back to bed. "If you promise to tell it. I've never had much luck in getting you to confide in me."

He chuckled. "You wouldn't this time either. We don't have any time." He stepped back and handed her the towel. "Get dressed. I'll wait outside for you."

"Now you tell me to get dressed. Why the hell did you come busting in here and make me—"

"I wanted to make sure you knew I wasn't going to let you make me a one-night stand." He smiled. "You're not going to be able to focus on me for a little while, but I'm going to be around every minute of your day. Don't forget it."

She stared at the door as it closed behind him. How was she supposed to focus on anything else *but* him? He had brought sensuality back into her life.

She was acting like some nympho. She would not be controlled by either her body or Joe Quinn. She could forget everything but what was important. It would just take will and determination.

She tossed aside the towel and began to dress.

JOE WAS SITTING in the chair beside the bed when she came out of the bathroom. His gaze searched her face and he slowly nodded. "I was expecting that reaction. No problem." He got to his feet. "Let's go down and get you some breakfast."

She had been girded for battle, and it was frustrating to have him sidestep before she could even say a word. "I'm not hungry."

"Okay, then you can watch me eat," He held out his hand and she realized he was holding her digital phone. "But first turn your phone back on. Dom may call and you'll need to talk to him."

Her gaze flew to his face.

"It's time to face him again," he said quietly. "Yes, I want to protect you, but I can't protect you from someone I can't see. We have to bring him out into the open."

"That's what I've been telling you all along."

"I was too scared for you to listen. Now I'm too scared not to listen. You're not going to stop, so I can't stop. We have to finish it. Turn on the phone."

She took the phone and pressed the on button.

It was silent.

Joe smiled. "Now, how's that for anticlimax? I think we both expected an ominous clash of cymbals." He gently pushed her toward the door. "Come on, let's get this show on the road."

Spiro was waiting in the living room when they came downstairs. "Where's the doll?"

"I put it in a box and slid it behind some books on a shelf." Joe crossed the room to the built-in bookcases. "I didn't want Jane to run across it."

"I can't see her flinching," Spiro said dryly. "Your Jane let me in when I rang the doorbell and she gave me the third degree. She even called security to make sure I hadn't leaped over the electric fence."

"Where is she?"

"After grudgingly allowing me to sit down, she said she was going to the kitchen to fix you something to eat." He took the box and glanced at the doll. "Ugly. It must have scared you."

"No. It made me mad."

"Did he make a follow-up call?"

"Yes, I hung up on him."

Spiro looked up. "That might not have been smart."

"I'm tired of being smart and cautious. What about the photograph? Can I see it?"

"Not before it's logged in."

"Can I get a duplicate?"

"Not before it's logged in."

Eve had very little patience left. "What about this Kevin Baldridge?"

Spiro smiled. "According to Charlie, Mrs. Harding remembers Kevin Baldridge and his brothers very well. Kevin was close-mouthed about where they were from, but one of his brothers mentioned Dillard."

"Where is that?"

"A small town in northern Arizona."

"Small enough to trace Kevin Baldridge?"

"Maybe. We have to hope the townsfolk have long memories."

"What about his brothers? Even if Kevin Baldridge has moved on, perhaps they might have gone back home."

"It's possible." Spiro stood up. "We'll soon find out. Charlie will call and check on birth and school records after he gets back with the photograph. And I'm heading up to Dillard today."

"Could we come along?"

He shrugged. "I suppose it wouldn't hurt. And if Dom is Kevin Baldridge, seeing you invade his turf might trigger him to act." He glanced at Joe. "I'm surprised that didn't arouse a reaction from you. No objections? No accusations that I'm using her?"

Joe ignored the mockery in Spiro's voice. "How soon can we leave?"

"Later this afternoon. I have to go back to the precinct, wait for Charlie, and make sure the photograph is logged in." He paused. "Mark Grunard came to see me at my hotel this morning. He said you were still cooperating with him." His lips tightened. "I told him that doesn't mean *I'm* cooperating. I've never approved of your involving him."

"He helped me," Eve said. "I owe him."

"I don't owe him and I don't like how he's been hanging around Charlie."

"He could have turned Jane and me in to the police a dozen times and he didn't do it."

"Why not?"

"Because I promised him an exclusive when we get Dom."

"Indeed?" He moved toward the door. "Whatever your deal with him, we're not bringing him along to Dillard."

"I fixed you an egg and bacon sandwich, Eve." Jane stood in the doorway. "Come on."

"I'll be right there."

Jane gave Spiro a cool glance. "He can talk to you while you're eating. Your food will get cold."

"Heaven forbid I interfere with your nourishment." Spiro mockingly bowed to Jane. "You'll be relieved to know I was just on my way out, young lady."

"Wait."

Spiro glanced back at Eve.

"How long will we be gone?"

"A few hours, a day. It depends on how much advance work Charlie is able to do."

"We're taking Jane with us."

Spiro shook his head. "For God's sake, I'm already sticking my neck out enough without being seen with a kidnap victim."

"She has to go with us."

"She's very well protected here."

"I wouldn't mind going without her if it's only for an hour or so. But you're not sure when we'll be back."

"Is taking her with us wise?"

"Dom wants her with me."

Spiro glanced from her to Jane. "But do you want him to see you with her? You're obviously on close terms."

"If Eve wants me, I'm going with her." Jane took a step closer. "And I wasn't kidnapped. How stupid can you get?"

"Evidently very stupid," Spiro said. "I don't recommend it, Eve."

"I'll take care of Eve and Jane," Joe said. "You handle tracking down Kevin Baldridge."

Spiro shook his head. "It's a mistake." He opened the door. "I'll pick you up at four this afternoon."

Was it a mistake? Eve wondered. She didn't want Dom to see her and Jane together, but what could she do? Jane was her responsibility. She couldn't leave her for hours or maybe days; she would never forgive herself if anything happened to Jane. She'd been down that road before.

She turned to Joe. "I have to take her."

"I know." Joe smiled.

"Of course I'm going," Jane said. "We're not going to let him tell us what to do. Now, come on and eat your breakfast." She started down the hall. "And then you can tell me *where* I'm going."

CHAPTER FIFTEEN

THE SMALL PLANE landed at a tiny airport north of Dillard, Arizona, at eight-thirty that night. There had been a recent snow in the mountain town, and the weather was icy. The airport had only two runways and the tarmac was bumpy. One taxi was parked outside the terminal.

Spiro got a call from Charlie in the taxi on the way to town. He didn't look pleased by the time he hung up.

"The courthouse burned down six years ago," Spiro said. "And there were no records of any Baldridge children attending the local school."

"Maybe they went to school in a nearby town."

"We're checking Jamison. It's thirty miles from here." He looked out the window. "But the schools will be closed until tomorrow morning. We'll have to stay overnight at a hotel . . . except Charlie said there isn't one. I think Dillard's population is only a little over four thousand."

"Six thousand five hundred," the cabdriver said.

Spiro reached into his pocket and drew out his notebook. "Charlie mentioned a bed and breakfast. Mrs. Tolvey's on Pine Street."

"Good choice," the cabdriver said. "Mrs. Tolvey puts on a great breakfast spread."

"Then that will be fine"—Eve looked at the driver's ID on the panel—"Mr. Brendle." She put her arm around Jane, who was leaning against her. "Anyplace with a bed."

"Bob. Good beds too. Mrs. Tolvey's been running the place for over twenty years, and she changes all the mattresses every five years."

"Incredible," Spiro said.

"Well, they don't get used that often."

"Twenty years," Joe repeated, looking at Spiro. "My, what a coincidence."

"Charlie's a good man. It's a long shot, but still we may find out something from Mrs. Tolvey."

"Will she have enough rooms for us?" Joe asked the cabdriver.

"Six rooms. All clean as a whistle." He nodded. "It's right up ahead. Two blocks."

The bed and breakfast was a large gray house with a wooden swing on the wide front porch. A light gleamed beside the storm door.

"You go on and knock." Bob got out of the car. "I'll get your bags."

"Wait," Spiro said. "Do you have a bar in this town?"

"You've got to be kidding. Four." Bob pulled the overnight cases out of the trunk. "You want to go get a drink first?"

"Is there one where all the regulars go?"

"Cal Simm's place on Third Street."

"Take me there." He turned to Eve. "I want to see if I can find out anything before tomorrow. Check me in and tell Mrs. Tolvey I'll be along in a few hours."

Eve nodded. To Joe, Spiro said, "You'll talk to Mrs. Tolvey?"

"You'd better believe it."

The taxi was pulling away when Mrs. Tolvey opened the front door. Dressed in a pale green chenille robe, she was in her late fifties with short, curly brown hair and a wide smile.

"I saw Bob drop you off. I'm Nancy Tolvey. Need a room?"

"Three." Joe picked up the bags and entered the foyer. "A twin for Ms. Duncan and the little girl, a single next door for me. We have a friend who will be back a little later. We'll check him in too."

"Fine. But we don't have any twins. A queen okay?"

Eve nodded.

"Suppose you show Eve and Jane upstairs and I'll stay down here to sign us in," Joe said.

Eve picked up her and Jane's bags, and Nancy Tolvey led the way.

The room she showed Eve was clean and bright with pale green ivy twining on cream-colored wallpaper. "No private bathroom. It's down the hall."

"You heard her, Jane," Eve said. "You shower first. I'll bring your pajamas to you as soon as I unpack them."

"Okay." Jane yawned. "I don't know why I'm so sleepy."

"The altitude," Nancy Tolvey said. "You must not be from around here."

"We came from Phoenix."

She nodded. "I visited there once. Too hot. I couldn't ever get used to that kind of climate after living here all my life."

All her life . . .

Joe had told Spiro he'd talk to Nancy Tolvey, but Eve might as well do it herself. "We're trying to locate a family who may have lived here a long time ago. The Baldridges?"

"Baldridges?" Nancy Tolvey was silent a moment and then shook her head. "I don't think so. I don't recall anyone by that name living here." She headed for the stairs. "I'll bring you up some more bath towels."

It had been worth a try, Eve thought. Maybe they'd find out something tomorrow.

NANCY TOLVEY WAS frowning as she came down the stairs.

"Something wrong?" Joe asked.

She sat down at the old-fashioned writing desk in the foyer. "It's nothing." She opened the guest book. "Sign here, please. Name, address, driver's license." She was still frowning as she watched him register. "You'll share the bath with your friends. We don't have—" She closed her eyes. "The candles . . ."

"I hoped you had electricity," Joe said dryly.

Her lids flicked open. "No, that's not what I meant. Miss Duncan asked me about the Baldridge family, and I told her I couldn't remember anyone around here by that name."

Joe stiffened. "But you do?"

"I didn't want to talk about it, but, yes, I remember." She smiled bitterly. "There's no way I could forget. And not talking about it isn't going to make it go away, is it? I've done that for years."

"The Baldridges lived here in town?"

She shook her head. "It was up north of Dillard."

"Near Jamison?"

"No, the tent was up farther in the mountains."

"Tent?"

"Old man Baldridge was an evangelist. A real fire-and-brimstone preacher. He had a big tent on this plateau in the middle of the mountains, where he gave his sermons." She made a face. "When I was in my teens, I slept around a little. Well, maybe a lot. My daddy thought I needed my soul saved. When he heard about Reverend Baldridge's tent show, he drove me up there one night. And believe me, it was quite a show. The reverend scared the daylights out of me."

"Why?"

"He looked like death warmed over. White face, dirty gray hair, and his eyes . . ."

"How old was he?"

"Sixty, maybe. He looked real old to me. I was only fifteen."

Then the evangelist couldn't have been Dom, Joe thought.

"He shouted at me," Nancy Tolvey continued. "He stood up there, waving that red candle, telling me what a whore I was."

"Red candle?"

"The whole tent was full of candles. No electricity. Just big iron candelabras filled with candles. We all got a candle when we came in. Children got white ones. The rest of us got red or pink." She shook her head. "I never forgave my daddy for taking me there and letting Baldridge drag me up to the altar and tell everyone what a sinner I was."

"I can see why it's impossible to forget."

"I remember crying and jerking away from him. I ran out of the tent and down the hill to our car. My father came after me and tried to make me go back, but I wouldn't go. He finally took me home. I got married and moved out six weeks later."

"Who else was in the tent that night?"

"There were so many people there. Why are you looking for him? Is he any relation?"

"No. Actually, we're looking for his family."

She shook her head. "I don't know about that. You'll have to ask someone else."

"Can you point me to anyone who might remember anything about the reverend?"

"Daddy heard about him through the Bloom Street Baptist Church. A lot of the members were driving up to the revival on weekends. Someone there might know something." She smiled crookedly. "That was the church where I was baptized, but I never went back. I was too afraid someone had been there when that old devil screamed out what a sinner I was."

"You never heard about the reverend again?"

"You think I'd want to hear or think about him again? I wasn't a bad kid. What's sex anyway? He shouldn't have done that to me." She drew a deep breath. "I'm getting all upset over nothing. It was so long ago. I've lived a happy life since then. Funny how the things that happen to you as a kid leave the deepest scars, isn't it?"

"Maybe not so funny."

She stood up. "I was going to bring up more towels. You're in the room at the top of the stairs, next to Miss Duncan and the kid."

Joe watched her walk down the hall. He had struck pay dirt.

"AN EVANGELIST," EVE repeated. "Dom's father?"

Joe shrugged. "Or grandfather. She said he was nearly sixty."

"Everyone over thirty looks decrepit to a fifteen-year-old."

"True."

"Candles had some sort of significance for the preacher. His flock's state of grace?"

"More likely degree of sin."

"And Dom carries on the judgment?" She shook her head. "He's very smart. He knows why he's killing. He likes it."

"But, as Nancy Tolvey says, things that happen in your childhood scar and stay with you."

"So what happened to him that could have turned him into a mass murderer?"

Joe shrugged. "Who knows? We'll go to the Baptist church tomorrow and see if we can find out anything else."

"Could Dom's father still be alive?"

"Possibly. He'd be pretty old." He bent his head and brushed a kiss on her nose. "Go to sleep. I'll wait up for Spiro and tell him what we've learned."

"It's more than I expected." Excitement tingled through her. They were getting close. Dom was no longer a complete enigma. "And tomorrow we'll know more."

"Don't get your hopes up."

"Don't be silly. Of course I'll get my hopes up."

Joe smiled. "I shouldn't complain. Hope's very healthy for you."

"Stop sounding as if I'm a nutcase and you're my psychoanalyst."

"Sorry. I've become accustomed to analyzing every move you make. It comes of standing wistfully on the sidelines."

"*Wistful* isn't in your vocabulary." She hurriedly looked away from him. "Jane's in bed. Will you keep an eye on her while I shower?"

"I won't take a step away from your door."

She could feel his gaze on her as she walked down the hall, feeling weak-kneed. Since the trip had begun, Joe had fallen back into the role of old friend. He hadn't said anything too personal until just then, and his words brought the memory of the previous night rushing back to her.

It was very unsettling to realize her feelings for Joe could almost overwhelm her eagerness at what they'd learned about Dom.

JOE WAS WAITING when Eve and Jane came down the stairs the next morning. "I'm afraid we'll have to skip Mrs. Tolvey's breakfast. I have a taxi outside. Spiro's waiting for us."

"He's not here?"

"No, he called me about three in the morning. At the bar he got a lead on Reverend Baldridge, and he's been up all night."

"Did you tell him we should go to the Baptist church?"

Joe nodded. "He said it's not necessary. After he found out about the tent revival, he tracked down Reverend Piper, who's the pastor of the Bloom Street church, and woke him up." Joe shrugged as she stared at him in surprise. "Nobody said Spiro isn't ruthless when he's on the trail."

"He found out something?"

"He found the place where the reverend gave his sermons. It's a fairly long drive. We're going to meet Spiro there."

SPIRO WAS STANDING alone on top of a hill. Patches of snow dotted the ground and gray clouds hovered over the mountains in the distance.

The driver parked at the bottom of the hill.

"Pay off the taxi, Joe," Spiro called out. "I'll drive you back. I commandeered Reverend Piper's car." Spiro smiled sardonically as he nodded at the brown Ford parked some distance away. "There are times when being FBI comes in handy."

Jane ran up the hill and looked around. The ground was utterly barren; tatters of seared cloth clung to the numerous blackened stakes driven into the earth. "A fire?"

"Yes," Spiro answered.

Eve felt suddenly cold. "What happened here?"

"Do you want to send the child to the car?" Spiro asked.

Jane was wandering slowly some distance away.

"No, I won't shut her out. She deserves to know everything we know."

"And what do we know?" Joe had joined them. "When did this happen?"

"Twenty-nine years ago."

"An accident?"

"It was presumed to be an accident. Everyone knew about all the candles. The tent was a fire waiting to happen."

"Any fatalities?"

"No bodies were found. Services were held here every Friday, Saturday, and Sunday. The fire must have happened earlier in the week, because the site was found exactly like this when the first carload of people came that weekend."

"Was there an investigation?"

"Of course. But no one could find Reverend Baldridge. It was decided that he had moved on. Evangelists are usually traveling men, and he wasn't very popular with the authorities anyway. He'd been warned about the candles being a fire hazard."

"*Did* he move on?"

"We'll have to find out, won't we?" Spiro glanced around. "Christ, this place is weird."

Eve felt the same way. "If the fire happened that long ago, why hasn't the grass grown back?"

"What else did you find out?" Joe asked. "What about his family? What did Reverend Piper tell you about Kevin Baldridge?"

"He doesn't remember a Kevin. His father was the pastor of the Bloom Street Baptist Church when Reverend Baldridge was preaching here. He was only a boy when his father brought him up here for services. He met Mrs. Baldridge once, but the only sons he recalls are Ezekiel and Jacob. He never met Kevin."

"But we know there's a Kevin. Mrs. Harding met him."

"If he was here, he was kept out of sight." Spiro shook his head. "Though why is a mystery. It seems old Baldridge kept everyone in the family busy at the services, handing out candles, passing the collection plates . . ."

"I don't like it here." Jane was standing beside Eve. "When can we go?"

Even Jane was feeling bad vibes, Eve realized. "Soon. Want to go wait in the car?"

Jane shook her head and moved closer. "I'll wait for you."

"We might as well all go," Spiro said. "There's nothing we can do right now. We'll hop back to Phoenix and I'll get a team to come here and go over the site."

"After two decades and a fire?"

"No one searched for graves in the area."

"You don't think Reverend Baldridge just moved on, do you?"

"I have to investigate every possibility. The old man seems to have been pretty unpleasant."

"Yes." Joe's gaze wandered around the campground. "Fanatics usually cause a lot of misery."

"Well, if Kevin Baldridge is Dom, he's created more than his share of misery." Spiro started down the hill. "Like father, like son."

"Maybe it isn't Kevin. Maybe it's one of the other brothers." Eve followed Spiro.

"But where was Kevin when the services were going on?" Spiro said. "It smacks of rebellion against the old man." He glanced over his shoulder. "What are you doing, Quinn?"

Joe was kneeling, digging into the soft soil with a hand. "Just checking something." He lifted a palmful of dirt to his mouth and touched his tongue to it. "Salt."

Eve stopped in her tracks. "What?"

"Like you, I was wondering why nothing had grown back." Joe brushed his palm clean as he stood up. "Someone plowed the area with salt either before or after the fire. He didn't want anything to live in this place again."

IT WAS EARLY evening when they arrived back in Phoenix. Spiro left them at the airport and Joe, Eve, and Jane arrived at Logan's house after nine o'clock.

To Eve's surprise, Logan himself was sitting on the couch, playing cards with Sarah, when they walked into the living room.

"It's about time." He threw down his cards and stood up. "Why the hell didn't you tell me you were leaving town?"

"I'm glad you're back," Sarah said. "He's been here for hours driving Monty and me bats. He wouldn't leave and then he wanted me to amuse him."

Logan scowled at her. "You cheated."

"I'm just a better poker player than you are. What do you think rescue teams do between searches?" She rose to her feet. "You deal with him, Eve. Monty and I are tired of watching him brood."

"I don't brood."

Sarah didn't argue. "Come on, Jane. You look as tired as I feel. Rough trip?"

"It was creepy there." Jane stooped to pat Monty. "Come on, boy. Let's go to bed."

The retriever stretched and then followed Sarah and Jane from the room.

Logan's gaze followed Sarah. "She's still holding a grudge."

"She played cards with you," Joe said.

"Because she wanted to beat my ass." He turned to Eve and went on the attack. "Didn't it occur to you that I'd be worried when Booker told me you'd left the house?"

"I was in a hurry. Spiro had a lead. I honestly didn't think of it." She supposed she should have called Logan, she thought wearily. "I'm sorry, Logan."

"Leave her alone." Joe was behind her, his hands resting lightly on her shoulders. "She has enough problems without trying to pacify you."

"Be quiet, Joe. He's been trying to help me. I shouldn't have made him worry."

"I don't mind worrying if I can get my teeth into a problem. I can't stand being shut out of—" Logan stopped, staring at Eve and then at Joe standing behind her. "It's over, isn't it? He's done it."

"What?"

"He's won. He's finally got what he wants. God, it couldn't be more clear." He smiled without mirth. "I should have known that I was fighting a lost cause. I could fight Quinn, but I can't fight you, Eve. From the time he came to the island, you wanted to follow him home."

"Because of Bonnie."

"Maybe." Logan looked at them for a long while. "You take care of her, Quinn."

"You don't have to tell me that."

"Yes, I do. Because I'm warning, not stating. If I can help, call me, Eve."

"She won't need your help," Joe said.

"You can never tell."

She couldn't stand it. She wouldn't let him leave like this. "Joe, I want to talk to Logan alone."

Joe didn't move.

"Joe."

"Okay." He left the room.

"Why do I feel that he's lurking in the hall?" Logan asked.

"Because he probably is." She tried to smile. "You should take it as a compliment."

"Should I?"

"He realizes how much you mean to me. How much you'll always mean to me."

"But evidently not enough."

"What's enough? It hurts me when you hurt. It makes me happy when you're happy. If you ever need me, I'll be there for you. Isn't that enough?"

"It's a lot. Not as satisfying as what I wanted, but I'll take it." He paused. "Just for my own curiosity, how did Quinn do it?"

"I don't know," she said frankly. "I didn't want it. It makes me uneasy. It's like being caught in some kind of whirlpool. It just happened."

"Nothing 'just happens' with Quinn. He's a major force. I've always known he was waiting in the wings for you."

"I didn't."

"I know. I hoped I'd have you wrapped up before he decided to make a move. I didn't manage to pull it off." He looked at her for several moments and then gave her a quick kiss. "But it was a good year, wasn't it?"

Tears stung her eyes. "The best."

"Not the best, or we wouldn't have reached this point, but pretty damn good." He took her arm and walked with her into the foyer, where Joe was waiting by the stairs. "Hello, Quinn. What a surprise."

"Not." Joe moved closer to Eve.

"You don't have to act as if I'm going to kidnap her. That's not my style." His lips tightened. "Though I'd like to break your neck."

Joe shook his head. "But you won't do it. That's the difference between us. You're tough, but you never reached the point of no return with Eve. I wonder if you ever have with anyone."

Logan took a step forward and said softly, "I'm tempted to prove you wrong."

"Logan," Eve said.

She didn't think he'd listen to her. Then he turned away from Joe and opened the door. "Good-bye, Eve. I'll be around. Don't close me out entirely. Okay?"

"That couldn't happen." They had become too close. She kissed his cheek. "Not ever."

"Remember you said that." The door shut behind him.

Joe gave a low whistle. "I don't like the sound of that. Am I going to have to be friends with him?"

"You don't have to do anything. But he's my friend, dammit. He always will be."

"I was afraid that was what you meant. I'll have to consider the way to—" He stopped. "You're upset. I'll shut up and leave you alone."

"That would be a first."

"You *are* upset." He scowled. "And I'm jealous as hell."

She used the word he'd once used with her. "Adjust."

He smiled. "I will."

"I've made you no promises, Joe. I still don't think we—"

"Time for me to leave," he interrupted. "You're starting to be introspective, and that could be dangerous. I'm going to the precinct and see about the picture." He paused. "I may not be back tonight. I think you could use some time alone."

She felt a mixture of relief and disappointment. "You don't have to stay away. If I don't want you in my bed, I can always say no."

"I'm trying to display my sensitive side." He leaned forward and kissed her hard and quick. "Sleep well. I'll see you in the morning."

She doubted she'd sleep well, she thought as she climbed the stairs. All the way back from Dillard she hadn't been able to forget the sight of that scorched, ruined hilltop. What had made Dom so bitter that he had ravaged the site? He had ripped and killed the earth as he had the bodies of his victims.

And then she'd faced Logan and hurt him. For the second time.

But she had never thought her feelings for Joe would shift and change. If she was smart, she'd close herself away from him, focus solely on her work. She'd never been this unsure and emotional when she was focused on her job. She had purpose and satisfaction knowing she was helping the lost ones.

Yes, that was the smart thing. Think only of work. Close Joe out . . .

"IT WON'T WORK, Mama." Bonnie was sitting in the chair beside her bed. "Joe won't let you do that. Besides, it's too late."

"I can do whatever I wish." Eve propped her head higher on the pillow. "He's interfering with my life."

"So am I, but you don't shut me out."

"You can't shut off your dreams."

Bonnie chuckled. "You always have an answer. The reason you don't shut me out is because you love me."

"Oh, yes," she whispered.

"And that's why you can't shut Joe out."

"That's different."

"You're darn right. Joe's alive."

"I'd hurt him."

"You're just depressed because of Logan. You shouldn't be. It was bound to happen. Remember I once told you that sometimes love started out one way and then became something else? You don't have to lose Logan and you won't lose Joe."

"Bull. Loss can happen anytime. I lost you."

"Silly. Then why am I here talking to you?"

"Because I'm nutty as a fruitcake. Another reason I should walk away from Joe."

"I'm not going to argue with you. You're smart, you'll do the right thing." Bonnie leaned back in the chair. "I just want to sit here and enjoy being with you. It's been a long time."

"Then why didn't you come sooner?"

"I couldn't get close to you. It was hard this time. So much darkness . . . Nothing but darkness around him, Mama."

"He's a terrible man." She moistened her lips. "Was he the one, Bonnie?"

"I can't see through the darkness. Maybe I don't want to see."

"I want to see. I have to see."

Bonnie nodded. "To protect Jane. I like Jane."

"So do I. But also because of you, baby."

"I know. But you're leaning more toward the living now. That's the way it should be."

Eve was silent a moment. "He tried to tell me Jane was you reincarnated. Wasn't that stupid?"

"I think it is. How could I be reincarnated when I'm here talking to you?" She smiled. "And you know she's nothing like me."

"Yes, I know."

"You wouldn't want her to be like me, Mama. We all have our very own souls. That's what makes every one of us so special and wonderful."

"Dom isn't wonderful."

"No. He's twisted and ugly." Bonnie frowned. "I'm frightened for you. He keeps coming nearer and nearer . . ."

"Let him come. I'm waiting for him."

"Shh, don't get upset. We won't think any more about Dom tonight. Will you tell me about Monty? I love dogs."

"I know. I was going to get you a puppy for Christmas the year that you—"

"And you've been regretting ever since that you didn't get me one sooner. Stop it. I was happy. But you should learn something from that. Live every moment. Don't put off anything until tomorrow."

"Stop preaching at me, dammit."

Bonnie giggled. "Sorry. Then tell me about Monty."

"I don't really know much about him. He belongs to Sarah and he's a rescue and cadaver dog. Jane loves him and trails after him every chance she . . ."

MARK GRUNARD WAS waiting in the lobby of Charlie Cather's hotel when Joe walked in. "Ah, back from the mountains?"

"What are you doing here?"

"Cather's promised to have a drink with me. He should be down soon. Any luck in Dillard?"

"No school records there, so we're checking a nearby town. It turns out the father was a traveling evangelist."

"Damn, I was hoping there would be school photos to compare with Mrs. Harding's snapshot."

"So were we." Joe sat down. "Spiro's not pleased you're sticking so close to Cather."

"Tough. I didn't get anything from him, so I had to zero in on Cather. He's a hell of an easier mark."

"He's tougher than you'd think."

"But he doesn't have Spiro's experience and just may let something slip." He added shrewdly, "Has he told you anything about the photograph? Is that why you're here?"

Why was he there? He'd gone to the precinct earlier about the picture and was told the duplicates weren't ready. That stone wall again. The Phoenix police were mad as hell at Spiro for not telling them who tipped him off about Debby Jordan's grave. So they were paying him back. A little tit for tat.

Even if Joe could persuade Charlie to describe the photo, he doubted it would help. Face it, he was really there because he'd needed to distance himself from Eve. His impulse had been to move quickly, push hard instead of waiting patiently. It would have been a stupid move. She had been close to Logan, and Joe should be grateful she hadn't been more upset. But he wasn't grateful, and he was tired as hell of waiting patiently. He'd come too close to her to take a step back.

"No one's told me anything," Joe answered Mark. "Have you seen Charlie since he picked up the photo?"

"Yesterday evening at the precinct." He paused. "Something's bothering him. He's trying to hide it, but he's not good enough."

"Maybe Spiro raked him over the coals for talking to you."

"Maybe." He shrugged. "But I didn't notice it until he came back from the Hardings' with that picture. I'm glad you're here. We'll gang up on the kid and try to find out what's making him so uneasy." He got to his feet. "Here he comes."

Cather was smiling as he walked toward them from the elevators. "I wasn't expecting you, Joe. Spiro said you just got back from Dillard. What is this? A conspiracy?"

Screw ganging up on Cather. If Charlie dropped something, he'd pick it up. But he wouldn't pressure him. Joe rose to his feet. "Yep, and you're the target."

Cather's smile faded. "I can't talk about the photo until I get clearance from Spiro. No way am I stepping on his toes again."

Grunard was right, something was bothering Charlie. But maybe he was just feeling the pressure. "If you can't, you can't. Then I guess if we can't bribe you, you'll just have to buy the drinks." He headed for the bar. "How's your wife?"

EVE WAS SLEEPING when Dom called her very early in the morning. The sound of his voice was hideously jarring, piercing the serenity she usually felt after dreams of Bonnie.

"You've been busy. How did you like the scenes of my childhood?"

"How do you know I was there?"

"I listen. I watch. Don't you feel me watching you, Eve?"

"No, I ignore you . . . Kevin."

He chuckled. "I prefer Dom. Kevin doesn't exist anymore. I've gone through so many transformations since then. And I've noticed you've been trying to close me out. It made me angry at the time. But I got over it. It only whetted my appetite."

"Kevin must have been a nasty little bastard. What happened to your parents?"

"What you think happened."

"You killed them."

"It was inevitable. My father saw Satan in me from the time I was a small child. He'd make me stand and hold a black candle in each hand and then he'd beat me until I fell to my knees. When the beating was over, he'd rub salt into the wounds. Maybe he was right about seeing evil in me. Do you think we're born with the seeds of evil?"

"I think you were."

"But you also think I'm insane. My father was insane and they called him a saint. The line is so thin, isn't it?"

"Did Ezekiel and Jacob think he was insane?"

"No, they were as frightened and fooled by him as all the rest. But I tried to make them see. I took them with me when I ran away. I was lonely then and needed people."

"And you brought them here to Phoenix."

"We were going to California. I'd talked the Harding kids into going with us. But then Ezekiel and Jacob got scared. They packed up one night and ran back to my father. I went into a rage."

"And killed the Hardings."

"It was beyond anything. The ultimate experience of my life. And at last I knew what I was and what I was meant to do. I went back to that tent on the hill and I butchered all of them."

"Your mother too?"

"She stood by and watched him punish me. Is cruelty less painful because it's passive?"

"And your brothers?"

"They made their choice when they went back to him. I had to start over."

"Where are the bodies?"

"You won't find them. I scattered their parts over half of Arizona and New Mexico and enjoyed every moment of it."

"And sowed that campground with salt."

"A melodramatic piece of symbolism, but I was only a boy at the time."

"Like leaving a candle with your victims? You're not a boy now."

"It's difficult to erase the teachings of childhood. Or perhaps part of my satisfaction is showing my father that I use his precious candles in my own way."

"Your father is dead."

"He was sure he was going to heaven, so he must be looking

down on me. Or do you think his soul was chopped up with his body? I've often wondered." He paused. "Do you believe Bonnie's soul was destroyed?"

She bit hard on her lower lip. "No."

"Well, you'll know soon. I haven't decided what candle I'll use for you. It's a terrible decision. White for Jane, of course, but your color must reflect—"

She hung up. He was in a mood for confidences, and perhaps she should have held on, but she couldn't take any more. He was dragging her down into the darkness that surrounded him. It was worse because it followed the wonderful dream of Bonnie. At this moment the evil seemed to be overpowering and she was helpless to fight it. It kept coming and coming . . .

You should learn something from that. Live every moment. Don't put off anything until tomorrow.

Bonnie's words.

Live every moment . . .

EVE HEARD JOE come into the house two hours later. She left her bedroom and waited for him at the top of the stairs.

He paused when he saw her. "Okay?"

"No, Dom called. Nothing is ever okay when he talks to me."

"What did he say?"

"Poison. Ugliness. I'll tell you later." She held out a hand. "Come to bed."

He slowly climbed the steps until he stood before her. "I'm being forgiven for not being sorry Logan bowed out?"

"It was never a question of forgiveness."

He took her hand. "You've discovered you can't live without me in your bed?"

"Will you stop joking?"

"Who's joking?" He reached out and touched her cheek. "I'm

probing. I have an idea something very important is happening here. Why, Eve?"

She swallowed to ease the tightness of her throat. "I never gave Bonnie a puppy. She wanted it and I put it off. And then it was too late."

His brows lifted. "And what's the connection? Is taking me into your bed the equivalent of giving me a puppy?"

She shook her head. "The puppy's not for you, Joe. It's for me. I'm being entirely selfish. I want to be near you. I want you to talk to me. I want you to make love to me." She smiled shakily. "And I won't put it off. I won't wait until it's too late. Will you come to bed and be with me, Joe Quinn?"

"Oh, yes." He slid his arm around her waist. His voice was as uneven as hers had been. "You're damn right I will."

CHAPTER SIXTEEN

WHEN SPIRO CALLED Eve that afternoon, she told him what Dom had told her of his childhood. "Did the technician monitoring the phone trace the call?"

"No, that's been a washout, dammit. But what Dom told you computes with the little we've learned," Spiro said. "We've contacted the schools in Jamison. No school records for the Baldridge boys. But I managed to track down a couple of reports about an official going out to see Reverend Baldridge and inquiring why the boys weren't in school. The reverend claimed his sons were being home-schooled. He didn't think the boys would get a godly education in public schools."

"Anything else?"

"One more thing. The reports were on Ezekiel and Jacob. No mention of Kevin."

"If he never attended the services, maybe they didn't know he existed."

"Judging by the destruction of that hilltop, I'd say he wanted to make his presence known."

"Not necessarily. He went for years and never seemed to need public recognition of his acts. It's only recently that he's changed."

"He was just starting out then. He hadn't learned. He hadn't evolved." Spiro paused. "But even though he's different now, he would still have traits that fit the usual pattern of the organized offender."

"Above average intelligence, for one," Eve said. "But all this talk isn't getting us anywhere. We need to know what he looks like. Where is that photograph?"

"Don't get your hopes up. The photo may not be the answer."

"What do you mean?"

"Just what I said."

"We're supposed to be working together. Stop being evasive. Tell me."

Spiro was silent.

Dammit, he was stubborn and FBI through and through. She was getting tired of prying information out of him. He had made a deal, but it was clear he wasn't going to budge on this point. Okay, pin him down at least on the time. "When?"

"Soon."

"When?"

"God, you're persistent. Tomorrow, maybe." He hung up.

THEY DIDN'T GET a duplicate of the photograph until two days later. Spiro came to the house and handed Eve a five-by-seven envelope. "Here it is. You're going to be disappointed."

"Why?"

"Look at it."

Joe moved to stand beside her as she opened the envelope and took out the photograph.

It had obviously been taken in a huge backyard. Two teenage boys sat in the foreground at a picnic table; a third was far in the background, coming down porch steps.

"According to Mrs. Harding, the kid on the steps is Kevin Baldridge," Spiro said. "The two at the picnic table are Ezekiel and Jacob."

Dammit, Kevin Baldridge was not only far away but the photo had been slightly overexposed, and because he was in motion, his figure was blurred and completely unrecognizable.

"No wonder the police didn't take this from the Hardings at the time," Eve said. "He's just a blur. He could be anyone. Joe told me that Charlie was troubled about this photograph. I can see why." She looked at Spiro. "Photo technology has improved enormously in the last twenty-five years. They might not have been able to clarify this photograph then, but you can do it now, can't you?"

"Probably. I've sent another duplicate to Quantico." He paused. "But I wondered if you'd like to take a shot at it yourself. You work with photographs too."

"My specialty is age progression, and that's completely different from what you need here."

"Oh." Spiro was disappointed. "Too bad."

Yes, it was, she thought with frustration.

"Nothing you can do?" Spiro asked.

She thought about it. "Maybe." She stood up and got a phone book. "If there's a film developer in town who does global corrections."

"Global corrections?"

"Air brushing and other kinds of— Here it is." She had found an advertisement in the yellow pages. "Pixmore. Now we'll have to see if they have the equipment and the experts to do the job."

"Glamour shots?" Joe was looking over her shoulder at the ad, which showed a close-up of a beautiful woman. "Not exactly scientific."

"How do you think companies like this make their money? They remove everything from zits and facial wrinkles to dark hair roots on photographs." She looked at the photograph again. "They *might* be able to do it. Correctors prefer to work with slides, but I'll take this to them, see if they have someone qualified." She put the picture back in the envelope. "These places are usually backed up for weeks. Can you put a little FBI muscle behind me?"

"I'll have Charlie meet you at Pixmore," Spiro said. "How long should it take?"

She shrugged. "I don't know. Maybe twenty-four hours. It depends on how good the technician is and what kind of overtime he's willing to put in."

"I'll ask Charlie to stay with him until it's finished."

"Good." She moved toward the door. "That will probably help."

"I'll drive you," Joe said.

"That's not necessary."

He made a face. "At the moment I don't seem able to make any other contribution. I'm feeling the need to be needed."

PIXMORE WAS THIRTY minutes from north Phoenix and perched on the summit of a curving mountain road. The one-story building was all glass and stone and gleamed in the sunlight. Charlie Cather pulled into the parking lot right after Joe and Eve.

"I'm glad you think we can get something done with that photo." He shook his head. "I was disappointed. I thought I'd really zeroed in on something."

"You did," Eve said. "It still may be salvageable."

"That's what Spiro said." He nodded at the Toyota driving into the parking lot. "There's Grunard."

"What's he doing here?" Eve asked.

"He was with me at the hotel when Spiro called. He's been bugging the hell out of me." Joe made a face. "But he's not a bad guy."

"Spiro won't like it."

"I cleared it with him. He said give him an appetizer but not the main course. He leaves before they start working on the photo."

Mark was coming toward them, smiling.

"Don't look now, but he appears ready for dessert," Joe said dryly.

"CAN'T YOU GET me a negative?" The technician's name was Billy Sung. He was under twenty-five and definitely not optimistic. "I'm not a miracle worker, you know."

"No negative," Eve said. "Your boss says you're the best technician he has. I'm sure you won't have a problem."

"Don't give me a snow job. I'll have a hell of a problem. This print has multiple errors. One would be easy to correct, but not all of them. You need one of those digital imaging companies in L.A. or a university think tank to enhance those pixels. Pixmore doesn't have the equipment."

"No chance?"

He shrugged. "Maybe. I have a college professor who has a government research grant, and his equipment is way beyond state of the art. He usually lets me use it."

"You're a student?"

"Yeah, I need a degree to get a job with one of those companies on the West Coast. I have to compete with all those whiz kids from UCLA and USC. Those companies are cutting edge. It's incredible what they do with digital computer and software equipment." He looked back at the photograph. "But I do damn well considering what I work with."

"I'm sure you do," Eve said. "Who is this professor and where's his lab?"

"Professor Dunkeil. Ralph Dunkeil. His lab's about five minutes from here on Blue Mountain Drive."

"Could I have it by tomorrow?"

He shook his head.

"Please, it's very important to me."

He looked at her face for a couple of seconds and then slowly nodded. "If you can clear it with Grisby. He's not going to like me putting everything on hold."

"Your boss has already okayed it," Charlie said. "He said that you're ours for the next thirty-six hours."

"That sounds like slave labor." He grimaced. "Though Grisby's pretty much of a slave driver himself. I had to threaten to quit last quarter to make him give me time off to take my finals."

"I'd be grateful if you'll try to hurry it," Eve said. "You'll call me?"

"I'll call you, Eve," Charlie said. "I'll go with Mr. Sung and help."

"I don't need your help." Sung gave Charlie a cool glance. "The government is too much into our business as it is. FBI, CIA, IRS. Now you come in here and try to pressure me."

"Hey, man, I'm only doing my job."

"Yeah, sure," Sung said as he sat down at the bench. "I've heard that before. It's always followed by the crack of the whip."

"Perhaps I could go with you instead." Mark Grunard smiled at Sung. "Do you have any objections to a little publicity? It might help you get that job in California."

Sung looked interested.

"No way," Charlie said firmly. "I told you that you couldn't stay, Grunard."

"But our friend doesn't like you as much as he does me."

Charlie jerked his thumb. "Out."

Grunard sighed. "Maybe I could come back after you've finished your work, Mr. Sung." He handed him a card. "Call me." He left the lab.

"The results are confidential, Mr. Sung," Charlie said.

"Yeah." Sung looked thoughtfully at the card before stuffing it in his pocket. "So were the atomic tests in Nevada that gave everybody cancer."

"Please call me as soon as possible, Mr. Sung," Eve said. "It means a great deal to me."

"I'll let you know."

"WHAT DO YOU think? Can he do it?" Joe asked as he and Eve got into the car.

"Maybe. He seems sharp." She leaned back in the seat. "And I think he likes a challenge. Though Charlie may have a tough time. Sung evidently hates government bureaucrats."

"Maybe you should introduce him to Sarah. So what do we do now?"

"Go home. Wait."

"That won't be easy."

"No." It seemed as if they'd done nothing but sit around and wait lately. "But at least Spiro gave us a chance to hurry the process along."

"He's taking a big risk dealing with us. He's impatient to have it over."

"So am I, Joe." She closed her eyes and tried to relax. "So am I."

IT WAS NEARLY three o'clock in the morning and the lights were still burning in the professor's lab on Blue Mountain Drive.

Eve must be happy she'd found someone passionate enough to work so hard on the photo, Dom thought. Passion could be dangerous.

But it could also be exciting. Every move Eve made was raising the stakes.

He probably should have gotten rid of that photo years ago, but he had moved on and he had not thought it important enough. But what was happening in that lab was important.

Time changed everything. Technology, morals, good, evil. Who would have known how much his needs would change? His priorities were so different now or he would not be sitting outside the lab.

What was happening in there? Were they getting close?

He felt excitement tighten his muscles. Go ahead, Eve. Come closer. Try to find me. . . .

"MORE COFFEE?" CHARLIE asked.

Billy Sung adjusted the computer. "Not right now."

"You didn't eat dinner. I could go out and pick up some fast food."

"No." He was coming close. Screw those L.A. bozos with all their fancy equipment. He was as good as them any day of the week. Just a few more adjustments and he might—

"Are you getting it?"

"You bet I am." He rubbed his eyes and bent forward again over the picture. "I wasn't sure I had a chance, but I'll be able to—" He stiffened. "My God."

"You've got it?"

"Shut up. I have to check the shift." He brought the picture in closer.

The shift was coming in clearer and then clearer still.

There could be no mistake.

THE PHONE RANG on Eve's nightstand.

"We're on our way to see you," Charlie said.

"What?"

"Sung wants to see you. He's all excited."

She sat up in bed. "He did it?"

"Not yet. He says he'll be done any minute. He was muttering about shifts and spectrums and he's bringing you the photo. He won't let me see it while he's working on it, but I'll take possession the minute it's completely finished."

"Why the secrecy?"

"Search me," Charlie said sourly. "He evidently thinks I'm the right arm of Big Brother. He made a phone call and then he said he had to see you right away. He seems to think this is only between you and him, but this is FBI business and he can't fool around with— Where the hell are you going?" He came back on the phone. "I've got to go. Sung must have finished. He just bolted for the front door. We should be there in thirty minutes." He hung up.

"Sung was able to do it?" Joe asked.

"That's what Charlie said, but Sung wants to talk to me." She put down the receiver and swung her feet to the floor. "He'll be here in thirty minutes with the photo. I'm going to get dressed."

Joe sat up in bed. "Why should he want to talk to you?"

"I told you, he doesn't like the government."

"Bad enough to wake you in the middle of the night?"

She headed for the bathroom. "I don't care if Sung comes up here and crawls in bed with us as long as he brings me that photo."

"I'd have a few objections," Joe said. "By all means, let's wait for him downstairs."

"WHERE IS HE?" Eve glanced at her watch again. "It's been forty minutes."

"Maybe they had to go back to the lab for something."

"Wouldn't Charlie have called us?"

"Car trouble?"

"Stop being comforting. Do you have Charlie's digital number?"

Joe nodded and reached for his phone. "No answer." He hung up. "It's time to go looking."

"I'll go with you."

"Stay here. What if all that comforting bullshit is really true and they drive up right after I've left? If they come, give me a call and I'll hotfoot it back."

He was right. She had to stay. But, blast it, it was going to kill her to sit there and wait.

EVE'S PHONE RANG forty-five minutes later.

"There's been a crash," Joe said. "A car went off the road and down into the ravine."

Her hand tightened on the phone. "Is it them?"

"I don't know." He paused. "The car's pretty messed up. It was over a hundred-foot drop."

She closed her eyes. "Christ."

"The medics and rescue team are going down to see if anyone survived. It's not going to be easy. The incline's very steep."

"How could anyone survive a drop like that?"

"It's possible. The car hasn't exploded yet. I have to go now. I'll call you later. I'm going down with the rescue team."

The car hasn't exploded yet.

Fear tore through her. "Let them do their job, Joe. Stay out of it."

"I like Charlie Cather, Eve." He hung up.

She liked Charlie too, but the thought of Joe going near that car terrified her.

She dialed Joe back.

No answer. He was already on his way down to the car.

She headed for the front door.

THE FLASHING RED lights of ambulances, fire trucks, and a half dozen police cars dotted the highway. A quartz spotlight was aimed down into the ravine. Yellow tape cordoned off the right lane.

Joe.

She parked on the side of the highway and jumped out of the car. She fought her way through the crowd, but dammit, she couldn't see *anything*.

"Eve." Spiro was coming toward her. He nodded to a policeman. "She's all right. Let her through."

She ducked under the tape and ran to the edge of the cliff.

Spiro followed her. "You shouldn't be here, Eve. What are you thinking? This place is crawling with highway patrol and—"

"I don't care. Where's the rescue team?"

Spiro pointed at the line of moving lights at the bottom of the ravine. "They're almost at the car."

What car? It appeared to be only a mass of twisted metal. "Joe's down there."

"I know, he called me. But he was already on his way down when I got here."

"Does anyone know what happened?"

Spiro shook his head. "No witnesses. We don't know yet if they were driven off the road or there was brake tampering. We're not even sure if it's Charlie's rental car. The rescue team is going to try to radio back the license number."

"But you think it is?"

"Don't you?"

"Yes." The lights were almost at the car now. "Do they know how long it's going to take?"

"It depends on what they find down there." He paused. "But I have to warn you. The rescue team is already smelling gasoline. Even worse, gas vapor will be hovering over the vehicle. All it would take is a spark."

She went rigid. "Then tell them to get out of there."

"They have to try to rescue whoever's in the car."

"They don't have to get blown up. I've seen burn victims and—"

"I know," Spiro said quietly. "No one wants that to happen. The squad leader will call off the attempt if it gets too dangerous."

"Joe won't listen. He won't take orders from anybody. He'll do what he has to do to get them out of that car." God, she wished she were down there so she could *do* something.

"Take it easy, Eve. The rescue team isn't going to make any mistakes that will get anyone hurt. They'll disconnect the battery and then steady the vehicle. And they'll use Hurst tools to force their way into the car to avoid sparks."

The lights were moving, weaving in and around the wreckage.

Ten minutes passed.

Fifteen minutes.

"Why aren't they coming back? Can't you find out what's happening?" she asked Spiro.

"I'll try." Spiro strode over to the command unit and came back a few minutes later. "They've got one man out. They weren't able to make a positive confirmation, but they think the other man is dead. The squad leader's made the decision to pull his team out."

"Why?"

He hesitated. "The car hood is crushed. They weren't able to get to the battery to disconnect it. They managed to turn off the ignition, but anything could blow the car. The catalytic converter, the wiring . . ."

"And everyone's coming up?"

"Look for yourself."

The lights below were moving faster, away from the wreckage, back toward the incline.

Please let Joe be one of those men running to safety.

Her gaze moved back to the wreckage.

One light still burned in the midst of the twisted tangle of metal.

"Joe."

She had known it. Damn him. Damn him.

"My God, he's crazy," Spiro said.

Joe, get out of there. Please.

One minute passed. Two minutes.

Don't stay. Don't stay. Don't stay.

The wreckage exploded into a fireball.

She screamed.

Joe.

She ran toward the cliff edge.

Spiro caught her.

She struck out at him. "Let me go."

"You can't help him. There's a chance he could be all right."

All right? She had seen that light inside the car when it exploded. "I'm going down there."

"No way." His grasp tightened. "Too many people have been hurt tonight. I'm not going to watch you tumble down that mountain."

She kneed him in the groin and his grasp loosened. She ran, but two highway patrolmen grabbed her and forced her to the ground.

She fought desperately, kicking, frantically striking out.

Joe!

Darkness.

"YOU SON OF a bitch. Did you have to hit her?"

"I didn't hit her," Spiro said. "It was one of Phoenix's finest. They were trying to keep her from sliding down that mountain and killing herself. She's not hurt badly. Only stunned."

"You could have stopped them."

Joe. That was Joe's voice. Her eyes flew open. Joe kneeling beside her. Joe's face, oil-streaked, a cut on his cheekbone—but he was alive. Oh, God, alive.

"How do you feel?" Joe was frowning. "Did they hurt you?"

Alive.

She shook her head.

"You're lying. Why are you crying if you're not hurt?"

She hadn't known she was crying. "I don't know." She sat up and wiped her cheeks. "I'm okay."

"You're not okay. Lie back down."

"Shut up, Joe." Her voice was uneven. "I said I was okay. No credit to you. God, you're stupid. I thought you were dead, you idiot. I saw the light in the car right before it blew up."

"I had to drop the flashlight when I wriggled out of the car."

Stop shaking. He was alive. "You shouldn't have been there."

"I know," he said wearily. "The squad leader is mad as hell at me, but I had to make sure." He glanced at Spiro. "I'm sorry, it was Charlie in the car. I thought he was dead, but I had to be sure."

"And he was dead?"

Joe nodded.

Spiro flinched.

"And Billy Sung was alive when we got him out of the car, but he died before we reached the top."

Dead. Both dead. Nice Charlie Cather and Billy Sung, with his plans for taking the world by storm. Joe could have died too. Joe . . .

"Eve?" Joe was gazing at her in concern.

"I heard you. They're dead. They're both dead." She wrapped her arms around her body, but she couldn't stop the shaking. "I heard you."

"You're cold." He reached out to her.

"Don't you *touch* me. I feel fine." Her voice was rising, and she had to stop to control it. "I wasn't down there. I didn't do that stupid—"

"Come on." Joe took her hand to help her to her feet. "I'm taking you home."

She jerked away from him and stood on her own.

"Yeah, get her home," Spiro told Joe. "Those officers may be focused on the wreck, but there's still an APB out on her." He grimaced. "I have to make a telephone call. I'm going to hate this."

Charlie's wife, Eve thought dully. Charlie hadn't survived, and

Joe had been so close to not surviving. Oh, God, she was going to throw up. "She's pregnant. Can you get someone to tell her in person?"

"I'll have someone from the field office go out to see her, but I'm the one who has to do the dirty work."

"Come to the house after you've finished," Joe said. "We have something to talk about." He opened his jacket.

Half of a five-by-seven envelope was stuffed into the top of his jeans.

"The photograph?" Spiro asked.

"I haven't had a chance to look at it yet, but it was on the floor of the car beside Charlie. It was caught under the drive shift, and it ripped when I jerked it out and ran for it."

Spiro held out his hand. "Give it to me."

Joe shook his head. "You'll get it after we take a look at it, and I'm not going to stop and do that now. I need to get Eve home. She's not doing well."

"The hell I'm not. I'd have to be dead before I'd wait to see that murderer's face." She tried to steady her hands as she took the envelope. Disappointment surged through her as she drew out the photo. "*No.*"

A third of the photograph was gone. The third with Kevin Baldridge sitting on the porch steps.

Two lives lost. All for nothing.

Spiro was cursing. "Why couldn't it have been the other half that was torn?"

"Murphy's Law," Joe said. "This is just a print, Eve. Can you do anything?"

She tried to think. "Maybe. Sung might have made copies. Or his work might have been saved on his computer."

Joe looked at Spiro. "Get us permission to go into that lab on Blue Mountain Drive."

Spiro nodded. "Meet me there in two hours."

"We'll be there," Eve said.

"Come on." Joe tried to wrap an arm around Eve's waist. "Let's go home."

"I don't need your help." She pushed his hand away and started toward the car. Put one foot in front of the other. Don't look at him. Keep control or you'll disintegrate into a million pieces. "I'll see you back at the house."

"I'm going with you. For God's sake, you just took a knock on the head."

"That doesn't mean I'm not capable of—"

"I'm not letting you drive."

"And what are you supposed to do with your car? Just leave it here?"

"Screw the car." He opened the car door for her.

"No, I don't—"

"Need my help," he finished for her. "But you're still not driving. Now get in."

HE WHIRLED TO face her as soon as they walked into the living room. "What the hell is wrong with you?"

"Nothing's wrong with me." Except she felt as if she were going to explode any minute. She wanted to scream and pound on him. Damn him. Damn him. Damn him.

"The hell there's not. You're shaking like a malaria victim."

"I'm fine." She couldn't hold on much longer. "Go wash your face," she snapped. "You have oil all over it. All over your hands and that—"

"I'm sorry it offends you."

"It does offend me." A single light in the wreckage and then the world exploding. "I hate it."

"You don't have to bite my head off."

"Yes, I do." She turned away, her back rigid. "Go away."

"Turn around. I want to see your face."

She didn't move. "Go wash up. We have to go to that lab and see if we can get another print."

"You shouldn't go anywhere in your condition."

"There's nothing wrong with me."

"Then look at me."

"I don't want to look at you. I want to go and look at that photograph. It's important, dammit."

"Do you think I don't know that? But there's something else happening here, and it may be more important to me than any picture."

The room seemed to be tilting, exploding beneath her feet.

Like the car had exploded.

Hold on. Don't break down. What had they been talking about? The photograph. "It couldn't be more important. Two men died because of that photograph."

"And I'm sorry as hell, but I'm not to blame." He spun her around to face him. "I did everything I could to help—"

"I know you did. Crawling into that— Stupid, idiotic—" The floodgates broke and tears were again running down her cheeks. "Charlie was already dead, dammit."

"I didn't know that."

"You could have died."

"I didn't die."

"Not for lack of trying."

"Will you please stop crying?"

"No."

"Then may I point out that you're being unreasonable."

"Go to hell." She walked over to the window and stared out into the darkness.

"Eve."

She could feel his gaze on her back. "Go away."

"Are you going to tell me why you're so angry with me?"

She didn't answer.

"Tell me."

She whirled on him, her eyes blazing. "Oh, yes, you're too mean to get killed. You're going to be around for the next fifty years or so. I don't have to be afraid, do I?"

He went still. "Oh, shit."

"You could have died tonight." The words tumbled over one another. "You had no *right*. You upset my life, you barged around and made me feel things I never wanted to feel. You said you'd be around for the next fifty years and then you try to get yourself— Don't you touch me." She backed away from him. "Charlie Cather and Billy Sung died tonight, and I hardly thought about them. I didn't care about the photograph. I didn't care about Dom. Do you know how that makes me feel?"

"I know how it makes *me* feel."

"Are you proud of yourself? You lied to me. You lied about—"

He was holding her, pressing her face to his shoulder. "Stop shaking. It's over."

"It's not over. It's going to go on. Because you'll never change. You'll keep on doing stupid, insane things because you have an ego that tells you that you'll live forever even if you—" Her whole body was trembling. "I can't *stand* it."

"Neither can I. You're turning *me* inside out."

"You shouldn't have done it. You shouldn't have done it."

He was lifting her and carrying her to the couch. "Shh, I'll do anything you say if you'll just stop shaking." He cradled her on his lap. "I thought I was prepared for anything, but I was wrong. I wasn't ready for this. It was always Bonnie who came first with you. I never thought—"

"Because you can't see farther than the tip of your nose."

He was silent a moment. "Are you telling me that you love me?"

"I'm not telling you anything, you bastard."

"It's hard to judge because of the verbal abuse, but I think that's what you're saying. It . . . heartens me."

"It doesn't hearten me."

"I know. It scares you." He was rocking her back and forth. "If you'll just stop shaking, I promise I'll try to live forever."

No one lived forever. His heart pounded strong and steady beneath her ear, but it could have been stilled tonight. Her hands tightened on his shoulders. "Idiot."

"Hush."

"You'll do it again. I know it. You're a cop."

He was silent.

She was silent too. Moments passed and she sat there, listening to the beat of his heart. Lover. Best friend. Center.

She gradually stopped shaking.

He gently pressed his lips to her temple. "Someday will you tell me you love me?"

"Probably not." Her arms tightened around him. "You don't deserve it."

"True." He was silent again. "I won't take chances I don't have to, Eve. I've never wanted to live more than I do at this moment. Okay?"

"It has to be okay, doesn't it? I have to accept it. That's life."

"Yes, that's life. Welcome back." He brushed her hair away from her face. "You're a mess. I've gotten grease all over you."

"It will wash off." But what had happened that night could never be eradicated. Every one of her protective barriers had been stripped away and she'd been forced to face her true feelings for Joe. But they were too intense, almost unbearable. She pushed him away and slowly stood up. "We've got to leave to go to Professor Dunkeil's lab. I'll use the powder room down here. You go upstairs and change. Those clothes are beyond hope."

"I'm on my way."

She watched him leave the room, not wanting to let him out of her sight. Get a grip. There were other things in life to worry about besides Joe Quinn. Two men had died tonight. Probably killed by Dom. He was getting nearer.

But so was she.

You haven't beaten us yet, Dom. I'll still find a way to see your face.

CHAPTER SEVENTEEN

EVE AND JOE were waiting across the street from the lab on Blue Mountain Drive when Spiro drove up.

"Professor Dunkeil's waiting for us. He was upset about Sung." Spiro studied Eve's face. "You look better."

"I'm fine. Did you reach Mrs. Cather?"

"Yes." His lips tightened. "I didn't talk to her very long. She broke down. She's only a kid herself."

"I know you were close to Charlie."

"I could have been closer. I thought I had to toughen him up." He shook his head. "Getting Dom is becoming very personal to me."

Eve started across the street. "Join the club."

She felt the tension rise as Joe rang the doorbell of the lab.

Please, don't let those young men have died for no reason. Don't let Dom win this one.

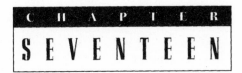

. . .

THE IMAGE OF Kevin Baldridge was still blurred. On the computer screen he was almost ghostlike, like a cadaver floating in a sea of light.

But his face was clear enough.

She couldn't breathe.

"Eve?"

"Tell me I'm crazy, Joe."

Joe was gazing at the screen and swore softly.

Spiro inhaled sharply. "Grunard."

Younger, thinner, but the charming, slightly cocky smile was the same.

Eve sank back in the chair, her mind whirling. "No."

"He's the right age. He's been close to you from the beginning," Spiro said slowly.

So close. "That guard at the welfare house . . ." She shuddered. "I told him to distract him if he ran across him."

Joe turned to Spiro. "He thinks he's safe. Pick him up before he learns what we've done here tonight."

"He may already know." Spiro took out his phone and punched in a number. "He's made some friends in the precinct the past few days."

Eve was thinking of the serial killer profile Spiro had given her in Joe's cottage.

They usually are aware of police procedures and may even associate with the police.

Joe had told her that Grunard hung out at the bar all the Atlanta police detectives frequented.

And a reporter could travel from place to place without suspicion. He had contacts and sources for finding out facts other people couldn't.

Mark had delayed going after Jane at the welfare house until eleven o'clock, giving him plenty of time to kill the security guard and make it to the alley where Mike had been. He would have had no trouble gaining access to Fraser all those years ago.

"No answer at Grunard's hotel." Spiro was punching in another number. "I'll send someone to the hotel."

Grunard. Dom.

He had wanted to stay at the lab last night. He had given Sung his phone number.

Spiro had finished his phone call and was heading for the front door. "I'll start a background check on Grunard. I don't know how much good it will do. There's no telling how many times he's reinvented himself. Go back to the house and stay there."

Grunard.

All the way back to the house, Eve couldn't stop thinking about Grunard and Dom being the same person. It was crazy and yet it made perfect sense. He had been there all the time and she had not felt an ounce of suspicion. My God, she had even felt guilty for not keeping him more informed. And he had warned her not to let Dom see Eve and Jane together in Phoenix.

She felt as if she had been kicked in the stomach. "Jane."

She had left Jane alone.

"How far are we—"

"Shit." Joe pressed the accelerator. "Take it easy. We're only a block from the house."

They tore through the gates and she jumped out of the car and ran into the house.

"Eve." Joe was running after her.

Jane was safe. Jane had two guards to protect her, and Sarah and Monty.

But Dom had gotten to the porch of Joe's cottage at the lake.

She took the stairs two at a time.

She flung open Jane's door.

The bed was rumpled, the covers thrown back.

Jane was not in the bed.

"Let's try Sarah," Joe said behind her.

Sarah sat up groggily when they barged in her room. "What is it?"

"Jane. We can't find—" Eve sat on the bed in relief. "Thank God."

Jane was curled up beside Monty on a blanket on the floor beside Sarah's bed.

"She came in a couple of hours ago," Sarah said. "She said she had a bad dream about Monty and asked if she could stay. It's okay, isn't it?"

Eve nodded, trying to quiet her pounding heart. "It's fine. I was just scared. Sorry I woke you."

"No problem."

Eve and Joe walked out. "God, I was afraid," she said.

"Me too." Joe put his arm around her. "Come on, let's go make some coffee. I could use a caffeine jolt."

SARAH CAME INTO the kitchen almost an hour later. "Okay. What's happening?" She yawned. "I tried to go back to sleep but couldn't because I got to thinking."

"We didn't want to bother you." Joe poured her a cup of coffee.

"Well, you didn't bother Jane and Monty. They're sleeping." She sipped her coffee. "The sleep of the innocent. It's a wonderful thing. Now, why were you scared about Jane?"

Sarah had finished her second cup of coffee by the time they'd filled her in. She leaned back in her chair. "So it's almost over."

"It's not over until he's dead or behind bars," Eve said.

"But you have a face and a name now. If he slips through the FBI's hands, put him on *America's Most Wanted* or some show like that. Someone's always finding murderers."

"You make it sound very simple," Joe said dryly.

"I have a very simple nature." Sarah smiled. "It comes from living with dogs. Everything's black and white, and you reach your goal by using the most direct path possible. That's why I work rescue instead of being a cop like you, Joe. I couldn't stand—"

The phone rang. Eve picked up the wall extension.

"Get out of there," Spiro said. "Tell Joe to get you and Jane away from there."

"Why? Dom?"

"No, there's no sign of Dom. But the Phoenix PD should be on your doorstep any minute."

"Why? Was I recognized at the wreck site?"

"They got an anonymous tip about where you could be found. Now, guess who would call that in?"

"Grunard."

"Right. He evidently wants to blast you out of your fortress."

"And he's doing it." She tried to think. "But if they put me in jail, he wouldn't be able to—"

"Jane won't be in jail. She'll go right back into Atlanta welfare custody."

If Jane was returned to welfare they'd be back to square one. "How much time do we have?"

"Zilch. Get out of there now."

She hung up. "The Phoenix PD is on their way here. They got a tip about Jane and me." She turned to Sarah. "You and Monty get out of here. Call Logan and tell him what's happened."

Sarah headed for the door. "I'm on my way."

Eve nodded. "I'll go get Jane. Throw some things into a suitcase, Joe."

THEY MADE IT only as far as the front gates. As the gates swung open, they saw the blinking lights of patrol cars just turning the corner onto the street.

Joe swore under his breath.

"Get out," Eve snapped at him.

"What?"

"Get out and hide in the bushes. It's Jane and me they want."

"And I'm supposed to leave you?"

"I'll be in jail. You're the one who'll have to keep an eye on Jane."

Joe muttered another curse but dove out the door and into the bushes beside the driveway. Eve slid behind the wheel and drove through the gates.

The headlights of the police car almost blinded her as it blocked her path.

"WELL, THIS IS a fine mess you've gotten us into," Logan said. "And that prison garb isn't at all becoming."

"You shouldn't have come here." Eve leaned forward to look at him through the glass. "And it's my mess, not yours."

"Not correct. Are they treating you okay?"

"As well as they treat any other felon. I've been in here only twenty-four hours, and that's enough to make me never want to even jaywalk. But there is a lot of time for thinking." Her folded hands clenched together in front of her. "I think that may be what Grunard wanted. He wanted to show me that even if he was on the run, he could still reach out and touch me. He wanted me to feel helpless and wonder what was happening to Jane. It worked. I nearly went crazy last night. Did Sarah call you?"

He nodded. "She gave me orders to make myself useful and bail you out."

"It's kidnapping, Logan. No one's going to bail me out."

"It might be possible. Extenuating circumstances. Barbara Eisley isn't being vindictive, and you're usually not a very dangerous character." He paused. "But it would be better if you told them where Quinn is. They want to question him about his involvement with you."

"I don't know where he is."

"And you wouldn't tell if you did." He stood up. "So I guess I'll see if I can find any judges in this town or in Atlanta I can influence."

"Logan, where's Jane?"

"She's being held in the local Family Services center. She's being returned to Atlanta as soon as a caseworker comes to pick her up. Spiro told me to tell you that he's got people watching her."

"That won't be enough."

"Grunard is on the run."

"He won't run far. It's getting too near the end of his game. If he ran away completely, it would mean he lost. He'll never admit that." She paused. "If he can't get to me, he'll kill Jane. It's the logical move for him. He wants both of us, but he'll take Jane because it will hurt me."

"Are you sure he knows it will hurt you?"

"Oh, yes." She smiled without mirth. "The bastard even warned me never to let Dom see us together."

"Nice." His gaze narrowed on her face. "I'm tempted to let you stay in here for a while. At least you're safe."

"And Jane becomes the target."

"I can surround her with protection."

"She was surrounded with protection in the welfare house and Dom could have gotten to her there." Her voice vibrated with desperation. "If you can get me out of here, do it, Logan. I don't know how fast he'll move."

He shook his head. "I don't like—"

"Please."

He muttered a curse and rose abruptly to his feet. "I'll see what I can do. It may not be today. It could be another twenty-four hours."

She stood up, and the guard moved forward to take her back to her cell. "Hurry."

Another twenty-four hours.

The words replayed in her mind as she walked down the long

corridor to her cell. The idea of any delay scared her to death. How long would Grunard wait?

It could be all right. Joe would be watching over Jane. He would take care of her.

And Grunard would be watching Joe. He would know that Joe was guarding Jane. Which meant Grunard would try to take out Joe first.

Sheer terror went through her at the thought.

I won't take chances if I don't have to. I've never wanted to live more than I do at this moment.

But she'd sent him to take a terrible chance. She'd made Joe a target.

Panic seared through her as the door of her cell clanged shut behind her. She was trapped there, helpless to do anything.

Calm down. She closed her eyes and drew a deep breath. Panicking would be playing right into Grunard's hands. He was probably sitting somewhere now, picturing her in her cell, feeding on her fear and frustration.

Don't give him what he wants. He wants panic. Give him coolness. He wants mindless emotion. Give him logic.

Twenty-four hours.

Spend that time thinking about Grunard, going over every minute, every conversation of the last weeks. See if she could find a lead to him, a weakness that could be exploited. Pretend he was one of her skulls that had to be measured and then reconstructed. Use her mind, talents, and instinct.

She sat down on the bunk and leaned against the wall.

Stay away from the people I love, Dom. Think of me shivering, brooding in this cell. Enjoy it.

Then maybe, just maybe, I'll have enough time to find a way to win your damn game.

• • •

SHE WAS RELEASED on bail at one forty-five the next afternoon. Logan met her outside the jail. "The good news is that I think all the charges will be dropped. Spiro's been discreetly putting pressure on Eisley." He paused. "But until we get you cleared, you can't go near Jane. One of the terms of your release is that you're not seen within fifty city blocks of her. If you violate it, you get tossed right back in the slammer."

"I expected that. She's all right?"

"She's okay. I have a man watching the local facility." He took her arm as they started down the steps. "The caseworker from Atlanta is arriving today to take her back."

"When?"

"Sometime this evening."

"Then they'll probably leave tomorrow morning."

His brows lifted as he held open the car door. "You're very calm."

"No, I'm not." She got into the car. "I'm scared shitless."

"Well, you're different from yesterday." He strode around to the driver's seat.

She took out her phone and dialed Joe's digital number. God, his voiced sounded wonderful.

"I'm out," she said.

"Thank God."

"Things are going to be happening. Soon."

"If you're out, that goes without saying."

"I'll call you." She hung up.

"Quinn?"

She nodded.

He smiled sardonically. "But you had no idea where he is."

"I still don't. I know only that he's guarding Jane."

He dropped the subject. "Where do you want to go?"

"Back to the house. I have some work to do."

"Work?"

"Telephone calls and then I need to get on the computer."

"You're not planning to hire a hit man to get Grunard, I trust?"

"It's an appealing idea." She shook her head. "But that's not what I had in mind."

"Am I allowed to help?"

"You bet you are."

SARAH PATRICK MET Eve as she walked into the foyer. "Welcome home." She glanced at Logan. "You evidently did something right."

"I didn't dare do anything else. I'm scared of Monty." He turned to Eve. "You'll have what you need in a couple of hours. Okay?"

She nodded. "Thanks, Logan. I owe you."

"Friends never owe friends." He smiled. "Remember that."

"Then is it okay if I'm grateful?"

"Same answer." He headed for the front door.

But she *did* owe him, she thought as she headed to the office. And she'd owe him even more if he came through with the information she needed.

Sarah trailed along with her. "You look a little jumpy. Anything I can do?"

"You can check with the welfare office and make sure Jane is all right."

Sarah nodded. "I've been calling a couple of times a day. I tried to go see her, but they wouldn't let me and Monty in the place."

"Too bad. Seeing Monty would have made her feel better."

"That's what I thought. Have you had lunch?"

Eve shook her head. "But I'm not hungry. I've got work to do."

"Really?" Sarah studied her face. "You're excited."

"Logan said I was very calm."

"On the surface. Beneath you're seething like a geyser. Want to talk about it?"

Eve shook her head. "But I think I've found a way to get him."

DONE.

Eve pushed her chair back from the computer and covered her eyes with her shaking hand.

I've got you, Dom. I've *got* you.

Her phone rang.

"The caseworker from Atlanta, James Parkinson, and Jane just got into a squad car with two officers and are on their way to the airport," Joe said. "I'm following them."

"I didn't think they'd leave tonight."

"I didn't either. Parkinson was in and out of that welfare house in fifteen minutes. I'll call you when we get to the airport."

Eve tried to think. It was logical that the caseworker wanted Jane out of Phoenix now that Eve had been released. But Jane was more vulnerable outside the home and on the road.

A twisted mass of metal at the bottom of the ravine.

That couldn't happen twice. Besides, Joe was watching.

But so was Dom.

James Parkinson.

She called Joe back. "How do you know Parkinson is the social worker?"

"The squad car radioed the pickup back to the precinct, and I heard it on my radio."

"What does Parkinson look like?"

"He's black, heavyset, plump face. He would have had to show ID to both welfare administration and the officers in the squad car."

"IDs are easy to get, and Grunard's had time to plan." But she did feel a little better. "Watch closely, Joe."

"You know I will."

"I GUESS YOU'RE glad to be going home, young lady." Officer Rivera glanced back at Jane over his shoulder.

Jane didn't answer.

"I have a daughter about your age. She's on the softball team."

Jane gazed through the window, closing out Parkinson and the officers. She hadn't said a word since she'd gotten into the squad car. Poor kid, Rivera thought. He looked at Parkinson. "Is she going to be okay?"

Parkinson nodded, his white teeth flashing in his brown face as he smiled. "Just fine."

Jane suddenly stiffened, her gaze flying to Parkinson's face.

"There, honey, don't be scared." Parkinson patted her shoulder.

Jane went rigid and then slumped to one side.

"What's wrong with her?" Rivera said. "Pull over, Ken."

"Oh, no, don't do that," Parkinson said softly.

Then he shot Rivera in the head.

SHIT.

Joe's hands tightened on the steering wheel.

Something was wrong.

The squad car was weaving in and out of the city streets, even backtracking.

What the hell!

The squad car roared over railroad tracks, driving through the signal just as the train approached, leaving Joe stranded on the other side.

He radioed the precinct for backup as he waited for the train to pass. "I don't care who comes. Just get someone, anyone."

He wasn't getting through to them. He closed his eyes. "Okay, if you won't stop the squad car, come after me. This is Joe Quinn."

Joe gunned his car as the caboose rattled past.

It took Joe ten minutes to locate the squad car again.

But he lost it again in the traffic near the stadium.

There it was. Two blocks ahead, turning left.

He lost it again.

It took five minutes to locate the squad car this time.

It was pulled over to the side of a deserted street.

"I HAVE HER, Eve."

Dom.

"You're lying. She's on her way to the airport."

"No, you'll get a call soon. I just wanted you to know that the game is almost over. It's time for me to claim the stakes."

"I don't believe you."

"You believe me. I can hear it in your voice."

"Let me talk to her."

"No, she's not able to talk. I drugged the little angel. Just a little pinprick. A rather boring old trick but effective. It was such a wonderful disguise, but I think she recognized my voice. Besides, I have a distance to take her and I needed her quiet." He paused. "Shall I tell you what I'm going to do to her before I kill her, Eve?"

"No." She closed her eyes. "Don't hurt her."

"Not yet. She's no fun at the moment. She can't feel anything."

Rage seared through her.

"That made you angry, didn't it? I can almost feel the waves of emotion through the phone. It's quite wonderful, but you really shouldn't indulge me this way."

"You don't want her. You want me."

"That's right. I want you to die first, knowing what's in store for her. Come and get her."

"Where are you going?"

"A place you'll remember. Earth to earth. Salt to salt. I thought it fitting. My most satisfying kills were done there. But don't worry, I won't chop you into pieces as I did them. I respect you too much."

"Will she be there?"

"I'm not a fool. You might arrange a trap for me."

"I won't come up to the tent site until I know she's alive. Until I hear her voice."

"You'll hear it. Be there at nine tomorrow night." He hung up.

Christ.

She had thought she was so close, and Dom had still managed to pull the rug right from under her.

Joe called her. "He's got her. I found both officers dead in the squad car and Jane gone."

"I know. Dom called me."

"Shit. I screwed up."

"It's not your fault," she said dully. "He was disguised. Even Jane didn't recognize him right away."

"Is she alive?"

"He says she is. Right now."

"Don't you move a muscle. I'm on my way over there." He hung up.

Joe would come and some of the fear would go away. She didn't have to face this alone.

Yes, she did. From the beginning she'd known that she'd have to face Dom alone. He was planning on having her walk right into his trap and killing her and Jane. He would butcher Joe if he was anywhere around.

Then flip his plan. Catch the hunter before the trap was sprung.

"Sarah! Will you come in here?"

Sarah appeared in the doorway. "What?"

She held up a finger. "One minute." She dialed Spiro's digital number. He answered on the third ring.

"Dom has Jane, and I know where he's headed. I want you to meet me there." She had to stop to steady her voice. "You wanted to use me as bait. Okay, let's find a way to do it."

CHAPTER EIGHTEEN

The following night
8:45 P.M.

CANDLES.

Everywhere.

Candelabras with tapers whose flames flickered in the wind. Lanterns. Oil lamps.

Eve parked her car at the bottom of the hill and looked up at the tent site.

Is this my welcome, Dom? Are you up there?

She dialed Spiro's number. "Where are you?"

"We're in a lay-by about two miles down the road to Jamison. We couldn't get any closer without risking him seeing us. That hill has a view for miles."

"I know. Can you see the candles?"

"Yes. Remember, press the radio signal as soon as you determine Dom's there, and we'll come in."

"You don't move until I'm sure Jane's alive and safe. He's supposed to call me."

"Stay locked in the car until you're sure. At least you're safe there. Do you have a weapon?"

"A revolver."

"Did Quinn give it to you?"

"No, I told you I didn't want him to know about this. Sarah had one and lent it to me. It's in my jacket pocket."

"We could have used Quinn."

"And chance having Dom butcher him? He's done too much for me already."

"I should have known that protective streak would raise its head. Don't hesitate to use that gun." He hung up.

She sat in the car, staring up at the candles on the hill.

Five minutes.

Seven minutes.

The phone rang.

"Are you enjoying my candles?" Dom asked.

"I want to talk to Jane."

"Do you doubt me? I told you I wanted you to die first."

"Let me talk to Jane."

"Oh, very well."

"Eve, don't you do what he says," Jane yelled into the phone. "He's a slimy creep and I—"

Dom took the phone away. "Is that enough? It's all you'll get. I've been very patient with Jane since she woke, but she's really beginning to annoy me."

"It's enough."

"Then step into my parlor. I'll be there in ten minutes."

She pressed the off button and quickly dialed Sarah. "Ten-minute walk from here."

"That could cover a lot of territory."

"Find her. If he manages to kill me and escapes, you can't let him get back to Jane."

"We'll do our best."

Nine minutes.

Stay in the car. Be safe for just a little longer. Sit and watch the flickering lights on the hill.

SARAH PUT ON her utility belt and Monty tensed.

"That's right, boy. Time to get to work." She let Monty sniff Jane's T-shirt. "Find her." She started down the trail at a trot. She'd already scoped out the lay of the land and come up with the two most logical possibilities.

He wouldn't keep Jane out in the open. So there was the stand of woods near the base of the mountains to the west.

Or there was the brush-covered ravine to the east.

Either was a fast ten-minute walk to the hill.

Which direction?

She'd make the decision when she got closer.

Pray to God she'd make the right one.

Monty was stretched out, almost running.

Child . . .

TEN MINUTES.

Eve opened the door and got out of the car. The air was knife sharp, cutting her to the bone. It was a moonless night, icy cold with a promise of snow.

She started up the hill.

Candles.

Flames.

Are you there yet, Dom?

She reached the top.

No one.

Just the candles and the flames and the flickering shadows on the desolate earth. It wasn't as brightly lit as she'd thought from down below. There was a patch of deep shadow at the far corner of the site.

She moved farther into the circle of light.

Was he watching her, or was it her imagination?

She whirled around.

No one.

Or was there?

Something in those shadows . . .

She hesitated and then moved away from the light toward the patch of darkness.

"Dom? You wanted me here. Come and get me."

No sound.

DECISION TIME.

Sarah paused to catch her breath.

The woods or the ravine?

Monty had already made a decision. He was tearing across the ground toward the woods. He stopped, sniffed, and took off again.

He'd caught Jane's scent.

THE SUBSTANCE IN the shadow was no standing figure, Eve realized. Something on the ground . . .

She drew closer.

She still couldn't make it out.

A few steps closer.

It was taking on a vague shape.

She was almost on top of it.

A body?

Oh, God.

Jane?

She screamed.

The man's body was tied spread-eagled to four pegs, and his eyes were wide open. His features were contorted in a silent howl of agony.

Mark Grunard.

"That's how I staked out my father."

She whirled to see Spiro behind her.

He smiled. "A little welcome present. It was going to be the little girl, but I knew you wouldn't come unless you thought you had a chance of saving her."

"You," she whispered. "Dom?"

"Of course it was me."

A man who stares at monsters.

But he was the monster himself. "God, what a fool I am. No trap. No FBI agents swarming in at the last minute to save me."

"Unfortunately not." He stepped closer and was almost lost in the shadows. "Don't put your hands in your pockets. I have a knife in my hand and I can reach you in a heartbeat, but I don't want it to end that soon. It's been a superb game, and I want to savor the win."

"You haven't won yet."

"That's what I admire about you. You never give up. But you should be more generous. I was very clever with every move. I deserve to win."

"You were clever. You set Grunard up perfectly. You even gave me the characteristics of the serial killer so I'd be able to associate them with Grunard later. It never occurred to me that they might also apply to you. You associate with the police as Grunard did, but even more, you're an FBI profiler. You could move from place to place. You liked to be in the field, you said. That means you were contacted by your digital phone and no one actually knew where you were at a given time. You could say you were in Talladega when you were in Atlanta."

"I do regard the digital phone as one of the most helpful inventions. And it was a real challenge to become an FBI agent. Background checks that had to be foolproof, psychological tests that had to show me as completely normal. I prepared for almost two years before I applied. Setting up the personal interviews with people from my supposed past was the most difficult. It took finesse, bribery, and a psychological sleight of hand that would fill you with admiration."

"No, it wouldn't."

"But it was all worth it. Who else would be in a better position to hide and change evidence? I had to keep an eye on where and when any of my kills surfaced so I could erase the records."

"But the VICAP report uncovered the Harding kills."

"Before I was able to sidetrack the search. Very annoying."

"But you led me here to find Debby Jordan."

"I'm a fatalist. I saw that everything was leading back to my roots. I wanted you here to help me start again, to revive that splendid surge of power." He smiled. "It did do that. When I killed Grunard, it was almost like the old days. But he wasn't you. It will be much better with you."

"Did you always plan to kill Grunard?"

"After I examined the situation and all the possibilities, I realized that his death would accomplish two ends, create a red herring and make our game more complicated. How could I resist? He would become Dom and disappear." He shook his head. "But that complication may cause me to have to move on and reinvent myself. Grunard's background is pretty solid. There may be questions." He shrugged. "Oh, well, I'll have plenty of warning and I've already set up an identity in Montana. It may be good for me. Being Robert Spiro made everything too easy for me. The kill, the cover-up . . . It may have been part of my problem."

"You'll move on and you'll kill again." Her voice was shaking. "Over and over."

"Of course, that's what I do."

"How many?"

"I really don't remember. I was drunk with the pleasure during those first years. I went out every night. Later everything blurred. More than thirty years . . . a thousand? I don't know. Maybe more."

"My God."

"But don't feel bad. You won't be like the others. I'll remember you."

"You have me. Let Jane go."

"You know I won't do that. She knows my face and the little bitch would try to find a way to hurt me. She's like you."

"But you were wrong about her being like Bonnie."

"But I set up an interesting scenario, didn't I? It pulled you in. The bones and then sweet little Jane."

"Whose bones were they?"

He was silent.

"*Tell* me. Were they Bonnie's bones?"

"I could let you go to the grave not knowing."

"Yes."

"But then you wouldn't realize how clever I've been. How wonderfully I'd set you up."

"They weren't Bonnie's bones."

He shook his head. "Doreen Parker's."

"Then everything you told me about your conversation with Fraser was a lie."

"Not entirely. I did talk to him. It was remarkably easy, since I was an FBI agent. He was a copycat and he was claiming some of my kills. We had a nice chat, and I told him to back off. Since he had the good sense to admire me enormously, he agreed."

"You knew about the ice cream. Did you find that out from the police records?"

"No, I told you, we had a nice chat. He told me a lot about Bonnie. Do you want to know how he did it?"

She clenched her fists as waves of pain washed over her. "No."

"Coward." His gaze narrowed on her face. "But you want to know where he buried her, don't you? You've always wanted to find her."

"I want to bring her home."

"It's too late. You're going to die without finding her. That hurts terribly, doesn't it? Your Bonnie is buried all alone in Chattahoochee National Park, and you're going to be buried here, hundreds of miles away from her. It cuts to the quick, doesn't it?"

"Yes."

"I can feel your pain."

"And you love it, you bastard."

"I have to squeeze as much as I can out of the moment. It's going to be over too soon." He paused. "You haven't asked me what color candle I'm going to give you."

"I don't care."

"It will be black. Black was the color of my candles, and I've decided to share it with you. I've never done that before. You should be honored. The candles are lying beside Grunard's head. Pick them up, Eve. Light them."

She didn't move.

"Pick them up or I promise you I'll make it very hard for Jane before I give her candle to her."

Eve hesitated and then walked over to Grunard.

How the man must have suffered. His expression . . .

"Pick them up and come back toward me."

He was standing in the shadow. There would be no chance if he stayed in the dark.

She picked up the black candles.

"Now come toward me."

She slowly started toward him.

One step.

Two.

Three.

"Hurry. I find I'm very eager for—"

She hurled the candles at his face.

"Eve!"

She took off running.

Out of the shadow into the candlelit center of the tent site.

"Stop running. The game's over, Eve."

She glanced over her shoulder. He was running after her.

Fast.

Closing on her.

Come on.

Faster.

Out of the darkness.

Into the light.

The single shot splintered the night.

Spiro jerked, stumbled, and collapsed to his knees.

The knife fell out of his hand.

He looked down in disbelief at his chest, which was bubbling with blood. "Eve?"

She turned to face him. "*Now* the game's over, you son of a bitch."

He touched his chest and brought his hand away. It was smeared with blood. "Who . . ."

"Joe."

"No, I—searched here before I lit the candles. There was nowhere he could hide . . ."

"He was a sniper in the SEALs. He told me once that he can hit a target from a thousand yards. It's not five hundred yards to that tree down the slope. I knew he could get you if he could see you, Spiro."

His eyes widened. "You knew . . ." He collapsed to the ground.

She walked over and knelt beside him. "Where's Jane?"

"Screw you."

"You're going to die, Spiro. What difference does it make?"

"It—makes a difference. How—did you know?"

"You made that anonymous telephone call and had me thrown in jail. I was there for forty-eight hours. For the first twenty-four hours I was a basket case. You would have loved seeing me. Then I realized I was letting you win. So I spent the second night thinking. I thought I was going to find a way to locate Grunard. I tried to divorce myself the way I do when I work on one of my skulls and just examine the facts and events. I started with something that bothered me at the time I learned about it, but I forgot about when I saw the photo. Charlie said that Sung was excited and talking about shifts and spectrums and that he made a phone call before he said he needed to see me. He could have called Grunard, but if he recognized Grunard as the killer, why call him? No, it had to be someone else. So I asked Logan to check phone records and find out who Sung called. It was to Multiplex, one of the digital imaging companies on the West Coast. Sung wanted to verify his findings on the photo. It was the middle of the night, but there's often a crew working at those big companies. You'd sent the photo out to Multiplex to have Grunard's image implanted in it so I could 'discover' it. That was why you stalled giving us the photo."

"Worked."

"But you didn't realize how sharp Sung was. State-of-the-art companies like Multiplex create their own software and the variance of the shifts in the light spectrums are almost like a fingerprint. Sung recognized that shift and he knew the picture had been doctored. Multiplex might not have been willing to confirm the specific job, but they would have no reason not to confirm the general technical aspects of the software. Did Charlie call you from the lab after he called me?"

"Of course. I trained him well."

"And then you killed him. What would you have done if Joe hadn't climbed down and retrieved that photo? Would that other picture you supposedly sent to Quantico surface?"

He didn't answer. He was having trouble breathing.

"But it was all guesswork, and I had to verify. Multiplex wouldn't talk to me. You'd probably told them to keep the job confidential, and everybody obeys the FBI. So I took the photo and did some work myself. I didn't have the equipment or expertise to do what Sung did, so I did a digital merge of the faces of your brothers." She smiled grimly. "And what to my surprise appeared? I came up with you."

"Lie. We look—nothing like each other."

"You're right and that was good. I was much more likely to pull up a completely distinctive face than if your brothers looked alike. I often use older family members' features for age progression for children. When I was studying at the National Center for Missing Children, I used to play with merging different familial faces and seeing what I could come up with. Even when the family members didn't look like one another, it was amazing how the similarities appeared when they were combined. The face I came up with didn't resemble you exactly, but it was close enough, and after I aged the image, it was even closer. It made me go over everything that had happened."

"I didn't make—mistakes. I didn't."

"No, you were almost perfect. But you were always there beside me or in the background."

"So was Grunard."

"Yes, and I stumbled over that conversation with Dom while you were in the same room with me at Joe's cottage. It was only later that I realized it wasn't really a conversation. Dom made a brief statement and hung up. A taped alibi set on a timer. Very effective." She shook her head. "There were so many things that became clear once I accepted that you were Dom. All the times you misdirected and lied to me and Joe. Why should we have suspected? You were Spiro of the FBI."

"You're so proud of yourself." His expression was full of malice. "You haven't won. I won't die. I'm feeling stronger all the time. I'll live and they'll say I'm insane."

"You won't live."

She looked up to see Joe standing beside her, staring down at Spiro.

"If there's even a chance of you living I'll put another bullet in you before the police get here," Joe said. "You'd be dead now if I hadn't decided not to risk a head shot. You were too close to her."

"Closer than you. Closer than anyone. She'll forget you. She'll never forget me." His gaze shifted to Eve. "The little girl will die. I've hidden her and it gets freezing cold up here at night. She doesn't have a coat and she's tied. You won't find her in time."

Fear rushed through her. "You lie. Sarah and Monty are looking for her now. They'll find her."

"What if I've laid a false trail? I knew you had Sarah and Monty at your disposal. You should know I never take anything for granted. Ah, I've scared you. You're not so—"

"Would you care to go down the hill and wait in the car?" Joe asked Eve. "I think it's time we said good-bye to the bastard."

"She won't let you. She's still too soft." Spiro raised himself up. "The girl will die, but I'll live forever. I'll live—" Blood gushed from his chest. "Stop the bleeding, Eve. You know you can't let me die."

"Screw you." She stood up and turned to Joe. "We have to call the local police and then ring Sarah and see if she's found Jane."

"I'll be right with you," Joe said.

"No." She looked down at Spiro. "I don't want it quick. Let the bastard bleed to death."

She turned and walked away.

"Eve!"

She stared straight ahead, ignoring Spiro's howl of disbelief and terror.

. . .

"WE HAVEN'T FOUND her, Eve," Sarah said.

"The temperature's falling."

"I know that. The bastard may have laid a false trail or even several."

"He wants her to die."

"Monty's moving in another direction. I have to go." She hung up.

Eve turned to Joe. "He has them running around in circles." She shuddered as a sudden gust of wind knifed through her jacket. "It must be down to zero. If he has her tied, Jane can't even move to keep herself warm."

ANOTHER FALSE LEAD.

How many had the bastard laid? Sarah wondered.

Child?

Monty was bewildered too. He was running around in circles trying to find the scent.

He suddenly stopped short and turned toward the east.

Child?

"What is it, boy?"

His head lifted as if listening.

Jesus, he was trembling, and the hair was rising on his back. What the hell was happening?

Other child.

He started at a dead run toward the east.

Other child. Other child. Other child . . .

"WE FOUND HER," Sarah said. "She was under some boulders on the slope of the ravine. We almost missed her."

"Is she okay?"

"She's cold but no hypothermia. Monty's lying beside her, keeping her warm. As soon as I get my breath, we'll start back."

"We'll come to you."

"No, I want her out of this cold. I gave her my jacket, and walking will be good for her."

Eve turned to Joe, who was coming down the hill. "She's okay."

"Thank God." He glanced back over his shoulder at the top of the hill. "Too bad Spiro isn't still alive so we could rub his nose in it."

"Did you . . . ?"

Joe shook his head. "Don't blame me. He was already dead when I went up to check on him."

"I wouldn't have blamed you if you had ended it for him. I would have killed him myself rather than chance having him go free."

"My, how you've changed."

"Yes, I've changed." She looked up at the hill still lit with candles. Dom had changed her. Not the way he had wanted to. He'd thought he could drag her down, close her away from life. He hadn't realized he'd caused her to reach out to life instead. How he would have hated knowing that.

"The police are coming." Joe's gaze was on the lights of two highway patrol cars coming up the road toward them. "There will be some tall explaining to do."

"Yes." She took his hand. His grasp was warm and strong and rock steady. See what you've given me, Dom? Life. Love. Light where there was darkness.

Burn in hell, you bastard.

She squeezed Joe's hand as they started down the road. "No problem. We'll manage to get through it together."

EPILOGUE

*"*YOU SHOULD GO *in. It may be March, but the lake breeze is still cool."*

Eve turned to see Bonnie sitting on the porch steps, leaning against the rail. "I'm not cold. Who's the mother here?"

Bonnie giggled. "I'm making up for all the times you said things like that to me."

"Ungrateful child."

"Yep." She shaded her eyes as she looked out at the boat on the water. "Joe's got Jane all bundled up in his sweater. Why didn't you go fishing with them?"

"I was feeling lazy."

"And you wanted to give Joe the chance to bond with Jane."

"If you knew the answer, why did you ask?"

"You shouldn't worry. He really likes Jane. It's not easy for him to let anyone else into his life. It will take a little time for him to adjust."

"I'm not worried." She leaned her head back against the rail. "Life's pretty good, baby."

"It's about time. You've been very difficult, Mama." She looked back at the boat. "You haven't told Joe about me yet."

"I will soon."

"Are you afraid he'll think you're crazy? You should know better."

"Maybe I just want to keep you to myself for a little while longer. Is that so bad?"

"Not to me."

"Or maybe I'm afraid if I tell anyone, you won't come back."

"That's pretty dumb. Why would I leave you just when you're so much happier? I love to see you happy."

Contentment flowed through Eve in a golden tide. "We're going to find you, Bonnie. Sarah offered to come here with Monty next month and search the Chattahoochee park. I have a good feeling. We're going to bring you home, baby."

"You know that never meant anything to me, but it will make you happy." She leaned forward and linked her arms around her knees. "I like Monty. He's nice and smart too."

"And how do you know he's smart?"

Bonnie didn't answer.

"Sarah said something weird happened to Monty up in the mountains that night."

Bonnie's gaze shifted back to the boat. "Did she?"

"You wouldn't know anything about that, would you?"

"Don't be silly, Mama. How could I?" The teasing smile Bonnie turned on her was brimming with love and mischief. "When you know I'm only a dream."

BOOK THREE

THE SEARCH

IRIS JOHANSEN

BANTAM BOOKS
NEW YORK TORONTO LONDON SYDNEY AUCKLAND

Many thanks to Sergeant John Hall and Danny Henderson, Technical Rescue Experts with the Clayton County Fire Department, and Captain Timothy Dorn, Commander, Maricopa County Sheriff's Office, for all their help.

My deep appreciation to Adele Morris, Shirley Hammond, and Bev Peabody of California Rescue Dog Association. Each was invaluable to my story with her rich store of information.

My gratitude to all search and rescue personnel who risk their lives so often to help those in need—and to all the Montys who work with search and rescue and offer their labor, love, and sometimes their lives without question.

THE SEARCH

1

Barat, Turkey
June 11

"Get out of there, Sarah," Boyd yelled from outside the house. "That wall is going to tumble any minute."

"Monty's found something." Sarah carefully moved over to the pile of rubble where the golden retriever was standing. "Be still, boy. Be very still."

Child?

"How do I know?" Monty always hoped it would be a child. He loved kids and all these lost and hurt children nearly killed him. They nearly killed her too, Sarah thought wearily. Finding the children and the old people was always the most painful. So few survived these catastrophes. The earth trembled and the walls fell and life was snuffed out as if it had never been.

Out.

"You're sure?"

Out.

"Okay." She absently patted Monty's head as she gazed at the rubble. The second story of the small house had caved in, and chances of anyone being alive beneath the wreckage were minimal. She could hear no groans or weeping. It wouldn't be responsible of her to bring anyone else from the search and rescue team into the building. She should get out herself.

Child?

What the hell? Stop wasting time. She knew she wasn't going to leave until she investigated more closely. She reached for a stool and tossed it aside. "Go to Boyd, Monty."

The retriever sat down and looked at her.

"I keep telling you that you're supposed to be a professional. That means you obey orders, dammit."

Wait.

She tossed a cushion to one side and tugged at the easy chair. Jesus, it was heavy. "You can't help me now."

Wait.

"Get out of there, Sarah," Boyd yelled. "That's an order. It's been four days. You know you probably won't find anyone alive."

"We found that man in Tegucigalpa alive after twelve days. Call Monty, will you, Boyd?"

"Monty!"

Monty didn't move. She hadn't thought he would, but there was always a chance. "Stupid dog."

Wait.

"If you're going to stay there, I'm coming in to help you," Boyd said.

"No, I'll be out in a minute." Sarah glanced warily at the south wall, then tugged at the mattress until she got it to one side. "I'm just looking around."

"I'll give you three minutes."

Three minutes.

She pulled frantically at the carved headboard.

Monty whined.

"Shh." She finally heaved the headboard to one side.

And then she saw the hand.

Such a small, delicate hand, clutching a rosary . . .

"A survivor?" Boyd asked as Sarah walked out of the house. "Do we need to send in a team?"

She numbly shook her head. "Dead. A teenage girl. Two days, maybe. Don't risk anyone's neck. Just mark the site." She snapped on Monty's leash. "I'm going back to the trailer. I've got to get Monty out of here. You know how upset he gets. I'll be back in a couple of hours."

"Yeah, it's only your dog that's upset." Boyd's tone dripped sarcasm. "That's why you're shaking like a leaf."

"I'm fine."

"I don't want to see you take a step out of that trailer until tomorrow morning. You've gone without sleep for thirty-six hours. You know exhausted workers are a hazard to themselves and the people they're trying to help. You were incredibly stupid to run that risk. You're usually smarter than that."

"Monty was sure there was someone—" Why was she arguing? He was right. The only way to stay alive in situations like this was to stick to the rules and not act on impulse. She should have gone by the book. "I'm sorry, Boyd."

"You should be." He scowled. "You're one of my best people, and I won't have you thrown off the team because you're thinking with your heart instead of your head. You endangered not only yourself but your dog. What would you have done if that wall had fallen and killed Monty?"

"It wouldn't have killed Monty. I'd have thrown myself on

top of him and let you dig the wall off me." She smiled faintly. "I know who's important around here."

"Very funny." He shook his head. "Except you're not joking."

"No." She rubbed her eyes. "She had a rosary in her hand, Boyd. She must have grabbed it when the quake started. But it didn't help her, did it?"

"I guess not."

"She couldn't have been over sixteen, and she was pregnant."

"Shit."

"Yeah." She gently tugged on Monty's leash. "We'll be back in a little while."

"You're not listening. I'm in charge of this search, Sarah. I want you to rest. We've probably found all the live ones. I'm expecting the order to pull out tomorrow. The Russian team can finish searching for the dead."

"All the more reason to work harder until the order comes. None of the Russians' dogs has Monty's nose. You know he's incredible."

"You're not so bad yourself. Do you know the other members of the team are making bets on whether or not you can actually read that dog's mind?"

"That's pretty dumb. They're all close to their own dogs. They know that when you live with an animal, you get to learn how to read them."

"Not like you."

"Why are we talking about this? The important thing is Monty is unique. He's found survivors before when everyone had given up hope. He may find more today."

"It's not likely."

She walked away.

"I mean it, Sarah."

She glanced back over her shoulder. "And how long has it been since you slept, Boyd?"

"That's none of your damn business."

"Do as I say and not as I do? I'll see you in a couple of hours." She could hear him swearing behind her as she picked her way through the rubble toward the line of mobile homes at the bottom of the hill. Boyd Medford was a good guy, a fine team leader, and everything he said made sense. But there were times when she couldn't be sensible. Too many dead. Too few survivors. Oh, God, too many bodies . . .

The rosary . . .

Did that poor girl have time to pray for her own life and the life of her child before she had been crushed? Probably not. Earthquakes took only a heartbeat to destroy. Maybe she should hope that death had come quickly and the girl had not suffered.

Monty pressed against her legs. *Sad.*

"Me too." She opened the door of the mobile home for Monty. "It happens. Maybe next time it won't be that way."

Sad.

She filled up Monty's water dish. "Drink, boy."

Sad. He lay down in front of the metal dish.

He'd drink soon, but she'd wait for an hour or two before she tried to feed him. He was too upset to eat. He never got used to finding the dead.

Neither did she.

She sat down on the floor beside Monty and put her arms around him. "It will be okay," she whispered. "Maybe next time we'll find a little boy alive like we did yesterday." Was it yesterday? The days blurred together when they were on a search. "Remember the child, Monty?"

Child.

"He's alive because of you. That's why we have to go on. Even if it hurts." Jesus, it did hurt. It hurt seeing Monty this upset. It hurt remembering that girl clutching the rosary. It hurt knowing there would probably not be another person found alive.

But probably was not certainly. There was always hope as long as you kept trying.

She closed her eyes. She was tired and all her muscles ached. So what? She'd have time for a long rest later. All she needed right now was a few hours of sleep and she'd be ready to go on. "Come on, let's take a nap." She stretched out beside the retriever. "Then we'll go see if we can find anyone else alive in this hellhole."

Monty was whining softly as he put his head on his paws.

"Shh." She buried her face in his fur. "It's okay." It wasn't okay. Death was never okay. "We're together. We're doing our job. We just have to get through the next few days. Then we'll be back at the ranch." She began stroking his head. "You'll like that, won't you?"

Sad.

He was hurting, but it wasn't as bad as usual. Sometimes isolated cases were worse for him. It wasn't that he became calloused to the massive loss of life he encountered in major disasters. It was just that they were working so constantly, the reaction was delayed. He'd be ready to go again in a few hours.

But would she?

She'd be fine. Just as she'd told Boyd. The last few days were always the worst. Hope was dimming, desperation growing, and the sadness lay in your heart and mind until you thought you couldn't bear it.

But she always did bear it. You had to bear it because there was always a chance someone was out there waiting. Someone who would be lost if she and Monty didn't find her.

Monty rolled over and lay on his side. *Sleep.*

"Yes, that's what we should do." Sleep, friend, and so will I. Let the memory of rosaries and unborn children fade away. Let death go. Let hope come back. "Just a little nap . . ."

Santo Camaro, Colombia
June 12

"How many dead?" Logan asked.

"Four." Castleton's lips tightened grimly. "And two men are in the local hospital in serious condition. Can we leave now? The stench of this place makes me want to throw up. I feel guilty as hell. I'm the one who hired Bassett for this job. I liked him."

"In a minute." Logan's gaze wandered around the scorched ruins that had once been a state-of-the-art facility. It had been only three days, but the jungle was already reclaiming its own. Grass sprouted among the fallen timbers, vines reached toward the site in a macabre embrace from nearby trees. "Were you able to recover any of Bassett's work?"

"No."

Logan looked down at the dark red carnelian scarab in his hand. "And Rudzak sent this to me this morning?"

"I guess it was Rudzak. It was on my doorstep with your name on it."

"It was Rudzak."

Castleton's gaze shifted from the scarab to Logan's face. "Bassett has a wife and kid. What are you going to tell them?"

"Nothing."

"What do you mean, nothing? You have to tell them what happened to Bassett."

"And what am I supposed to tell them? We don't know what

happened to him. Not yet." He turned away and headed back toward the jeep.

"Rudzak's going to kill him," Castleton said, following Logan.

"Maybe."

"You know it."

"I think he'll try to make a deal first."

"Ransom?"

"Possibly. He wants something, or he wouldn't have bothered to take Bassett."

"And you're going to deal with that bastard? After what he did to your people?"

"I'll deal with the devil himself if it will get me what I want."

It was the answer Castleton expected. John Logan had not gotten to be one of the foremost economic forces in the world by avoiding confrontation. He had made billions with his computer company and other enterprises before he'd reached forty.

And he had risked the lives of several scientists to realize the gigantic rewards this project offered. Some people would say that no man with a conscience would have set up this facility when he knew what the consequences might—

"Say it." Logan was staring at him. "Let it out."

"You shouldn't have done it."

"Everyone in this facility chose to be here. I never lied to them about what they were facing. They believed it was worth it."

"I wonder how they felt when the bullets hit them. Do you think they still thought it was worth it?"

Logan didn't flinch. "Who the hell knows what's important enough to die for? Do you want out, Castleton?"

Yes, he wanted out. The situation was becoming too deadly and complicated. He didn't deal well with either, and he cursed the day he'd become involved in it. "Are you firing me?"

"No way. I need you. You know how things work down here. That's why I hired you in the first place. But I'll understand if you want out. I'll pay you and let you walk away."

"Let me?"

"I could find a way to keep you on the job," Logan said wearily. "There's always a way to do anything you want to do. You just have to decide how far you want to commit yourself. But you've done a good job for me and I'm not willing to force you to stay on. I'll try to find someone else."

"No one could force me to do anything I don't want to do."

"Have it your way." Logan got into the jeep. "Take me back to the airport. I've got to get busy. Am I going to have trouble with the local police?"

"You know better than that. These hills are deep in drug country. It's not safe to ask questions. The police just look the other way." He smiled bitterly as he started the jeep. "Isn't that why you built the facility here?"

"Yes."

"And they won't help you get Bassett away from Rudzak. He's a dead man."

"If he's not dead now, I'll get him back."

"How? Money?"

"Whatever it takes."

"It's impossible. Even if you pay a ransom, Rudzak may kill him anyway. You can't expect to—"

"I'll get him back." Logan's voice suddenly vibrated with harshness. "Listen to me, Castleton. You may think I'm a son of a bitch, but I don't shrug off my responsibilities. Those were my employees who died and I want the man who did it. And if you think I'm going to let him kill or use Bassett to get at me, you're wrong. I'll find him."

"In the middle of the jungle?"

"In the middle of hell." Logan's voice was flint sharp. "Now you've been telling me how sorry you are and how guilty I should feel. Well, I don't have time for guilt. I've always found it counterproductive. You do what you have to do, but don't tell me anything's impossible until you've tried and failed and tried again. I won't buy it."

"You don't have to buy it. I'm not asking you to—" His gaze narrowed on Logan's face. "You're trying to manipulate me."

"Am I?"

"You know damn well you are."

"Smart man. You should have expected it. I'm just as ruthless as you think I am, and I told you I needed you."

Castleton was silent for a moment. "Do you really think you have a chance of saving Bassett?"

"If he's alive, I'll bring him back. Will you help me?"

"What do you want me to do?"

"What you've been doing all along. Grease palms and take care of my people. By the way, I want them out of that hospital and on their way home as soon as possible. They're too vulnerable here."

"I was going to take care of that for you anyway."

"And keep your ears open and your mouth shut. If I'm not in the area, Rudzak will probably contact you first." He smiled crookedly. "Don't worry, I'm not going to ask you to put your neck on the block. You're much too valuable to me in other ways."

"I'm not a coward, Logan."

"No, but this is out of your area of expertise. I always get the right person for the right job. I assure you I wouldn't hesitate to rope you into it if I thought it necessary."

Castleton believed him. He had never seen Logan like this. Most of the time he kept that streak of hard ruthlessness buried beneath a layer of easy charisma. He suddenly recalled the many stories about Logan's shady associations in the early years he had spent in Asia. Gazing at Logan now, he could believe there was more truth than fiction in those wild tales of smuggling and violent power struggles with local gangs who had tried to sell him "protection."

"Well?"

"Okay." Castleton moistened his lips. "I'll stay."

"Good."

"But not because of anything you've said. I just feel guilty as hell that I was in town and not here when it happened. Maybe I could have done something, anything to prevent—"

"Don't be an idiot. You'd have been dead too. Now, do you know of any contact Rudzak might have that we can tap?"

"The talk is there's a dealer named Ricardo Sanchez in Bogotá who's been acting as a go-between for the Mendez cartel and Rudzak."

"Find him. Do anything you have to do. I want to know where Rudzak's camp is located."

"I'm not a thug, Logan."

"Then would it hurt your delicate sense of ethics to hire a thug?"

"You don't have to be sarcastic."

"No, I don't," he said wearily. "If I weren't pressed for time, I'd go to Bogotá and pressure Sanchez myself. Never mind, I have a man who can find out what I need to know."

"I hope you succeed."

"So do I. But even if Sanchez proves useless, I'll still find Bassett."

Castleton shook his head. "No one around here is going to tell you where he is or go into that jungle to look for him."

"Then I'll find him on my own."

"How?"

"I know someone who might be able to help me."

"The right person for the right job?"

"Exactly."

"Then God help him."

"It's not a man." Logan glanced back over his shoulder at the ruins. "It's a woman."

Logan called Margaret Wilson, his personal assistant, the minute his jet was airborne out of Santo Camaro. "Pull the file on Sarah Patrick."

"Patrick?" Logan could visualize Margaret mentally going over the files in her head. "Oh, the dog lady. I did that research on her about six months ago, didn't I? I thought you'd gotten what you needed from her."

"I did. Something else has come up."

"The same lever won't do?"

"Maybe. But this situation has complications. I need to review the file because I'll probably have to use everything we know about her. Not just how to make her jump when I whistle."

"I don't think Sarah Patrick is going to jump when anyone whistles," Margaret said coolly. "And I'd like to be around when you pucker your lips, John. I have an idea that you got lucky the last time. Serve you right if you go around—"

"Lay off me, Margaret," he said with a sigh. "I'm not up to defending myself right now."

"Why not?" She paused. "Is Bassett dead?"

"No, I don't think so. He was alive when they took him."

"Shit."

"I need that file, Margaret."

"Five minutes. Do you want a fax or should I give you the information over the phone?"

"Call me back." Logan hung up, leaned back in his chair, and closed his eyes.

Sarah Patrick.

Her image was there before him: short dark hair streaked by sunlight, high cheekbones, olive skin, and a lean, athletic body. Features more interesting than pretty and a wit as sharp as her tongue.

That sharpness had stung him innumerable times during the time in Phoenix. Sarah was not one to forgive and forget. But the sharpness had been for him only. She had become good friends with Eve Duncan and Joe Quinn after Logan pressured Sarah into working with Eve. The three were still good friends, according to Eve. She had called him last month and told him that Sarah had visited them in Atlanta and had—

His phone rang.

"Sarah Elizabeth Patrick," Margaret said. "Twenty-eight. Half Apache Indian, half Irish. Grew up in Chicago, except the summers she spent with her father on the reservation. Mother and father both deceased. The father died when Sarah was a child, her mother five years ago. High IQ. She studied veterinary medicine at Arizona State University. Inherited a small ranch from her grandfather in the foothills of the mountains outside Phoenix at about the same time the mother died. She still lives there. Oh, you know that. You visited her ranch. She's something of a loner but got along well with students and professors. After school, she started working with the K9 training unit of ATF. She can do anything with animals. She's affiliated with a volunteer search and rescue group based in Tucson, and evidently ATF has given her permission to work with them on both man-made and natural disasters. She and her dog, Monty, have also been lent out to several police departments to find cadavers and also to detect explosives. Monty is something of a wonder dog."

"I know."

"That's right, he found that body in Phoenix." She hesitated. "You know, I think I'd like her, John. Those search and rescue people are pretty wonderful. When I was watching the television coverage of the Oklahoma City bombing, I wanted to give every one of those guys a medal. Or my firstborn child."

"You don't have a child."

"Whatever." She paused. "She doesn't deserve to be pulled into this thing with Bassett."

"Bassett didn't deserve what happened to him either."

"He made a commitment and a choice."

"She can always tell me no."

"You won't let her. It means too much to you."

"Then why are you trying to argue me out of it?"

"I don't know. Yes, I do. Did I mention that Sarah Patrick was one of those rescue workers at Oklahoma City? Maybe this is my try at giving her my firstborn child."

"She doesn't need it. She has her dog."

"And you're not going to listen to me."

"I'm listening. I wouldn't dare do anything else."

"Bull. I'm not asking you to give her a medal. Just give her an out."

"Where is she now?"

"On her way home from Barat. She's been there five days. Earthquake."

"I've not been totally in my own world, Margaret. I heard about the earthquake before I left Monterey."

"But it didn't rock you like the news about Bassett. So what do I do? Do you want me to phone her? Set up a meeting?"

"She'd tell you to go to hell. Since I'm a true gentleman and want to spare you that indignity, I'll take care of it myself."

"You're afraid I'll bond with her and we'd gang up on you."

"You guessed it."

"Okay, then where can I reach you? Are you flying direct to Phoenix?"

"No, I'm going to Atlanta."

Silence. "Eve?"

"Who else?"

"Oh."

"I believe I have you speechless. What an accomplishment. I'll take pity on you. No, I'm not going in sentimental pursuit of a lost love. Eve and I are friends now."

"Heaven forbid anyone would mistake you for being sentimental. You don't have to explain to me about—"

"No, but you'd die of curiosity and then I'd have to break in a new personal assistant. Such a bore."

"I'm not nosy. Anyone would be curious," she said tartly. "After all, you spent a year with her. I thought you might—"

"You can reach me in Atlanta at the Ritz Carlton in Buckhead."

"If you're not going directly to see Sarah Patrick, I'll keep tabs on her."

"That's not necessary. I'll see her in Atlanta."

"No, she's booked back to Phoenix."

"She'll change her plans. By the way, I'm calling Sean Galen after I hang up. If he needs funds, give him—"

"Carte blanche," Margaret finished for him. "As usual. I thought you'd pull him into any rescue attempt. Is he to go directly to Santo Camaro?"

"No, I'm sending him to Bogotá on a fact-finding mission."

Margaret made a distinctly skeptical sound. "Pretty words. Who's he going to beat up?"

"Maybe no one. I just need him to find someone and ask a few questions."

"Yeah, sure."

"If Castleton calls, I want to hear from him immediately.

He has my digital phone number, but he's too cautious for my taste. He may try to reach me on it only in case of emergencies. But as far as I'm concerned, everything is an emergency at this point."

"No problem."

"Wrong. I see nothing but problems looming. I'll keep in touch." He hung up.

He should have known Margaret would champion Sarah Patrick. Margaret was an ardent feminist who admired tough, smart women who boldly ran their own lives and careers. She had liked Eve Duncan for that same reason. Eve was a top forensic sculptor who had overcome tremendous odds in both her personal and professional life. A very special woman . . .

He hadn't seen her in almost six months. Had he made the transition from lover to friend as he'd told Margaret? Who knew? He had felt something for Eve he'd never felt for any other woman, and he'd tried to analyze it in these last months. Respect, pity, passion . . . Hell, maybe all those emotions had been present. She had certainly caught his imagination from the moment he had met her.

No, he wasn't being honest. He had loved Eve. What was love but respect, pity, passion, and a hundred other emotions? Joe Quinn had said Logan didn't love her enough and deserved to lose her. Well, he had lost her, so maybe the bastard was right. Maybe he'd never make a total commitment to a woman. Totality was for the young and the daring.

Christ, that sounded like a soap opera.

Okay, forget personal problems. Eve was going to marry Joe Quinn, a fact that he'd accepted months ago. His commitment now was to Bassett, and he had to concentrate all his efforts on bringing him back.

That's where Sarah Patrick came in.

He could force her to help him as he'd done the last time,

but he'd prefer not to do that. Was there anything else in her background he could use to manipulate her?

He had time to think about it. He should have at least a day to decide what to say to her.

It might take every minute of that time, he thought ruefully. Sarah was tough as nails and Margaret was probably right. This time when he tried to get her to jump when he whistled, there was every chance the situation would explode.

And the situation was explosive enough without Sarah. He had been uneasy ever since he had left Santo Camaro. His instincts told him that something was not as it should be, and he trusted his instincts. What the hell was bothering him?

He was filled with anger and sadness and the usual adrenaline-charged eagerness to jump into the fray—emotions that were getting in the way. So put those emotions on hold. He had to clear his head and analyze Rudzak's opening move. Why had Rudzak taken Bassett? Ransom or revenge was the obvious answer, but Rudzak was seldom obvious.

He pulled the scarab from his pocket, the one Rudzak had sent him via Castleton. His thumb rubbed its carved surface. The scarab was from such a long time ago, a time of pain and torment and regret. . . . Rudzak had meant to send a message with it, but what did the message have to do with Bassett?

He leaned back in his chair. Think. Play the scenario out. Put everything together before you call Galen.

The shrill howl echoed eerily in the night.

Sarah stopped at the top of the hill, her breathing labored from the hard uphill run.

Another howl, more mournful than the first.

A wolf, Sarah thought. Probably one of the Mexican gray wolves that had been recently released in western Arizona.

There had been stories of a few migrating to this area, much to the anger of the local ranchers. That howl had sounded very close. She stared at the crags spiking the mountain behind her.

Nothing. The night was clear and still and the wolf was probably farther away than he sounded.

Beautiful. Monty was staring at the mountain.

"You wouldn't think so if you ran across one of those wolves, Monty. They have no manners. Ask the ranchers around here."

Another howl echoed through the night.

Monty's head lifted. *Beautiful. Free.*

Dogs were supposed to be descended from wolves, but she had never noticed any savage qualities in Monty. No animal could be more gentle or loving. Yet was he feeling some buried instinct as he listened to that wolf? The idea made her uneasy, and she dismissed it immediately. "I think it's time we went back to the cabin. You're getting moonstruck." She started at a run down the path toward the cabin in the valley below.

Clean wind.

Clean air.

Firm earth.

Silence that had nothing to do with death or sorrow.

God, it was good to be home.

Good.

"You bet. Beat you to the cabin."

She didn't, of course. Monty had already jumped through his dog door and was lapping at the water in his dish when she threw open the front door. "You're supposed to be tired from that job in Barat. Give me a break."

Monty gave her a scornful look and then leisurely walked over to his rug in front of the fireplace.

"Okay, don't give me a break. But remember who pays for the groceries."

Monty yawned and stretched out.

The fire was welcoming and her easy chair beckoned. She would like to stretch out herself.

She reluctantly glanced at the blinking red light on her answering machine. She had ignored it when she'd arrived at the cabin two hours before and was tempted to do the same thing now.

Retrieve the messages or take a shower and then curl up in front of the fire? She knew what she wanted to do. Close the world out and go back to the routine with Monty that soothed and sustained them during these off periods. Even the telephone was an intrusion when all she needed was rest, exercise, and no more mental stress than was involved in reading a good book.

But that red light wouldn't stop blinking. She might as well get it over with.

She crossed the room. Two messages.

She punched the button.

"Todd Madden. Welcome back, Sarah."

Shit. She didn't need this.

Her hands clenched into fists as she heard Madden's smooth, faintly mocking tone. "I hear you did a magnificent job. The team earned grateful praise from the Turkish government, not to mention nice coverage by CNN. I think we may have to bring you and Monty up to Washington for a few interviews."

"The hell you will, you asshole," she muttered.

"I can almost see your expression. You're so predictable. Unfortunately, Boyd's mandatory report to ATF on you mentioned that you disobeyed orders on one occasion. He was obviously trying to protect you, but he had to do his job. Are you becoming unstable, Sarah? You know we can't permit instability at ATF. And you know the consequences of your expulsion from ATF." He paused. "But I'm sure you can persuade me that this was just an isolated incident. Come up to Washington for those interviews and we'll talk about it."

Slimy bastard.

"Call me and tell me when you'll arrive. No more than two days, I think. We don't want to be old news." He hung up.

She closed her eyes as waves of rage poured through her. Damn him. Damn him.

She drew a deep breath and tried to control herself. Madden would love to know that he had upset her. He preferred cowed obedience and he didn't like it when she refused to give it to him. He might have the upper hand, but she had let him know what she thought of him any number of times in language that was both abusive and explicit.

Screw him. There wasn't any question she'd have to go to Washington, but she wouldn't call him back and she'd take at least a three-day rest before she left the ranch.

She punched the button for the second message.

"It's Eve, Sarah. We've finally got it. It's confirmed. We'll wait for you. Please come right away." Eve hung up.

So much for rest, she thought resignedly. She would never phone Eve to ask her to wait a day or two. Eve had waited too long already. "Looks like we have another plane trip tomorrow, Monty. We have to go see Eve in Atlanta."

2

"I'm here," Logan said as soon as Eve picked up the phone. "I've checked in at the Ritz Carlton in Buckhead."

"Thanks for coming, Logan. I wasn't sure you would."

"I always told you I'd come when you called." He hesitated before asking, "How's Quinn?"

"Wonderful. He's very good to me."

"That's no great chore. Who could help it? I'll see you tomorrow morning."

"You could come to the cottage tonight."

"No, I'm here to support you, not irritate Quinn. Take care of yourself." He hung up.

She had sounded calm and there was a ring of truth in her words when she spoke about Joe Quinn. It was clear all was going well in that quarter. Was he disappointed? It surprised him that he felt a tinge of regret but no pain. Well, you got over everything in time, and he had never really felt that Eve belonged to him even when they were living together. Their bond had been fragile, and Quinn had no trouble barging in and—

His phone rang.

Margaret?

"Hello, Logan, it's been a long time."

Logan's hand tightened on the receiver. "Hello, Rudzak."

"You don't sound surprised to hear from me."

"Why should I be surprised? I knew it was only a matter of time."

"You don't know the meaning of time. Neither did I until I lived in that hell you threw me into. It was like being buried alive. Every minute was a decade. Did you know my hair turned white in that prison? I'm younger than you and I look twenty years older."

"How do you know how I look?"

"Oh, I've kept tabs on you. I saw you once on the street and several times on television in the last two years. You've done well for yourself. You're a very big man."

"Where's Bassett?"

"I don't want to talk about Bassett. I want to talk about you . . . and me. I've waited a long time for this moment, and I'm savoring it."

"I'm not. Talk about Bassett or I'll hang up."

"No, you won't. You'll stay on the line as long as I want to talk to you because you're afraid of what will happen to Bassett if you don't. You haven't changed. You still have that streak of softness. I'm glad you're not completely hard. It's going to make it easier for me."

"Is Bassett alive?"

"At present. Do you believe me?"

"No, I want to hear his voice."

"Not now. Bassett is such a small part of what's between us. Did you know the first thing I did after I got out of prison was visit Chen Li's grave?"

"This isn't about Chen Li. This is about Bassett."

"It's about Chen Li. Everything is about Chen Li. You allowed her to be buried in that disgustingly simple grave like a thousand others in that cemetery. How could you do that?"

"She was buried with quiet dignity and grace. The way she lived."

"The way you made her live. She was a queen and you made her common."

"Don't talk about her."

"Why not? What can you do to me that you haven't done? Am I making you feel guilty? You are guilty."

"And you're a crazy son of a bitch."

"I wasn't crazy when I went into that prison. If I'm crazy now, it's because of you. You knew what I did was right and you let me rot in that cell. But I'm not insane, and when this is over I'll be able to live again. Do you know why I hit that research facility?"

"You knew it was important to me."

"No, that wasn't the reason. Think about it. It will come to you. I'll even help you along. Did you get the scarab?"

"I got it."

"Good. I thought it was a fitting signature to Santo Camaro. It was the first Egyptian piece I gave to Chen Li. It wasn't very expensive or important, but she didn't care. I was able to give her much nicer pieces later."

"That you stole and murdered to get. Do you think she would have accepted them if she'd known how many people you killed to get those artifacts?"

"But she didn't know and those people didn't matter. She was the only one who mattered. She deserves the best. I'll always give her the best."

"You're talking about her as if she's still alive."

"She'll always be alive to me. Every day in that prison she was with me. She kept me sane. I talked to her and told her how much I hated you and how I was going to hurt you."

"You can't hurt me, Rudzak."

"Oh, but I can." His voice lowered to a silken murmur. "I may be white-haired, but Chen Li would still think I'm handsome. I remember how she would stroke my face and tell me how beautiful I was, how kind and—"

"Shut up."

Rudzak chuckled. "You see, it's easy to hurt you. I'll be calling you again. I've gotten a great deal of satisfaction out of this conversation." He hung up.

Bastard.

Keep calm. The anger pouring through him was counterproductive. Rudzak would enjoy knowing how that jab had pierced his defenses. He did know. Logan had been caught unprepared and let Rudzak see his rage and pain.

You are guilty.

Chen Li.

Don't think of her. Think of Bassett and the problems Rudzak was causing now.

Don't think of Chen Li.

Rudzak pressed the disconnect on the phone and looked down at the tiny round box in his other hand. He wiped the raindrops from the lid. It was a lovely thing, studded with ivory and lapis lazuli. He'd been told that it had once belonged to a princess of Egypt, but he'd embroidered the tale for Chen Li when he gave it to her.

"This belonged to Meretaten, the daughter of Nefertiti. She was supposed to be even lovelier and more clever than her mother."

"I never heard of her." Chen Li held the box up to the window to see the sunlight glitter on the blue stones. "I love it, Martin. Where did you get it?"

"A collector in Cairo."

"It must have cost the earth."

"Not so much. I made a good deal."

She chuckled. "That's what you always say."

He smiled. "I told him it was joining the collection of a woman who should have been born a queen in the time of the pharaohs. There were no rules then but the ones they made for themselves."

A shadow crossed her face. Things had been going so well that he had moved too fast. He pretended to misunderstand the withdrawal. "You were just being polite? You don't really like it?"

She walked into his arms. "I love it. I always love everything you give me."

She leaned back and looked up at him. Her eyes were night dark and he could see himself mirrored in them. His reflection was always better, almost godlike when he saw himself in Chen Li's eyes.

She was gazing at him uncertainly. "Martin?"

Don't scare her. She was closer to him than ever and there would soon come a moment when she would be his. Just don't scare her.

He lifted her hand to his lips. "Happy birthday, Chen Li."

One of her last birthdays.

He could feel warm tears blend with the rain on his cheeks.

"Rudzak." He turned to see Carl Duggan coming toward him. "I've set the timer. We've got to be out of here before someone trips it."

"In a minute. I want to leave Logan a present." He carefully placed the box behind a boulder where it would be sheltered from the blast. He whispered, "Happy birthday, Chen Li."

Rest in peace, Bonnie Duncan.

The minister's words echoed in Sarah's mind even as the casket was lowered into the grave. It wasn't only Bonnie who was at peace now, she thought as she looked at Eve Duncan, who stood between Joe Quinn and Eve's adopted daughter, Jane MacGuire. After all these years of searching for the remains of her child who had been murdered over a decade ago, Eve had brought Bonnie home. The DNA report that had just come through had confirmed these bones were her daughter's.

Tears were running down Eve's mother's face, but Eve was not weeping. Her expression reflected peace, sadness, and completion. She had wept her tears for Bonnie long ago. Her daughter was home now.

But Sarah felt tears sting her own eyes as she tossed the rose in her hand on top of the casket.

Good-bye, Bonnie Duncan.

"I think we should leave the family alone to say their good-byes," John Logan said in a low voice. "Let's go back to the cottage and wait for them."

Sarah hadn't been aware that he had moved to stand beside her. She instinctively shifted away from him.

Logan shook his head. "I know how you feel about me, but this isn't the time to burden Eve with it. We've got to help her get through this."

He was right. She hadn't been pleased when she had seen him drive up to the cottage a few hours before it was time to go to the burial site, but she couldn't fault his behavior toward Eve and Joe. He had been both sympathetic and supportive. And he was also right about leaving the family alone now. She turned away from the grave and started the short walk around the lake toward the cottage. It was pretty here, she thought. Eve had chosen a lovely spot on a small hill overlooking the lake to bury her daughter.

"Where's Monty?" Logan asked as he caught up with her.

"I left him in the cottage. Being at the grave site would have upset him."

"Ah, yes, I'd forgotten what a sensitive canine your Monty is."

"More sensitive than some people."

"Ouch." He grimaced. "I didn't mean to slam your dog. I'm actually trying to be pleasant."

"Are you?"

"And evidently not succeeding."

"Right."

"I'll start again. Eve told me that it was you and Monty who found Bonnie. She said the two of you must have gone over every foot of that national park until you discovered where that murderer buried her."

"We did. But I almost gave up."

"But you didn't."

"Eve's my friend."

"Then don't you think you could forgive my rather unscrupulous methods of bringing the two of you together?"

"No," she said coldly. "I don't like being forced to do anything. You're as bad as Madden. Always trying to manipulate everyone and every situation."

"I'm not quite as black as you're painting me. I do have a few virtues."

She was silent.

"I'm patient. I'm responsible. I can be a good friend. Ask Eve."

"I'm not interested. Why are you making this futile attempt to convince me you're a decent human being?" Her eyes narrowed. "You're up to something."

"Why should I be—" He shrugged. "Yes, I'm up to something, besides failing to convince you that I'm anything but a son of a bitch. Too bad. It would have made it easier on both of us."

"Why the hell are you here?"

"I'm here for the same reason you're here. I wanted to support Eve when she needed her friends."

"You weren't her friend. You were her lover and it won't do you any good to come here and try to lure her away from Joe. She loves him and you're past history, Logan."

"I know, but thanks for reminding me. I can see it's only your dog that has any sensitivity. I'm not here to stir up old embers. Is it too hard to believe that I want only the best for Eve?"

"I don't have to believe or disbelieve you." Her pace quickened. "As I said, I don't care. It doesn't matter if you—"

"Sarah!"

She turned to see Jane MacGuire running down the hill toward them, her red hair gleaming in the sunlight. The ten-year-old's expression was pale and strained as she stopped beside Sarah. "Hi, can I walk back with you?"

"Sure. But I thought you'd want to wait for Eve."

She shook her head. "She doesn't need me. She has Joe." She looked straight ahead. "Neither of them wants me there right now."

Sarah could see a problem looming. "You're part of Eve's family. She always wants you with her."

"Not now. I don't belong here. It's Bonnie's time." She shifted her glance to Logan. "You knew it. That's why you took Sarah away."

Logan nodded. "At least someone appreciates my sensitivity. But Sarah is right. You're part of the family."

Jane's lips tightened. "You're trying to make me feel better. I don't need your pity. I know Joe and Eve care about me, but I'm not Bonnie. I'll never be Bonnie to them. So don't tell me they want me there when they're saying good-bye to her. Can't you see how hard it is for them having me here right now? All they want to think about is Bonnie, but they have to try to make me feel all cozy and wanted because they don't want to hurt me."

"Talk to them," Sarah said gently.

"No." Jane looked away from them and repeated, "It's Bonnie's time." She changed the subject. "May I go on ahead and take Monty out for a walk?"

"I think that would be a very good idea."

Sarah frowned, troubled, as she watched Jane run down the path toward the cottage.

"Will Monty go with her?" Logan asked.

She nodded. "He adores her. They got to know each other very well in Phoenix."

"You like her too. She's not the easiest kid to get to know."

"She may look like a kid, but she's more grown-up than most adults. That's what happens when you're raised in foster homes and on the streets." She nibbled at her lower lip. "She's right, isn't she? Having her here is going to be a strain on Eve and Joe."

"Probably. It seems Jane has good instincts." He was studying her face. "What are you thinking?"

"None of your business." They had reached the porch of the cottage. "Are you leaving now?"

"Not yet. I thought I'd leave for the airport after lunch. You're on the three o'clock flight, aren't you?"

"How do you know that?"

"Eve told me on the phone. She said they picked you up at the airport. Could I give you a lift?"

"Joe's going to drive me."

"But shouldn't he stay with Eve? It won't hurt you to occupy the same car with me. It's only an hour's drive."

It wouldn't hurt her, but she didn't want any favors from him.

It was as if he'd read her mind. "I'm not doing you any favors, Sarah. Considering your opinion of me, you should know better."

No, she could see Logan doing favors for Eve but not for her. Why should he? She didn't know why he had made the attempt to bridge the gulf between them, but it wasn't because he regretted what he had done. Logan never looked back after he had made a decision.

"Eve needs Joe right now," Logan said. "We both know it."

"And does that sting, Logan?"

"Would you feel sorry for me if it did?"

"Hell, no."

"I didn't think so. So do I take you to the airport?"

She shrugged. "Okay. I should leave by one."

He nodded. "I'll be ready. But shouldn't you be there earlier to board Monty in the cargo?"

"Monty always travels in the cabin with me."

"I thought only small animals or dogs for the blind were permitted in the cabin."

"He has special ATF clearance."

He smiled. "And if he didn't, you'd probably insist on traveling in the baggage with him."

"You've got it." Sarah opened the front door. "I'm going to start making sandwiches and coffee. There's Reverend Watson coming down the path. Why don't you make yourself useful, say something charming and send him on his way?"

"I'm surprised you think I'm capable of being charming."

Oh, he had never tried it on her, but she had seen him work that charisma. It was probably one of the more potent weapons in his arsenal. "Why should it surprise you?" As she entered the cottage, she glanced at him over her shoulder. "I understand that most of Germany's population thought Hitler was charming."

• • •

"Thanks for coming, Sarah." Eve sat down in the porch swing and looked out at the lake. "I know you're tired. But it meant a lot for me to have you here."

"Don't be silly. I wanted to come."

"I think Bonnie would have liked you to be here. After all, you did find her."

"We were lucky."

"Don't give me that. You worked your butt off."

"That doesn't always mean that Monty and I find what we're looking for." She studied Eve's face. "Is everything okay with you?"

"It will be soon. It feels very strange right now." Her gaze moved to the hill across the lake. "She's home now. That means everything. Even though she never really left me."

Sarah nodded. "Memories can be very precious."

"Yes." She smiled faintly. "But that's not exactly what I meant." She changed the subject. "I'm worried about Jane."

"I thought you would be."

"Most of the time I think she's happy with us. She knows we love her." She sighed. "But Jane's not easy."

"The situation's not easy." Sarah paused. "How would you feel about Jane spending a few weeks with me at my cabin?"

Eve didn't speak for a moment. "Why?"

"A change will be good for her. She loves Monty and she likes me. I'd take good care of her."

"I know you would." She frowned slightly. "Has she talked to you about Bonnie?"

"The important question is if she's spoken to you about her."

"Not since you found Bonnie. I tried a couple of times, but she shuts me out. I've been hoping that time— I don't know. It's hard for me to think right now."

"It's a period of adjustment for all of you. You've been obsessed for years with the thought of bringing Bonnie home. I know you're happy that she's here now, but it will be—"

"Jane thinks she's second best," Eve interrupted. "I tried to tell her how different— She won't accept it. She's not resentful, but I can't talk her out of it."

"With her lousy childhood, it's possible you may never be able to convince her. But that doesn't mean you can't have a good life together."

"Don't tell me that. I want her to feel special. Everyone should feel special."

"Jane *is* special. She's tough and independent and smart as a whip. So smart she knows that you're confused and sad right now and she can't help you. It hurts her. Send her to me for a while, Eve."

"I'll think about it." Eve tried to smile. "I never thought I'd have this kind of problem adjusting when I found Bonnie. It's not that I'm not relieved, it's just . . ."

"You've lived your life a certain way because Bonnie was lost. Now she's found."

Eve nodded. "It will take a little time, but God, I'm lucky, Sarah. I've got Joe. Everything will fall into place as long as I have Joe." She reached over and took Sarah's hand. "And friends like you and Logan."

"Speaking of Logan, it's time I left for the airport. Where is he?"

"He walked down to the lake."

"Alone?"

Eve nodded. "Which is just as well. He and Joe are still not too friendly."

Sarah grinned. "Because you're such a femme fatale."

"Yeah, sure." She straightened her glasses and got to her feet. "Let's go find Jane and Monty. You'll have to pry her away from him."

"It won't be so bad if you tell her that she'll see him soon."

"I said I'd think about it." She made a face. "You're obstinate as hell, Sarah. What makes you so sure you're the best thing for Jane right now? If you get a call, you and Monty will be trekking off to some outlandish part of the world. What would you do with her?"

Sarah shrugged. "We'd make out."

Eve shook her head. "For that matter, what would you do if you had a child of your own? Talk about adjustments."

"I'd deal with the problem when I had to face it."

"Kids are more demanding than dogs."

"That's why I stick to dogs. I'm happy living just as I am. Can you imagine me with a husband and a bunch of kids?"

"No, not really. But it must be a lonely life."

"Why? I have Monty and my friends in the unit."

"Who you never see unless you're on some rescue mission."

"It's enough."

"Why is it enough? Why won't you get close to anyone?"

She smiled. "Eve, stop trying to make me into some kind of scarred drama queen. I'm not like you. I've no dark, brooding past. I'm just a normal woman who happens to be a little more selfish than most people. My life suits me just fine."

"And I'm to mind my own business."

"Do what you like. But you surprise me. You were once one of the most isolated women on the planet, and you think *my* lack of social interaction is a problem."

"Touché." Eve smiled. "I guess I just want everyone to be as happy as I've been lately."

"I'm happy as a clam." She tilted her head. "You know, I've always wondered about that phrase. How does anyone know how happy a clam is? And why should a clam be particularly happy?" She chuckled. "Okay, I'm as happy as Monty when he's getting his belly rubbed. It doesn't get any better than that."

• • •

Fifteen minutes to one. It was almost time to go.

Logan started back toward the cottage. He could see the shadowy figures of Sarah and Monty silhouetted in the windows. They looked like two fantasy figures on the cover of a novel.

But there was nothing fanciful about Sarah Patrick. Damn, she was hardheaded. She would neither forgive nor forget, and she was tying his hands. He had only another hour to find a way to get her help on a voluntary basis; after that he'd have to—

His digital phone rang.

"I've heard from Rudzak," Castleton said. "He wants to deal."

Logan's hand tightened on the phone. "Did you talk to Bassett?"

"Not yet. He says that all you have to do is come up with fifty thousand dollars and he'll let you talk to Bassett. I'm to leave the money at a drop near the research facility."

"And how much cash to release him?"

"He wants to negotiate that with you personally."

Logan had expected that. "Have you found out anything more about Rudzak's location?"

"I told you that you'd have to take care of that. I gave you a lead. Hasn't your man found Sanchez yet?"

"He's working on it, but it wouldn't hurt if he had help."

"Dammit, I'm doing everything I can on this end. When are you coming?"

"I'm leaving this afternoon."

"And what do I do about the money?"

"Give it to him. I've told Margaret to give you anything you need."

"It could be a bluff. Bassett could be dead."

"Give it to him."

"What if he doesn't let you talk to Bassett?"

"We'll worry about that when it happens."

Castleton paused. "I gave him your number when he asked me for it. I hope you don't mind."

"No, you did the right thing. If he wants to talk to me, make it easy. I want to keep on with the dialogue. The more we're in contact, the better our chance of finding out something."

"I think he's killed him, Logan. What if he's dead?"

"Then Rudzak will be dead too."

He hung up and shoved the phone into his pocket. He needed to get down to Santo Camaro. He had learned long ago that you played by the rules of the game in progress and this game was shaping up to be very nasty.

His gaze went back to Sarah and Monty waiting on the porch. Too bad. He had no more time. He took out his phone again and quickly dialed a number.

"Take care of yourself." Logan brushed a kiss on Eve's forehead before he got into the car. "If you need me for anything, give me a call."

"I'm fine." She looked at Sarah, who was sitting in the passenger seat. "I'll let you know about Jane."

"I have to fly straight from here to Washington, but that should take only a couple of days. After that I'll be at the cabin."

Eve waved and stepped back as Logan started the car.

Sarah turned her head and saw Eve still standing there, watching them as they started down the gravel road. For a moment she looked very lonely, but then Joe came out of the cottage and stood behind her with his hands on her shoulders. No, Eve wasn't lonely. She had Joe and her mother and Jane. She would never have to be lonely again unless she wanted to be. But wasn't that true of everyone? You made choices, and to be alone was one of them.

What was she thinking? She wasn't alone. As she had told Eve, she had Monty and a job that fulfilled her. She didn't want anything or anyone else.

"What did she mean about letting you know about Jane?" Logan asked.

"I may have Jane visit me for a few weeks."

"When?"

"As soon as possible."

"No."

She turned to stare at him. "What?"

"Not now."

"What the hell are you talking about? Now is when Eve needs my help. The sooner the— Why am I even talking to you about it? It's none of your business."

"It's my business. I need your help. And I need it now."

The arrogance of the bastard. "Go jump in the lake, Logan."

"I'll pay you anything you want. Name your price."

"You don't have enough money."

His lips tightened. "I was afraid you'd say that. Sorry. I can't let you walk away from this job, Sarah. It's too important."

"To you. I don't give a damn about what you need, Logan."

"I know. That's why I called Todd Madden and asked him to arrange for ATF to lend you to me."

She stared at him, stunned. "What?"

"You heard me."

"My God, you're doing it again."

"I tried to avoid it." He shrugged. "But I couldn't get through to you. You're still holding a grudge."

"And you wouldn't? I can't see you being railroaded and then forgiving and forgetting."

"I'm not saying I don't understand, I'm just explaining why I had to call Madden. He told me to tell you to forget about that press conference for the time being. You and Monty belong to me for as long as I need you."

Her surprise was turning to fury. "The hell we do."

"Madden assured me you'd do whatever I asked."

"And what did you promise him?"

"My gratitude. And all the influence that goes with it. Your Senator Madden is very ambitious, isn't he? Is he eyeing a cabinet post?"

"I can't believe he canceled the press conference. He likes to see his face in the newspapers too much."

"Oh, I had to be very persuasive."

"You son of a bitch."

"I was worried that you'd turn me down in spite of Madden's orders, but he said there was no way you'd refuse him." His gaze narrowed on her face. "He has something on you, doesn't he? Some kind of hold?"

"What do you care? It was nothing to you how Madden got me to do what you wanted the last time. All you wanted was results. That's all you care about now." She was shaking with anger. "Is that why you came here?"

"I came here because Eve wanted me to be here. The same reason you came."

"But you knew I'd be here. Two birds with one stone."

"Yes, I knew you'd be here."

"And what do you want me to do? Find another corpse for you?"

"I don't think he's dead." He smiled crookedly. "I know how you hate using Monty as a cadaver dog. You should be pleased that I'm asking you and Monty to work on rescuing a real live person."

"Pleased?"

"Wrong word. I'm trying to put a tolerable light on a bad situation."

"It's not tolerable."

"It will have to be."

"Screw you." She took out her phone and dialed Madden's number. "What the devil are you doing to me?" she asked as soon as he answered.

"Now, Sarah, it's for the best."

"Whose best, damn you?"

"Logan tells me the job is very important and it may not be all that long."

"Did it occur to you that Monty and I just came back from a job that wore us down to the bone? We need to rest."

"You need to do what I tell you to do. I'm sure Logan will take care of you. Let me know when you're available again." He hung up.

Her hand clenched the phone so tightly, her knuckles turned white. Bastards. They were both bastards.

"Satisfied?" Logan asked.

"I'd like to castrate him." She glared at him. "And you too."

He flinched. "I gather he verified what I told you. Now, shall I tell you about the job?"

She tried to control herself. A long time ago she had accepted the fact that she couldn't beat Madden. The card he was holding was too high. But, dear God, she hated the idea of being under Logan's thumb. She wanted to pound someone. No, not someone. Logan.

Monty whimpered in the backseat and she reached over to stroke him. "It's okay, boy. It's okay."

"It's not okay, but you'll do it," Logan said. "Right?"

"Damn you."

Monty whimpered again.

"Shh."

"He senses that you're upset." Logan smiled. "I remember how close you are. He's a good dog."

"I should have him go for your throat. Do you know how tired he is?"

"Monty doesn't impress me as being a very vicious guard dog."

"He makes an exception when he thinks I'm in danger."

"But you're not in danger yet."

Her gaze flew to his face. "Yet?"

His smile faded. "There are a few problems with this job, but I'll try to keep you both safe."

"Just what do you want me to do?"

"I need you and Monty to find one of my employees who has been kidnapped. One of my research facilities in Colombia was attacked and four of my employees killed. Tom Bassett was taken hostage."

"Do you know who kidnapped him?"

"Martin Rudzak. He's a very nasty fellow."

"How nasty?"

"About as nasty as they get. He dabbles in everything from drug running to terrorism."

"Terrorism? Why is he targeting you?"

"We had a run-in several years ago when I was in Japan. He doesn't like me very much."

"Then he should have kidnapped you."

"I'm sure you'd prefer that, but there are reasons why he picked Bassett."

"And you're not going to tell me."

"Not at the moment."

"I don't track criminals, Logan."

"You work for ATF."

"These days my primary job is search and rescue."

"You'd be rescuing Bassett."

"Just pay the ransom. You've got plenty of money."

"The percentages are high that after I pay it, Bassett will be killed anyway. I need to find him and get him away."

"And how am I supposed to find him? Do you know the specific locality?"

"Not yet. Somewhere in the jungle near Santo Camaro, Colombia."

Her eyes widened. "South America?"

"Last time I checked."

"You want me to go to South America? You want me to wander around the jungle until I find—"

"I have someone working on pinpointing Rudzak's location. I'm hoping to have more information by the time we reach Colombia."

"And when will that be?"

"My plane is waiting at the Atlanta airport now."

"And you think I'll hop on the plane and go meekly with you."

"Not meekly. Never meekly."

She drew a deep breath. "You're not only risking my neck, you're risking Monty. If those scumbags see Monty trying to track them, the first thing they'll do is shoot him."

"I'll be very careful with both of you. I'll do everything I can to keep you safe."

"And you expect me to trust you?"

He shook his head. "No, but it doesn't make it less true."

"I'll never trust you. You're a user, just like Madden. I'm the one who'll keep Monty safe. You don't care about anyone or—" She broke off. Why was she arguing? She knew she didn't have a choice. He and Madden had backed her into a corner. "How long?"

"I don't know."

She closed her eyes as the anger and frustration poured through her. "I'll do the job. I'll find your man." Her eyes opened and she added with soft venom, "But then I'll find a way to get you. And if you get my dog killed, you'll wish you'd never been born."

"I believe you." He pulled off the freeway into the lane leading to the airport. "You know, even using Madden as a lever, I wasn't sure you'd go with me. Whatever Madden has on you must be pretty powerful stuff. You wouldn't care to tell me what it is?"

"Go to hell, Logan."

3

"It's been over an hour since we took off," Logan said. "It would be nice if you said a word or two. Maybe even three."

"We've said everything that needed to be said and I don't feel like being nice."

"Would you like something to eat?" Logan asked.

"No."

"What about Monty? Do you suppose he might be hungry?"

"Monty eats only twice a day. I fed him at the cottage." Sarah curled up in the wide leather chair and stared out the window. "And you don't have to be concerned about Monty. I always take care of him."

"That's obvious. I just thought I'd play the gracious host and offer."

"Offer us food and then put our lives on the line?"

"I can do only what I can," he said wearily. "I told you I'd try to keep you safe."

"Trying isn't good enough." She reached down and stroked Monty's head, then said through gritted teeth, "Do you know how this makes me feel? It's not only you who's responsible for putting Monty in danger. He's my dog. The bottom line is always me. He never says no, so if I make the wrong decision, I have to bear the blame."

"Even if I blackmailed you into it?"

"That makes you a bastard, but I'm the one who makes the final decision."

He was silent a moment. "You find the camp and you're done. You won't be within a mile of any firepower. Nothing will happen to you or Monty."

"I know," she said sarcastically. "You'll try to keep us safe."

"No. It won't happen. I promise you."

She turned to look at him.

"You don't believe me?"

"Should I?"

"I suppose not. Sometimes fate takes a hand and there's nothing anyone can do to change what happens. But if I'm still alive when we get out of that jungle, you and Monty will be too." He grimaced. "I assure you that's not a promise that's easy for me to make. I have a keen sense of self-preservation." He stood up. "I'm going to the cockpit to talk to our pilot. You might make a list of your needs on this job, and I'll call my assistant and have her make sure they're waiting for you in Santo Camaro. There's a pad and pencil in the drawer of the table next to you. I won't be gone more than fifteen or twenty minutes, but then, I'm sure you won't miss me."

"No, I won't." She watched him walk down the aisle before she reached for the pad and pencil and started making her list. Why had he tried so hard to convince her he'd protect her and Monty? They were nothing to him. Just tools to get him what he wanted. Yet for a moment she had believed him. She had faced crooked bureaucrats and power figures in disaster sites around the world, and she could recognize sincerity when she saw it.

Or could she? Logan had learned manipulation in a hundred corporate boardrooms. Maybe he was a little out of her league.

Bull. Either she trusted her judgment or she didn't. Was Logan a complete son of a bitch or was there a trace of softness that she could exploit?

She finished her list, then closed her eyes. She didn't want to exploit anyone or anything. She just wished she could go home and forget about Logan and Madden and everything connected with them.

"Coffee?"

She opened her eyes to see Logan holding a cup out to her.

He smiled faintly. "It's only coffee. It's not like eating at your enemy's table. Besides, you should really take me for all you can get. Food, drink, money." He looked down at Monty. "Isn't that right, boy?"

Monty's tail thumped, and he rolled over on his back.

Logan reached down and scratched his belly. Monty gave a soft woo-woo from the back of his throat.

Good.

"Traitor," she muttered.

Nice.

"The hell he is."

Logan raised his brows. "Am I missing something?"

"You're not going to convince me you're a great guy just by petting my dog."

"But he likes me."

"Don't flatter yourself. He likes everyone. He's a golden retriever, for God's sake. They're known for being affectionate . . . even with someone who doesn't deserve it."

Nice.

She looked down at Monty in disgust. No discrimination.

"Why do I feel out of the loop here?" Logan thrust the cup

at her. "The reports I had on you said that you could almost read that dog's mind. I'm beginning to think he may be able to read yours too. Drink your coffee while I go get your familiar a bowl of water."

Before she could argue, he was strolling back to the galley.

Monty wriggled over onto his belly. *Nice.*

She ignored him as she took a sip of the coffee. She had been tempted to refuse, but she was so tired she could scarcely think, and what he said made sense. Why shouldn't she use him as he was using her? She suddenly stiffened as a thought occurred to her. My God, why not? Why sit there feeling sorry for herself when she had a chance to—

"Good. I was afraid you'd pour that coffee on the floor." Logan set a delicate china bowl down before Monty. "I'm glad you're being sensible."

"And being sensible is doing what you want me to do?" She took another drink of coffee. "I wanted this coffee, so I took it. I'm not into futile gestures."

"Why isn't Monty drinking?"

"He won't take food or drink from anyone but me." She reached down, touched the rim of the bowl, and Monty started thirstily lapping up the water. "That's fine china. Monty may break it. He has a tendency to push his bowl around when it's empty."

"It's all I had and he deserves the best."

"Yes, he does. Screw your china." She looked around the luxurious interior of the jet. "This is beautiful. I've never seen one like it."

"I like to be comfortable. I do a lot of traveling and there's nothing worse than being tired and irritable when I get off a plane. One mistake in protocol or financial misstep and the entire trip could be blown." He sat down beside her. "And do you see the inside of a lot of corporate jets?"

"A few. The government seldom pays for transporting search and rescue groups, and the current administration has given us zilch." Her lips twisted. "Though they're very willing to take advantage of any publicity we generate. We rely heavily on corporations to give us a ride when we need it."

"I'm surprised. Billions of dollars in foreign aid and not a dime to search and rescue?"

"We get along." She shrugged. "It's probably better that the government doesn't get involved. We'd probably have to fill out requests in triplicate and deal with strings attached."

He was silent a moment. "Like the ones Madden has you dancing on?"

She stiffened. "You don't have an aversion to pulling the strings yourself. You're both into power trips."

He quickly changed the subject. "You have a job with ATF, don't you? Don't they foot the bill to send you and Monty to disaster sites?"

"Only when there are explosives involved. ATF doesn't have search and rescue missions."

"Then why did you take the job?"

"I had to live." She glanced out the window. "And after the first year I was only loosely affiliated with ATF. Monty and I were permitted to go with volunteer search and rescue groups when we weren't being loaned out to police departments to use in particularly difficult cases."

"Cadaver searches?"

"Yes."

"Why did you do it? You hate them. I had to twist your arm to get you to help Eve."

"I did what I had to do."

He studied her closed expression with narrowed eyes. "And why would you have to do it? Why not just quit?"

"I told you, I had to live."

"I don't think that's the reason." He said thoughtfully, "You live simply and seem to enjoy it. I offered you any amount you wanted for this job. So it's not money. Blackmail? Now, what kind of crime could you have committed to put you under Madden's thumb?"

She stared him directly in the eyes. "I murdered a manipulating bastard who pried into my business."

He chuckled. "Sorry, I'm cursed with an inquiring mind. You're an interesting enigma, Sarah. The temptation to solve you is almost irresistible."

"Because you think you may need another hold on me?"

His smile faded. "No."

"Bullshit. You're thinking all the time, weighing advantages and disadvantages, bad moves, good moves. This was a bad move, Logan."

"It was the only one I had."

"There are always choices. You chose Monty and me. It may be the worst choice you've ever made. Because if anything happens to Monty, I'll hunt you down and tear you limb from limb." She finished her coffee in one swallow. "I've been sitting here, doing some thinking myself. For some reason you want my willing cooperation to find this Bassett. I don't know why. Maybe you're smart enough to realize that working smoothly together as a team will increase the chances of getting him out."

"Perish the thought that I might dislike using force."

"That never occurred to me. You're a user, like Madden. If force was needed, you'd be there with your little hatchet." Her lips tightened. "Well, I'm tired of being used. It's not going to happen again. Not by you and not by Madden."

"Really."

"You want cooperation, I'll give you cooperation. I'll get your man out, but I want a payoff."

"I told you I'd give you any amount you wanted."

"I want Madden out of my life."

He was silent a moment. "I've no doubt he's very unpleasant, but I hope you don't want me to take a contract out on him. That could be very awkward."

"What if I said I did?" she asked, curious.

"I'd have to think about it."

Her eyes widened with shock as she realized he wasn't ruling out the possibility. "Don't be stupid. I just want him out of my life with no holds on me."

"That's a great relief. You wouldn't care to confide what hold he has on you?"

She didn't answer.

"I didn't think so. You don't trust me. You're afraid I'll just take over the reins from Madden. Did it occur to you that you'll still run that risk?"

"It occurred to me. That's part of the deal. I'm free of both of you."

"Then it seems you trust me more than you do Madden."

"Eve trusts you. You might keep your word. And once this job is over, you won't have any other use for me. You can afford to let me go."

"True. But I can hardly help you if I go at it blind."

"I'll tell you when you need to know."

"And why do you think I can help you?"

"I don't have the kind of clout I need to get away from him or I'd have done it years ago. Is it a deal?"

Logan slowly nodded. "As long as you give me your best effort, Madden's out of your life whether we get my man out or not. You have my word on it."

She felt a flicker of surprise.

"I'm not quite the bastard you think me," Logan said roughly. "Ask Eve. As you said, she trusts me."

"She's prejudiced. You were lovers. You probably behaved differently with her than you do with other people."

"Yeah, I made a really big effort to treat her like a human being. It was a great strain on me." He stood up. "I need to go and make some telephone calls. Why don't you stretch out on the couch and try to sleep? We're going to hit the ground running when we reach Santo Camaro." He picked up the list on the table. "Is this all you need?"

"That's it."

"I'll see that you get it," he said, and strode down the aisle.

She had made him angry and his response had been uncharacteristically vulnerable. Maybe he wasn't quite the steely man she had thought. But it didn't matter how hard or soft he was as long as he could get Madden out of her life.

A life without the threat of Madden . . .

The thought brought an unbelievable surge of relief. For years she had lived without hope, and suddenly the possibility was there before her. Win or lose, Madden would be out of her life if she just did her job. Logan had given his word.

Monty whined softly and put his head on her knee, sensing her excitement.

"We've got a chance, boy," she whispered. "If he's not lying, we may be able to come out of this with something pretty good."

Nice.

"He's not nice, but it doesn't matter if he keeps his word."

Nice.

Stubborn dog. She got up and moved over to the couch. "Come on, we have to get some sleep. We want to be in top form and get through this fast and get home."

Monty settled on the floor in front of the couch, but his

gaze went to the back of the cabin, where Logan had disappeared.

Nice . . .

"Then you've got her?" Margaret asked after Logan had rattled off Sarah's list to her. "I was hoping maybe you'd strike out."

"I know you were. You made that pretty clear," Logan said. "Find out everything you can about Todd Madden. I want a complete report."

"How complete?"

"I want to know the name of every kid he mugged in kindergarten."

"Oh, that kind of report. I gather we're no longer playing on the same team with him?"

"He's on the funding committee for ATF, but I don't think that's how he's pulling Sarah Patrick's strings. It's something else."

"You've got her. What difference does it make?"

"It makes a difference. Any messages?"

"Galen called from Bogotá. He said it's not urgent, but he wants you to phone him."

"As soon as I hang up. Did he mention any problems?"

"No, he said to tell you the team was in place." She paused and then added grudgingly, "You know, I really like him."

"And that surprises you? Oh, yes, it would. You're not supposed to like men like Galen. It violates your code."

"Yes, it does, but Galen is . . . different."

"That's indisputable. Nothing from Castleton?"

"No. And it may take a while to get the dirt on Madden. He's a politician and they bury their skeletons pretty deep."

"Just get it."

"How's the pooch?"

"Easier than Sarah."

"Well, you can hardly blame her for—"

"I'll call you when we get to Santo Camaro." He ended the call and dialed Galen's number.

"What's happening?"

"No greeting? No small talk?" Galen drawled. "After all those years in Tokyo, I'd think you'd have learned some manners."

"Do you have a location?"

"Have I ever failed you? I got a general location, but Sanchez says Rudzak moves camp every few days. And he's going to set up a decoy camp as bait."

"We have to find the main camp now. We can't afford any extra time. We have to get in and out fast or we'll have a dead hostage. You're sure you got the truth from Sanchez?"

"I'm truly hurt. Not only a lack of manners, but doubt? I admit Sanchez was stubborn, but eventually his good sense prevailed."

"Money?"

"No. Sanchez already makes a tremendous amount in the drug trade. There's millions floating around down here. I had to convince the scumbag he'd be safer running from Rudzak than from me. Can you imagine, he wasn't taking me seriously?"

"I'm sure that didn't last long."

"Almost thirty minutes."

"You're slipping."

"Now insults?" He made a *tsk-tsk* sound. "And while I was at it, I did that little research project you heaped on me."

"And?"

"Confirmed."

Logan's hand tightened on the phone. "Son of a bitch."

"Do you want me to take care of it?"

"No, I'll do it myself." Dammit, he had known it. "But I can't have Sanchez ratting to Rudzak."

"He won't. I sent him out of the country with a suitcase of Rudzak's money he was laundering. He's neatly boxed."

"Good," Logan said. "We'll be arriving in Santo Camaro shortly."

"I'm already on my way. I should be there in about an hour, and I'll contact Castleton to pick you up at the airport."

Logan hung up. Everything was in motion. As usual, Galen had succeeded and had the information he needed. Logan had Sarah and Monty in hand and had found a way to get Sarah to voluntarily work with him.

Yeah, sure. Actually Sarah had taken control. She'd turned a situation that made her a victim to one in which she had control. How many times had she had to do that with her life on the line?

Christ, what was he doing? He had made his decision and it was no time for regrets. He shoved his phone in his pocket, left his office, and started back up the aisle toward the cockpit.

Sarah was asleep on the couch and didn't stir as he stopped beside her. Monty opened one eye and his tail thumped lazily.

"Shh."

But Sarah didn't wake, and even in slumber she was curled up in a defensive position, her muscles locked and stiff.

Search and rescue. What made anyone embrace a career that involved not only danger but constant despair? All the dossiers and reports in the world never really told you what made a person tick. Logan knew Sarah was strong, smart, streetwise, and had a wicked sense of humor with everyone but him. But he was beginning to realize that there might be a whole lot more beneath that tough facade. What kind of woman was Sarah Patrick?

Well, he was not likely to find out. She was wary and he had established himself firmly in the enemy camp. What the hell. It didn't matter. He didn't have to know her. It was better if he didn't. He had learned a long time ago that it was dangerous to get close to people in dangerous situations. It hurt too much if you lost them.

Chen Li.

He shunted the thought back into the darkness, where it belonged. He had been younger, less experienced then. This situation didn't have to end as that one had. Sarah Patrick wasn't Chen Li.

He could keep Sarah alive.

Santo Camaro

"This is Sarah Patrick," Logan told Castleton at the airport. "Ron Castleton. He works for me."

"Don't we all," she murmured. She gestured and Monty jumped into Castleton's car. "How do you do, Mr. Castleton. This is Monty. I don't have any health papers for him. Are we going to have any trouble with the authorities?"

Castleton was staring wide-eyed at the dog. "What's happening here? If I'd had any warning, I could have—"

"We won't need papers," Logan said. "We'll be in and out before anyone knows we've arrived."

"And what if we aren't?"

"I'll take care of it." Logan got into the front passenger seat. "Have you heard from Galen?"

"He's at the facility. He said you'd want to start out right away."

"He's right." He looked at the sky, which was already darkening to twilight. "But we should probably wait until morning. Did you hear any more from Rudzak?"

"Not since I left the money where he told me." He glanced sideways at Logan. "But he has informants everywhere. He's probably got someone watching us now."

"Then let's get moving."

Castleton started the car. "The dog's a dead giveaway. He'll know you're trying to find Bassett. He has contacts who can trace—"

"That's why we have to move quickly."

"Did you get the supplies on the list I made out?" Sarah asked.

Castleton frowned. "What supplies? I didn't receive any list."

"Galen has the supplies, Sarah," Logan said. "I had Margaret call him while he was on the road and give him your list."

"I don't like bringing a woman into this." Castleton looked over his shoulder at Sarah. "Has Logan explained how dangerous this situation is? I hope you know what you're getting into."

She didn't really know anything, dammit. "Thanks for your concern, but we'll be okay." Although Castleton wasn't making her feel any better. And the heat . . . it was going to make the search twice as difficult. It was hard to breathe and Monty was already panting. She reached down and stroked Monty's head. "I think it's time for a clip, boy."

"We don't have time," Logan said.

"I'm not suggesting taking him to a groomer. I'll do it myself." Her lips thinned. "I won't take him into the jungle until he's more comfortable. He's a long-haired dog and we don't know how much time this search will take."

"If it takes enough time for the heat to cause him a problem, then we're in trouble."

"It's causing him trouble now. I'm clipping him."

Logan opened his mouth to protest and then thought better of it. "Okay, we'll work around it."

"You bet we will." She looked out the window. They'd turned onto a bumpy dirt road and the jungle foliage was crawling over the road, encroaching on both sides of the car. It was not only the weather that was oppressive. "Who is this Galen? Another employee?"

Logan nodded. "Sort of a freelance agent."

"Sort of?"

"We're here." Castleton turned a curve in the road and then screeched to a halt to avoid hitting the man standing in the middle of the road. "What the hell! Are you crazy, Galen?"

"That's been debated for decades." He grinned at Logan. "What am I going to do with you? You're always late. I have dinner on the table."

"You almost caused me to run off the road." Castleton turned off the ignition. "I wasn't expecting you to—"

"I didn't think there'd be any real danger. This is private property and you're the cautious type, Castleton. I knew you'd be meandering along at a snail's pace." He opened the back door of the car and gave a low whistle as he saw Monty on the floor. "Ah, the recipient of the dog biscuits in my backpack. I admit I'm a little disappointed. I thought they might be for you, Logan. I was hoping you'd acquired more adventurous tastes. Remember when you refused to eat those delicious grubs in that Maori settlement in—"

"This is Sean Galen," Logan interrupted. "Sarah Patrick and her dog, Monty."

"Delighted." Galen smiled as he helped her out of the car.

He was in his mid- to late thirties, a little over medium height, with a lithe and athletic body. His dark hair was cut close, but it persisted in curling and his eyes were as dark and irrepressible as his hair. Energy emanated from him in waves. "Do you like ham and macaroni casserole?"

British? He had a faint cockney accent. "Yes."

"Good. That's what's for dinner." He glanced down at Monty. "I might sneak some to you too. That dog food and vitamins I brought don't look awe-inspiring."

"So much for adventurous dining," Logan murmured.

"Well, I didn't know about the lady, but Castleton didn't impress me as being anything but a meat-and-potatoes man." He strode off to the side of the road. "This way. I set up camp some distance from those ruins. They depressed me."

For the first time, Sarah's gaze turned to the burned-out facility a few hundred yards ahead. She had been so filled with anger, worry, and resentment, she hadn't really thought about the people who had lived and died here. All those promising lives cut off by assassins' bullets . . .

"See? The lady's getting depressed too," Galen said. "Come on, Castleton. You can help me dish up."

"I have to get back to town."

"After dinner. Do you want to hurt my feelings?"

"I should . . ." Castleton shrugged and then followed Galen into the brush.

She stood looking after them for a moment. She felt as if she were being swept away and she wasn't sure she liked it.

"It's okay." Logan took her elbow. "He won't poison you. Galen's actually a gourmet cook."

"In the middle of the jungle?"

"In the middle of a hurricane. He adapts to any situation."

"I wasn't afraid of his poisoning me. He just surprised me."

"I can understand the feeling." He pushed her gently toward the side of the road. "He's surprised me a few times."

They were obviously old and good friends. "The grubs?"

"He didn't tell you I actually ate the damn things. He backed me in a corner where I had to do it or insult the Maoris."

"Just what are grubs?"

"Larvae. And they look disgustingly like worms."

"I thought so." She smiled. "I think I'm beginning to like your Mr. Galen."

"I thought that story would endear him to you." He was silent a moment. "You can trust him, Sarah. If anything happens to me, do what he says and he'll get you out."

She felt a chill she tried to ignore. "I'm not used to trusting anyone else to take care of me. Just what does he do for you?"

"I suppose you might call him a problem solver."

"Problems like this?"

"It's his specialty. So don't feel bad about letting him take over if things get rough."

"Do you let him take over?"

"Hell, yes."

She gazed at him skeptically. "I can't see you trusting anyone but yourself."

"I learned a long time ago how to delegate." He smiled. "Why else would I have gone after you?"

"I don't see you stepping aside and turning me loose to do my job."

"In spite of what you think of me, I can't shrug off responsibility."

"How long have you known Galen?"

"Fifteen years or so. I met him when I was in Japan. He was fresh out of the service and working for a local businessman."

"So you hired him away?"

"At that point in my life I couldn't afford him. I was struggling to keep a fledgling business afloat. We became involved in several projects together in the next few years. Then, when I began having personal problems, he helped me out."

What kind of personal problems? she wondered. She wasn't about to ask. She didn't want to know anything about his personal life. She just wanted to do the job and walk away. "And he's worked for you ever since?"

"On occasion." They had come into the clearing where Galen had set up camp. To her amazement, there was a table beside the fire with a damask tablecloth and colorful china. "What the hell?"

Galen looked up and grinned. "My mum always told me that you should never use a picnic as an excuse for ignoring the finer things in life."

"And you think this job is going to be a picnic?"

"It depends on how you look at it."

"How do you intend to transport all this stuff?"

"I don't. It's disposable. Isn't everything?"

"No."

He raised his brows. "Good. It's refreshing to meet someone who's not a cynic." He carefully dished up the macaroni. "Tell me, Logan, do these squiggly bits of pasta remind you of grubs?"

The casserole was excellent and the coffee Galen served afterward was even better. "I'm sorry, there's no dessert. Next time perhaps." He lifted a brow. "Are you going to wash up, Castleton? It's only fair."

Castleton got to his feet. "I have to get back to town. I've got to make final arrangements to get our people out of the hospital. Thanks for the meal. It was really very good."

Galen made a face. "Words of praise don't get those dishes done."

Logan stood up. "I'll walk you to the car, Castleton. There's something I want you to do for me."

"Sure." Castleton turned to Sarah. "Take care of yourself. Good luck."

"Thank you."

She watched Castleton and Logan stroll across the glade and into the trees, then she stood up and began stacking the plates.

"Sit down and have another cup of coffee," Galen said. "I was joking."

"I'm not. Fair is fair."

"Right. And you said you have to clip the pup." He nodded at Monty. "That's going to be quite a job with all that golden fluff. I want you to get some sleep tonight."

"It won't take that long. Monty's very good."

"Clip the pup," he said firmly as he took the dishes from her. "You might break my fine china."

"It's plastic."

"Oh, you noticed? The catalogue swore no one would be able to tell the difference."

She smiled. "They took you, Galen."

"The story of my life. Do you want me to get your clippers for you? They're in a backpack, along with all your supplies."

She wasn't going to win this one. In spite of Galen's easygoing manner, it was clear he also had a streak of iron. "I'll get them."

"That was quite a list you gave Logan."

She knelt and rummaged in the backpack. "I had to leave

without my equipment. You got all the bottled water? I can't have Monty getting sick."

"So the water is all for Monty?"

"Most of it. I can get along on less than he can." She sat down beside Monty. "Come on, boy. Let's get this stuff off you."

He sighed and rolled over on his stomach.

Galen chuckled. "You're right, he's good with it. Nice dog."

"Do you have any pets?"

He shook his head. "I'm on the move too much. I had a parrot once, but I gave him away. He was abusive and my ego couldn't take it. Now, your Monty would never be abusive."

"Don't count on it."

"Well, not verbally. He might lift his leg on something he shouldn't."

She nodded. "He always makes his displeasure known."

"But you're obviously soul mates. How long have you had him?"

"Four years. He was a year old when I saw him at the ATF training school." She smiled reminiscently. "He'd just flunked out of guide dog school and ATF picked him up."

"He flunked out?"

"Not because he wasn't smart enough," she said defensively. "He would just get distracted and that could have been a danger."

"Attention deficit disorder?"

"It's his nose. He was only a puppy and his sense of smell is probably the keenest ATF has ever run across. When he's constantly bombarded with scents, it's natural that he'd become distracted."

He held up his hands. "I didn't mean to insult your dog. I have too much respect for dogs. I've seen them work during combat conditions and I'd rather have one of them as a buddy than anyone on two legs."

"Sorry. I overreacted. Roll over, Monty." She started clipping his belly. "You have an accent. English?"

"I was born and raised in Liverpool."

"Logan says you met years ago in Japan."

He nodded. "When we were both young and green. Well, younger and greener. I was hard as nails and Logan was no pussycat even before Chen Li died."

"Chen Li?"

"His wife. She died of leukemia a few years after I met Logan. Not an easy death and not an easy time for him either. He was crazy about her."

Personal problems. Yes, that would be classified as personal problems. She wished she hadn't asked the question that had led to this revelation. So he'd had a tragedy in his life. Life was full of hard knocks. She would not feel sorry for him, dammit. "I'm sure he was able to handle it."

"Oh, yes, he handled it." Galen finished washing the last plate. "It turned him a little nuts for a while and then the scars formed and he was okay. We batted around the Pacific for about a year before he went back to Tokyo."

"That's when you introduced him to grubs?"

He smiled. "No, that was later. After the first edge had dulled. He would have broken my neck if I'd tried that the first year after Chen Li died." He looked at Monty appraisingly. "He looks like a big yellow bear without all that hair."

"At least he's cooler." She sat back on her heels and began to pick up the shorn hair on the ground. "I wonder where Logan is. He's been gone longer than I thought."

"He might have walked over to the ruins after he left Castleton." He frowned. "Nasty. They must have been like sitting ducks for Rudzak."

She shivered. "Why would he go there?"

"Maybe he didn't. But I'd bet on it. Logan feels very bad about what happened here. Perhaps he's trying to make some sense of it."

"I can't see Logan being that sensitive."

"But then, you don't want to see him like that, do you?" He wiped his hands on a towel. "Never mind. I'm bored with all this meaningful chatter. It offends my shallow soul. I need a bit of mindless recreation before I hit the sack. Do you play poker?"

"Why did you want to come back here?" Castleton swallowed hard as he glanced around the charred ruins. "God, it's hard for me. We're not going to find anything. I told you I'd retrieved every bit of information that wasn't destroyed. I didn't slip up, Logan."

"I believe you. I know how efficient you are." He didn't look at Castleton as he knelt and picked up a scorched wooden box. "What do you suppose was in this?"

"I don't know. Computer disks, maybe."

Logan was silent a moment. "Four dead. Carl Jenkins, Betty Krenski, Dorothy Desmond, Bob Simms. Did you know Betty Krenski was trying to adopt an HIV baby from an orphanage in South Africa?"

"Yes, but I didn't know that you did."

"She asked for my help. She said that someone had to care for those children. I tried to talk her out of it. Assuming responsibility for a baby with HIV is a heartbreaker."

"But you agreed to help her?"

"People have to make their own decisions. We can influence but we can't dictate. I told her if she still wanted to do it at the end of the year, I'd help her."

"I wish she'd gone through me. It was my job to take care of personal problems."

"Did you think I stopped being responsible for the people I sent down here when I hired you?"

"You're a busy man."

"Not that busy. This was a very special project to me. I read every one of their dossiers when you hired them, and I can quote passages from your monthly reports. I never met those people, but I felt as if I had."

"They were all good people. No one knows that better than me." Castleton paused. "I don't mean to be unsympathetic, but I have to go. I can't do anything about the people who were killed, but I can get those wounded into a hospital in the States."

"Yes, I know. You're in a hurry." He stood up. "And coming here must upset you."

"Why are we here?" Castleton repeated.

"I thought it fitting. Galen says I have no sense of ceremony or protocol, but that's not quite true. Not when it comes to this particular business."

"What business? What did you want me to do, Logan?"

"Just die." He whirled and smashed the ball of his hand upward under Castleton's nose, splintering the bones and driving them into his brain.

4

"Done?" Galen was standing in the middle of the path as Logan strode through the trees toward the campsite.

Logan nodded.

"What about disposal?"

"No one will find him."

He gazed at Logan curiously. "It's been a long time since you did a job like this. Did it bother you?"

"No."

"Not even a little? You've been a respectable businessman so long, I'd think you'd find it hard to revert to the old ways."

Logan's lips twisted. "I enjoyed it."

"I don't like traitors either. I told you I'd do it for you."

"I know. But it was my job. I chose him. If I'd kept a closer eye on Castleton, maybe I'd have sensed he'd turn Judas." His face darkened as he glanced over his shoulder. "All those lives . . ."

"It was probably a crime of opportunity. Castleton might have walked the straight and narrow if Rudzak hadn't tempted him."

"How tempting was it?"

"Sanchez said he was paid one million for helping them set up the attack on the facility, and he was to get another two when he lured you into the trap. How did you guess Castleton was in Rudzak's pay?"

"I didn't guess. I was just exploring every possibility. Castleton was conveniently in town when the attack occurred. I started from there. It could have been coincidence, but I couldn't take a chance on coincidence in a situation like this. I had to make sure. If he was dirty, then the lead he gave me to Sanchez would be bogus. Sanchez would be set up to give me the wrong information on how to find Rudzak, and I'd be led down the garden path straight into a trap. That's why I sent you to Sanchez."

"Because you knew how efficient I am."

"Because I couldn't have any more deaths on my hands. I thought the research center was safe here. But it wasn't safe. Rudzak found out about it."

"Stop beating yourself on the head. You didn't know Rudzak would turn up again. You thought he was in that prison in Bangkok."

"You're wrong. I always had a feeling he'd show up again."

"Then you should have had him killed in that prison. I offered to have it done." Galen glanced sideways at him. "Why didn't you?"

Logan didn't answer.

"I never could understand what went on between you and Rudzak. For a while I thought he was your best friend."

"So did I. Then he started to hate me. But he never let me see it until the end." He shrugged. "And he hates me more now. So maybe he was meant to get his shot at me."

"Fate?" Galen shook his head. "We make our own fate."

Logan agreed with that premise. He'd lived too long in the

Far East not to have acquired a healthy respect for the patterns life seemed to weave. But he believed only to a degree. "Maybe. I only know I was dead certain I'd be Rudzak's prime target when I heard he'd finally managed to bribe himself out of that prison two years ago."

"Two years is a long time. I was hoping he might have forgotten you."

"Be for real. After what I did to him? I've been waiting for him. I knew he'd have to reestablish contacts before he'd go after me. But, Christ, I was hoping he wouldn't find out about the research facility."

"How long has it been operating?"

"Three years."

"Progress?"

"Early stages, but promising. Very promising. Bassett was brilliant."

"Was?"

"Freudian slip. He may still be alive. But since money isn't Rudzak's prime motivation, it could go either way."

"That was my reading. We're going in regardless?"

Logan nodded. "I won't have Rudzak killing my people or hovering over me like a dark cloud any longer. We're taking him out."

"When we find him. Just how good is Sarah and her dog?"

"Do you think I'd be taking a chance on anyone I didn't think could perform? But I want you to watch out for her, Galen. If anything happens to me, get her and Monty out."

"I'll do everything I can." He was silent a moment. "You do know if Rudzak survives, she may be on his hit list too."

"I'm not a fool. That's one of the reasons I didn't tell Castleton about her and Monty. I'll make sure from now on that she's kept out of sight of any of Rudzak's men and hope for the best."

"And if the best doesn't happen?"

"I'll worry about it then. I need her." He changed the subject. "Something's been nagging at me. Rudzak may be playing games with—" He shook his head. "I don't know. I just feel uneasy. When he called, I felt he was giving me some kind of puzzle to solve."

"The decoy camp?"

"Maybe." He thought for a moment. "You know, he sent me a scarab just before he hit the facility. Chen Li's scarab."

"You didn't tell me that."

"I wasn't sure it had any meaning. I still don't."

"How did he get ahold of it?"

"He stole the entire collection from her bedroom before he left Tokyo. The police in Bangkok looked for it but didn't find it. I thought maybe he'd sold it and stashed the money. It would have been enough to get him out of a dozen prisons."

"Evidently he didn't sell it or he would have gotten out of that prison a lot earlier. It must have meant something to him."

"It meant something to him all right. He talked to Chen Li for years about ancient Egypt, tried to brainwash her for years. He bought her books and took her to museums. He gave her that scarab when she was only fifteen."

"Why go to all that trouble to—" Galen gave a low whistle. "That scheming asshole."

"And then I came along," Logan went on. "I think if Chen Li hadn't gotten sick, I would have had an untimely accident. And he might have gotten away with it." His lips twisted. "Like you said, I thought he was my best friend."

"Then maybe the scarab was some kind of taunt."

"Maybe. But I feel as if— Who the hell knows? That scarab just makes me uneasy. Has Sarah turned in?"

Galen grimaced. "After she beat me three games at poker. She could make her living in Las Vegas. Sharp."

"I know. She took me to the cleaners once when I first met her. She told me poker is the game of choice when the rescue teams are waiting to go to work at a disaster site."

"Well, let's hope this job doesn't qualify as a disaster." They had reached the campsite and he lowered his voice to avoid waking Sarah, who was lying with Monty beside her across from the fire. "What are the chances?"

"I bought time tonight. I figure we have two days before Rudzak gets suspicious. If we move fast and have surprise on our side . . . seven out of ten."

Galen dropped down on his bedroll. "We'll have to make sure of both. I have a lot of living to do. There are millions of people out there who haven't yet experienced my intelligence and charm."

"I'll keep that in mind." Logan stretched out on his bedroll and closed his eyes.

Death.

Galen was right. It had been a long time for Logan, but he hadn't felt a moment of hesitation. He had always believed in an eye for an eye. Primitive but fair.

Rudzak understood that philosophy. He had waited almost fifteen years to get Logan, and he was out there now, salivating.

Logan had gone over and over in his mind the possible targets. Which one would Rudzak pick next?

Screw him. No use worrying about future targets until Bassett was free and he had Sarah, Monty, Galen, and his team to help do that job.

And seven out of ten odds weren't that bad.

Seven out of ten.

Sarah stared into the darkness as she heard Logan lie down

across from her. Those were good odds, better than what she had gone up against in a dozen situations in her life. And the chances of survival for her and Monty had to be even greater because their part would be finished the moment Rudzak's camp was located. She would have no part in the attack, and even if Logan and Galen were captured or killed, she and Monty had the training and experience to survive alone in the jungle.

Jesus, that was cold.

No, it wasn't. She had a perfect right to preserve her life and that of Monty with no sense of guilt. She liked Galen, but he had been hired to do a job and evidently he was a mercenary who was paid well to take his chances. As for Logan, he was the one who had drawn all of them into this web. Even if his motive in rescuing his employee was compassionate, his methods were certainly not. No, she was in this alone and would act accordingly.

Monty whimpered and put his head on her arm, sensing her tension. She reached out to stroke, quiet him. No, she wasn't alone. Not as long as she had Monty. "Go to sleep, boy."

Scared?

She was scared. She'd been scared since the moment she'd caught sight of that burned-out research facility. *Premonition?*

Hell, no. Imagination.

But Monty wouldn't believe that, not when he could feel the tension tightening her muscles.

She gently stroked his throat. "A little, but it's okay."

He relaxed. Monty knew about fear. How sometimes you had to keep on going even if you were scared. Once he'd crawled down a tunnel in a crushed parking garage when he'd caught scent of a victim. She'd gone in after him and the shaft had crashed down behind them. There had been no going back, and there had been nothing but darkness and fear ahead. She had felt Monty trembling beside her and could smell his fear and her own. He could have frozen, but he'd crawled on his belly through the long tunnel, guiding her until she could see light ahead.

If they survived that nightmare, they could survive anything.

And seven out of ten odds weren't bad at all.

"Wake up. It's time to leave."

Sarah's eyes flew open to see Logan's face above her. "Okay." She sat up and threw aside her blanket. "Monty."

Monty stretched and then trotted over to the nearest tree to take care of morning business.

"Here's your backpack." Logan dropped it beside her. "I took a few bottles out and put them in mine. I didn't have room for many."

"I don't need your help. I could have managed."

"I wasn't being gentlemanly." Logan was smiling, but the words were crisp. "I can't afford to have you falling behind."

She put on the backpack. "I won't fall behind. You worry about keeping up with me. This stroll through the jungle is going to be a little more demanding than playing tennis at one of your fancy country clubs." She looked around and suddenly realized they were the only two in the clearing. "Where's Galen?"

"He went on ahead."

"Why?"

"To take care of a few things. We have information that Rudzak may have set up a decoy camp about ten miles to the west. Galen will join us later."

"And what direction are we taking?"

"East." Logan was putting out the fire. "We should reach the search area by noon. After that, it's up to you and Monty."

"Right. Do you have anything belonging to Bassett?"

"Margaret expressed me an old baseball cap he'd left in his locker at the Silicon Valley plant. But he hasn't been home in six months. Will the scent still be strong enough?"

"Probably. But couldn't Castleton have gotten you something down here belonging to him?"

"No." Logan turned away. "That wasn't an option."

"Why wasn't it—"

"Does Monty eat this early?"

She shook her head. "He can do that after we've been on the trail for a while."

"Then let's get going."

No question about breakfast for her. He was as cold and efficient as a surgeon's scalpel and she didn't like the fact that he hadn't told her earlier about the decoy camp. "Do you suppose I could brush my teeth and go to the bathroom?"

The sarcasm didn't faze him. "If you hurry."

She stiffened when she saw his gaze go to the trees at the edge of the clearing. "What are you looking at? Do you think someone's watching us?"

"No, Galen reconnoitered the area before he set up camp, and he didn't think it was necessary to take turns on guard duty last night."

She hadn't been aware there had even been a discussion about setting up guards. She had thought they were safe for at least that one night. "Then why are you behaving as if you think someone is—"

"It doesn't hurt to be careful. Rudzak seldom does the expected." He moved toward the trees. "But this time neither are we."

• • •

They stopped to eat at ten and reached the search site at twelve forty-five. By that time Sarah's shirt was plastered to her body with perspiration, but Monty was still moving swiftly. She gave him his third bowl of water and sank down beside him as he drank it.

"We need to hurry." Logan had come back to stand beside her.

"Fifteen minutes. Monty needs rest." She took off her backpack, then took a drink of water herself. "From now on we'll be leading, not following. Give me Bassett's cap."

He reached into his pack, pulled out a faded Giants ball cap, and tossed it to her.

She put it aside and dug into her pack for the canvas utility belt. It was a little large, and she took out her knife and cut additional holes. Then she got out Monty's leash and tossed it on top of the utility belt.

"Why do you need the utility belt?" Logan asked.

"I probably won't need it this time, but I always wear it when I'm on a search. When I put it on, it's a signal to Monty that we're going to go to work." She leaned back against a tree. "I'd advise you to rest. If Monty catches the scent, we'll stop only to give him water."

He sat down across from her and took off his hat. "Okay, I could use some rest."

He didn't look tired. He looked tough as hell. His shirt was as damp with perspiration as hers was, but she could feel the waves of energy and tension he was emitting. Was the tension caused by fear? Maybe. But if he was afraid, he wouldn't give in to it. He was totally relentless as he had led her through the jungle.

She stroked Monty's head. "You set a pretty hard pace."

"I told you we were in a hurry." He smiled sardonically. "I'm sorry if you were disappointed. I know you would have enjoyed leaving me in the dust."

"You're in good shape," she said grudgingly.

"It must be all that tennis at the country club."

"Maybe." At that moment she couldn't imagine him in a country-club setting. He looked more like a scruffy gunrunner than a tycoon. After a short silence she asked, "What's Galen up to?"

"What?"

"You said Galen was taking care of a few things. What's he planning on doing? Or aren't I supposed to know?"

"You want details? I thought you weren't interested in anything but your and Monty's involvement."

"This does involve us. If you manage to get yourselves killed, I want a decent chance of getting out of this jungle. What's Galen doing?"

"Attacking the decoy camp."

Her eyes widened. "By himself?"

"No, Galen's good, but he's not Superman. When he's ready, he'll radio for his team to come in by helicopter."

"How many are in his team?"

"Twelve."

"Against how many of Rudzak's men?"

"Our informant, Sanchez, said at least twenty. That leaves eight at the real camp, where Bassett should be."

"And the plan?"

"Galen's unit hits the decoy camp and makes Rudzak think we've fallen into the trap. Galen pretends to get out by the skin of his teeth and proceeds to the main camp to rendezvous with us. We get Bassett out, hop on the helicopter, and head for home."

Her lips twisted. "Very simple."

"Not simple at all. If Galen's not convincing enough,

Rudzak will head back to the base immediately and we'll be in deep shit."

"Why even go after the decoy?"

"Rudzak will be getting suspicious that he hasn't heard from Sanchez or his man in Santo Camaro. If an attack on the decoy doesn't occur by tonight, then he'll think we're onto him and we'll lose the element of surprise." He glanced at Monty. "That's why Monty has to find this base by nightfall."

"I can't promise that. What do we do if we don't find it? What if Rudzak isn't fooled by Galen's attack?"

"Then we try to get out of the jungle before Rudzak tracks us down."

There were too many things that could go wrong. She didn't like it.

"I don't like it either." He was reading her expression. "But it's our best shot." He got to his feet. "Monty's had his fifteen minutes. Let's go."

She slowly stood up and looked at the sun. Seven, maybe eight hours until nightfall.

"Ready?"

"Yes." She didn't look at Logan as she picked up the utility belt and fastened it around her middle.

Monty froze, his gaze on the belt. Then he jumped to his feet.

"Time to go to work." She took Bassett's hat and let him sniff it. "Find."

He whirled and took off running.

"Won't we lose him?" Logan asked.

"No, he'll keep coming back. When he catches the scent, I'll put on his leash and run with him."

"You're afraid he'll get excited and not come back?"

"No." She started in the direction Monty had taken. "I'm

afraid some son of a bitch will shoot him, and I want to be there to protect him."

Two hours later Monty had still not caught the scent.

"I think we're going around in circles," Logan said with a frown.

"We might be." Sarah pushed through a screen of palms. "But Monty knows what he's doing."

"Does he? He's not even sniffing the ground."

She gave him an impatient glance over her shoulder. "He's scenting the air. He doesn't always have to keep his nose to the ground. Air scenting is much more accurate in cases like this. He lifts his nose high and waves it back and forth until he catches the large end of the cone."

"Cone?"

"Bassett's scent will be dispersed downwind in a cone-shaped pattern. The smaller end will be centered around his body, and as the distance from him grows, the cone widens over a large area. Monty will find the large end of the cone and then work back and forth as it narrows until it leads him to Bassett. Are you sure they're encamped and not moving?"

"So my source told Galen. Would that make a difference?"

"Of course it would," she snapped. "Even if Monty finds the scent, he could lose it again and have to start all over again."

"Sorry. Just asking. This is all new to me."

It would have been new to most people, and she wouldn't have snapped at him if she hadn't been so frustrated. It wasn't unusual for a search to take this long, but she had found herself looking behind every tree, afraid to let Monty out of her sight. God, she wished this were over.

"Will you jump on my ass again if I ask you how long this could take?"

"Monty can't go by your time schedule. It will take as long as it takes. He's doing his best, dammit."

"I know," he said quietly. "Is there anything I can do to help?"

She drew a deep breath. "No, there's nothing either of us can do. It's all up to Monty. We're lucky it's so hot. Bassett's body will be producing a stronger scent."

He grimaced. "At the moment I don't feel lucky."

Neither did Sarah. She felt acutely on edge and so hot, she couldn't breathe.

Find him, Monty. Find him and let's go home.

It was over an hour later that she heard Monty bark.

Relief surged through her. "Thank God."

"He's found something?" Logan asked.

"I think so. I taught him not to bark until he caught the scent. If he comes back to get me, we'll know that he's—"

Monty bounded toward her, barking up a storm, tail wagging with excitement.

"He's got it." She took the leash out of her backpack and fastened it to his collar. "Come on."

"Can you stop him from barking? We don't want to alert—"

"He barks only to signal me when he's on a search. If I'm with him, there's no need for him to bark." She broke into a fast trot to keep pace with Monty. "Keep up, Logan. We can't wait for you."

Christ, she was tough, Logan thought.

Sarah was moving at almost a run ahead of him, weaving, pushing through the brush, pausing occasionally to let Monty sniff the air before taking off again. She must be as tired as he was, but she had kept going at this speed for over an hour.

During the last ten minutes the pace had picked up and Monty's eagerness had intensified.

Logan's own breath was coming in gasps, and he could see Sarah's shoulders rise and fall as she struggled to force the hot, muggy air into her lungs. She was covering the ground with the same speed and concentration as her dog.

Then she skidded to a halt.

Logan froze in place as she motioned him to stop. Monty was silent but pulled eagerly, frantically, at the leash. Sarah put her hand on his head, and he instantly quieted. Then she turned and strode back to Logan. "There's something up ahead. I think he's found the source."

"How do you know?"

"I just know, dammit." She glared at him. "And I'm not going to take Monty any farther and chance having some guard shoot him."

"No one's asking you to." He took off his backpack and set it on the ground. "I'll go ahead and make sure before I radio Galen."

"And probably get shot yourself." She scowled. "You don't have to check for yourself just because I don't have any proof that the camp's up ahead. I tell you, Monty *knows*."

"And you know what Monty knows." He opened his backpack. "I believe you. I have a great respect for instinct. Just stay here."

"Of course we'll stay here. Why should I—" She stopped as she saw the assault weapon he pulled out of his backpack. "Shit. No wonder you had room for only a couple bottles of water." She moistened her lips. "Do you even know how to use that thing?"

He smiled. "Oh, yes, I know how to use it. I took lessons at the country club."

Thirty minutes passed.

Then fifteen minutes.

Why the hell wasn't he back? Sarah wondered. He'd probably been caught or killed. Just because she hadn't heard anything didn't mean anything. Not all weapons were as loud as that gun Logan had handled with suspicious familiarity. It was clear his time with Galen had been spent in more deadly pursuits than recovering from grief over his wife's death.

Monty whimpered, his gaze on the dense foliage where Logan had disappeared. He wanted to go too. His search had been cut short and he didn't understand why he couldn't bring it to a satisfactory end.

Find?

"No, it will be okay. We don't have to go after him. Logan will do it."

But where was Logan?

Why was she so worried? She and Monty could find their way out of this jungle. She didn't care about Logan. He had caused her nothing but trouble.

But he didn't deserve to die when he was trying to save a life. He might be totally relentless, but he wasn't a murderer like those men in the camp.

No sound but the shrill sound of birds.

Then Monty's tail started to wag and he rose to his feet.

Relief surged through her. He was coming. She couldn't hear him or smell him, but Monty could.

It was another five minutes before Logan appeared through the leaves. "The camp's there." He moved toward his backpack as Monty ran to him, whimpering in an ecstasy of greeting. "About a mile ahead."

"I told you. What took so long?"

He knelt down and gave Monty an affectionate pat, then reached into his backpack for his radio. "I don't flatter myself that you were worried about me."

"No," she said coolly. "Monty was worried. I was just curious. Could you tell if Bassett was there?"

He gave Monty a hug and then pushed him away. "There's a tent with a guard posted out in front. I'm assuming Bassett's inside. The camp's small. Six tents and the numbers Sanchez gave us seem accurate."

"Did you run into anyone patrolling the area?"

"One man. I managed to avoid him."

"Obviously, or you wouldn't be here."

"Not so obviously. Another pinprick at my ego. But if I'd taken him out, it might have triggered an alert."

"So now you call Galen and get him here? Won't the people in the camp hear the helicopter?"

"The pilot will drop Galen and his men off at the clearing we passed about a mile north. We'll rendezvous with them there. Then the pilot will pick us up at Rudzak's camp when it's clear."

Her mouth tightened. "You mean when everyone's killed."

"I mean when we've gotten Bassett out." He looked directly into her eyes. "Whatever that takes." He bent over the radio. "You can lecture me later. We'll have plenty of time. I figure at least an hour before Galen gets here. Now I've got to talk to him and tell him to attack the decoy camp."

"Six dead. One wounded," Carl Duggan told Rudzak. "But we managed to repel the attack and save the helicopter. And I think we got one of their men. Shall we go after the rest?"

Rudzak gazed around the camp. Two tents were in flames and Duggan was wrong. Rudzak could see seven dead. It had been a savage attack and brilliantly executed. "I didn't see Logan. Did you?"

Duggan shook his head. "But Galen was there and he's Logan's hired man."

Rudzak gave him a scathing glance. "I know that."

"Shall we go after them?" Duggan repeated. "It doesn't have to end here. Give me a chance and we'll still capture them."

"Shut up, I'm thinking." Galen and not Logan. The attack had been brutal, but had Galen been repelled too easily? Seven deaths but no push to completion of the mission.

"I have the men waiting," Duggan said. "We don't want to lose them."

Duggan didn't realize they had probably already lost them. They had not heard a helicopter, but no doubt Galen had one if he intended to get his men out alive.

And transport them quickly to another location.

Ah, Logan, you think you've fooled me.

"We won't lose them." Rudzak turned away. "I know where they're going."

It was almost nightfall when Galen and his men were dropped off at the glade where Logan and Sarah waited. They streamed out of the helicopter like a Delta Force. Galen's expression was grim as he waved the helicopter to leave before turning to Logan. "Let's go."

Logan turned to Sarah. "Stay here until you hear the helicopter come back. Then come to the camp. We won't radio the pilot until it's safe for him to land."

"How long do you estimate that taking?" Sarah asked.

"At least forty-five minutes." He shrugged. "Maybe longer. Just don't come until you hear the helicopter."

"I've no intention of getting close," Sarah said. "My involvement in this is over. We've done our job."

"Come on, Logan." Galen was moving down the path into

the forest, closely followed by his men. "I lost a man to Rudzak. Let's get this bullshit over." The words were curt and his attitude was different from when she had first met him. This was Galen the mercenary, and it was an intimidating change.

The entire situation was intimidating, Sarah thought as she watched the men disappear from view. What was she doing in the middle of a jungle with a bunch of mercenaries and Logan, who carried that damn assault weapon as casually as if it were a briefcase?

Monty pressed closer to her, his gaze on the path.

"No, we wait here, Monty." So many others could die to save a man who might already be dead. Galen had said one of his men had already been killed.

Logan could die.

Don't think about it. Just sit here and listen for the helicopter.

Ten minutes.

Twenty.

Thirty.

Thirty-five minutes passed before she heard the helicopter.

Faint.

Far away.

But coming closer every second.

She snapped the leash on Monty. "Come on, boy."

He eagerly bounded down the path in front of her, dragging her forward through the brush. He knew exactly where he was going even if she didn't.

Gunshots.

Explosions.

She caught sight of the camp and it looked like a war zone. Acrid smoke. Bodies. Blood. Fighting. She stopped on the path, staring in astonishment. What was going on here? When the helicopter came back, the battle was supposed to be over. It wasn't over.

"What the hell are you doing here?" Logan was beside her. "Never mind. Just don't come any closer." He said over his shoulder, "Bassett, stay with her."

The tall, lanky man behind him nodded. "I'm not moving a muscle until you come back for me. That's a promise."

Logan turned and ran back toward the camp.

5

"This is no time for introductions, but I'm Tom Bassett," the man standing beside Sarah said. "And you are?"

"Sarah Patrick." Her tone was abstracted, her gaze on Logan.

What the hell are you doing here? Logan had said.

"I've no idea why you're here, but I'm very glad to see you. Hell, I'm glad to see anyone but those stooges of Rudzak's." Bassett shook his head. "I thought my goose was well and truly cooked. When I saw Logan burst into my tent, I wanted to kiss him."

"I believe that would have upset him."

If Logan had not expected her, then they had not radioed for the helicopter?

But the helicopter was coming. She had heard it.

Dear God.

"Stay here." She ran toward the camp. She could still see Logan making his way through the smoke toward where Galen was standing. She and Monty dodged across the campsite to stand next to them.

Logan was not pleased to see her. "I told you to—"

"Shut up. Do you think I came here just because I wanted to see you kill and maim someone? Did you radio for the helicopter?"

"Not yet."

"Well, I heard a helicopter, dammit. And if it wasn't Galen's pilot, who do you think it was?"

He stiffened. "Shit. Rudzak. You're sure?"

"I've ridden in enough helicopters to know that sound in my sleep. Your red herring didn't work."

"How close?"

"Not close then, but they could be almost on top of us by now."

Galen turned away. "I'll radio for pickup." He waved his arm and shouted to his men. "We're pulling out."

"Tell the pilot to go to the clearing," Logan said. "We have to make a run for it back there."

"Take Bassett and get out of here. We'll be right behind you. It's not—"

Rotors. Loud. Close.

Sarah's heart jumped. She couldn't see the helicopter through the palms, but it must have been near and getting nearer every minute.

Logan took her arm. "Run for it. I'll get Bassett."

She didn't have to be told twice. "Monty!"

Branches hit her in the face as she tore through the jungle with Monty beside her.

The helicopter flew over her, almost on top of the camp.

Bullets.

The helicopter was spraying firepower on the camp below.

Logan and Bassett were next to her now.

More shots from the helicopter.

Galen and his men were behind them, then passing them as they raced toward the clearing.

It was scarcely a mile. It seemed a thousand.

Her lungs ached as she tried to force air into them. God, she was afraid. Stop it. Fear was always the enemy. She had been afraid before and survived. She'd survive now.

The clearing was up ahead. Would the helicopter be there?

It was landing as they burst out of the jungle. Galen's men weren't even waiting until it hit the ground to jerk open the door and tumble into the aircraft. Galen was standing by the door waving his men inside before he jumped in himself.

Bassett reached the helicopter and Galen pulled him inside. "Logan," Galen called. "Hurry. Get the hell inside. They must have spotted us. I hear them coming."

"So do I." Logan was looking up at the sky. "Get Sarah and the dog inside."

She glanced over her shoulder and saw Rudzak's helicopter flying low and fast toward them.

"Hurry." Galen reached for Sarah's hand.

"Monty," she called, and the retriever jumped inside the helicopter with her.

Bullets. Spraying the clearing from Rudzak's helicopter.

Logan moved away from the helicopter, lifted his weapon, and released a hail of bullets at the approaching helicopter.

Another spray of bullets.

"Logan!" Galen shouted.

Logan was down, blood streaming from his thigh. "Get out of here, Galen."

"The hell I will." Galen jumped out of the helicopter.

But Monty was ahead of him, already running toward Logan.

"Monty!" Sarah screamed.

Monty began tugging at Logan's shirt, trying to move him.

Sarah dove out of the helicopter.

More bullets.

Monty. Still. Bleeding.

"No!" She sank to her knees beside Monty. He was still breathing. Thank God.

"Get back in the helicopter." Galen was squatting beside her. "I'll take care of Logan."

"She'll never leave Monty. Get the dog first, Galen," Logan said. "Dammit, get the dog first."

"He's my dog. I'll do—" Sarah broke off when Galen picked up Monty.

"Go take care of your dog," Logan told her. "Galen will—"

"Shut up." She picked up Logan in a fireman's lift and struggled to her feet. Jesus, he was heavy. Three steps and she had him in the helicopter. "Lift off."

More shots.

What if they hit the fuel tank?

"Cover fire," Galen snapped.

Sarah was only dimly aware that Galen's men were shooting as she cradled Monty in her arms. He opened his eyes and licked her arm. The helicopter lifted and headed north, barely skimming the trees.

Oh, God, Rudzak's aircraft was right behind them.

Then, suddenly, it was gone.

"Got him." Galen's gaze was on Rudzak's helicopter, which was slowly spiraling to the ground. "We must have hit something crucial. He's trying to get back to the clearing to land. I hope he gets a palm tree up his ass. Too bad we used the last of our missiles back at the camp." He turned to Logan. "You always did cause me trouble. Somebody pass me the first aid kit and I'll try to stop the blood."

"How's the . . . dog?" Logan whispered.

"I'm tending to him." Sarah was pressing a compress to Monty's wound. "I think he's going to be okay. The bullet only skimmed his shoulder and he's not bleeding much." She glanced at Galen. "Do you need help taking care of Logan? I've had training."

Logan tried to smile. "Yeah, she went to vet school. She can take care of my fleas at the same time."

She ignored him and spoke to Galen. "I've also had EMT training."

"Galen can handle it," Logan said. "Just make sure—the dog's okay. I know I'll be on your hit list if anything happens to him."

"You're right." She felt angry and scared and, yes, guilty that Monty had been hurt. She had placed him in harm's way. There was no doubt Logan was ultimately responsible, but he had ordered Galen to save Monty first even though his life had been in danger. "I'll care for Monty. Worry about yourself."

His eyes closed. "Too—much trouble. Galen, you—do it."

He passed out.

Logan didn't regain consciousness until they were transferring him to the jet at Santo Camaro.

"About time you came back to us," Galen said. "You've caused me no end of trouble and made a mess of my copter. Of course, the pooch didn't help."

"He's alive?"

"In better shape than you. Sarah's bandaged him and is trying to keep him still."

"Where is she?"

"Inside the plane with Monty and Bassett." Galen paused. "You still have a bullet in your thigh. I didn't think there'd be any additional damage if I let you go back to the States and have it taken out there. Sarah didn't think so either. So we plugged you up and she'll give you a shot of morphine once you take off. Where do you want to go? Monterey?"

He tried to think. His mind was so blurry, he already felt as if he had the morphine. "It depends on whether Rudzak's alive. Go back and check and phone me. It would be nice if the bastard crashed and burned, but we're probably not that lucky."

Galen nodded. "I was going anyway. I thought you'd want to be certain one way or the other."

"And don't let her give me the morphine. Tell her you just remembered I'm allergic to it or something. I need to know about Rudzak as soon as possible."

"Why not tell her the truth?"

"And let her find out this may be only the beginning? I promised her when we found Bassett, her part would be over, but the situation's changed and I don't know how it's going to affect her. I'm not up to handling her right now. I have to stall."

"And what do I tell the pilot?"

"Just tell him to get us out of South American airspace and I'll give him his orders when I hear from you."

"Okay, but it's a long flight and you're going to hurt like hell."

"I'm hurting like hell now, but Rudzak had to have seen her and Monty. If he's alive, then he may try to take her out first. She's an easier target and it's pretty clear he doesn't want me dead before he can make me suffer."

"Are you going to tell her that?"

"Not if I can help it. It may get in the way and she's pissed enough at me. I just have to be wherever she is to keep Rudzak in check."

"You're not exactly in prime condition to keep anyone in

check. You could get protection for her. You don't have to do it yourself."

"I made her a promise." He smiled crookedly. "And, hell, I probably owe her for more than Bassett now."

"You mean for picking you up and throwing you into the helicopter? It's possible. Seconds were counting at that point." Galen grinned. "And it was an interesting role reversal. Do you suppose she has Amazon blood?"

"All I know is that I could have done without that particular guilt trip." He closed his eyes. "Get me in that plane and go back and check on Rudzak. I have to know."

Logan's eyes were closed, but Sarah knew he wasn't asleep. His mouth was compressed and deep lines were engraved on either side of his lips.

She sat down on the bed beside him. "Take this."

Logan's eyes opened and looked at the glass in her hand. "What is it?"

"Tylenol." She popped two tablets on his tongue. "You're not allergic to that too, are you?"

He shook his head as he swallowed the water. "Thanks."

"Tough luck about the morphine allergy. The Tylenol may help a little. I gave some to Monty too."

"Then I know it's a surefire remedy. You might take chances with my health but never with Monty's. How is he?"

"Better than you."

"That must give you some satisfaction. After all, I was responsible for his being hurt."

"It doesn't give me any satisfaction. I hate violence. I never wanted you to be shot." She glanced away from him. "And you told Galen to save Monty before you. Not many men would have done that for a dog."

"Don't give me too much credit. I'm not the selfless type. I wanted to tell Galen to get me the hell on that helicopter."

"But you didn't." She was still not looking at him. "And I've always found it's what you do and not what you think that's the bottom line. Fear's always there."

"Is it?"

"If you're not stupid." She rose to her feet. "I have to get back to Monty. You're probably in too much pain to sleep, but you can try."

"I'm expecting a call from Galen. If I do fall asleep, will you see that I wake up to take it?"

"It's that important? You need to sleep."

"Will you wake me?"

She lifted her shoulders. "Sure. Why not? You're the one who's going to suffer for it."

"How's Bassett doing?"

"Okay. He's covered with mosquito bites and he's got a bad case of nerves. He wants to call his wife."

Logan shook his head. "Not now. Tell him not to worry. She wasn't told he was missing."

"But why can't he call her?"

"It could cause problems. He may not be able to go home yet."

"Isn't that his choice? He's had a rough time." She rubbed her temple. "We've all had a rough time. I'd spit in your eye if you tried to keep me from going back to the ranch."

"Would you?"

"You bet your life. Why shouldn't he go home?"

He didn't answer.

She said slowly, "You're worried about Rudzak?"

"He could still be alive, and he thought Bassett was valuable enough to take as a hostage before. I may have to find a secure place for him for a while."

"What if he won't go? His nerves are already shot, and it would be like being put in another prison."

"Maybe it won't be necessary. I hope not."

"It should be Bassett's choice. Not yours."

"It became my choice when Rudzak destroyed that research facility. Everything Rudzak does is aimed directly at me. I'm the only one who can deflect him."

"You talk as if it's some kind of contest."

"It's no contest. It's a war and Rudzak's as tenacious as a bulldog."

"Don't malign any dog by comparing him to that murderer. He tried to kill Monty."

He smiled. "I wonder what it would take to make you care as much for a human being as you do that dog."

"Unswerving loyalty, courage, humor, companionship, intelligence, and the willingness to give his life for me."

He gave a low whistle. "You're tough."

"You asked me. Total commitment is almost impossible between individuals. That's why I like dogs more than I do most people. It's a hell of a lot safer."

"You've found that?"

"Haven't you?" She felt his gaze on her back as she walked away from him. He was wounded and in pain, and yet he was still trying to pull Bassett's strings. What a surprise. He'd probably have to be in his coffin before he'd give up control.

Maybe she wasn't being fair. He was trying to help Bassett.

Well, she was too tired to be fair, she thought as she sat down beside Monty. Her emotions were in shreds and she was so tired, she was almost numb. She wanted only to go home and rest.

She glanced at Bassett, who was curled up asleep in the chair across the aisle. He deserved to go back to his wife and kid. He should never have gotten caught up in any project with a man as dangerous as Logan. What was she thinking? But she had not really thought of Logan as dangerous until the past few days. On the surface he was a powerful and eminently respectable businessman. Bassett had probably thought himself lucky to hitch his wagon to a star of Logan's magnitude. Well, not Sarah. She had done her job and was through with Logan.

Monty made a sound deep in his throat and she quickly bent to stroke his side. "I know it hurts. It will be over soon. We're going home."

"I think it's a displaced clavicle," Duggan said. "It must hurt like hell. You'd better not walk any farther."

"Don't be an idiot. I have to keep going. Give me a minute and I'll be able to go on." Rudzak leaned back against the tree, closed his eyes, and let the waves of pain wash over him. He had learned in prison that it was better to accept pain than to fight it. Another lesson he owed to Logan. "Did you radio Mendez and ask him to send another helicopter?"

"Yes, he said that he'd have it waiting for us at the cliffs."

The cliffs. Five miles away. It might as well be fifty in the shape he was in. Dammit, why did the helicopter have to crash? All his plans blown in a moment. "You told him I was hurt?"

Duggan avoided his glance. "He said this wasn't company business and that he wouldn't chance involving his men in a confrontation with Galen. He'll be glad to help you if you reach an area that's relatively safe."

He should have known. Company business was the only passion in Mendez's life, and as long as Rudzak kept the profits coming in, the drug baron would continue to pour unlimited funds into his bank account. If Rudzak did anything that harmed business, he'd be cut loose quicker than the blink of an eye. Mendez needn't worry. Rudzak would do nothing to damage their relationship. Money was God in this world, and he needed money to unleash a lightning bolt at Logan.

"I could call him back," Duggan said. "Maybe he didn't realize—"

"He realized exactly what he was doing." Which meant he had to get to those cliffs before Galen and his team returned. "Help me up."

Agony shot through his upper body as Duggan got him to his feet. It would be all right, he told himself. Accept the pain. Make it work for you. Turn it into hate.

He knew all about hate. Fifteen years . . .

"Do you want to lean on me?" Duggan asked.

"No." He staggered down the trail. Keep going. Ignore the pain. Think about Logan. Plan the next move. "As soon as we get to Bogotá I want you to arrange transport to the U.S."

"We have to get you to a doctor before—"

"That won't take long. If it's a displaced clavicle, it can be put back. I want to be en route by tomorrow. I don't want Logan to feel safe."

"And we're going to Silicon Valley?"

Duggan was zeroing in on his principal interest. No harm; it would keep him focused. But there were so many more facets to revenge than he was capable of seeing. "Yes, but first I have to check and see if—" He stopped to get his breath as another wave of pain shot through him. Fight it. Clear your mind. "I saw a woman and a dog. . . . She helped Logan get to the helicopter. Find out who she is."

"As soon as I can."

"Right away. I know Logan. He can be very soft when he's grateful to someone. I've exploited that weakness myself." The pain was getting hard to suppress. But he mustn't be discouraged just because one thing had gone wrong.

I'm coming, Logan. Do you feel my hate? You will soon. It will burn you and everyone around you to cinders.

"He's alive," Galen said over the phone. "We found the helicopter, but he'd managed to land it. No sign of him or any of his men."

Logan cursed. "Keep looking."

"I am, but it's my bet he's safe in drug heaven somewhere in the hills."

"Not for long. He'll be on the move as soon as he can."

"But we may have a break for a little while. What's the plan?"

"I'm working on it. But right now we have to wait for him to make a move. Have Margaret contact the FBI and ATF and tell them we've had an anonymous threat and to give my plants and research facilities additional protection."

"Including Dodsworth?"

Logan didn't answer for a moment. "No, not Dodsworth. She's not to tell them about Dodsworth. I've already tripled the security there. Dodsworth will be safe."

"Don't sell Rudzak short."

"You don't have to tell me that."

"Easy."

"I don't feel easy." Dammit, Logan had hoped that Rudzak had been taken out. "Try to find him. If you can't locate him, find someone who can point the way. We need to know what he's up to." He had to think through the pain throbbing through him. "Oh, and tell Margaret to make the pilot head for Phoenix and have a surgeon ready in my house there to take out this damn bullet."

"Phoenix?"

"The house has security. I'll double it and set up quarters for Bassett there."

"What about Sarah Patrick?"

"My chances of getting her to stay at the house are slim to none. Arrange surveillance and protection for her cabin, but make sure she's not aware of it."

"Done. And what about you? You're the one Rudzak wants to slaughter and hang out to dry."

"I'm safe for now."

"Oh, yeah? You have a bullet in your leg to prove how safe you are."

"I think Rudzak would have been very upset if that bullet had killed me. He wants to torture me first. He told me so."

"Just hope he doesn't change his mind." Galen hung up.

Rudzak wouldn't change his mind, Logan thought wearily. He had planned his revenge too long.

"Monty wanted to come." Sarah was standing beside him with Monty in her arms and carefully placed the dog on the floor beside Logan's couch. "He's got that sore shoulder, and I couldn't stop him from trying to crawl over to you. He knows you're hurt and he wants to comfort you. Now that you've gotten your call, will you go to sleep? I don't want Monty disturbed any more than he is right now."

"I'll go to sleep." He reached down and stroked the retriever's head. "I wouldn't want Monty disturbed."

She took the phone from him and put it on the end table. "What about Rudzak?"

"Alive."

"And what are you going to do about it?"

"Wait. Watch. Try to find him." He paused. "But Bassett will have to go to the secured house in Phoenix for his own protection."

"Why there?"

"Why not? It's a pleasant enough place. You stayed there yourself for a while with Eve. I don't suppose you'd want to live there until Monty has recovered?"

"No way. I want to go home."

That's what he'd been afraid of. "Do you mind if we go to the house first before I have you taken home? I need to get this bullet out."

"The house instead of a hospital?"

"Hospitals ask questions."

"Doctors are bound by law to report gunshot wounds."

"But they can often be persuaded to delay or forget the report."

"Money?"

"Or influence. Or even a charitable donation. Doctors see so much suffering, sometimes they weigh legalities against a contribution that can help heal thousands."

"And risk their license."

"It's their choice, Sarah." He closed his eyes. "Now go away and let me and Monty sleep. I'm tired of defending myself."

"In a minute." He heard the sound of pouring water and opened his eyes to see Sarah setting down the carafe. She handed him two more Tylenol. "You can take these now. I don't want you restless and disturbing—"

"Monty," he finished for her. He swallowed the pills and closed his eyes again. "I'll try not to thrash around and bother your dog."

"Monty wouldn't care. It's his nature to want to comfort." She tucked the blanket around him with a gentleness that belied the briskness of her tone. "But I care for him. Go to sleep."

He was already half asleep as he heard her move away from him. It wasn't only Monty's nature to want to comfort. In spite of Sarah's resentment toward him, she found it impossible not to try to ease his pain and equally impossible to admit to that softness.

A truly remarkable woman . . .

"Bring him into the living room. It's already set up as an operating room." A plump, fortyish woman in a pinstriped suit was standing outside the house, waiting, when the ambulance doors opened and Logan was lifted to the ground. "How are you doing, John?"

"Okay."

"You don't look okay. You're pale as a tombstone. This was incredibly stupid of you." She walked beside his stretcher. "And you've caused me a great deal of trouble. Do you know how difficult it is to arrange this kind of thing with any kind of confidentiality?"

"Sorry." He looked back over his shoulder at Sarah. "This is my assistant, Margaret Wilson. Ask her for anything you need."

"I'll be fine. Stop worrying about me."

To her surprise, he reached out his hand to her. She took a step closer to the stretcher and enfolded his hand in hers.

His grasp tightened as he looked up at her. "Stay," he whispered. "Stay, Sarah."

"I'm not going anywhere right away."

"I'll take that as a promise." He glanced at his assistant. "Take care of her, Margaret. She needs to—"

"Shut up," Margaret said. "I'll take care of everything. You just let Dr. Dowden take care of this stupidity you've gotten yourself into before you lose that leg."

He released Sarah's hand. "Yes, ma'am."

Margaret turned back to Sarah as Logan was whisked into

the living room. "They're going to operate at once. How bad is he?"

"The bullet didn't shatter the bone, but it tore through some muscle. Infection is always the problem. He'd be better off in a hospital."

Margaret shook her head. "He won't do it. Where's your dog? I heard he was shot too."

"Still in the ambulance. He's okay. Just a little sore. He hasn't wanted to leave Logan since he was hurt, so we rode here with him. Bassett is being driven here by the pilot and the security guard you arranged to meet the plane." She turned, lifted Monty out of the ambulance, and carried him into the house. "We'll stay until the operation is over."

Margaret lifted her brows. "Because Monty's worried?"

"I'm not so hard that I can't feel compassion for someone in pain. Even Logan." She carried Monty through to the kitchen. "Will you get down a bowl? I need to give Monty water."

"Sit down. I'll do it." Margaret went to a cabinet, got a bowl, and filled it with water.

Sarah took the bowl and pushed the water toward Monty. When he started to drink, she straightened and asked, "Is this Dowden a good doctor?"

Margaret nodded. "You don't know me or I'd be insulted that you'd think I'd put John in some quack's hands." She looked down at Monty. "How about him? Does he need a vet?"

Sarah shook her head. "I'm used to taking care of him unless it's something serious. He's fine. He could walk, but that shoulder is sore. I want him to rest it. He'll be back to normal in a day or so."

"So you're lugging him around like a baby." Margaret grinned. "A seventy-pound baby at that."

"No problem. I'm strong. In my job I have to be."

"I know. I did the research on you." She sat down across

from Sarah. "You have a perfect right to be pissed at me, but I'm still going to tell you that I admire what you and Monty have done."

"Why should I be angry with you? It's Logan who pulls the strings."

"That's very fair." Margaret's gaze searched her face. "But you're not as angry with John as I thought you'd be. Why not?"

Because he'd kept his word. Because though she disapproved of his methods, she couldn't fault his motives. Because she'd grown to know him in that jungle, his strength and his determination, even a little of his past. It was difficult hating anyone but a total ass once you understood them.

"It's over." She rose to her feet. "It's a waste of energy being angry. Will you keep an eye on Monty? I want to be at the door to meet Bassett. This is pretty difficult for him. He thought he was going home."

"Sure." Margaret reached down and patted Monty. "I love dogs and he's a sweetheart."

Bassett arrived at the front door five minutes later.

He smiled with relief as soon as he saw Sarah walking toward him. "Am I glad to see a friendly face. When I went through those electric gates, I felt as if I was at Alcatraz."

"So did I the first time I came here. And then there were only two security guards, not the four I saw when I drove through the gates."

"You've been here before?"

"Several months ago."

He nodded. "I should have known you and Logan were old friends. The intimacy is pretty obvious."

Intimacy? A ripple of shock went through her. "Why do you say that?"

"As I said, it's fairly obvious watching you together. You

saved his life, and you kept an eagle eye on him all during the trip, though I could see you were trying to be offhand about it. Logan's not a man who likes being coddled, is he?"

"I wouldn't know. I don't coddle."

He held up his hands. "Sorry. Did I make a mistake?"

"Yes. Logan and I aren't old friends. I didn't save his life. I just gave him a boost into that helicopter so we could take off. And I did a job for a friend of his and then this one for him. That's the extent of our 'intimacy.' " She turned and moved toward the stairs. "You're probably tired. I'll show you to a room."

"You're upset. I didn't mean—"

"I'm not upset." It was true. She wasn't upset with Bassett. It wasn't his fault he'd read the situation wrong. That she had felt concerned for Logan was entirely natural. She would have felt the same for anyone who was hurt and helpless. By instinct and training she was a person who tried to save.

If it was entirely natural, then why was she justifying her reaction?

Because at that moment she was tired and vulnerable. No other reason. She'd be better after a little rest.

"This is a nice room. It overlooks the garden." She threw open the door at the top of the stairs. "The telephone is on the bedside table. I assume Logan is letting you at least call your wife."

"Sure. Though he asked me not to tell her I'd left Santo Camaro."

"Asked?"

"Well, strongly suggested." He glanced at Sarah. "But don't get me wrong. I came here voluntarily. Logan offered to fix up a lab for me here so I can get on with my work."

He might have thought the choice was voluntary, but what Logan wanted, Logan generally got. "I thought you wanted to go home."

"He pointed out that I didn't want to compromise the safety of my family. He's put a guard on them, but I'd just be a threat to them right now." He entered the room and looked around. "Private bath. Nice. A lot better than the living quarters at Santo Camaro. Castleton did his best, but he concentrated more on lab equipment than on little luxuries. The damn hot-water heater had to be replaced four times in the time I was there."

"Then why did you stay?"

"It was my dream," he said simply. "You don't give up a dream because you have to take cold showers."

"What kind of dream?"

He made a face. "I didn't mean to pique your curiosity. I'm sorry, you've been very kind, but I can't talk about my work. It's in my contract."

"And was it in your contract to risk being killed?"

"No, but we all knew there might be repercussions. It went with the territory."

"What do you—" Why was she asking questions when he'd already told her he couldn't discuss it? She wasn't interested anyway. It was time she distanced herself from Logan and everyone around him. "Margaret Wilson is in the kitchen downstairs and I'd bet she's had it fully stocked. Do you know her?"

"No, I worked through Castleton, but I've heard of her. Tough, efficient, and bossy as hell." He grinned. "She's something of a legend in Logan's empire. But you can't expect anything else. He's a legend himself."

"Well, that legend is downstairs having a bullet dug out of his leg. When they're through, maybe they should look you over."

"I'm fine. All I need is to talk to my wife and son."

"Then I'll leave you to it."

"Thanks." He was already heading for the phone as she closed the door.

She returned to the kitchen, where Margaret updated her on Logan. "The doctor just stuck his head in. The operation's over and John's doing fine. He's under sedation, but he should be waking up in a few hours."

Relief surged through her. She had known Logan's injury wasn't critical, but operations were always serious. "Good." She sank down in the chair. "No signs of infection?"

"A little. They're giving him megadoses of antibiotics to combat it. The doctor didn't like the fact that the bullet stayed in him all those hours."

"It was safer to bring him back to the States."

"I'm not saying it wasn't the right thing to do. There are always pros and cons." Margaret stood up. "How about some lunch? I've got a lot of canned stuff. Soup? Stew?"

Sarah shook her head. "It's time for Monty and me to go home. Will you arrange for someone to drive me back to my ranch?"

"Now?" Margaret frowned. "What's your hurry?"

"I want to go home."

"You told him you'd stay."

Stay, Sarah.

She had agreed because Logan's moment of vulnerability and need had caught her off guard. But he was neither vulnerable nor in need. He was surrounded by people who would take care of him and protect him. He certainly didn't need her. "I did stay. He's out of danger now."

"John won't like it. He told me to take care of you. How can I take care of you if you're miles away?"

"I don't need anyone to take care of me. I can take care of myself." She bent down and stroked Monty's head. "He's hurt and he needs to be in familiar surroundings."

"John won't like it," Margaret repeated.

"Do you get a car for me, or do I do it myself?"

"I'll do it." Margaret sighed. "But you're making my job very difficult."

"I think you'll bear up. You don't seem very intimidated by Logan."

"We've been together a long time. Familiarity generally casts out fear, but I do have a healthy respect for him."

Sarah studied her. "And you like him."

"Hell, yes. He's tough, but he's always been fair with me. And if life gets a little complicated around him, at least it's not boring." She went to the telephone. "I'll call one of the security men on the grounds and tell him to bring a car around front. Sure you don't want to have lunch before you leave?"

"I'm sure." She listened to Margaret put through the call. In a few minutes she'd be on her way back to the life she loved best—silence, simplicity, and serenity. Let Logan spin his complicated webs around someone else. She was going home.

6

The howl was eerily exquisite floating on the still night air.

Monty lifted his head. *Beautiful.*

"It looks like our wolf is still around." Sarah knelt to pour vitamins into Monty's food. "I hoped it would be gone by the time we got back."

Hungry?

"Maybe. Those Mexican gray wolves have had a pretty rough time since they were released. Eat your dinner."

Monty nosed the bowl away from him. *Hungry.*

"You need to eat. You're not going to heal without food, and you can't save that wolf by starving yourself."

Monty stretched out beside the untouched food bowl. *Hungry.*

The wolf howled again.

"Shut up," Sarah muttered. "Do you want those ranchers to come looking for you? Your best bet is to keep a low profile and—"

Hungry.

"That wolf is a hundred times better equipped than you to find food in the wild."

Sad. Alone.

The wolf shouldn't be this far east. He might well be alone, separated from his pack. "We can't help. They were released to make their way in the world." She sat down at the table and started to eat the stew she'd just heated. "See, I'm not worried. Now eat your dinner." She glanced over her shoulder and saw him staring at the door. "No, we are not going out to try to find—"

A knock.

She stiffened as the door swung open.

"Sorry." Logan was leaning against the jamb, his face pale, a small suitcase at his feet. "Do you mind if I come in? I think I need to sit down."

"What the hell are you doing here?" Sarah jumped to her feet and ran over to the door. She slung his arm around her shoulders and helped him to the easy chair in front of the fire. "Idiot. They just operated on you this afternoon. Are you trying to break open those stitches?"

"You promised me you'd stay. I woke up and you were gone." He settled back in the chair and closed his eyes. "So I came here."

She got a hassock from across the room and lifted his leg to rest on it. "Who brought you?"

"Margaret. I told her to drop me off and leave."

"I bet she loved that."

He smiled faintly. "Oh, you've gotten to know Margaret. She wasn't pleased."

"Neither am I. What are you doing here?"

"I decided I needed a little rest and seclusion. You have lots of that here."

She blinked. "What?"

"You have a couch." His voice was slurred. "I can sleep there."

"You're not making sense."

"I'm not? I'm a little fuzzy right now. Must be the medication the doctor gave me. I'm trying to ask you to either come back to the house or let me stay here."

"I'm not coming back and you cannot stay here. You can get all the seclusion you want in your house in Phoenix."

"It's not only—I promised you I'd deal with Madden for you."

"Yes, you did, and I'm holding you to it, but you didn't have to get out of a sickbed. And you didn't need to come here. Madden's not been here since the day I threw him out."

"Like you want to throw me out."

"Right."

"Safer. I'm—responsible."

"You're mumbling. I can't understand you."

"I don't mumble." Logan opened his eyes as Monty put his head against his hand. "Hello, boy. I'm glad someone is rolling out the welcome mat."

"Don't be flattered. Five minutes ago he wanted to roll out the same mat for a wolf."

"Wolf? I heard him when I was in the car. Beautiful . . ."

"Not you too?" She turned away and reached for the telephone. "What's Margaret's cell phone number? I'll call and tell her to turn around and come back for you."

He shook his head. "I told her not to pay any attention. You're . . . stuck . . . with me."

"The hell I am. I'll call an ambulance and have them— Dammit, listen to me."

"Sorry." His eyes had closed again. "Tired . . ."

He was asleep.

"Logan!"

No answer. He was probably so heavily drugged, it was a wonder he had been able to stir himself to come here. No, not really a wonder. She knew how determined Logan could be.

But why had he been so determined to come here?

Well, it would do no good to fret about reasons, when his presence was an accomplished fact. It would serve him right if she shipped him back to Phoenix in an ambulance.

Monty mournfully looked at her.

"Okay, okay, we'll let him stay until he wakes up. Maybe it will take your mind off that blasted wolf."

Monty settled down beside the chair.

She sighed in exasperation as she brought Logan's bag inside, then she lay down on the couch. She had thought she was done with him. Yet here he was again, only hours later, and she was sleeping on this lumpy couch instead of in her comfortable bed to make sure the idiot didn't thrash around and hurt himself.

"Wake up."

Logan was dimly aware that Sarah was shaking him.

"Dammit, wake up."

He fought his way through the fog of sleep and opened his eyes. The cabin. She wanted him to go. . . . "I'm staying."

"And I'm leaving. So call Margaret and tell her to come get you."

"What?" He sat up in the chair as he realized she was shrugging on her jacket. "Where the hell are you going?"

"Taiwan. They've had torrential rains for the past two weeks. A mudslide just buried a village. They think the fatalities are going to mount to over five hundred." She crossed to the kitchen counter and poured steaming coffee into a thermos. "God, I *hate* mudslides. The chances of pulling anyone out alive are so slim, they may as well be nonexistent. They're death searches, not life searches."

"Then why are you going?"

"Hundreds of people are buried underneath that damn sludge. Maybe Monty and I can cut that number down by a few."

"How did you find out about this slide?"

"Helen Peabody, our rescue group's coordinator, called ten minutes ago. You were so zonked, you didn't even hear the phone."

"You're dead tired. You have no business going anywhere."

"It's my job. It's a long flight. I'll be able to rest on the plane."

"What plane?"

"Helen is calling around now to see who'll lend us a plane and pilot. She'll get them." She tucked the thermos into her duffel. "Now, get on the phone and call Margaret."

"What about Monty? He's been wounded. You were so concerned about him and yet you're willing to take him on a rescue like this?"

"It's his job too. He's sore but he'll make it. If I see he's hurting too much, I'll pull him."

"I never thought you'd be that tough on Monty. You're crazy about that dog."

"If there's a chance of saving anyone, neither Monty nor I have any right to hold back. We've been hurt before and gotten through it." She reached in the cabinet, got Monty's vitamins, and threw them in the duffel. "We'll be there for only a few days. After that we'll let the other teams take over the search. Monty's had enough death for a while after Barat."

"What about you? Haven't you had enough?"

"Oh, yes." She turned away and wearily arched her back. "I've had enough. But it just keeps coming."

"Did you ever think about saying no?"

"How can I say no when there's someone waiting for help?"

"I guess you can't." He should argue with her, but he was having trouble thinking. He shook his head to clear it. "Taiwan. Where in Taiwan?"

"A place called Kai Chi. Do you want some coffee?"

"No, thanks."

"Are you sure? You look like you could use it."

"Five hundred dead?"

"That's the estimate."

"Then I guess you need some help." He reached for his digital phone. "Though you're making things difficult for me. How many people are in your team?"

"Six."

"And six dogs?"

She nodded.

"Call back this Helen Peabody and tell her you've found a plane and pilot." He wrinkled his nose. "My upholstery and carpets may never smell the same after six dogs running around the cabin."

Her eyes widened. "You're lending us your plane?"

"How soon can you have the team at the Phoenix airport?"

"Most of them are in Tucson. Five hours tops."

"That's too long if the conditions in Taiwan are as bad as you say. We'll fly down to Tucson, pick up the team, and go direct to Taiwan from there."

"We?"

"I'm going with you."

"Are you out of your head? To Taiwan? Why?"

"Maybe it's my way of trying to make up for having Monty hurt in Santo Camaro."

"Then just give us the plane and pilot."

He shook his head. "It's my plane. I call the shots." He dialed Margaret. "Margaret, I'm going to Taiwan. Have my plane and documents ready within the hour." He cut her short when she started to protest. "Not now. Just do it." He hung up.

Sarah was shaking her head. "You can't go with us."

"Why not?"

"This is a rescue mission. We have work to do. You'd get in the way."

"No, I wouldn't. I know the language. I have a small plant on the coast, so I have contacts in the country and I have the plane. What else could you ask for?"

"That you stay here and give us the plane and pilot."

"No deal."

"You've just had that leg operated on. You don't know what kind of conditions we're going to face. What if you get an infection?"

"Then you'd have to take care of me as well as Monty."

"That's what I'm afraid of."

"Don't be. It won't happen. I won't be a burden." He struggled out of the chair and had to suppress a wince as pain shot through his thigh. "If I am, then I promise I'll stay out of your way. Now, make the call while I go to the bathroom and throw some water on my face."

She stood there, undecided.

"Go call Helen Peabody." He limped toward the bathroom. "You know I'm the best game in town."

"Look at you. You can't even walk without hurting."

"What do you care? Serves me right, doesn't it?"

"I don't want you to lose your damn leg."

"I'll take care of me, and you and Monty take care of the suffering millions of the world. I'd say that's fair." He glanced at her over his shoulder. "Wouldn't you?"

She slowly nodded. "You're right. Why should I worry about you?" She turned away and picked up the telephone. "Come if you like. But don't blame me if you get more than you bargained for in Taiwan."

"I won't blame you." He closed the door and leaned against it, fighting the waves of agony. He should take some more painkillers, but he couldn't afford to be fuzzy right now. Once they left Tucson, he could let go for a while. In spite of her toughness, Sarah was a caretaker, and she would find a way to keep him from going if she realized he was hurting like hell. And sick. God, he felt sick. When the pain dulled to a throbbing, he pulled out his phone and called Galen. "I'm at Sarah's cabin, but we're leaving for Taiwan right away. Have you found out anything?"

"Not yet. I'm still tracking Sanchez. Taiwan?"

"It seems there's a mudslide in Taiwan. Her rescue team has been called out. I'm going with them."

"Christ. How do you feel?"

"I just had a bullet cut out of me. Not good."

"I don't envy you."

"Just find Rudzak. Even if he's hurt, I'll bet he's somewhere plotting and planning his next move."

He hung up and closed his eyes, gathering his strength. He'd gotten through the call. He could get through the flight. The trick was blocking the pain, operating on automatic, and not allowing himself to think.

He bent over the sink and splashed cold water on his face.

"Nice guy." Susie Phillips sat in the leather seat, her gaze on Logan at the front of the plane, talking to Boyd Medford. "You'd never know he was some kind of tycoon, would you?"

"Look around." Sarah's tone was dry. "I think anyone would be able to hazard a guess by this plane."

"You know what I mean. He's pretty down-to-earth. Have you known him long?"

"Not long."

"Then he must be a good guy to volunteer to do this for us. Particularly after he had that accident."

"Did he tell you he'd had an accident?"

"No, but it was, wasn't it?"

Sarah changed the subject. "How's Dinah been doing?"

"Fine. But she misses the searches. She looks so mournful when I take Donegan here out to my pickup." She reached down and stroked her German shepherd's head. "She doesn't understand that retiring after years of service is a reward, not a punishment." She glanced at Monty. "I know Monty's nowhere near that point, but it will be hard for him too. Maybe more than any other dog in the group. You should think about it. You'll need time to train another dog."

Sarah didn't want to think about it. She couldn't imagine working with another dog after all these years, and the thought of Monty growing old hurt her. "There's plenty of time to think about that." She rose to her feet. "Logan's looking a little tired. I think I'll go see if he needs anything."

Susie nodded. "Good idea." She took a paperback book out of her tote. "I'll see if I can read myself to sleep. It's going to be a long flight, and I'd love to spend it unconscious."

"So would I." Sarah could feel weariness dragging at every muscle as she walked down the aisle, stepping over dogs and carry-on baggage on the way to Logan. She couldn't wait until she was able to curl up and sleep as the other members of the team were doing. Actually, there was nothing to prevent her. Logan didn't need her. He could take care of himself.

If he was sensible. But if he'd been sensible, he'd have stretched out on one of the couches when the jet had left Tucson an hour before. Instead, he'd continued talking to

Boyd, listening politely and growing more wan and exhausted-looking by the minute.

Men.

Boyd looked up and smiled as she stopped before them. "Hey, Sarah. Pretty nice digs, huh? Remember that cargo plane we hopped to Barat?"

"How could I forget?" She gazed directly at Logan. "You look like death warmed over. Go to bed."

"In a few minutes. Boyd was just telling me about the rescue operation in Nicaragua."

"He can tell you when you wake up." She turned to Boyd. "I'm kicking you out of here. He should have that leg elevated. He probably didn't tell you he had an operation yesterday."

"Hell, no." Boyd stood up. "I'm gone. See you later, Logan."

Logan nodded and watched Boyd walk down the aisle and settle down by Susie. "You know him well?"

"Years."

"I thought as much. You can be rude only to very old friends."

"You'd have been better off if you'd been rude to him. He's a great guy, but he talks a lot when he's not on a search."

"I liked him." He smiled. "And I'm fully capable of being as rude as you, Sarah. He interested me. He was giving me an insight into your work."

"And?"

"It was like a glimpse into hell. Intriguing to hear about, but I wouldn't want to live there."

"You don't have to live there. I do."

"Not unless you—"

"Stop talking. I'm dead tired, and the last thing I wanted was to have to run interference between you and my friends because you were too macho to admit you were in pain. Now, will you go and lie down so that I can get some rest?"

"Sure." He struggled to his feet and stood swaying with one hand on the back of the chair. "If you'll give me a minute to get the kinks out. I've stiffened up."

He probably just didn't want to admit that the long walk down the aisle was intimidating in his present state. "Do you want me to help you?"

He grimaced. "You won't let me get away with anything, will you?"

"Pride's pretty dumb if you're hurting."

"No one can ever accuse you of mincing words. Two minutes. If I'm not okay then, I'll let you sweep me up in a fireman's lift and carry me to my couch. Tell me why you hate mudslides so much."

"I told you, they're death searches. In an earthquake you have more of a chance of finding air pockets. When a mountain of mud comes down on you, you suffocate."

"Like a snow avalanche?"

She shook her head. "Snow is easy because it's porous, scent travels through it. Mud is different, the scent is sealed inside. It's almost impossible for a dog to pick up the cone. And the dog thinks he can walk on mud, which leads to trouble. He can get stuck, get carried away, or go under, and sometimes you can't get to him to help him. You have to watch him every minute."

Her words were shooting out like machine-gun bullets. "You can't search alone because you have to use one person as a spotter in case a searcher gets in trouble. And that happens frequently. Just getting a boot full of mud can be a death sentence. A handler has to make sure her rubber boots are well fitting and duct-taped on. Plus, it's still raining in Taiwan, and we can't search until the rain stops because the mud can shift at any time. So you sit and wait while the victims' relatives stare and curse at you. Is that enough problems for you?"

"Shit."

"Exactly. Are you sure you don't want to stay on board the plane instead of going to the village?"

"I'm sure." His gaze wandered over the occupants of the plane. "Nice people, but they must be as crazy as you to be willing to go through that. I'm afraid I was a little out of it when you introduced me. Tell me about them."

Her gaze followed his. "The fiftyish man with the black Lab is Hans Kniper, he's a vet and dog trainer. The small young man asleep by the window is George Leonard. He works at a supermarket in Tucson and trains dogs on the weekends. You met Boyd Medford, our team leader. I guess I know him best. He was with the ATF K9 unit before he bailed and bought a ranch. Theo Randall is the blond man with the black-and-tan German shepherd. He's an accountant with a luxury hotel. Susie's a stay-at-home mom with two kids and four German shepherds."

"None of you have much in common."

"Except a love of dogs and the willingness to train them to help. That's enough of a bond."

"Monty's the only golden retriever. Three German shepherds, two Labs, and Monty. Are some breeds better suited than others for this kind of work?"

"You'd get an argument from every owner on the team. I think the only true qualifications are intelligence, the search instinct, and a good nose. Are you ready to move now?"

"Slowly." He started carefully down the aisle. "Very slowly. Good night, Sarah."

She watched him walk haltingly, stopping for a moment to step around Susie's dog, Donegan. Susie looked up from her book, and he exchanged a few words with her.

Lie down, you idiot. You don't have to charm everyone on the damn plane.

He had gone past Susie and was sitting down on the couch.

He took a vial of pills from his pocket and swallowed a couple with a glass of water. Painkillers? If they were, he should have taken them before. At that moment, when he wasn't aware he was being watched, his expression was haggard . . . and tormented. She could understand the haggardness—but torment? What devils were driving Logan?

Monty got to his feet, walked stiffly to Logan's couch, and plopped down in front of it. He could always sense illness and pain, which was only another signal that Logan had no business on this trip.

And Sarah would have no business on this mission either if she didn't stop worrying about a man who was too stubborn to worry about himself and get some rest. She sat down in the chair Logan had vacated and pushed it back until it was almost fully reclining.

Sleep. Don't think about Logan.

Don't think about that suffocating mud.

Taiwan would come soon enough.

God, she hoped it would stop raining.

The sun was shining brightly and there was not a cloud in the sky. All was right in Dodsworth, Rudzak thought with amusement.

"Why did you want to come here?" Duggan asked. "I told you it was too well protected to hit right now."

"I just wanted to see it." He gazed at the small brick building surrounded by ivy-covered stone walls. "What do the townspeople think is going on here?"

"Agricultural research."

Rudzak chuckled. "Trust Logan to pick a lie that would appeal to America's heartland." He turned away. "I suppose he's reinforced security?"

"Inside. Outside. Patrols, surveillance cameras, sensors, and personnel checks."

"Have you been able to get a blueprint of the building?"

"Not yet. But I won't need it."

"*I* need it. I want to know every structural strength and weakness in that building. Make it a priority."

"The security is too tight. You'd do better to hit one of Logan's other facilities."

"I'll consider it. But Dodsworth is such an interesting challenge, and it's clearly Logan's crown jewel. There's usually a way around security if you study the situation enough." He paused. "And that's what we're going to do. Study the situation and see what we come up with." A new element had appeared on the horizon. Sarah Patrick. He had learned quite a lot about her in the last couple of days, including the fact that Logan had extended his protection to her cabin outside Phoenix. What place did she occupy in his life? Was it worthwhile to remove her now? What about Eve Duncan, who had occupied a central place in Logan's recent past?

So many choices. So many paths to explore. But he had time and leisure to find the answers. He was the one setting the pace. Logan could only counter. He could hardly wait to get going again, but it took time to set up interesting scenarios. *It's coming closer, Chen Li. Just be patient.*

"I've seen what I need to see." He strode toward the car. "Let's go. I want to be in Phoenix tonight."

7

"Hurry. Into the bus." Logan stood in the road, the rain hammering his face, his local contact, Sun Chang, beside him. "The village is only a short distance from here, but Chang says the road there is going to be washed out any minute. If it's not gone already. The soldiers won't let anyone in or out of the area after the road goes."

"Great." Sarah scrambled onto the bus. "That's all we need. What about air support?"

"No place to land. The terrain is too rough. The best they can do will be supply drops. The village was terraced on the side of a mountain."

"Have they been able to get medical equipment into the village?"

"Yes. And they've set up tents."

"Any other search and rescue teams arrived?" Boyd asked.

"One from Tokyo. They've been here since last night."

"Survivors?"

Logan's lips tightened. "They've dug out six . . . so far."

Sarah leaned her head against the window, staring blindly out at the driving rain. Six out of five hundred. Dear God.

Logan dropped down in the seat beside her. "I don't suppose there's any chance of you staying here instead of going to the village?"

"No, but you could do it. You won't be any help after we start work. You can barely walk."

"You'd be surprised how helpful a man like me can be. I haven't failed you yet, have I?"

"No." From the moment he had gotten off the plane, Logan had been a dynamo of energy, checking with the handlers to make sure they had everything they needed, talking to Chang, who had met the plane and arranged for the bus. "But there's not much you'll be able to do from now on unless you're a doctor or trained in rescue. It will be—" The bus bounced and skidded across the road, throwing mud on the windows. "And you won't be able to get out if that leg needs more medical attention than the doctors here can supply."

"It's amazing what I can accomplish with a cell phone."

"Don't be flippant. It's not funny."

"Funny is the last thing I'm trying to be." He straightened his bad leg. "I'm trying to reassure you that I'll not be a—Shit."

They had rounded a curve of road and a mountain of mud spread out before them. The village was gone. No sign of houses or streets . . . or life. Through the driving rain Sarah could see a few search and rescue handlers and their dogs plodding through the mud on the lower slope and a bevy of men digging furiously while balanced on boards placed across the mud to the safe stone banks on either side. Tents ringed the area, and she located the hospital tent with a large red cross.

"Christ," Logan murmured. "Where the hell can we start?"

"Where we always start." She reached down, checked Monty's bandage, then fastened his orange halter with the red cross on both sides. "With the dogs."

Logan's face had turned pale. "My God."

"I told you mudslides were the worst."

"Yes, you did." He took a deep breath and dragged his gaze from the mountain to Monty. "He didn't wear that halter when we were in Santo Camaro."

"It wouldn't have done any good there. On disaster sites it identifies him as a lifesaver, not one of the wild dogs that often scavenge among the ruins. I've seen starving families kill those dogs for their next meal." She put up the hood on her poncho and tied it under her chin as the bus slithered to a stop in front of the hospital tent. "That's not going to happen to Monty."

Logan watched Sarah and the rest of the team disappear into the tent to be briefed by the military. It was getting dark, and the slide looked like a monstrous obscene mass in the half-light.

No screams . . .

No sobbing . . .

No children singing . . .

Silence.

Silent as a tomb.

"You're getting wet, Mr. Logan." Chang was standing beside him. "There's hot food in the mess tent."

"Not now." He gazed up at the mountain. "Where did the slide start?"

"They're not sure. It happened in the middle of the night." He pointed to a spot near the top of the mountain. "Close to that area."

"I want to go there."

"The military isn't letting anyone up there. The mud is still shifting and the rain—"

"Then take me around it." He jerkily moved toward the mountain. "I want to go there."

The rocks were slippery underfoot as they neared the top of the mountain.

Death.

A monument to death.

No coincidence. It couldn't be a coincidence.

"What are you looking for?" Chang asked.

"I don't know."

It would be protected. He would want Logan to find it.

The beam of his flashlight flared on the rocks around him.

Nothing.

"We should go down," Chang said. "The military wouldn't like it if they knew—"

"You go down." Logan scrambled over the rocks, the light from his flashlight weaving back and forth. The scarab had been small. . . .

So was the blue and white box shining in the beam of the light.

Chen Li's box. He had seen her handle it a hundred times, her fingers tracing the lapis lazuli flowers on the lid.

He sank to his knees beside it.

He wanted to shout. He wanted to pound his fists on the stone.

All he could do was stare at the exquisite jeweled box glittering in the beam of his flashlight.

Five hundred people.

Buried alive.

Rudzak called him six hours later. "Is it still raining in Kai Chi?"

"Yes."

"I saw the news bulletin that you were on a mercy mission. The rain didn't stop you from finding Chen Li's box, did it?"

"No."

"Because you knew it would be there. You're a smart man, Logan. You finally realized what I was doing with Chen Li's treasures, didn't you?"

"Funeral gifts."

"You sound a little numb. Did I wake you?"

"No."

"I didn't think so. You were probably lying awake, staring into the darkness. Isn't that what guilty men do?"

"You should know. You were the one who did this."

"I feel no blame. It's not in my makeup. But now you've been thinking and I'll wager you've figured out why I hit Santo Camaro and Kai Chi."

"Her grave."

"I was very angry when I saw her grave. Chen Li was a queen and you buried her like a pauper. The passing of a queen should be marked by the blare of trumpets and the clash of cymbals."

"So you gave her Santo Camaro and Kai Chi."

"I would have gone after you anyway, but as I stood by her grave, it came to me how it must be done. It was so beautifully clear to me. Santo Camaro was fine for a beginning, but

Kai Chi is special. Chen Li was born there, and we spent every summer playing on those slopes."

"After she died and I'd earned a little money, I endowed an orphanage here in her name. Did you know about the orphanage?"

"Of course. Did you think it would make a difference?"

"I suppose not."

"And I remembered that you and Chen Li spent your honeymoon there," Rudzak said. "All the more reason for it to die with Chen Li."

"Is it over? I'd think five hundred people would be enough even for you."

"Of course it's not over. She was a queen and a queen must have her due."

"She would hate you for this."

"She could never hate me. You tried to make her hate me, but even when you met her, she was already mine."

"I never tried to make her hate you. I actually liked you until I found out what a son of a bitch you were."

"You kept her away from me."

"She was dying. I didn't want her hurt. And she didn't argue. By that time she knew what you wanted from her. She didn't want to see you."

"You're lying. It was you who—" He drew a deep breath, and when he spoke, the anger was gone. "I won't let you upset me. I'm winning, Logan. I fooled you, didn't I? You never expected Kai Chi. You thought I was in Colombia when I called you. I set the timer right after I talked to you on the phone."

"You're right, I never expected even you would be this sick. You won't fool me again."

"Don't be so certain. I found it interesting that you brought Sarah Patrick with you to Kai Chi."

"*She* brought *me*. This is her job."

"Then it's doubly interesting. You two seem to be walking the same path, don't you? By the way, do you know that I still have eight more of Chen Li's artifacts?" He hung up.

Logan wanted to lie down again and shut the world out, but he had to call Galen. Galen had to know so he could try to protect—

Protect what? Who? Where was Rudzak going to strike next?

"I've been wondering when you were going to call me." Galen's voice was uncharacteristically sober when he answered the phone. "You didn't tell me you were going to Kai Chi."

"I didn't want it to be true. I wanted it to be an act of God, not Rudzak. But I knew that wasn't likely."

"It was Rudzak?"

"Yes, I went looking and found another of Chen Li's artifacts and some blasting caps on the mountain where the slide started. Christ, I was hoping I wouldn't find it. But when I saw that mountain of mud, I knew. It couldn't be a coincidence. Everything came together. Funeral gifts."

"Funeral gifts?"

"Pharaohs were entombed with the treasures they held precious in life. Chen Li loved her collection. If it couldn't be buried with her, why not use it to honor her passing?"

"Are you guessing?"

"I was until Rudzak just called me and confirmed it. He's got some twisted idea that all these deaths are a tribute to Chen Li."

"So he killed four at Santo Camaro and over five hundred there?"

"In several ancient civilizations it wasn't uncommon for the servants and wives to die with the ruler. Rudzak wouldn't see the difference. Even if he did, it wouldn't matter to him."

"Shit."

"I didn't expect Kai Chi. I never thought about it happening here. I don't want to make another mistake like that."

"Don't be an ass. How could you know?"

"From now on I have to know. He reminded me that he still has eight more artifacts to spread around."

"Your plants?"

"Maybe." He paused. "And he mentioned Sarah."

"Are you going to tell her about the mudslide?"

"And have her hate me more than she does right now?"

"You didn't cause that slide."

"Keep telling me that. I need to hear it. Get back to me if you spot anything that's even a little suspicious." He hung up.

He lay back down on the cot. He should try to rest though he knew he wouldn't be able to.

You were probably lying awake, staring into the darkness. Isn't that what guilty men do?

It's what he had been doing. Lying there and thinking about that sarcophagus of mud only yards away. Was he feeling guilt? Hell, yes. If he'd had Rudzak killed in that prison, he'd never have been free to cause this carnage. So, yes, the blame was partly his own, and he felt as if that entire mountain were lying on top of him.

As it was lying on top of that orphanage.

He had visited the orphanage many times over the years, and the nuns always had the children sing for him.

He closed his eyes.

He could almost hear them singing. . . .

Mud.

Sheets of rain.

Death.

How long had it been?

Two days? Three?

It didn't matter.

She had to go on.

Monty had caught the cone. Maybe this one would be alive.

Not likely. She and Monty had found only five survivors. The rest had been dead.

That didn't mean this one wouldn't be alive. You had to keep hope alive. Otherwise the ones who waited might never be found.

She staggered on the makeshift bridge across the mud after the dog.

The man wasn't alive. The pouring rain had freed him from the coffin of mud but not in time. His mouth was wide open in a silent scream.

Monty was whimpering. Too much. Take him down. Get him away from the death.

"Come, boy." She put a stake in the mud beside the body and marked it with orange flagging tape, then started down. She could see Logan below, looking up at her, a shovel in his hands. He was covered in mud like all the rest of the rescue workers trying to dig out the ruins of the village. He shouldn't be there. She had caught only brief glimpses of him in the past few days as he moved around the camp, helping in the medical tent, assisting the handlers, besides spending hours digging. He seemed driven. But she had been vaguely aware of his growing exhaustion, the gauntness of his face, and his worsening limp.

He wasn't looking at her anymore. He was bent over, digging at the mud. But he glanced up as she and Monty passed by him. "Boyd says we're pulling out tonight," he told her. "The team hasn't found a survivor in twelve hours."

"Is the road open?"

"The army's built a bridge over the washout. We got a shipment of food and blankets while you were up there on the search. There will be a truckload of volunteers here within a few hours. Not that it will do any good." His shovel dug viciously into the mud. "None of it is any good. No matter how hard I try, it's useless. I hate it that it's so goddamn hopeless. Why can't we find anyone? Christ, I'll be glad to get out of here."

So would she. It had been an even more heartbreaking search than usual. The rain stopped and started in a seemingly neverending cycle, keeping them from taking the dogs out, and there had been two other slides since they arrived. "I have to go up and try one more time. There might be someone alive out there."

"I'm not arguing." He didn't look at her. "At least get some rest first. I know I can't convince you to be easy on yourself, but Monty looks like he could use it. How's his wound?"

"Almost entirely healed. Do you think I'd let him work if he wasn't okay?" Not waiting for an answer, she walked away from him toward the tent the rescue team shared. Logan had no room to talk about being easy on herself when he was staggering around with that bad leg.

Only Hans Kniper was asleep on his cot with his Lab beside him when she went into the tent. She didn't bother being quiet as she watered and fed Monty. No danger of waking Hans. They were all operating on practically no sleep and fell unconscious when they got the chance to rest.

She washed enough mud off Monty to make him a little more comfortable and then scrubbed her own face. No use doing anything else when they'd be back in the mud within a few hours. She lay down and cuddled next to Monty. It was raining again. She could hear it pounding on the canvas of the tent. God, she wished it would stop.

"Sarah."

Logan. She came instantly awake.

Logan was kneeling beside her. He nodded at the Asian woman standing in the entrance of the tent. "This is Ming Na. She wanted me to ask one of you to find her baby."

Sarah felt sick as she looked at the young woman's desperate expression. "Did you tell her how hard we've been trying?"

"She says we've been looking in the wrong place for her child. He wasn't in the village. They were walking down the mountain after visiting Ming Na's grandparents. A flash flood took him away from her and swept him down the mountain to the creek that runs beside the village."

"How old is her baby?"

"Two."

"The chances of his surviving a flash flood are practically nil."

"She said he did survive. She saw him thrown up on the bank and crawling away. She tried to run after him, but the mudslide came and she couldn't get over to get him. She heard him crying."

"It's been four days," Sarah whispered. "If he survived the flood, who's to say he would survive the exposure? You're grabbing at straws."

"Hell, yes, I want that baby to be alive." His lips twisted. "I want a miracle. After these last few days I need a miracle."

She could see that in his face. She needed a miracle too. You never knew when you'd find one, so you kept trying. "I'll go take a look." She got to her knees and put Monty's halter on. "Ask her if she'll take me to the place where she heard the baby crying."

Logan turned to the woman and spoke to her in rapid Taiwanese. She nodded and answered. He turned back to Sarah. "She'll take us."

"Us?"

"I'm going," he said firmly. "I promised her I'd bring back her baby."

She shook her head.

"I want to do something besides pull corpses from beneath that goddamn mud. I want to find that baby . . . alive."

She opened her mouth to protest and then closed it. She understood his desperation and weariness; how many times had she felt the same way? How many times had she tried to fool Monty into thinking there was life in a sea of death? "Come if you like. But if you can't keep up, I'm not going to wait for you."

"I'll keep up."

"Over there." Logan pointed over the lake of mud to the rocks on the other side.

"The child was thrown on the bank there?" Sarah asked.

Logan nodded, then moved toward the boards that bridged the mud. "Let's get the kid."

"Let Monty and me go first, give him a head start." She and Monty carefully picked their way across the narrow bridge to the safety of the rocky ground on the other side. She took off the leash and let Monty run down the mountain.

She tried not to look over her shoulder at Logan but couldn't resist a glance before she started after Monty. He was okay, she saw with relief. Though God knows how he was keeping his balance on the wet boards with that bum leg. "Don't try to hurry. Monty may come back to me a dozen times before he gets the scent." She set off after the dog. "If he gets the scent."

Monty was running around in circles as he tried to pick up the cone. The rain had increased in the last few minutes and she could barely see him.

"Monty's not picking up anything," she told Logan when he was beside her. She watched the retriever barrel down the bank.

Logan limped ahead of her to follow Monty. "Let's go."

She saw his expression and felt a ripple of shock. He was tense, totally absorbed, completely driven, and desperate.

I want to find this baby alive.

Oh, God, I hope you do, Logan.

Monty wasn't picking up the scent. He was running around in circles.

"What the hell is wrong with him?" Logan's tone was harsh. "Can't you do something?"

"He's doing the best he can."

Logan drew a deep breath. "Sorry. I know he is."

Fifteen minutes later Monty barked. He came running back in a delirium of joy and then took off running down the mountain.

"He's found him." Quickly following, Logan slid and slipped down the bank. "He's found him!"

Sarah muttered a prayer as she stumbled after Logan.

The rain was so heavy, she could no longer see him or Monty, but they had to be straight ahead. "Logan!"

No answer.

"Logan, where—" Then she saw him.

And she saw Monty standing over a mound of mud beside the creek, whimpering.

"Sweet Jesus, no," she whispered.

"It may not be the kid." Logan fell to his knees and clawed

desperately at the mud. "It may not be—" He stopped, staring down at the delicate arm of a child he had uncovered. "Shit." He dug frantically until he'd uncovered the still, small body. "Shit. Shit. Shit." He sat there, his shoulders slumped as he gazed down at the baby. "It's not fair. He's only a little kid."

"One of the later mudslides must have gotten him." Sarah knelt beside Logan. Poor baby. Poor Ming Na.

She couldn't move for a few minutes and then she slowly struggled to her feet and got out her flagging tape. "Come on, Logan. We've got to get back to Ming Na."

"What are you doing with that tape?"

"You know what I'm doing. You've seen it before. Marking the spot."

"Not him." Logan reached out, picked up the little boy, and rose to his feet. "I promised Ming Na I'd bring back her baby. I'm not going to leave him here in the mud."

"You can't carry him up that mountain. You barely made—" She stopped as she saw his face. The cords were standing out in his neck, and tears were running down his cheeks. "Can I help?"

"No. I'll make it." He started up the mountain. "I promised her."

She stood there with Monty, watching him struggle up the slippery slope. Why was it so heartbreaking to see a strong man like Logan with that baby in his arms? She wanted to rush forward and help him, comfort him. She knew what agony he would face when he handed the baby to Ming Na. She had faced that agony any number of times in a hundred different places over the years.

But he wouldn't let her help.

"Come on, Monty." She slowly started up the mountain after Logan.

• • •

The team washed their dogs, showered, and changed at the airport before they boarded Logan's plane. They took off at a little after eight that evening.

Logan was quiet. Too quiet. He'd spoken only a few words since he'd placed the baby in Ming Na's arms and walked away. Well, she hadn't been very talkative herself. There was a pall over the entire team. It had been a nightmare of a search operation. She started to settle down for the night.

Oh, what the devil. She strode over to the chair where he was sitting. "Are you okay?"

He smiled faintly. "You held out longer than I thought you would."

"You shouldn't have come. I warned you that you didn't belong on the search."

"I had to come."

"Just as you had to go after that baby."

He nodded.

"It happens. Searches don't always turn out as they should. You have to think about the good ones."

"Since this is my first, I don't have a happy experience for comparison. And I don't think I want to try another one." He looked out the window. "How the hell do you take it?"

"Hope. And the knowledge that almost always there's someone waiting for us to come. Maybe it's only one or two, but those lives are precious." She rubbed the back of her neck. "But this was a rough one."

"Yes, it was." He looked back at her. "So stop trying to make me feel better and go lie down and sleep. I'm okay. It's not as if I haven't dealt with death before. It's just that babies are . . . different."

"Yes, they are."

"I wanted that kid to live."

"I know."

"But he didn't and I have to put it aside. I'll bounce back. I always do." He closed his eyes. "So go take care of your dog and let me sleep."

She stood looking at him uncertainly.

"Sarah." He didn't open his eyes. "Scat."

They heard the wolf howl as they were driving to the ranch. Monty sat upright in the backseat, looking eagerly at the mountains.

"I'd forgotten about the wolf." Sarah's gaze followed Monty's. "At least he's still alive."

Beautiful . . .

"But dangerous, Monty. And you don't need a challenge after what you've gone through lately."

The wolf howled again.

"Call of the wild," Logan murmured. "Incredible."

"And the National Wildlife Federation wants him to stay wild. So do I. I wish the damn wolf would quit coming down and raiding the ranches." She parked in front of the cabin and jumped out of the jeep. "Come on. I'll give you a cup of coffee and then you can call Margaret or whoever is available to come get you. I don't know why you didn't let me drop you off at your Phoenix house."

"I had to deliver you to your door. Galen would have said it was the polite thing to do. I'll take that cup of coffee." He got out and limped into the house. "I can use it."

She flicked on the lights and went to the cabinet. "You don't look so good. You need more than a cup of coffee. I didn't see you taking any of your painkillers on the plane."

"I ran out yesterday. I guess the doctor thought I wouldn't need any more."

"He didn't know you were going to abuse yourself like you did these past five days." She started the coffee. "I don't think he would have recommended all that digging, much less sliding down that mountain."

"It had to be done." He settled himself in the easy chair and propped up his leg on the hassock. "You should understand. I've never known a more passionate advocate of that philosophy."

The wolf howled again.

She stared out the window into the darkness. "I wish he'd stop. He's unsettling Monty."

"We wouldn't want that to happen. I seem to have a calming effect on him. Why don't I stick around for a while?"

She had been half expecting that suggestion from him. She should have followed her instincts and dropped him off in Phoenix. If she hadn't been so tired, she would never have let him get his foot in the door. "Nothing's changed since the night you first came." She brought him his coffee. "I don't want anyone staying here."

"Things have changed. We've gone through a lot together. I don't think you regard me as the enemy any longer."

"That doesn't mean I want you in my house. Why the hell did you come anyway? When you first showed up I thought you were just out of your head. We both know any action you take against Madden doesn't have to be done from here. Something's weird."

"Can't we argue about this in the morning? I'm pretty tired."

"Then finish your coffee and call Margaret."

"I'm too tired." He set his cup on the table beside him and smiled faintly. "You wouldn't kick a wounded man out of your house."

"Maybe I would." She let her breath out in a resigned sigh.

He was playing on her feelings, but he did look terribly pale, and she knew what he had gone through in Taiwan. "Okay. Tomorrow. But that chair isn't as comfortable as those cushy recliners on your plane. By morning you may be ready to leave."

He closed his eyes. "You can never tell. . . ." He was asleep.

She sank down on the couch and gazed at him in frustration. Déjà vu. Why couldn't she get rid of him? She didn't want him there. That he had become too much a part of her life in these last days made her uneasy. She had seen him tired and discouraged and hurting. She had seen his tears. He disturbed her, and she had enough disturbance in her life. This was her home, her haven, and she wanted no strangers—

But that was the crux of the problem. He was no longer a stranger. She didn't know exactly what Logan's place was in her life now, but he could never be a stranger again.

The wolf howled.

Monty lifted his head and whimpered deep in his throat.

She couldn't blame him. The wolf's cry was terribly melancholy and heartbreakingly wistful.

And closer.

Stay in the mountains, she prayed. Those ranchers will shoot you. There's danger here. They think you're a threat and don't care if you're wild and free and beautiful.

Monty put his head on his paws. *Beautiful* . . .

8

"Get up, Sarah."

She opened her eyes to see Logan standing over her. She had been sleeping hard and for a moment she thought she was back in Taiwan.

"Come on. He's gone. I can't go after him by myself." He half walked, half hopped toward the door. "Hell, I couldn't catch up with a turtle."

She sat up and rubbed her eyes. "What is it?"

"Monty. He took off out that dog door like a bat out of hell. He heard something."

She swung her feet to the floor. "What?"

"I don't know. I didn't hear anything. I'd just opened my eyes and saw Monty get up. He listened for a minute and then took off." He opened the door. "Does he go out much at night?"

"No, but it's not completely unusual."

"I tell you he heard something. We'd better go after him."

Logan was clearly worried, and his concern was infectious.

Monty had probably just gone outside to relieve himself, but she had to check. She grabbed a flashlight and followed Logan. "Monty!"

She waited.

"Monty!"

For the first time, fear iced through her. Monty always answered her.

Unless he couldn't.

She heard something in the distance. Not a bark. A moan?

"I hear something." She set out at a run. "Go back to the house."

"The hell I will. Where are the keys to your jeep?"

"I always leave them in the ignition."

"Well, that's safe."

She paid no attention as she ran west, where the sound had come from.

Darkness.

Silence.

"Monty!"

No sound.

"Answer me!"

A low moan in the distance.

Monty. She knew it was Monty. She flew over the hard-baked sand, the beam of her flashlight spearing a wide circle from side to side in front of her.

Then she saw him.

Blood.

Monty was lying in a pool of blood.

"Oh, God." She flew toward him, tears running down her face. "Monty."

He looked up at her, his eyes full of pain.

She was almost to him when she saw what his big body had blocked from view.

Gray fur, silver eyes staring fiercely in the light, and lips drawn back from gleaming white teeth.

And a front paw caught in an iron-jawed trap. The blood was trickling from the wolf, not from Monty.

Monty nestled closer to the wolf. *Pain.*

"Get away from him, Monty. He'll hurt you."

Monty didn't move.

She knelt down beside them. "I'm going to release the trap. Just get out of the way."

He didn't move.

"Okay, be stupid." He wasn't the only one who was stupid. Trying to free the wolf from this trap without putting him to sleep first was asking for trouble. She took off her shirt and wrapped it around the arm nearest the wolf. "I'm going to get you out of this," she said softly. "Give me a break, will you?"

The wolf snapped. Sarah snatched her arm out of harm's way just in time.

"Okay, no break." She reached for the iron teeth of the trap. Quick. She had to be quick.

The wolf snapped again. This time he drew blood.

She sat back on her heels. "Look, do you want to bleed to death? Let me help."

The wolf lunged toward her and then collapsed with a cry of pain.

Monty crawled closer to the wolf.

"No!"

Monty ignored her and laid his head across the wolf's throat.

She held her breath. "What are you doing, boy?" Any minute she expected the wolf to rise up and slash at Monty.

But the wolf lay still.

Unconscious?

No, she could see the gleam of his slitted eyes. What was she doing, sitting there? It didn't matter what weird thing was happening between Monty and the wolf. Seize the moment. She started working at the trap, every moment expecting the wolf to make a move.

Lights suddenly speared the area.

The jeep.

"Stop, Logan." She froze, her gaze on the wolf.

No motion. As if Monty's touch on his throat were paralyzing him.

"Can I help?" Logan called from the jeep.

"Get the first aid kit under the front seat and then come and help me with this trap. I'm not strong enough to do it alone."

A moment later Logan was kneeling beside her, his gaze on Monty and the wolf. "What's happening here?"

"I've no idea. I think Monty's hypnotized him or something." She opened the medical kit and withdrew a hypodermic and sedative. "Get ready to spring the trap after I give him this shot."

"Why not afterward?"

"He'll run away. I have to take care of that leg before he bolts." She kept her eyes fixed warily on the wolf as she gave him the injection. No movement. Maybe the pain of his leg dwarfed the little pinprick.

Monty was the one who gave a low moan as if in sympathy with the wolf's agony.

"Just keep him quiet a minute more and we'll have him out, Monty," she murmured. "I don't know what you're doing, but keep doing it." She said to Logan, "Be ready to jerk open that trap when I tell you." She put her hands beside Logan's on the iron. "On the count of three. One, two . . ." She glanced at the wolf. He had gone limp. "Three."

She and Logan pulled with all their strength. The iron jaws slowly parted. "Can you hold it open while I get his foot out?"

"Do it," he grunted.

Carefully she freed the wolf's leg. "Let it go."

The trap snapped shut with a lethal click. How she hated those traps. She unwound the shirt from around her arm, formed a pressure bandage, and bound the wolf's leg. "Get in the jeep, Monty."

Monty hesitated, then got to his feet and ran toward the jeep.

"What now?" Logan asked.

"We get the wolf back to the cabin, where I can tend him."

"A wild animal?"

"A wounded animal." She picked up the wolf and carried him toward the jeep. "Come on. I need your help. You'll have to drive while I keep an eye on him."

"Okay." He struggled slowly to his feet as she settled the wolf in the backseat. "There's blood on your arm."

"He barely broke the skin." She jumped in the passenger seat. "Hurry. I'm not sure how long he'll be under, and I want to work on him without giving him another shot."

"Right."

Logan pulled the jeep in front of the cabin in less than five minutes and Sarah jumped out. "Go on ahead and open the door beside the fireplace. It leads to a small screened-in back porch."

He limped into the cabin. "Anything else?"

She followed him. "Grab that throw on the back of the couch and put it on the floor of the porch."

He did, then asked, "Next?"

She set the wolf carefully on the throw. "Bring me the bag with the medical supplies in that first kitchen cabinet."

She knelt down and gently stroked the wolf's muzzle.

"What a beautiful boy you are. Don't worry, we're going to take good care of you."

Monty settled himself beside the wolf.

"You'll have to get out of the way," Sarah told him. "I'm going to stitch up that cut and set the leg. It's fractured."

Monty laid his head on his paws, his gaze on the wolf.

"Here's the bag." Logan fell to his knees beside the wolf. "Tell me what to do to help."

She looked across the wolf's body at him. So far he had taken orders without question, and heaven knows she needed help. "First we have to clean the wound."

"Are you going to leave Monty in there with the wolf?" Logan asked as he followed Sarah from the porch an hour later.

"I don't think I could budge him." Sarah set the medical bag on the counter and washed the blood from her hands at the sink. "Not until he's sure the wolf's okay. Coffee?"

"Yes." He carefully lowered himself into the easy chair and raised his leg onto the hassock. "I could use it. How long will he sleep?"

"I hope another hour or so. And it's she, not he. I assumed it was a male too, until I started working on her. I'm surprised you didn't notice."

"I was preoccupied." His gaze shifted to the fire. "Aren't you a little cold?"

"No."

"Well, neither am I. Will you go put on a shirt?"

She glanced at him in surprise. "I'm wearing a bra. That's no different from wearing a bikini top."

"Trust me, there's a difference."

She inhaled sharply as she met his gaze. She quickly averted her eyes. "Oh, for God's sake. I suppose I should have expected it even in a situation like this. It's a guy thing. I read an article once that said men think of sex once every eight minutes."

"Then I must be a cold fish. I'm sure it doesn't pop into my head more than every ten minutes."

His tone was flippant, and the disturbing moment was gone, she realized with relief.

She went into the bedroom and came back pulling a white T-shirt over her head. "Satisfied?"

"No." He changed the subject. "What are you going to do with the wolf?"

"Get her well and then turn her back over to the Wildlife Federation to relocate." She made a face. "If I can keep my rancher neighbors from busting in here and trying to kill her again."

"Maybe I can help there."

"What are you going to do? Pay them off?" She shook her head. "These ranchers are independent as the devil and they're not about to be bought. They've lost livestock and they're mad as hell."

"I'll think of something." He drew a quick breath. "I wonder—if I could—trouble you to get out your medical bag again. I may need a little first aid myself. I believe kneeling beside that wolf may have been the last straw."

Her gaze flew to the leg propped on the hassock. A wide dark stain was spreading on the inner side of his thigh. "Dammit, you tore open the stitches." She grabbed the bag off the counter and moved over to the chair. "Why didn't you tell me?"

"You were busy. We were both busy. You seem to live in a constant state of emergency. I'm almost afraid to close my eyes around— What are you doing?"

"Taking off your jeans."

"You seem to have no compunction about nudity in yourself or others."

"There's nothing shameful about nudity." She wriggled the trousers off his hips and down his legs. "I can repair those stitches—unless you want me to call an ambulance."

"No, you do it." He closed his eyes and smiled faintly. "Just please don't enjoy sticking that needle in me too much."

"I never enjoy inflicting pain." She bent over his thigh. "You didn't break all the stitches. This shouldn't take long."

"That's good. I've never been good at—" He inhaled sharply as the needle went into his flesh. "I should have asked for a shot like our wolf friend."

"I would have given you one, but I have only morphine, and you're allergic to it."

"Oh, shit. I knew that would come back to haunt me."

"Just a couple more."

Actually, it was three more before she was able to rebandage the wound. "That wasn't so bad, was it?" she asked as she pulled up his jeans and fastened them.

"It wasn't good." He opened his eyes. "But since most of it was my fault, I guess I can't complain. Could I have that coffee now? I need it."

"Sure." She moved toward the counter. "I could use a cup myself."

"I can see how you would. It's been a difficult night for you."

She poured the coffee, gave him a cup, and then sat down on the hassock with her own. "And for you. And it wasn't your fault that you broke open those stitches. You were trying to help Monty and then the wolf. If anyone's at fault, it's me."

He shook his head. "No, my responsibility."

"You said that before. You're big on responsibility."

"It's one of the few codes I never break. Whatever I do, I shoulder the responsibility for my actions."

She took a sip of coffee and was silent a moment. "Why did you come here, Logan?"

"Why do you think I came?"

"I don't know. I thought it might be the medication that caused you to stumble here from a sickbed. But I can't see you being that woozy even under drugs. So it was something else."

"Go on."

"Tell me."

"I'm enjoying watching you work it out. Did I ever tell you how much I admire that fine brain of yours?"

"Don't flatter me, Logan."

"I wouldn't presume. We may have had our differences, but I've never underestimated you."

"Just used me."

"That's done. I'll never use you again, Sarah."

She studied his expression.

"Believe me."

She did believe him. "If that's true, then it narrows down the reasons you'd show up here. You made me a promise about Madden, but you wouldn't have thought it necessary to drag yourself here to keep it."

"I would if you'd told me you wanted it done immediately."

"But I didn't tell you that." She tilted her head, thinking. "And you were more scared than I was when Monty ran out of here tonight. You were afraid something would happen to him."

He was silent, waiting.

"Responsibility." She met his gaze. "You were afraid someone would hurt Monty."

"Or you. You nearly gave me a heart attack when you took off running. I knew I'd never catch you with this bum leg."

Her eyes widened. "Rudzak? Why?"

"He had to have seen you when you jumped out of the helicopter after Monty."

"And that's enough to target me?"

"More than enough. You helped me, and no one believes more in revenge than Rudzak. He'll regard his defeat as a humiliation, and you both participated in and witnessed that humiliation."

Her hands clenched into fists. "I thought I was out of it."

"Will you come back to Phoenix with me?"

"No, I think you're off base about any threat to me, but if there is, I'll take care of myself."

"I thought that would be your response. I told Galen to get some security out here, but it would be much easier if you go back to Phoenix."

"I want my life back. I don't want to make it easy for you."

"Then if you're going to stay here, let me stay too. I'll be chief cook and bottle washer. You have your hands full with the wolf and Monty."

"I told you I don't want you here."

"Just imagine me humble and at your beck and call. Doesn't the picture appeal to you?"

"Like a dream come true. But you'd probably break open the stitches again and I'd be waiting on you too."

"I trust your stitches." He grimaced. "They hurt too much not to be tight as a drum."

"And you'd be more danger to me here than behind those gates in Phoenix. Rudzak would probably crawl up to my cabin and blow it up just to get you."

"No, my presence will actually make you safer. Rudzak doesn't want me dead yet. He wants me to suffer first."

"What the hell did you do to him?"

"I took away fifteen years of his life. I should have killed him, but things didn't work out." The words were cold and the tone without feeling. Then he smiled. "But that's the past. We have to worry about the future. Just let me stay until you get the wolf in shape. Maybe by that time we'll have located Rudzak. And I have some strings I can pull to get the IRS to persuade the ranchers not to go after the wolf again."

"I wouldn't sic the IRS on my worst enemy."

"Just a mild attack? To save the wolf?"

"Maybe." She stood up. "I've got to check on her."

"Don't you think we should give her a name? Something exotic, perhaps. Ivana or Dest—"

"I hate cutesy names." She headed for the porch door. "Her name is Maggie."

"Margaret will be flattered . . . I think."

"It's not about her. I just like the name."

"Sarah."

She glanced over her shoulder.

"I'm making sense," he said soberly. "I know Santo Camaro seems far away and unreal. But it's not. Believe me, Sarah."

He was right. The threat from Rudzak did seem completely unreal to her. "You could be wrong."

"I'm not wrong. Let me stay. Let me help you. I promise I won't be a disturbance." He made a face. "And just think how you'll love ordering me around."

"It might almost be worth it."

"Then think about it."

She was silent a moment. "I will."

He watched her disappear to the porch. Had he been persuasive enough? He had laid the facts out before her with complete honesty; anything else would have been the height of idiocy. She would never accept deception in herself or anyone else. She had a directness he had seen in very few women and a passionate caring for the helpless he had never experienced. She had worked over that wolf as if it were her child, stroking it, talking to it, soothing even though the animal couldn't hear her. There had been something beautiful about Sarah Patrick in those moments. Fine-boned hands that were gentle as well as deft, tousled hair that she'd had him push back once so she could better see what she was doing. Strong shoulders, breasts lifting and falling with the intensity of her emotion . . .

Oh, shit. He didn't need this physical response right now. He certainly didn't need it in connection with Sarah Patrick.

Then forget it, block it out.

Easier said than done. Every time he looked at her, he'd remember how he'd felt at that moment.

Nothing was easy. Do it. Forget how she'd looked in that simple white bra.

Remember only what he had to do to keep her alive.

Monty was stretched out next to the sleeping wolf, almost nose to nose. He didn't lift his head when Sarah walked into the room. Good. She was glad she had a moment to herself. Too much had happened that night and she was upset and off balance. Logan had thrown her another curve and now she had to deal with it.

This cabin was her haven; she didn't want anyone here. Particularly a presence as strong as Logan. He had said he wouldn't disturb her, but there was no way a personality that forceful wouldn't prove a disturbance.

Yet he hadn't exerted that strength when he helped her with the wolf. He took a backseat, ready to help but not interfere, same as in Taiwan.

But living comfortably with him wasn't the real issue. Was it safer for her and Monty to have him there? Did she trust his judgment and motives? He was a complicated man, but she had grown to know something about him and she had believed him when he had said he would never use her again.

She stared across the room at Monty and the wolf. "We have a problem, boy."

Monty lifted his head and looked at her inquiringly. *Okay?*

"Me or the wolf? We're both going to be fine. You shouldn't have gone out looking for her, you know. You're not in top shape yourself, and there's no telling what could have happened. She's no gentle soul."

Monty put his head back down. *Beautiful.*

"Yes, she is, and she's clearly a maiden in distress, but she could take you apart in minutes. You don't have the killer instinct."

Hurt.

"Right now, but in a few weeks she'll be well again. And I don't want you pulling that trick of putting your head on her throat again. It's a good way to get mauled and you—"

The wolf opened her eyes and stared directly into Monty's.

Beautiful.

"Oh, shit." Sarah's heart sank as she watched them together. "No, boy. She's definitely from the wrong side of the tracks. Hell, the wrong side of the universe. Believe me, you have nothing in common."

Beautiful.

"If you had a domestic squabble, she'd take you apart."

Beautiful.

"And what kind of kids would you have?"

Beautiful.

They might be at that. Golden retriever and this gorgeous

wolf . . . "It would definitely be a one-night stand. The Wildlife Federation has other plans for Maggie."

Monty delicately licked the fur beneath the wolf's eyes.

Maggie drew back her lips in a snarl.

Sarah tensed, ready to jump forward to protect him. "Stop."

Monty didn't stop.

And Maggie's snarl slowly disappeared. She closed her eyes, accepting.

"I'll be damned." Sarah shook her head. "Maybe it's mutual after all." She moved forward and knelt by the wolf. "I have to give her another shot, boy. Try to distract her."

Maggie opened her eyes and snarled at Sarah when the needle entered, but she didn't attack. A few moments later she was asleep again.

Once more Monty stretched out beside her.

"You're not listening," Sarah said. "It's strictly Montague and Capulet stuff. Her folks would never accept you."

Monty sighed, his gaze never leaving the wolf. *Beautiful.*

Logan was asleep in the chair when she left the porch.

She marched across the room and shook him awake. "You can stay. But you'd better get well fast. I'm going to work your tail off and enjoy every minute of it."

He yawned. "I'm glad you informed me in such a gentle manner."

"I don't feel gentle. I have problems." She headed for her bedroom. "I have to get Maggie on her feet and out of here quickly and I may need your help with some repercussions."

"What repercussions?"

"Monty's ga-ga over her."

Logan chuckled. "So?"

"It's not funny. I have to get them apart before they decide to mate. Wolves mate for life, and Monty . . . I won't have him hurt."

"Isn't it unusual for a rescue dog not to be fixed?"

"ATF wanted to do it, and I told them to leave it to me. I meant to . . . but then I didn't." She glared at him. "Okay?"

"Maybe for Monty it will be only a fling."

"That's crazy. Monty's the most loving dog I've ever known."

"I can see the problem."

She scanned his expression. He wasn't laughing or mocking any longer. He did understand. "Most people would think I'm being weird, but it's . . . important to me."

"Then it's important to me. And I can understand why you wouldn't want your best friend to make a bad match." He closed his eyes. "But could I go back to sleep now? If you're going to work my tail off, I'm going to need all the rest I can get."

He waited until the bedroom door shut behind her before he reached into his pocket for his phone and called Galen. "I'm at Sarah's cabin and I'll be here for a while. Have you heard anything?"

"Not yet. I'm still tracking down Sanchez. How were those last days in Kai Chi?"

"Hell."

"Is Sarah okay?"

"As good as can be expected. She's having a few domestic problems. Monty's in love with a wolf."

Galen burst out laughing. "That ball of fluff?"

"Believe me, it's not funny to Sarah. Call Margaret and have her find out everything she can about the Mexican gray wolves that were released in this area."

"Why don't you call her yourself?"

"She was pissed at me for coming here, and Taiwan won't

have made her temper any better. I've had a rough night and I don't want to deal with her right now."

"Say no more. I wouldn't want to contact her either."

"Have you secured the cabin?"

"Six of my best men."

"I haven't seen anyone."

"They can see you. They're camped up in the mountains and they can see trouble coming for miles. I'll give you Franklin's number."

"Tomorrow. I don't have a pen and I don't want to move. I'm hurting like the devil. Bye."

He had to get a few hours' sleep. It was almost dawn, and he hadn't the slightest doubt Sarah would soon be up and tending the wolf. As usual, she'd be fighting any softness toward him and would have no compunction about putting into action her threat to "work his tail off."

9

"Just what do you think you're doing?" Sarah stood in the bedroom doorway with her arms folded across her chest.

"Feeding Monty." Logan patted the dog on the head. "He was hungry, and I didn't want to wake you."

"No one feeds Monty but me. I've trained him not to accept food from anyone else." But Monty was eating, she realized with a mixture of amazement and annoyance. "Damn."

"He was hungry," Logan repeated as he filled up Monty's water bowl. "I thought I'd give it a try."

"I can't have you interfering with Monty's training."

"I can see why you wouldn't want to have strangers feed him, but I'm no threat."

"Practically no one is a stranger to Monty. He loves everyone. That's why I can't have him fed by anyone but me."

"Maybe he has better judgment than you think." He put down the water bowl. "Here you go, boy."

"I can't take the chance. So please leave my dog alone."

"Okay. Just trying to help. Anything else I can do?"

"You can go sit down and rest that leg. You haven't been off it in the last three days."

"Whatever you say." He limped back to his chair. "But it's getting better. Did you notice I was able to do a lot more yesterday?"

"Yes." Since the night they'd brought home the wolf, Logan had kept himself busy doing everything from sweeping the cabin to helping nurse Maggie. When they weren't working side by side, he was cooking or cleaning or on the phone, trying to wield influence to keep the ranchers away from the wolf. She scowled. "Too much."

"Do I perceive a softening?" He stretched his leg out on the hassock. "You're the one who wanted to work me to the bone. You asked, I obeyed."

"I know."

He grinned. "But you don't like the fact that I didn't mind it."

"Nonsense. I just didn't—" She smiled reluctantly. "You've not been any fun at all. What good is a slave if he's so obliging? It takes all the joy out of the situation."

"Sorry."

She studied him. "And you've been doing a heck of a lot more than I ask. I don't like that."

"I'm just a self-starter."

"You're also a prime manipulator. You knew it would bother me to see a wounded man overextend himself."

He gazed at her innocently. "Did I?"

"Knock it off."

"I'm surprised it took you this long to call me on it."

"I'm not that soft." She made a face. "And I thought you'd stop. I knew you were hurting."

"Just doing my job, ma'am."

"And getting a little of your own back."

"I admit I have a problem with total subjugation."

"Any subjugation."

"I do prefer partnerships. I think we've proved we work pretty well together, don't you?"

She didn't speak for a moment. "Yes."

"Then why not call a truce? You don't have to force me to do anything. I'd go nuts if I didn't have something to do. Even nursing your wolf is better than twiddling my thumbs. We're living together, let's do it as painlessly as possible."

"I'm not in any pain. I could go—" She broke off as the phone rang. "And we're not living together," she said as she crossed the room and picked up the phone. "Hello."

"You didn't call me," Todd Madden said. "How did the Logan job go?"

"What do you care, Madden? It's over. That's all that's important."

"Good. Then you can come up to Washington for the weekend. I've set up a press conference about the Barat earthquake, and what about this Taiwan mudslide? That will be excellent copy."

"Go to hell."

"Don't be ugly, Sarah." Madden's voice was silky smooth. "You know it doesn't do you any good to be nasty to me. Shall I make your reservations or will you?"

"I'm not coming to Washington. I'm busy."

"You know how I hate to pressure you, but I can't tolerate—"

"Screw you." She hung up the phone.

"You should have let me talk to him," Logan said.

"I got too much satisfaction out of telling him to go chase himself."

"That wasn't exactly the term you used," he said lightly.

The phone rang again.

She didn't answer it. "It's him again. He can't believe I'm not jumping through his hoop."

"Are you going to answer it?"

"No. I'm burning my bridges. If you don't keep your promise, I'm going to go down in flames."

"But you trust me to keep it. Or you wouldn't have burned that bridge."

She was silent a moment. "Yes, I trust you."

"How much time do I have?"

"A few days, maybe a week. Madden will have trouble believing that I won't change my mind. Then he'll get angry and want to punish me."

"And then what happens? What will he do to you?"

"He'll take Monty away from me."

"What?"

"Monty doesn't belong to me. ATF owns him. I do what Madden wants or he uses his influence to have them take Monty away and give him to someone else."

Logan swore softly. "Can't you buy him from ATF?"

"Don't you think I've tried? They won't sell him. Madden wants that hold on me."

"Are you sure he can get them to take Monty away?"

"He's done it before. Two years ago I'd had enough and told him to go jump in the lake. ATF snatched Monty out of my jeep while I was in the supermarket getting groceries. They left a very businesslike note. They were sending him to a handler in Europe and I'd be notified of the new dog I'd be assigned."

"Europe?"

"The K9 Corps trains dogs for other law enforcement bodies overseas." She continued bitterly. "Madden was very clever, wasn't he? He didn't even tell me what country. I was frantic. I begged everyone from mail clerks to senior officers in ATF to tell me where they'd shipped Monty. It took me over a month to find out they'd sent him to a police department in Milan. I thought it might be too late."

"Too late?"

"It's not only that he won't eat or drink for anyone else. Monty loves me. We're . . . close. He would mourn. A dog as loving as Monty can die of sadness." She blinked her stinging eyes. "He did mourn. He was sick, so sick, when I found him in Milan."

"And what did you do?"

"What do you think I did? I called Madden and told him I'd do anything he wanted if he'd give me back my dog." She looked straight into his eyes. "I won't let that happen to him again. If you can't find a way to get Madden off my back, Monty and I will just go away and disappear."

"I'll find a way." Logan's lips tightened grimly. "Count on it."

"I am. Heaven help you if you let me down."

"I won't let you down." He took out his phone. "Now go tend your wolf while I take care of Madden." He looked up after he'd dialed a number. "Since we're joined in putting Madden down, couldn't you ignore all my sins and give me my truce?"

"Maybe." She smiled. "If you promise not to feed my dog again."

"Only if he's starving." He spoke into the phone. "Margaret, what's the word on Madden?"

Sarah was still smiling as she and Monty moved toward the back porch. There was something very comforting about Logan's immediate and focused response to her problem.

Monty looked back at Logan. *Nice.*

"Cupboard love. You shouldn't have eaten until I fed you. You know better."

Trust.

"You still shouldn't have broken the rules." But she, too, was breaking the rules and trusting Logan. How had he managed to get past her defenses?

Nice.

Charisma? No, heaven knows he hadn't tried to charm her during these last days. He had just been straightforward and hardworking.

Why was she worrying anyway? All she had committed herself to was a truce for the next week or so.

Beautiful. Monty was trotting toward Maggie, who looked at him balefully. He plopped down beside her. *Love.*

She curled her lips in a snarl.

Sarah shook her head. "She's not feeling very romantic, boy. That wound's giving her a fit." She moved toward Maggie. "Come on, let's see if I can make it feel better. No snapping. Let's see if we can have a truce too."

The dog was romping and playing, his golden tail wagging happily as it ran circles around the Patrick woman.

Duggan sighted down the rifle squarely on the dog's head. His finger slowly caressed the trigger.

"What are you doing?"

He looked up to see Rudzak coming toward him over the ridge.

"The Patrick woman and the dog are outside the cabin. I'm going to give her a little surprise. I didn't do a good job of getting the dog at Santo Camaro. I'm going to blow his fucking head off now."

Rudzak looked down at the cabin. "That's not why we're here. We just managed to avoid Galen's men patrolling this area. They're all over the place. You'd think they were protecting Fort Knox. We may have only a short time before they come back. Have you seen Logan?"

"He's standing in the doorway."

"Ah, yes," Rudzak murmured. "His attitude is very protective, isn't it?"

"You told me we weren't going to touch him or the woman yet. But there's no reason I shouldn't kill the dog, is there?"

"Do you think you can do it? We weren't able to get very close. It's way out of range for most shooters."

"I can do it."

The golden retriever was lifting his head in the air and joyously barking.

"I've always hated barking dogs." Duggan sighted down the barrel again. "What do you bet I can put him down with one bullet?"

"No bet." Rudzak smiled. "I know you're an excellent marksman."

Yes, Rudzak always appreciated him, Duggan thought. Ever since he'd joined Rudzak a year earlier, he'd been given due respect. "Then watch me blow that pooch away."

"I'm looking forward to it." Rudzak crossed his arms across his chest. "Actually, this may be a stroke of genius on your part. I imagine Logan is feeling very safe in that little cabin with Galen's men protecting them on that far ridge. What better way to shake him up than this little statement? By all means, shoot the dog."

Duggan could almost see the after scene play out before him. The dog falling, covered with blood. Sarah Patrick staring at her dog, screaming, and then she and Logan running toward him.

"Wait a minute."

He followed Rudzak's gaze to the woman. She had whirled around and was looking up at the mountains.

"Interesting," Rudzak said. "Do you suppose she senses something? She's calling the dog."

"Goddammit." The dog and the woman were moving quickly toward the cabin, Duggan realized with frustration. He had to act fast. "Don't worry. I can still kill that dog."

"No."

He glanced up at Rudzak with a frown.

"I've found out what I wanted to know, and Galen's men aren't fools. They'd be able to locate the direction of the shot and be down on us in a heartbeat. It would be worth the risk if it was important, but it's not." He shrugged. "Besides, killing a dog would hardly be a worthy follow-up to Kai Chi."

"But it wouldn't hurt anything to—"

"No, Duggan," Rudzak said gently as he turned away. "Trust me. We'll just have to think of something more fitting."

"What's wrong?" Logan asked as Sarah shooed Monty in the front door. "What did you see?"

"Nothing."

His gaze narrowed on her face.

"Nothing," she repeated. "I just felt . . . something wasn't right. I know it sounds crazy. But I've learned to go with my instincts."

"It doesn't sound crazy at all. I imagine you've developed very good instincts over the years." He took out his phone. "I'll call security and ask Franklin to check out the area for any sign of Rudzak."

"If there's any threat, it's more likely that ranchers have found out I'm taking care of Maggie. They might have decided to teach me a lesson." She made a dismissive gesture. "As I said, it's probably nothing but maybe I'll take Monty out after dark from now on."

"Good idea." He spoke into the phone. "Franklin, what's happening up there?"

"Come on, Monty." Sarah headed for the kitchen. "I'll get you some fresh water."

Logan hung up as she finished filling Monty's dish. "No one's been sighted but they're checking."

"I told you, I didn't *see* anything." She moved toward the back porch and Maggie. "But if it was one of those ranchers, it won't hurt for them to know they're not alone out there."

"Are you letting me win?" Sarah leaned back in her chair and gazed at Logan suspiciously. "I'm good, but you can't be this bad."

"Believe me, I am. Poker's not my game. I've never been into instant gratification. I'm better at chess."

She studied him and then nodded slowly. "I can see it. Strategy and war games. I've never gotten into chess. I vote for instant gratification every time."

"Who taught you to play poker? Someone on the search team?"

"No, my grandfather. When I was a kid, we'd sit here before the fire and play for hours."

"What about your mother?"

"She lived in Chicago. She didn't like it here."

"But you did."

"I loved it." She grimaced. "And I loved getting out of the city. It was dirty and crowded and—" She stood up. "I'm thirsty. Want some lemonade?"

"Please."

"It's not as cool as it usually is this evening." She went to the refrigerator. "Maybe we should put out the fire."

He crossed to the fireplace. "Your mother liked the city?"

"She liked lights and movies and bars and people. Lots of

people. She got bored a lot." She gave him the frosty glass. "She was married four times."

"Tough for you."

"I survived." She sat down and stretched out her legs. "In fact, I was lucky. I got to go to my grandfather for a while every time she got married. I liked that. The third time she let me stay for two years."

"Why didn't she just turn over custody?"

"She'd get lonely. She had to have someone around."

"Nice."

She looked at him over the rim of the glass. "Look, I'm not complaining. That's just the way things were. I wasn't abused. Some people are just needy."

"But not you."

"Who'd take care of the needy people if we were all the same? It all balances out."

"Did your grandfather need you?"

She didn't answer right away. "I think he did. It was hard to tell. I know he loved me. He told me so at the end."

"Not before?"

"He didn't talk much. He worked his fingers to the bone to get the money to buy these few acres. When he moved into this cabin, he swore he would never leave until the day he died."

"How did he make a living?"

"Training horses and dogs. He was wonderful with animals."

He sipped his lemonade. "So are you."

"Animals are easy. They don't demand anything. All you have to do is love them."

"Some people are like that too."

"Are they? I haven't found that to be true."

"Why? Because you had a selfish mother who obviously didn't know how to take care of her own kid? You've been around enough to know there are plenty of great people in the world."

"I don't resent— It's none of your business, Logan."

"I know. It was just an observation."

"Screw your observations. You don't see me asking you the story of your life and then judging you."

"Go ahead. Turnabout is fair play."

"I don't want to know anything about—" She stared at him challengingly. "What were you doing with a research facility in Santo Camaro?"

"That's not the story of my life."

"So you won't tell me."

"I didn't say that." He looked down at his drink. "It's a medical research facility. We're making some interesting breakthroughs."

"Medical?"

"It's a field of research I've been funding for some time."

"Breakthroughs in what?"

"Artificial blood."

Her eyes widened. "What?"

"A substitute for blood. You haven't heard about it? There's been some news coverage about the research."

"I've heard a little." Her eyes narrowed. "It's because of Chen Li, isn't it? Because of her leukemia."

"It started off with Chen Li. It nearly killed me when I couldn't help her. But I'm not so selfish that I can't see the application to other diseases."

"But why bury the facility in the jungle? What's the big secret?"

"Industrial espionage. We're so damn close. The company that gets there first will control both development and the market."

"Money?"

"Control," he repeated. "I haven't devoted all these years to finding answers to give up control now."

"And that's what Bassett's working on?"

"Yes, he's trying to reconstruct the last month of research by the Santo Camaro team. They sent reports every month, but we didn't get the last report, and a hell of a lot was done right before the attack at Santo Camaro."

"Does Rudzak have anything to do with industrial espionage?"

"Rudzak doesn't give a damn about anything but getting me where it hurts the most."

"How was he able to find out what you were doing and about the facility? Did he know about your wife and how she died?"

"Oh, yes, he knew about Chen Li." He set his glass down on the table beside him. "See how I trust you? I've told you all my secrets."

Not all his secrets. "You must have loved Chen Li very much."

"Yes, she knocked me for a loop the first time I saw her. She was half Old World and half new technology. She was a computer whiz, but there was something serene and gracious about her. We were married a month after I met her." He paused. "She died three years later."

"And you're still hurting." She added brusquely, "That's why it's safer to love dogs."

"That was a long time ago and I was a different man. And I don't think you're totally devoted to the canine species or you wouldn't do the work you do."

"Think what you like. I knew from the first search I ever went on that this was what I was meant to do. A little girl got separated from her folks in the mountains near Tucson." She looked down into her glass. "She was only five and it was freezing cold. I wasn't sure we'd find her alive, but we didn't give up. Three days later Monty zeroed in on her, and she was alive. When I picked her up and wrapped her in a blanket, she whispered that she knew someone would come. She had been waiting. And I knew that she'd been waiting for *me*. I was the one who had saved her. There's nothing like that feeling on the face of the earth."

"Sometimes you can't save them."

"No, but then I can bring them home."

"You sound like Eve."

She shook her head. "I keep telling you, I'm nothing like Eve. Stop trying to dig into my psyche. Look, I'm just what's on the surface. I don't have a tragic past like Eve and I don't harbor resentments. I accept people as they are and go along with it. Understand?"

"I understand. But I don't believe you. If I've learned anything about you in the past weeks, it's that you're more complicated than you'd ever admit."

She snorted with disgust. "Bull."

"You're intelligent, hardworking, and crack a mean whip. And beneath all those prickly thorns, you're probably the most loving and giving woman I've ever met."

She glanced away from him. "Don't be sappy."

"You don't like that. Why not?"

"Because I just do what needs doing. Everybody has a purpose, a job to do. This is my job."

"You don't admit that your job is more selfless than most?"

"No more than a firefighter's or a policeman's or any number of other—"

"And you're embarrassed that I'd suggest you care for people as much as you do your four-legged friends?"

"I'm not embarrassed." She stood up. "I've got to check on Maggie."

"Are you running away?"

"No." She gave him a steady glance over her shoulder. "You couldn't make me run away, Logan. I'll check on Maggie and then I'll come back and give you another trouncing in poker."

"And I'll accept it. Do you know why?"

"You're a masochist?"

"No." He picked up his glass and lifted it in a toast. "I'm a friend."

She stared at him.

"Resign yourself. It was bound to happen after the time we've spent together and now, we've exchanged confidences. That seals it. I'm very impressionable. Don't worry. I'm not going to demand anything of you. Just pretend I'm a dog or a wolf."

She didn't know what to say.

"It's okay, Sarah," he said gently. "Really."

It wasn't okay. She felt awkward and uneasy and oddly . . . warm. "Are you trying to kid me?"

He started to stack the cards. "No way."

Two days later Logan got a call from one of the security men camped out in the foothills.

"Okay. No, just keep watch. I think I know who it is." He turned to Sarah. "We have a visitor. He should be here within a few minutes."

She stiffened. "Rudzak?"

He headed for the door. "I think it may be your friend Madden."

"What?" She followed him. "Why the devil should he come here?"

"If Margaret did her job, he should be hopping mad." He shaded his eyes to watch the approaching Buick. "Though I expected him to call you, not come here."

"Why should he be mad?"

He grinned. "It was taking too long to find the dirt on the prick so I hit him where it hurts. The wallet. He has an election coming up, and I called two of his biggest campaign contributors a few nights ago and persuaded them to drop their support. Then I had Margaret call Madden and tell him that would only be the beginning if he didn't persuade ATF to sell you Monty."

Her mouth fell open. "I'll be damned." Her gaze went to the Buick. "No wonder he's here."

"Like I said, I thought he'd call."

"No, that's not Madden. If he's frustrated, he's going to want to strike out and see my pain."

"Go inside. I'll talk to him."

She shook her head. "Stop trying to protect me. He'll be ugly, but it's nothing I can't handle." She braced herself as the car screeched to a halt before the front door. She hoped she was telling the truth. Madden was an expert at inflicting pain, as she'd learned all those years ago. But she wasn't that young, inexperienced girl any longer. She stepped forward as Madden got out of the driver's seat. "I told you never to come here again, Madden."

"You bitch." His face was flushed with anger. All the smoothness he usually showed Sarah was gone. "What the hell do you think you're doing?"

"A little more respect, please," Logan said softly. "And I think you're aware of what we're doing."

Madden's gaze shifted to Logan. "And what are you doing here? I did you a favor, dammit. You were supposed to help me."

"Circumstances changed. As a politician, you know how empty promises can be. Have you called ATF?"

"I won't be pressured by you."

"If you want to keep your seat in the senate, you will. We've only just begun to play. I'll stop your contributions cold and if you've even jaywalked, I'll find out about it and put it on every front page in the country."

"You son of a bitch."

"I want this, Madden. Give it to me and I may let you survive to run again."

"May?"

"I don't know if I can stand the thought of you sitting fat and healthy in the capitol, but it will definitely make my mind up if you turn me down."

"I will turn you down, you asshole."

"No, you won't. You're an ambitious man and I'm probably the biggest obstacle you've ever run across. Think about it. Why risk everything just for a little goodwill and publicity? Go get them somewhere else. You've used her and Monty enough."

"Have I?" Sarah could see him struggling to contain his rage as he whirled on her. "Have I used you enough, Sarah?" His voice was thick with malice. "Speak up. It's not like you to stay in anyone's shadow."

"Go away, Madden."

"Now you're giving *me* orders?" His gaze went from her to Logan and back again. "You think just because you're sleeping with the big man, you can pull the strings."

"I'm not sleeping with Logan."

"He's just staying in this crummy shack because he likes it? I'm not an idiot. I can see how he looks at you. Money and sex make the world go round. You couldn't give him money, but sex is no problem for you, is it?"

"Shut up, Madden," Logan said.

"So protective." He shot him a mocking glance. "I can't blame you for letting her talk you into—"

"Shut up."

"She fucks like a wild animal, doesn't she? She's the only woman I ever screwed who never said no. It didn't matter what I asked her to do, she—"

Sarah's fist connected with his nose. Blood spurted and he staggered back against the car.

"Go away, Madden," Sarah said. "Now."

"Whore." He reached for his handkerchief and covered his nose. "You *are* an animal."

"Maybe. I know I'm tempted to go for your throat."

"Hit the road." Logan's expression was grim. "And get on your phone the minute you hit the highway. I want a call from ATF within thirty minutes offering to sell Monty to Sarah."

Madden began cursing.

"I'm not going to repeat myself." Logan took a step closer. "Listen to me. I was annoyed with you before, now I want to break your neck. Do what I tell you."

"I'm not afraid of you." But Madden backed away. He gave Sarah one last malevolent look as he got in the car. "You think you're so clever. Oh, you've got him now, but he'll get tired of you and I'll still be around."

"I don't doubt it," she said. "Cockroaches are great survivors."

"Unless they get stepped on," Logan said.

Madden opened his mouth and then closed it without speaking. A moment later he was in the car, streaking down the road.

"God, that felt good," Sarah said. It felt better than good, as if a gigantic weight had been taken off her shoulders. "Do you think he'll make the call?"

"I almost hope he doesn't." Logan turned on his heel and went into the house.

She stared at him in surprise before following him. "Why?"

"Because I want to crucify the son of a bitch." His tone was savage. "But you're feeling just fine because you punched that bastard in the nose, aren't you?"

"Yes. Why are you so angry? Madden attacked me and I took care of it."

"Did it occur to you that I would have done it for you?"

"No."

"I didn't think so."

"Why should you? It was my job."

"The hell it is."

"Stop pacing around the room and sit down. You've been on your feet too much today."

"I'll sit down when I feel like it."

She held up her hands. "Whatever you say. I don't care if your leg aches all night. It would serve you right." No, it wouldn't; he had just done her a great favor. She tried to hold on to her patience. "Look, I'm sorry I involved you in that ugliness with Madden. I owe you and I—"

"You don't owe me shit. We made a deal and I paid it. Do you think that's what this is all about?"

"All I know is that you're not behaving reasonably. It's not my fault that Madden is the bastard he is."

"It's your fault that you didn't let me help you. You're not alone in this world, you know. Would it have hurt you to let me protect you? Just once?"

She blinked. "I didn't need protection."

"No, you don't need anyone, do you? You're not wounded. You haven't got a scar to your name. Bull*shit*."

She stiffened. "Shut up, Logan. I'm sorry if your ego was hurt, but don't take it out on me."

"You should have let me help you."

"You did help me."

"Is that why your knuckles are bleeding?"

She looked down at her hand in surprise. "It's nothing. Just a graze."

He stopped before her. "And you're so tough that it didn't faze you."

"No, dammit, I was too busy trying to understand why you were overreacting to a little— Let me go, Logan."

His hands tightened on her shoulders. "Why? Will you sock me too?"

"Maybe. If you deserve it." She looked up at him. "What the hell is wrong with you?"

"Nothing's wrong with me. No, that's a lie." He shook her. "You're driving me crazy. You're not alone in the world, dammit. You don't have to do everything for yourself."

"Let me go."

His hands opened and closed on her shoulders. "What's the matter? Are you afraid I'll jump you like your friend, Madden?"

"I know you better than that."

"Do you?"

Her chest tightened. He was gazing at her with an intentness that made her feel . . . She hurriedly looked away from him. "You're not Madden. And you said you were my friend. Was that a lie?"

He went still. "No." His hands dropped away from her shoulders. "It wasn't a lie." He walked back to the open doorway and stared at Madden's car, which was faintly visible in the distance. "And I'm not Madden. Why didn't you tell me you were lovers?"

"You didn't need to know to help me. It wasn't important."

"No? It feels damn important."

"It shouldn't. That was a long time ago and doesn't affect the present situation. The only use he has for me these days is to help his career."

"And what about you?"

"Get real."

"What about you?" he repeated.

"For God's sake, I was only a kid. I met him right after I joined ATF. I was lonely and I thought he— He was very smooth. He fooled me for over six months. Then I broke it off. He didn't like it."

"Evidently." He didn't look at her. "He clearly found you very entertaining."

She felt heat rise to her face. "So?"

"Just commenting. I take it he's been fucking you in other ways since you stopped letting him come to your bed."

"That was crude."

"But true."

She didn't speak for a moment. "Yes. He always wanted to be the one holding the whip."

"I trust you're not speaking literally. I think even you would have said no to—" He broke off and shook his head. "Sorry. That wasn't necessary."

"No, and that was crude too. And none of your damn business."

"You're right. As I said, I'm sorry." He turned around to face her. "I suppose I felt a little hurt that you'd close me out. Friends don't do that."

The tension between them was gone, she realized with relief. Or had it just eased? She'd take it either way. "I never said I was your friend."

"But you are, aren't you?"

Days of closeness and working together. Nights of tending Maggie. Jokes, humor, familiarity. "I suppose I am," she said slowly.

"You're damn right you are. I've worked too hard to make sure you—"

The phone rang.

"I'll get it." Logan crossed the room in four steps and picked up the phone. "She's not available. This is John Logan. Talk to me." He listened for a few moments. "I'll have someone stop by your office with a certified check within the hour. Give him a notarized bill of sale in exchange. Thanks." He hung up the phone and turned back to her. "Sanders with ATF. He said he's the head of the K9 unit. You know him?"

"He's my boss." Excitement was surging through her. "Madden called him? He's going to sell me Monty?"

He nodded. "Tomorrow you'll have the papers on him."

Oh, God, it was too good to be true. After all this time and heartache, it was going to happen. "Really?"

He smiled. "Really."

Her knees felt weak. She sank down in the easy chair. "I was afraid he wouldn't do it. I couldn't believe . . ."

"Believe."

Monty was hers. No more threats. He was safe.

Logan's gaze was on her face. "You're . . . radiant."

She felt radiant. She felt as glowing as the sun. "He's safe."

"Yes."

She closed her eyes. "I've been so worried about him. Dogs are helpless. They can't protect themselves from cruelty."

"But you protected him."

She opened her eyes as she felt his handkerchief touch her cheek. "What are you doing?"

"You're crying." He wiped her tears and then handed her the handkerchief. "Why do women always cry when they're happy? It doesn't make sense." He went over to the sink. "And it's disconcerting as hell."

"Why?"

"Tears are a sign of sorrow, and it's primitive instinct for a man to try to heal sorrow in a woman." He was returning to her carrying a damp dish towel. "It messes up our minds when there's no sorrow to heal. Give me your hand."

"What?"

"You're bleeding." He took her right hand and gently dabbed her bruised knuckles with the towel. "And that's a wound I can heal."

"It's barely a—"

"Hush. You've got a wicked right hook. Where did you learn it?"

"Ray Dawson."

"Who's Ray Dawson?"

"He's a fireman, one of my EMT instructors. He said that in natural disasters or tragedies people sometimes go crazy. Looters, relatives of people you can't manage to save. You have to be able to protect yourself."

"I can see that." He lifted her hand to his lips and kissed the bruised knuckles. "To make it better. Not scientific, but it satisfies my primitive instinct." He rose to his feet. "I have to call Margaret and make sure that she gets a man out to ATF headquarters right away. Anything else I can do for you?"

She shook her head.

"Sure? Dragons to slay? A diamond tiara?"

"You've done enough. Thank you."

"Enough for you, but what about me?"

"What about you?"

"I like this. It makes me feel ten feet tall making you look like you do right now. I think it may be addictive."

She swallowed. "You'll get over it."

"I'm not sure. We'll see." He pulled out his phone. "But evidently it's making you uneasy, so I'll go outside and make my call."

As soon as he walked out the door, she released the breath she hadn't known she was holding. Christ, she was actually shaking. The last thirty minutes had been too charged with emotion: anger, relief, bewilderment, joy.

And lust.

Don't dodge it. It was lust she had felt, lust for Logan. Strong and hot and basic.

He had felt it too.

But he hadn't pushed. He had stepped back and turned away.

And she had been disappointed. Stupid. God, that was stupid. A sexual involvement was the last thing she needed with a man like Logan. He was too strong and dominant and would interfere with her life.

But why would he interfere? They could be just ships that pass in the night. There was no way he would want any kind of commitment. She was really nothing to him.

Stop thinking about it. Stop thinking about him.

She got to her feet and moved toward the back porch. Monty was lying next to Maggie as usual but looked up and lazily wagged his tail.

"Some friend you are." She knelt beside them. "Here Logan and I have been working to get you out from under Madden, and you're in here making eyes at Maggie."

Beautiful. Love.

"How do you know? Maybe it's sex."

Love.

"Maybe." She stroked his head. "But you'll have to convince Maggie. She'll demand a commitment. She'll mate for life." But the bond between men and women wasn't as unshakable. A long time ago she had hated her mother's emotional instability and been determined to marry for life. But that was a child's dream. She had learned in a hard school that relationships between men and women were often casual and fleeting.

Love.

Not for her.

And not for Logan.

"I'll get right on it," Margaret said. "This is a good thing, John. I thought the pup belonged to her."

"So did I."

"Shall I stop the investigation into Madden's background?"

"No, I want to know everything I can about him."

"You sound grim."

"I feel grim. I want to hang him out to dry."

"Why?"

Because he was jealous as hell. Because he'd never had a stronger urge to destroy someone than at the moment he'd learned Madden had been Sarah's lover. "Why not? He's a sleazeball."

"You run into a lot of sleazeballs. You usually ignore them unless they get in your way."

"I'm not ignoring this one. I'm taking him down."

"Okay, okay. I'll try to have more information on him in a few days."

He hung up and dialed Galen's number.

"Where the hell is Rudzak?" he demanded when Galen picked up the phone.

"Hello to you too. Where are your manners, Logan?"

"Have you found Sanchez?"

"Last night. He didn't know where Rudzak was, but I persuaded him to make a few phone calls. He was told Rudzak had returned to the U.S. a few days ago."

"Where?"

"Destination unknown. But before he left he made a buy from a Russian dealer for a hell of a lot of explosives and detonators."

"Shit."

"He's through playing penny ante and it's a good bet he's going after his prime objective. We should be able to make a guess. Dodsworth?"

"Probably. But I've got seven factories and twenty-two research facilities in the U.S. I've increased the security on all of them and ATF is making regular checks."

"Not enough."

"I know that, dammit."

"But you're lucky. You have me flying to your aid even as we speak. I should be landing in San Francisco in a couple of hours. I'll go check out the plant in Silicon Valley tomorrow, since that's your largest facility, then Dodsworth. After that I'll tap my contacts and see if I can get a lead on Rudzak. If that meets with your approval, of course."

"And if it didn't, you'd do it anyway."

"What can I say? So I have an overabundance of initiative. How's the dog lady?"

"Fine."

"Do I detect a sour note? That was a distinct growl."

"I don't growl."

"Well, you might come to a better understanding with her if you did. She seems to have an affinity for animals. But I thought you've been on friendlier terms lately."

You are *an animal.*

Logan's hand tightened on the phone as Madden's words to Sarah came back to him. "Just find Rudzak. Fast."

"I'll find him." Galen hung up.

Logan shoved the phone into his pocket, his gaze on the sun setting behind the mountains. He should go in, find Sarah, and smooth over the ripples of discord he had stirred after Madden left. He'd bungled it badly. With Rudzak no longer a continent away, he must not be forced to leave Sarah.

He couldn't go back in the cabin. Not yet.

Damn Madden. With a few sentences he had blasted through Logan's composure and shocked him into losing control.

She fucks like a wild animal.

He closed his eyes. "Jesus." He could feel his body ready again even while fury and jealousy coursed through him.

She's the only woman I ever screwed who never said no.

What erotic games had she been willing to play?

Get control. This almost painful lust wasn't natural to him. Sex had always been an exquisite pleasure, not a driving obsession.

It wasn't obsession. He wouldn't let it be. He had reacted with instinctive arousal to Madden's words, but any man would have had the same response.

And as soon as he could get his body in check, he'd go back in the cabin and make Sarah forget that he'd made that slip.

10

"Something's happening," Bonnie said. "I don't like it, Mama."

Eve glanced away from the skull she was working on to look across the room. Bonnie was curled up at one end of the couch. The little girl was dressed in jeans and a T-shirt, as she always was when she appeared to Eve, her red hair wildly curly and her expression radiant and full of life. Eve's heart leaped with joy.

She quickly looked back at the skull. "Well, hello. I wondered if I was going to see you again." She changed the tab on the skull to a different depth. "I mean, dream of you again."

Bonnie chuckled. "Of course that's what you mean. You never give up, Mama. But someday you'll admit I'm who I say I am. You're already halfway there."

"To the funny farm? No, thank you."

"You know you're not crazy. Where are Joe and Jane?"

"They went to a matinee in town. Jane wanted to see some new Matt Damon movie. I had work to do, so I passed on it." She paused. "But I must have gotten sleepy and stretched out on that couch for a nap. Or you wouldn't be here."

Bonnie grinned. "Isn't it great how much work you got done on that skull while you were sound asleep?"

"Shut up, brat. I don't care what you say. You're not a ghost, only a figment of my imagination. I created you, and as soon as I no longer need you, you'll fade. I'm already on the way. You haven't appeared for months." She kept her eyes on the skull. "I thought when Sarah found your body and we brought you home that maybe you'd moved on."

"And that made you happy?"

"Yes, of course." She closed her eyes. "No, I'm lying. I've missed you, baby."

"I've missed you too."

She cleared her throat. "Then why haven't you come to see me?"

"You were all confused about me. You know, for a smart woman, sometimes you don't think so clearly. I thought I'd stay away until you and Jane got everything straight."

"How diplomatic of you."

"I want things right for you, Mama. I would have stayed away longer, but I got worried." She fell silent a moment. "Something's going to happen."

"You said that before."

"Because it's true. Something bad."

"And I'm supposed to believe you?" Her hand was shaking as she placed another tab. "Joe? Jane?"

"I don't think so. Maybe. You know I can't see what's going to happen. I just get glimpses or feelings."

"A fine ghost you are. Get me all excited and then tell me you don't know any details."

"Sarah . . ."

"What?"

"There's darkness all around Sarah. Death. So much death."

"She just got back from Barat. There was plenty of death there."

Bonnie shook her head. "Something's going to happen."

"Then go visit her dreams."

"Mama."

"What can I do? Tell her my daughter who we just buried is worried about her?"

Bonnie nibbled at her lower lip. "It's not only her. Some of the darkness has to be near you or I wouldn't be able to feel it." She cocked her head, listening. "I have to go now. I hear Joe's car."

"I don't." Eve wiped her hands on a towel and moved toward the window. Joe's car was just turning the far curve in the road. "How do you do that?"

"There are some advantages to being a ghost. I love you, Mama."

"And I love you, baby." She turned her head. "But you can be very—" The end of the couch was empty. No small jean-clad form, no bright, mischievous face. No Bonnie.

She closed her eyes as disappointment surged through her. Most of the time dreaming of Bonnie brought her a sense of peace, but this time she had a nagging feeling of disquiet. Why?

Something's going to happen.

Darkness.

She had thought she had left darkness behind. These last months with Joe had been filled with joy and light. The only cloud had been Jane's attitude, and Eve had been sure that could be remedied. If there were something menacing coming, she wouldn't believe the fates would let it come to them.

She was whistling in the dark. When Bonnie had been murdered, she learned there was no justice in the world. She could only cling to the people she loved and hope.

Joe parked beside the cottage and he and Jane were getting out of the car. They were laughing and Eve suddenly felt better. She headed for the front door to meet them. She wasn't going to let her imagination depress or panic her. Bonnie was not a ghost, only a dream. She had no power to see danger on the horizon. Sarah was perfectly safe, and no darkness was near either Eve or the people she loved.

Darkness was falling, but Rudzak could still see the eager, loving look on Eve Duncan's face as she moved across the porch toward Joe Quinn and the child. It told him all he needed to know. It appeared Logan's affair with Eve Duncan was as dead as yesterday's news. Duncan had a new man and Logan wasn't one to accept the role of second fiddle.

Too bad.

He lowered the binoculars and turned to Duggan. "Start the motor. We can go now." He settled back in his seat as Duggan piloted the speedboat across the lake.

The dossier on Logan had told him that the relationship with Eve had faded, but Rudzak had had to see for himself. It would have been exquisite to destroy a woman Logan loved. However, he might reconsider Eve Duncan if nothing more interesting appeared on the horizon.

His fingers touched the ivory and jade comb he'd slipped into his pocket when he'd left the hotel that morning. He'd thought perhaps . . .

Not yet, Chen Li.

He would be glad to rid himself of the comb. It was one of the last gifts he'd given her and the memories were bitter.

"You shouldn't give this lovely thing to me." Even as Chen Li spoke, her forefinger ran delicately over the yellowed ivory teeth of the comb. "It's too expensive. John never says anything, but I think it makes him feel bad that he can't give me gifts like this."

"Logan isn't that selfish. You like it, don't you?"

"It's wonderful." She reluctantly handed it back to him. "But John's feelings are more important. You do understand, Martin?"

Fury tore through him. He turned away so she wouldn't see it. "Of course I understand." He moved toward the cabinet where she kept her treasures. "But it belongs to you. Suppose we just put the comb in the back of the case and not mention it to Logan? He'll probably not even notice it."

"I—I suppose that would be all right."

"I'm sure it will." He closed the case and smiled at her. "After all, he does want you to have the things that make you happy."

"It's not things that make me happy, Martin. John makes me happy."

"That's good. That's all I want."

And to see Logan dead.

She had gone to the doctor the next week and he diagnosed her with leukemia. After all those years he had been cheated.

Logan had cheated him.

"Are we coming back?" Duggan asked.

"Maybe. But not right now."

"Where do we go from here?" Duggan asked. "Sacramento? Dodsworth?"

"Patience," Rudzak answered. But Duggan had no patience; in many ways he was like a child.

"Dodsworth?" Duggan persisted.

"Eventually. But there are other things to do first. I've waited a long time for Logan. I've always found that anticipation can almost be more rewarding than the act itself."

"For you," Duggan said sourly. "It seems to me all that trouble we went through in Phoenix was a waste of time."

He was really incredibly dense, Rudzak thought with amazement. And stupidity was dangerous. Already Rudzak had decided that Duggan would not survive the blast he was so eager to engineer.

But that was down the road, and Duggan's usefulness was not plumbed fully yet. So keep him on an even keel, don't show him the scorn. Push the right buttons. With Duggan it was his self-love and conceit. "I know it's difficult for a man of action like you to hold back," he said gently. "It's one of the qualities I admire in you. But give my way a try. I think you'll be surprised."

He watched the words work on Duggan.

Finally the man shrugged. "If you say so. I guess I'll go along with you."

"Thank you." Rudzak smiled brilliantly. "I promise this job will be the ultimate experience of your lifetime."

Eve called Sarah at nine-thirty that evening.

"Is everything okay?" Sarah asked. "How's Jane?"

"Not much better. Though you'd never guess if you didn't know her. She's just . . . quiet."

"And how are you?"

"Fine. I knew you'd be worrying, so I thought I'd give you a call."

"The offer is still open. I'm having a few problems right now, but they should be settled soon and I'd love to have Jane for a while."

"We're a family. We'll work it out."

Sarah shook her head. "You're so stubborn. It's not a crime to ask for help from a friend."

"We'll work it out. How's Monty?"

"In love. With a wolf."

"What?"

"Don't ask." But that gave her an idea. "Maggie, that's the wolf, has a fractured leg and I could use help tending her. Jane is really good with animals."

Eve laughed. "And that's going to make me send Jane to the rescue? Only you would think a wounded animal is a perfectly good reason to send a child into a wolf's den."

"Hey, it's my den. The wolf is just a guest."

"No deal."

"Jane would love her. Maggie's not easy, but she has character. Come to think of it, she reminds me a little of Jane."

"Does she?"

"I can tell you're not convinced. Keep thinking about it and let me know."

"Take care of your own wolf." Eve hesitated. "How are things with you? What kind of problems? Besides the wolf."

"Isn't the wolf enough?"

"You're being evasive."

"Maybe a little." She looked at Logan sitting in his chair across the room. "But any problem I have isn't anything that won't go away. I'll call you in a week and see if you've changed your mind about sending me Jane. She really would like Maggie."

"That's what I'm afraid of. All I need is to have her heart broken when she has to leave your damn wolf." Another pause. "You're sure everything is under control with you? I've been uneasy about you lately."

"Why on earth?"

"I don't know. I just feel . . ."

"You're crazy. Nothing ever happens to me. Or, if it does, I always come out of it."

"Yeah, sure. Well, I suppose you wouldn't tell me anyway. But if you don't call me next week, I'm calling you. Give Monty a pat for me." She hung up.

"You tried to give away my job," Logan said as Sarah turned away from the phone. "And I thought I was doing pretty well with Maggie."

"You'll do." She sat down on the couch across from him. "But Eve would be better off with Jane here."

"So you'd throw me out. It's not a good idea. Not now."

"If you get rid of Rudzak, I could go on with my life."

"I'm trying. I have to find him first." His gaze narrowed on her face. "It hasn't been so bad having me here, has it?"

"No." She looked away. "But it's time for it to be over."

"Why now?"

You're sure everything is under control with you?

It was odd Eve had asked that question. For the first time in years, Sarah was feeling out of control. Hell, for the past two days she had done everything under the sun to keep herself busy just to avoid Logan.

"Why now?" Logan repeated.

She got to her feet. "I think I'll check on Maggie and then turn in."

"Aren't you going to tell me why Eve called?"

"She said she was uneasy about me."

"And you told her nothing could put you down."

"If you're going to eavesdrop, get it right. Any number of things can put me down, I just usually manage to work out of them."

"I stand corrected. Why was she uneasy?"

"No reason. She doesn't know anything about Rudzak or that you're here. The situation with Jane probably has her on edge."

"Maybe." He thought about it. "But it's not like her. She's been through too much to let one worry carry over to another."

"You should know." She headed for the porch. "Since you

lived with her for a year. Don't worry about Eve. It's Joe's job to take care of her now."

"For God's sake, I'm not worrying about Eve."

The harshness of his tone startled her, and she looked at him.

He held her gaze with an intentness that made her lose her breath. "I'm worried about you. Is that too much to believe?"

She breathed deeply to ease the sudden tightness in her chest. "Yes. I don't know . . . I mean . . . naturally, you'd feel concerned about Eve."

"Naturally."

"You care about her."

"Of course I do. That doesn't mean I can't feel anything for any— Where the hell are you going?"

"I told you, I'm going to bed."

"Look at me."

She didn't want to look at him. She was feeling the same mindless heat she'd felt that day Madden had come. "I don't want to talk anymore. Good night."

"Then don't talk. Listen." He was out of his chair and standing before her. "You know what we both want. If you refuse to take it, I'm not going to force you. But don't throw Eve between us. She has nothing to do with this."

He wasn't touching her, but he was so close, she could feel the heat of his body. She felt dizzy, tingling . . . She wanted to step closer. He was so big. What would it feel like to have that body against her own? The next moment she knew.

He inhaled sharply and went rigid. "What are you doing?"

She wasn't sure. The movement had been purely instinctive. "I don't know. I wanted . . . I think I made a mistake."

"You'd better make up your mind fast. I'll count to five."

How could she make up her mind when she was so dizzy

she couldn't put two coherent thoughts together? "It probably shouldn't happen. We're not really compatible."

"The hell we're not." His hands dropped to her hips and he pressed her to him, rubbing in an undulating, catlike motion. "You can't be more compatible than that."

She bit her lower lip as a wave of sheer lust surged through her. "You'd try to control me. You're a manipulator. You like things your own way."

He kissed her. "Doesn't everyone? But I'm willing to negotiate, and I know better than to get in the way of your precious job."

"What about Taiwan? There are jobs I have to do alone and you'd—"

He kissed her again. "I promise."

"You said—you'd count—to five."

"I did. Internal clock." He stepped back and took her hand, pulling her toward the bedroom. "And it's still ticking. God, is it ticking. Want to hear it?" He put her hand on his heart. "If you're going to say no, it better be now."

She could feel the rapid thump of his heartbeat beneath her palm. It was sending shock waves through her with every beat. It filled her body. It filled the room. It filled the world.

"It's going to be good. Can't you feel it? Don't you—"

"Stop talking," she said unevenly. "I'm not going to say no. How the devil could I?" She followed him down on the bed and covered his mouth with her own.

"I really have to go check on Maggie." Sarah yawned and cuddled closer to Logan's naked body. "I should have done it hours ago."

"You were busy." He brushed a kiss on her forehead. "And you're going to be busy again in about . . . two minutes."

She chuckled. "Your internal clock again?"

"You bet. It's wound tight and ready to spring forward."

She reluctantly pushed him away and sat up. "Maggie."

"I'll do it." He swung out of bed. "You stay here. I don't think you've had much practice at balancing duty and pleasure. I wouldn't want those weights to swing in the wrong direction."

She felt a ripple of heat go through her as she watched him walk naked across the room. The very first time she had seen him she thought he was beautiful as a cougar. He was muscular, big, strong, fit, as comfortable in this bedroom as he had been in the jungle.

He had swept her away with his bawdy eroticism and dynamic energy, totally surprising her. She had thought sex with him would be intense, overpowering, and it had been. But it had also been fun. If she had been overpowered, it had been by her own sexuality. Logan had not tried to dominate her. He had led, offered, tempted.

But wasn't that the height of power and manipulation? To seduce was a thousand times cleverer than to force, and Logan was the most seductive man she had ever met.

To hell with it. She didn't want to analyze what had happened. It was sex, not brain surgery. She had enjoyed her body and his. That was all. No harm had been done.

"Maggie's fine." Logan was coming back toward her. "I changed her bandage."

"You were quick. It usually takes me longer."

"I had incentive." He sat down on the side of the bed. "Scoot."

She moved over. "Is Monty okay?"

"If you call mooning at Maggie okay. I've never seen an animal more lovesick. She's leading him on a merry chase."

"She has to be careful. It's forever for her. Not that I'm defending her. Poor Monty is— What happened to your hand?"

"Nothing much." He looked down at his left hand. "Maggie nipped me a little. She barely broke the skin." He put his hand on her breast. "Not her fault. I was in too much of a hurry."

She felt a tingle of heat go through her. "Go wash and put antiseptic on it."

"Later." He moved over her and parted her legs. "The clock's ticking."

"Now." She pushed him away. "Never mind. I'll do it myself. I won't have you bleeding all over me."

"That's tender."

She got up and hurried across the room. "I'm not into kinky sex. Well, maybe I am a little, but blood doesn't turn me on."

"You say something like that and then expect me to be patient and keep my—"

"Hush." She came back a moment later with the medical bag. "It will take only a minute."

He watched her bent head as she swabbed the wound with alcohol. "This isn't necessary. I think you're only trying to torture me."

"It's a thought. Or maybe turnabout is only fair play. You cleaned up my knuckles after I decked Madden."

"But you weren't in the shape I am right now."

"Yes, I was. Not right away, but you were angry and I could sense . . ." She lifted her gaze. "What Madden said excited you. You looked at me and I could see you thinking about the things you'd like to do with me. And then I started thinking about them and I became excited too."

"Madden had nothing to do with this."

"Of course he did." She looked down again and began rubbing antiseptic on the cut. "Madden called me an animal. Was I animal enough for you, Logan?"

He said gruffly, "You were damn wonderful." He tilted her head so she could look into his eyes. "I wanted to kill Madden when he called you that, but there's nothing wrong with being an animal. Not if they're as clean and bold and beautiful as you are. And maybe Madden was the catalyst, but this would have happened eventually anyway. Remember?" he teased. "It's a guy thing. What else can you expect from a man who thinks about sex every ten minutes."

"Eight minutes," she said unevenly. "After tonight, I have an idea that magazine article was dead on the money."

"Tonight wasn't a fair test." He pulled her back into bed. "What do you expect me to think about when I'm making love to you?"

She looked away from him. "Turn out the light."

"I like to look at you."

She liked to look at him too. "Turn it out."

He did and pulled her into his arms. "If you didn't like it, why didn't you tell me before?"

She did like it. It was just easier to say some things in the dark. "You said you were making love to me. But you're not making love to me, it's just sex. We both know that. You don't have to pretend anything else."

"Oh, I don't?"

"It's better not to confuse the issue. I know you couldn't love me any more than I could love you. We're like fire and water."

She could feel his muscles stiffen against her.

"I . . . see."

"I'm not like Eve."

"No, you're not."

"And I'm sure I'm not like Chen Li."

"Not the slightest."

"So sex is enough." She buried her face in his shoulder. "I . . . like this. I like you. I thought—I'd like it to go on for a while. But it can't if we're not honest with each other."

"Well, no one could say you're not being honest enough." He was silent a moment. "Tell me, did you ever tell Madden you loved him?"

"What difference does—"

"Did you?"

"Yes."

"Anyone else?"

"No."

"That son of a bitch really did a number on you, didn't he?" He pressed her head into his shoulder. "Never mind. We've talked enough about Madden tonight to last me a lifetime. I just wanted to get the picture straight."

"You can't think I'm pining for that bastard?"

"Perish the thought. You're not scarred. I'm the one who's carrying all the baggage. Right?" He didn't wait for an answer. His mouth covered hers and he moved over her. "Now shut up and let's have sex. I promise I won't make love to you. I wouldn't want you to think I'm dishonest."

He was angry, she realized. This time it was rougher, deeper, harder, and yet she found herself responding with a passion even stronger than before. It went on for a long time before he collapsed on top of her.

His chest labored as he struggled to get his breath. "Isn't it lucky this is just sex? It might damn well kill me if it was anything more serious."

11

It was almost ten o'clock when Sarah opened her eyes.

Monty.

She had to feed Monty and Maggie.

She usually fed them at seven, and she was surprised that Monty hadn't been pawing at the door.

Logan's arm was draped across her breasts and he was still asleep. One more minute wouldn't matter. She lay there, looking at him. It was pleasant seeing Logan with his defenses down. He looked younger, more vulnerable. It gave her a warm, cozy feeling to know he trusted her to see him like this.

Monty.

She carefully got out of bed. No need to wake Logan yet. She'd feed Monty and Maggie, shower, and maybe fix them breakfast. She grabbed her robe, gathered her clothes, and shut the bedroom door silently behind her.

Monty greeted her with reproachful eyes and a soft woo-woo when she came out on the porch.

"Don't give me that." She set his bowl of food down beside

him. "I deserve a life too, you know. You're not the only one who needs a little companionship." But it hadn't been companionship, or her body would not have this delicious lethargy and sensitivity. She set Maggie's bowl down before her. "And you weren't very nice to Logan last night. I thought you'd stopped that snapping."

Maggie gave her an enigmatic look from silver eyes, then started to eat.

It had been her fault. Maggie was Sarah's responsibility and she had let Logan do her work. It had been easy to let Logan take over.

Much too easy. She frowned as she slowly rose to her feet. Wasn't it possible she would start unconsciously trying to please him?

There wasn't anything wrong with trying to please a man who was obviously trying to please her. She could guard her feelings and take the pleasure.

Guard her feelings? Where had that thought come from?

"No," she whispered.

Monty looked inquiringly at her.

She shook her head. "Not you, baby." She left the porch. That tiny ripple of panic had no reasonable basis. There were no feelings to guard except liking and respect. She didn't have to give up going to bed with Logan as long as she could keep her head straight and her life as independent as it always had been. That was the only sensible way to—

The phone rang.

Howling.

Logan's eyes flicked open.

It had to be Maggie.

And Sarah was no longer beside him.

He tossed the sheet aside. "Sarah! What's wrong with Maggie?"

No answer.

He went cold. "Christ." He ran out of the bedroom. "Sarah!"

She wasn't in the living room.

The porch.

No one was on the porch but Maggie. No Monty. No Sarah. Maggie gave him a baleful glance, then lifted her head and gave another mournful howl.

Where the devil was Sarah?

Don't panic. He doubted that she'd taken Monty for a run. He'd dress, go check to make sure the jeep was still there, and if it wasn't, he'd go after them.

He saw the note on the kitchen counter on his way to the bedroom.

Logan,

I got a call from Helen Peabody. They need Monty and me for a water-search job. It's local, so I should be back tonight or tomorrow. You take care of Maggie.

Sarah

Shit.

He punched in Franklin's number. "Sarah's left the cabin."

"I know. About thirty minutes ago."

"Did you have her followed?"

"You've got to be kidding. Galen told me he'd have my ass if we slipped up on this one. Smith's tailing her. She's on Highway 60 heading east. There's no one following her."

Relief surged through Logan. "Good. Tell Smith not to lose her." He hung up.

It could be all right. The call had come from Peabody, someone she knew and trusted.

And it could be a trap.

He dialed Margaret. "Get Helen Peabody, Tucson Search and Rescue, on the line. I need information. Make her cooperate any way you have to." He went into the bedroom and threw on his clothes. The phone rang as he was buttoning his shirt.

"Helen Peabody," Margaret said as she patched him through.

"I'm sorry to disturb you, Ms. Peabody, but I need your help."

"Certainly. How do you do, Mr. Logan? I want to thank you for your help in getting our group to Taiwan. And now Ms. Wilson said Sarah had persuaded you to make a donation to our organization. I'm sure you're aware how desperately we need it."

"Sarah was very convincing. But she left before we were able to finalize the donation. I believe she talked to you before she ran out the door."

"I'm sorry, but Monty is the only dog in our group who does water search. I didn't like to bother Sarah since she just returned from Taiwan, but when Sergeant Chavez called, I gave in. It shouldn't take more than a day or two. But I could discuss the contribution with you. Actually, it's really my job. Sarah is in the field."

"I started the talks with her and I'd like to continue. But my time is at a premium right now. Perhaps I could reach her through this Sergeant Chavez? Do you know him personally?"

"Several of our group have worked with Richard in the past. He's with the Maricopa Sheriff's Department and works with the lake patrol. Nice guy. He was terribly concerned about those kids."

"What kids?"

"Haven't you seen the stories on TV? Three teenagers were picnicking in the Tonto Basin forest near Apache Lake and they disappeared. Search parties have been looking for them for the past two days. Thank God it's summer. It increases the chance of survival enormously."

"No, I didn't see the story." Sarah didn't have a television set. "Is Sarah going directly to Apache Lake?"

"Yes, she's to meet Chavez at the rest stop."

"Can you give me his phone number?"

"Sure. But he's hard to reach. In emergency situations he's usually out on the trail or water with the search teams."

"I can try." He took down the number. "Thank you. I'll have Sarah get back to you about my donation." He hung up and called Margaret. "Get in touch with the Maricopa Sheriff's Department and check on Sergeant Richard Chavez. Make sure he's on the up-and-up. Then get me any information on the search going on at Apache Lake."

"Got it."

He hung up the phone.

Maggie was still howling.

Maybe she was hurting. He went to the porch and checked her bandage. It was fresh; Sarah must have changed it before she left. Maggie snapped and he barely eluded those powerful jaws. "I can't help it, dammit. I didn't send them away."

She glared at him and then raised her head and howled.

He got to his feet when the phone rang.

"Chavez checks out. Been with the patrol for fifteen years and has a chest full of commendations. He's working the Apache Lake case. Anything else?"

"Not right now." He hung up and sank down in his easy chair.

Everything looked okay. It was a valid case, Chavez had checked out, no one was following Sarah but Smith.

Okay, hell. Just the fact that Sarah had not woken him to tell him she was going was significant. She had reasserted her independence and delicately thumbed her nose at him. It was a reaction he had half-expected, one he couldn't ignore. Now what was he going to do? The situation appeared safe and she was only doing her job. If he went after her, she would have grounds to claim he was interfering with her freedom.

Maggie howled.

And she had told him to take care of Maggie. He couldn't leave the wolf alone or under the care of someone Sarah didn't trust. Any other action would really blow any gains he'd made the previous night.

Maggie howled again.

He felt like howling too, in frustration, anger, and panic. What appeared smooth on the surface might be nasty underneath. He didn't know Smith. Was he sharp enough? And there were too many things Logan didn't know about the job Sarah was going on.

Just what the hell was a water search?

She was being followed.

Sarah glanced at the rearview mirror again. Black Toyota SUV. It was the same car she'd noticed behind her a few miles after she'd left the cabin. And he was closer. Her hands tightened on the steering wheel.

She was going through the last small town before she hit that twisting road down to the lake. Time to check out the

SUV before she got to a more isolated area. She pulled into a busy Texaco station and got out of the car. "Stay, Monty."

She took six steps back to the road, directly in the path of traffic. The SUV screeched to a halt only a few feet from where she stood.

"Jesus." A sandy-haired man stuck his head out the window. "I almost hit you, lady."

She glanced over her shoulder at the service station. They were attracting enough attention. Several motorists had stopped pumping gas to watch them. "Who almost hit me?" She moved to the side of the car. "Who are you? And why are you following me?"

"I wasn't following you. I was—" He stopped and grinned. "Okay, I'm busted. I'm Henry Smith. Franklin sent me after you when you left the cabin."

"And who hired Franklin?"

"Galen. Who else?" He glanced over his shoulder. "Could I pull into the service station?"

"The other cars can go around you. This should take only a minute. Call Galen. I want to talk to him."

He dialed the number and handed her the phone when Galen answered. "Galen, do you know a Henry Smith?"

"Sarah?"

"Henry Smith—do you know him and what does he look like?"

He answered crisply, "Yes. Thirty-something, light brown hair, brown eyes, small scar in the hollow of his throat. If you have any doubts, ask him where he got the scar. It was in San Salvador."

He did have a small round white scar in the hollow of his throat. "Where did you get that scar?"

"San Salvador, 1994."

"It's him. Thanks, Galen."

"Sarah, what are you doing? Logan called me and—"

"I'm doing my job." She hung up and handed the phone back to Smith. "Sorry. Actually, I expected one of you to follow me. I don't take much stock in this threat Logan seems so sure of, but it would have been dumb of me not to be careful."

"No problem. I'm glad you're on your guard. But you could have told us you were going to Apache Lake."

"How did you know I was?"

"Logan. He called Franklin and told him where you were headed."

She was relieved Logan hadn't come himself. It seemed he had taken her words seriously. "I'm supposed to meet Sergeant Chavez in the rest stop at the lake. If you're going to keep an eye on me, stay out of my way and let me do my job."

He touched his forehead in a casual salute. "You won't even know I'm around."

"You don't have to take it that far." She turned and moved back toward her car. "Just don't get in my way."

"Ms. Patrick? I'm Richard Chavez." The man in the brown Maricopa Sheriff's Department uniform got out of the 4x4 Tahoe patrol vehicle as she walked toward him. "It's good of you to come." He handed her his badge and photo ID as he glanced at Monty. "Hi, boy, I've heard a lot about you. Helen says you're a wonder dog. Can I pet him?"

"Sure." She checked the ID, glanced at the corresponding ID in the patrol vehicle, then returned the badge. "But let him stretch his legs first. It's been a long trip. Go, Monty."

He bounded out of the jeep and tore around the parking lot.

"He's a beauty." Chavez's admiring gaze followed the dog.

"I've got a mutt I adopted from the pound. Lots of character, but no one could say she's any beauty queen. Not that I'd want any other dog."

"Hey, everyone says mutts are the brightest. And I wish more people adopted from the pounds." She looked at the forest beyond the rest area. "When were the kids seen last?"

"Three days ago. They came up here camping. Josh Nolden called his father on his cell phone and said they'd be back before midnight. They never showed. We found their campsite about ten miles from here but no sign of them." He rubbed the back of his neck. "Late yesterday we found tire marks just beyond those pines near the lake."

"You think the car may have gone into the lake?"

"We don't know. We hope to God not. But the incline is steep along there and the water's deep. If they went off the bank, they could have skidded right down into the water."

"Wouldn't there be tire marks on the incline?"

He shook his head. "Shale."

"Have you sent out divers?"

"Not yet. Not until we have more to go on." He made a face. "A water search can take days, weeks."

"I know." And it became a nightmare for the friends and relatives of the victims. "Where are the tire marks?"

"I'll take you. It's about a mile through the forest to the lake. I have a speedboat tied a short distance from the last place we saw the tracks."

She put on her utility belt. "Monty."

Monty bounded over to her and she put his leash on him. "Time to get to work, boy."

"Do you need the leash? He seems very obedient."

"He is." She followed him down the trail and into the forest. "But that doesn't mean he won't jump out of the boat and try to rescue them if he finds them."

"Even if they're dead?"

"Monty doesn't give up. He's an optimist. He doesn't want to believe it."

Chavez sighed. "Neither do I. Those kids are only sixteen and seventeen. The Nolden boy's an honor student, going to MIT this fall. Jenny Denkins goes to the same high school as my daughter. They know each other."

"Don't tell me about them."

"Why not?"

Because it broke her heart. "It's hard enough to try to find a stranger. It's worse to have a picture in your mind."

He looked at her in understanding. "Maybe you and your dog are a lot alike. I think you might jump in the water too if we find the bodies."

"Not anymore. The first couple of times I did a water search I was tempted. There's something terrible about someone's life ending underwater. You want to bring them up out of that darkness."

"But you're tougher now?"

"No, but I have to control myself for Monty. My job is to find them. Someone else can bring them to the surface."

"Like me."

"Like you. But I won't be here when you do. I'm taking Monty home if we locate— What's wrong?"

Chavez had stopped and was looking over his shoulder. He shrugged. "Nothing. A goose went over my grave."

"What?"

"I had a funny feeling in the back of my neck." His gaze raked the trees around them. "Like something's watching us."

She scanned the trees. She couldn't see anything and, unlike Chavez, she didn't sense anything threatening.

"Sorry. It's probably nothing." He shook his head. "There are bears up here, you know. And they like to roam near the rest stops and pick up food from the trash barrels."

More likely Henry Smith was keeping his promise to keep out of sight. "Or it could be my friend who followed me here. I told him not to interfere."

"Someone followed you? Why?"

"He's a little overprotective. It's a long story, and you wouldn't be interested."

"The heck I wouldn't." His expression was sober. "You've got to be careful of people following you around. A lot of women discover that overprotectiveness is a sign of a stalker."

"I'm not worried." Time to change the subject. She could see Chavez was getting protective himself. They had reached the top of the hill, and the lake was spread out before them. "Beautiful. I'd almost forgotten . . ."

"Have you ever been here before?"

"Years ago. My grandfather brought me. He loved it here." She looked down at the blue lake. It seemed impossible such still, serene beauty could hide the bodies of those children. The thought was incredibly sad. Just do your job and get out of here. "Where's the boat?"

Chavez pointed down the incline about fifty yards from where they were standing. "The last tracks we were able to trace were right here. But the shale is harder packed from here on, and they could have traveled for another mile or two." He started down the incline and reached back to take her hand. "Let me help you. This stuff's slippery."

His hand was warm and firm and it felt good. She was still feeling a little chill from that first sight of the lake, and it was nice to have someone to hold on to. She looked back over her shoulder but could see no sign of their footprints on the rocks.

She could understand what Chavez was up against in determining where the car went into the water.

"Did you hear something?" Chavez's gaze was following her own.

"No, just looking at the shale." She added teasingly, "No bear in sight."

"I thought I heard— It must have been our footsteps. This shale is damn noisy." Chavez helped her into the boat and Monty jumped in after her. "Where do you want to start?"

"You tell me." Her gaze went to a point at the far end of the lake. She could barely discern a few highway patrol cars and sheriff's vehicles and officers moving around. "Is that your command post?"

"Yep." He waved his hand at one of the officers and the man waved back. "The parents are there too. I'm glad we're a good distance away. I told the guys to keep them away from the lake so they wouldn't see you. Not that they'd know what you were doing with the dog anyway. Not many people have heard about dogs that can find cadavers underwater."

"Bodies, not cadavers. I hate that word. It dehumanizes." She shaded her eyes. "How far out could a car hit the water?"

"It depends on how fast the car was going." He pointed to a hill a few miles away. "If it bounced and went off that incline at a high speed, it could be thirty, forty feet out. If it went into the water here, it could be right underneath us."

"It's not right underneath us. Monty would tell me." She settled back in the boat. "But we'll start close to the shore."

12

"It's about time you got here." Logan came out of the cabin as Galen parked by the front door. "Hurry. I need to take your rental car."

"I've been exactly two and a half hours," Galen said as he got out of the car. "And that's extraordinary considering I was in Dodsworth when you called. Really, Logan, you can't yank me around all over the country if you expect me to find Rudzak."

"This is important."

"She's all right, you know. I told you she called me to verify Henry Smith's identity. She's not being stupid and Smith will watch her."

Logan got into the driver's seat. "I want to go myself."

"Then why didn't you? Why bring me here?"

He started the car. "Maggie."

"Maggie?"

"The wolf. Someone Sarah trusts has to take care of her."

"You want me to baby-sit a wolf? That's not in my job description."

"You don't have a job description. And if you had one, it would be censored. Maggie's on the back porch. I just changed her bandage, but if I'm not back in a few hours, check it again."

"You'd better be back. I'm not too enthusiastic about—"

Logan was gone.

Galen shook his head as he watched the taillights disappear. It wasn't like Logan to roar off in a panic when there was no clear-cut danger. But then, Rudzak had always been the exception to any rule with Logan. Ever since that time with Chen—

Galen jumped as a piercing howl broke the silence.

"Jesus." He turned and went into the cabin. Back porch, Logan had said.

Maggie lifted her head and snarled when he appeared in the doorway. What the hell had Logan gotten him into? Change a bandage? The wolf wouldn't let him near her.

He'd better find a way. "Hello." He moved slowly toward her. "Aren't you a beauty. It seems we've got to become each other's best friend." Maggie didn't take her malevolent gaze from him. "I don't blame you for not trusting me. I don't trust many people either." He sat down a short distance away and crossed his legs. "But we're probably a lot alike. So I'll just sit here and talk a bit to you."

The last rays of the setting sun were casting scarlet streaks over the lake and Monty still hadn't indicated a find.

"Does Monty need to go ashore again?" Chavez asked.

"I don't think so." Monty's concentration was so intense on water searches that he had to take frequent breaks to prevent burning out. "It's been only about forty minutes."

"It seems longer."

It seemed longer to her too. Time was dragging as the tension built.

"Should we go in and start again tomorrow?" Chavez asked.

"No, not unless we've covered all the territory. Darkness doesn't make any difference to Monty."

"I hoped you'd say that. I want to go back and tell those parents we searched the entire area and didn't find anything." He guided the boat out farther into the water. "I'll stay as long as you will. But are you sure Monty can tell if there's anyone under the water?"

"As sure as I can be," she said tersely. "If you didn't think Monty could do it, why did you send for me?"

"Sorry." He held up his hands. "I don't know much about the technicalities of water rescue. I just wanted to do what I could for those parents."

"I know." She rubbed the back of her neck. "I guess I'm kind of tense. Maybe they're not in the lake. God, I hope not."

"But if they're here, Monty will find them? How does he do it?"

"The body of a drowning victim releases invisible skin particles. The particles have their own vapors and oil and gas secretions that are lighter than water and rise from any depth to the surface. The minute they come into contact with air, the particles form the narrowest point of a widening scent cone. Monty will recognize the cone and follow it back to the area of heaviest concentration."

"Incredible."

"Training. Monty and I spent an entire summer learning how to locate underwater victims. We were both pretty waterlogged by the time we got it right." She patted Monty's head. "He is pretty incredible. His ability to pick up a scent is fifty-eight times greater than any human's and his sensitivity to particular molecules may be thousands of times greater."

"Impressive. Then, if he doesn't find a scent, we can assume they're not here?"

She shook her head. "If there's heavy algae, it could trap the scent. Layers of cold water can do the same thing. There are other factors that can interfere, but Monty's been able to locate the—"

Monty barked.

"Shit." So much for hoping those kids were safe.

Monty began running back and forth in the boat, his head down, pointing at the water.

"He's found something." Her hand tightened on the leash. "Cut the motor and let the boat drift." When Chavez obeyed, she sat still, watching. Monty was excited, but he hadn't found the source yet. "Start the motor, but keep it very slow. Go first to the right and then to the left."

When they'd turned left and gone a few yards, Monty went crazy. He strained at the leash, trying to paw and nip at the water.

"Here." She swallowed to ease the tightness of her throat. "Throw out a buoy to mark the spot."

Mark the spot. Mark this spot so those parents could find their children. Lately it seemed as if she always had to just mark the spot and go on.

"Are you okay?"

Her gaze left the yellow buoy floating on the water to see Chavez staring at her sympathetically. "I'm fine." She smiled crookedly. "No, I'm lying. I was hoping I wouldn't find anything. Let's get out of here. I'm having trouble holding Monty."

"You warned me he'd try to jump in the water." He started the motor. "Do you need my help?"

"No. As soon as the excitement passes, he'll realize they're dead and he can't save them."

And neither could she.

"It doesn't have to be those kids," Chavez said. "Couldn't it be an animal or—"

"No, Monty knows the difference. It's at least one human being."

Monty had stopped fighting the leash and was looking back at the spot marked by the buoy.

Save.

"You can't save them, boy."

He was already realizing he couldn't save them, and she could sense the sadness.

Help.

"You did help."

Monty lifted his head and howled mournfully.

She stared at him in surprise. She was used to hearing him bark, even whimper, but he'd never given vent to that eerie sound before.

Maggie's influence?

He howled again.

"Christ," Chavez muttered. "He gives me the creeps."

"He's upset." She reached out and stroked Monty's head. "He'll be better soon."

"Sorry." Chavez grimaced. "Let him howl. I suppose we owe him a big debt."

"We'll know that when you get a scuba team out here."

"I'll put in a call right away." Chavez cut the motor as they neared the shore. He jumped out of the boat and guided it onto the bank. "Though I'd better tell them to report tomorrow morning. It's dark now, and trying to locate wreckage underwater can be dangerous enough in daylight."

"Will you tell the parents tonight?"

He shook his head as he helped her from the boat. "It won't hurt to give them one more night of hope. Hell, maybe your

Monty is wrong. Maybe that million-dollar nose has a cold or something."

"I hope you're right." She nibbled at her lower lip as she urged Monty from the boat. His tail was tucked between his legs, and he lay down on the bank and stared out at the water. This wasn't good. She constantly had to fight to keep Monty from going into deep depression. Sometimes it took weeks to bring him out of it. She turned to Chavez. "Will you do me a favor?"

He looked at her inquiringly.

"Go hide in the woods."

"What?"

"Go hide and let Monty find you."

"I haven't got time for games. I have to go and make my report."

"Ten minutes. That's all I ask. It will help Monty. It's a form of therapy. A rescue dog gets terribly depressed when he finds only the dead. Monty needs to find someone alive."

"I shouldn't waste—" He looked down at Monty. "Poor mutt."

"Just ten minutes."

"Okay." He took out his phone. "I guess I can phone in a preliminary report while I'm hiding." He made a face. "Though you can bet I'm not telling anyone I'm playing hide-and-seek with a golden retriever. Do you need anything of mine to let him sniff?"

"Your cap will do. I'll give you five minutes' head start. Just hide in the woods somewhere. But don't make it too easy."

He took off his black cap and handed it to her. "Ten minutes."

"Right. Thanks, Sergeant."

He smiled. "No problem. We wouldn't want him to have psychological problems." He started up the incline. "Jesus, what am I saying?"

She watched his shadowy figure disappear into the darkness. Nice guy. He had made the search as easy as possible, and not many officers would have been willing to go out of their way to accommodate a dog.

Monty whimpered, his gaze still on the water.

She knelt beside him and put her arms around his neck. "It's okay. You did good work today. In a few minutes we'll go find someone else and then we'll go home. You'll see Maggie. Won't that be nice?"

Monty nuzzled his head against her shoulder. At least he wasn't staring out at the water any longer. She held Chavez's cap beneath his nose. "Smell. He's lost. Soon we're going to have to go find him."

Gone?

"No, he's alive. Only lost."

She felt a little lost herself just then. Lost and discouraged and alone. She wanted to go back to the cabin and see Maggie and then curl up beside Logan and close out the world.

Logan. She had tried to shut out the thought of him all afternoon; only now and then had the memory of the night before filtered through. But now it would do no harm to think about him, and she needed warmth and passion to shake off the knowledge that those poor kids were—

Stop thinking about them. Take care of Monty and then leave and go home to Logan. She stood up and took out her flashlight from her utility belt. "One more sniff." She unhooked his leash and passed the cap beneath Monty's nose. "Find."

He bounded up the incline toward the road.

She caught up with him deep in the woods a few minutes later when he paused to scent the air. He was quivering, excited, his whole being concentrating on the job at hand.

Good. That's what you need. Forget death. Find life. She held out the hat, but he ignored it and turned and raced off to the south. He'd caught the cone.

She ran after him, her flashlight spearing the darkness ahead.

Bushes.

She ducked around them, but one branch caught her arm as she passed.

A gnarled fallen log.

Jump over it.

The ground on the other side of the log was muddy, and she slipped. She caught herself and ran on.

She could see Monty ahead, stretched out, in a dead run up the hill ahead. He reached the top and stopped, his head lifted, silhouetted against the night sky. He looked back at her and barked.

We've got you, Chavez.

A moment later Monty disappeared as he tore down the other side of the hill.

Sarah stopped a moment to catch her breath. She could afford a minute before she went down to praise Monty. He'd be so proud and happy that maybe he'd forget—

Someone was behind her.

She whirled around.

No one.

Nothing.

But someone was there.

Something is watching, Chavez had said.

She had laughed and made a joke about a bear. She didn't feel like laughing now. The fine hairs at the back of her neck were lifting.

"Smith?" It had to be Henry Smith. He had said he was going to keep an eye on her.

No answer.

Her hand tightened on the flashlight, and she forced herself to cast the beam slowly over the terrain. Trees, shrubs, boulders. So many places to hide. Anyone could be—

Monty howled.

He'd found Chavez. Relief surged through her. She wasn't alone. She had Monty and Chavez. She bolted up the hill and then down the other side. She could see Monty now. He was sitting near a pile of boulders, his head lifted. Chavez must be behind the—

Monty howled again.

She skidded to a stop. It wasn't right. Monty always indicated a find by barking and running back to her. He shouldn't be sitting there, howling.

She moved forward slowly, her flashlight focused on the boulders. "Monty?"

He didn't move. His gaze was fastened on something hidden behind the boulders.

"Sergeant? He's found you. It's all right to come—"

Then she saw him.

His uniformed body was facedown on the ground.

And the hilt of a knife was sticking out of his back.

Monty edged closer. *Help.*

She couldn't help Chavez, she realized, sick. That knife had been driven through his body, pinning him to the ground. Who could have—

A twig cracked on the path behind her.

Her heart leaped to her throat.

Something is watching.

"Monty!" She flew down the hill, past the boulders. "Monty, come!"

Running footsteps behind her.

Knife. Knife in the back. Knife tearing through flesh.

All she had as a weapon was the flashlight.

Monty was running ahead of her down the path.

Suffocating darkness. Where was she going?

It didn't matter. Follow Monty.

Footsteps pounding behind her.

Faster. Go faster.

A break in the trees up ahead. She could see light.

The rest stop. Relief tore through her as Monty stopped and looked back at her, waiting.

"Go." She spurted ahead and out on the concrete tarmac. A car she recognized was parked beside the building. Henry Smith's car, and he was sitting behind the wheel.

Thank God.

She glanced over her shoulder as she ran toward Smith's car.

No one.

But someone was there. She knew it. She could feel it.

She pounded on the window of the car as Monty bounded excitedly around her.

Smith didn't look at her. Why the hell didn't he—

Because there was a small round hole in his temple.

She backed away from the car.

Dead. Dead. Dead.

Smith dead. Chavez dead.

And someone was back there in the woods, watching, coming closer.

"Sarah."

She whirled and threw her flashlight at the man coming toward her.

Logan grunted as the flashlight struck him in the chest. "Dammit, that hurt. Why couldn't you—"

"Logan." She threw herself into his arms. "Dead. They're

all—" She couldn't stop shaking. "And he's out there. He was running after—" She tore out of his arms. "We have to get out of the light. I thought I was safe. He has a knife. . . . But Smith was shot. He must have a gun too."

"Easy," Logan said. "No one's going to hurt you."

"The hell they're not." Logan. No one must hurt Logan. She couldn't bear it if— She pulled him toward the building. "Get inside."

He only moved to stand in front of her. "It's safe." His gaze raked the woods surrounding them. "Look up the road."

Headlights. Two Sheriff's Department patrol cars were coming toward them.

She went limp with relief.

"I called them when I started down that screwed-up road. I wanted to be able to find you without scouring the entire lake area. They said they'd meet me here." He turned to face her. "Now talk to me. Slowly and clearly. Who's dead?"

Her knees felt as if they wouldn't hold her. She leaned back against the fender of the car. "Chavez. And Smith. He's in the car. I thought he was the one following me. He said no one but him had followed me from the ranch, but there must have been—"

"Shh, just a minute." He went around the car, took out a handkerchief, then carefully opened the driver's door and looked inside. "Christ." He slammed the door and turned back to her. "And Chavez?"

"In the woods. Behind some boulders. My fault. I sent him out there alone."

"Show me."

"I don't know if I can find it." She rubbed her temple. "But Monty can." Poor Monty, he would hate going back to Chavez's body. She had promised him life and brought him only more death. "If it's safe for him. I'm not going to have some crazy loon shooting at my dog."

"He's not crazy. And when he sees all those troopers, he'll leave as quickly as he can."

"How do you know? You think it's Rudzak, don't you?"

"Don't you?"

She didn't know what she thought. She was finding it difficult to think at all. But evidently the question didn't need answering, because Logan was walking away from her toward the patrol cars that had just pulled into the parking lot.

Monty stopped ten yards from the boulders and wouldn't go nearer. She didn't force him. She had no desire to see that bloodstained knife again.

She gestured with her flashlight. "There he is."

Logan and the four troopers moved closer, scanning the area with their flashlights before they took each step. She knew they were afraid of destroying evidence, but it seemed to take them forever to cover those last few yards.

Please. Get it over with and let's go home.

She averted her gaze, but she could still hear the murmur of their voices as they knelt beside Chavez's body.

"Sarah." Logan was back beside her. "Lieutenant Carmichael wants you."

"Why should I—"

"Just come, okay?"

"No, it's not okay." But she started for the boulders anyway. "Stay, Monty."

"Walk on the rocks so you won't disturb the—"

"I know." She was standing beside Chavez's body, staring over it at Lieutenant Carmichael. "You wanted me?"

"We can't move the body, but his head is turned to one side." He motioned for her to kneel down beside him. "Look at him."

She didn't want to look at him. She did anyway. His eyes and mouth were open. Death must have come suddenly and—

She stiffened in shock. "It's not Chavez."

"You're sure?"

"Of course I'm sure." She stared dazedly into the heavy features of the dead man. "It's not Chavez."

"Thank you." He motioned to Logan, who lifted her to her feet. "You can take her back to the rest stop now. But don't leave until after we've questioned her."

She stood there staring down at the dead man.

"Come on, Sarah." Logan gently nudged her up the hill toward Monty.

"It's not Chavez. I thought I'd sent him straight into the hands of that murderer. But it's not Chavez."

Logan was silent. Too silent.

"What is it?"

"It was Chavez, Sarah."

"No."

"Those policemen knew him, worked with him every day. It was Chavez." His hand tightened on her elbow. "And he's been dead for a long time. Rigor mortis has started to set in."

She stared at him in bewilderment. "I spent the entire afternoon with Chavez. He was with—" She drew a deep breath as realization hit her. "Rudzak?"

"What did he look like?"

"Tall, forty-something. Fine features, gray eyes, white hair." She looked at him. "Rudzak?"

He nodded.

"But I . . . liked him."

"Everyone likes Rudzak. It's one of the things he does best.

I'm sure Chavez liked him too. The lieutenant thinks Chavez was forced to call Helen Peabody this morning to request you to come here and then was murdered. He wasn't seen at the command post after ten this morning."

She shook her head. "But he waved at one of the troopers on the other bank and the officer waved back."

"How close were you?"

He was right. The officer had been too far away to realize the man he was waving at wasn't Chavez. My God, the boldness of the man. "Smith. I told him about Henry Smith when he said he thought we were being followed, but he couldn't have killed him. We were together on the lake."

"Did he use his telephone?"

She thought back and then nodded. "At least once. When we went ashore to give Monty one of his breaks. I thought he was reporting in to the command center. You believe he called someone to kill Smith?"

"I don't doubt it."

She shivered. "I was alone with him all afternoon. If he'd wanted to kill me, he could have done it anytime. Why didn't he do it? And why lead me to Chavez?"

"I don't know. Cat and mouse? Maybe he didn't intend to kill you. Maybe he just wanted to show me he could do it."

"This is all about you, isn't it?"

"You mean it's all my fault. Hell yes, do you think I'd deny it? I don't blame you for being angry."

"I am angry." She had been frightened and stunned, but now those emotions were being supplanted by pure rage. "That son of a bitch. He used me. And manipulated me."

"Rudzak has always prided himself on being able to push all the right buttons."

"And was killing that poor officer one of the buttons he pushed?"

Logan nodded.

"He's got to be crazy."

"I'm not sure he's insane. I think he was born with something missing. He has no concept of right or wrong as we know it. What benefits Rudzak is right, what gets in his way is wrong."

"A sociopath."

"You can't pigeonhole Rudzak that easily." They had reached the rest stop, and his hand tightened on her arm when he saw the forensic team going over Smith's car. "Why don't we go inside? You don't want to see this."

He was right. She didn't need to see another dead body, and neither did Monty. She headed for the building. "How long do we have to stay here?"

"The lieutenant wants to talk to you and take a statement, but I'll see if he can send someone to the cabin to do the formal statement. You're not classified as a suspect."

She hadn't thought she would be. "And what am I classified as?"

"Witness." He shrugged. "Or maybe . . . victim."

She remembered the terror and helplessness she had felt as she ran through the woods. She had felt like a victim then, and the memory filled her with anger. "The hell I am."

They weren't permitted to leave the rest stop for another four hours; by then Sarah was almost as drained as Monty.

"I'll drive," Logan said as he got into her jeep. "You rest."

"I can do it. You have your own car to—"

"It's Galen's rental car. He'll arrange to have it picked up." He started the jeep. "Stop arguing and climb in. You know I'm in better shape emotionally right now. You wouldn't want to crack up on that ugly road and hurt Monty."

She hesitated and then got into the passenger seat.

"The one irresistible argument," he murmured. "Lean back and close your eyes."

She didn't feel like closing her eyes. She was numb with exhaustion, but her mind wouldn't stop working. Her gaze focused on the winding road ahead as the jeep slowly crept up the incline. "How'd you get Galen's rental car?"

"I phoned him to come and wolf-sit and then took his car."

"Galen's at the ranch?" So many things had happened that she'd forgotten about Maggie. "You shouldn't have left Maggie. I told you to take care—"

"Shut up," he said roughly. "There was no way I wasn't going to come after you. And you know Galen will be able to care for Maggie."

Yes, Galen would be capable of doing anything he wanted to do. "I suppose she'll be okay."

"Better than you. She has a keen sense of self-preservation."

"She walked into a trap too, like me with Rudzak. He knew I had to try to find those kids."

"And if you got another call from Helen Peabody, you'd go traipsing off again."

"Yes."

Logan muttered a curse beneath his breath. "Stupid."

"I wasn't stupid," she said, stung. "I got a call to do my job, and it seemed a legitimate search. How was I to know Rudzak would take advantage of those kids' disappearance to set a trap? He would have had to plan everything ahead with Chavez, the call from Hel— Oh, God." She closed her eyes. "The kids. Maybe he didn't just take advantage of circumstances. Could he have killed them, Logan?"

"Yes."

She opened her eyes and turned to look at him. "He'd kill three innocent kids just to set me up?"

"I think it's likely. He's very precise about his planning. He wouldn't want the kids to show up and spoil everything after he'd gone to so much trouble."

"I feel sick." The image of a yellow buoy floating on the water came back to her. "The lake . . ."

"Lieutenant Carmichael told me he was sending a scuba team out to the buoy. I asked him to call me if he found out anything."

"Kids . . . And you say he's not insane."

"He doesn't enjoy killing, he just does it when it benefits him." He smiled grimly. "Though I may be the exception to the rule. He'd definitely enjoy killing me."

"I hope they don't find the kids," she whispered. "Dear Jesus, I hope he didn't kill them to draw me here."

He covered her hand clenched on her lap. "So do I, Sarah."

Logan's phone rang when they were only a few miles from the ranch. "Yes, Lieutenant."

She tensed, watching his expression, but she couldn't tell what Carmichael was saying to him.

He hung up. "There's no trace of Rudzak. They think he's gotten away."

"What about the teenagers?"

"They found them under the buoy." He looked straight ahead. "They haven't gotten them out of the car yet, but the scuba divers say all three were bound with rope."

She felt as if she'd been stabbed.

"Say something."

She shook her head. What could she say? She just wanted to curl up and make the world go away.

"None of this is your fault, dammit."

"I know."

"Then stop looking like—"

"I can't help how I look." Her hands clenched into fists. "Were they alive when they went into the water? No, they couldn't know that yet, could they?"

"No."

"No one could be that terrible. To tie them up and then—"

"Don't let your imagination run wild. It might not have been that way."

"But it could have been." She leaned her head against the window. "I don't want to talk anymore, Logan."

"Then don't talk, but don't think either, dammit."

"I'll try," she whispered.

He muttered a curse and jammed his foot on the accelerator. A few minutes later he drew up before the cabin. She jumped out of the jeep and started for the front door.

"Wait a minute." Logan came around the car. "You dropped something."

She shook her head.

"I saw you kick something out of the car. It must have been on the floorboards." He knelt in the dirt.

"What is it?" she asked dully.

"Nothing. Go inside."

He had something in his hand. "What is it, dammit?"

"A comb." He held out his hand and revealed the delicate ivory and jade comb. "A present from Rudzak."

She shuddered. "Do you suppose it belonged to one of the kids?"

"No, it belonged to Chen Li."

"Why would he—" She stared at him. "You expected it?"

"I didn't expect it, but I'm not surprised. Go on to bed, we'll talk about it later."

"You bet we will." But she couldn't cope with anything more

just then. Her nerves were shredded. She turned and went inside the house.

"Hi." Galen came out of the back porch. "It's about time you came home. I was beginning to feel like a— You look like hell."

"I'm tired. I'm going to bed." Monty. She had to take care of Monty. But Monty was already heading for the back porch and Maggie. "Good night, Galen." She closed the door of the bedroom behind her.

She threw off her clothes, crawled into bed, and drew up the covers. The sheets smelled of Logan and their intimacy, she realized dimly. Sex and life and a joy those kids would never experience.

"Move over." Logan slipped naked in bed beside her and pulled her into his arms.

"I don't want you here."

"Tough. You've got me." He brushed his lips on her temple. "My God, have you got me. Now relax. I don't want to do anything more than comfort you."

"I just want to go to sleep."

"And have nightmares?" He pushed her head into the hollow of his shoulder. "Talk it out."

"What do you want me to say? That three kids died because some maniac wanted to draw me into his damn web."

"That's not your fault. I thought we agreed that I was to blame for everything."

"I did what he wanted. He analyzed me like some Machiavellian shrink and then decided to kill innocent kids because that would make me do what he wanted. And he was right. He called and I came."

"What else could you have done? You went there to— Stop crying. No, don't stop. It's probably good for you. It's just hell for me."

"It doesn't feel good for me. It hurts."

"That's because you don't do enough of it. You're out of practice. When's the last time you cried? When your grandfather died?"

"No, I promised him I'd be strong. It was when I found Monty at that police department in Italy."

"I should have known."

"Is Monty all right?"

"Monty's with Maggie."

"That's right, I forgot. But he usually senses when I'm sad and comes and sleeps by my bed."

"The poor mutt's hormones are raging. You'll have to make do with me."

"I'm glad he has Maggie. Maybe it will distract him from what happened tonight."

"It's you we're trying to distract."

"It shouldn't have happened. I try so hard to find the living and bring closure to the dead. It's what I do, what I am. And he used that and killed those kids." She was shaking. "He twisted everything I am and made it ugly and—"

"Shh."

"You just told me to talk."

"That's when you were making sense. There's nothing ugly or twisted about you. You're clean and beautiful and straight as an arrow. Ask me, I'm an expert on twisted and ugly. I've been there."

She shook her head.

"You don't believe me? It's true. I've done things that—" He stroked her hair. "You don't want to hear about me."

She did want to hear about him. It was important, she realized. When she had seen Logan at the rest stop, she had known then that everything concerning him was vitally important to her. If he died . . . She didn't want to think about that now. She was too confused and numb. She just wanted to be held by Logan and pretend the nightmare at Apache Lake had never happened.

"Go to sleep now," he said. "I'll stay awake and be here for you if you have a nightmare."

Had he read her mind? Did he know what a rare gift he offered her? Never in her life had she ever had anyone to keep the nightmares at bay. . . .

"Is she asleep?" Galen asked as Logan came out of the bedroom.

"Right now. I've got to get back. I promised I'd stay with her."

"She looked like hell."

"She went through hell." He went to the sink and got a glass of water. "Henry Smith is dead. Rudzak killed him."

Galen stiffened. "Why didn't you tell me right away? Franklin has been trying to reach him since you returned with Sarah."

"I'm telling you now. You couldn't do anything about it and she needed me." He drank the water. "Or someone."

"It was a trap?"

"Yes, and Rudzak used the death of three teenage kids to spring it. Do you know how that makes her feel?"

Galen's lips tightened. "I know how it makes me feel."

"Then make sure Dodsworth is ready. Or find Rudzak. He could have killed her tonight."

"But you came just in the nick of time?"

"No, I would have been too late if Rudzak had wanted to kill her. He didn't want her dead . . . yet."

"Then what was his little trap all about?"

"To let me know he could do it and to find out how high she was on his list of the things I value."

"And did he find that out?"

"Probably. If he was watching us. He's always been able to read me."

Galen lifted a brow. "And is she high enough on the list to be worth his while?"

"He struck pay dirt." Logan put the glass down and turned away. "So we've got to find the son of a bitch before he kills her. Because next time he'll do it."

Sarah was sleeping deeply, like a child after a hard day.

Logan stood staring down at her.

Tenderness. Protectiveness. Love. Passion. Fear.

She wasn't the first woman in his life. He had felt all these emotions before. But not like this. Not with this single-minded intensity and desperation. When had admiration and friendship become obsession?

It didn't matter. It was here, it had come.

And Rudzak knew it had come.

Sarah stirred and whimpered something in her sleep.

Nightmares? He had promised to keep the nightmares away.

He slipped into bed beside her and drew her into his arms. She felt soft and womanly, but he knew how strong she was. Strong and stubborn and yet terribly vulnerable and guarded. It was a wonder he had even gotten into her bed. It would be a superhuman task making her accept any other relationship. He would have to be careful not to rush her.

She whimpered again, and he brushed his lips across her brow.

"Shh, it's okay. I'm here. I'll never let anything hurt you." He drew her closer and whispered the words he knew she'd never believe if she was awake. "I'll always be here, Sarah."

Logan was still beside her when Sarah woke the next morning. His eyes were open and he was obviously wide-awake.

"Good morning." He planted a kiss on her forehead and sat up in bed. "You hit the shower while I go and see about breakfast."

"What time is it?"

"Nearly noon."

"I have to feed Monty and Maggie."

"Already done." He stood up. "I left you long enough to take care of Monty, and Galen had already fed Maggie. You'll be glad to know that Monty wouldn't let him feed him."

"But he let you feed him again."

"Don't be mad at him. I'm special. We've gone through a lot together. Santo Camaro, Taiwan, and then last night. It's natural that—" He stopped as he saw her expression change. "Don't think about it right now. Get your shower and something to eat." He grabbed his robe at the foot of the bed and left the room.

Easy to say, she thought as she slowly sat up in bed. How could she help thinking about those poor kids? The events of yesterday were rushing back to her with every sickening detail, clear and dagger sharp.

Like the knife in Chavez's back.

She shuddered as a chill iced through her. Five lives wasted for no reason other than the desire to draw her to Apache Lake. How could anyone do that?

But he had done it. And he had gotten away with it.

Suddenly the chill was gone, replaced by burning anger.

Son of a bitch. Son of a bitch. Son of a bitch.

No way, you bastard.

13

Sarah, dressed in khaki shorts and a T-shirt, walked out of the bathroom twenty minutes later.

Galen looked up from the stove at her. "I still have to make the gravy and biscuits."

"Where's Logan? I thought he was going to cook breakfast."

"Get real." His expression was pained. "Much as I'd like to have Logan wait on me, there's no way I'd sacrifice my digestive system. Over the years I've become accustomed to fine cuisine."

"So where is Logan?"

"Outside with Monty."

"I thought Monty would be with Maggie."

"He's sulking. He doesn't like the rapport I've developed with his lady friend."

"What?"

"He's afraid Maggie likes me best. She totally ignored him when I was changing her bandage and feeding her. Anyone could see she's besotted with me." He shook his head as he added a flour mixture to the hot skillet, then he winked at her. "Just joking. It took me a long time to get her to stop howling while you two were gone. I think she's in a snit and playing hard to get with him. Of course, I could be wrong. My modesty gets in the way at times, and I—" He broke off, studying her. "You look better than you did last night but still pretty grim."

"I feel pretty grim."

"Then go talk to Logan. I need calm and good thoughts to reach sublimity in cooking."

"Did Logan tell you that Smith had been killed?"

"Oh, yes, and I had some grim thoughts myself." He stirred the gravy. "But after I put some wheels in motion, I felt much better."

"What wheels?"

"Determining and then verifying who was the logical person with Rudzak at Apache Lake. It's always necessary to be sure before action is taken." He opened the oven to check on the biscuits. "It was almost certainly Carl Duggan."

"How can you be sure?"

"I have great contacts. Everybody loves me. Did I mention that?"

"I got the gist. And what action are you planning on taking?"

He said softly, "Why, an eye for an eye. What else?"

She had a sudden memory of him running through the jungle, as much a predator as Maggie ever could be. She didn't find the idea repulsive. It would be a clean kill and well deserved. Not like Rudzak, who—

"You're thinking bad thoughts again." He clucked reprovingly. "I told you I couldn't tolerate that. Go out and talk to Logan. I'll call you when breakfast is ready."

Logan was leaning against the fence, talking on his phone. He lifted his hand in greeting but kept on talking. Monty was lying at his feet until he saw Sarah, and then he leaped up and bounded toward her, his fluffy tail wagging his whole body in joyful greeting.

"Now you're happy to see me," she murmured as she crouched to pet him. "Where were you last night, when I needed you?"

But she had not really needed him. Logan had been there, holding her. Maybe Monty had derived the same comfort from being with Maggie.

"Is breakfast ready?" Logan had hung up his phone and was watching her and Monty.

"Not yet. I was disturbing Galen and he sent me to you."

"I'm surprised. It takes a lot to disturb Galen. But I'm glad he has his priorities straight."

"Who were you talking to?"

"Lieutenant Carmichael. He's sending someone to take your statement this afternoon."

"Any word on Rudzak?"

"No."

She hadn't thought there would be. "What about the kids? How did they die?"

He shook his head. "You don't want to know."

"The hell I don't."

"One was shot. The others drowned. They were alive when they went into the water."

She flinched. "Christ."

"I told you that you didn't want to know."

"I had to know." She closed her eyes and held tight to Monty. "I have to know everything."

"Why? So you can tear yourself apart?" he said roughly.

"Because Rudzak hasn't been real to me. I knew he had killed those people in Colombia, but I couldn't really make the connection from him to me or my life." She opened her lids and stared at him with tear-wet eyes. "I'm making the connection now, Logan."

"And it's killing you."

"No, that would mean that Rudzak had won. I won't let that happen. I won't let him hurt me." She rose to her feet. "And I won't let him hurt anyone else. Not ever."

His gaze narrowed on her face. "What does that mean?"

"It means I'm going to find him before he kills anyone again."

"And then what?"

"You tell me. You said Rudzak was smart. Even if he's caught, it doesn't mean he'd get convicted. And if he was convicted, he got out of prison once. He could do it again, couldn't he?"

"It would be more difficult."

"But he could do it."

"Hell, yes, he could do it. What are you getting at, Sarah?"

"You know what I'm getting at." Her voice was shaking with rage. "Galen believes in an eye for an eye. You do too."

"But you don't. It's not your nature."

"How do you know? I've never been this angry before."

"You were angry when Madden took Monty away and you didn't kill him."

"Monty didn't die. I was able to save him. Rudzak didn't give me the chance to save those kids. He killed them and then he took me to that spot and let Monty find them. He told me how sorry he was, and all the time he'd put them in that car and sent them—"

"You're taking this personally, but it was me he was really aiming at."

"You're damn right I'm taking this personally. I don't care if he meant to get at you through me. He used me and he used those kids and Chavez and Smith. He smiled and told me about the dog he'd adopted from the pound, and I liked him. He played me like a—"

"Shh." He was standing before her, his hands on her shoulders. "You're scaring me to death, and I'm choosing the wrong words to try to reason with you."

"How are you going to reason with me? Are you going to tell me I should just forget about that—"

"I'm trying to tell you that this is my battle, not yours. I'll find a way to get Rudzak."

"You haven't found him yet."

"And you're going to?"

"I'll find him." Her hands clenched into fists. "That's what I do. I find people. I'll search him out."

"That's what I'm afraid of." His hands tightened briefly on her shoulders and then dropped away. "I'm not going to be able to talk you out of it, am I?"

She shook her head.

"Then I suppose I'd better make the best of it." He stepped back. "If there is a best. I trust you don't intend to leave me out of this entirely?"

"How could I? I need you."

"That's comforting . . . barely."

"I don't intend to be comforting. You're the one who knows everything about Rudzak. Now I want to know what you know."

"Can we wait until after breakfast?"

"No."

"Okay." He led her toward the bench against the wall. "Sit down and fire away."

"Why did Rudzak put that comb in my car?"

"Is that going to help you find him?"

"Maybe. It will help me to know him and what he might do."

He was silent a moment. "He wanted to show me that he was the one who had killed those kids and that he could have killed you too. He gave the comb and several other ancient Egyptian artifacts to Chen Li, and now he's using them as a kind of signature when he makes a kill."

"What kind of signature?"

"A symbolic death gift. Egyptian rulers had their treasures entombed with them, and he wants to honor Chen Li's passing with other deaths." His lips twisted. "And make a stab at hurting me at the same time."

"Then all this is about Chen Li? Were they lovers?"

"No, they were half brother and sister."

She stared at him in shock. "And you had him put in prison?"

"Yes."

"For God's sake, why?"

"He killed Chen Li."

"What?"

"He went into her hospital room and he broke her neck. He called it a mercy killing."

"And what did you call it?"

"Murder. She was in remission and the remission could have lasted." His lips tightened. "He didn't give her that chance."

"Did he know she was in remission?"

"I told him. He didn't believe me. He didn't want to believe me. He'd lost her and he didn't want her to live if he couldn't have her."

"Lost her?"

"He loved her. He wanted to go to bed with her."

She gasped.

"That's why he tried to draw her into the Egyptian mystique. It was common then to go to bed with close relatives.

He wooed her like a lover and never took a wrong step. But I think she guessed it toward the end and he sensed her revulsion. He couldn't accept it, so she had to die."

"And you sent him to prison?"

"If I'd caught him before he ran off to Bangkok, I would have killed him. Instead, I told the authorities in Bangkok when and where they could find the drugs he'd smuggled into the country. Then I bribed the judge at his trial to give him a life sentence in one of the worst prisons in the world. Galen assured me that even the cockroaches bailed out of that place after they got a look around." His smile was chilling. "That made me very happy."

"Rudzak smuggled drugs?"

"His father owned an import-export house in Tokyo. Rudzak began by taking advantage of his father's contacts to do a little art smuggling. That's where Galen met him and introduced him to me. We did a few runs together and he brought us home to meet his family . . . and Chen Li."

"You were a smuggler too?"

"I told you my life hasn't been squeaky clean. I was broke and trying to make a stake. I stopped when I married Chen Li. Rudzak told me he was quitting too, but he just shifted his focus. Galen came to me two years later and told me Rudzak had started smuggling drugs throughout Asia. It was much more profitable but a hell of a lot more dangerous. I knew it would kill Chen Li if she found out, so I tried to convince him to quit. He assured me he'd do it right after the next run."

"But he didn't."

Logan shook his head. "He was making money hand over fist and there was no way he'd stop. So I turned a blind eye and just tried to protect Chen Li. Everything I did at that time was aimed at protecting Chen Li. I'd just found out that she had cancer and I was searching desperately for a cure for her. I was so young, I didn't believe anything could beat me."

No, Logan wouldn't believe anything could beat him, she thought. And as a younger man he must have been even more willful and determined to get his own way.

"So now you know what a bastard Rudzak is and you have a better picture of me too. Why don't you bow out and let me go after him?"

She shook her head.

"You're being a fool," he said roughly. "You're not equipped to go up against him. He's studied you. He knows your weakness."

"What weakness?"

"Humanity. If you're needed, you'll go to help. Just as you did at Apache Lake."

"And what am I supposed to do? Just sit here?"

"Would that be so bad? It won't be for long. He's evidently done his homework and he'll be on the move now. Things will be moving fast."

"What homework?"

"We think he's found out about Dodsworth. Galen planted a man at the courthouse and he says someone's been nosing around the records."

"Dodsworth?"

"That's my medical research facility in North Dakota. It's been doing less sensitive work than Santo Camaro. As soon as Bassett gets his notes in order, he'll be going up there to complete the project with that team."

"You never explained how Rudzak found out about Santo Camaro. If it was top secret, how did he do it?"

"Money. He zeroed in on someone and bribed him for information."

"Who?"

"Castleton."

She stiffened in shock. "Castleton? Are you sure?"

"I'm sure."

She thought about her meeting with Castleton and couldn't recall anything suspicious about him. But looking back and knowing Logan as she did now, she could see there had been something in his attitude that wasn't quite right. "You knew that evening we arrived."

"Yes."

"And you let him go?"

He didn't answer for a moment. "No."

After all she'd learned about Logan, she wasn't even surprised. "Because you were afraid he'd tell Rudzak about Monty and me and spoil the surprise attack?"

"Partly. But I'd have done it anyway. He'd betrayed those people at the facility. He was responsible for their deaths. An eye for an eye. Remember?"

She slowly nodded. "Then that's how Rudzak knows about Dodsworth?"

"What Castleton knew, Rudzak knows. The first thing I did was increase the security in all my plants and research facilities."

"All of them? But you think he'll target Dodsworth."

"Probably. But who's to say that's the only one he'll pick? I can't take a chance. Besides, we know he bought enough explosives to blow up a small town."

"Explosives," she whispered.

"You were at Oklahoma City. You know what explosives can do."

She knew very well. She had helped take out those pitiful babies from the wreckage. "You can't let it happen. Why haven't you notified ATF?"

"I have notified them and the FBI."

"Did you tell them about Dodsworth?" She could see the answer in his face. "You didn't tell them."

"Not yet."

"Call them."

"No one will be hurt at Dodsworth."

"How can you say that?" She could still see the tragedy at Oklahoma City before her. "You just said Rudzak has explosives."

He shook his head. "It's the first time we've had an inkling where Rudzak may strike. We may have a chance to trap him."

"It's too big a risk. Let ATF trap him."

"There can't be an obvious official presence at Dodsworth if I want to draw him. He'd regard my security people as a challenge, not a deterrent. But security is as tight as a drum there. No one could get through."

"Call them."

"Not yet. Not until I'm sure it's necessary. Not until I'm certain we can't stop him. Trust me. I'll act if I have to."

"How many people do you have in that installation?"

"Fifty-seven."

"And do they know what danger they're in?"

"Yes. I told the head of the project to tell everyone what happened at Santo Camaro and that they might be next. I gave them the option of staying or leaving. Six left. The rest stayed."

"You should shut down the facility."

"Rudzak would just change his target." He stood up. "If you want ATF called, do it yourself."

"I will."

"But be sure you're ready to accept the responsibility of another Kai Chi."

She could feel the blood drain from her face. "Kai Chi?"

"That was Rudzak. A tribute to Chen Li. Do you want another Kai Chi or do you want a chance to catch the bastard?"

"Kai Chi." She stared at him in horror. "Why didn't you tell me?"

"Because I knew you'd look at me as you're doing now and run to the opposite end of the earth. You don't understand anyone who would kill five hundred people to make a sick statement."

"Do you?"

"No, but I'm part of the problem, and every time you look at me, you'll see Kai Chi."

"Please, call ATF," she whispered. "You saw the baby who died in Taiwan. It's nothing compared to what a bomb did to the children in Oklahoma."

He was silent for a moment, a multitude of emotions crossing his face. Then he shook his head. "I'll give you anything else in the whole world, but I can't give you this, Sarah. I have to have a chance of catching him."

"It's wrong, Logan."

"Then make the call. No one's stopping you." He started into the house. "But think long and hard about it. And remember Kai Chi. It could happen again."

No one was stopping her? The hell no one was stopping her.

Oklahoma City. Oh, God, she couldn't stand to be responsible for another disaster like that.

Kai Chi.

If Logan was right, could she bear being responsible for the death of even more people than those at Dodsworth?

She had to have an answer and soon.

Monty whimpered and put his head on her knee.

"It's okay." She stroked his head. "Go on back to Maggie."

He didn't move. He was there giving her comfort and companionship as Logan had done the night before. But in the morning Logan had offered nothing except loneliness and despair.

Sarah tried to ignore the pain. Stop feeling sorry for yourself. She had told him she expected nothing but sexual pleasure. It was too bad she had let him slip beneath her defenses. But it would be okay. She had been alone most of her life and she had made out fine.

He asked her to trust him. Could she? Because of the way she felt about him, or because she truly believed the risk was worthwhile? She had always thought for herself, but she had never been as emotionally involved as she was with Logan.

When she had come out to speak to him, everything seemed simple. She was filled with rage against Rudzak and determination to find and punish him for the atrocity at Apache Lake. Now an even greater atrocity was looming at Dodsworth and nothing was simple anymore.

Nothing but the fact that whatever decision she was about to make could be the wrong one.

"My biscuits and gravy are ruined," Galen told her when she walked into the cabin an hour later. "And Logan wouldn't eat either. But out of the kindness of my heart, I'll make you both a new batch. You'll have to wait though. Perfection takes time."

"I'm not hungry." She looked at Logan sitting in a chair at the table. "Something's sticking in my throat."

Logan met her gaze. "I don't doubt it. The question is whether you'll be able to swallow it."

"I'm going to try. I don't see any other solution." She crossed her arms across her chest. "I'll wait awhile before notifying

ATF about Dodsworth. But the minute I see any danger to the facility, I'm going to blow the whistle and I won't let you convince me otherwise."

"I didn't think you would."

"And I'm not willing to sit here, twiddling my thumbs, until I hear Rudzak's blown it to kingdom come. You said you think Rudzak's ready to move. I want to go to Dodsworth and be there before he decides to set his explosives."

"I told you, the target might not be Dodsworth."

"But it's your passion and he knows it. You don't think he'd pass that up."

"No."

"And you on site would be another reason for him to zero in on it."

"Yes."

"And evidently he also wants to target me. Right?"

"You couldn't be more right." His mouth lifted in a crooked smile. "Or more terrifying."

"Then the multiple targets should draw him." She turned to Galen. "You're sure the security at Dodsworth is unbreakable."

Galen nodded. "I'd set up shop there and I value my neck more than I do any of those scientists. Science may save the world, but where would it be without charm and fine cuisine?" He glanced at Logan. "It seems plans are escalating. We were planning on waiting a bit."

"I don't want to wait," Sarah said. "I want Rudzak now."

Logan nodded. "I'd hoped to keep you out of it."

"Rudzak doesn't want to keep me out of it."

"Then why give him what he wants? Stay here and be safe."

"Makes sense to me," Galen agreed.

"When do we go to Dodsworth?" Sarah said.

Logan sighed. "When Bassett is ready to join the team up there. I think Rudzak will want to eliminate all hope of success for the project with one roll of the dice. He can't do that if Bassett is left alive."

"And you said Bassett will be ready to go within a week?"

Logan nodded.

"Good. Then I have plans to make myself." She went into the bedroom and shut the door.

"So much for keeping her out of it," Galen said. "I'll try to take care of her at Dodsworth, but I can't promise you anything if she goes off on her own the way she did at Apache Lake. You can't protect someone if they don't want to be protected."

"I know."

"And I detected a coolness in her attitude that may make things more difficult."

"Can you blame her? I'm surprised she doesn't want to cut my throat. I had to tell her about Kai Chi or she would have gone off on her own after Rudzak."

"True." Galen turned back to the stove. "But I'd stop brooding about how she feels and go in there and see what she's doing. If she says she's making plans, I don't think you want any of them to surprise you." He looked down at the gravy congealing in the frypan. "Pity. The two of you have spoiled everything. It was going to be a masterpiece of a breakfast."

"What are you doing?"

Sarah looked up to see Logan standing in the doorway. "What does it look like?" She threw a load of underwear into the duffel she had set on the bed. "I'm packing. I want to be ready when Bassett is ready."

"We won't have to walk out the door the minute he does."

"I know." She tossed a cardigan and two pairs of jeans into the duffel. "But I'll go crazy if I don't do something. You and Rudzak may have all the patience in the world, but I don't. This isn't some kind of contest to me."

"It's not to me either. You're not being fair, Sarah."

"Maybe not. Ask me if I care."

"You care. That's the problem. You care too much." He crossed the room and stood next to her. "It's playing hell with my plans, but I wouldn't have it any other way."

He was too close. She could feel the heat of his body. She took a step away and went back to the bureau. "I care about those people at Dodsworth. Not about you."

"I never meant anything else," he said quietly. "I know I'm not in your good books right now. It will be different once this is over. I'll make it different."

She didn't answer.

"We have to work together, Sarah. You can't let your feelings get in the way."

That was exactly what she was trying to prevent. She had to keep him at a distance. She couldn't let the way she felt about him cloud her judgment. Not with all those lives in the balance. "I'll work with you." She met his gaze across the room. "But don't expect anything else from me. I can't give it to you."

"You will. As you said, I can be very patient."

"By the time this is over, you may have changed your mind."

"I won't change my mind."

Her hand closed tightly on the knob of the bureau drawer as he walked out and closed the door behind him. Finish packing. Don't think about him. Don't let him be important to you. Even if he seems to care about you now, how long can it last? You're too different from him.

And that's okay. She didn't want to change. She didn't want

to be anyone but herself. She was a woman who could make decisions and run her own life to suit herself.

Don't think about him. Think about Rudzak and how to protect Dodsworth.

"You want me to come there?" Eve repeated. "Why?"

"Maggie. She's much better, but I need someone to take care of her while I'm gone."

"I thought it was a joke when you said you needed Jane to nurse your wolf."

"It was at the time. But not now. I need your help. Can you come?"

"Do you have to ask? You came when I needed you; you found my daughter. I'll be there on the next plane."

"Thank you. Will you have your mother take care of Jane and bring Joe?"

"I'll see if he can get away. But why should I bring Joe?"

"I'd feel better. I don't think there's any danger for you as long as we're not here, but I'd like to know Joe is with you."

"We? Who's with you?"

"Logan."

A pause. "Are you going to tell me what's happening?"

"As soon as you get here. But bring Joe if you can. Though I probably shouldn't tell you to do that. He's going to make you get right back on a plane to Atlanta as soon as I tell him about Rudzak." She rubbed her temple. "Well, maybe he should. We'll leave it up to him."

"You're being as clear as mud."

"That's what I'm wading in. I want you to know if you decide not to help me that it's okay. I'll understand and you mustn't feel obligated to—"

"Shut up. I'll call you when I find out when my plane will arrive in Phoenix." Eve hung up.

Sarah headed for the door to the living room. It was done. Now to find Galen.

But the living room was empty. "Galen!"

"Out here," he called from the back porch. "I've just fed Maggie."

"I called my friend Eve, and she's—" Her jaw dropped as she stopped in the doorway. Galen was sitting on the floor close to Maggie and her head was on his thigh. "That's a good way to lose a body part. One you may treasure highly."

"We understand each other." Galen stroked Maggie's head. "We talked it over and decided we're a lot alike. Isn't that right, Maggie?"

"How are you alike?"

"Same background. From the cage, to the wilds. Same instinct for survival." He winked. "And we're both so damn smart, it's enough to stun the senses."

"I'll brace myself against the shock. Will you please shift a few feet away from her? You may understand each other, but I'm the one who brought her home and I'm responsible for any damage she might do."

"If it makes you feel better." He carefully moved his leg from beneath Maggie's head so he wouldn't jar her, then continued to stroke her. "You do know that I have to leave this beauty and go to Dodsworth? My job is there now."

She nodded. "I called someone to take care of her. Eve Duncan and Joe Quinn are coming today."

"Indeed? It's going to be a bit cozy in this little cabin, isn't it?"

"I want to make sure you're not pulling your men away from here. I want Eve and Joe protected."

"I was going to send them to Dodsworth."

"Get someone else. Logan has plenty of money."

"Money can't buy training and the skill to—" He grinned. "What am I talking about? Of course it can. Isn't it lucky that I already have enough men at Dodsworth?"

"Then why were you giving me a hard time?"

"I felt obligated to try to get you to stay here. Logan does pay me, and it's what he wants."

"Where is Logan?"

"Out for a run with Monty. I think he needed to blow off a little steam after he left you."

She started to leave, then stopped. "You might call Franklin and tell him that I'm going to leave within the next fifteen minutes and head for Logan's house in Phoenix."

"Why?"

"I'll be closer to Bassett and I can wait there until he finishes his work. Logan appears to think he's important to Rudzak."

"You could wait here."

"It's also closer to the airport. I want to pick Eve and Joe up."

"Let one of my guys do it."

She shook her head. "I want to talk to her and Joe at the airport. They might decide to get right back on a plane."

"And if they don't, you'll bring them here?"

"No, I'll send them. As you pointed out, there's not much room here."

"Logan's going to be right on your heels."

"I'm not trying to run away from him. He can come with me if he likes. I'm going to have to go after him to pick up Monty anyway."

"I'm sure he'll be grateful."

He wouldn't be grateful. He'd be impatient and probably angry that she had taken the initiative.

Eve set down the phone after making her flight reservations and crossed over to the window to look out at the lake.

Joe was strolling along the bank with Jane at his side. He was looking down at her, listening intently to something she was saying. It was a bittersweet fact that Jane had grown closer to Joe since Bonnie had been found. But the slight estrangement might be for the best. Eve would overcome the problem with Jane and then they would be a true family.

Perhaps as soon as she got back from Phoenix the three of them would take a little trip together. In a vacation atmosphere Jane might talk more readily to her and they could get misconceptions ironed out.

After Phoenix. What was happening to Sarah and why was Logan with her?

Something bad is coming.

Her gaze lifted to the hill across the lake. "I hope not, baby. I hope not."

14

Sarah and Logan met Eve at the Phoenix airport that evening. Joe Quinn was not with her.

Eve held up her hand when Sarah opened her mouth to protest. "Jane is disturbed enough. I didn't want to take Joe away from her."

"Do you have luggage?" Logan asked.

Eve shook her head as she knelt to pet Monty. "I hoped I wouldn't need more than my carry-on." She looked at Sarah. "Will I?"

"I don't think so." Sarah frowned. "I wanted you to bring Joe. Did you tell him—"

"I told him you needed me to wolf-sit." She smiled as she rose to her feet. "After all, that's all I know. Right?" She started for the exit. "He didn't like the wolf bit, but he would really have been worried if I'd told him you wanted me to have a bodyguard. Joe's a little protective."

Logan snorted. "A little?"

"Maybe more than a little. That's not a bad thing." She

glanced at Logan. "You're pretty protective yourself. I'm surprised you let Sarah get into a mess that—"

"I had no choice." Logan took her carry-on. "But she has one right now, and if you can talk her out of going to Dodsworth, I'll put you both on a plane to Atlanta."

"Dodsworth?"

"I'm not going to Atlanta." Sarah looked him in the eye. "And it's a dirty trick to try to use Eve to change my mind."

"Not nearly as dirty as what you're going to find at Dodsworth."

Eve said, "It would be nice if you'd let me know what's going on."

"I will." Logan swung open the door of Sarah's jeep. "I'm dropping Sarah off at the Phoenix house and I'll drive you to the cabin. There will be plenty of time to fill you in on the way."

"I'll drive her," Sarah said. "I brought her here. I should be the one to explain what's happening."

"Too bad. Joe's not here to ride shotgun, so I take over," Logan said. "And I want you under lock and key until I get back." His lips twisted. "You're the one who wanted to stay on top of Bassett. Maybe you can push him to finish a little faster."

"Eve's more important."

"Yes, she is." He started the jeep. "And I'll take good care of her. Do you doubt it?"

Sarah looked from one to the other. She could almost see the bond of memories and experiences that linked them together. She slowly shook her head. "No, you always did take good care of her."

"Then trust me to care for her now."

Her gaze shifted to Eve. "If you think there's any hint of

danger after Logan tells you about Rudzak, I want you to go home. Don't stay. Okay?"

Eve smiled. "Don't worry, I'm staying clear of trouble these days. Life's dealt me a very good hand lately. I want to savor every play."

But Eve had come when Sarah had asked. "Remember that when Logan tells you about Dodsworth."

Fifteen minutes later Sarah stood outside the Phoenix house and watched Logan and Eve drive out the electronic gates. They were chatting casually as old friends . . . or lovers always did. She felt suddenly empty and alone. It was dumb to stand there, looking after them.

She would call Eve at the cabin and talk with her. Perhaps she'd call Joe too, and tell him what was going on. She'd make that judgment after she talked to Eve.

Another judgment. She didn't want to weigh lives and choices. She wasn't Solomon. She was just a search and rescue operator who tried to do the best she could. How had she gotten roped into—

"Thank heaven someone else is here to take over baby-sitting." Margaret marched toward her across the foyer. "I've got a thousand things to do, and I'm stuck with Bassett."

"Has he been a problem?"

"I guess not. He just doesn't know what's good for him and he won't listen to me."

"I'll help all I can."

"Well, at least a little. Logan placed the responsibility on me and I won't shirk it." Her gaze scanned Sarah's face. "Things not so good with you?"

Sarah shook her head.

"Well, then it's just as well that you're here. Nothing like regular meals and exercise to keep your nerves in check. I'll go dig Bassett out of his lab and we'll all go for a brisk walk around the grounds."

"I don't need—"

But Margaret was gone. Sarah shook her head resignedly. It seemed she was being established firmly under Margaret's wing. She should never have admitted anything was wrong.

Bassett came down the hall a few minutes later. "Hi, I'm glad you came back. It gets kind of lonely here."

It was the first time she'd seen him. He had been in his laboratory when Logan and Sarah had dropped off their suitcases. His hair was tousled and there were circles beneath his eyes. Evidently he'd been burning the midnight oil.

"I don't see how anyone could be lonely with Margaret around," she said.

"She's a cross between a mother and a dictator. She makes me eat, go for walks, and constantly interrupts my work."

"Good for her."

"But I could use some company who doesn't nag me twenty-four hours a day."

"Well, you shouldn't be lonely long. Logan says you're almost finished and should be heading for Dodsworth soon."

He went still. "Logan told you about Dodsworth?" A smile lit his face. "I'm glad. I didn't like closing you out after you helped me, but it was necessary. Artificial blood is a prime target for industrial espionage and—"

She held up her hand. "I've been over that with Logan. As long as there's no danger of anyone at Dodsworth being hurt, I'm not going to blow the whistle."

His smile faded. "We all knew what we were getting into when we took the job."

"You didn't know about Rudzak."

"No, I guess I didn't, but I'd still hire on to get in on the ground floor of this research."

"How close are you to completing your notes?"

"At least another five days. I'm working as hard as I can, but there are only so many hours in the day."

Her gaze narrowed on his face. "And you haven't spent very many of them sleeping."

"I told you, it's my dream. Maybe you can understand now that you know how important the project is."

"I do understand." She shook her head. "But you don't have to kill yourself."

"I'll survive. People are dying every day who could live if we meet our goal. It's worth a little exhaustion." He rubbed the back of his neck. "I try to take a walk every day to work out the kinks and clear my head. Want to come with me?"

"I thought that was Margaret's job. I don't want to hurt her feelings."

He made a face. "I guess she can come with us. I like to amble and she sets a pace like a Nazi drill sergeant."

"I'll come if you can wait until I give Monty some water."

"I'll wait. Maybe we'll even have a real conversation." He leaned against the doorjamb. "You know, I get a little lonesome with no one to talk to. My wife says I'm way too gregarious for a scientist." He chuckled. "Which means she thinks I'm a chatterbox. I tell her my work is so solitary that the floodgates just break open when I leave the lab."

"How is your wife?"

"Fine. I miss her. I call her every day, but it's not the same. She's taking our son to the Bahamas for a vacation this week. We went there on our honeymoon. I wish I were going with them. Do you know the scuba diving is fantastic off— I'm babbling, aren't I?"

"Well, you can babble all you please as soon as I get Monty his water. Neither one of us is a talker, but we're both good listeners."

"You say that as if your dog is human." Then he nodded. "Why not? He's part of your work and your work is your passion too."

"He's more than that. He's my friend."

"Lucky Monty," he said wistfully. "I haven't had much time for friends. I've barely had time to be a decent husband and father."

"You're young. You've got plenty of time." She motioned for Monty to precede her into the kitchen, then added grimly, "If you don't let Logan bulldoze you into another project like this one."

"Logan never bulldozes me. It's not his way."

"Not unless he thinks it's necessary." But she knew what he meant. Logan's usual way was charm and subtle maneuvering, which invariably got him what he wanted. Who should know better than she how powerful that spell could be? She had been caught and was still held fast by Logan.

"You're still angry with him? I hoped you'd realize what a great guy he is."

"I'm not angry." But she wanted to be. It would be so much easier if she didn't know Logan so well. But she'd seen his vulnerability, his humor and determination. Walking away from him would be difficult. What was she thinking? He would probably be the one to walk away from her. Their sleeping together meant nothing. Even now he was with a woman he'd had a relationship with not even a year ago. Who would be next year's woman?

"And I do admire him," she told Bassett. "I just don't think he's a hundred percent right a hundred percent of the time." She followed Monty into the kitchen. "I'll be back in a minute. I'll give Monty his drink and then we can get Margaret."

"If I didn't know you better, I'd swear you have no conscience, Logan," Eve said sternly. "You shouldn't have involved Sarah."

"You're preaching to the choir." Logan parked the car next to the cabin and turned off the ignition. "But it's too late now. I just have to do what I can to protect her."

"As long as you can also protect this Dodsworth. I wouldn't want that responsibility."

"Neither do I." His hands tightened on the steering wheel. "You know I'm no saint, Eve. I'm arrogant and selfish and more bullheaded than any man has a right to be. Years ago I made a mistake and let Rudzak live, and now I have to correct it. Dodsworth is the bait, and I have to run with it."

"If Sarah lets you."

"She'll let me. I'll make sure that security is so tight, she won't believe Rudzak has a chance."

She was silent a moment. "You said that Rudzak would target anyone close to you. Does that include me and my family?"

"I don't think that's likely. I've had two security guards watching your cottage since Rudzak surfaced, but it was only a precaution." His lips twisted in a wry smile. "He's not interested in past history."

"You'll always be my friend, Logan."

"I know, and that's enough for me." He paused. "Call Quinn and tell him to come. Sarah will feel better about it."

"What about you?"

"You'd probably all be safer here. You're under surveillance from the foothills and it's a clear view to the cabin. It's hard to guard that cottage in the woods. You found that out when you were dealing with that murderer who stalked you."

She shivered. "Rudzak couldn't be as clever as Dom."

"Don't bet on it. He fooled Sarah, and she's pretty canny."

"Yes." She frowned. "I'll think about it." She got out of the jeep and reached for her suitcase. "Don't get out. I'll introduce myself to Galen. I know you want to get back to Sarah. You seem worried about her."

"I am. All the time."

"But the guards at the Phoenix house are very—" She stopped, her gaze on his face. "My God."

He nodded. "No possibility that she's not a target." He said, mockingly, "Quinn would laugh. He always told me I didn't love you enough, that it had to be an obsession. I didn't understand then, but he was right, you know. It's an obsession."

"If anything happens to those people at Dodsworth, she'll hate you, Logan."

"I'll hate myself." He started the jeep. "Call her and tell her you're going to ask Quinn to come. She's worried enough about Dodsworth. She doesn't need to worry about you."

Logan's phone rang on the drive back to Phoenix.

"I met your Sarah," Rudzak said. "Did she tell you what an entertaining time we had together? She's an interesting woman. Not nearly as fascinating as Chen Li, but then, you never had the sophistication to appreciate her. It doesn't surprise me that you've formed an attachment to someone as blunt and straightforward as Sarah Patrick."

"She did a job for me. There's no attachment."

"It's too late to lie to me. I saw you together and I read you so well."

"You don't know jack. You haven't been around me for a long time. I'm not the man you knew all those years ago."

"You've matured, you're sharper, but the basics are still

there. You become involved and you're pitifully sentimental when your sympathies are aroused. Look how unreasonable you became when I did what was best for Chen Li."

"I agree. It would have been far more reasonable to have broken your neck then. I'll have to do it now."

He laughed. "Then come and get me, Logan. Find me. I'm waiting for you. Oh, by the way, the comb wasn't for Sarah or anyone at Apache Lake. That was just a mere exercise, not worthy of Chen Li."

Logan stiffened. "Then why throw the comb in her jeep?"

"It wasn't for Sarah, Logan." He hung up.

15

"Where's Jane?" Eve fired the question at Logan as soon as he picked up the ringing phone the next morning. "You said they'd be safe. Damn you, where's Jane?"

"What?" Panic spiked through him. "What are you talking about?"

"I'm talking about Jane. Joe just called me and told me that Jane's missing."

"Missing from where?"

"My mother's house in Atlanta. Joe dropped her off there last night when I asked him to fly out here today. When my mother went into Jane's room to call her for breakfast, she was gone. Goddammit, you said they'd be safe."

"Was there any sign of forced entry?"

"No, I don't think so. Joe's on his way over there to talk to my mom and check out the house."

"Could she have run away? She's been upset lately."

"Not enough to run away."

That was Logan's impression too, but he'd been reaching. Any other explanation scared him shitless.

The comb wasn't for Sarah.

Rudzak's words had been clawing at him since the previous night.

Had it been for little Jane MacGuire?

"Why aren't you saying anything?" Eve demanded.

"I was thinking. Let me get off the phone and call Galen. He wouldn't have let Jane be dropped off without putting a guard on your mother's house."

"Then phone him and call me back." Eve's voice was uneven. "You get my Jane back, Logan. I won't lose another daughter." She hung up.

"What's wrong?" Sarah had come into the living room. "What about Jane?"

"She's disappeared from her grandmother's house." Logan was punching in Galen's number. "Eve's nearly frantic."

"Of course she is," Sarah said. "It must bring back Bonnie's kidnapping and all the horror that—"

"Galen, who the hell do you have in Atlanta? Jane MacGuire's missing."

"The kid? No way. I stationed two good men at her grandmother's last night. They would have reported anything wrong."

"Well, your two good men fouled up. She's missing. Call them and see what the hell they know." He hung up. "Galen didn't know anything about it. He said the house was guarded."

"Rudzak," Sarah whispered.

"I don't know."

"She's only a little girl, Logan." She shuddered. "But those kids at Apache Lake were just children, too, weren't they? He doesn't care."

"No, he doesn't care." His lips tightened. "But we shouldn't jump to conclusions."

"Why not? With that monster out there?" She reached for the phone. "I've got to call Eve."

"Not now."

"I brought her here. If she'd stayed with Jane, this might not have happened."

"And what are you going to say? That you're sorry? Is that going to make her feel better? Keep her line open in case someone needs to reach her."

"Like the police," she said dully. "Isn't that what they say when a child is missing?"

"Quinn is on the job, trying to find Jane. He'll be calling Eve as soon as he hears even a whisper." He paused. "It doesn't have to be Rudzak, Sarah."

"And this is just a coincidence? Isn't that what you told yourself about Kai Chi?"

He couldn't deny it. "Don't jump to conclusions."

She headed for the door. "Not until we find one of Chen Li's artifacts beside Jane's body?"

He was glad that she had left the room. He wasn't about to tell her what Rudzak had said, but she might have read something in his expression.

The comb wasn't for Sarah.

"Any news of the kid?" Margaret asked as she walked beside Sarah to the front door.

Sarah shook her head. "Galen's men swear they didn't see anyone near the house."

"That's good news."

"It only means Rudzak's smart. I can't wait any longer. I'm going to drive out to the cabin to see Eve."

"You can't do any good there."

"I can be there for her. For God's sake, it's almost dark and they found out she was gone this morning. I was hoping we'd hear something right away."

"Wait a little longer," Margaret coaxed. "We'll go for a stroll with Bassett, and if Logan hasn't found out anything by the time we return, you can scoot out of here and I'll cover for you with Logan."

"I don't need anyone to cover for me."

"Then you can cover for me for not doing my job and keeping your mind off Jane."

"Is that what Logan told you to do?"

Margaret shook her head as she opened the door. "Some jobs are implied. There's Bassett waiting already."

Sarah shrugged. Another fifteen minutes would do no harm. "Okay, once around the grounds."

"Super." Margaret passed Bassett at a fast clip and started for the back of the house. "Get the load off, Bassett. Get that circulation moving."

"Yes, ma'am." Bassett winked at Sarah as he followed Margaret. "Here I go again. The woman's the bane of my life." He sobered. "Logan told me about the little girl. Have you heard anything?"

Sarah shook her head as she fell into step with him. "Galen flew to Atlanta this afternoon." And he and Joe should be meeting by now.

"She may be okay. Kids are funny. Maybe she's hiding or trying to make them worry about her."

"That's not Jane."

"Well, maybe her grandmother is making—"

"Hurry up." Margaret waved at a security guard standing by the front gate some distance away. "Hi, Booker. Did you ever see two worse wimps in your life than these two?"

The security guard grinned. "Do you really expect me to answer that?"

"Coward." Margaret started to turn onto the path leading around the house. "Come on, exercise isn't any good unless it raises your heart rate."

"Coming." Bassett's pace quickened. "Right behind you."

They weren't right behind her. Margaret actually was yards ahead of them. She turned and gave them a scornful wave. "I told you that you had to hustle to—" She stiffened, her gaze on the front gate. "Booker?"

The wolf was howling again. Eve felt like howling too.

Oh, God, let Jane be all right.

Go check on Maggie, make sure she's okay. It was something to do. She moved toward the back porch and stuck her head in the door. The wolf glared at her resentfully and raised her head to howl again.

"I can't help you," she whispered. "I can't bring them back."

And she couldn't help herself.

Or Jane.

Dammit, Logan, find her.

She stiffened as she heard a knock on the door.

She slowly moved across the room.

If they'd found her, they would have called immediately. People came in person to give you bad news. Policemen knocked on the door and said how sorry they were that your little girl was dead.

Bonnie.

No, this was Jane, and God wouldn't let it happen to her again. There had to be some universal law that forbade—

Another knock.

The wolf howled.

She leaned her forehead on the door for a moment. Face it. She stepped back and threw open the door.

Herb Booker was clinging to the gate, staring straight ahead. Blood was pouring from his shoulder. His whole body suddenly jerked.

"Christ, he's been shot." Bassett ran past Margaret down the driveway. "We've got to *help* him."

A shot? Panic surged through Sarah. "Bassett, stay away from the gates!"

"Drop to the ground." Margaret was already running toward Bassett and the fallen Booker. "Stay low, Bassett."

"What the hell's happening? Booker's been—" Bassett spun around clutching his wrist.

Another shot.

And Sarah saw blood gushing from Margaret's chest as she slowly sank to her knees. "Sarah?" she whispered in disbelief.

Sarah screamed and ran toward her.

"Call security," Bassett said, dazed. He was clutching his wrist and blood was running through his fingers. "For God's sake, call—"

"Hit the ground and stay there," Sarah yelled at him. "You can't help. Monty, stay with him."

A bullet whistled by her cheek as she knelt beside Margaret, who had slumped to the ground. "Margaret?"

Margaret's eyes were staring straight ahead. "Stay . . . low . . ."

She was still giving orders, Sarah realized. Should she move her? What if the bullet shifted?

Help. She needed help.

She opened her mouth and screamed.

• • •

"I know you're going to be mad at me." Jane straightened her shoulders belligerently. "That's too bad. I'm here and I'm going to stay here. You can't just go away and not expect— Let me go. I can't breathe."

"Too bad." Eve's arms tightened around Jane's thin body. "I'm not letting go." She cleared her tight throat. "Well, not for a minute or two. Then I'm going to murder you."

"I knew you'd be mad. I would have told Joe or your mother, but I knew they would have stopped me from coming. They think I'm a kid."

"You are a kid, dammit."

Jane looked at her.

"Okay." Jane was no more a child than Eve had been at her age. They had both grown up on the streets where youth had been stolen from them. "Then you should have been adult enough not to worry me to death."

"You wouldn't have let me come." She stepped back. "And I'm here now. You should call Joe and tell him I'm here, shouldn't you?"

"Yes." She didn't want to move. She didn't want to stop looking at her daughter. "How did you get here?"

"I bought an electronic ticket on the Internet and charged it to your credit card. I owe you money."

"They let you on the airplane by yourself?"

"I managed. Is that the wolf howling? Where is she?"

"On the back porch. And how did you get here from the airport?"

"I hitchhiked." She held up her hand to stop Eve's protests. "I know it's dangerous. I picked an old man and his wife and they lectured me all the way here. They stayed outside in their truck until you opened the door. I want to see the wolf." She started toward the door Eve had indicated. "You call Joe and then you can yell at me later."

"Count on it." She headed for the phone. "And stay away from Maggie. She's crabby."

"Why?"

"I think she's lonely."

Jane looked at her over her shoulder. "That's a bad thing to be. It . . . hurts."

"Yes, it does."

Jane looked away. "Call Joe."

Another shot tore by Sarah's ear as she huddled over Margaret's body, both hands pressing above the wound.

"Sarah!" Logan was running toward her from the house with Juan Lopez behind him. "Get yourself and Margaret into the trees, dammit."

"I'm going to. Go take care of Bassett and Booker. They've both been shot."

"Lopez, call 911," Logan shouted.

There was a screech of tires outside the gate, and a dark Camaro tore down the street.

Lopez ran out the gate and stood looking after it. "Son of a bitch."

"Forget him. Call 911."

"Is she going to be okay?" Bassett was standing over Margaret, still clutching his wrist. "This shouldn't have happened. I thought we were safe here. Is she going to live?"

"She's going to be fine." Oh, God, she couldn't stop the blood. "Don't you dare fall asleep, Margaret. Stay with us."

• • •

Eve walked to the back porch and stood beside Jane in the doorway. "I called Logan but couldn't get an answer. I left a message on his voice mail. You've caused him a world of trouble. I was able to get hold of Joe. He's hopping the next plane. He says he's going to scalp you. I told him I'd tie you to the stake for him."

"She's beautiful, isn't she?" Jane's gaze was fastened on the wolf. "But you're right, she's crabby. It's a good thing I'm here to take care of her."

"You?"

"Joe didn't like you being here with the wolf. I could tell. So I came to take care of her."

"And me?"

Jane's gaze shifted to Eve. "Sure. This is something I can do. I'm not Bonnie. I'll never be Bonnie to you. I don't think I'd want to be her. I talked to your mother about her, and Bonnie was so nice, I don't even know if I'd have liked her."

"You'd have liked her."

"Maybe. But I know I like you." She looked back at the wolf. "Maybe I even . . . love you."

"That's nice. I know I love you."

Jane nodded. "I went up on the hill and visited Bonnie's grave after you left yesterday afternoon."

Eve went still. "Why did you do that?"

"I don't know. I just did. And I decided it doesn't matter that you still love her. I'm not nice like she was, but I can do things for you that she couldn't. She wouldn't have been able to take care of you like I can. I'm smart and I know the same things that you do. That's got to mean something."

"It means a great deal."

"So you're lucky to have me."

"Oh, yes."

Jane gave her a disparaging glance. "You're not going to cry?"

Eve shook her head. "I wouldn't think of it." She cleared her throat. "When you're only being sensible."

"Good. Crying would be silly." Jane walked toward the wolf. "Now show me what to do to take care of Maggie."

Sarah tensed as Logan walked into the hospital waiting room. "Is she going to live?"

"I don't know. They were able to get the bullet out, but she's in critical condition. It'll be touch and go for a while." He sat down and buried his face in his hands. "I just don't know."

She was silent a moment. "She's been with you a long time."

"Almost fifteen years." He raised his head to reveal a haggard face. "We've worked together for so long, she's like family. But I didn't think Rudzak— I thought she'd be safe."

"She was behind electric fences with security guards."

"It shouldn't have happened. I should have been more careful. I should have stopped her and Bassett from taking those walks."

"It was safe as long as they stayed away from the gates. That's the only place where there's a clear view to get a shot. You couldn't know that the shooter would target Booker first to draw us to the gates."

"That doesn't mean I'm not responsible. I should have—"

"Shut up, Logan." She took his hand and held it between hers. "You did the best you could. You're not a fortune-teller and you're sure not God. So stop blaming yourself."

He smiled with an effort. "Thanks for the sweet words."

"You want sweet?" She blinked the tears back. "Sorry. I can only be myself. If I could take this away from you, I would. At least Booker and Bassett are going to be okay. The doctor said Booker is being taken off the serious list, and Bassett's only got a nasty wound in the hand."

"He's pretty shaken up. He wants to finish the research at Dodsworth."

"He knows Dodsworth may not be safe either."

"He'd rather take his chances there. I tend to agree. Dodsworth is safer." He stood up. "I need to move. Do you want some coffee from the machine?"

She shook her head.

"I'm having Lopez pack your bag. Galen's going to pick you and Bassett up and take you to Dodsworth."

"Me?"

"I have to stay here, and I want you where Galen can protect you. He has to be at Dodsworth."

"Did it occur to you that I might want to stay with you?" she asked unevenly.

"It occurred to me. In spite of your lack of tender feelings for me." He gently touched her cheek. "But if you want to help me, you'll go to Dodsworth. I don't need to worry about you too."

"I don't want to—"

"What about all those people at Dodsworth? Have you forgotten you may have to blow the whistle on me?"

"I haven't forgotten."

"Then go and make sure Galen is doing his job. I'll be there as soon as Margaret takes a turn for the better."

Dammit, he was in pain and she didn't want to leave him. She wanted to hold him and get him through this horrible night as he had held her after Apache Lake.

"Rudzak is going to be at Dodsworth, Sarah. I couldn't be more sure. And I don't need you or want you here." He left the room.

She caught up with him halfway down the corridor. "Don't you dare try that bull with me." She spun him around, her arms around his waist, and she hugged him with fierce strength. "I won't let you. You do want me here. I know you care something about me and I could help you." Her arms fell away from him. "But I'm going to Dodsworth. To make sure nothing happens to those people so you won't end up feeling guilty for the rest of your miserable life." She stepped back. "I'm going to Bassett's room. Tell Galen to pick me up there."

The ivory mirror was in the shape of an ankh. An asp was intricately carved around the teakwood handle. It had been his last present to Chen Li.

It would be his last present to Logan.

"An ankh?" Chen Li held up the mirror. "It's the symbol of immortality, isn't it?"

"That's why I brought it to you. To show you that you'll live forever."

She made a face. "I don't feel immortal at the moment, Martin. Though I'm much better than I was last week. Maybe I am getting well after all."

She wasn't getting well. Sitting there in that chair by the window, she looked thin and weak and pale. She would never be the same Chen Li again. Death was stealing her from him just as Logan had stolen her. And Logan would keep her his until the very end, giving her hope and yet telling Rudzak that she was not well enough to see him. "Did you go to sleep early last night? Logan said I couldn't come in."

She looked away. "I was a little tired."

"The weariness will go away soon." He stepped behind her and put his hands on her shoulders. "This mirror is very special. It belonged to a high priest. It will make you live forever."

"Perhaps we should tell my doctors about it. They could use a little help." She leaned forward and his hands fell away. She was trying to avoid his touch, he realized with incredulous fury. She was already lost to him.

But he could get her back. He could take her away from Logan.

"Let's try it," he said. "Look in the mirror."

"I don't like what I see in any mirror these days."

"But you should. You're beautiful."

"Yes, sure. That's what John says."

He didn't want to hear what Logan said. This moment was his alone. "Because it's true." He bent over her and put his hands on her nape. "You can see it in my eyes. Look in the mirror. If you won't look at your reflection, look at mine and you'll know that you'll live forever and always be as beautiful as you are to me at this moment. Lift the mirror."

She slowly lifted the mirror. "Why, Martin, what's wrong? There are tears in—"

The mirror fell from her hand as he snapped her neck with one violent twist.

"Good-bye, Chen Li." He tenderly kissed her cheek, then picked up the mirror. "Good-bye, my love."

He tucked the tissue paper carefully around the mirror and placed it in the box. He slipped the note he'd written on top of the mirror and closed the lid.

He addressed the box to Sarah Patrick at Dodsworth.

Municipal Courthouse
Dodsworth, North Dakota

Had he heard something?

A door swinging shut?

Probably not. He'd been imagining sounds in this creaky old building all evening, Bill Ledwick thought. When you were as bored as he was, your imagination had a field day. He'd be glad to get back with the guys at the facility.

Better check the sound. Galen didn't like anyone taking anything for granted.

He got up from his chair and moved down the long, dark corridor.

Silence except for the soft thud of his rubber soles on the marble floor.

He paused at the glass door of the record room. He stepped to one side and threw open the door. He waited a minute and then reached in and flipped on the light.

No one was in the room.

Of course not. Imagination.

Check. Just to make sure.

He moved to the file cabinet across the room and pulled open the drawer. He knew exactly where the file was kept. He'd checked it often enough.

He opened the file folder.

Shit!

"I heard from my man at the courthouse," Galen said when he called Logan the next day. "The blueprints of the facility disappeared from the record department."

Logan was silent a moment. "I thought that would happen. Rudzak's not the type to rely on a truckload of dynamite parked near his target. No random hits for him. He wants to be sure of me."

"Then he should have had his hired gun shoot you instead of Margaret."

"That wouldn't have satisfied him. It's not a big enough statement. He wants to bury me at Dodsworth like I buried him in that prison. A final tribute to both him and Chen Li."

"How is Margaret doing?"

"Not out of danger, but better. They're going to let me see her in a few minutes. Her folks got in from San Francisco last night and they let her brothers visit her in intensive care." He paused. "How's Sarah?"

"A pain in my ass. She and Monty have been over every inch of the facility looking for cracks in my security. She knows emergency procedures better than my second-in-command, and I think she's memorized every corridor in the damn building."

"Did she find any cracks?"

There was a hesitation. "One. But it was more of a hairline fracture."

"So she's satisfied that Dodsworth's safe?"

"Yes, but now she doesn't see why Rudzak would persist in targeting it."

"Tell her about the blueprints."

"I'll tell her. She may still worry about all your other facilities."

"Your job is to keep her from worrying."

"Until she makes another one of her four A.M. inspection tours." His tone was distinctly sour. "I'd rather take care of Maggie. When are you coming to get her out of my hair?"

"I'll be there as soon as I can, but I assure you that Rudzak isn't going to start without me. No word from him?"

"Just the missing blueprints. That's a pretty decisive statement. Give Margaret my best." He hung up.

Logan slipped the phone in his pocket and headed for intensive care. It was no surprise that Sarah was giving Galen a hard time. She wouldn't care how much she liked someone if it got in the way of her job and, in this case, her job was to keep Dodsworth from becoming a disaster area.

"What are you doing here?" Margaret's voice was only a breath of sound, which he could barely hear from where he stood in the doorway.

He crossed the room and took her hand in his. "How are you feeling?"

"Like shit." She glared at him. "And mad. Why are you here moaning and groaning instead of going after the asshole who shot me? Did you think I was going to die?"

"The thought never occurred to me."

"Liar. But I'm not going to die and"—she had to pause to get her breath—"and I have enough problems with my brothers being overprotective. So get out of here."

He stood looking at her.

"Okay, okay, I promise I won't die, John." She showed her teeth with tigerlike ferocity. "And instead of flowers, why don't you send me Rudzak's head?"

"I'll do my best."

"Good." She closed her eyes. "Now get out of here. I'm tired."

"Shall I call a nurse?"

"His head, John." She didn't open her eyes. "Stop standing there worrying and just get out of here and bring me his head."

"Yes, ma'am." He turned toward the door. "Right away, ma'am."

7:45 P.M.

"Joe got here yesterday," Eve told Sarah on the phone. "He's going to be here as long as you need me. Do you have any idea yet how long that will be?"

"I wish I did."

"No problem. I just like the idea of being home with my family."

"Jane is okay now?"

"No thanks to me. She worked it out for herself . . . I think."

"What do you mean?"

"It's funny how clear and simple everything is when you don't let baggage get in the way. What are you doing there at Dodsworth?"

"Keeping myself busy."

"Is the security as good as you hoped?"

"Better. And that bothers me. Why would Rudzak think he could take down this facility?"

"You're afraid he'll target another place?"

"I seem to be the only one. Galen and Logan think the stolen blueprints are cast-iron proof. I'm afraid it might be a red herring."

"Logan's nobody's fool."

"I know that. It's just—" She stopped, frustrated. "I'm afraid we're on the wrong track. It doesn't smell right."

Eve chuckled. "You sound like Monty on a search."

"Monty's usually right."

"I'm the last one to disagree. You should follow your instincts. I've got to go. Time to feed Maggie."

It was time to feed Monty too. "Come on, boy." Sarah hung up the phone and headed toward the cafeteria with Monty at her heels. She'd packed one of the kitchen cabinets with his food and vitamins, and she tried to feed him in the evening when he wasn't distracted by the constant attention of the scientists. Monty was already practically a mascot, and he'd rather have gotten belly rubs than eat.

Bassett was sitting at a table, and he looked up when Sarah came into the room. "Got time to sit down and have a cup of coffee with me?"

She shook her head. "I just came to feed Monty. I'm nervous enough without the caffeine."

"Are you? I feel a lot safer here." He got to his feet and followed Sarah and Monty into the kitchen. "Funny. I felt fine until that last day in Phoenix. Have you heard how Margaret's doing?"

"She's still alive."

"I complained a lot about her, but I really liked her."

"I know. How do you like your lab here?"

"Fine. They've assigned Hilda Rucker to work with me. She's brilliant." He wrinkled his nose as he looked down at his bandaged left hand. "And she's got two good hands to operate the computer. That's nothing to sneeze at." He finished his coffee in one swallow. "I'd better get back to the grind. Hilda's no Margaret, but I can't let her get ahead of me. Let me know about Margaret."

"I will."

Galen passed him at the kitchen door and gave him a casual nod before coming toward Sarah. "Logan's on his way. He just called and told me that Margaret had kicked him out. He should be here within a few hours."

"Good." She leaned down and put Monty's dinner before him. "Then she's better?"

"Well, it's clear she's functioning in her usual manner." He made a face. "I'm glad she's in Phoenix. I don't need another high-powered woman here."

"Yes you do. But you'll have to be satisfied with me. Speaking of high-powered females, I talked to Eve a little while ago. She thinks Maggie is either pouting or mourning. She won't stop howling."

"Then why don't you go home and take care of your wolf yourself?"

She gave him a sly glance. "Maybe I should send for Maggie and Eve, have them come here instead."

"Forget it." He headed for the door. "I'm out of here."

"Can't take the heat?" But he'd already gone.

The large kitchen was suddenly cavernous and lonely. Her smile faded as she leaned on the counter and watched Monty eat. Sparring with Galen was an outlet she badly needed. The tension was growing with every hour, and she needed it over.

Monty looked up at her. *Sad?*

She shook her head as she filled his water bowl. Not sad, uneasy. And lonely. It was strange how lonely you could feel when you're apart from one special individual. "Eat your dinner. You haven't eaten decently since we left the cabin."

Sad.

"This is our job. I had to take you away from Maggie."

Sad.

"Heaven save me from a lovesick—" Why was she blaming Monty, when she'd been mooning around herself only a few minutes before? "It's okay," she whispered as she reached down to scratch behind his ear. "I know it's bad, but we've got to go on. Now eat your dinn—"

"Sarah."

She turned to see Galen standing in the doorway. "Why did you come ba—" She stiffened. "What's wrong?"

"A package for you." He crossed the room and handed her a neatly wrapped box. "It just came. Special delivery."

All packages coming into the facility were X-rayed. "What is it?"

He shrugged. "I couldn't tell. Something weird. But it's not an explosive."

She slowly took off the wrap and opened the lid. The object inside was old, very old, the ivory yellowed by time, but the gold-sheeted mirror still shone. She felt her stomach clench. "Chen Li."

Galen stiffened. "I was afraid of that. Don't read the note. Maybe we'd better save it for Logan."

"It's addressed to me." She unfolded the paper.

Sarah,

As I told Logan, the last gift wasn't for you. This one is far more fitting. Notice the asp? You can share it with Logan.

Martin Rudzak

16

8:20 P.M.

Just one more charge to go.

Duggan carefully set the plastic explosive high in a cleft in the column so it wouldn't be visible.

Now get down.

Get out.

And watch the damn place blow.

10:05 P.M.

"Just what am I sharing with you?" Sarah asked as she and Galen watched Logan read the note. All the blinds were drawn in the first-floor conference room, and Monty lay a few feet from Sarah. "Is the mirror Chen Li's?"

"Probably. But I've never seen it. The nurses told me

Rudzak was carrying a box when he went into Chen Li's hospital room the night he killed her."

"And what does it mean?"

"If it's the last thing he gave her, it means he's growing impatient. He wants to put an end to this." His hand tightened on the mirror. "Thank God. So do I."

So did Sarah, but the idea also terrified her. "Then is Dodsworth—"

Logan's phone rang. He listened to the caller for a moment. "Right. I understand." He hung up and turned to Galen. "Rudzak's going to move. Clear the building. How many people are working tonight?"

"Twelve."

"Get them out of here. Then tell your guys to do a tour and get out too."

"I'm on my way." Galen headed out of the room at a run.

"Shall I call the bomb squad and ATF?" Sarah asked.

"Galen will do it." He touched her cheek. "It's okay, Sarah. The building will be cleared before anything happens. We have a little time."

"How do you know? Is that what Rudzak told you on the phone? Then you can expect the liar to blow it in the next few minutes."

"Rudzak's been planning this a long time. There's no one more methodical. He's taking it step by step. Trust me. No one's going to get hurt."

"How can I trust you, when you never tell me anything? Why didn't you tell me about Rudzak saying that comb wasn't for me?"

"Why worry you? I was worried enough for both of us."

"Are there other things you haven't told me?"

He didn't answer.

"Ever since I met you, I've been fighting your secrets. You didn't tell me about Kai Chi either."

"Don't do this to me now, Sarah."

"Why not? It's important. You always have to be the big, strong hero. Well, I'm tired of it. What about sharing? And treating me as a partner? I'm not fragile like Chen Li. You don't have to take care of—"

"Be quiet." He gripped her shoulders and shook her. "Don't throw Chen Li in my face."

"I don't have to. Dear God, Rudzak is making sure that neither one of us forgets her."

"Listen to me." He stared directly into her eyes. "I'm no longer the person who married Chen Li, but I'm grateful for what she gave me."

"I know you are. You and she were—"

"Dammit, shut up. You don't know anything. I love you. I want to spend my life with you. I've never felt like this about anyone else, and I'm not going to let anything happen to you." He kissed her hard. "And I'm going to take care of you whether you like it or not. You go out when the security team does."

She watched dazedly as he walked away from her. "The hell I will," she called after him. "Rudzak wants me here. He may not come if I leave."

He walked out the door without looking back.

"Where are you—" She ran after him, Monty at her heels, but Logan had vanished around the corner.

She had no intention of leaving, but there was no time for arguing. There were people to get out of the building.

"Come on, Monty. Let's get everyone out of here." Monty followed her as she walked quickly to the lab on the ground floor where Kevin Janus was working.

Her uneasiness was growing. The whole situation was like a puzzle with key pieces missing. It shouldn't be happening like this. It didn't smell right.

You sound like Monty on a search.

You should follow your instincts.

She had no choice. There was no time to do anything but rely on instinct.

Okay, put your uneasiness on the back burner. But try to find the cone, try to find the source.

Before it is too late.

10:35 P.M.

The building was emptying. The parking lot was almost deserted.

"You shouldn't have sent them the warning," Duggan told Rudzak as they sat in the car watching. "They're scattering like scared mice."

"And you prefer the mice caught in the trap." Rudzak lowered the binoculars. "I'm willing to let a few unimportant people scamper away. The mice that count are still inside, Duggan. Where did you set the charge?"

"Where you told me. In the basement lab. The drainage tunnel was right where the blueprint said it would be. I was in and out in fifteen minutes. But you should have had me put the charge on a timer. That would be a lot safer."

"I don't want it to be safe. I want to be there, looking at his face when I tell him what's coming." He smiled. "You can understand that. You get a thrill from pressing the trigger yourself."

"Not while I'm sitting on top of a pile of explosives."

"But you said I'd have no trouble getting out the drainage tunnel. In and out in fifteen minutes?"

Duggan nodded.

"And you have the switch in the trunk? Get it for me, will you, Duggan?"

"Sure." He got out of the car, and when he returned, he handed the switch over. "It's real sweet. And I made sure it wasn't hair trigger. I didn't want you blowing yourself up by accident."

"Thank you for your concern, Duggan." He leisurely got out of the driver's seat. "But I really don't want you to have to worry about me anymore."

Rudzak shot him in the head.

11:10 P.M.

Darkness.

Logan stopped in the doorway, tensing. He knew what was ahead in that darkness. When his eyes became accustomed to the blackness, he'd be able to see Rudzak. He could almost feel the waves of hate bombarding him from the depths of that room.

But the verbal threat didn't come from the darkness. It came from behind him.

"Go on." The barrel of a pistol was suddenly pressed against his spine. "Move, Logan."

11:45 P.M.

Four labs cleared. Three to go.

Sarah and Monty hurried down the hall.

Galen's men had already cleared the seven scientists out of the second-floor lab by the time she and Monty got there. Next stop—Hilda Rucker and Tom Bassett on the third floor.

She ran into Hilda Rucker on the stairs. The gray-haired woman was carrying a boxful of files. "I know. They told me to get out and I will be in two minutes."

"You stopped to grab those files?"

"Do you think I want my work blown to smithereens?"

Logan was right. These people were as committed to the project as he was. "Where's Bassett?"

"Right behind me. He came back to the lab just after Galen's men left and I told him about the evacuation. He was dumping computer disks into his briefcase when I left."

"And probably throwing files into boxes like you did. I'd better get him out of there right now." She continued up the stairs.

She'd get Bassett out and then—

Get Bassett out.

Protect Bassett.

She stopped short.

Sweet Jesus.

Her phone rang as she started up again.

"Get out of there, Sarah," Galen said as soon as she picked up.

"Damn you, Galen. You and Logan both knew, didn't you?"

Silence and then, "Get out of there, Sarah."

"Go to hell." She hung up and took the rest of the stairs two at a time with Monty at her heels.

Protect Bassett.

Keep Bassett safe.

"Bassett!"

He came out of the lab carrying his briefcase. "Sarah, I was just going to call you. I ran into Logan a few minutes ago and he wants you to come with me to—" He stopped as he saw her expression. "I see. It's not going to be as easy as I thought, is it? You're a very smart lady. I was afraid you might figure it out. Too bad you did."

"You're the Judas, aren't you? Rudzak had you planted from the beginning. He wanted us to rescue you. He wanted us to get you out of Santo Camaro so that he could use you to set up Dodsworth." And set up Logan. Her heart stopped. "Where's Logan? It was you who called him, wasn't it?"

He nodded. "I told him I'd received a threat from Rudzak and asked him to meet at the basement lab. Naturally, he came." He smiled. "We all know how Rudzak's targeted me in the past." He took a gun out of his jacket pocket. "But Rudzak also wants you with Logan, so I'll have to oblige."

"How much did he pay you?"

"More than Castleton. Even though Castleton brought me on board. I deserved it. Rudzak suddenly got impatient so he gave me an excuse to leave Phoenix right away. The bastard didn't tell me he was going to shoot me too." He motioned with the gun. "We'd better get going. Rudzak doesn't want to blow this building without you, but he may get edgy. I don't want to be here if he does."

She didn't move.

"Should I shoot your dog first?"

"No!" She started down the steps. "If I agree to go with you, is it all right if I send Monty to Galen?"

"You're afraid he'll be blown up?"

"There's no reason for him to be hurt." She stopped and turned to face him. "Let him go."

He shrugged. "It doesn't matter. I don't want to deal with him anyway. Send him away."

"Monty! Go to—" She launched herself up the stairs and dove low, grabbing Bassett's gun hand. "Monty!"

Monty buried his teeth in Bassett's wrist as Sarah grabbed his bandaged hand and pushed the fingers back.

He screamed in agony and dropped the gun. She scooped it up and hit him in the face with the butt. Blood spurted from his gashed lip. "Bastard." She hit him again with the gun. "Son of a bitch."

He doubled over in pain.

"Sarah!"

She saw Galen running toward them. She told Monty, "Release."

Monty reluctantly let go of Bassett's wrist.

"Excuse me." Galen stepped in front of her and gave Bassett a lethal chop on the carotid artery. "We don't want him interfering. My, that felt good." He looked down at Monty. "I never thought I'd see that ball of fluff on the attack."

"He doesn't like guns pointed at me."

"Maybe I shouldn't have worried so much when I ran into Hilda Rucker at the front door and she told me you were going to see Bassett. You and Monty seem to have everything under control."

"Nothing's under control." She started down the steps. "Logan's in the basement lab. If you didn't know already."

"I knew."

"And you and Logan knew all about Bassett."

"Not at first. We only suspected. But we confirmed when we found out that his calls to his wife were being forwarded to another number."

"That's why no matter how tight the security, you knew Rudzak would strike here. He had someone on the inside feeding him information about security checks and opening all the doors."

"Yes, that's what tipped you off, wasn't it? I knew it bothered you."

"Then why the hell didn't someone tell me?"

"Sarah, you're many things, but deceitful isn't one of them. You'd never have been able to look Bassett in the face and pretend you didn't know."

"So Logan is down there alone with Rudzak."

"You can't go down there, Sarah. That's what Rudzak wants."

"Watch me."

Galen's hand closed on her shoulder. "I promised Logan that I'd get you out of here."

"Then you lied through your teeth, because I won't—"

Darkness.

12:05 A.M.

"You're being very docile, Logan," Rudzak said. "I wonder why."

"It could be the gun in your hand."

"Yes, that would have a dampening effect. Then there's the fact that your feet and hands are tied up. And you're lying on the floor like an animal ready for slaughter."

"Or it could be that this building is crawling with security men and one of them will come bursting in here any minute and butcher you." Logan smiled. "I'm visualizing that possibility with great pleasure."

"I'd kill you first." He smiled back. "But that's not going to happen. I've planned this too well. We'll just wait for your Sarah and then begin. I'm hoping the blast won't kill you immediately, but it probably will. If the blast doesn't kill you, then you'll still be crushed. I had Duggan plant the explosives at the top of those columns. The girders holding up this section of the building will topple like dominos."

"Another tribute to Chen Li."

"The last one."

"No, you'll be the last one. They'll catch you and send you back to prison. You'll die there."

Rudzak shook his head. "I'll get away from here the same

way I got in—through an old trapdoor leading to a drainage tunnel beneath the building. I have a plane waiting for me at a small airport outside town. I'll be gone before anyone bothers to look for me. They'll be too busy trying to dig your body out of the wreckage."

"Don't count on it. Galen's smart and he's my friend."

"I was very tempted to include Galen in my plans, but it wasn't practical. Perhaps I'll have a chance at him later." He checked his watch. "Bassett is being very slow."

"Maybe he's tipped his hand. Sarah's not stupid."

"No, but Bassett says she likes him, and it's hard to suspect people you like." He smiled again. "You liked Bassett too, didn't you?"

"Wouldn't he have been here already if something hadn't gone wrong? Galen was ordered to clear the building. That would include Bassett. If Bassett objected, it would have sent up a red flare. Galen's not like Sarah, he suspects everyone."

Rudzak frowned. "You're trying to make me uneasy. Are you willing to give up your final moments to save the woman?"

Logan didn't answer.

"Maybe you are. You always were a fool." His frown cleared. "I'll wait a little longer. It may be worth it."

"Good." Push him, make him uncertain, make him uneasy. And hope Galen managed to get Sarah out of the facility. "Every minute you spend here will make it easier for Galen to catch you."

Rudzak hesitated and then shook his head. "We'll wait."

Five minutes.

Ten minutes.

Logan was staring at him. Where was his fear? Rudzak had wanted him afraid. Would he be afraid at that final moment?

And where was Bassett?

"He's not coming." Logan was reading his expression. "But Galen will come. He should be wondering now where I am."

Rudzak made a decision. "I don't need Sarah Patrick. I can always get her later." He walked over to Logan. "And I will get her, Logan. Think about that when those columns come crashing down." He opened his duffel bag. "I have a present for you. I was going to make the mirror my final gift, but I changed my mind. I decided that this should be the final resting place for all my other gifts to Chen Li." He pulled out a large teakwood box. "So I put the other six treasures I gave her in this box and a little something else besides." He opened the lid to reveal four sticks of dynamite beneath the artifacts.

Logan stiffened. "I hate to pun, but isn't that overkill?"

A response at last. Logan was trying to hide it, but the shock was clear.

"When I'm in the drainage tunnel, I'll blow the charges Duggan set in here. But that's a little unimaginative for me. So I want you to watch this fuse creep closer and closer." He placed the box beside one of the columns nearest Logan and unwound the fuse as he made his way across the lab toward the door. He stopped there and leaned down to light the fuse. "It's a slow-burning fuse. You won't know which one of the charges will take you out first, Duggan's or mine. You have about three minutes. Lie there and count the seconds." He took a last look at Logan. Logan's expression was grim, but he still didn't see fear, he realized in frustration. "Good-bye, Logan, you're going to die."

"If I do, then Chen Li will welcome me. I did all I could to save her. She wouldn't welcome you, Rudzak. You murdered her. She'd hate your guts."

"You lie. I *saved* her." He slammed the door and ran down the steps. Moments later he was in the drainage pipe.

• • •

Shit.

Logan stared at the bright glow of the burning fuse.

Think. Don't panic.

Don't panic when the damn lab might fall down on top of him any minute? His heart was pounding so hard, it felt ready to jump out of his chest.

Find a safer spot.

He started crawling across the floor.

Rudzak's footsteps echoed as he ran down the drainage tunnel.

What Logan said wasn't true. Chen Li would never hate him. It was Logan, not Chen Li, who thought that everything Rudzak and she had together was ugly and strange.

Another two minutes and it would be safe for him to press the switch. Logan would die.

And the memory of Logan and Chen Li together would die with him. Then Rudzak would remember only Chen Li, the way she had been before Logan had come along.

One minute.

He reached in his pocket and took out the switch. One more minute, Chen Li.

He ran faster.

Only a little while longer, Chen Li.

Soon, beloved.

Soon . . .

Sarah opened her eyes to black sky and trees overhead. She was lying on grass and Monty's head was on her arm.

And Galen was towering above her, talking to someone.

He must have felt her gaze on him, because he looked down. "Sorry." His tone was tense. "I had to get you out of there."

She vaguely remembered his hand on her shoulder. A pinprick . . . "You drugged me."

"Only the lightest sedative, or you'd still be out."

"You drugged— Logan!" She sat upright.

"I think Logan's fine."

"You think?" She looked around her. Grass. Men. A concrete drainage pipe. "Where are we?"

"Outside the facility."

"And Logan's still inside?"

"It's been only ten minutes."

"With Rudzak." She scrambled to her knees. "Why haven't you gone after him?"

"We're waiting."

"Waiting?"

He nodded at the drainage pipe. "That was the way Rudzak got into the facility."

"Then go after him, dammit."

"Logan told us to wait."

"What do you mean? He's going to blow—"

The earth shook beneath her before she heard the blast.

The drainage pipe erupted into a fireball of flying concrete and smoke.

"*No!*" She was on her feet and running toward the drainage pipe.

Galen tackled her before she reached it. "Sarah, it's okay. This is what Logan wanted."

She gazed at him in horror. "He wanted to be blown to bits? Are you crazy?"

"Logan's not suicidal. It wasn't the facility that blew, it was the drainage pipe. We knew about the explosives planted in the basement lab and we moved them to the pipe. Rudzak should have been in the pipe when he pressed the switch."

Hope surged through her. "The lab didn't blow?"

"No, just the drainage tunnel."

"You knew Rudzak was coming through that pipe, but you didn't call the police."

Galen was silent a moment. "Logan didn't want him caught and put in a jail somewhere. He wanted him dead. He made the mistake before of not killing him. He wasn't going to do it this time."

"So he made himself bait? What if Rudzak killed him before he left the lab?"

"Logan didn't think that's what he had in—"

"What if Logan was wrong?" She was starting to shake. "How can anyone guess what that son of a—"

Another explosion rocked the earth.

Sarah stared in shock at the building. The smoke was clearing to reveal that not only the drainage pipe had been blown. She whispered, "Is it the lab?"

Galen was cursing. It was answer enough.

12:55 A.M.

The firemen were blowing out the drainage pipe, trying to clear it of dust and lethal gases. Sarah's nails dug into the palms of her hands as she watched them.

"It shouldn't have happened," Galen said. "My guys aren't careless. They wouldn't have missed any of the charges in that lab."

"Well, it did happen," she said dully. "And Logan will be lucky if he's not underneath a ton of wreckage. Even if he's alive, I don't know how the hell anyone's going to get to him. That corner of the building collapsed."

Monty pressed closer to her legs and looked up at her. *Find?*

She reached down and stroked his head.

Find?

Yes, keep hope alive even if she was scared to death. So, stop standing there, shaking. There might be a way. Sweet Jesus, she hoped there was a way. "Find." She started toward the fire department rescue command post with Monty trotting after her.

"Where are you going?" Galen called.

"To do my job."

Christ, it was dark.

Monty was crawling ahead of her through the rubble in the drainage pipe. She could barely see him, but he was crawling steadily. He knew where he was going, he had the cone.

But that didn't mean Logan was alive.

Don't think about that. When they got through this pipe, they'd find Logan and he'd be alive. Repeat it like a mantra.

He is alive.

He is alive.

He is alive.

She could hardly breathe. She checked the monitor she wore around her neck. No lethal gases. It must be the concrete dust . . . and fear.

Digging her elbows into the rubble, she slowly made her way forward.

"Okay, Sarah?" It was Donner at the command post, speaking through her wire.

No, it wasn't okay. She was terrified. But she said, "No problem. There are more air pockets than I thought there'd be. And I haven't found any weak spots I wasn't able to shore up."

"That doesn't mean you won't. Don't be a hot dog. You should get out of there and let us go in."

She couldn't do that, not when she knew they'd be forced to take precautions that would eat up time. Logan's time. "No problem," she repeated.

Monty gave a low moan.

She knew that sound. Oh, God, he'd found something.

And it wasn't alive.

"I can't talk anymore, Donner. I hear Monty. . . ."

She crawled until she saw Monty standing still.

Standing next to a body crushed beneath slabs of concrete.

Dead.

Please, Jesus. Let Monty be wrong.

Let Logan have a spark of life so she could save him.

She crawled closer.

Blood. She was crawling through blood.

"Easy, boy. Move just a little. I've got to help him."

Monty whimpered and shifted to one side.

Her flashlight speared the darkness, and her stomach wrenched. Blood. So much blood.

Puddled around the head.

Oh, God, not Logan.

Rudzak.

Eyes wide open, blood on his white hair, on his face and throat.

Dead.

Not Logan.

The relief was so strong, it made her light-headed.

"Find, Monty."

He looked at her, confused. Then he started down the pipe again.

Five minutes.

Ten minutes.

Darkness.

Dust.

Monty barked.

"Logan!"

No answer.

But she could see Monty ahead of her, and there had been eagerness in his bark.

"Logan! You answer me!"

"Sarah, what the hell are you doing down here?"

She almost fainted. She had to close her eyes for a moment before she could speak. "What do you think I'm doing? I'm rescuing you."

"Then get out of here and tell Galen to dig me out."

"Stop giving me orders. Where are you? I can't see you."

"I can't see you either, but I can hear you. I'm behind one of the collapsed columns in the lab."

"How many collapsed?"

"Two, one is still holding."

She wriggled closer to the sound of his voice. "There's a blockage."

"That's what I told you."

"But I think I can wriggle around it."

"Stay where you are."

"Shut up. Are you hurt?"

"A few cuts and bruises."

"Better than you deserve." She squeezed into the blocked passage. Monty whimpered eagerly and tried to come after her. "No, boy, you found him. Good boy. Now go tell Galen and Donner."

"*You* go tell Galen," Logan said.

"Go, Monty."

Monty looked at her uncertainly.

"Go."

He turned and started crawling back through the tunnel.

She spoke into her wire. "I've found Logan. I think he's okay. I've sent Monty to show you the way back." She switched off her wire, then turned the flashlight on Logan. "Now, where are these cuts and bruises that— You liar." She crawled closer to where he was lying. "It's broken?"

"I suspect."

"Anything else?"

"Isn't that enough?"

"Yes." Her hand trembled as she took out her first aid pack and got a good look at his arm. She cut the ropes binding him and then opened her pack. "It's not a compound fracture. I'm surprised because you never do things simple, do you?"

"The pot calling the kettle black."

"It could have been your idiotic head."

"That occurred to me. I didn't expect Rudzak to set a surprise charge before he left. I thought I had everything covered. I had the blueprints changed before he stole them to make the basement lab seem the perfect target. I knew he'd choose to—"

"Shut up and grit your teeth." She splinted the arm and then bound it. "Okay. It's done."

"I'm very . . . glad."

"So am I." She sat looking at him. "But I'll break your other arm if you ever try to keep anything from me again."

"It was necessary."

"Bull. Even if you didn't know about the second charge, you had to blow that pipe, didn't you? You had to take a chance that could—"

"I couldn't let him live. Not after Kai Chi. I just hope I got him."

"You did. Monty found him before we got here."

"Thank God."

"I thought he was you. I thought you were dead." She lay down beside him, not touching him. "I don't want you ever scaring me like this again."

"I think you could call this an extraordinary circumstance."

"I don't care what you call it. It's not going to happen. I don't want you hurt or broken or dead."

"Neither do I."

"Then you should take better care of yourself. You can't expect Monty and me to come after you whenever you get into trouble."

"I'll keep that in mind."

"Because we'll have to do it. We won't have a choice."

"Why not?"

She was silent a moment. "Because we . . . love you."

He stiffened. "You do?"

"Not that you deserve it. But that doesn't seem to make a difference. We're stuck with you."

"My God, what a romantic declaration. I'm not sure whether it's you or Monty who's—"

"It's me. Monty has more sense." She moistened her lips. "And I don't care how many women you've loved in the past. Because I'm going to be the best and the last. We match. We could have a great marriage. I'll work at it and make you work at it until we have something that's really special."

"Are you asking for my hand in marriage?"

"No, I'm telling you that you should marry me because you're not going to find anyone who's better for you and I'm not going to let you go for the next hundred years or so."

"You don't have to be so argumentative." He cleared his throat. "I believe I made the first confession of affection. I could wish you hadn't chosen this hole in the ground in which to reply."

"I had to get it out."

"Could you at least take my hand?"

"No, I might hurt you. You broke your damn arm."

"I'll suffer."

She reached out and carefully linked her fingers with his. She whispered, "I do love you, Logan. I never thought I could love anyone like this. I hope you know it's not going to go away."

"I'll resign myself." He leaned his head on her shoulder and his weight felt dear and solid and wonderfully right. "There's only one other thing I want to know. It's of supreme importance."

"What?"

"Do you love me as much as you do your dog?"

EPILOGUE

They heard the wolf howl as soon as they got out of the jeep.

"Thank heavens." Eve had flung open the front door of the cabin and stared at them now in exasperation. "I never want to hear another wolf for the rest of my life. I may even cancel my subscription to *National Geographic*. I was tempted to give the animal a sedative just so we could get some sleep."

"Sorry." Sarah looked sheepish. "We'll take over. Where are Joe and Jane?"

"Out for a run. I think they wanted to get away from Maggie."

"That bad?"

"That bad." Eve glanced at Logan. "That cast on your arm may come in handy."

Maggie howled.

Monty barked joyously and disappeared into the house.

"You'd better monitor that encounter," Eve told Sarah. "She's very bad tempered. He may get his throat sliced."

"I think it will be okay," Sarah said. "She usually tolerates him. But we'll take a look."

"What are you going to do with her?"

"That's a big question," Logan said. "Do you think she'd like California?"

"No." Sarah frowned. "You can't take her out of the state. The authorities wouldn't permit it."

"I think I can guarantee that they'll cut us some slack."

"Even if you pull strings, what are we going to do? Let her roam among all those mansions on the seventeen-mile strip? She's better off here."

"And risk having your rancher friends shoot her?"

"No, of course not." She sighed. "It's just that Monty . . ."

"I know," Logan said. "He's got a problem." He tilted his head. "What's that?"

Sarah heard it too, a cross between a growl and a warble.

"Monty?" No, that wasn't Monty. She strode quickly to the back porch. "What's happen—"

Monty was on his back with his feet in the air. He gave an ecstatic woo-woo of a yodel.

Maggie growled in disgust but continued to lick Monty's face.

"I'd say that absence definitely made the heart grow fonder," Logan murmured. "That's more than toleration. Unless you want to turn Monty loose to roam with her, I believe we have to find a domestic solution. I can see a second generation on the horizon."

"Good luck," Eve said. "You'll need it."

"I'm not worried about luck." Sarah's gaze shifted from Maggie and Monty, and she smiled into Logan's eyes. "If we don't have it, we'll make it. Isn't that right, Logan?"

"I plead the Fifth Amendment. You've already accused me of blatant manipulation, and I've had enough problems convincing you to take a chance on me. If I rouse your suspicions, you might take your dog and head for the hills."

"What would you do then?"

"Go after you. Maggie and I would track you down. We both know what we want and we wouldn't give up. You told me that once Maggie committed, she'd mate for life."

"And what about you?"

He smiled. "Try me."